THE SWORD OF
ANGELS

JOHN MARCO

D1344893

GOL
LONDON

The right of John Marco to be identified as the author of
this work has been asserted by him in accordance with
the Copyright, Designs and Patents Act 1988.

First published in Great Britain in 2005 by
Gollancz
An imprint of the Orion Publishing Group
Orion House, 5 Upper St Martin's Lane, London WC2H 9EA

A CIP catalogue record for this book is available
from the British Library

ISBN 0 575 07635 6 (cased)
ISBN 0 575 07779 4 (trade paperback)

1 3 5 7 9 10 8 6 4 2

Typeset at The Spartan Press Ltd,
Lymington, Hants

Printed in Great Britain by
Clays Ltd, St Ives plc

www.orionbooks.co.uk

THE SWORD OF ANGELS

Also by John Marco in Gollancz:

The Eyes of God
The Devil's Armour

THE TYRANTS AND KINGS TRILOGY
The Jackal of Nar
The Grand Design
The Saints of the Sword

This one's for Jack, with all my love

PART ONE

THE BLACK BARON

1

The Desert of Tears seemed eternal, like an ocean, stretching to the corners of the world. Beyond the white sands and mirages stood the nothingness of dunes, ever shifting in the hot winds. Light poured from the cloudless sky, blinding the lone rider as he loped across the earth, his fair skin shielded from the sun beneath a headdress called a gaka. His drowa bounced slowly through the desert, unhurried, unconcerned for the mission of its rider, which had taken the young man from the safety of a fabled city toward the unknown dangers of the northern world. The young man had lived in the desert more than a year now, but he had never grown accustomed to the lung-searing air or the way the sun could peel his skin. Today, the sun tracked him without pity, making him long for home.

For Gilwyn Toms, home was Jador, the city of his beloved White-Eye, a city that had opened its arms to him and his companions when the world they knew – the world up north – had gone insane. Like his companions, Gilwyn Toms was an exile now. The Desert of Tears, that vast sea of sand and wicked heat, had protected Jador from the continent and most of their enemies, and had been a good home for Gilwyn. He had missed his land of Liiria, but he had found solace in Jador and love in the arms of White-Eye. And he had not wanted his time in Jador to end, but rather to go on untroubled, undisturbed by the upheaval racking the world beyond the sands.

Gilwyn raised his face to heaven, squinting at the sun. He could bear the brightness only for a moment, but noon had passed and that comforted him. Lukien had taught him the art of reckoning, and by his amateurish calculation he guessed that he had six hours more before the sun abated and he could rest for the night. It had been three days since he had left Jador. At least two more days remained before he reached Ganjor, the gateway to the north. Alone, he had only his silent drowa for company, but if he calmed himself he could reach deep within his mind and find Ruana. She was with him always now, a pleasant current running through his brain. She was like Teku, the pet monkey he had left in Jador, perched on his shoulder, always there if he took the time to look for her. Gilwyn looked for her now, sensing her sublime presence. Closing his eyes, he saw her pretty face.

Ruana had been young when she died, falling from a boat into a lake and drowning. In life she had been an Akari, when that race had ruled the land called Kaliatha. She was an Akari still, but now she was a spirit, bound to him, pledged to aid him and bring out the 'gift', that strange summoning power he was only now beginning to understand. Most Inhumans had such a gift, and now Gilwyn was one of them. He had been an Inhuman all his life, in fact, from the day in his crib when Minikin had kissed his forehead, forever marking him. But only a few months ago had he been introduced to Ruana. Though she had been with him from that moment in infancy, she was still new to Gilwyn, still an enigma to unravel. Keeping his eyes closed, he glimpsed her fair face and slight smile, like looking in a wavy mirror. Her ears turned up in elfish points.

I can feel your tiredness, she said. *Take your ease now, for a while at least.*

The words were soundless, yet resonated like a spoken voice from her dead realm. Gilwyn had only to think his answer to reply.

The heat, he reminded her. He tried to flex his clubbed left hand, an appendage that matched his clubbed left foot for uselessness. *My hand aches. And I'm itching like mad under this gaka.*

Though the desert garb shielded him from the sun, it also set his skin on fire. Ruana's sympathy came over him like a mother's pity. Instantly her strength buoyed him. They were one, Gilwyn and his Akari, and though he still did not fully grasp their bond he knew that Ruana did more than guide his gift. She shared his thoughts and, sometimes, his pains, and when he was weak she shouldered him. So far, she had helped him mightily to cross the desert. Gilwyn was not strong like Lukien, the Bronze Knight. At eighteen, he was no longer a child, but he had lived a sheltered life in Liiria, one of books and fantasies. Even now it was hard for him to grasp the enormity of his task. No one had wanted him to cross the desert, not Minikin and certainly not White-Eye, but they had not stopped him, either. They had tried, but in the end they had relented, letting him go on his desperate mission.

'We'll make it,' he said aloud, more to himself than to Ruana. Beneath him the hairy drowa ignored his boast, twitching its ears. He could barely see the horizon, but he knew that Ganjor awaited him. It would be an oasis after his journey, but he would have to be cautious there. He was Jadori now, and the Jadori were not welcome in the city by everyone. If he could find the Ganjeese princess he might be safe, but if he could not he would simply enter the city as quietly as possible, hiding under his gaka, and leave just as soon as he could.

4

Princess Salina will find you, said Ruana confidently. *Remember Dahj and Kamag.*

Gilwyn nodded, reminded now of Lorn's advice. Lorn, who had been helped across the desert by Salina, had told him to ask for men named Dahj and Kamag. They could be trusted, Lorn had said. They would take him to the Ganjeese princess.

But could Salina be trusted, Gilwyn wondered? Still, after all that had happened? Or had she since been discovered? It was a crime to help northerners across the desert but Salina had disobeyed her father, aiding the desperate from the war-torn continent in their bid to reach Jador. She had even warned Minikin and the others of danger, sending her doves across the Desert of Tears with their tiny hand-written notes and allowing them to prepare for Aztar's attacks. Of all Gilwyn's companions, only Lorn had actually seen Salina. He had described her as breath-taking and courageous. She was, to Gilwyn's thinking, certainly made of iron, for she was but a girl in a realm where females were subservient, and if her secret were ever discovered she would surely be imprisoned. Or worse.

Do not fret for her, said Ruana. *The girl can take care of herself.*

But is she safe? Gilwyn asked.

Ruana hesitated. *I cannot tell.*

'Of course you can tell,' said Gilwyn. 'You just won't say.'

You are right, said Ruana. There was a laughing quality to her tone. *I can tell, but I cannot tell you.*

It was not her place to reveal such things, nor predict the future nor tell him of the afterlife. The Akari existed beyond the world of the living and so had many secrets. From the realm of the dead they saw with eyes of gods, but they were wise beings and knew the virtue of silence. Unlike the Akari, Gilwyn was *alive*. He existed in the realm of the living, with all its choices and possibilities. His possibilities. The choices were not Ruana's to make. She had explained that to him, and so had Minikin. If Salina were dead or imprisoned, it was not for Ruana to say, though surely she could have searched the living world for the answer.

'If she's alive I'll find her,' said Gilwyn. Then he shrugged, his confidence waning. 'If I can.'

He licked his dry lips, trying to put aside his fears. It would be a month until he made it as far north as Liiria. He had so very long to go. He needed to be a man now, not the boy he had been in Liiria, surrounded by books. Only a man – a truly brave man – could save Baron Glass from the Devil's Armour.

Too much, chided Ruana gently. *You think too much of all these things. Quiet yourself. Rest now.*

Gilwyn shook his head. 'Can't.'

He took a skin from the drowa's tack and squirted a stream of water into his mouth. His aim was expert now, but he carefully conserved the precious liquid. The water, hot from the desert, stung his throat as much as cooled it.

Rest so that you do not waste yourself, urged Ruana. *It is hours yet until the sun goes down. And the drowa cannot go on forever. It needs rest, too.*

Though not without sympathy for the beast, Gilwyn ignored Ruana's suggestion. A drowa could go for hours without rest or water; that much he had learned from the Jadori. And if the poor creature expired when they reached Ganjor . . .

Gilwyn thought about that a moment. He reached down and patted the drowa's muscled neck. So much of what was happening seemed unfair. Even this ugly animal had got caught in the whirlwind. Surely it didn't want to die, but like Gilwyn it went on because it had to go on.

There was no choice.

At sundown, Gilwyn finally rested.

He was pleased with the day's progress, and by the time the sunlight slackened he and his drowa were exhausted. He didn't wait for the sun to complete its decent, but rather took advantage of the last slivers of light to make his camp. He was more than halfway through the desert now, and had come to a place were the ground was firmer and some dry plants grew in scrubby patches. Ugly, mis-shapen hills of baked earth shadowed the distance. A few cacti huddled nearby, but Gilwyn saw nothing of water or any real shade. As he had done the past two nights, he unloaded his belongings from the drowa and arranged his meagre camp, mostly a bedroll, some food, and a knife for eating. With the sun going down he had no need for shade, for soon the temperature would drop. The thought of the cool evening made him smile.

Before settling down Gilwyn tended to the drowa, first removing the saddle and striped blanket, then feeding it from a bag of fruits and mixed grains. Since the drowa could eat cactus and gain water from it, he led the beast to the small stand of piny plants. Drowas were browsers, he knew, and got much of their nourishment from the things they found in the desert. Gilwyn held the beast's tack as it fed, using its long snout and powerful teeth to slowly devour the plants. By the time the drowa had finished, the sun was almost complete gone, and with it nearly every speck of light.

'Soon the stars will come,' he said. Already some were twinkling through the twilight. He led the drowa back to his camp and eased the beast down. Now sated, the drowa bent easily to his will. Or was it his gift? Gilwyn couldn't say for sure, but the drowa had surprised him with its compliance. Usually, they were haughty, independent beasts, but this one had obeyed his every command. He had not even found the need to stake it down at night; the drowa simply stayed with him. 'Good boy,' he crooned, patting the drowa's back.

Famished from the ride, the meagre items in his travelling back seemed like a banquet. Mostly they were staples, like flat Jadori bread, dates and figs from the gardens around the palace, and goats cheese made by some of the city's northerners. The cheese smelled particularly bad to Gilwyn as he unwrapped it, but it had hardened with dryness and he had been assured it would do him no harm. Since he had no need to cook, and since he welcomed whatever cold the night would bring, he didn't bother making a fire. The stars, he knew, would provide all the light he needed.

So Gilwyn ate, all the while watching the stars come alive above him. Back in Koth, when he had been apprenticed to Figgis, they had watched the stars together from a balcony in the city's great library. Figgis had taught him about the movements of the heavens and Gilwyn had remembered everything. But here in the desert the constellations seemed different. They had actually *moved*, and he knew it was because he was so far south, so very far away from his homeland.

Still, he could make out his favourite constellations, and as they slowly appeared he studied them, calling out their names one by one, whispering to himself. His voice seemed to go on forever. Suddenly he wished for company, anyone with warm blood and real flesh, but all he had was Ruana, floating around him – inside him – like an invisible ghost.

Ruana, however, remained silent. Gilwyn could feel her, but she kept her distance while he ate, allowing him privacy. Finally, his hunger satisfied, he rolled a blanket into a pillow and propped it beneath his head, then looked up again into the star-filled sky. Like a theater, the night exploded with life. Gilwyn felt lost in its enormity. His thoughts turned to Salina again, and what she might look like.

Beautiful. That's what Lorn had said. Gilwyn dug into his pocket and pulled out the only real thing of value he carried. The lump of gold felt sturdy in his hand, like the man who'd given it to him. He held the ring up above his face, studying it in the starlight. It was Lorn's kingship ring, proof that he still lived. Gilwyn considered the prize, wondering what Jazana Carr would do when she saw the ring. He was to give the ring to her with Lorn's promise to reclaim it someday. Gilwyn had met Jazana Carr only once, but he suspected the message would craze her.

'Ruana,' he whispered. 'Are you there?'

Always.

'What do you think will happen? When Jazana Carr gets the ring, I mean?'

It was the kind of question Gilwyn often posed, the kind Ruana could not answer. The spirit seemed to chuckle.

The ring is nothing. It is Lorn that concerns you, Gilwyn, not Jazana Carr.

7

The reply annoyed Gilwyn, who playfully slipped the ring onto his finger. Much too big for him, it quickly slid to his knuckle.

'I trust Lorn, Ruana,' he said.

You worry, said Ruana, *about Lorn and what he will do to Jador.*

'He'll do nothing. I left him to look after things, that's all.'

He is King Lorn the Wicked.

Gilwyn nodded. 'I know.'

He had never asked Ruana's advice on the matter, and now it was too late. Jador needed a strong leader. Baron Glass had stolen the Devil's Armour and fled north to Jazana Carr. Lukien had gone after him, and might well be dead. White-Eye was blind now, the victim of the armour's accursed spirit, and Minikin . . .

Thinking of Minikin broke the boy's heart.

'I had no choice,' said Gilwyn. 'Lorn knows how to deal with any troubles that come up. White-Eye needs him, even if she won't admit it.'

White-Eye is Kahana, Ruana reminded him. *She has the blood of Kadar in her veins. She is strong.*

'She's blind now, Ruana,' said Gilwyn. 'She's lost her Akari, and I don't know what that will do to her. She needs help to rule Jador. She needs Lorn, because there's no one else left.'

His logic was inescapable. Ruana remained silent. Gilwyn took Lorn's ring off his finger and stuffed it back into his pocket. He intended to keep the promise he'd made to Lorn, to give the ring to Jazana Carr and tell her that King Lorn the Wicked would return for it. Then, if the Great Fate willed it, he would deal with the demon who had blinded White-Eye.

Enough now, said Ruana suddenly. *No more black thoughts. Clear your mind.*

'My mind is clear.'

Oh? Now is a good time, then.

'For what?'

To stretch your mind. The desert can teach you things, Gilwyn.

Gilwyn lifted his head from the blanket, listening. To him the desert seemed dead.

Not with your ears, argued Ruana. *Stop being silly and do as I say.*

'Ruana, I'm tired. Do we have to do this now? In the morning, maybe . . .'

You can sleep soon enough. The spirit paused a moment. Though he could not see her face now, Gilwyn could feel her sly smile. *Open your mind, Gilwyn. Use your gift to search the desert.*

Gilwyn closed his eyes. 'All right,' he agreed, admitting some curiosity. He had opened his mind to the desert before, but mostly to search for kreels, the giant lizards the Jadori rode. There would be no kreels this far from the city, he was sure. 'What should I look for?'

Suddenly he wasn't just in the desert any longer. He was over it, his mind soaring across the warm sand and rugged hillsides. The sensation amazed him. It came with such ease.

You see? Freeing your mind here is different from in the city, said Ruana. *Here there are no other beings to interfere.*

Untethered, Gilwyn let his mind fly through the night. He felt weightless, as if he himself were a bird on wing. The cool air made a mantel for him, wrapping him, bearing him up in every direction. He laughed with delight, and his concentration did not falter the way it had in the past.

'What's out here?' he asked, excited to know. 'What am I looking for, Ruana?'

Control the gift, Gilwyn. You shall see.

Gilwyn steadied his senses. Some Inhumans had amazing strength. Others, like the hunch-backed Monster, had the grace of a dancer. Gilwyn's gift lied in other creatures, and the ability to communicate with him. He had always had this gift, Minikin had told him, from the moment he'd been given a monkey to help him with the smallest chores. That strange bond had grown into an infinity of powers, and Ruana had brought them out in him. With her help, he could control the amazing reptilian kreels or snatch a hawk in flight and see the world below through its keen, soaring eyes. With Ruana, he was never alone. Now she had sensed something worth finding.

But what?

Gilwyn slowed his thinking. Whatever was out there would come to him. His mind would draw it out. He would feel its coursing blood.

'Rodents,' he said. Their small brains and clicking language tickled his brain. Focusing, he realized they were everywhere, hidden in the darkness. But he knew they were not why Ruana tested him.

What else? asked the Akari.

Gilwyn paused. The whole sensation was pleasant but confusing. 'I don't feel anything,' he said. 'Just—'

A presence struck him like a wall. In the darkness moved something massive, far away but determined. Prowling, on the hunt. Unspeakably cold. There was no mistaking it.

'A rass,' he whispered.

The great snakes of the desert. Hooded like a cobra. Enemy to the kreel. The terror of their desert realm. Gilwyn had seen them hunting for kreel eggs in the twilight. He had even touched one's mind. They were giants, with skulls like boulders and coiling, muscled bodies that could easily squeeze the life from his drowa. This one was far away, too far to catch his scent on its flicking tongue.

'It doesn't know we're here,' said Gilwyn, more than slightly relieved.

Remember the gift, Gilwyn. Speak with the beast.

The notion made Gilwyn recoil. 'What? No . . .'

Command it, Ruana insisted. *You are its master. Make it believe.*

'Are there others?' Gilwyn asked. He probed the desert looking for rass, frightened at the prospect of being surrounded.

Concentrate.

'I am.'

No, you are not. You are afraid.

'Ruana, if it senses us it might come looking for a meal.'

It will not, because you are its master.

Gilwyn laughed. 'Does it know that?'

You must tell it so. Make it believe. Go deeper.

Gilwyn steeled himself, then touched the serpent's mind again. The first time he had proved a rass had been months before, out in the kreel valley with Ghost. The encounter had drained and frightened him, and he had hoped never to do it again. Now, this new rass entered his brain. He could feel it hunting, slithering across the earth, its slivered eyes scanning the terrain, its tongue darting out to taste the air.

'I can feel it,' he said softly. 'I can feel its mind.'

Slowly, he unlocked its brain. A carnal picture of the hunt appeared. The snake's thinking filled Gilwyn, and when it noticed him it paused. Its great body ceased slithering. Its hooded head rose to look around. Confused, its leathery eyelids blinked.

It knows you're here now, said Ruana.

Gilwyn nodded but could not speak. The serpent's thoughts mesmerized him. He struggled to keep his distance, to keep the gleaming eyes from withering his resolve. Ruana forced him forward. He could feel her hand at his shoulder, comforting him.

It is afraid of you, she said. *It cannot see you. It cannot smell you. Yet it knows you are here.*

Gilwyn's confidence crested. If the beast were afraid of him . . .

He bored deeper into its brain, making himself known, allowing it to sense him fully.

You are powerful . . .

'Powerful,' Gilwyn echoed. And as he said the word he believed it, making the rass believe it too. A shrinking sense of dominion overcame the serpent. Its ancient mind twisted. Gilwyn fixed his thoughts. Magically, unspoken words passed between them.

I am your master, he said. *Do not come hunting here.*

The effort made him shake. Holding their minds sapped his strength.

Know me, he continued. *Know my presence.*

He saw the serpent rear back, opening its fanged maw and hissing in anger. Hatred filled its tiny brain. Its rope-like tongue darted out to search for him, probing the night. Its muddled thinking startled Gilwyn.

He felt his control begin to slip. Ruana quickly bolstered him, thrusting him further toward the rass. The strength of the bond startled the snake, making it lower its glistening head.

It obeys, said Ruana. *It knows you are its master, Gilwyn.*

Gilwyn forced himself to continue, feeling every fibre of the creature, sensing every instinct. Its anger diminished, its hissing ebbed. The beast's shining eyes calmed, watching the night for the thing it now feared.

'What now?' Gilwyn asked.

You may release it, Ruana replied. *It will not hunt here now.*

Slowly, Gilwyn let his grip slip away, drawing back across the dark sands. He opened his eyes, then felt the thunderous pounding of a headache. He felt exhausted, completely spent from the brief encounter. But he felt exhilarated, too.

'Ruana,' he said softly. 'That was incredible.'

Ruana's voice resounded with pride. *You had done it before. You only need to practice.*

'It's difficult,' Gilwyn confessed. 'I was afraid.'

I will never tell you to do something that you cannot do, Gilwyn. You need only trust me – and yourself.

The answer comforted Gilwyn. 'I'm tired,' he sighed.

Ruana's reply was sweet. *Sleep now. The rass will not harm you.*

Gilwyn put the serpent from his mind, trusting Ruana. Within minutes he was asleep.

The next morning dawned as hotly as the one before.

Gilwyn did not bother breaking his fast in camp, but rather mounted his drowa early and resumed his long trek toward Ganjor. As he rode he took some flat bread from his bags to stem his hunger, washing it down with warm water from the skins that jangled off his saddle. The night's sleep had energized him, and being more than halfway to Ganjor put bounce in his stance. Already his skin was beginning to itch beneath his headdress, and the stubble of a light beard irritated his face. He rubbed at the beard, wondering what White-Eye would think of it. Most Jadori men wore beards, a sign of virility and source of great pride, and since he had been Regent of Jador he thought a beard might be a good idea.

'When I return, maybe,' he said with confidence, sure suddenly that he would see White-Eye again.

Gilwyn rode on for nearly an hour before coming upon a stand of cacti. Not knowing when more of the water-bearing plants would appear, he decided to stop and feed his drowa. Without using the tack, he led the huge beast to the plants. The drowa munched happily while Gilwyn stood aside, studying the horizon. He could still not see Ganjor, but he didn't expect to, really. The city was large, larger by far than Jador, but it was still many miles away.

'Tomorrow, then,' he told himself. Staring off across the sands, he contemplated the distance to Ganjor, and how many hours of scorching heat he had left to endure. By nightfall tomorrow, he might see the city. Then, at last, he could meet Salina.

He was about to turn back to his drowa when something in the distance caught his attention, the movement of two dark shapes against the white sand. Gilwyn squinted hard, focusing against the dazzling sun. He hadn't seen anyone since leaving Jador, and it took a moment for him to realize that, yes, these were people riding toward him.

'Look,' he said excitedly, wondering if Ruana had noticed them. 'Riders.'

And riding quickly, too, Gilwyn realized. Toward him. They had seen him, no doubt, but there were not many who came across the desert these days. There had been no more Seekers since the battle with Aztar. Nor had anyone seen the remains of Aztar's army. Still, Gilwyn had seen the likes of these riders before, and his heart froze over.

'Raiders.'

Fear nailed him in place. His mind groped for an explanation. Aztar's raiders had all been defeated, soundly trounced by Minikin's magic. Aztar himself was dead, no doubt, yet these were raiders, unmistakably, Voruni fighters from Aztar's own tribe. Their dark gakas, visible now as they drew near, flared out behind them like comet tails as they rode. Gilwyn stumbled backward, into the still-feeding drowa.

'Ruana,' Gilwyn called. 'What should I do?'

Ruana was with him instantly. *Get on your drowa, Gilwyn. Do it now.*

Poor advice, thought Gilwyn, but he snatched the beast away from its meal and pulled himself onto its back. Mounting the drowa took effort for him, though, for his clubbed appendages slowed him. Finally able to throw over his leg, he wheeled the drowa around to face the coming riders. He could hear the powerful hooves of their drowas beating on the sand. Out-running them was impossible, and in the desert there was no place to hide.

Turn around and ride, Ruana urged, *back the way you came.*

Gilwyn obeyed, urging the drowa on. The beast exploded beneath him. Over his shoulder, Gilwyn saw the raiders pursuing, tucked low in their saddles. With nowhere to go, Gilwyn's mind numbed to the possibility of capture.

'They'll catch us,' he gasped.

Ruana's voice stayed firm. *Find the rass, Gilwyn,* she commanded. *It's very near.*

'The rass?'

Find the rass and bring it here.

'Yes!'

Gilwyn drove the fear from his mind, closing his eyes and summoning the gift. Behind him, he heard the shouts of the raiders urging him to surrender. They were Aztar's men; he knew that surely now. And if they caught him they would kill him, revenge for what Minikin had done. But even this he pushed aside, thinking instead of the open desert and of the cold-blooded monster hidden in its folds. The feeling of the rass was unforgettable. He homed in on it, sensing it easily. This time he entered its brain like a knife, slicing past its primeval thoughts into its very core. The rass was near, no more than minutes away. It had sunned itself and was ready to hunt, and when Gilwyn entered its mind it reared up to spread its coloured hood.

'I have it,' he said. Opening his eyes, he focused both on the rass and his blurring surroundings. Soon his drowa would tire, he knew, and the blood-thirsty quartet would catch him.

Unless he called the rass.

Obey me, he said, speaking only to the serpent, drilling into its brain and seizing its thoughts. *I am your master. Yield to me.*

He had done it with Teku, and he had done it with kreel. But this was different, far more difficult. The serpent, confused by his commands, lifted itself up to search for him. Somehow, it knew he was coming, and though they could not yet see each other, it waited.

Down! Gilwyn commanded. *Into the sand. Hide yourself.*

Time slipped quickly as the raiders sped toward him. Gilwyn forced himself to concentrate.

Enemies come, he told the rass. *Hide yourself.*

Remarkably, the creature understood. Though he still could not see it, Gilwyn knew its location now. Up ahead lay a cradle of rocks, blown-over with sand and studded with brush. Hidden there lay the rass, waiting for him. Gilwyn directed his mind at the creature, filling it with his presence, speaking in a language it somehow understood. As he drew near the rocks, he felt the serpent bend to his will. Its dark eyes dawned with understanding. Then, at last, it obeyed. Moving with a quickness that seemed impossible, it burrowed its long body beneath the rocks and sand, shielding itself in shadows.

And Gilwyn rode right toward it.

Trust yourself, Ruana told him.

With little choice, Gilwyn urged his drowa toward the rocks. Now the raiders were gaining again, their own mounts lathered with effort. Peering over his shoulder, Gilwyn watched the raiders draw their weapons. The rocks were only yards away. He braced himself and raced toward them.

Hear me, he commanded. The hidden rass opened its mind for him. *The four are your prey.*

The serpent understood. Confident, Gilwyn entered the rocks. His drowa slowed, then wheeled about at Gilwyn's order, snorting in anger as the four raiders approached. Gilwyn drew the dagger at his belt and held it aloft. Up ahead, he could barely see the outline of the enormous rass, tucked in waiting at the base of the rocks.

'Come, then, damn you!' he cried. The raiders were clearly visible now, four burly Voruni with scimitars and oily beards combed to sharp, black points. The first man, a Zarturk by the looks of him, held up a hand and brought his men to a halt. Gilwyn cursed when he saw their strategy. Zarturks were leaders among the Voruni, tribal warriors who had proven themselves in battle, and this one wasn't stupid. He looked at Gilwyn across the rocks, lowering his blade curiously and leaning back in the saddle of his drowa. Gilwyn put his thumbnail to his front teeth and flicked a vulgar gesture at them. He had not learned a lot of their language, but because the Voruni spoke a tongue similar to the Jadori he knew how to curse them.

'Aztar moahmad!' he shouted. The words meant 'filth of Aztar,' and when the Zarturk heard the insult he bristled. He barked back across the rocks, calling Gilwyn a stupid boy and ordering him to surrender. Gilwyn shook his head, refusing to budge, but he knew he could not hold the rass much longer.

'Come and get me!' Gilwyn cried, then turned his drowa and rode off, sure that the raiders would follow. Half his brain stayed connected to the rass. The other half turned to see two of the raiders riding to pursue. The other pair rode round the rocks, trying to reach him the long way. Gilwyn quickly reigned in his drowa. The first men were riding past the rocks. Sure that he had no choice, he shot an order to the waiting serpent.

Now!

A swale of black flesh and shaking sand burst from the rocks. The shocked riders reared back on their mounts. The great rass unfolded its leathery hood, opened its forbidding maw, and lunged. Gilwyn watched, horrified, as the nearest drowa stumbled back and spilled its rider in the monster's shadow. His comrade, dumbstruck, barely raised his blade. The rass was on them instantly, quickly coiling round the fallen man, then bearing him up in its vise-grip tail. The head jolted forward, knocked the other rider from his mount, then reared back in leering delight before clamping its jaws around him. A moment later both men were in the air, one suffocating in the serpent's tail, the other punctured and bloody, dangling from the creature's fangs.

'Fate above . . .'

Nausea spiked in Gilwyn's throat. The remaining raiders stopped, as stunned as Gilwyn by the shocking sight. The Zarturk turned to look at Gilwyn, his dark eyes furious. Quickly he and his remaining warrior retreated, circling around the rocks and safely away from the raging serpent. The rass, occupied with its still-living prey, barely noticed them. Sickened by what he'd done, Gilwyn lost control of the rass. When he did, Ruana slammed into his mind.

Get control or get away from it!

Confused, Gilwyn squeezed his legs and urged the drowa away. With nowhere to go he rode away from the raiders, begging the drowa to hurry. He left the rock behind, left the rass to feed on the two men he had trapped, and was soon out in the open again, racing helplessly away from the raiders, who shouted after him.

'Unless there are more snakes out here I'm in trouble!' he gasped. 'Ruana?'

The Akari gave no reply, because nothing could be done and Gilwyn knew it. With only a dagger and an exhausted drowa, he had no hope at all. He looked over his shoulder and saw the relentless raiders bearing down fast. Behind them, the rass had dropped the man from its tail and craned its neck skyward to swallow the other man whole.

'All right, enough running,' spat Gilwyn. 'They have me. Damn it!'

He jerked back the drowa's reins and spun to a halt, facing the Zarturk and his man. The Voruni pair brought their own mounts to a stop a few yards away. Thunder filled the Zarturk's face. A jagged tattoo across his cheek twitched with fury.

'You want me, you pirate trash?' Gilwyn held up his dagger. 'You want to rob me? Then come and get me!'

The Zarturk and his underling smirked at his small weapon. Then, surprisingly, both men put their blades into their belts. The Zarturk shook his head contemptuously, pointing to the distant rass.

'That's right,' Gilwyn taunted. 'Big snake. Bad death. Do you understand me, you stupid beasts?'

The Zarturk frowned. 'Aztar.'

Gilwyn's dagger trembled. 'What?'

'Aztar,' said the man again, then pointed eastward. 'Aztar.'

'Aztar? Aztar's dead,' said Gilwyn. He pretended to draw his knife over his throat. '*Dead.*'

The Voruni understood the gesture, but shook his head in denial. 'Aztar bis arok.'

'Arok? Alive?'

The Zarturk nodded, then put out a finger and bid Gilwyn forward. 'Aztar.'

They want you to follow them, said Ruana.

Gilwyn couldn't speak. There was nowhere to go and no one to aid him. Helpless, he put the dagger back in its small sheath. He rode toward the Zarturk warily, unsure what else to do. His heart thundered in his temples, muddling his thinking and his connection to Ruana. Aztar would kill him, and probably not quickly. The thought of torture smothered him. As he rode he took no notice of the nearby dune, partially blocking the horizon. The angry face of the Zarturk filled his vision. Like Gilwyn, the big man and his companion remained oblivious to their surroundings. Having forgotten the nearby rass, not even Gilwyn saw it in time.

A black shadow fell across the dune. Sand exploded amid the terrible cries of frightened drowa. Ruana burst into Gilwyn's mind, but amidst the sudden chaos he barely noticed her. He saw only a great wall of rising flesh . . . and then, darkness.

2

A young woman on a horse entered the broken city of Koth just as twilight fell. It had been a long day's journey from the farm up in Borath, and the woman, who was not much more than a girl, felt depleted. Around her, all of Koth's past majesty seemed to lay in ruins. Norvan soldiers patrolled the streets along with bands of mercenaries. The fires of the battle two weeks before had finally died away, but the smell of smoke still lingered over Koth, reminding everyone of the terror that had happened here. Not far ahead, the woman could see Library Hill. At the top of the hill stood the once-great Cathedral of Knowledge, devastated now, its timbers and stone walls split by Norvan catapults. Torches burned brightly on the road winding up the hill while men camped and rested on the grounds, still recovering from the bloody siege. In the middle of a wide avenue, the woman drew her horse to a halt. Bad memories swarmed over her as she stared up at the library.

Her name was Mirage. Once, not long ago, her name had been Meriel, but she had swapped that name for the beauty of a magical mask. She was an Inhuman, a person of Grimhold, and the Akari bound to her mind had given her a splendid gift. As a teen she had been burned, nearly dying in a fire. She had lived with the scars of that event for years, but no longer. Now she was lovely, as beautiful as the woman she would have been if the fire hadn't raked her flesh away. Her first Akari, a sweet-tempered spirit named Sarlvarian, had controlled the pain of her tortured skin, but even he could not quell the pain in her heart. She had looked in mirrors for years and had always seen a monster staring back at her, and so she had changed her Akari, letting go of Sarlvarian's hand and inviting a new Akari into her life, a spirit named Kirsil who had made her appear beautiful again. On that day, Meriel had died. And Mirage was born.

As Mirage, she still felt the old pains. Beneath the veneer of beauty, her skin remained ravaged, but no one could see the woman she had been. Nor did Mirage ever speak of it, or complain about the searing pain that accompanied her everywhere. Over the years she had learned to control her agonies, and now all the world saw only her beauty.

Mirage took the time to look around, trying to ignore her hunger. Her long blonde hair hung loose around her shoulders, and she noticed now that the soldiers in the street watched her. Mirage made sure not to look at them. The lust of men was unknown to her, mostly. No one had longed for her, not when she was burned.

No, she corrected herself. That wasn't exactly true. Thorin had loved her. He had loved and longed for her when no other man had, and that was why she had returned to Koth, to find him.

But where?

She glanced around. Vendors had abandoned most of the shops months ago, long before the Norvans had come. Before the arrival of Jazana Carr and her horde, it was civil war that had split the city, but Breck and the others had quelled the worst of it. Now Breck was gone, dead like most of Koth's defenders. Dead like Vanlandinghale, the young lieutenant who'd been so kind, so thoughtful to Mirage that he had never asked her why she had come to the library or why she loved Lukien so much. Of the thousand men who had defended the city, barely three-hundred had survived, and all of them were scattered now. At first they had hidden at Breck's farm up north, just as Mirage herself had done, but even remote Borath was too near to be safe, and the soldiers had gone, leaving their homeland for any safe haven.

But not I, thought Mirage.

She had not the sense to leave with Thorin's son, Aric, or any of the others. Even Lukien had refused to return to Koth, going off on a mad quest instead. Of all of them, only Mirage had returned, and suddenly she was not proud of her decision. She was simply afraid. The soldiers in the avenue took more notice of her, passing comments and leering. Mirage turned her face away and trotted deeper into Koth. She realized how few women were in the city. Those that remained had obviously locked themselves in their homes, fearing the rapes that so often accompanied a sacking. Mirage considered her plan. She had come to Koth because there was nowhere else for her, and because Lukien had shunned her love. She could not return to Grimhold, for to do so would mean defeat, and she could not admit defeat to Minikin. Only Thorin had really shown her love. Though the Devil's Armour had maddened him, Mirage was sure he would welcome her.

If she could find him.

He may not even be in the city, she realized. Looking up again at the battered library, she knew he would not be there. *He'll be at Lionkeep.*

Lionkeep had been ruined too, though not as badly as the library. And Mirage had heard rumours that Thorin had set up a command post there.

Still, it was a longshot to find him, and she wondered what she would say to gain an audience with him. Already her presence was arousing suspicion. She didn't want anyone's attention, especially not one of the Jazana Carr's greasy mercenaries.

A strange sense gripped her then, forcing her to look over her shoulder. Except for the soldiers she saw no one, yet all day she had felt the cold appraisal of unwanted eyes. She calmed herself, told herself that no one was following her, then proceeded across the avenue. Lionkeep was on the other side of the city, and if she was to reach it before darkness fell completely she would have to make haste. But she had not eaten since morning and was wildly hungry now, and knew that she could not go on without a little food, at least. Ahead of her, she spotted a tavern. Amazingly, it looked open. A pair of soldiers sat by the doors, sharing a pipe and a bottle of liquor. Mirage reined in her mount, keeping to the shadows while she studied the place, reading the battered sign over the door.

'The Red Stallion,' she whispered.

The name sounded familiar to her. They would have food, probably, and give her a chance to rest. Mirage wondered if she should stop or go on to Lionkeep. Stopping would make it that much later – and darker – when she finally asked for Thorin. But her bones ached and her stomach roared to be filled, and she knew she could not go on much longer. Screwing up her courage, she trotted back into the light and headed for the tavern. Outside, other horses had been bridled and a boy had been hired to look after them. Despite the obviously drunk Norvans at the threshold, the place seemed safe enough, at least enough to draw Mirage forward. The Norvans looked up from their drink when she approached, staring at her through the pipe smoke. In Liiria, a woman riding alone was a rare sight, but in Norvor it was unheard of, and the two soldiers blinked in disbelief. Mirage dismounted and tied her weary horse at the post. She had left Borath with precious little money, but her horse was important and she couldn't afford anything happening to the beast.

'Here,' she told the boy, dipping into the pockets of her riding pants and fishing out a coin. 'Look after him and don't let anyone touch him. All right?'

The boy nodded dumbly, as struck as the Norvans by her appearance, and quickly took the coin. Mirage felt the eyes of the men on her backside as she sidled toward the door. The Red Stallion was a large place, and as she entered she immediately noticed the crowd, laughing and drinking, playing cards by the fire, and teasing the prostitutes with promised coins. Mirage felt herself blush. The only women in the tavern were whores. Her eyes darted about, wondering if she should leave. A man hurried into the side of her vision.

'You want a table?'

Startled, Mirage stared at him a moment. He was a stocky man with a kind, round face. Obviously the proprietor, his skin gushed sweat from the rushing he'd been doing.

'Uhm, yes. Do you have food?'

'Food, yes, we have food.' The man looked at her peculiarly. 'Are you alone?'

Mirage nodded. 'That's right.'

The proprietor's smile was awkward. 'You're not looking for work, are you? I mean, you're not a . . .' His grin broke down. 'You know.'

'I certainly am not,' said Mirage indignantly. Flustered by the question, she thought again of leaving, but the man hurried an apology.

'No, of course you're not,' he said. 'Forgive me, but a lovely lady like yourself . . . well, you probably shouldn't be on your own, especially at night.'

'I have no choice,' Mirage replied. 'I'm in the city looking for some-one.'

Sympathy suffused the man's chubby face. 'Ah, the war. You've lost someone.' He looked suitably sad. 'Come, I'll find you a table away from the noise.'

When he turned, Mirage followed reluctantly. An empty table sat in the corner of the room, away from the worst of the men and commotion, beneath a quickly darkening window. The proprietor wiped the wooden chair with his towel and held it out for her. Mirage took her seat, glancing around. Not surprisingly, the men in the room noticed her. She averted her eyes.

'You've been on the road all day, I can tell,' said the barman. 'We have good food for you.'

'And beer,' added Mirage. She reached into her trousers and pulled out two more coins, one slightly larger than the other. 'Whatever this will buy.'

'That won't buy you much,' said the man. 'But you bring elegance to the Stallion, pretty thing like you. Don't worry – I'll take care of you.'

'Thank you,' said Mirage as the barman turned away. She sat back, trying to get comfortable while she waited for her meal, feeling remark-able suddenly. She was *free*. No longer tied to Lukien or the library, she could go anywhere she wanted, and not answer to anyone. During her long years in Grimhold, she had craved freedom, almost as much as she craved her old, unscarred face. Now she had both. She dared to look at the men in the room, noting with satisfaction the way they stared. They frightened her, yet it was so much better to see hunger in their eyes than revulsion.

But they're the enemy, she told herself. They conquered Liiria.

The bar girl brought her a tankard of beer and laid it sloshing on the table. She was gone in an instant, Mirage barely noticed her. She lifted the beer and tasted it while she scanned the tavern's patrons.

I'll have to live among them if Thorin will have me, she realized.

While Mirage drank she noticed a man in the opposite corner, looking at her. He sat alone, nursing his own tankard and spinning a coin on the tabletop. The taut skin around his face pulled back in a sharp smile when their eyes met. The man did not wear the uniform of a soldier but rather dressed himself in black, a long cape draped around his shoulders. He had a strangely familiar face. Mirage was sure she'd seen him before, probably at the library. Was he a Liirian, one of Breck's men? She was nearly certain she had seen him at the farm, where the survivors of the siege had fled, but she did not know his name or even remember speaking to him. The stranger's smile faded and he went back to spinning his coin.

If he was at the farm, what was he doing here, Mirage wondered? As though deliberately ignoring her curiosity, the man stood, pushed back his chair, and walked out of the Red Stallion, leaving his coin spinning on the table. He hadn't eaten – there were no dishes near his seat. Mirage wasn't even sure he'd been there when she entered. But when the proprietor finally brought her plate of food, she forgot about the stranger entirely.

'For you,' the man said proudly, laying down a feast of meat and bread. 'This should get your strength back and then some.'

Mirage nearly melted when she smelled the food, the odour of which rose up from the plate like a steaming bath. 'All this?' she exclaimed.

The man winked at her. 'Enjoy it. Stay as long as you like.'

Mirage picked up her fork and dug into the buttery beef. Already there were benefits to beauty, she realized, and she smiled secretly as she ate, her confidence soaring. Thorin would take her in, she was sure.

Mirage stayed in the Red Stallion for more than an hour, far longer than she intended, taking her leisure while the innkeeper occasionally refilled her tankard, free of charge. He was plainly smitten with her and stopped by to chat from time to time, mostly, he claimed, to protect her from the other patrons. Once they had got used to her, the Norvans in the tavern stopped leering and offered to buy her drinks, all of which Mirage politely refused. She also got dirty looks from the Stallion's prostitutes, but these she ignored as well, realizing none of them were a danger.

By the time she left the tavern the night had gone completely dark. The boy she had left outside with her horse had slumped into something like sleep at the edge of the cobblestone street. Mirage untied her horse without disturbing him, guiding it quietly down the lane. Her belly full, she felt wonderfully contented as she walked, lost in the effect of all the beer she had drank and loving the cool night air. The streets had thinned of people. A few soldiers straggled along, most of them mercenaries and most of them far more drunk then she. She was a long way from Lionkeep, and the dark streets intimidated her. Only the Red Stallion seemed open for business. The other shops and taverns were either abandoned or locked for the night. Mirage peered down the wide, gloomy avenue. Years ago the city had bustled with commerce, or so Lukien had told her. Now it was just a hulking corpse, with no spirit to animate it.

'Maybe we should go back,' Mirage whispered to her horse. The Red Stallion had rooms, and she was sure she could convince the kindly barkeep to give her one for the night. But despite the darkness it wasn't really late, so Mirage continued down the lane, away from the soldiers, until the merry noise of the tavern faded far behind her. Being a main thoroughfare, the street would take her toward Lionkeep, she was sure. After long minutes of walking, she reached a corner and paused, not sure which direction to take. Koth's tall buildings obscured her vision.

'West?' She thought for a moment. 'North?'

Straight would lead her down the same broad lane. Turning right led to a narrower, darker street, but it seemed to be the direction she wanted. She peered down the narrow street, focusing her eyes through the gloom. Koth's skyline beckoned darkly. She saw hills in the distance, bordering the city.

'That way,' she whispered, not liking the choice at all.

Then, she glimpsed something unusual in the road, draped in shadows, hidden by the neglected buildings. A horse. And a rider, facing her and not moving. Mirage caught her breath and froze. The snorting of the horse echoed down the lane. The mounted man barely stirred, nearly invisible in the blackness. His great beast clopped at the broken cobblestones. Mirage drew back, first one step than another, wondering if she'd been seen. As she moved the horseman flicked back his cape and took something from his belt.

'Do not run, girl,' he ordered. 'If you do it will be worse for you.'

Forgetting her horse, Mirage bolted back down the avenue. At once she heard the horseman pursue, his thundering mount coming fast behind her.

'Leave me alone!' she shouted. Up ahead the road was empty. 'Someone help me!'

Running made the world a blur, and soon Mirage felt the horseman's shadow. His gloved hand shot down, grabbing up her blond hair and yanking her back. She screamed as his cape fell over her eyes. His hands were everywhere, lifting her, jerking her up, then silencing her scream in smothering flesh. Mirage's head pounded with pain. An odour seared her mouth and lungs. She was in molasses suddenly, her body slack, her panicked thoughts quickly fading. Unable to stop her arms from dropping, Mirage sagged in the violent grip.

Mirage's consciousness waned swiftly. Before it fled, she heard the man again, happily triumphant, telling her to be a good girl.

She awoke to a thunderous headache and the world swaying beneath her. Heat stroked her skin, the feeling of sunlight on her burning neck. It was more than the usual pain in her flesh, and it awoke her with a gasp. Her eyes fluttered open, glimpsing the ground moving below her and the thick coat of her horse against her face. She fought the pain and fog, struggling to reason, to even raise her head.

'Where . . .'

The word dribbled from her dry lips. A foul flavour coated her mouth and throat, burning when she breathed. Forcing her eyes wider, she realized she was riding. Daylight streamed down from the sky and the sounds of horse hooves reached her ears.

Am I drunk?

She had been drunk before, but it had never hurt like this. Again she raised her head, straining against the nausea squeezing her skull. Another sharp pain grabbed her wrists, and she realized her hands were tied to the saddle. Startled, she bolted upright, then felt a rope around her waist as well, keeping her from tottering off her horse. The same panic from the night before overwhelmed her.

'What's this?' she moaned. 'What's happening?'

Up ahead sauntered another horse, huge and black. A caped rider straddled the beast, barely turning his head to regard her. Mirage knew instantly it was the man from the bar, then remembered the brutal way he'd chased her down. Fear rose up in her as she fought the bindings on her wrist. Her horse was tethered to the dark man's own, riding slowly along the deserted road.

'Tell me who you are,' she hissed, 'and what you're doing to me.'

'My name is Corvalos Chane,' said the man, 'and you are my prisoner.'

The unnerving casualness of the statement horrified Mirage. 'What?' The rope bit into her thrashing wrists. 'Prisoner?' Speaking took effort, and her words boomed in her aching head. She leaned forward to steady herself against her horse. 'What did you do to me?'

The man chuckled. 'It's an unpleasant feeling, I know.'

'You drugged me. You chased me down . . .'

Mirage could hardly talk or keep her head up. Sweat beaded on her forehead, stinging her eyes. They were not in Koth any more, or even anywhere near the city. An unfamiliar landscape of hills and conifers met her blurry gaze. The urge to vomit overwhelmed her.

'I'm going to be sick.'

'Then be sick.'

'Who are you?'

'I am Corvalos Chane.'

The useless answer broke Mirage's resistance. 'Please,' she cried, 'How can I be a prisoner? I didn't do anything!' Then another, more ghastly thought entered her mind. 'Gods . . . you're a slaver . . .'

Corvalos Chane shook his head but did not bother turning to look at her. 'Wrong.'

'What, then? You mean to rape me?'

'Will you wail like this all the way to Reec?'

Mirage tamed her breathing, trying to understand his riddles. 'You're taking me to Reec? Why?'

'Because I am a Reecian,' said Chane, as if that explained everything.

'I've done nothing!' Mirage raged. 'Listen to me, you're the man from the tavern, yes? You saw me there; you know I've done nothing wrong!'

'Is that why you recognize me? Because of the tavern?'

Mirage thought hard, pushing her puzzled mind past the pain. The harder she concentrated the sicker she got, but then she remembered what she had thought the night before, how she was sure she'd seen the man somewhere else.

'No,' she groaned. 'Or yes, maybe. I can't remember.'

Corvalos Chane, amused, laughed as he trotted along. 'I am good at making myself disappear. It's my job, you see. And the drug makes the mind weak. Think, and in time you will remember.'

'Tell me now, damn you!' Mirage glared at the back of his head. 'Turn around so I can look at you!'

At last the stranger brought his horse to a stop, letting Mirage's mount catch up a bit. He turned to regard her with his iron eyes. He was not a young man, but there was power in his frame like an unsprung catapult. Mirage could see the taut muscles beneath his tightly fitting tunic. His clean shaven face tilted with a jeering smile as he allowed her a close inspection. Through her swimming brain Mirage made the connection.

'I've seen you,' she said. 'You were at the farm.'

'And at the library before that,' said Chane.

'Yes, you were one of Breck's men.'

The stranger pretended to blush. 'Thank you. I'm an excellent actor.'

'I don't understand,' said Mirage. She was quickly losing stamina and longed to lay her head down. 'Please, tell me who you are. Tell me what you want from me.'

There was no pity on Chane's weathered face. 'Your name is Mirage,' he stated. 'You came to the library with the Bronze Knight.'

'That's right.'

24

'And you're a friend to Baron Glass. You were returning to Koth to see him.'

Mirage still didn't understand. 'Get to your point.'

'My point? You still can't figure it out? Why I was in the library, watching you and everyone else?'

'You're a Reecian,' Mirage sighed, trying to piece things together. 'You're a spy.'

Chane's face brightened. 'I love that word. But I'm not just a spy, pretty child. I am an artist. I do miraculous things to make people believe. I made Breck believe I was a Liirian, from Koth even, who wanted to fight with him.'

'But you were spying for the Reecians.' Mirage closed her eyes. Some of the tale began making sense. She knew the Reecians were watching Liiria, as well as Jazana Carr's Norvor. In the days before the siege, Breck had even hoped the Reecian king might aid them, but he never did. 'You fought for the Library, though,' she said. 'I saw you there.'

'I did,' admitted Chane. 'And I was proud to do it. Jazana Carr and her new lover are my enemies. That makes you an enemy of Reec as well.'

'What? I'm not even a Liirian. My family came from Jerikor . . .'

'But you came from Jador, looking for Baron Glass. Do not deny it, girl, for I know the truth of you. You are a friend to Baron Glass. All the others from the siege have fled, but not you. You've come back to find him.'

'Yes,' Mirage admitted. 'Because I have nowhere else to go.'

'Because you are his ally. That means you know about him. That means you are valuable.' Chane reached out and tapped her head. 'In here.'

'I don't know anything that can help you,' said Mirage miserably. 'You have to believe me. Please, I'm not what you think.'

Chane flicked his hand dismissively. 'I am not your interrogator, girl. You may tell your lies to Asher when we reach Reec. He will get the truth from you.'

'But there is no truth! Haven't you been listening? I don't know anything. I only came back here to save Thorin from the Devil's Armour.'

'Thorin?' Chane's smile stank of arrogance. 'You see how familiar you are with him? I know of the Devil's Armour, as you do.'

'It's not a secret,' spat Mirage.

'No, but you have knowledge of it. You are from Jador, just like the armour, and you have come to help your friend. You should hold your tongue, girl, at least until the drug wears down. You incriminate yourself with everything you say.'

Frustrated, Mirage pulled madly at her bindings, trying to rip free of the saddle. But Chane had bound her well by the waist and hands, and without a knife she had no way to cut free. And even if she did, then what? They were alone on the road, far from Koth now. Mirage forced herself to stay calm, to think of a way to convince Chane of her innocence.

'Listen to me,' she pleaded. 'You're right . . . I am a friend of Baron Glass. We were together in Jador.'

'I know this already.'

'Yes, you've been watching me. You watched everyone at the library, yes?'

'As I have said.' Chane looked bored. 'Continue.'

'Then you know the truth already. I'm just a friend to him, nothing more. And I can't go back to Jador. It's too far. That's why I was going to Thorin. Not to ally myself with him, but to save myself.' Mirage stopped herself before she went too far. There was no way she could reveal the whole truth to him, about Grimhold and its magic. Just mentioning magic would have her dissected when they reached Reec. She looked imploringly at her captor. 'A lot of people went to Jador, you know that. I was a Seeker,' she lied, 'just looking for a way to escape the war.'

'There is no war in Jerikor.'

Mirage caught herself. 'No, but my family died and I was afraid. I heard about the Seekers and joined them.'

'And then you went to Jador and found Baron Glass and befriended him.'

'That's right,' said Mirage. 'And that's all.'

'Lies.'

Chane finally turned and returned to riding, dragging Mirage's horse along.

'It's not a lie!' Mirage protested. 'It's the truth!'

'I saw you with the Bronze Knight at the library,' Chane said. 'The way you both talked, so secretly. You know more about Glass and his armour than you are telling me, girl. But never mind. I am the dark arm of Raxor. I will not fail my king. In the right hands you will yield your secrets.'

The statement chilled Mirage. 'You mean to torture me?'

'Not I, no.'

'Who then, damn you? Who is this Asher you spoke of?'

'We're very near the border. We will be in Reec soon enough.'

Mirage lost her fragile control as fear and nausea surged together. Unable to stop herself, she leaned out over her horse and retched.

Remarkably, Mirage fell asleep again. Her captor, Corvalos Chane, had hardly spoken at all over the next few hours, and the hot sun and sickness mingled to make her drowsy. Mirage's dreams were full of nightmares as they rode toward Reec. She dreamt of torture and iron bars, and of never seeing Lukien again. She had been foolish to try and find Thorin on her own. Her bad dreams echoed that realization, filled with images of Thorin laughing and calling her a whore. Her stomach, which she had filled to bursting the night before, had been thoroughly emptied by vomiting, but she had no appetite at all. In her groggy state of illness, she thought only of her dire plight.

Occasionally, Corvalos Chane stopped by a brook or pond to refresh their horses. He offered her water, which he forced down her throat when she refused to drink, but never untied her bindings to let her down from the horse. Mirage's spine and backside ached from the riding. Her skin burned with sunlight, and beneath her magic mask she felt the sting of her old wounds. Without Sarlvarian she could do nothing to stem the pain, and her new Akari was impotent to help. Through her sickly fugue, Mirage called to her.

Kirsil . . .

The Akari fluttered through her brain like a butterfly, just on the surface. She was a young Akari and not very powerful, just strong enough to change Mirage's appearance. A feeling of gentleness and comfort settled over Mirage as the spirit stroked her.

I am afraid, Kirsil.

There was nothing the Akari could do but comfort her. The sweet voice spoke like a lullaby.

I am with you, Mirage. You won't be alone.

Mirage began to weep. And Corvalos Chane, who heard her sobs, said nothing.

By the time twilight came, they had travelled many miles and came to the river Kryss, the ancient border between Liiria and Reec. Here they turned north, toward greater Reec and its capital, Hes. The sickness that had plagued Mirage the entire trip had finally passed, and the cool air coming off the wide river revived her. Her body continued to ache from the ride, but her appetite had at last returned. Still, she would not beg any favours of her cruel captive, not even a morsel of food. Mirage sat up as tall as she could, looking at the darkening horizon. They would never make it to the capital by nightfall. Hes was still days away. Expecting to bed down for the night, Mirage wondered what Chane would do with her while they slept.

'There,' said Chane. It was the first thing he'd said in hours and his voice startled Mirage. He sat up, peering northward, and sighed with contentment.

Curious, Mirage looked past him. Up ahead she saw a mass of lights and movement near the river bank. On the west side of the Kryss – the Reecian side – lay a large camp of men and tents and animals. Mirage's heart sank when she saw them. Red Reecian flags blew over the camp, still visible in the failing sunlight.

'Soldiers,' she whispered dreadfully.

'Reecians,' said Chane happily. 'Home.'

Mirage felt the familiar terror cresting. Ridiculously, she had hoped that they wouldn't make it this far, that something – or someone – would see her plight and rescue her. Now that silly notion fled like the wind, faced with an army of Reecians. There were hundreds of them, spread out along the riverside, armed with lances and armoured horses, prancing or huddling around cooking fires, waiting for night to fall. Waiting, Mirage suspected, for her.

'Those men – what are they doing here?' she asked.

'The same as me,' Chane replied. 'They are keeping an eye on Jazana Carr and your good friend Baron Glass.'

'An invasion?'

Chane laughed. 'If it comes to that. But not yet.'

'Why are you taking me there? What's going to happen to me?'

They continued riding, Chane refusing to answer her queries. The camp grew larger as they neared, finally crossing a bridge and entering Reecian territory. The simple act of fording the river snuffed Mirage's last hopes. Now she was in Reec. A handful of men dressed in Reecian uniforms greeted Chane as they rode into camp. They seemed to recognize him, at least by reputation. As they spotted Mirage they grinned. Chane halted both their horses and dismounted. Finally, he undid the rope binding their mounts together, then told one of the soldiers to care for his horse. At last he went to Mirage.

'What will happen to me? The man you called Asher – is he here in camp?'

Maybe it was the fear in her tone that made Chane finally soften. He shook his head. 'Asher never leaves Hes. This is just a resting place, girl.'

'Resting place? For how long?'

'Just a day or two.' Chane took out his dagger and cut the rope from around her belly. The soldiers around him stared with a mix of desire and curiosity. 'There are others going to Hes as well. We'll ride with them.'

Relieved, Mirage let out an imprisoned breath. But when she looked at all the men, waiting for her to dismount, she wilted. Chane shook his head slightly as he gestured for her to get down. It was a reassurance of sorts, an unspoken promise to protect her. It was the first real kindness he had shown her. Hesitantly, Mirage put out her bound hands and let her captor guide her down from the horse. The Reecians rushed in closer, but a bark from Chane kept them back.

'Leave her,' he ordered. 'She's mine.'

A single soldier with a silly grin stepped forward. 'Come on, Chane,' he joked. 'You can share her at least.'

Chane faced him, laughed at his joke, then kicked him sharply in the groin. The man bellowed in agony. As he collapsed, Chane snatched his hair and pulled his face closer.

'*Mine,*' he said menacingly. 'Got that?'

Twisted with pain, the soldier moaned his understanding. Chane dropped him, letting him fall. His fellows kept back. Chane looked at them each in turn.

'Find us a place to sleep for the night. And tell the company commander I want to see him. We'll be travelling on to Hes from here.'

The soldiers hurried off. Following them, Chane dragged Mirage deeper into the encampment, stepping past their crumpled comrade.

'I had to make a point of him,' he said. 'They've been out here too long, and seeing a pretty woman makes them crazy. They are jackals, some of them, but I am their tiger.'

Helpless, Mirage let Corvalos Chane take her into camp.

3

Jazana Carr's arrival in Koth was not what she expected.

After riding the one hundred miles from Andola, enduring rain and the usual hardships of the road, she came to the outskirts of the city at sundown, watching as the light disappeared behind the crumbling sky-line. It had been a four day ordeal to reach the Liirian capital and Jazana Carr was exhausted, slumped across the back of her horse, her damp hair dangling in strings in front of her runny eyes. The fifty men she had brought with her – all trusted Norvans from her own country – rode in two lines behind her, following their queen without complaint, and when at last they saw the city the train let out a happy exclaim. They could rest now, at last, and enjoy what little comfort Koth could offer. Yet Jazana Carr was disappointed. Her lover, Baron Glass, had not come out to meet her as expected. Instead, she saw a party of Norvan mercenaries riding toward her, led by the familiar figure of Rodrik Varl. Jazana sank a little. She adored Rodrik Varl but she hungered for Thorin, and the pain of his absence was like a knife in her.

Her party came to a stop in the muddy road as the small band of Norvans approached. Behind them, the city of Koth looked ill. Jazana had heard stories of the Liirian capital from the time she was a girl, about its grand buildings and vigour, and how it was a beacon for the world, spreading its wealth and influence to every far-off port. She had not expected its slack exterior, poisoned by war, drooping under the weight of its own great history. She felt sad as she looked at it, sad because she and Thorin had fought so hard for it, and sad because she knew – *knew*, without knowing why – that even her great fortune would not be enough to lift the city from its ashes.

'It's Varl,' said her man Garen, pointing toward the riders. He sidled closer to his queen, hoping to lighten her mood. 'You see, my lady? They come to greet us.'

Garen, a mercenary like Varl, had served Jazana loyally for years. She had hand-picked him to accompany her from Andola, another Liirian city they had conquered only months before. Jazana wondered what news Varl would bring her of Koth, and if the city was as quiet as it seemed. It had been only three weeks since the capital had fallen to their overwhelming army, and it surprised Jazana that reports of resistance and uprisings had been almost non-existent. A good omen, surely.

Rodrik Varl smiled broadly as he approached his queen. He lifted off his beret and placed it over his heart, bowing his red head. He was a handsome man who loved Jazana dearly. More than once he had confessed his love for her, but he was an underling – a hired lance. He was also Jazana's only friend. He led his horse up to her confidently, then gestured at the city behind him as if presenting her with a fabulous gift.

'My lady,' he said proudly. 'Welcome to Koth.'

Jazana barely hid her disappointment. 'Where's Baron Glass?'

Rodrik Varl's boyish grin slackened. 'In the city. Waiting for you.'

'I've ridden a hundred miles in the rain. I already hate this country. Could you not have told him I was here? I sent a herald, Rodrik.'

'Aye, and the Baron awaits you, my lady,' said Varl. The men accompanying him looked away. 'He's anxious to see you, I'm sure.'

His last words rung with anger; Jazana could sense his jealousy. Rodrik Varl had always vied with Thorin for her attention, but Thorin had won out, easily. She supposed she should at least show him some gratitude.

'Roddy,' she sighed, 'I'm tired.'

Varl smiled lightly. 'We've made every comfort ready for you, my lady. In Lionkeep.'

'Lionkeep? I thought it had burned.'

'Not all, my lady, no. A small fire, in the east wing. King Akeela's chambers were unharmed, and still splendid, I should say. You'll be right at home, I think.'

'A barb, Rodrik?' Jazana snorted in annoyance. 'Very well.' She looked up into the dark sky, wondering if the blackness masked more rain clouds. 'Take us there before the sky opens up again, if you please.'

Rodrik Varl nodded, then gave his queen a surreptitious look. 'Yes, my lady. If you'll ride ahead with me . . .'

He wanted to talk – privately. Jazana turned toward Garen. 'Almost there at last, Garen. Hold back a few paces, will you?'

Garen contained his smirk. 'Yes, my lady, we'll do that.'

Varl told his men to do the same and the small party joined the queen's own, allowing Jazana and Varl to ride off ahead. Too weary to hurry, Jazana let her horse canter slowly toward the vast city. Rodrik Varl kept pace with her, riding alongside. He said nothing until they were a good distance from the others, then finally spoke.

'I wanted to warn you,' he said.

Jazana glanced at him. 'Oh?'

'About Thorin.'

'I expected you to speak against him. But so soon? You surprise me.'

'Jazana, listen to me now . . . Thorin has changed since you saw him last. That armour he wears has maddened him. And he spends all day at the library—'

'Yes, the library! Would you like to explain that?' Jazana leered at him. 'Hmm?'

'Aye, it's true. I had my men attack the library. But to save lives, Jazana. Thorin would have slaughtered them to get what he wanted. He claims otherwise, but—'

'So you let them flee? We're trying to accomplish something here.'

'I let them go to save lives,' asserted Varl. 'Even you can't fault me for that.'

'Watch your tongue. I didn't want this war any more than you did. And I certainly didn't want to see those people slaughtered. But you're judging Thorin too harshly, and the library is too valuable to be destroyed. You had no right.'

Varl kept his eyes on the city as they rode, but the tension rising in him made his neck pulse. 'You're not listening. Thorin has changed.'

'So you've said.'

'And you refuse to hear me. Because you love him. Don't be blinded, Jazana.'

Jazana kept riding, unsure how to respond. Of all her thousands of soldiers, only Rodrik Varl talked to her so plainly. She allowed it because she cared for him, and because she knew the value of honest counsel. Worse, he was right; she could not face the truth about what had happened. She loved Thorin too much, had waited for him too long to let anything get between them.

'Thorin is a good man,' she said. 'He'll bring order to Liiria. He just needs time. And he needs our loyalty, Rodrik.'

Varl grimaced. 'Count Onikil was loyal. And I sat by and watched Thorin murder him.'

'Onikil was too ambitious.'

'That's a lie and you know it.'

Jazana didn't allow herself to think much about it. Count Onikil's murder had shocked her, but she had chosen to believe it was necessary.

'Thorin knows I have arrived, yes?'

'He knows. As I said, he awaits you.'

Jazana nodded. 'At Lionkeep.'

'No, Jazana.' Varl hesitated. 'Thorin is at the library.'

'Still? Why?'

'Because he spends every bloody moment there, alone in one of the chambers. The one with the machine.'

'Ah,' said Jazana, smiling slyly. It was the thinking machine that had first attracted her to Liiria. 'He has made progress with it?'

'None at all. He is most always in a foul mood and won't discuss it with anyone. And he has many of our men cleaning up the library, moving away the debris.'

'Which would be completely unnecessary if you hadn't tried to destroy the place.'

Rodrik Varl changed the subject. 'It is good to see you, my lady. Koth can do with your presence. Something pretty to liven it up. Now, what news from Norvor?'

'Bad news only,' replied Jazana. 'Trouble. Things to discuss with Thorin.'

'Rebellions,' said Varl. 'I've heard. I told you this would happen, Jazana.'

'Gods, I'm begging you not to lecture me, Rodrik.' Jazana rode her horse a little harder, a little faster toward the city. 'I need rest. And I need to see Thorin. No more talk. Tomorrow, when I am stronger.'

She did not say another word, but instead rode into Koth, anticipating her reunion with Baron Glass.

Alone in a warm, windowless room, Baron Thorin Glass sat on a plain wooden chair and stared at the vast contraption before him. Stale air wafted up his nostrils and his eyes burned from the smoke of a trio of candles, the only light penetrating the chamber. A great, brooding silence surrounded him. In the candlelight, the contraption glowed. Its vast network of armatures – like the legs of a hundred giant spiders, disappeared into the darkness. It took a giant room to contain the machine, and Baron Glass could barely see the end of it. Before him sat a console, a flat desk of worn wood curved up at the edge. Once, the console had been used to hold books for reading, but now it had been fitted with a rectangular hole ringed with iron. Inside the hole was a box, and inside the box were small metal squares that the machine had long ago punched with answers. Similar squares littered the room, stacked in corners and on shelves, the arcane answers to a thousand questions. In all of the great library, an edifice filled with knowledge, this room alone held the place's greatest prize. A machine that could *think*. And nowhere, not in the millions of papers housed in the library, had Baron Glass discovered a single word about its use. The machine had vexed him since he'd arrived, tantalizing him with its gleaming armatures and sprockets, the sheer complexity of its construction. Housed in its own huge chamber, the machine had been blessedly unharmed in the bombardment that had so ruined the rest of the library. Yet though it was undamaged, Baron Glass had been unable to make the thing respond. Despite hours spent studying the machine, he had not even been able to make it move, not even the smallest degree.

Essentially, the machine was a catalogue. That's what Gilwyn had told him back in Jador. Figgis, Gilwyn's dead mentor, had built the machine himself. An unquestionable genius, it was Figgis who had overseen the library's construction for King Akeela, and it was Figgis who had filled it with countless volumes. Then, seeing the need to catalogue the gigantic sums of information, Figgis had somehow made his miraculous machine. According to Gilwyn, every scrap of intelligence within the library was somehow contained within its endless network of rods and spinning plates. If asked a question, the machine could answer, punching out its inscrutable replies on the metal squares that were everywhere in the room.

At least theoretically.

Baron Glass leaned back on the chair and breathed the warm air. The door to the chamber remained locked behind him, preventing unwanted visitors. Figgis' catalogue machine was too great a prize to be shared with anyone. Worse, the confounding machine had brought Baron Glass to the edge of exhaustion. Only the armour encasing his missing arm gave him strength, allowing him to work through the night without sleep or go days without food. The Devil's Armour – only a small part of which he now wore – had given him the eyes of a hawk and the vitality of ten men. He was more than a man now, because Kahldris shared his mind and body. In many ways, he was invincible. But he was not infallible or a genius like Figgis, and he realized that he alone would never make the machine run.

Baron Glass closed his eyes and felt the touch of Kahldris on his shoulder. The ancient Akari had been with him throughout the day, guiding him, lending his own peculiar sciences to the task. In life, ages ago, Kahldris had been a great Akari summoner. Like a sorcerer, he could speak with the dead, and upon his own death had encased himself in the armour. Not a blade existed that could scratch his creation, and when he wore the armour Baron Glass knew immortality. Kahldris had renewed Baron Glass. The Akari had given him the strength to ride back from Jador and reclaim his troubled homeland. With Jazana Carr they had conquered Koth, and now had armies marching on other Liirian cities as well. Liiria belonged to Baron Glass.

Still, Kahldris knew no satiety.

Thorin opened his eyes. Turning, he saw the demon standing behind him. Kahldris's ethereal hand felt cold on his shoulder. He did not appear in armour, the way he had in Thorin's dreams. Instead he wore a glowing tunic and wide leather belt, shimmering the way a ghost might in the darkness. Through him, Thorin could see the wall beyond. He was not a young man; he had 'died' when he was fully mature. Straight, white hair fell neatly around his shoulders. Ancient lines edged his face. His cool eyes sparkled with unearthly light as he regarded Thorin. It was not normal for an Akari to appear this way to a host; Thorin knew that much about Akari lore. But Kahldris was unlike his brethren.

'We must continue.'

The spirit's voice was like an echo, wide and ringing, sounding as much in Thorin's mind as it did in the dark chamber. Thorin wasn't even sure it was sound at all. Like everything about the spirit, it seemed unreal. He nodded, acknowledging the Akari's command.

'We will go on,' said Thorin, 'but I don't know where to start. I have tried, Kahldris. Without the boy to help me . . .' Thorin shrugged. 'It may be impossible.'

Kahldris drifted closer to the machine, inspecting its odd construction. His people – the long dead Akari – had been scientists and architects, but Kahldris confessed he had never seen the like of the machine before. Its potential fascinated him. Somehow, according to Gilwyn Toms, it had helped to locate the Eyes of God. To Kahldris that seemed like a miracle. Surely, then, it could locate his brother.

'I still cannot sense the boy,' said Kahldris.

The news worried Thorin. He knew that Kahldris had lured Gilwyn north to the library, though the Akari had refused to explain how. But for days now Kahldris had been unable to feel Gilwyn's presence, despite exhausting attempts. It was not at all easy for Kahldris to stretch himself across the dimensions, and he did so only reluctantly. Always weakened by the efforts, he had so far been unable to locate Gilwyn.

'If he is dead . . .' Kahldris shook his white head in frustration. 'Then this machine will be useless to us.'

'He is not dead,' grumbled Thorin. 'He is blocking himself from you, surely.'

'Such a thing would take great ability. Too much for the boy. He is not on this realm, Baron Glass.' Kahldris moved his hands over the machine, caressing one of its long, peculiar rods. 'This great puzzle might be ours to unravel. Alone.'

Thorin considered the enormous task. There was power in the machine but only Figgis had been able to use it, and he was long dead. He had passed some instruction on its use to Gilwyn, or so Gilwyn had claimed, and that was why Kahldris had lured the boy out of Jador. Perhaps to his demise. The thought wrecked Thorin. He loved Gilwyn like a son, had done everything he could to protect him. And he would not allow the demon to harm the boy; he had made that clear to Kahldris numerous times. But Kahldris needed Gilwyn, and because Thorin needed Kahldris he had agreed to the unsavoury plot. They would use Gilwyn and make him operate the machine. And then they would find Kahldris' brother, the only Akari capable of destroying him and his invincible armour.

Thorin had seen Kahldris' brother once before, in a vision when he had first stolen the Devil's Armour. Kahldris had forced him to watch, to make him understand their bitter relationship. Kahldris had forged the Devil's Armour for his brother, so that his brother might defeat the invading armies of Jador. And his brother had promised to wear the armour in battle – but never did. He had simply left Kahldris locked away inside the miraculous metal suit, unwanted, scorned by the other Akari, even while the Jadori slaughtered them.

Still, Kahldris' brother lived on. Somewhere. Because he was an Akari he did not die like the last rose of summer. Hidden for millennia, he had survived.

'Yes, Baron Glass, but where?' asked Kahldris, easily reading Thorin's mind. The demon grew frustrated, his old eyes sparking with rage. 'I have waited a thousand forevers to find him, and now the means sits here before me. I must find the damnable key to open it!'

'Gilwyn is alive,' Thorin asserted. 'And he will help me if I ask him.'

'He will help us or he will suffer.'

Thorin rose to his feet. 'You won't harm him.'

The visage of Kahldris wavered under Thorin's withering glare. 'Baron Glass, we must have the means to protect ourselves. You are special now. The laws of normal men do not apply to you.'

'I have already murdered for you, demon.'

'And I have given you so much!' Kahldris came to stand before the baron, his strange body rifling through angry colours. 'Not just your arm, not just your manhood. A kingdom I have delivered you!'

'You will not harm Gilwyn,' said Thorin evenly.

'Bah! He is already harmed.' Kahldris turned his frightening face away, staring absently into the darkness. The long days of effort had made him sullen. 'He holds the secret of this thing, Baron Glass – the only means to find my brother. I cannot stretch myself far enough to find him. Wherever Malator hides, it is beyond me.' He came closer again, this time touching Thorin's arm, the arm that had been missing for decades. Now encased in the fabulous armour, the arm held life again. 'I will give you everything your heart desires. You worry about the enemies on the border but you must trust me. They are nothing. They cannot even nick you. But my brother can bring an end to everything, Baron Glass. You must not let fondness weaken you.'

Thorin stared into Kahldris' imploring gaze. It was not like looking at a man. If one could see heaven and hell, that was Kahldris.

'I will make Gilwyn understand,' Thorin promised.

At last, Kahldris nodded. He surprised the baron by showing something like grief. 'You do not know what it is like to be betrayed by a brother, Baron Glass,' he said in a sanguine voice. 'We could have saved our whole world.'

Thorin sympathized with the demon. It was why Kahldris hated the Jadori so much, and why he hated his brother, too. He wondered why the other Akari had feared him, when his motives seemed so pure.

'But,' added Kahldris, 'we will not let the same thing happen to Liiria. We will save Liiria, Baron Glass. You and I together.'

'Yes,' Thorin agreed. Again he felt that inexplicable bond. 'If this machine really works as promised, we'll find Malator.'

Before he could return to his chair, a knock at the door intruded. Thorin hesitated before answering, watching as Kahldris dissolved from view. Suddenly alone, he went to the door, turned the lock and opened it a crack, just enough to see a trio of Norvan soldiers waiting there. The men looked nervous, as if they knew the stupidity of interrupting him.

'What is it?' Thorin asked.

The young man in the lead spoke up. 'News, my lord, from Lionkeep. Jazana Carr has arrived. She awaits you at the keep.'

Thorin opened the door all the way, pleased at the news. 'Then why look so gloomy? That is excellent news!' He laughed delightedly. 'Fetch my horse at once. Tell the queen I'm on my way.'

Happy to be dismissed, the three Norvans scurried off to do the baron's bidding. Thorin waited in the threshold for them to go, then turned back to the catalogue machine. Tonight, at least, his work would have to wait.

The woman?

It was Kahldris again, this time speaking in his mind. Thorin felt his growing appetite.

'I'm going to her,' said Thorin. 'We can return here tomorrow.'

The demon filled Thorin with lusty energy. *Indeed, Baron Glass,* he crooned. *We are men, after all.*

Jazana Carr waited more than an hour for Thorin to arrive, standing under a wall of torches near Lionkeep's ancient gate. She had rested, briefly, but had not eaten or changed her clothes. She was too anxious to see her lover and nothing could keep her inside, not even the promise of food and a warm bed. Rodrik Varl waited with her in the quiet courtyard. The mercenary had already made arrangements for the fifty men that had accompanied the queen from Andola, and Jazana herself had dismissed Garen and her other protectors, preferring instead to wait for Thorin alone with Rodrik. Her stomach tripped like a school girl's at the prospect of seeing him. It had been almost a month, corresponding through letters and the occasional messenger, promising each other in love notes that they would soon be together.

Interestingly, Lionkeep was much as Thorin had described it. When Thorin had been a true nobleman of Liiria – nearly twenty years ago now – he had spent countless hours in the keep, arguing with King Balak and later his son, Akeela. Once it had been grand, like everything else in the old city, but time had eroded its vaunted beauty, leaving a kind of sad ghost behind. Still, the keep impressed Jazana Carr, for despite neglect and the recent fire it remained oddly stupendous, a lovely relic of a bygone age. Now, Lionkeep would be Thorin's home. When he was not with her in Andola or Hanging Man or Carlion or any other of a dozen conquered cities he would rule from this ancient edifice, the way he had always dreamed.

Jazana looked up into the sky and saw the moon struggling through the clouds. The courtyard echoed with the sounds of night and the constant groans of the city. The keep itself was on the outskirts of Koth, over-looking the city and braced by rows and rows of gardens and orchards. Jazana tried to see the gardens from the courtyard, peering through the gloom and oily torchlight. Tomorrow she would walk through them, she resolved, and tell Thorin about the troubles plaguing Norvor. So far, she had not even confessed these things to Rodrik Varl. She stole a glance at him, standing a pace or two away from her, quietly keeping her company as he puffed on a fragrant pipe. He smiled, sensing her eyes on him.

'He'll be here,' quipped the mercenary.

'I wasn't thinking that,' replied Jazana peevishly. 'I was thinking of—'
She stopped herself, but too late.

'What?' Varl asked, turning toward her. He took the pipe out of his mouth, waiting for her answer.

'Home,' said Jazana. 'The way you're standing there reminds me of it.'
She felt childish suddenly, as if she'd just confessed something ridiculous. 'This isn't our home. We belong in Norvor.'

Varl looked troubled. 'Now that surprises me. What will you tell Thorin? He expects—'

A call from across the yard cut off Varl's words. He and Jazana twisted to see a horseman riding quickly toward them. Jazana's heart leapt at the sight, so beautiful in the orange glow. Moonlight dappled Thorin as he rode, playing off his armoured arm, glistening with unholy blackness. He had come alone, without a single bodyguard. His smile beamed at Jazana, then shrank when he noticed Rodrik Varl. Varl put his pipe back in his teeth and bit down hard as Thorin rode up, jerking back his horse and staring at Jazana. She gazed up at him, and for a moment could not speak. He simply looked magnificent, much younger, with a confident vigour that hadn't been in him a month ago. His eyes dazzled her, mesmerizing her with their magic, and for the briefest moment the Diamond Queen felt afraid, for she knew it was Jadori sorcery that animated her lover, born of his strange armour. But then, when he spoke, her fear fled.

'Jazana,' he sighed. 'My love.'

She stepped up to him, leaving Varl behind, staring into his strong face. Her hand reached out to touch him, and when he lowered his own hand she grabbed it, putting it to her face.

'My love,' she echoed. Overwhelmed, she tried not to weep, closing her eyes against the flood of emotion. From atop his snorting horse, he bent to stroke her cheek.

'Great Fate, how I have longed for you,' he whispered. 'So beautiful . . . you have haunted my dreams, Jazana!'

'Come down,' she urged, pulling his hand. 'Come inside with me now.'

Thorin glanced around the courtyard. His eyes came to rest on Rodrik Varl. He grimaced, then shook his head. 'No. I want to be alone with you.'

Jazana laughed, confused. 'We are alone, Thorin! At last we are together! Come down and greet me properly . . .'

Her lover grinned, and at first Jazana did not recognize the strange look in his eyes. He pulled her powerfully toward him, lifting her from her feet then using his other arm to scoop her body up. Jazana cried in alarm, then found herself looking up into Thorin's shadowed face. And then she knew what it was in his eyes – strapping, unbridled lust. Unable to stop herself, she felt her body yield to him, wilting in the cradle of his grasp. Her arms wrapped around his neck as his head bowed to kiss her. The world fell away as their lips met.

He held her like that for a long moment. Jazana trembled in his arms. She saw Rodrik Varl watching her in shock, the pipe slack in his mouth.

'Where are you taking me?' she asked Thorin.

'Away,' was all he would answer. He lowered her to the saddle, allowing her to sit in front of him on the beast. She leaned back to nest against his chest. She didn't even bother waving to Rodrik Varl as Thorin sped off, spiriting out of the courtyard toward the dark gardens. At once blackness blanketed her eyes. She strained to see in the feeble moonlight, catching glimpses of tangled vines and misshapen trees as they bounded down a narrow lane. Thorin moved with ease, unencumbered by the darkness. Confident that he would not harm her, Jazana allowed herself to relax. The cool night air struck her face and made her hair blow back against Thorin. He stuck his nose into it and took a deep breath, smelling her lilac scent and growling.

'Thorin, tell me now,' she goaded. 'Where are we going?'

Thorin laughed, 'You are dressed for riding, my lady! I am taking you for a ride!'

'I have ridden all day,' she cried. 'I want to rest. I want to see you, Thorin!'

'Wait, my dear,' he crooned in her ear. 'We shall see *all* of each other soon.'

She knew what he meant and it thrilled her. The sweet air made her pulse race. The horse continued deeper into the gardens, letting Lionkeep fall far into the distance. Up ahead, Jazana spied long lines of apple trees as they neared an orchard, spread out like a huge, rolling blanket. The perfectly spaced trees let the moonlight seep between them, lighting the loamy earth. At last Thorin drew back the reins to stop his horse. And all fell silent.

Jazana waited, hardly breathing, spying their bare surroundings. Even in the darkness the orchard was beautiful, overgrown now but still like a sliver of heaven. She could feel Thorin's heart pounding against her back. His hand – the one of flesh – touched her neck.

'Thorin . . .'

'Hush.'

He kissed her neck, nearly biting her tender skin. His hard breathing reached her ear, full of thirst.

'We should get down from the horse, at least,' she joked, her own appetites quickly rising. Thorin tossed himself down from the steed's back, then reached up and took her by the waist as she slid into his arms. He led her away from the horse, near the stand of trees. The damp earth glistened. Thorin tore the cape from his shoulders and laid it over the grass, then pulled her down onto it.

His armoured hand worked her buttons, snapping the threads as he pulled open her riding shirt. His face thrust itself against her, searching for her breasts. Jazana's fingers clawed his back. She became lost in him, smothered by his strong body. The cool air braced her naked skin as he peeled free her clothing. His own shirt came off in a grunt of lust. Tossing it over his shoulder, once again he fell on her.

For a month now Jazana had craved this moment. Her body opened to it like a flower.

Exhausted, Jazana opened her eyes.

For a moment she had been dreaming of drowning in cold water. But it was only the rain, which had begun again to fall in cool drops. She felt warm in Thorin's embrace, wrapped in his cape and sheltering arms. He was already awake and turned his eyes on her. His smile spoke of his satisfaction, but he did not say a word. The orchard remained dark. Jazana Carr did not know how long they had slept or how many times they had made love. Her hair drooped over her wet face, matted with rain water and bits of grass. Shreds of her shirt covered her shoulders, and her riding trousers were soaked, laying an embarrassing distance away. The apple tree they lay under shielded some of the rain. Jazana thought she should be cold, but wasn't. Thorin's body warmed her like a hearth.

'It will be morning soon,' she whispered. Then she puzzled. 'I think.'

Thorin put her head down on his chest. Wiry hairs tickled her cheek. 'We can watch the sunrise.'

It seemed an absurd notion, so romantic and unlike him. Jazana barely stirred. Part of her wanted to return to Lionkeep, to get dry or take a hot bath. More powerfully, though, she wanted to lie with him forever. At last they were alone, completely, without spies or bodyguards to bother them. They could be silly and whisper like children to each other.

'Thorin, I'm happy,' she said softly. She kept her head on his warm chest, her hand tucked beneath him. 'I want it to be like this forever.'

'It will be, my love.' Thorin bent to kiss her hair. 'Now that you're here, everything is perfect.'

Jazana hesitated. She had planned to speak with him at Lionkeep, perhaps over supper, but she would never have a better time, with no one around and Thorin already in a fine mood.

'I can't stay,' she said.

Thorin stopped breathing for a moment, then lifted himself off the ground a little. She looked at him, resting her chin on his shoulder.

'You can't?' he asked. 'Why not?'

'There's no good time to tell you this, but Norvor needs me, Thorin. There's trouble back home and I need to be there.'

'What trouble? Rebellion?' Thorin laughed, trying to ease her worry. 'I have heard these stories already, my love. It is as I have told you – these skirmishes happen always. Men are ambitious.'

Jazana sat up to confront him, pulling the wet cape over her bosom. 'No, Thorin, it's worse than you think. I get reports from Andola every week. They say that in Carlion men are following Elgan now. My own capital! They wait for Lorn to return. They say I am not their queen. I need to return, Thorin. My people need to see me.'

'But I need you here, Jazana,' Thorin said, putting his hand to her face. His long fingers brushed her skin. 'You make me strong, and I need to be strong for the work ahead.'

'Will you listen to me, my love? Elgan has a movement now. The loyalists to Lorn are growing everyday. They say I have abandoned them. They call me the Whore-Queen.'

Thorin's eyes flashed. 'They should die for the things they say about you. And they will, my love, all in time. But for now we have Liiria to secure. Let Lord Gondoir and the others deal with Elgan. He is nothing but a gnat and I am sure your men can deal with him.'

'They have tried, Thorin,' said Jazana hopelessly. 'Gondoir tells me he has Carlion in control, but Elgan hides in the mountains around the city, waiting for Lorn to return and—'

'Lorn will never return, Jazana. He has gone to Jador.'

Jazana nodded, though the story hardly comforted her. It had taken time for Thorin to confess this to her, because he knew the news would trouble her. King Lorn the Wicked had indeed escaped her death-trap in Norvor, and had gone to Jador seeking magic to save his infirm daughter. He had even spent time in the library before its fall. Thorin himself had never encountered Lorn, but he had learned about him from Breck and the other defenders at the library, Thorin's own son Aric among them. Jazana wondered if Thorin was thinking of Aric now.

'Lorn still has power,' lamented Jazana. Now she grew chilled and nestled closer to her lover. 'They know he's alive. He was a tyrant and a butcher and yet they want him back, and they see me here in Liiria. My people think I have abandoned them, Thorin.'

'With all your wealth, all you have bought them . . .' Thorin shook his head, exasperated. 'If they want Lorn back then they do not deserve you, my love.'

'They are my people, Thorin. And I must keep my promise to them.'

'But you have!' said Thorin, sitting up suddenly. 'You have given everything to Norvor. You freed them from Lorn, ended the famine and the war. And they repay you with treason?'

'No, not all of them,' Jazana corrected. 'Just some. Just Elgan and a few others.'

'And who is this Elgan to challenge you? Nothing! A minor noble.'

'A friend to Lorn, and as loyal as the day is long,' said Jazana miserably. 'I've tried to convince him, but he won't have a woman govern him.'

'Then he'll die,' Thorin growled. 'When I am through here I will ride to Carlion myself and smoke him out of whatever hole he's hiding in. And then I will cut out his heart and eat it.'

Jazana leaned back against the tree, the wet bark scratching her naked back. It was true that Elgan was only a gnat now, but insects like him had a way of chewing up entire houses. And in truth, Jazana longed to return home. She missed Norvor, and hated what her pride had led her into. It was pride that made her launch the war on Liiria, all to draw her beloved Thorin out of hiding.

'I don't want to ignore this problem, Thorin. I'm not asking you to come with me, but I must return to Norvor myself.'

'No, not yet,' said Thorin.

'Soon, then.'

They looked at each other. Thorin's features grew troubled. 'Not too soon, Jazana. I need you with me. Do you hear? I need you.'

She inched closer, putting her arm around his neck and pulling him near. 'Because you feel alone? Because you're thinking of your son?'

'No.' Thorin let her kiss his forehead. 'I do not think about Aric. He is with the traitors now, or dead.'

'It is all right to be thinking of him, Thorin, and I can always tell when you're lying. You're troubled. Do you miss him?'

'Of course I miss him,' Thorin admitted. 'He's my son. I thought we were finally together again.' For a moment, the dark mask that covered his face evaporated, and Jazana glimpsed the old, sweet man he had been. 'I call him a traitor, but I should not. He's young. He just doesn't understand.' Thorin smiled. 'Only you understand, Jazana. You're the one who gives me strength. I need strength now, because my enemies are everywhere.'

'What enemies?'

'On the border, near Reec. King Raxor has men stationed on the Kryss. There aren't many of them yet but they grow in numbers. At first I thought they meant to spy on us, but I know better now. They mean to invade, Jazana, to topple us, you and me both.'

Jazana grimaced at the news. 'You're sure of this? They could be defending themselves, Thorin. In their eyes we're the invaders.'

Thorin shook his head. 'Raxor is cunning. I know him from years ago, and he's a man that holds a grudge. He was never as peace-minded as his brother, and when Akeela made the treaty with Karis, Raxor was against it.'

'As were you,' Jazana reminded him.

'True, because I didn't trust the Reecians then and I do not trust them now. They mean to destroy us, Jazana, and I will not let that happen. I need troops to defeat them, troops and money.'

He paused, looking at her straight. Jazana got his meaning.

'Troops and money from Norvor, you mean.'

Thorin smiled crookedly. 'We cannot spread our forces too thinly, my love. Gondoir is doing well in Carlion. He and Manjek and the other lords can deal with Norvor while you are gone. Elgan is hardly a threat, after all. But the rest of our men must remain here in Koth. The city needs protection, and Raxor must know that we are strong. You see that, don't you, Jazana?'

The queen gave a grudging nod. 'I do,' she admitted. 'But we cannot forget Norvor, Thorin. I must have your promise that you will deal with Elgan soon.'

'Soon, yes,' Thorin agreed. 'When this business with Reec is done and Liiria is secure, I will ride with you to Norvor and deal with Elgan myself.' He took her hand and kissed it. 'But you will stay with me, won't you?'

Feeling torn between the two things she loved the most, it took a moment for Jazana to reply. She loved Norvor; she had fought for it for years, and now that it was hers she could not let it slip away. Somehow, though, she convinced herself that Thorin was right. Elgan *was* a minor noble, and she had enough forces in place to deal with him.

'Promise me that Norvor will not slip away,' she begged. 'Promise me that Lorn will never return. If you promise those things, I will stay.'

Baron Glass, naked in the darkness, lay before her confident and unashamed. Squeezing her hand, he said, 'I promise it, my lady. Norvor is yours, and no one shall take it from you. Not even Lorn the Wicked, wherever he is hiding.'

Relieved, Jazana leaned back again against the tree. His words comforted her, as did his very presence, so solid she knew it would never break. She spoke a soft thank you to Thorin, then watched as the eastern horizon began to glow with the first inklings of morning.

4

A lonely man sat upon his dust-laden horse, peering through his single eye, pondering the dead city rising before him. His body, worn thin from hunger and endless days of solitary riding, bore the dirt of a thousand roads and the countless, nameless towns he had encountered. A month of beard sprouted from his face. His battered leather jerkin bore stains of sweat and sand. Beneath his shirt he wore an amulet hidden from view, priceless and ancient, its gold encrusted jewel pulsing with unnatural light, a light that had kept its weary bearer alive despite mortal wounds and a body desperate to collapse. The rider drew a breath, unsure what he was seeing. He had ridden for days without seeing a soul, not even the hint of human habitation, and the visage of the city startled him. Across the rugged plains he heard the wind whisper in the grasses, but from the city he heard nothing. From his place in the tall weeds the city appeared a purplish-black, a broken silhouette with the sun dropping behind it. His long hair – once blond but streaked with grey now – stirred in the breeze as he studied the city. The city had died millennia ago, along with the race that had built it. Its towers and tall aqueducts crumbled in the failing light. Vermin and shrubs had overtaken its deserted streets.

Lukien, the Bronze Knight of Liiria, looked upon the city and was silent. Dreams had guided him here, but he knew the city was not the Serpent Kingdom, the object of his quest. The city was Akari. Finally, his long journey was nearing its end. Lukien took water from the canteen at his saddle, carefully drinking the precious stuff. Beyond the city he could see forests, lush and alive, and he knew that there would be streams there and game to hunt. In the shadow of the sad ruins, he felt grateful for the shade. It had been a mercilessly long journey from Liiria and he had endured every hardship to get this far. Driven on by dreams he could not explain, he had ridden south and east, through Marn and the nations of the continent, then on through the badlands bordering the Desert of Tears, into lands that would not welcome him and did not speak his northern tongue. Against hunger and thirst and crushing loneliness, he had left behind civilization, riding here to the end of the world.

And he did not know why, except for the dreams.

Lukien's body had mostly healed in the weeks since leaving Liiria. His battle with Baron Glass had left him near death, but the amulet around his neck had snatched him from the grave. His body was stronger now, though desperately weary, and he knew that Amaraz, the spirit in the amulet, had not only saved him but had gifted him with the dreams. Each night when he lay himself down, Lukien heard the words in his mind, urging him westward, pointing him in directions he would not have guessed to travel. Because of the dreams he knew which roads to take and which stars to follow. At last he put his hand over his chest, feeling the Eye of God beneath his jerkin.

'Is this what you wanted me to see?'

The great Akari Amaraz, encased within the Eye, Amaraz did not respond.

'I know it is,' Lukien told the spirit spitefully. 'Be silent, then.'

He did not know why Amaraz always ignored him, or why the Akari had spoken to him in dreams instead. Perhaps Minikin might know, but he had not seen her for entire seasons, nor sought her counsel in the matter of the sword. He had only his vision of Cassandra to guide him. And the dreams.

Thinking of Cassandra now, his heart broke once more. It was she that had told him of the Sword of Angels. After his battle with Lorn, his body shattered and dying, she had appeared to him. They had actually talked, like living people, and looked into each others' eyes. She had told him that only this strange weapon could defeat the Devil's Armour. She had been the first to guide him this way.

'Beyond the desert . . .'

He was well beyond the desert now, he knew. Beyond Grimhold and Jador too. All because the dreams had told him where to go. Sadly, Cassandra had not come to him again, but Lukien knew she was with him. Death was just a veil, and beyond it was Cassandra, waiting for him.

'And when this is done, Amaraz, I will see her again.'

He partly expected the Akari to rage at his oath, the way Cassandra had. He would find the Sword of Angels and he would defeat Baron Glass, and when that was done he would strip away his hated amulet and join his beloved in death.

'But not today.'

Today he had the city to explore. With daylight quickly fading, Lukien pressed onward. His weary horse eyed the city suspiciously as he trotted over the hard grassland. Behind them, the world stretched forever with similar features, nearly barren and devoid of people, but up ahead the lushness of the forest called to the horse, urging it forward. As they neared the city, Lukien spied the fabled architecture of the Akari. They had been a race of scientists and sorcerers, a people who had worshipped knowledge and had built great monuments to it. The city itself was at least the size of Koth. In its day it had no doubt dominated this part of the world.

Until the rise of the Jadori.

How far was Jador, Lukien wondered? He knew that the Jadori had ridden their kreels to this place and had vanquished the Akari. Lukien turned his gaze south, knowing that somewhere, lost over the horizon, lay Jador. His heart ached to return there. He looked toward the city and imagined the battle. On this very plain, his peace-loving Jadori had murdered countless Akari, and if he tried very hard Lukien could hear their ghosts on the breeze. Before him, a great, twisting tower rose up, stretching its shadow over him. He entered the city to the sounds of his own breathing and the clip-clop of his horse on the ancient paving stones. There he stopped again, unsure where to go.

The city was called Kaliatha, and every Inhuman and Jadori knew of it. None had ever returned, though, not even Minikin. It was a holy place to some, worthy of avoidance. Distance and rugged terrain had sealed it off from the rest of the world, and as Lukien gazed upon its decayed splendour he realized that he alone was the only person to have looked on it for centuries. The notion staggered him. His eyes bounced from one magnificent edifice to the next, all crumbling yet all somehow remarkably whole, still standing against the brutal elements. An empty gathering square greeted Lukien, a round collection of polished stones surrounded by archways and long-closed shops. Near the square stood a dried-out fountain. Statues of beautiful men and women lined the square, most missing limbs but all with the same exquisite Akari faces. Enchanted, Lukien guided his horse closer, inspecting the figures one by one. A woman in a gown with one breast exposed studied a dove perched on her finger. An imposing soldier reared back on a snorting horse, trampling a reptile beneath his angry hooves. Lukien paused to stare at the reptile, thinking it a dragon at first.

'A kreel,' he whispered in amazement. He smiled, delighted with the sculpture and wondering what Gilwyn would think of it. He continued, and soon came across a statue smaller than the rest, of a tiny girl at prayer. Locked forever in a kneel, her eyes eternally closed, she seemed perfect in the square, totally silent and reverent. Lukien moved on.

Deeper into the city, he left the square behind and entered an avenue of homes and overgrown, abandoned gardens. With daylight quickly fading, he considered going into one of the homes for shelter, but then decided against it. None of them looked particularly stable, and the thought of being surrounded by ghosts unnerved him. He stopped his horse at the gate of one of the homes, somewhat grander than the rest, with a large garden out front and the pillars of a gate, the wood from which had long ago turned to dust. Lukien dismounted, studying the place as he tied his mount to one of the pillars. The two-story structure held the familiar markings of Akari architecture, with long, graceful arches and rounded turrets. A rich man's house, Lukien supposed. The garden itself was at least a half an acre in size and studded with tall trees that had grown up through the carefully laid bricks. Birds nested in the trees. For the first time, Lukien noticed their songs.

'Here, then,' he declared, supposing it as good a spot as any to wait out the night. He could not make it through the city in the dark, and he was bone-tired from his long day of riding. Tomorrow he would continue on, searching for the Serpent King, but tonight he would rest among the Akari ruins. And, if he was lucky, he would have another dream to light his way. Deciding to explore the garden before settling down, he walked to the threshold of the old home. Where once a wooden door had stood, now only iron hinges hung, uselessly rusted. Lukien peered inside.

'Hello?'

The darkened interior echoed with a cavernous yawn. Lukien didn't bother stepping inside. In his younger days he might have enjoyed exploring the home, but now he was tired, and the emptiness of the place only made him feel more alone. He retreated from the threshold, stepping back into the garden. An iron trestle, rusted and dilapidated, caught his eye at the far end of the yard. A clearing had been made there. Lukien studied it as he neared the flat ground. Once, the area had been lovingly tended, or so he imagined, full of roses and fragrant plants. Even now, a few hearty ancestors of those plants rose up from the weeds, bursting brightly into colour. It was the only real life Lukien had seen in the city, and the flowers made him grin. He went to them, pushing past some thorny shrubs, and stuck his nose into a yellow bloom. Along with the birdsongs and light breeze, he heard bees making music. Because no one had told them the city had died, they went on about their busy work, hopping from flower to flower.

Lukien returned to his horse to collect his saddle bags and bedroll. He had a meagre meal planned for himself, just the dried out things he had collected in the last town a week ago, but he knew that soon he would be able to hunt in the forest. Tomorrow, he would have fresh meat, and this thought buoyed him as he laid out his bed for the night. He would make a small fire, too, have his poor supper, and sleep well in the garden of this dead rich man. But as he began unpacking his bags, he noticed another feature of the garden he hadn't seen before, near the trestle. What looked like a grave marker jutted from the earth, mostly hidden behind bramble.

Lukien pushed aside the thorny sticks with his boot, kneeling down in front of the stone. It did indeed seem like a tombstone, but it was rectangular, like a pillar. About half as tall as Lukien, it had been carved with hundreds of words, long lines of them travelling its entire surface. Lukien ran his hand over the rough stone, feeling the carvings. They were Akari words, he supposed, similar to Jadori symbols. Since he couldn't read Jadori, either, he couldn't guess at their meaning. Names, perhaps. He looked down at the ground.

'Of the people buried here?'

He backed away from the marker, unsettled by it but unwilling to find himself another spot for the night. He was too tired, and whoever might be buried here was too long dead to trouble him. Deciding it better to stay put, he sat himself down on his bedroll and stared up into the darkening sky. He had already laid some food next to him, and as he watched the stars he ate of his dried meat and hardtack, sipping water in between bites to soften the unpalatable fare. The sky quickly darkened as the sun finally faded completely. Lukien chewed slowly, listening as the birds fell silent and the insects took over, chirping and buzzing. An orchestra of stars came out, one by one twinkling to life. They were different stars then he'd seen up north in Liiria, though much the same as they appeared in Jador, and seeing them comforted Lukien, for he knew that he was not far from Minikin and Gilwyn and all the others he had left behind. As he stared into the sky, he imagined their faces in the constellations – little Minikin, with her upturned ears and sharp, knowing smile, and Gilwyn, too, so quickly becoming a man. Lukien, whose left eye was gone and covered with a patch, focused his good eye on the stars and tried to picture Cassandra. She was there, he knew, somewhere.

'In the land of the dead,' he whispered to himself.

That's what she had said when she had come to him. And he had been with her there, so close to death himself that he had breached the wall between their worlds.

'Cassandra, are you there?' he asked the stars. 'I know you are. I know you can see me. I'm close now. I've made it to Kaliatha. Soon I'll find the Sword of Angels.' He smiled, sure that she heard him. Cassandra was like an Akari now, out of sight but only just beyond his reach. He continued, 'I'll find the Serpent Kingdom, Cassandra, just like you told me. I'll defeat Thorin so we can be . . .'

He stopped himself, blinking at the sky. She didn't want them to be together, not that way. Not until his time had come.

Lukien swallowed his last bit of beef and closed his eyes. Feeling sleep quickly overtaking him, he wondered if Amaraz would come to him again, the way he had so many nights before. It was not like being talked to, but rather a feeling of being pulled. In all their time together, Amaraz had never addressed Lukien directly. Being so ignored had embittered Lukien, but tonight he welcomed the Akari into his mind.

Lukien slept.

Hours passed quietly, and Lukien did not awaken while he slumbered. His exhausted body craved the rest, making him sleep deeply and dreamless. At well past midnight he finally stirred, sensing a presence around him. He tried to open his eye but could not. Then a voice sounded, sweet and calming. Not Cassandra's voice, and not Amaraz' mighty boom, either. It was a voice Lukien had never heard before, and it snatched him from sleep into something just on the verge of wakefulness.

He sat up, looking around, and yet he knew he had not truly awakened. A man stood in front of him, smiling, his face and hands shimmering like light on water. Neither old nor young, his features bore the same sharpness as the Akari statues Lukien had encountered in the square, with a long, dimpled chin and slightly turned-up ears. His clothing seemed Akari too, mostly loose-fitting robes pinned with a broach at his chest and sandals on his feet. His eyes were wide with curiosity.

'What is this?' Lukien asked. At once he heard his voice, echoing the way it had when he'd encountered Cassandra. 'Is this the place of the dead?'

'No, it is not,' the man replied. 'You are in your world, the world of men.' He laughed happily. 'You are the first to come here in more years than I could ever count! Who are you?'

'Who am I? Who are you?' Lukien got to his feet, keeping his distance. 'I'm not awake, am I? This isn't real.'

'It isn't a dream, if that's what you're thinking. You are still asleep, my friend. And you were the one who came to me, remember?' The man pointed at the grave marker. 'You touched my story stone.'

'I'm sorry,' Lukien offered, not really sure why he was apologizing. 'I didn't know . . . story stone?'

'There,' said the man, again gesturing at the marker. 'But you're not an Akari. You don't know what a story stone is, do you?'

'It looked like a tombstone to me. I didn't mean to disturb it.'

'You delight me, friend. You didn't disturb me – you called to me.' The man who was not quite a man came closer. 'My name is Raivik. I am an Akari. You know what that is, don't you?'

Lukien nodded, still confused. 'You are an Akari? Yet I can understand you. How is that possible?'

'You wear something around your neck,' said Raivik. 'A relic of my people.'

'You mean the Eye of God.' Lukien touched the amulet immediately. In this dreamscape, his hand felt real and unreal at the same time. 'Yes, I see. You are speaking in my mind.'

'That's right,' the man assured him. 'You have an Akari with you now. I sensed it the moment you called to me. I can feel him now. He makes my words real to you.'

'You mean he's translating?' asked Lukien, pleased at the prospect of Amaraz helping him. 'That could be, yes. But I didn't call to you. Or at least I never meant to. I'm just travelling through here. I didn't even think this city still held life.'

'It does not,' said Raivik. 'We are all dead.'

'Then this is the realm of the dead.'

'No,' the Akari corrected. 'This is your world. You summoned me here. I am Raivik, and that is my story stone.' He pointed at the marker. 'And there is my house and this is my city, such as it is. When I was alive, like you, I dwelt in this place.'

'I'm sorry, I don't understand,' said Lukien. 'If this isn't the realm of the dead, then how are you able to speak to me? You are not my Akari; you're not bound to me. I'm confused, Raivik.'

'Yes, I can see that,' laughed the spirit. 'You carry an Akari with you, yet you do not understand our ways? Strange.' Again he gestured to the odd piece of rock. 'That is my story stone. My family planted it there when I died, so that they could speak to me. They were summoners. Do you understand that much?'

'I think so,' said Lukien, remembering what little Minikin had told him of the Akari. The Akari of Grimhold were all dead members of Raivik's race, willing to bind themselves to the living to help them. Summoners were the magicians among them. Amaraz had been a summoner, as had Kahldris. 'A summoner was someone who could commune with the dead. But I'm not a summoner – how can I be talking to you?'

'Through the story stone. That's how it is here. If a summoner makes a story stone . . . well, look here . . .' Raivik moved easily through the plants, pushing them aside, then knelt down next to the marker. 'Come, friend, let me show you.'

Lukien went to stand beside the man. The whole thing seemed unbelievable, yet he had experienced so many oddities since meeting Minikin that this one seemed almost prosaic.

'Those words,' he said, pointing out the symbols carved along the stone. 'What do they mean?'

'That's my story,' Raivik declared proudly. 'All about me. My family made this stone. They told my story here.'

Intrigued, Lukien knelt near the stone. 'What does it say?'

'It says that I am Raivik and that I was a great merchant. I sold garments and fabrics from all around this part of the world, and that I was trusted by my customers.' Raivik's face grew calm as he told the tale. 'I had two sons and two daughters, and a wife named Jinia, my beloved. I brought this house for her when we were married.'

The story delighted Lukien. 'Go on.'

Raivik caressed the stone as if it were an infant. 'It says that I was loved.' There was an odd silence as the Akari stared at the stone. He seemed to sigh. 'But that is all over now. All gone.' His hand fell away from the stone. 'What is your name?' he asked.

'I am Lukien, from Liiria,' Lukien answered. 'But I'm also from Jador and Grimhold. You know those places, yes?'

Raivik wrinkled his nose. 'I know those places, but how can you be from both of them? Grimhold is an Akari place, an outpost. Jador is, well, Jadori. The Jadori are our enemies.'

The statement puzzled Lukien. 'Enemies? No, not any more. Not for hundreds of years.'

'Because they killed us.'

'No, because they have changed,' said Lukien. 'They're not warlike any more. They're peaceful. Don't you know that?'

'Lukien of Liiria, I know nothing more than what happened to me when I died. When the Jadori killed my people there were no more visitors to my stone to tell me what had happened in this world. You are the first.'

'But how can that be? You're an Akari. All the Akari know what's happened. They—'

He stopped himself, remembering what Minikin had told him. Only the Akari of Grimhold lived in both worlds. It was one reason why they helped the Inhumans, so that they could live on in the normal, living world they adored.

'Apologies,' said Lukien. 'I didn't know. In Grimhold, where I come from, the Akari speak to the people. They have hosts, like me, and they live in the world.' He gestured to the dark landscape and stars. 'This world.'

The news enchanted Raivik. His face grew curious, then sad as he touched his story stone. 'The people of Grimhold were slaughtered by the Jadori. They were among the first to die. Some of us could put ourselves into objects, but they were the summoners. Only the strongest of summoners, in fact.' He reached out and nearly touched Lukien, letting his fingers hover over his chest. 'This amulet you wear – it holds a summoner.'

'That's right,' said Lukien. At last he pulled the Eye of God out from under his shirt, letting it dangle freely on its golden chain. 'The Akari inside this amulet keeps me alive. He was a great summoner named Amaraz. Do you know of him?'

Raivik the dead merchant smiled. 'May I touch it?'

Lukien nodded, and Raivik carefully held the amulet in his dream-made hands. A look of serenity filled his eyes.

'I can feel him,' he said. 'He is very strong.'

'Yes, he is,' said Lukien. 'I should have been dead a long time ago, many times, but Amaraz keeps me going. I have been told he was well known among your people.'

'Indeed he was,' said Raivik, 'but I knew of him only through the stories I was told, here in this place. Amaraz lived after I died. I never knew him in life.'

'And so you don't know what else happened? After the Jadori killed your people, I mean?'

'No, stranger, I do not.' Raivik rose from his knees. 'I know only what my family told me when they visited this place. Now they are with me in the world beyond this one. They are ignorant, like me.' He looked imploringly at Lukien. 'But you know all these things. You can tell me, Lukien, so that I may tell the others. Will you do that?'

Lukien laughed. 'That's a lot of history to explain, Raivik. And really, I don't know much about your world. I do know that the Jadori have changed. They regret what they did to your people. They protect the people who live in Grimhold now. They're called the Inhumans. I'm one of them, in a way.'

'These Inhumans – they have Akari hosts?'

'Many of them do, yes. They're good people and the Akari help them. And because of what they did to your race, the Jadori protect Grimhold from the outside world. Once it was a secret, but no more.' Lukien hesitated, unsure how much he should reveal. 'The rest of the world knows about Grimhold now, but the Jadori still protect it. They've given a lot of blood for Grimhold, Raivik.'

'Amazing,' sighed the spirit. 'I want to hear more, Lukien. I want to know everything!'

'I don't know everything, Raivik. I barely understood the things you told me, even. I'm not an expert on the Akari of Grimhold, or even about the Jadori.' Lukien tried to be congenial, noting the change in Raivik's expression. 'I am sorry. I didn't mean to summon you, though I am glad that I did. I didn't expect to encounter anyone in the city.'

'But you did come here,' said Raivik. His curious eyes searched Lukien's face. 'Why?'

Lukien wandered back to the place where he had been sleeping, the place where – in the waking world – his body still lay asleep. 'That's rather hard to explain, Raivik. I'm looking for a place called the Serpent Kingdom.'

When he turned around again, Raivik was right behind him. 'I know this place you seek,' he said eagerly. 'The Kingdom of the Serpents – Tharlara.'

'I don't know what it's real name is,' said Lukien. 'I was only told to seek the Serpent Kingdom. Here, beyond the desert.'

'There is only one place that could be called the Serpent Kingdom, and that is Tharlara,' said Raivik. 'The place of the giant snakes. The riverland.'

'Giant snakes?' Lukien recoiled. 'You mean rass?'

'Yes, the rass,' acknowledged Raivik. His glowing hand pointed eastward. 'You will find a river beyond the city. The river will take you to Tharlara.'

'Toward the rass? I don't know . . .'

'Tharlara is safe for you, Lukien. The people there will not harm you. They are quiet, though, and I do not know much about them.'

'Forgive me, Raivik, but you've been dead for . . . what? About a thousand years? You don't know much more about the Serpent Kingdom than I do.'

The Akari looked wounded, but nodded. 'You are right, of course. I can only tell you what I remember. The Tharlarans were never bothersome to us, though they did not trade much with us, either. They kept to themselves. I do not know what became of them.'

'You've already helped me greatly, Raivik,' said Lukien. 'I'm grateful to you. I will follow the river as you have said.'

'Forgive me, but I am curious. For what purpose?' asked Raivik. 'Why do you seek Tharlara?'

'For a sword,' said Lukien. He sat down again on his bedroll, remarkably calm despite the strange happenings. 'I was told I could find it in the Serpent Kingdom.'

'This is a special sword?'

'Very. I need it to defeat someone, someone dear to me that's been corrupted by a bad Akari.'

'Bad Akari?' Raivik's eyes crinkled playfully. 'There are no bad Akari, my friend. We are a great race. You must have discovered that by now.'

'Oh yes,' said Lukien. 'Your people have impressed me, Raivik. But there is one Akari that's not like the rest of you. Have you ever heard the name Kahldris?'

The spirit paled. 'Kahldris.' He spat the name like a curse. 'Kahldris was a madman and butcher. He is not to be spoken of, Lukien.'

'Kahldris has my friend in his control, Raivik. With his Devil's Armour.' Lukien leaned forward. 'Do you know about the armour?'

'All Akari know of the Devil's Armour. It is an obscenity. Kahldris is part of the armour. He is encased in it, the way your Akari is encased inside your amulet. Kahldris made the armour for his brother, Malator, to use against the Jadori.'

Lukien's eyebrows went up. 'Malator? You do know a lot about the armour!'

'It is known among us all,' said Raivik. 'The armour was taken to Grimhold to be hidden, so that no one would ever use it.'

'That's right. That much I know already. Please, Raivik, tell me more.'

'Kahldris lived in the time of the Jadori wars. He was a general. He fought the Jadori.'

'After you died?' asked Lukien.

Raivik nodded. 'Kahldris lived while I lived and beyond. I left this world before he did. My people were at war with the Jadori for years, Lukien. Kahldris and his brother battled them.'

'This brother – Malator. I never heard of him,' said Lukien, surprised that Minikin had never mentioned his name. 'Tell me about him.'

'Malator was a good man, not like his brother. But he was strong like Kahldris. He was a powerful summoner. When Kahldris made the armour, it was so that his brother might use it to defeat the Jadori. But Kahldris was already a butcher by then.' Raivik closed his eyes in revulsion. 'You would not the believe the stories of his brutality. Malator told his brother that he would wear the armour, but only so Kahldris would encase himself within it.'

'Which he did,' offered Lukien. 'So it was a trick?'

'Yes. Once Kahldris was encased in the armour he was no longer a threat. All Akari rejoiced when he was gone.'

'And then the armour was moved to Grimhold, so that no one would ever use it.' Lukien considered the logic of the move. 'So what happened to Malator?'

'I do not know. Nobody knows. Like you, he went off to seek the Serpent Kingdom, to ask the Tharlarans for their help against the Jadori. He never returned, though. Not long after . . .' Raivik looked around and shrugged. 'All of this happened.'

There was a sad pause in Raivik's story, as if there was no more to tell. But Lukien still wanted answers.

'Raivik, how can it be that none of your people know where Malator is now? He must have died not long after you did. Yet you've never felt his presence? None of you have?'

'It is not always that way, Lukien. If Malator wanted to come to us, then perhaps he could. I do not know for certain. I dwell in the world of the dead. Malator dwells in the world of the dead, too. But he need not come to me, or seek out another. His place is not my place. It is as I told you – I am bound to my world. I see my family and loved ones because they are part of me. They lived here, in my house. Do you see?'

Lukien tried gamely to understand, but it was all too arcane for him. He knew only that Malator had left for Tharlara, and that no one had ever heard from him again. At least not according to Raivik. And should he believe this long dead apparition? Lukien wasn't sure.

'Everything you've told me is like a huge text, Raivik,' he admitted. 'And I'm not studied enough to understand it all.' Suddenly he felt the pull of his physical body, urging him to return. 'I can't stay much longer. Something doesn't feel right.'

'Your body is waking,' said Raivik. 'It is unused to all of this.'

'This dream has to end,' said Lukien. 'You have to let me go now, Raivik.'

The Akari smiled sadly. 'I have so enjoyed this, Lukien of Liiria. To talk to someone about the world – it has been magnificent. I wish you could stay forever and talk to me, but I know you cannot.'

Lukien shared the spirit's remorse. He regretted having tantalized Raivik with the small gift of his presence. 'Maybe we will see each other again someday,' he said. 'If I find the sword, I can return this way, perhaps.'

'I would like that,' said Raivik. 'There is so much I want to know about the world. I miss it. Now, remember, my friend – follow the river.'

'I will,' replied Lukien, fighting to stay in the dream. The world around him began to dissolve, the house and trees slowly melting. 'Thank you, Raivik. You have helped me a great deal.'

Raivik, the dead merchant of Kaliatha, raised a hand in good-bye as he shimmered out of view. A second later, Lukien felt his body again, falling into blackness before consciousness arrived. His eye fluttered open, feeling heavy and real. He saw the stars above, felt the cool air on his face. He breathed, sat up, and looked around the empty garden.

Without Raivik, the city seemed more dead than ever.

5

'Lady White-Eye, will you come?'

The question lingered a long time, ignored as White-Eye distracted herself. She had not expected the invitation. She had thought – hoped, in fact – that her fellow Inhumans had given up asking her. She pretended to toy with the spinning wheel Minikin had given her, though she still did not know how to use it and hadn't really tried. It was work to keep her mind busy, after all, and distract her from her loss. She shrugged as she sat on the stool, pretending to move the wheel with her hand.

'I am just learning this, Monster,' she replied. 'Tomorrow perhaps.'

The man called Monster inched a bit closer. White-Eye heard his shuffling feet on the stone of her chamber. She was completely blind now, and without her Akari could not see his chiseled face, a face she had always found comforting and oddly handsome. Monster, who was hunch-backed, had served her for years. His forwardness surprised her.

'My lady, I should reconsider if I were you. You have not been down to see any of us in weeks. You are missed.'

White-Eye frowned. It was the same thing Minikin had been telling her. Since her blinding, she had spent precious little time out of her chambers, taking her meals alone and speaking to no one. Losing her Akari had not been what she expected. It had been far, far worse, and White-Eye had not recovered from the violence of it or been able to understand the crushing blankness of the truly blind. She had not been born with normal eyes. Instead, she had two milky, sightless orbs, but Faralok had showed her the world with his Akari magic, saving her from a life of walking into walls. Without him, blackness had enveloped her. Every sound, strange and familiar, made her fearful.

'You should get downstairs, Monster, before all the food is gone or cold.'

She didn't like refusing him, but there was no choice for her. She was a shut-in now, and too old to learn the ways of the blind. She would not have them all staring, pitying her.

'Will you sup alone again, then?' Monster probed. 'It is not good to eat alone, my lady. My dear mother taught me that when I was just a child.' She could hear him smile, and knew the anecdote was meant to coax her out. 'Eating alone does strange things to the stomach, she would say. She didn't want me to feel different from others, you see.' Again he stepped closer, coming to stop in front of the spinning wheel. White-Eye could feel his kind eyes looking down at her. 'It's that way for you now, my lady. You need to be with the rest of us.'

White-Eye felt terror knotting in her stomach. Why was he pushing her so? As kahana, she could order him away, but even that was too much for her. How could she possibly give orders now, so weak and useless she couldn't even feed herself? She was no kahana, not any more.

'I cannot, Monster,' she said. She shook her head, trying to rid herself of the desperate feelings. 'I am not ready.'

Monster's face came very close to her as he whispered, 'We are all Inhumans, my lady. This is Grimhold. No one will judge you.'

'They will,' said White-Eye. 'They will not mean to, but they will. I do not want them to see me like this, blind and weak.'

'You are afraid, I know,' said Monster gently, 'but I am here, right here with you. And anyone who laughs will have to deal with me!' He punched his thumb into his chest so that White-Eye could hear the thump. 'Now, shall you walk or will I have to carry you? I can do it, you know. Not very fitting for a Jadori kahana.'

He was only half-joking, and White-Eye didn't laugh. Though horribly hunched from birth, Monster's Akari had given him amazing strength. He could easily hoist her over his shoulder and carry her down to the dining chamber. Since Lukien had gone and Gilwyn after him, Monster seemed to have pronounced himself her protector. White-Eye, though, had trouble trusting him. He was, quite probably, just one more man who would leave her.

'And what will you do when I stick a fork in my eye instead of my mouth?' she asked. 'Make a joke to cover my clumsiness? Thank you, no.' She went back to distracting herself with the spinning wheel, pretending to feed it wool and hoping Monster would leave. When he did not, she looked up at him again. 'You may go now.'

Monster hesitated. Then she felt his rough hand guiding her own, easing the strands of wool into the wheel.

'You could do this if you wanted to,' he said, 'but you have not even tried, I can tell.'

White-Eye froze under the accusation. She sat back on the stool, her shoulders slumping.

'I did not want this thing,' she said. 'Minikin brought it here to distract me.'

'No, to teach you,' Monster corrected mildly. 'Minikin knows you can do things if you will try.'

'I am blind, Monster!'

'Yes, I know,' said the Inhuman evenly. 'Does that mean you have no friends here?'

The words struck White-Eye. She breathed to steady herself. There would be no convincing him, not this time. So she put out her hand.

'Take it,' she commanded. 'And do not let go.'

Monster was good to his promise. He carefully led White-Eye to the dining chamber of Grimhold, the place where the young kahana had always taken her meals and conversed with her fellow Inhumans. Tonight, the chamber was filled with familiar voices, most of which hushed when she entered. Monster ignored the silence, leading White-Eye to her familiar chair. Since losing Faralok, White-Eye had yet to be surrounded by so many people. She gripped Monster's hand a little tighter as she took her seat.

'Who is here?' she whispered.

'We're all here, my lady,' replied Monster.

It was true, White-Eye knew, because even their stares were familiar to her. Next to her, she heard Monster sit himself down. His misshapen body could not comfortably accommodate a normal chair, so he always used a stool. White-Eye put her hands down to feel the table, a sturdy slab of rectangular marble stretching out into the chamber. There were others like it in the hall, too, enough to seat hundreds of Grimhold's odd inhabitants. White-Eye did not have to listen hard to hear them all – they're anxious breathing assaulted her.

'Welcome, my lady,' came a sudden voice.

White-Eye turned toward the sound, wondering who had spoken.

'It's me, Dreena,' the voice offered.

'Oh, Dreena,' White-Eye replied. She licked her lips, feeling flushed suddenly. 'Hello.'

Like most of Grimhold's people, Dreena was an Inhuman, another blind girl who Minikin had found in Farduke as a child. She was about White-Eye's age now, but still had an Akari to help her see.

'Welcome, kahana,' said another voice, and then another and another greeted her, overwhelming White-Eye. She sat leaned back in her throne-like chair, nodding as she tried to recognize the voices. Most of them were easy for her to recall; she had spent years with these people. One voice, however, remained absent. White-Eye turned to Monster.

'Is Minikin here?' she whispered.

'No, my lady.'

White-Eye frowned. 'No? Why not?'

The hunchback sighed before answering. 'She has gone to Jador.'

'Jador?' White-Eye puzzled over the comment. She was kahana of Jador, but had abdicated her responsibilities now. Still, she missed her homeland and its dark-skinned people. 'Minikin said nothing of this trip to me. Why did she go?'

'I do not know, my lady. She left early this morning. She took no one with her, only Trog.'

'She has gone to do my work for me,' said White-Eye sullenly. 'What I should be doing.'

'No, my lady.'

'Yes, Monster, yes,' White-Eye insisted. 'First I let Gilwyn take charge of Jador, and now that he is gone a foreigner is looking after Jador.'

'Minikin did not say why she was going to Jador,' said Monster, fighting to contain his impatience. 'But it was not to look after Lorn, I am sure.'

'You are sure? How can you be?' asked White-Eye angrily, though she was more angry at herself than anyone else. She sank back into her chair, her appetite all but gone. Lorn was a man of terrible reputation, Gilwyn's decision to leave him in charge of Jador had shocked her. He had not even asked her opinion. He had simply left Jador in Lorn's hands, then fled north to rescue Baron Glass. White-Eye felt the weight of guilt crushing her shoulders. 'Minikin should have told me she was going,' she said.

Around her, her fellow Inhumans had begun their meal. Servants began moving plates and setting pots down on the tables. White-Eye heard knives carving and the tinkle of glassware. She disappeared into the noise, hoping no one was watching her. The thought of Minikin riding to Jador saddened her, because she knew the little woman was unwell. The battle against Aztar had weakened her, sapping her good nature, making her feel old. And in truth, Minikin was old, far older than anyone else in Grimhold or Jador. She was hundreds of years old now, and amazingly, she was only now showing her age.

'My lady? You should eat something,' Monster suggested. He put some food into her plate, then pushed it closer to her. 'Your fork is near your right hand.'

'Monster, I'm not hungry. Let it be enough that I have come to be with everyone.'

'You need strength, my lady, to recover.'

'I am fine. And I can never recover from what's happened to me.'

'That is not true. You should not tell yourself such lies.'

White-Eye felt trapped suddenly, not wanting Monster's help but unable to get back to her chambers without him. She muttered, 'You have your Akari still. I can never have another, and you have no idea what that is like. I have come because you asked me to come, because everyone wanted to see me. And here I am! But I cannot see them, Monster, and you cannot guess how horrible it is.' She gave a heavy, lamenting sigh. 'I am sorry, but that is the truth.'

Monster did not argue with her. Instead he took her hand and wrapped it gently around her fork.

'There is meat and carrots on your plate. Eat.'

'I am not a child!'

'No. You are kahana. Act like it.'

Furious, White-Eye stabbed her fork down, skewering a piece of meat. Feeling it securely on the utensil, she carefully raised the fork to her mouth. The meat was too large, so she nibbled at it, wondering how grotesque she looked and reminding herself that she was indeed kahana.

They are friends, she told herself. *They will not laugh.*

And indeed they did not. The other Inhumans kept up with the meal they way they always did, though this time they gave the kahana the space she required. Instead of barraging her with anecdotes, they left her alone to eat. White-Eye chewed her food absently, listening to the chatter at the table. Dreena was speaking, talking about her day with the sheep. There were new lambs born today, three of them. One was black and smaller than the rest.

'A runt,' Dreena proclaimed. 'Like Emerald. I wish Gilwyn was here to see it.'

White-Eye stopped chewing, and for a moment the conversation stopped. She hadn't heard Gilwyn's name mentioned previously, for they all knew he had left and no word had been heard from him.

'Continue, please,' White-Eye told her companions. 'I know Gilwyn is well. I am not worried about him.'

It was a lie, but it helped to alleviate the tense mood, and soon Dreena went back to talking about the little black lamb that reminded her so much of Gilwyn's kreel. Monster leaned over then and spoke gently to White-Eye.

'You see? Isn't it better to be with us, instead of alone in your chamber? You are doing well, my lady.'

White-Eye smiled, happy at the compliment. Forgetting her blindness, she reached out for her goblet . . .

And promptly knocked it over. The noise abruptly halted the conversation. White-Eye felt wine dripping into her lap, soaking through her gown. Heat rushed through her face in embarrassment. She lifted her hands carefully away from the table, holding them up to shield herself from the pitying looks.

'It's nothing,' Monster hurried to say. 'Just a spill. It's *nothing*.'

To White-Eye, though, the wine was scalding water. With her hands still out before her, she pushed back her chair and stood up.

'Monster, take me upstairs, please.'

'Kahana . . .'

'*Please.*'

The Inhumans said nothing as Monster relented, taking White-Eye's hand and guiding her out of the room. White-Eye's rubbery legs carried her slowly away. Crushed with embarrassment, she wanted only the four walls of chamber and the quiet blackness of her dead eyes.

Minikin arrived at Jador at dusk, along with two Jadori warriors as escorts and her bodyguard Trog. The desert evening was closing in on the city, blushing scarlet on the cloudless horizon, and the minarets of Jador glowed with a golden aura. The city was blessedly peaceful, a welcome sight after the long ride through the desert, and because Minikin had not announced her arrival there were no Jadori guards to greet her or children to cheer her arrival. Instead, the streets near the palace were wonderfully quiet. In fact they were always quiet lately, for the city was still licking its wounds, rebuilding from both the battle with Prince Aztar and the war with Akeela a year before. There were fewer Jadori warriors now than ever and far too many widows, and Jador was recovering slowly from the blow, still mourning their dead and the terrible thing that had befallen their kahana, the beloved White-Eye.

Minikin slowed her kreel as they rode into Jador, bidding her escorts to do the same. Now that she was in the city she was in no hurry. The warriors accompanying her kept back a few paces, leaving her and the mute Trog to study the city by themselves. Trog's kreel was an enormous beast, by far the largest in Jador, with a back broad enough to support Minikin's giant bodyguard. Trog himself was not an accomplished kreel rider, not like the warriors, but the kreel he rode was gentle and intelligent like all of its breed, and had carried him effortlessly to Jador, without any guidance from the giant. Still, Trog looked eager to dismount, tottering on the beast's back as he surveyed the city with his saucer-like eyes.

'Yes, it's good to be back,' said Minikin wearily.

They had not been to Jador since the battle with Aztar, when she had summoned the magic to incinerate the prince's army. It had been a galling, exhausting thing to do and it had sapped the little woman's strength. It had even made her doubt her purpose, for she had never taken so many lives before. She was old now and she knew it, and the time had come to give up a bit of her authority. But Gilwyn was no longer in the city, and White-Eye was teetering on the brink of hysteria, driven to depression by her new-found blindness. There seemed little any of them could do.

Minikin looked west, toward the entrance of the city that bordered the Ganjeese township. She could barely see the city gate or the tower where she had watched the battle, summoning the Akari fire that had scorched the earth and taken so many of Aztar's men. Aztar himself had mostly likely perished in the flames, a small blessing for the horror she had unleashed, Minikin supposed. She rode forward a bit, surveying the quiet streets near the palace. Without Gilwyn in residence, the area around the palace had become desolate. It was said that King Lorn had the Jadori working hard in the Ganjeese province, building new and better homes for the Seekers who had come across the desert and strengthening the defenses around Jador. The rumbles about his harshness had reached Minikin all the way in Jador. She looked around, trying to determine if the complaints were true. In fact, Jador did look more orderly to her. The streets had been cleaned of rubble and debris, and the distant tower stood proudly against the horizon. Squinting, Minikin could see people down the avenue, dark-skinned Jadori walking casually in the twilight. Riding a bit further, she heard the gurgle of a fountain. She turned, surprised to see the pretty thing spouting water again after being so long neglected. Because she was approaching the palace now, she and her escort were easily sighted by a pair of Jadori guardians patrolling near the garden. Usually, the Mistress of Grimhold was greeted by a procession of well-wishers. As the guards hurried toward her, she girded herself.

'N'jara,' she said, telling them in their own tongue to stay quiet. She held up her hands as she spoke. 'N'jara, bisa.'

The Jadori looked around, confused, then quietly approached her, beaming smiles at the adored mistress. They asked if she was well and why she had not told them she was arriving. Minikin smiled at the men, explaining that she had come to speak with King Lorn and that she was very tired. She did not want the people of the township to know she had come. Both men nodded, understanding her concerns. She was always swamped with questions by the Seekers in the township, people from the north like King Lorn who had come across the desert in search of healing magic.

'King Lorn; is he in the palace?' Minikin asked in Jadori.

'No, Mistress,' replied one of the guards. 'Lorn is at the gate. Shall we take you to him?'

Realizing that riding near the gate would expose her arrival easily, Minikin politely shook her head. She loved the Seekers and admired them. They had all gone through remarkable hardships to find their way to Grimhold, and she had been forced to refuse them, making them live outside Jador's white wall because there was simply no room for them in the city, and no way to cure their ailments. They had come to Jador on a rumour, calling it Mount Believer, sure they would find magic in the city to straighten their bent limbs and clear their sightless eyes. And they had overwhelmed tiny Jador. Without meaning to, they had stretched the city and its meagre resources to the breaking point.

'I will wait for King Lorn in the palace,' said Minikin. 'His child, Poppy – she is well?'

The warrior nodded. 'Yes, Mistress, the baby is well. She grows stronger. The woman who tends to her is with her now in the garden. We can take you to her.'

'Yes, that would be fine,' said Minikin eagerly. She had never spoken to Eirian before, but knew it was her chance to find out how Lorn was faring. Lorn was deeply fond of Eirian, a woman from the north like himself though far younger than the deposed king. She had even taken to raising Lorn's daughter Poppy, feeding her from her own breast and seeing to her every need. 'I will await King Lorn with the girl.'

'Lorn may take his time,' the warrior warned. 'He spends much of the day working.'

'Does he?' asked Minikin brightly. 'I have heard complaints about him. I have heard that he is working everyone else too hard, but not himself.'

The warrior's expression grew embarrassed. 'Forgive me, Mistress, it is not my place to speak against Lorn.'

'But you have, yes?'

The man nodded. 'Yes. He is a foreigner.'

'Gilwyn was a foreigner,' Minikin reminded the man.

'Yes, Mistress, but Gilwyn was regent,' the guard replied.

'Yes, regent,' his companion agreed. 'He was chosen by Kahana White-Eye.'

'And Lorn has been chosen by Gilwyn,' said Minikin. By now the warriors who had escorted her were listening intently. Minikin looked at each of them. 'I do not mean to scold you, truly. I wish only to know what is happening here.'

The guards became sheepish. Finally, the first one to speak nodded. 'Lorn works as hard as any man. Harder than most, even.'

'To defend us,' added his fellow guardian. 'That is what he claims.'

'And you believe this claim?'

The guards looked at each other, wondering what each was thinking. None of the palace guards had ever been comfortable speaking frankly with the mistress, not in all the years she had been coming to Jador. The boldest of the pair shrugged and confessed what he was thinking.

'Some say he is building a new kingdom for himself,' said the man, 'because he no longer has his own.'

The other Jadori remained silent at the accusation. Minikin supposed they were equally as suspicious. She saw it in their eyes.

'I will have words with King Lorn when he returns,' she said. 'For now, take us to the garden, please.'

The guards bowed, then turned and walked off, leading Minikin and her companions back toward the palace and the lush, quiet gardens bordering the barren desert.

Along with the setting sun, the ache in Lorn's back told him it was time to quit.

He had spent the day the way he had spent so many since coming to Jador, laying bricks and digging holes. It was difficult work, even for a man half his age, but Lorn attacked it with vigour, renewed by the challenge Gilwyn had given him to look after the city and thrilled to be useful again. Two battles, both in the space of a year, had set Jador back on its heels. There were shortages of everything and only meagre defenses to protect the city. Manpower was scarce, horses were almost non-existent, and the people of the township – northerners like Lorn himself – lived in comparative squalor to the Jadori themselves, secure behind their gleaming white wall. Because most of the Seekers who had come to Jador were not able-bodied, they were of little use to Lorn's rebuilding efforts, though they tried gamely to help by bringing water and supplies. It was the Jadori themselves who did most of the toil.

Lorn stepped away from the bricks he had laid and admired his handi-work. In Norvor he had been a king, but Jazana Carr had reduced him to poverty and sent him fleeing from his homeland with only his daughter and the clothes on his back. Along with Eirian and the others, he had eventually found himself here in Jador, seeking the protection of the city and its healing magic, magic he had hoped would cure Poppy of deafness and clouded, nearly useless eyes. Instead, he had found only excuses in Jador, a thousand unfathomable reasons why his daughter could not be healed. But Lorn had not been angered. Though Minikin claimed she could not heal his daughter, she and the Jadori had welcomed him and his fellow travellers, thanking them for their help in defending the city by allowing them to live in the palace. Now, with Gilwyn gone, the palace was Lorn's to protect – just like everything else in the ancient city.

So Lorn began by building walls.

While others worked hard to construct housing for the Seekers, the refugees who had come across the desert, Lorn had decided that the township itself needed a wall, just like the one its big sister Jador wore. He had enlisted the help of every able-bodied northerner and Ganjeese trader willing to help, and so far they had made commendable progress. It surprised Lorn how ill prepared Jador had been for Aztar's attack. They were amateurs at defending a city, all of them, and though young Gilwyn had tried gamely he had been a very poor regent by Lorn's reckoning. The Jadori were slack. And the township, a huge, sprawl of houses that had sprung up over the decades for Ganjeese travellers, had almost no defenses at all. Not even a wall.

'But not for long,' said Lorn, clapping the dust from his hands. He had finished the fifth course for this section of the wall, using brick made in the township and washed the same, gleaming white as the wall around Jador. It would take months to finish, he knew, but it didn't matter. The wall was needed. More importantly, it gave the desperate Seekers of the township something useful to do.

Lorn ran a dirty hand through his matted hair and wiped the sweat from his brow. He had worked longer than almost anyone else. With night falling, most of the others had gone back to their families to eat and rest. The rumbling in Lorn's stomach told him it was time for him to eat, too. Satisfied, he took a breath and listened to the still desert air. Amazingly, he was growing accustomed to the heat and dryness.

'Enough now,' he called, signalling his fellows workers to stop. Three men had remained with him at the site, all of them brothers from Marn, and all of them afflicted with a blood disease that weakened their bodies and made their bones brittle. Yet despite their ailments and the hopelessness of their plight, they had worked tirelessly alongside Lorn, because their father had been a brick-layer in Marn and had died from the same inexplicable disease. 'We can start again tomorrow, but right now my back aches like I've been stabbed and if I don't get some decent food I'm going to collapse.'

Tarlan, the nearest of the siblings, slung a dipper through a bucket of water and offered it to Lorn. Grateful, Lorn drank, then handed the dipper back to Tarlan. The brothers had sprung from the same womb at the same time and all had the same blonde, cow-licked hair. They were much younger than Lorn, too, barely half his age, though their desperate ailments meant they could only do half the work, as well.

'Come back to our house tonight, Lorn,' said Harliz. The most ill of the triplets, Harliz stooped considerably even when he walked. He liked to joke that he had the perfect position for laying bricks. Whenever Lorn looked at him, he could see the considerable pain on his face. 'It's late and you look about to die. Our house isn't far.'

'*I* look about to die?' countered Lorn. 'You should get a mirror for your home.'

'We have a mirror,' said the third brother, Garmin. 'Harliz loves to look at himself.' He went to his stooped brother and playfully mussed his hair. 'See? He's the prettiest of us all!'

'And I have a prettier one still, waiting for me back at the palace,' said Lorn. 'I would rather spend time in her bed than with any of you mutts.'

The brothers laughed, relieved to be done for the day. They had worked hard for Lorn, and he was grateful. Like most of the Seekers, the brothers accepted their lot. There would be no healing for them. Lorn stretched his back and tried to work the aches from his muscles. In Norvor, he had never had to work so hard. While he bent to touch his toes, he heard his name being called from a nearby street. He rose to see a man hurrying toward him on a kreel, one of the Jadori warriors named Amarl who guarded the palace. In the failing light Lorn could barely make out his dark features wrapped beneath his flowing gaka. The people in the street parted as the kreel loped past them. The brothers from Marn gaped at the beast.

'Amarl?' Lorn called. 'What is it?'

Amarl reined back his kreel. The hot night made the reptile's skin glisten. Its long tongue darted out to taste the dusty air. Amarl unwrapped the black cloth from around his face. He was one of the few inside the palace who could manage the language of the continent, and that was why Lorn depended on him so much.

'The mistress has returned, King Lorn,' said the warrior. He had a throaty, commanding voice. Like most of his race his eyes were black and fierce. 'You should come.'

'The mistress?' asked Lorn. 'You mean the little one?'

'She awaits you in the gardens. She is sitting with your woman.'

The news surprised Lorn – and excited him. He had only spoken to Minikin once, when he had first arrived in Jador with Poppy. She had thanked him for his help against Aztar, then promptly denied his daughter access to Grimhold. There were reasons, of course, and Lorn understood them. But he held out hope that his good deeds for the city might change her mind. Lorn turned toward Harliz and his brothers.

'Tomorrow,' he told them. 'Get well rested. I'll be back in the morning.'

The brothers nodded, watching in awe as the Jadori swept Lorn onto the back of the kreel. Lorn fought for balance then held tightly as the great beast hurried toward the palace.

The sun had gone completely by the time Lorn reached the palace. He stepped carefully into the garden, hiding behind broad-leafed plants and listening for Minikin. Torches had been lit and the garden glowed a pleasant yellow. The flowers and light swayed in a warm breeze. Lorn noticed Eirian first, sitting in their usual spot, a place where they could see the desert beyond the outskirts of Jador. Tonight the desert stretched darkly into nothingness. Eirian held Poppy in her arms, swaddled in white cotton as the baby nursed from her breast. Lorn peered around the plants, then saw Minikin seated across from Eirian. The little woman's feet dangled like a child's from her chair. The shadow of her brutish bodyguard fell across her shoulder. She was talking gently to Eirian, admiring the child in her arms. Lorn smiled, proud of Eirian and the way she had handled the interruption. Not even this magical midget could upset his Eirian.

Lorn smoothed down his grey hair and straightened his rumpled shirt. A lane of cobblestones led to the sitting area. Lorn stepped onto the lane and adjusted his pliant face to greet Minikin. As he approached she looked up at him, a strange grin splashing across her elfish face. She made to rise, but Lorn quickly stopped her.

'No, do not get up,' he told her. 'Sit, please.' He paused at Eirian's chair, resting a hand on her shoulder. Eirian greeted him with a smile.

'You were quick,' said Eirian. 'The mistress only just arrived.'

'As quick as I could be,' Lorn said. He bowed slightly at the tiny woman. 'I'm honoured to see you again, my lady.'

Minikin sat back and closed her coat around herself. The coat swam with colour as if alive. Around her neck she wore a golden amulet, most of it hidden beneath the coat's miraculous fabric. His grey eyes seemed haunted, though happy too that Lorn had come.

'It is good to see you, King Lorn,' she said, her voice like music. As Lorn stood next to Eirian's chair, so too did the giant Trog stand beside his mistress. 'You have been busy, apparently.'

Lorn glanced down at his filthy clothes. Mud caked his boots. 'Forgive me, my lady. This is the second time I have not been given time to pre-pare for you! Did Eirian tell you? I have been working at the township.'

'I know,' said Minikin. 'You have been keeping everyone in the city occupied, King Lorn.'

There was a trace of reproach in her tone. Lorn grinned at her.

'There is much to do here, Lady Minikin. A lot of work was left undone. I am only doing the things that were left neglected for too long.'

Minikin sharpened her own smile, then looked at Eirian. 'Child, would you leave us to talk alone, please? I have things to discuss with King Lorn, private matters.'

Her request didn't surprise Lorn. Nor did it surprise Eirian, who gladly accepted the invitation to leave, sensing the coming clash.

'I do not mind at all,' said Eirian as she rose from her chair. 'I should tend to my father anyway. It was good to meet you, Lady Minikin. I hope we can speak again some time.'

She had the politeness of a princess at court, and her manners delighted Minikin, who gave Eirian a cheerful good-bye as she left the garden. Her almond eyes watched Eirian as she left.

'A beautiful woman,' the mistress commented. 'You are fortunate, King Lorn. She adores you. It is so plain to see.'

'And I her,' said Lorn. He took the seat Eirian had vacated, relaxing in the ornate iron chair. 'I was truly blessed to find her. She's a tiger. She reminds me of my wife, Rinka. Rinka wasn't afraid of anything, and neither is Eirian.'

'And she loves the child,' Minikin added. 'She is like the babe's mother.'

'Aye, I couldn't be more fortunate. This is a good place for Poppy.'

Lorn studied Minikin's expression for any sign of hope. 'Unless, of course, you have a better place for her.'

It was the same argument they had gone through in their first meeting, and just like that time Minikin shook her head, shattering Lorn's hopes.

'No, King Lorn, that's not why I have come. Nothing has changed in Grimhold. There is still no Akari for Poppy.'

'Pardon me, but I have heard about what happened to White-Eye. Before he left, Gilwyn explained it to me. She was severed from her Akari, and it is tragic. But would that not free up her Akari for Poppy?'

'No, because it does not work that way. You are a stranger here, King Lorn, and I do not expect you to understand the bond between Akari and Inhuman. White-Eye's Akari was taken from her in violence.' Minikin dropped her gaze a little. 'Faralok is lost to us.'

'I'm sorry,' said Lorn. 'But for my daughter's sake I had to ask.'

'I have not forgotten Poppy, or my promise to you. She is always in my thoughts, and if the time comes I will make arrangements for her. But I have explained this to you already, King Lorn. There are many like Poppy, and they have been here longer.'

'I understand,' said Lorn, unable to hid his disappointment. Over Minikin's shoulder, the brooding Trog stared at him. The great bald giant with the overbite didn't seem to understand anything that was being discussed, but his gaze unsettled Lorn. 'So,' Lorn continued, 'if you have not come to talk of Poppy, then you have come to talk about what I have been doing here. I assure you, Lady Minikin, you have nothing to worry about.'

'Good, because I want your assurances, King Lorn. I want to know that Gilwyn made the right decision when he gave Jador over to you.'

'Let me correct you. Gilwyn did not give me the city. He asked me to look after it for him, because of what happened to White-Eye and because of what has happened to you, as well. Forgive this impertinence, but you have not been well. Your heart aches from what you did in the battle with Prince Aztar. I know. I was there, remember.'

Minikin's normally placid face grew stormy. 'I have no regrets.'

'My lady, I was King of Norvor for sixteen years. I killed people just as you did, and I never regretted it either. I did what had to be done, just like you. But I never enjoyed it. So you need not pretend with me. Believe it or not, I know what guilt feels like.'

'So,' sighed Minikin, 'that is why Gilwyn asked you to look after things. I thought as much. And he is correct. I am old now, King Lorn, far older than you can imagine. And I need young people like Gilwyn and White-Eye to look after things. I cannot do it on my own, not any longer. Jador has grown too much, and with Grimhold's secret out in the world . . .' She shrugged. 'Others are needed. And that's why I have come here.'

'I'm not certain I understand you, Lady Minikin. You have not come to speak about Jador?'

'In a way, yes, but I haven't come to criticize you, or even to curtail you.'

'That is good, because I made a promise to young Gilwyn.'

'And you intend to keep it.'

Lorn nodded. 'Precisely right.'

'I have no argument with you, King Lorn. Not yet, at least. You promised Gilwyn you would look after things in the city. That is good. Gilwyn is young, but wise. He is concerned about Jador, and he is concerned about White-Eye. I am concerned about White-Eye as well. Gilwyn was only regent of Jador. He and White-Eye are not married. Only her desire made him regent over Jador.'

'I know that,' said Lorn. 'My lady, your meaning is clear. I know that I am not Jador's rightful ruler . . .'

'No, you misunderstand me, King Lorn. I have not come to talk about you. I have come to talk about White-Eye.'

'White-Eye? I do not even know the girl.'

'But I do, and I can tell you that she is not well, not at all,' said Minikin. At last the mistress sat back, looking remarkably old. The torch-light wavered on her face. 'I have known White-Eye since she was born. Her father, Kadar – he gave her to me to look after. Did you know that?'

'Yes,' said Lorn. 'Gilwyn told me that. You are like a mother to the girl, that's what he said.'

'A mother?' Minikin brightened. 'I like to think that's true. I have tried to make her strong. And she is strong, King Lorn. White-Eye is like her father. Even when he died, White-Eye was strong. But not now. She has lost her Akari.'

'I confess, I do not really know what that means,' Lorn admitted. 'Gilwyn has tried to explain it to me, but this bond between people and spirits; it vexes me.'

Minikin gave a knowing chuckle. With Trog's big hand still on her chair, she reached over her shoulder and patted it. 'The Inhumans use their Akari to help them. Without her Akari, White-Eye is as blind as your daughter, Poppy. But Poppy has never known sight, while White-Eye has had it robbed from her.'

Lorn tried to look moved. 'It must be terrible.'

'Terrible? At least that. White-Eye has not only lost her sight but also part of her soul. That is what an Akari is like – they become part of their hosts. She has never been so alone, and it has damaged her. She no longer thinks of herself as kahana. And she must, King Lorn, because she must rule here someday.'

'But how can she? She never even comes to Jador because of the sun. How can she rule the city?'

'White-Eye made Gilwyn regent so that he could look after things while she stayed in Grimhold,' said Minikin. 'But what if Gilwyn never returns?' She looked hard at Lorn. 'Have you not considered that?'

'I have,' said Lorn. 'He is young, and I warned him when he left that there would be dangers. That is why I am trying to prepare Jador, Lady Minikin. The city needs to be strong.'

'Indeed, and it needs a strong leader. You are strong, certainly, but you are not Jadori and you were not chosen by White-Eye. The city needs its kahana. And White-Eye needs to be whole again. She needs to see that she is strong, that she can lead.'

'I'm sorry, my lady, but I am still lost. What is it you want of me?'

Minikin at last got out of her chair. She padded over to stand before Lorn, who looked up in confusion into her troubled face. She returned his gaze directly, her eyes gentle and encouraging.

'You have done a great deal for Jador, King Lorn,' she said. 'Some think you are ambitious and that you only agreed to help us for your own self-interest. I do not believe that about you. Gilwyn believes in you, and so do I.'

Lorn wanted to look away, but forced himself to meet the lady's gaze. 'You are naïve to say that,' he replied. 'You are speaking to King Lorn the Wicked.'

'That is what they call you up north. Not here.' Minikin touched his hand. 'I have a great favour to ask of you.'

A day later, White-Eye remained in her bleak chambers, waiting for sleep to come. The spinning wheel Minikin had given her sat neglected in the corner of the room. White-Eye sat near a windowless wall, listening to the deaf-making silence.

Alone.

The profoundness of her solitude frightened White-Eye. While Faralok was with her, she was never really alone. He had been her constant companions, even making her dreams vivid. Now, closed or open, her eyes surveyed the same blackness. The sound of her own breathing grated loudly on her brain. She did not know the time, for time moved like syrup now, dripping slowly in frozen drops. Occasional footfalls outside her door told her that it was not yet very late, but to White-Eye the time didn't really matter. One moment was like the next or the one before, and to sleep meant nightmares. So she remained in her chair, brooding, neglecting to grope her way toward her bed.

She would be 'all right.' In time. That's what they all were saying, and it angered White-Eye. She had nothing but time these days, and no way to help herself or her people. Even Gilwyn was lost to her.

71

'How much time?' she wondered aloud. In her stark chamber, her voice rang hollow.

Then, remarkably, she heard a knock at her door. White-Eye sat up and turned toward the door, cocking her head to listen.

'White-Eye? I'm coming in.'

The door opened. A pair of little feet entered the room. White-Eye tried to smile, feeling the presence of her beloved Minikin. There was another with her, too, bigger and larger. White-Eye puzzled, for the sense of the person felt unlike Trog.

'White-Eye, I've just returned,' said Minikin. She went to stand beside White-Eye's chair, to touch the girl's arm. A gentle kiss caressed her head. 'How are you?'

'The same.' Though she was glad Minikin had come, she could give no other answer. 'Minikin, who is with you?'

White-Eye felt her pull away. The other – a stranger – stepped into the room.

'Kahana,' said the voice, a man White-Eye did not recognize. 'I am Lorn of Norvor.'

White-Eye got unsteadily out of her chair to face him. 'I know you,' she said. 'Gilwyn told me about you.'

She felt Lorn step closer. Even in her blindness his presence felt enormous. Minikin did not touch White-Eye again, but stayed near her.

'What happened to you is a great tragedy,' said Lorn. 'You have my sympathies.'

White-Eye nodded, confused. 'King Lorn, you have surprised me. I did not expect you to be coming here.' She turned toward Minikin for an explanation. 'Is there a reason?'

Minikin shrunk under the question. 'White-Eye,' she sighed, 'please listen to me. Lorn is here to help you.'

'Help me? How?'

'You are going back to Jador with me,' said Lorn. 'To be Kahana.'

White-Eye was in no mood for jests. 'Be serious, now . . .'

'I am serious, my lady,' said Lorn. 'It is what Minikin has asked of me, to make you into a ruler.'

'What?' White-Eye asked furiously. 'Minikin, what is this? Tell him to leave at once.'

'Child, it is necessary,' said Minikin. 'Jador needs you.'

White-Eye put up her hands, shaking her head and backpeddling until she hit her chair. 'No! Go away!'

'Listen to me,' Minikin insisted. 'You think you are useless because you are blind. But you are Kahana! You cannot sit forever in this room. You must learn things, things that Lorn can teach you.'

'Him?' White-Eye shrieked.

'I will be as gentle as I can with you, Kahana.' She felt Lorn stalking closer. 'I will teach you how to lead your people, and how to overcome your terrors.'

'This is madness!' White-Eye collapsed into her chair, turning away from them both. 'Look at me! How can you do this to me?'

'It is necessary,' Minikin said, her voice pleading. 'This is not to hurt you. It is to make you strong. You must see that you can still do things.'

'I do not want to do things! I want to be left alone!'

Minikin took a breath to quiet down them all. Finally she said, 'Lorn will not leave without you, White-Eye. You must go with him to Jador.'

'Minikin, I cannot! I cannot stand the light!'

'It is dark now, Kahana,' said Lorn. 'And I will not allow any harm to come to you. We will travel through the night, and while the sun is up you can stay within the palace.'

'And what will you do with me in the palace?' White-Eye asked. 'Tutor me? Like I am some dullard?'

Lorn quickly seized her hand in his own. 'Do you feel that?'

White-Eye could not break from his grasp.

'Do you feel that?' he asked again.

'Your hand?'

'Aye, my hand. Do you feel the strength of it, girl? I have been through a hundred heartaches like yours.'

He yanked her to her feet. She stared blankly, frightened.

'You and I are special, girl. We are rulers. I'm going to teach you what that means.'

White-Eye felt herself shaking. She tried to pry his fingers free, but they were like corded ropes.

'King Lorn, I am afraid!'

His grasp wouldn't slacken. 'You have dragons,' he said. 'Together we will slay them. I will teach you.'

White-Eye turned hopelessly toward Minikin. 'Minikin, I do not want this. Please . . .'

The mistress would not comfort her. 'He won't harm you, White-Eye. He has promised it and I believe him. There are kreels and warriors waiting to escort you.'

The madness of the moment seemed inescapable. White-Eye nodded, not really agreeing, not wanting to struggle. Lorn's hand remained strong. She kept hold of it even as he took his first slow steps toward the door.

6

Mirage was dreaming of Grimhold when the carriage came to a halt.

At first she did not remember where she was, but then the chains around her feet reminded her. She lifted her head from the hard floor, groggily searching the dark interior. The airless, windowless carriage stifled her breathing, but she knew they had stopped and her stomach rumbled with hunger. Finally, there would be food. Her companions inside the prison carriage – all of them women – began coming alive in the darkness. She had spoken barely a word to any of them over the past few days. She didn't even know their names. Mirage prepared herself, ready to fight the way an animal might. Days of darkness and hunger had driven her to madness. The chains around her ankles had made the skin chafe and bleed. Her eyes stung from tears and dirt and the sheer stink of captivity.

'Mine,' muttered one of the women insanely. She was a small, Norvan woman with jet hair who had positioned herself near the carriage door, the first to leap whenever food was given. The other women – less than a dozen in all – shuffled near to her, to beg for the morsels their captors pressed through the portal. They were all Norvans, Mirage had guessed, captured in Liiria just as she had been. After Chane had taken her to the Reecian camp, she had been shoved into the prison carriage for the long ride to Hes, the Reecian capital. Without explanation, she had learned on her own that there were scores of prisoners, mostly men. Mirage rubbed her red eyes with her dirty hands. The food was always terrible, but hunger made her choke it down. She could barely believe her misery.

She had been having a good dream, and had awoken to a nightmare. For days now she had endured the humiliation of captivity, fighting for scraps and wondering against logic how her life had taken such a turn. At first she had thought it a sick joke, but then Chane had taken her to the camp across the border, and she knew with awful certainty that it was no joke at all, and that she truly was a prisoner. And she had cried. Like the other bewildered women, she had sobbed lonely tears as the carriage bumped toward Hes, away from her old life toward the frightful unknown.

At last she heard the bolts being thrown open and saw the door crack with moonlight. It was still late, and she had no real notion of the hour. The women shouted and crowded toward the door, but before Mirage could make her move the figure of their gaoler appeared, his angry face barking at them to back away. He had no food, this giant Reecian, just a chain of keys around his wrist and a stout stick in his meaty fist. He beat the little Norvan woman back until she yelped like a dog.

'Norvan sluts,' he cursed. 'Get back, the lot of you. We're here.'

Mirage crept forward to see outside the little door. Were they in Hes? The gaoler stepped away and let a team of his companions into the carriage. One by one they hauled the chained women out, dropping them to the cold earth. When it was Mirage's turn she tried hard to keep her balance. Suddenly she was tumbling, the fresh air pricking her skin, the hard ground rattling her jaw. With her bound wrists she tried to right herself, looking around in horror. Her body was always in pain, and stretching it now made her wince. A dark city rose up around her, quiet and still. The other prison carriages had also stopped to unload their human cargo. Mirage got to her knees, pausing uncertainly. The big Reecian with the stick knocked the other women into the same position, his thick accent barely understandable. Around them, ancient Hes twinkled with torchlight, its magnificent towers soaring into the black sky. A courtyard spread out around them, full of soldiers and activity. Mirage glanced up to see a forbidding structure blocking her sight, a rambling edifice of grey stone and iron. Her heart iced over, sure that her undoing lay inside.

'That one,' said a voice.

Mirage turned toward the voice and saw Corvalos Chane. He was pointing at her, conversing with the gaolers. When their eyes met he smirked. One of Mirage's captors approached and lifted her roughly to her feet, dragging her toward Chane. Barely able to walk, Mirage struggled not to fall when the Reecian released her. She stood before Chane, filthy and broken, her eyes locked hatefully on his own.

'I will take her inside myself,' said Chane.

The big man with the stick backed away, not questioning Chane as he took hold of Mirage and led her away. Mirage's head swiveled in confusion. Throughout the courtyard, men were tumbling out of prison carriages.

'My feet,' she gasped. 'I can't . . .' She paused, nearly falling, coughing up dirty spit. For days she had barely used her voice, and now it failed her.

'Keep up,' Chane demanded. 'Little steps, girl.'

Mirage forced herself to walk, her steps shortened by the chain around her ankles. Chane's strong hand clamped around her arm guided her painfully away from the others, toward an open, spiked gate and the dark recesses of the keep.

'This place,' she rasped. 'What is it?'

Chane did not answer.

'Is this Hes?' she asked angrily. 'Is this where Asher is?'

The name Asher had haunted her the whole miserable journey. Chane had used the name like a weapon. The nightmarish castle of slimy moss and tangled iron tortured her thinking, making her beg for answers. Before Chane could pull her through the gate, Mirage planted her feet and grit her teeth, refusing to go further.

'No!'

Chane's free hand shot across her mouth, stunning her.

'You will have your answers . . . *inside.*'

He pulled her bodily through the gate, nearly lifting her from her bound feet as he dragged her into the keep. Remarkably strong, he barely broke a sweat as he half-carried her through a sleepy hall, dimly lit with oily lamps and smelling badly of humanity. Mirage gave up her struggle, fighting instead to keep from falling, her booted feet skipping across the stone floor as Chane bounced her along. Soldiers leered, ignored by Chane as he led her deeper into the keep. She heard the cries of other prisoners echoing through the halls, the ghastly music punctuated by the noise of scraping metal. Nausea swam through Mirage's mind as she imagined the torture the Reecians had arranged for her. Chane's special interest in her snuffed out the last of her confidence.

'I don't know anything,' she said again, her voice breaking. 'This is madness. I swear . . .'

Unmoved, Corvalos Chane ignored her pleas. He moved with urgency, and in time took her to a rounded turret overlooking the courtyard. A bank of dingy windows afforded a perfect view of the yard. Though they had not climbed any stairs, the turret stood above ground level, low but imperious. A figure waited near the windows, his body draped in plain grey clothes with an apron wrapped around his mid-section, the kind a butcher might wear. His back turned toward them, he nevertheless raised a hand to bid them forward as he stared intently out the windows, studying the newly arrived prisoners.

'I saw you come in,' he said, still not turning. Dread-filled, Mirage watched him, his features obscured in shadows. 'What have you brought me?'

'A special captive,' Chane replied. He pushed Mirage forward. She wobbled on her toes, managing to remain upright. At last the man at the window turned to face them. The first thing Mirage noticed were the blood stains on his apron. The white cloth was soaked with gore. He stepped out of the shadows to reveal his frightful face. The eyes, too far apart, leapt with intrigue when he sighted Mirage. His bent nose leaned to one side and the curve of his mouth turned up in an unnatural grimace. Long, stringy hair writhed down across his bulbous forehead, white like snow. Deep ruts ran down along both cheeks, the scars of some long ago injury. Mirage stared at him, mesmerized by his manic eyes and deformities. His feet stepped gingerly across the floor as he approached her.

'A gift,' he said. 'For me?'

Mirage shifted back on her chained feet. The man's blood-caked hand reached to take her collar.

'Oooh, don't fall now,' he cooed, pulling her closer. He cocked his head, inspecting her. A little pink tongue ran across his lips. 'Beautiful. What is your name, pretty lady?'

Mirage shook under his leer, too afraid to reply. The man put his ear closer to her mouth.

'What's that? Speak up, child.'

'Mirage,' she managed, forcing herself.

'Mirage?' The man's permanent grimace twisted into a smile. 'What an exotic name. You are Norvan?'

'She is from Jador,' said Chane. 'I found her in Liiria. She knows Baron Glass.'

'Really? Now that is interesting. Allow me to introduce myself, pretty Mirage. My name is Asher, and this is my church. I am the lord high god of this keep. I am your master, your saviour, and your only hope. Be warned – if you displease me . . .' Asher put his hands together as if in prayer. 'It will be unpleasant for you.'

'Asher, enough,' said Chane. 'You're scaring her.'

The gaoler raised his heavy brow. 'Forgive me, pretty Mirage. I have the face for this work, don't you think?' He turned toward Chane. 'Tell me about her.'

'She wasn't with the others,' Chane replied. 'I followed her myself, from the library at Koth. She spoke of Baron Glass openly. They're friends.'

Asher looked at Mirage. 'You admit this?'

Mirage didn't know what to say. Deciding it better not to lie, she nodded.

'There is no way for her to deny it, Asher. I saw her, as did hundreds of others. She's from Jador, as I said. That means she knows about Glass, and probably his plans. Find out for me.'

'Don't leave me here!' begged Mirage.

Chane sighed, as though he didn't like the idea of abandoning her, either. 'You can make this easier on yourself, girl. If you tell us what you know about Baron Glass and his plans, I can spare you from this place.'

'Oh no, please,' said Asher. 'Don't yield so easily, child. We'll have fun!'

'I don't know anything!' Mirage cried.

Chane said, 'Baron Glass has plans for Reec. What are they?'

'I don't know!'

'Chane, can't you see the girl is exhausted?' said Asher. 'She needs rest. Leave her with me a little while.'

Mirage looked pleadingly at Corvalos Chane. 'Please don't . . .'

Asher glanced hopefully between them, wiping his hands on his dirty apron. 'You're wasting my time, Chane. I have a lot of work to do tonight.'

Finally, Chane turned and walked away. 'Find out what you can,' he said over his shoulder. 'I will be at Castle Hes.'

The dark hall swallowed him, and as it did the man named Asher sidled closer to Mirage. The deformed flesh of his eyelids closed incompletely as he blinked. 'I'll call my gaolers, have them make a place for you,' he said. Then he pulled at her bindings. 'Let's get these chains off you. I want you to be comfortable.'

Only a single lamp swatted back the blackness. Just outside Mirage's cell, the lamp light wavered as the oil burned away, threatening to leave the hall completely dark. Mirage watched the flame, concentrating on it, gleaning sanity from its feeble warmth. She had arrived at the keep hours ago, dumped into the cell by one of Asher's rough gaolers. Free of her chains, she had been given water and bread and a pot in which to relieve herself, and that was all. The bars of her freezing chamber rattled as a breeze moved through the dark corridor. Amid the darkness, she could hear the distant shrieks of others like herself, screaming somewhere in the enormous prison, their cries echoing forever through the labyrinthine halls. Mirage wrapped her arms around her shoulders, fighting to keep warm. So far, Asher had left her alone, but she knew the reprieve would be short. She had seen hunger in his eyes, a kind of warped lust that frightened her. Beneath his misshapen flesh he was not like other men, content to merely leer.

Mirage braced herself for the morning, sure of the torture it would bring. She had already told the Reecians all she really knew. She had confessed her friendship with Baron Glass, and in truth she did not know his plans. The secret of the Akari, though, she could never confess, because deep in her soul she was still an Inhuman – one of Minikin's beloved – and would never betray that trust. But Mirage did not know what kind of torments Asher would deal her, or if she was strong enough to resist them. Under his skilled torture she might crack like an eggshell, she told herself.

'Pride,' she muttered. 'Stupid, stupid pride.'

How clear it was to her now that pride had brought her to this place. How much better her life would have been, if only she had listened to Minikin's warnings. In Grimhold she had been safe. Now she was trapped in the most unsafe place a woman could imagine, surrounded by bars in a foreign land, in the clutches of a mad and lustful monster. She closed her eyes, wishing someone – anyone – might find her. She called to her Akari, Kirsil. The spirit lilted across her brain, young and as frightened as her host. Together they had already tried to summon help, but Kirsil was not like Sarlvarian, so old and strong, and they were too far away from Jador to make any kind of contact. Even the realm of the dead was off-limits to callow Kirsil. Still, Mirage took comfort in the spirit's presence. As long as the Akari remained, she would not be completely alone.

Alarmed, Mirage opened her eyes as she suddenly heard footfalls approach. The pit of her stomach lurched. She leaned forward, trying to hide and see down the corridor at the same time. The light from the bare flame stirred in the breeze. Mirage held her breath as the footfalls drew nearer. The outline of Asher appeared before the bars.

'Good evening.'

His voice trembled with delight. His malformed face remained in shadow. In his hand he held a wooden stool. The pockets of his butcher's apron bulged with unseen tools. With his free hand he produced a key from his apron, using it to open the padlock on the iron bars. He worked gingerly, as if he'd done the manoeuvre a thousand times, then opened the cell door. When he was inside he placed the stool on the floor, closed the gate behind him and once more locked it closed. Mirage watched, shaking, as Asher took a seat on the stool, staring at her in the dim light. With the lamp behind him, she could barely see his poisoned features.

'*Mirage.*'

He crooned the name, and the sound of it brought a smile to his ravaged face. Resting his hands on his dirty apron, he relaxed. Mirage noted the oily stains on his garb, the shining blood of new victims. Gore crusted his fingernails. His shoulders slumped slightly.

'I've been busy tonight,' he said wearily. 'I did not mean to keep you waiting so long.'

Should she speak? Mirage didn't want to plead. That was what he craved.

'I have a whole prison of people like you to deal with now,' he continued. 'I wish I had a twin to share the work with, but alas there is only me. I suppose this interview could have waited till the morning, but I wanted to see you. You're so . . .' He searched for the word. 'Stimulating.'

'What are you going to do?' Mirage asked.

'Talk,' replied Asher. He grinned, a peculiar expression for someone soaked in blood. 'So many of the women they brought from Liiria are cows. They've spent their lives with mercenaries, eating swill and sleeping on straw. But not you. You're very beautiful, Mirage. Tell me – how did you come about such a name?'

'It was given to me,' said Mirage guardedly.

'Of course it was. By your parents?'

Mirage hesitated. She knew answering his questions would be like walking a tightrope. 'No. In Jador.'

'But you are not from Jador, not originally. You do not have the dark skin of a Jadori woman. So you are from the northern lands?'

'Yes.'

'And you found yourself in Jador.'

Mirage nodded. The lord of the prison relaxed, oblivious to the moans rattling the corridor. His head cocked a little as he looked at her, admiring her with his wild eyes, the lids of which sagged with deformity. The scars on his cheeks reminded her of her own.

'Corvalos Chane thinks much of you,' said Asher. 'To have brought you here on his own; you should feel honoured. He is the right hand of Raxor, our king. He would not waste his time with you if he was not sure your skull held secrets. Do you know why he brought you to me, Mirage?'

'Don't make me answer that,' Mirage implored. 'I already told you what I know.'

'Stand up.'

Shaken by the order, Mirage got slowly to her feet. She stood before the torturer, her hands at her sides, and could not look at him.

'Do not look away,' he ordered. 'Look at me always. Your eyes will tell me if you lie or not. Now answer me.'

'What?'

'Tell me why Chane brought you to me.'

Mirage swallowed hard. 'To be questioned.'

'You could have been questioned by anyone. Chane could have questioned you. He brought you to me because I am the best at what I do. I have a gift, you see. Look at all these people on my apron!' Asher proudly pulled at the garment, showing off its numerous stains. 'I learned a lot tonight.'

The sickening boast turned Mirage's legs to rubber. As she began to waver, she steeled herself.

'I think you are insane,' she said, 'to hurt people the way you do.'

'We all have to make a living, pretty Mirage. That is my answer when someone looks at me the way you do, with such disdain. Do you know, all of Raxor's men think they are my better. Even Chane, that miserable cutthroat. Why? Because what I do is distasteful? Someone has to bash in the sheep's brains before the mutton can be served.'

It was a demented argument. Mirage forced herself not to look away.

'You want to torture me,' she said. 'I can't stop you, because you'll never listen to reason, will you?'

'I want the entire truth,' replied Asher. 'Please do not make the mistake so many others have about me. We do not choose our gifts in life, girl. Mine were thrust upon me, just as beauty was thrust upon you.' He leaned closer, examining her face and the curves of her figure. 'What is it like to be so lovely? In my work, I do not see many pretty young women. It's my face, you see. They shun me. I want to know what it's like for you. So easy, I'd wager.'

Mirage didn't know how to answer the odd question. Mere months ago, she had been as scarred and damaged as Asher.

'Would I be here if I weren't beautiful to you?' she asked.

'I don't know. I don't know if Chane would have paid enough attention to you.' Asher laughed, delighted at the irony. 'You see? Beauty is a curse sometimes.'

His laughter angered Mirage. 'What are you going to do to me?'

Asher stopped chuckling. 'There was a woman brought in with you, a little one from Norvor. Dark hair. Do you remember her?'

'Yes.'

Asher inspected his apron, found the appropriate bloodstain, and pointed at it. Mirage blanched as her bravado drained away.

'I have a favourite knife to use on people like her,' said Asher. He reached into the pockets of his apron and took out a thin knife with a long, hooked blade. 'You would be amazed at how long someone can live if you use the right tool. I asked her what she was doing in Liiria. She was the whore of a mercenary named Devyn. It was the usual, tiresome questions. She told me nothing useful.' Asher held the knife close to his face, turning it so that Mirage could see its fine edge. 'She didn't look anything like you, Mirage. She was ugly, like me. I did her a kindness by killing her.'

He looked sad suddenly, like a little boy with a broken toy. The madness on his face ebbed a little, replaced by something like shame.

'I wish Chane hadn't brought you to me,' he said. 'You don't belong in this butcher's shop. That's what this place is, you know. I kill cows here. But you're not a cow, Mirage. You are a beautiful butterfly.'

Asher touched his face, brushing the narrow blade against his uneven cheek.

'I've seen you looking at me. You don't realize how you stare, do you?'

'I'm sorry,' groped Mirage. 'I didn't mean to.'

'I've been stared at all of my life.'

'I'm sorry.'

Asher shrugged. 'It isn't your fault. You couldn't know what it's like to be me.'

How little you know, thought Mirage. Instead she asked, 'What happened to you?'

Asher shrugged. 'Who knows what happens in the womb of a whore? My mother was a drunken slut. She was diseased, a gift from all the men she bedded. I was born like this – that was her gift to me.' He laughed. 'Can you imagine such a woman? A bitch.'

'And the scars?'

'Beatings. I told you, my mother had many men. One of them favoured a horsebrush.'

'I'm sorry.'

'Stop saying that,' spat Asher. 'Your pity won't save you.' His face softened. 'But I do regret this. I want you to know that. I'm going to get the truth out of you, Mirage. All of it, everything you know about Baron Glass, even things you've forgotten. It will be like magic!'

The knife held against his haunting face made Mirage wither. Her mind ran with images of blood and her own mangled body. So far she had been strong. Now, though, she could not be strong. Faced with Asher and his cherished knife, she crumbled.

'I don't know anything,' she moaned, dropping to her knees. 'I swear to heaven, I don't know.'

She could not look at him any more. She faced the floor as tears overcame her, shaking and hating herself for it. Asher rose from his stool, watching her. He said nothing, letting her sob. Unable to control herself, Mirage dropped lower to the floor, like a frightened house cat. She glanced up, waiting for the torturer to fall on her, to feel the slice of his hook blade. He glared at her, completely unemotional, then buried the blade of his knife upright into the seat of the stool.

'I will leave this here to argue with you,' he said.

Then, to Mirage's great relief, he unlocked the padlock to her cell, let himself out, and closed and locked the gate behind him. He spared her one last, longing look before disappearing down the dark corridor.

Choked with tears, Mirage stared at the knife protruding from the stool. Unable to move, she could not avert her eyes from it. She knew it wasn't mercy she had witnessed. Asher would return, and when he did he would bring his lustful appetite with him. It might be an hour or a day. Either way, it would be an eternity.

7

To Gilwyn, the world was like an ocean, black and featureless. He felt its tug. He struggled to awaken. His eyes fluttered open to the darkness of the ocean, but the ocean was like space, cold and completely without end. He could not feel his body, but he did feel afraid, and he knew that he was somewhere immortal, trapped in a place of magic where he should not be able to tread. His eyes – if indeed they were eyes – studied the darkness. He gazed down to glimpse his hands, but although he felt them moving they were nowhere to be found.

Gilwyn fought to remember. He could not recall his last conscious thoughts, and he considered that he was sleeping, and that he had been asleep for a very long time. He knew his name, and he knew his mission, and it all came suddenly back to him, how he had fled across the desert, being chased by Aztar's men.

And then?

He could not remember.

'Hello?' he called. He felt a presence in the darkness, straining to reach him. A familiar tremor coursed across his disembodied mind. 'Ruana?'

He had only to speak her name, and she was there. Ruana's sweet face shimmered in the darkness near him, shining with relief. Her hand reached out but did not touch him.

'Gilwyn, you are alive.'

Puzzled, Gilwyn felt himself shrug. 'Ruana, where am I? What is this place?'

'Gilwyn, you must go back,' said Ruana. 'You are alive.'

'Go back? Where? I don't understand. Why did you bring me here?'

'I did not bring you here, Gilwyn. This is not the place of the dead.'

She had read his thoughts, and her answer confused him. 'No?' Gilwyn looked around, but could see nothing familiar, only darkness. 'Where, then?'

'Your mind, Gilwyn,' said Ruana. 'This is your mind.'

The emptiness seized him. 'My mind?' He groped through the blackness. 'What's happened to me?'

'You must awaken, Gilwyn. You must try very hard. Do you understand? Try *now*.'

It was like a horrible dream, but this time there were no monsters chasing him or molasses to slow his feet. Ruana's words meant little to Gilwyn, yet they frightened him. His lungs filled with air, yet still he couldn't breathe. If this was his mind, then it was an empty void he couldn't fill.

'Gilwyn, you must rouse yourself,' Ruana continued. 'You are very close. That is why I can reach you now. Are you listening? Can you wake yourself?'

'From sleep? Am I sleeping?'

'You are ill, but you are coming out of it. Wake yourself now, Gilwyn.'

'Ill? What's happened to me?'

'Find your body. Connect it to your mind.'

Ruana's urgings made breathing unbearable. Gilwyn searched his empty mind – a great field of nothingness – for the mortal part of him. He felt a wave of nausea, then pain.

'That's it,' said Ruana, noting his fear. 'That is your body, Gilwyn. Go back to it.'

'What's happened to me?' Gilwyn asked. 'Ruana, I'm afraid.'

Ruana's face suffused with kindness. She stopped urging him and gently smiled. 'You will be all right soon. I promise. But you must return. That pain you feel – it is necessary. It is your body calling you back. Go to it, Gilwyn.'

'Don't leave me . . .'

'I am always with you, Gilwyn. When you awaken I will be there.'

There was no sense to her riddles. Gilwyn surrendered to his puzzlement. The pain he felt was growing enormous, and though he wanted to flee, he felt it calling to him, dragging him into its nauseating maw. Before him, he watched as Ruana shimmered and dimmed, her beautiful face yielding to the darkness. He began to cry, yet as she vanished she smiled.

'Ruana!'

Then she was gone, and the strange, empty world began to fade with her.

8

Gilwyn awoke to the sounds of his own cries. His ears heard the noise, and when his eyes snapped open he saw figures overheard, swarming in a fuzzy haze. He breathed hard, struggling to find his breath. His head swam with pain. Trying to move, he felt a thousand stinging needles prick his naked skin. A swollen tongue filled his mouth, dry and tasting of medicine. Sweat drenched his face and matted his hair. Barely lifting his head, he fought to focus his eyes, squinting at the figures, but they were unfamiliar to him, their features distorted by his broken vision. He coughed, a great hacking series that shook his body. The effort made his lungs burn. A dark figure stooped to touch his forehead. The touch of the soft hand made him whimper.

'White-Eye . . . ?'

The hand cupped his forehead, gently caressing it. He smelled perfume. Had he been sleeping? If so, awakening was exhausting him. His vision faltered and his eyes shuddered closed. As he drifted off he remembered something of Ruana, and how she wanted him to wake.

For hours more, Gilwyn slept, and when at last he awoke again he could not remember when he had taken to bed. This time when he awoke his vision had cleared. His head still ached and his body still burned with pain, yet his breathing had relaxed and his terror had subsided. He wakened peacefully, in a chamber darkened with night and lit by golden oil lamps. Alone and naked in a bed of soft blankets, he slowly turned his head to study his surroundings, realizing with surprise that he was in a tent. Moonlight sifted through the fabric walls. The air of the pavilion smelled of flowers and scented oils. Outside, Gilwyn heard voices, softly murmuring. He raised himself off the bedding, barely an inch. Finding the effort too depleting, he collapsed.

'Hello?' he croaked.

From the corner of the pavilion a figure stirred, coming toward him. Gilwyn felt no fear as he noted the woman, young and pretty, with dark skin like White-Eye's and the silken garb of a desert lady. She looked at him and smiled, obviously pleased he had awakened. Looking deeply into his eyes, she nodded. She touched his forehead, reminding Gilwyn that she had done it before. Her touch soothed him. He tried again to talk.

'Who are you?' he asked, his voice gravelly. 'Where am I?'

The woman frowned at his questions. She was older than he was, though not by much. Suddenly his nakedness embarrassed him.

'Where are my clothes? Who are you?'

Again his queries went unanswered. The woman knelt beside his bed and dipped a bronze ladle into a shining bowl of water. With one hand she lifted his head. With the other, she gave him drink. Gilwyn sipped carefully, grateful for the water. His parched tongue cooled immediately. He coughed to clear his throat.

'No, no more. Tell me where I am.'

'In a good place,' said the woman.

Gilwyn had not expected her to speak his language. Again he tried sitting up. 'You understand me,' he said with surprise. 'Tell me what's happened to me.'

'Too many questions. Lay quietly now.'

'No . . .'

Gilwyn tried to keep himself up but could not. Overwhelmed with fatigue, he put his head back to the silk pillow and looked pleadingly at the young woman. Weary-looking marks darkened her eyes. She had obviously been with him for hours. Yet she was beautiful to Gilwyn, if only because he felt so alone.

'Am I sick?' he asked. He began to remember what Ruana had told him, though it seemed so long ago.

'Sleep,' directed the woman. She rose from his bedside and turned to go.

'I won't sleep,' he warned her. 'I'll keep you up all night unless you start answering my questions.'

The woman sighed heavily, and for the first time looked annoyed. 'You have kept me awake for days already.'

'Days? How long . . .' He broke into coughs. 'How long have I been here?'

'Long. We have tended to you.'

'Yes, I remember others.' Gilwyn closed his eyes, recalling the figures gathered over him. 'I need to know where I am.'

'You are in a good place.'

'You told me that already,' said Gilwyn sourly. 'It doesn't help.'

He sagged at the empty conversation. Seeing this, the woman came closer. Because his bed lay very near the floor, she took an emerald pillow from a nearby pile and sat down next to him, cross-legged. Almost unable to lift his head, Gilwyn managed to smile at her.

'I am called Harani,' she said. 'I speak the tongue of the continent. There are not many of us who do. That is why I was chosen to care for you.'

'Harani.' Gilwyn liked the way she spoke her name, almost musically. 'Are you Ganjeese?'

'I am Voruni,' said the woman. 'Do you remember what happened to you?'

Gilwyn shook his head. 'Not really. You're Voruni?' He thought a moment, then became frightened. 'Are you one of Aztar's people?'

'You are in the camp of Aztar,' said Harani. 'Perhaps we should not talk about this. If you do not remember . . .'

But suddenly Gilwyn did remember. 'The rass.'

'Yes.' Harani smiled. 'You are blessed by Vala, truly. To have survived the rass you must be blessed.'

'I was riding,' Gilwyn recalled. 'There were raiders. They attacked me. And then . . .'

He stopped himself. It was he who had summoned the rass. He remember that now, but he could never confess such a thing. He opened his eyes to see Harani nodding at him earnestly.

'Good that you remember,' she said. 'Your mind is clearing. You have been very ill. We did not think you would survive.'

'Because of the rass?' Gilwyn asked. 'Did it bite me?'

'Your arms and legs – they burn, yes?'

Gilwyn nodded. His limbs burned like fire.

'That is the poison of the rass,' explained Harani. 'You were stiff like a branch when they brought you here. On your chest you have the scar.' Harani traced her finger lightly over his chest, pushing the blanket. 'Here. That is where the fangs cut you.'

Even the gentle pressure made Gilwyn wince. 'Who brought me here?' he asked. 'The men chasing me?'

'They were Voruni men,' said Harani. 'You were still alive when the rass attacked. They escaped with you and brought you here.'

'They were trying to kill me. Why would they save me?'

Harani touched his face to calm him. 'You are safe.'

The answer did little to relax Gilwyn. Suddenly he remembered everything, even how his captors had claimed they were taking him to Aztar. 'Is Aztar alive?' he asked. 'Is he here?'

'Aztar lives. You will see him when you are stronger.'

'No,' Gilwyn protested, forcing himself up onto his elbow. 'I can't wait. I have to go. I have to get to Ganjor.'

'Not until you are well and not until Aztar speaks with you. That is why the others brought you here.'

'They captured me for Aztar?'

'There are others outside. If you try to go they will stop you.'

Desperate, Gilwyn gripped the blankets. 'Harani, I can't stay here. Aztar wants to question me – you said so yourself. When he's done he'll kill me.'

'The prince did not keep you alive to kill you,' Harani assured him. 'And if you do not lay back you will not get well.' She pushed him back into the soft bedding. Gilwyn yielded, mostly because he hadn't the strength to fight. Whatever had happened to him had left him weak, too weary even to argue. Harani fixed the blankets around him, covering him against a feverish chill that suddenly swept through his body. Then, she surprised him with a simple question. 'What is your name?'

'My name? Gilwyn. Gilwyn Toms.'

'Gilwyn.' Harani grinned. 'That is a strange name.'

'Not where I come from.'

'You have been here for many days, Gilwyn. You need to know how close to death you were. Do you remember anything more?'

Gilwyn shook his head. 'Just the rass. After that . . .' He shrugged. 'Nothing.' He looked earnestly at Harani. 'How long?'

'Many days. Nearly twenty.'

'Twenty?' Gilwyn gasped. 'In bed like this?'

'Yes. Do you understand now? The rass poison should have killed you, but it did not. Aztar says that you are blessed, Gilwyn, and I believe him. No one should have survived it, but you did. Aztar told me to care for you, to keep you alive.' Harani eased back from the bedside. 'And now that you are awake, I must tell him.'

Gilwyn but didn't argue. For some reason he couldn't quite fathom, Aztar wanted him alive. It might be for information, or the simple sport of watching him squirm, but Gilwyn was determined to face the prince bravely. The mere fact that Aztar still lived earned him a certain respect.

'I'm ready,' said Gilwyn. 'Go and bring him.'

Harani laughed. 'One does not summon Prince Aztar. I will tell him you have awakened and that you can speak. He will come when he is ready.'

For three more days, Gilwyn waited for Aztar. Mostly, he fell in and out of sleep, comforted by Harani who was always there with a dipper or water or offer of food. When he was sweaty, Harani bathed him, and when he was despondent she smiled, reassuring him even as she avoided his questions. Gilwyn gradually felt himself grow stronger, and by the third day he was able to sit up and dangle his legs from the ends of the bedding. He ate very little, for his stomach still rebelled with nausea, but he discovered an insatiable thirst for water that required him to relieve himself in a pan that Harani and the other women emptied for him without complaint. The days in the pavilion were unbearably warm, and though the fabric walls shielded them from the worst of the desert sun Gilwyn nevertheless longed for night to fall each day. He had very few visitors while he recovered, among them Harani's husband, who had come to check on his wife and the upstart boy she was looking after. He was a fierce man, so like the image of a Voruni raider, with suspicious eyes that barely left Gilwyn even as he spoke to his wife.

Aztar, however, was not among those who came to the pavilion, and by the end of the third day Gilwyn began to wonder if the prince truly had survived, or if Harani was merely playing a ruse to keep him in bed. It seemed an elaborate pantomime, especially from the woman whom Gilwyn had come to trust. She was, as she had explained, one of the only people in the camp who could speak the language of the north, having learned it from her father, a Ganjeese merchant who had traded with the continent before his death. Harani had learned well from him, but then she had met the Voruni named Mazal, who became her husband. Together they had heard the call of Aztar. Harani adored Prince Aztar.

That night, Gilwyn found himself alone in the pavilion. Harani had left for a rendezvous with her husband, and Gilwyn had let her go with a promise that he would not get out of bed or try to leave the tent. Leaving, Gilwyn had already discovered, was impossible, for the Voruni guards posted at the exit would have no trouble at all stopping a groggy boy with a clubbed hand and foot. So he lay awake in his bed of colourful pillows, watching as moonbeams slanted through the walls and wondering how much longer he would have to remain. He had not forgotten his mission to find Thorin. Thoughts of his old friend plagued him. It had been weeks since he'd left Jador. By now, he should have been halfway to Liiria.

'I may never get there,' he whispered. 'Or see White-Eye again.'

Being morose wouldn't help him, Gilwyn knew, but he had already struggled for days to find an answer. Maybe there wasn't one, he realized. He was still weak. Worse, he remained in the clutches of a sworn enemy. He supposed Prince Aztar – if indeed he was still alive – was simply playing a cruel game with him and would kill him as soon as he was strong enough to walk up a gallows. Did the Voruni hang their prisoners the way Liirians did? Or did they just behead them with scimitars? Gilwyn rolled onto his side, thinking he would try to sleep, then glimpsed a shadowy figure entering the pavilion. It wasn't Harani; Gilwyn knew that instantly. He held his breath, squinting for a better view. The figure paused in the threshold, then reached out a hand to pinch out the oil lamp, leaving only the one by Gilwyn's bed lit.

'Hello?' Gilwyn called. He sat up, alarmed but curious. 'Who's there?'

The figure – clearly a man – took a silent step closer. Gilwyn could barely see his face, shadowed as it was by darkness. Moonbeams and lamp light shone off his richly textured vest. A thick belt of gold surrounded his middle. He was tall, but stooped. He moved with effort, hiding himself in the darkness. An air of importance followed him into the tent. Gilwyn sat up tall, unsure what to expect.

'You look well,' said the man. His voice boomed in the silence, sounding neither pleased nor angry. 'Better.'

Gilwyn didn't know whether to speak or stay quiet.

'I am Aztar,' the man pronounced. 'And I live.'

The words chilled Gilwyn. Aztar moved no closer.

'Your name is Gilwyn Toms. You are from Jador?'

'Yes.'

'You are blessed by Vala.'

'Your men saved me.'

'You are blessed by Vala,' repeated Aztar. 'His hand is on your shoulder. It must be so for you to have survived the rass.'

'Harani told me your men brought me here. I'm grateful for that.' Gilwyn shifted, uncomfortable under the gaze of Aztar's unseen face. 'They could have left me to die.'

'And you're wondering why they didn't.'

'They saved me because you willed it,' said Gilwyn. 'That's what I'm wondering about.'

Prince Aztar stepped closer, still keeping himself in shadows. He was called the Tiger of the Desert, but he did not move like a tiger. His legs worked stiffly, as he compelled himself across the floor, going half the distance toward Gilwyn before pausing. When he stopped he looked at Gilwyn, studying him. Gilwyn stared back but could not make out Aztar's features, except to note his beardless face, an odd thing among desert men.

'You have a question,' growled Aztar. 'Ask it.'

'I'm surprised is all,' said Gilwyn. 'You speak my language – I didn't expect that.'

'Voruni are not stupid.'

'That's not what I meant.' Gilwyn struggled to see Aztar's face. 'You hate northerners.'

Aztar seemed to sag. 'Vala has taught me.'

Gilwyn barely understood his meaning. 'The battle of Jador,' he said. 'We thought you died.'

'Disappointed?'

'Yes.'

'I have waited months to speak to someone from Jador,' said Aztar. 'That is why my men pursued you. Not to kill you, but so I might speak to you.'

'Speak to me? About what?'

'I wronged Jador.'

The confession shocked Gilwyn. 'What do you mean?'

'Look at me, Gilwyn Toms. Have you not seen yet? Do you not know how beautiful I was before Vala's fire?'

Gilwyn asked, 'You think it was Vala who made the fire?'

'Your leader, the little one – she commanded the fire. I know that. But only Vala could have created such a thing. It was Vala's hand coming down from heaven . . . to teach me.' Aztar sighed, then finally stepped into the light of Gilwyn's lamp. Instead of a handsome, confident face, Gilwyn glimpsed an ugly mask, reddened with scars and painful burns. 'A lesson learned.'

'I'm sorry for you,' said Gilwyn. Beneath the scars and obvious confusion, there was kindness on Aztar's face, even regret. 'And I am grateful for you saving me.'

'The rass would not have attacked you if my men had not given chase. You were theirs – and mine – to protect. Vala would have it no other way.'

'Harani told me I've been here for twenty days,' said Gilwyn. 'I haven't been out of this tent in all that time. I don't even know where I am.'

'We have kept you safe here,' replied Aztar. 'This is my place – my kingdom.'

The boast made Gilwyn grimace. 'The desert doesn't belong to you, Prince Aztar,' he said. It was why Aztar and Jador had warred in the first place.

Aztar laughed, mocking himself. 'Indeed no. Vala has already made that plain to me. But this camp is mine. This camp is my kingdom. It is all that's left to me. And there are still those who follow me.'

'Like Harani,' said Gilwyn. 'I've seen the way she speaks about you, like a god.'

'Harani has a loyal heart. Not everyone is like her.' Aztar shuffled closer, as though he were finally comfortable being seen by Gilwyn. 'In the battle with Jador many were lost. Many others left soon after.' The desert man paused in front of Gilwyn, cocking his head. 'You look weary. Lay back while we speak.'

Before Gilwyn could comply, Aztar sat himself down on the pillows near the bedding, just as Harani had many times before. Surprised, Gilwyn let himself relax. Still weak, he was happy to ease into the cushions.

'Why have you come here?' he asked. 'Why do you want to speak to me?'

Before she had gone, Harani had refreshed Gilwyn's water, leaving two clean, golden cups near the basin. Aztar picked up one of the cups, filled it with sparkling water, and handed it to Gilwyn.

'You are here to listen to my confession,' Aztar replied, now filling his own cup. 'I want you to know that I am no longer your enemy. I want you to know that Vala has changed me, and that I see his wisdom. And I wanted to see for myself the people He has chosen to touch.'

Gilwyn held his cup but did not drink. 'Chosen? I don't understand.'

'Do you know why I battled your people in Jador?' asked Aztar. 'Because I loved a woman. And because I thought the Serene One would allow me to spill the blood of innocents to get what I wanted.' The prince looked contemplatively into his cup of water, frowning at his own reflection. 'And now I am cursed. Vala has taken away my pride. But he has taught me much, too. He has humbled me.'

Frustrated, Gilwyn leaned over and put his cup on the floor. 'Prince Aztar, the people of Jador aren't chosen by Vala. Many of them don't even believe He exists. A lot of them are northerners, like me.'

Aztar smiled. 'You see how wise are the works of Vala? I could live a thousand years and never glimpse all his greatness. The Jadori do not even know the Serene One favours them, but he does. He allowed your people to summon the fire. He burned me and took away my pride.'

'None of this makes sense to me,' sighed Gilwyn. He knew it was Minikin who had summoned the fire, and that the fire had come from the great Akari, Amaraz. 'I was riding through the desert. I don't understand anything you're talking about.'

Prince Aztar finally drank his water. He seemed endlessly patient. He sipped his water like tea, and when he was done placed the cup on the floor.

'The woman I spoke of; she is no more than a girl, really. Her name is Salina, and you have never seen a more beautiful creature in all of creation. I craved her, and made a deal with her father to have her.'

'Salina of Ganjor?' Now Gilwyn was intrigued. 'Yes, I know of her.'

'Salina's father Baralosus rules Ganjor. You must know that as well. And Baralosus is an ambitious beast. He loves his daughter dearly, but would cut her up and sell the pieces if it earned him the key to Jador and its powers. I had an argument with Jador and a burning passion for Salina. Baralosus knew this and bargained with me.'

'A bargain. You would conquer Jador for Baralosus, and for that he would give you Salina.'

'Just so. And I did not regret this bargain at all, because to me your people – you northerners especially – were rodents. You were soiling my desert, bringing disease. You needed to be destroyed, and truth be told I would have done so without the prize of Salina.'

'But you were wrong?' probed Gilwyn.

Aztar nodded. 'I was wrong. Before the battle, I prayed to Vala for victory. But I did not tell Him that I was doing this to win Salina, that I was killing in His name to slack my lust.' He stuck his face out for Gilwyn to inspect. 'Look at me. I have no beard. It does not grow now.'

It was a profound admission. Aztar was Voruni, and Voruni men all had beards. They grew them from the earliest possible age, a sign of manhood and virility. Gilwyn knew that Aztar's fire-smoothed face was an abomination to him.

'Is that why your men have left you?' he asked.

'Some. Others left because their brothers died in the fire. More others because they felt the wrath of Vala on their own souls.'

'But not everyone. Some have stayed.'

'Yes. Even now Vala blesses me. He has not forsaken me. He teaches me. That is what I want you to know, Gilwyn Toms, and what I want you to tell the others. When you return to Jador, you must tell them that I am no longer their enemy. I release my claim to the desert. I will not kill those who come across it.'

Gilwyn hesitated. He was relieved by the man's words, but still afraid to tell too much. 'Prince Aztar, that is difficult . . .'

'Because of what I have done,' said Aztar, nodding. 'I do not expect you to trust me. But when you are able to return to Jador, tell them what I have said. Tell Shalafein.'

'Shalafein? You mean Lukien?'

'The one you call the Bronze Knight. Your protector. Many of my men have sought his head, but I have released the bounty. Tell Shalafein he is free now.'

'I will when I can,' said Gilwyn evasively, 'but I am not going back to Jador, Prince Aztar, not yet. I have to go to Ganjor.'

'When you have finished your business in Ganjor, then.'

'No. When I am done in Ganjor I am going back north to Liiria, my homeland.'

Aztar looked crestfallen. 'But you will go back to Jador someday, yes?'

The question saddened Gilwyn. 'Yes. If I can.'

'Good. Then you can give them my message when you return. I cannot tell them myself. I am too disgraced to face them.' The prince rose from the floor. 'I will not leave this camp.'

'Ever?'

'This is where I must remain, Gilwyn Toms. Alone.'

'But what about Salina? What about your pact with Ganjor?'

'My dealings with Baralosus are dead,' Aztar declared. 'And I will not see Salina again.'

Aztar turned to go. And Gilwyn, feeling lost, looked blankly at his back as he retreated from the pavilion.

'That's it?' he blurted. 'Nothing more?'

Aztar paused. 'I have told you everything, boy. When you are able you can be on your way. I will not stop you.'

'But I am going to Ganjor, Prince Aztar.' Gilwyn thought for a moment, considering his words carefully. 'If I can, I am going to meet with Princess Salina.'

The mention of her name made the prince's face slacken. 'You know her?'

'No. But she has helped us. She warned us of your attack. She was an ally to us, Prince Aztar, and I was told to seek out her help once I got to Ganjor.'

Aztar blinked at the news, and Gilwyn could not read the strange expression on his face. Though he had just been told of betrayal, he simply looked empty. 'If her father ever knew . . . he would kill her.'

'I'll be careful,' said Gilwyn. 'There are men in the city I'm supposed to find, agents who work with Salina. They can take me to her.'

'And what will you do when you find her?' Aztar asked.

Gilwyn shrugged. 'Ask for her help. I'll need a horse to take me the rest of the way north. Food and water, too.'

'I can give you those things. You need not endanger Salina.'

'You still care for her, then.'

The prince's face grew stormy. 'Rest. And when you are ready be on your way.'

Aztar left quickly through the tent flap. Gilwyn watched him go, confused by everything that had happened.

A week later, Gilwyn was at last ready to leave Aztar's camp. He had not seen the prince since that first moonlight meeting, and could not get any more information out of Harani. She cooked his food, mended his body, and entertained him with gossip from the camp, but when the subject turned to Aztar she refused to indulge. Only once did she hint at her master's love for Salina, and only then obscurely. Eventually, Gilwyn gave up pursuing her. Deciding he needed to be on his way, he put his energies toward healing himself, alternating between rest and exercising his sore muscles, until at last he could walk without getting winded. The rass poison had done a remarkable job of weakening him, but the kindness of Harani and the generosity of Prince Aztar had healed him.

And for that, Gilwyn was grateful.

He had been in Aztar's camp for almost a month, and knew it was time to leave. This he explained to Harani, who prepared for his departure the next morning. Good to her promise, she had a horse waiting for him and all the things he had brought with him from Jador, including the kingship ring Lorn had given him. His own horse had died in the rass attack, but the new one Aztar provided was a prize, indeed, a great, stout-hearted stallion of obvious breeding. Certainly, the horse had been worth more than Gilwyn could ever pay for it, and he puzzled over the grand beast as he prepared to leave the camp. Harani and her black-eyed husband watched as he studied the animal. Other Voruni had gathered as well. They had all grown accustomed to seeing Gilwyn in camp, and Gilwyn had grown to like them. Despite losing many of his followers, Aztar still had hundreds of people calling him master.

Still, Aztar himself had not come to bid Gilwyn farewell. For a reason that confused Gilwyn, the prince's absence disturbed him. He fiddled with the stallion's tack, making sure his belongings were secure while Harani looked on, confused. The morning sun was already hot on his back, and when he looked eastward he saw the great expanse of desert still needing to be crossed.

'Be well on your journey,' said Harani, 'and when you return, you will be welcome here.'

Gilwyn smiled at her, pleased to see her husband agreeing with a nod. He had hardly spoken to Mazal at all, but had found him to be less fierce than his appearance.

'I will,' said Gilwyn. 'Thank you for everything, Harani.' He looked around at all the gathered faces. 'Thank you to everyone.'

'You are well enough now?' asked Harani. 'You are sure?'

'Yes,' said Gilwyn. 'I'm sure.'

'Then why do you wait?'

Gilwyn didn't answer. He wasn't sure why he hesitated. It might have been fear, he supposed, but then he realized it was not. It was unfinished business that kept him.

'Harani, I want to see Prince Aztar,' he said.

Harani blanched at the suggestion. 'No, Gilwyn.'

'Please. I want to speak with him. It's important.'

'Tell me what you want to tell him. I will speak for you after you have gone.'

'That won't work,' said Gilwyn. 'I want to talk to him about Salina. Please . . .'

Harani looked at her husband, who shrugged in confusion. The request left them both uncomfortable, but seeing that Gilwyn would not leave, Harani relented.

'Come, then,' she said, and started off into camp. Gilwyn followed eagerly. Aztar had been good to him, despite the plans he had laid against Jador. Gilwyn picked his way carefully across camp, trying to keep up with Harani, the special boot for his clubbed foot sinking heavily into the loose earth. Soon, Harani had taken him through the centre of the camp, across the outskirts and toward an outcropping of rock surrounded by desert sand. Here the morning sun beat down hotly, sending up a blinding reflection from the shimmering land. Gilwyn slowed, squinting to see better. They were alone now, a good distance from the pavilions. The noise of the Voruni and their animals fell away under the whisper of the wind.

'Where are we going?' Gilwyn asked.

'To Aztar,' said Harani. She pointed toward the outcropping. 'There.'

The rock itself rose out of the rugged desert, its jagged silhouette cutting the daylight. It was, Gilwyn realized, the tallest structure for miles, like a tiny mountain that had somehow wandered away from its mother range. There were no other people in the distance, only the sweeping dunes, but on the crest of the hill Gilwyn spotted a lone figure, cloaked in plain robes and kneeling, his head bowed, his hands flat against the stone.

'Is he praying?' asked Gilwyn.

'Every morning he comes here to be near Vala,' Harani answered.

Gilwyn stared, struck by Aztar's devotion. He seemed so alone on the rock – and so lonely. He took no notice of his visitors far below, but instead raised his voice in a musical chant, singing mightily as he turned his face toward the cloudless sky.

'What is he praying for?' Gilwyn wondered aloud.

Harani looked melancholy. 'For understanding. That is what I think.'

'Should we wait? How long will he pray?'

'Until his prayer is done.'

The sun baked the top of Gilwyn's skull. He waited, cultivating patience, waiting for Prince Aztar to finish his devotion. At last the prince ceased his song, bent low to kiss the rock, then straightened his stooped spine. It occurred to Gilwyn that the effort to climb the rock had been enormous for Aztar, whose body was racked with burns. Aztar slowly turned his head to regard them from his perch. A mild annoyance flashed across his face.

'Stay,' commanded Harani. 'I will leave you now.'

'What? Harani, wait . . .'

The woman ignored Gilwyn's plea, turning and walking back toward the camp. Gilwyn thought of going after her, but Aztar was already making his way down the jagged slope, painfully coming toward Gilwyn, his head and face protected by a brilliant white gaka. The dark skin of his cheeks glowed with redness. His eyes flashed when they met Gilwyn's.

'You are to go,' he grumbled. 'Why are you here?'

'To speak with you, Prince Aztar. I've been thinking.'

Aztar remained perturbed. 'On your way, boy.'

Gilwyn shook his head. 'I can't go, not yet. I've been thinking about what you told me, about Princess Salina. I'm going to speak to her, Prince Aztar.'

'So you have said.'

'That's right. And when I told you, you got angry. I don't understand why.'

'Why? That is none of your concern.' Aztar drilled Gilwyn with his gaze. 'Is that why you came here?'

Gilwyn spoke carefully. 'Prince Aztar, you've been kind to me. I didn't expect that. I expected you to kill me.'

The prince's suspicious eyes barely softened. 'You were wrong about me. Perhaps we were wrong about each other.'

'Yes, we were. But I wanted to repay that kindness if I can. I want to bring a message to Salina for you, tell her you're still alive. She thinks you're dead, probably. You know that, don't you?'

'To her, I am dead,' said Aztar. 'I have nothing to offer her, and nothing to say.'

'But you love her. She should know that you're alive, at least. When I see her, I can tell her that for you.'

Behind his cloak, Aztar looked regretful. 'I cannot stop you,' he said. Pulling the hood close around his face, he brushed passed Gilwyn on his way back to camp. 'Go.'

Gilwyn hobbled after him. He had been so sure Aztar would welcome his offer. 'Don't you want to tell her you're alive? That you still care for her?'

'It makes no difference. I cannot see her again. Not ever.'

'But why?'

'Because I am forbidden!' Aztar roared. He whirled on Gilwyn, ripping back his hood and exposing his burned and furious face. 'Look at what Vala did to me! My love for her is a curse, boy. It must never rise again.'

'But what if she loves you? What if she's suffering because she thinks you are dead? That isn't fair, Prince Aztar.'

'Why do you pursue this?' Aztar groaned. 'Why must you torture confessions from me?'

'To repay you,' said Gilwyn. 'Because you've been kind to me. And because I think you're wrong. I know about Vala, Prince Aztar. I know that He is a kind and loving god. Maybe he did punish you for attacking Jador. But not because you love Salina. That can't be.'

Aztar snarled, 'You know nothing of Vala, boy. You are a northerner; you do not even believe. I have devoted my life to the Serene One. And I know my crimes. Let me suffer them in peace.'

Gilwyn looked at the man, stunned by his refusal. He had wanted to repay Aztar's kindness, but now he realized he had stumbled into a hornet's nest.

'All right,' he said softly. 'I'll go. And when I see Salina I won't say anything about you. I won't tell her that you're alive or that you were kind to me. I'm sorry, Prince Aztar. I only meant to help you.'

He started off, wandering past Aztar on his way back to camp, leaving the prince in the shadow of the hill. He went five or six paces before Aztar called after him.

'Wait.'

Gilwyn paused, turning hopefully. Aztar's pained eyes faced the ground.

'Tell her that I am alive,' he said. He lifted his gaze toward Gilwyn. 'Tell her that I love her still.'

'But you won't go to her?'

'No. I can never go to her. Tell her that as well, Gilwyn Toms, and that I will never forget her beauty.'

Prince Aztar covered his head again, then turned and walked quietly back toward the hill. Gilwyn waited a moment, wanting to say more but having no words. As Aztar again began climbing his sacred hill, Gilwyn walked slowly back to camp, where the magnificent black stallion waited for him.

9

A chorus of song birds greeted Salina as she made her way through the palace gardens. Already the sun had risen, but Salina's mind still slept, and as she padded across the cobblestones she let out a long, unlady-like yawn. The brightly coloured birds who had risen with the sun ignored her outburst as they sang, clinging happily to the fruit trees in the garden. The first rays of sunlight shone through the green leaves, warming the small balls of sweet-smelling citrus. The palace itself was already humming with activity, but the garden remained blessedly quiet, and Salina took satisfaction in the silence. Tonight was the last night of Oradin, the week-long festival of the new year's moon. That meant legions of revelers and a long night pleasing her father's many friends, and Salina was already dreading it. When she was a girl, she had loved Oradin and the sweet-tasting moon cakes that came with the holiday. For a week she and her sisters would choose pretty clothes to impress the boys, painting their nails and polishing their jewelry until it sparkled. Of all the Ganjeese holidays, Oradin was not the most holy or important. It was simply the most fun, and for that reason alone the people or the city looked forward to it all year. But Salina took no joy in this year's holiday, nor in the tedious task her father had assigned her for the morning.

Princess Salina of Ganjor was the youngest of five daughters, and often described by her father as the prettiest rose in his garden. Until recently, King Baralosus had indulged Salina, favouring her with liberties he had never granted her older sisters. She had been independent, able to make up her own mind as to her education, her friends, even her manner of dress.

Until now.

At the end of the garden, Salina glimpsed the woman who had come to the palace to instruct her. Her name was Fatini, and Salina had seen her around the palace many times before. Fatini was the wife of Toran, the silk merchant who supplied the fabric to all of the king's tailors. She was a woman of great stature among the servants, certainly rich by Ganjeese standards, but when she came to instruct the king's daughters she lost the haughtiness she displayed in her own shop. Salina slowed her pace, sure that Fatini had not yet seen her. Around the woman were wooden tables burdened with bales of fabric and tools. Fatini herself fiddled with tools, testing and arranging them as she waited for the princess to arrive. All five of Baralosus' daughters had been instructed by Fatini, patiently taught how to make their own mejkith. Now, it was Salina's turn. She was to wear the veil tonight, hiding her pretty face from all of the hungry male onlookers. Salina cringed at the thought, wondering how thunderously mad her father would get if she simply turned around.

A bird in the tree above Salina's head began to sing, getting Fatini's attention. Spotting Salina in the grove, Fatini smiled and urged her forward. Except for the two of them, they were alone in the garden. Grateful no one else had come to watch her, Salina reluctantly proceeded. Fatini had arranged their work area under a beautiful, wide-spreading orange tree. A carpet of fallen leaves softened the ground beneath the tables. Salina looked around, dazzled by the colours of the many fabrics Fatini had brought with her. The display softened Salina's mood. She would be able to choose her own colour for her mejkith. The thought brought out the child in her.

'Good morning, Princess Salina,' said Fatini, rushing forward to greet her with a smile. Though many merchants and their wives spoke the tongue of the continent, Salina had never heard Fatini speak anything but Ganjeese. She had a practiced, aristocratic accent that made the language sound beautiful.

'Good morning, Lady Fatini,' replied Salina, giving the woman a slight bow. Even though she was a princess, she could still be intimidated by her father's lordly friends.

Fatini reached out and took Salina's hand. She had long, dainty fingers laden with rings that dug into Salina's skin. 'Look!' she pronounced, making a sweeping gesture at the tables. 'I've brought only the best for you, Princess. This is a special day for you. Your formal mejkith!' She sighed dramatically. 'I am happy for you, child. No, not a child! A woman.'

'Yes, a woman,' Salina agreed, though the distinction was not what it should have been. In Ganjor, becoming an adult was not the same for women and men.

'Here, sit yourself down, child,' said Fatini, steering Salina toward a chair near the largest table. 'First we will choose a colour. Have you thought of what you would like?'

Salina sat down, staring at the bales of fabric. 'No. I have a green dress for tonight. A mejkith that is green should do fine.'

'Oh, but this is your first mejkith. The dress you wear is less important.' Fatini happily started going through the fabric. Like most Ganjeese ladies of means, she wore a dress of velvet, the colours slightly muted yet nonetheless beautiful. Silver and gold threads rounded the cuffs, all perfectly stitched. 'You should choose a colour that makes your heart sing,' said Fatini. 'Something that will make men wonder about you.'

'Lady Fatini, this is my father's pride,' said Salina. 'I do not mean to be unkind, but I have not given this much thought.'

'Then it is time you did think of it, child. You are a woman grown now, and tonight is a formal night. You cannot act like a little girl any longer. Consider what people will say about you, and your father. Always consider that, Salina.'

Salina nodded, concealing her anger. Everything she did was carefully considered so not to embarrass her father. That was the duty of all daughters – to make their fathers proud, and never, never to embarrass them. People like Fatini simply never noticed the contortions Salina put herself through to please her father. Still tired from being woken up so early, Salina felt her lips twisting in rebellion.

'We'll choose the best colour for your face,' said Fatini. She had a large swatch of lavender silk in her hands, which she helped up to Salina's face, just below the eyes. 'Look how pretty this is. Do you think so?'

Salina shrugged. 'It's nice.'

'Nice?' Fatini seemed hurt. 'Child, do try to understand what we're doing here. The mejkith will give you mystery. It will mark you as a woman, ready for a husband.'

'Husband?' Salina shook her head adamantly. 'No.'

The lady laughed. 'Oh, yes. There will be many fine men at your father's celebration tonight. Do not be surprised if one has his eyes on you.'

'One already *had* his eyes on me,' said Salina. She knew it was an open secret. The entire palace knew of Aztar's interest in her. And now that Aztar was gone – maybe even dead – no other suitors had come forward.

'Prince Aztar would have made a man for you,' said Fatini softly. 'Your father spoke of him often.'

Did he speak of Jador too? Salina wondered. *Or how he simply bargained me away for it?* She wanted to ask these questions with an acid tongue, to pin Lady Fatini down like a butterfly, but she did not. She simply pushed the lavender silk aside. She had already settled on green.

'If Prince Aztar would have had me,' she grumbled, 'it was not my father's place to speak of it. I am a woman grown – I should be able to choose my own time of marriage. And my own husband.'

'That is northern nonsense,' said Fatini. She looked at Salina gently. 'Your father is very wise, Princess. Let him make these decisions for you. You will see – he will not fail you.'

'But I do not wish it, Lady Fatini.' Salina pushed herself away from the table. 'I do not wish to be bartered as my sisters were, or share a bed with a man three times my age.'

'That is how marriages are made, child. That is how I met my husband, and Toran is a good man. He has provided well for me and our children. He works hard to make a fine life for us all. Do not fret so. Your father will choose wisely. Your husband will have the means to make you happy.'

Salina glanced up at the woman. 'We are so different, you and I,' she sighed. 'You take joy in the mejkith. I do not.'

Fatini put down a bale of silk she was about to unravel, pulling up the only other chair to sit beside Salina. She did not seem offended by the girl's words, but rather confused. In the shade of the orange tree, she smiled the way a mother might, plaintively and without judgement.

'Princess, if you were my daughter I would tell you things, about how a man shivers when he looks at a woman in a mejkith, and how he hungers, wondering what beauty lies beneath.'

Salina laughed, feeling her cheeks flush. 'Fatini, please . . .'

'It's true,' said Fatini with a grin. 'Men love mystery. You see? The mejkith is not a prison, Princess. It is a mighty shield! It gives you power. If I was your mother I would tell you these things.' Lady Fatini sat back. 'But I am not your mother, so I never told you that, did I?'

'No,' chuckled Salina. 'You never did.' She reached out and took the fabric Fatini was about to show her, a rich silk the colour of sparkling emeralds. 'Now, show me how to make a mejkith.'

Happiness flashed through Lady Fatini's dark eyes. In the still cool air of morning, the merchants wife lined up her needles and cutting tools and began her teaching. Salina listened intently, still not wanting to wear the mejkith but not wanting to disappoint the sweet, surprising woman, either. She had misjudged Fatini, she decided, and cheerfully let Fatini guide her hands across the fabric, using a sharp blade to cut the delicate silk. The first would be only practice, Fatini told Salina. There was no need to worry about mistakes.

'We have all day,' said the woman.

Salina settled into her work, and after an hour she had learned to work the little tools. She was already an accomplished seamstress, a skill all the women of the palace learned from an early age. As she worked some golden thread into a long needle, Salina began to sing to herself. It was a glorious morning in the garden, too lovely to retain a foul mood. Then, from the corner of her eye, she glimpsed someone waving at her. Salina put down her sewing.

'Nourah?'

Her friend and handmaiden stood a few paces away, partially hidden in the grove, staring at her sheepishly. Nourah gestured nervously for Salina to come. Salina frowned, surprised at the girl's forwardness. Nourah was a close confidant, and smart enough not to interrupt unless something important had arisen.

'Lady Fatini, your pardon, please,' said Salina, getting up from her chair. 'That is one of my maidens. She must need something.'

'Of course, Princess,' said Fatini, preoccupied with her own projects. 'Do not be too long, though. You still need work.'

'I won't,' Salina promised, then excused herself to go to Nourah. One of her youngest handmaidens, Nourah was nevertheless among Salina's most trusted. Salina was closer to Nourah than to any of her sisters, and had confided her deepest secrets in the girl, who had kept them all safely locked away. Nourah's brown eyes jumped nervously as Salina approached, obviously bursting with news. Anxiously she waved for her princess to hurry, keeping herself partially hidden in the grove.

'Why are you here?' Salina asked crossly. 'Nourah, you shouldn't have come . . .'

'I had to,' Nourah insisted. She waited until Salina was well within earshot, keeping her voice to a whisper. 'Salina, Kamag came to see me.'

Salina started at the name. She took Nourah's shoulder and turned both their backs toward Fatini. 'Kamag? When?'

'This morning, when I was shopping in the market. He wants you to come.'

'Did he say why?'

Nourah bridled at the question, bracing herself. 'Salina, he said it was about Aztar.'

Princess Salina felt her heart race. She had not had news of Aztar for months, nor had she heard from Kamag, either. From his place in his safe little tavern, Kamag had helped Salina ferry Seekers across the desert, keeping them safe from Aztar as they sought Jador. Like she, he had risked his life to help the desperate northerners, always using Nourah as a messenger. Since Aztar's defeat, there had been no need for them to talk, and very few Seekers who needed their help anyway.

'Aztar . . .' Salina put her hand over her chest. The news had winded her. 'What did he say?'

'Nothing else,' said Nourah. 'But he wants you to come tonight.'

'Tonight? I cannot come tonight! It's Oradin!'

'Kamag knows, but it is urgent. I told him of the gathering at the palace, but he insisted that it cannot wait, and that you would want to know.' Nourah looked helpless, like the young girl she was. 'I'm sorry, Salina. I do not know more.'

Salina simply wilted. 'Aztar. I can't believe it . . .'

Nourah looked at her expectantly. 'What will you do?'

'What can I do? I have to be at that cursed gathering tonight.' Salina felt exasperation rising like a cobra. 'My father will skin me if I miss it.'

'Tell him you are sick,' Nourah suggested, 'that you have your moon time.'

Salina rolled her eyes. 'He is wise to that one. So is everyone else.'

'Think of something else, then. Eat a bad fish or some spoiled milk.'

'I don't want to really be sick. Seriously, now, think . . .'

Salina turned back to Lady Fatini, who waved at her impatiently. Salina waved back with a face that begged indulgence.

'I have to get back,' she groaned. 'Nourah, I have to see Kamag tonight.'

'I know,' Nourah nodded helplessly. 'We will get you there. Stay at the gathering as long as you can, then be ill. I will say you've gone back to your room. Everyone will be too busy to look for you. By the time they do, you will be back.'

Salina considered the plan, confident it would work. Her father always got too drunk on Oradin to notice anything unusual, and with so many people to entertain, it was certain she would not be missed.

'All right,' Salina agreed, smiling nervously. 'Go now. I'll be done here when I can.'

Salina squeezed her maiden's shoulder, then turned and walked back to Fatini and her table full of fabrics. Over the next hour she struggled hard to concentrate on her work, but her mind was a thousand miles away, over Aztar and what fabulous news Kamag might have for her.

Just past midnight, Salina found herself in the streets of the city, surrounded by revelers still celebrating Oradin. Overhead, the moon that was the holiday's namesake glowed a brilliant ivory, lighting the avenues of Ganjor while men and boys moved between the shrana houses and played card games, enjoying the parades of brightly garbed women as they too enjoyed the merriment. At her palatial home, Salina had managed to convince her father of a sudden illness, excusing herself from the gathering even as hundreds of guests still stalked the palace's halls and banquet chambers. King Baralosus' guests had come from miles, paying him tributes of gold and spices and enjoying his famous kitchens and wine cellars. Salina had endured the night gracefully, wearing the mejkith she had made and doing her best to please the young men her father introduced, smiling just enough not to encourage them. It had been a tedious function, and Salina was glad to be gone from it. With Nourah's help, she had slipped out of the palace in the dress and sandals of a commoner. Because she was the king's daughter and seldom allowed out of the palace, almost no one in the city knew what she looked like, making it surprisingly easy to walk the streets anonymously.

Kamag's shrana house lay in a dark and quiet corner of the city's marketplace. Normally, there were few people in this part of Ganjor so late at night. Tonight, however, the streets were filled with happy people and market stalls that had stayed open for the holiday, selling sweet and spicy foods that filled the avenue with aromas. Salina's head swam with excitement as she hurried toward the place. To be out so late at night, without a chaperone to pester her, was a rare treat she always savoured. So far, she had managed to keep her meetings with Kamag secret and rare. It had been months since she had spoken to him.

Salina tugged the fabric of her head wrap closer around her face. Normally, women were not permitted in shrana houses unless escorted by a man, but tonight was Oradin, and that meant the holiday would give her cover. She pressed passed the inn's beaded curtain, hiding her face from a pair of men who were leaving. Entering, her eyes scanned the busy house. Kamag was having a good night, indeed, for every one of his tables were full. Luckily, she spotted Dahj darting about the place, taking orders from the patrons. Another of her confidants, Dahj often worked for Kamag to earn much needed money. He was a young, friendly man, and brave like Kamag, too. Both of them had risked much to aid the Seekers. When Dahj glanced in her direction, Salina waved. Dahj quickly dropped his tray of shrana cups on a nearby stool and hurried toward her, pushing his way through the crowd.

'Princess,' he whispered, not smiling and not wanting to draw attention.

Salina nodded, holding her wraps high against her face. She was pleased to see Dahj, but had no way of showing it. 'Kamag?'

'Waiting for you.' Dahj looked around. 'Busy tonight. Be careful.'

Salina understood, careful to avoid the stares of others. She followed Dahj through the busy inn, keeping her eyes low. Dahj moved quickly to the back of the tavern, toward the hall that lead to the upstairs sleeping chambers. A few other servers darted past them with trays of steaming shrana and the popular moon cakes. When they reached the hall, Dahj paused.

'Wait here,' he directed. 'I will bring Kamag.'

Dahj disappeared quickly back into the main room, leaving Salina alone in the hall. The servers ignored her, too busy with the work to pay the girl much notice. Salina shifted uncomfortably, anxious to see Kamag and hear his news. Overhead, she heard the boards creak from the rooms upstairs, obviously rented for the evening. Salina smiled beneath her wraps, imagining the romance going on above her head. A minute passed, and then another, but before too long Kamag appeared, alone, skidding into the hall and beaming when he saw Salina.

'You came,' he pronounced happily. 'I knew you would.'

'Nourah told me it was important,' said Salina. 'What is it? What's happened?'

Kamag came closer, tossed a glance over his shoulder, and said softly. 'Princess, someone has come. He is upstairs, waiting for you.'

Salina trembled. 'Aztar?'

'No,' said Kamag. 'But someone with news of Aztar. A young man from Jador.'

'Jador? I don't know anyone from Jador,' said Salina. Though she had sent the Jadori doves warning them of coming Seekers, she had never met any of them. 'This young man – he knows of Aztar? He has seen him?'

Kamag waited for one of the servers to pass before answering. 'He was with Aztar in the prince's camp. He said he had a message for you.'

'Take me to him,' said Salina. 'I want to see him.'

The top floor of the house had about a dozen small bedrooms patrons could rent for the night. Salina had never spent much time in any of them, except to meet secretly with Kamag and give him money to help the Seekers. Knowing the way, she followed Kamag up the stairs toward the landing, where the first beaded curtain was drawn closed, light spilling out between its braids. Kamag went ahead and parted the curtain. He spoke softly to someone inside, then held the curtains open for Salina. When Salina stepped past them, she noted the tiny room, dimly lit by a few well-placed candles. A young man seated on the bed rose stiffly to greet her. Dressed as a northerner, he had the red complexion of sunburn, with sandy hair that fell into his eyes and a curious, trusting expression. His left hand dangled at his side, palsied into a club. A heavy, strange-looking boot surrounded his left foot. A slight smile crept over his boyish face when he saw Salina.

'Hello,' he said, shuffling forward and staring. His eyes went to their host. 'Kamag?'

'This is she, Gilwyn,' said Kamag. 'Princess Salina.' Kamag gestured toward the stranger. 'Princess, this is Gilwyn Toms, from Jador. He has come to speak with you.'

'I do not know you, Gilwyn Toms,' said Salina. 'Nor have I ever heard your name. Yet Kamag tells me you have a message for me, and news from Prince Aztar. Tell me, please.'

'I should go,' said Kamag. 'Princess, you will be safe with him. Keep your voices down, yes? When you need me, come downstairs.'

Salina said nothing as Kamag left, wanting only to hear from the stranger. The young man named Gilwyn Toms offered her the only chair in the little room, which Salina declined. 'Please tell me,' she asked. 'I want to know about Aztar.'

'Aztar is alive, my lady,' said the stranger. 'I was with him just two days ago in his camp.'

'He sent you here?'

'No,' said Gilwyn. 'Not really. I'm from Jador, my lady. I was heading home to Liiria. A man named Lorn told me to ask for you when I got here to Ganjor. Do you remember him?'

'Lorn? Yes, I remember,' said Salina with a smile. 'Lorn of Norvor. He made it to Jador, then?'

'He did, my lady, and he says he has you to thank for that. He wanted me to see you, to thank you for helping him and his people make it across the desert. They're all safe, my lady.'

'That is good news,' sighed Salina. 'I did not think they would all make it alive, especially the little one, the baby.'

'You mean Poppy?' Gilwyn Toms laughed. 'She's well, too.'

The two strangers looked at each other. Salina shrugged helplessly.

'I am desperate for news, Gilwyn Toms,' said Salina. 'What of Aztar? Is he well?'

The young man seemed reluctant. 'He lives, my lady,' he said gravely. 'But he is not well, no. You warned us in Jador about the battle . . .'

'Yes,' said Salina. 'What happened?'

'Aztar was hurt . . . badly.'

Salina felt her legs go weak. She went to the chair Gilwyn had offered and sat down, unraveling her stifling face wraps. Gilwyn Toms stood over her, concerned. It took a moment for Salina to find her voice again.

'Tell me more,' she said softly. 'Tell me everything.'

'There was a fire during the battle,' said the young man. 'Aztar and his men were pushing their attack. They were winning. They would have overrun us.' Gilwyn's face darkened. 'Something had to be done.'

'You do not need to make apologies,' said Salina. 'Some of Aztar's men came to Ganjor after the battle. They told of the magic fire.'

'So your father knows about it too, then?'

'Yes,' replied Salina, confused. 'What does that matter?'

Gilwyn shrugged if off. 'Maybe it doesn't mean anything,' he said without explaining. 'But Prince Aztar survived the fire. We didn't think he did, but he managed to escape.'

'But he was burned,' said Salina. 'Yes?'

Gilwyn nodded gravely. 'He has trouble walking sometimes. He is in great pain. He hides it, but I know he suffers. The fire burned much of his body. He probably looks nothing like you remember, Princess Salina.'

The statement shattered Salina. She tried to speak, but her throat constricted and her voice died. The joy of simply knowing Aztar was alive fled in an instant, replaced by a horrible guilt.

'It's my fault,' she gasped. She could barely bring herself to look at Gilwyn. 'I warned you of his coming. I sent him to this fate.'

Gilwyn Toms came closer, falling to one knee in front of her. 'He knows that,' he said gently. 'Aztar knows you warned us.'

'You told him?'

'I did. I told him what I knew about you, my lady, and how much you've helped us, and helped the Seekers.' Gilwyn gave an encouraging grin. 'He knows all about it, and he isn't angry. He just wanted me to come and see you.'

Salina gaped at him, stunned. 'He is not angry? That is unbelievable . . .'

'He's not what I expected, that's true,' said Gilwyn. 'He took care of me, made sure that I was well enough to travel before I left camp.'

'Yes, tell me about that – you were in his camp? That I do not understand.'

'It didn't make sense to me either at first,' said Gilwyn. 'I woke up there, after being attacked by a rass on my way through the desert.'

He went on to tell her about his time in the camp, waking up from an illness that nearly killed him. Aztar's women had cared for him, he told Salina, nursing him back out of a sleep that had lasted for weeks. Then, finally, Aztar himself had come to see him. Salina listened intently, watching Gilwyn's face in the candlelight, amazed by his tale of Aztar's kindness. She had always thought there was a part of Prince Aztar that could be gentle; she had even glimpsed it on occasion, when he came to visit her with flowers or quoted Ganjeese love poems. It broke her heart to hear it.

'When I told him I was coming here, it saddened him,' Gilwyn went on. 'I told him I was coming to see you if I could, because I had been told by King Lorn that you would help me. He loves you, Princess. He wanted me to tell you that.'

Sitting in her chair, Salina felt like a little girl, all alone and wanting to weep. Aztar had loved her from the moment they had met, and she still didn't know why. Then, when her father had tried to bargain her away to him, she had resisted because she wanted only independence for herself and the chance to choose her own husband. Yet Aztar's memory tugged at her, always like a little bird on her shoulder, chirping and reminding her that he cared for her.

'Even though I betrayed him,' she whispered darkly. 'Even still he loves me.'

'He does,' Gilwyn echoed. 'And he's changed. He wanted me to know that and tell the others in Jador, too. He claims he's not our enemy anymore, that he's been changed by Vala and that . . .' Gilwyn stopped himself, looking unsure.

'What else?' urged Salina. She could tell he was holding back.

'Aztar thinks Vala's punishing him,' said Gilwyn. 'He thinks Vala made the fire to teach him a lesson.'

'What lesson?'

Gilwyn finally rose from his knee and made his way to the edge of the bed. There he sat contemplating his words.

'Aztar told me about the bargain he made with your father, Princess Salina. He said that if he conquered Jador for him, your father would give you to him for a bride.'

'That is true,' Salina admittedly sourly.

'But Aztar didn't tell this to his god. He didn't tell Vala he was attacking Jador to win your hand. That's why he thinks Vala punished him, because he spilled innocent blood for his own lust and desires. He's convinced of it. That's why he won't leave camp, not even to go to Jador to explain himself. He feels disgraced.'

Salina got up from the chair and went to the room's lone, dingy window. Outside the small square of glass she could see the streets of Ganjor filled with people. Beyond Ganjor, the Desert of Tears loomed, dark and lonely. A spike of despair impaled her as she thought of Aztar, tortured and confused, sure that the god he loved so mightily had struck him down.

All for her.

'That's why you asked about my father,' Salina surmised. 'Because you knew about his plans for Jador.'

'That's right,' said Gilwyn. 'Pardon me for saying so, Princess Salina, but I do not trust your father.'

'Nor should you.' Salina turned from the window to face him. 'My father is a good man, mostly. But he is a Ganjeese king, and there are always jackals around him. He needs to stay strong, and do what he must to grow his power. I do not hate my father for the plans he laid against Jador, or even for trying to bargain me away. I am a girl, and in Ganjor that does not mean much.'

Pity flashed through Gilwyn's eyes. 'I'm sorry for you, Princess. I'm sorry I had to bring this news to you. But Aztar is still alive. That should bring you some comfort, at least.'

'It does. But then I think of him burned and pained and lonely. And then . . .' Salina turned hopelessly back to the window. 'Then I do not know what to think.'

She saw Gilwyn's reflection in the glass, slowly approaching her. 'My lady, I cannot stay long. I have things to do in Liiria, and I am so late already it may be too late.'

'Do you need my help?' asked Salina.

Gilwyn shook his head. 'No. Aztar gave me money and a good horse. I should be able to make the rest of the trip on my own. I only stopped to tell you his message, and to thank you for the help you gave Jador.'

'That help has cursed me, Gilwyn Toms. I saved strangers at the cost of someone who cared for me.' Salina turned to look at him. 'I want to go to him, Gilwyn. I want to see him.'

'You can't,' said Gilwyn. 'He made that clear. He doesn't want to see anyone, especially not you.'

'But he loves me. You said so yourself.'

'Aye, he loves you, my lady, but he's convinced his love for you is what brought down his punishment from Vala. Don't you see? He thinks his love is a curse, and that Vala had forbidden it.'

'That is madness,' hissed Salina. 'Love is never evil. *Never.*'

'It's what he believes. He won't leave his camp, and he won't have any more contact with you. He only wants you to know that he's alive, and that he still cares for you.'

'And that is all? That is why you came here?' Salina stormed across the room, feeling trapped. 'You bring me this message, then expect me to do nothing. Am I to live with this guilt forever, then?'

'I don't know,' Gilwyn admitted. 'I only wanted you to know that he's alive.'

'Yes, alive. Alive and burned and hidden from the rest of the world. And all because of me. Well, I cannot live with that, not without seeing him.'

'He won't see you, Princess,' Gilwyn insisted. 'He has already told me that.'

'Tell me where to find his camp. Please, that is all I am asking.'

'And how will you get there? Just coming here tonight was difficult for you. I know; Kamag told me. You won't be able to ride off into the desert.'

Salina wanted to scream, because his logic was unassailable. How could she go to Aztar? Without her father's blessing it would be impossible, and that was something the king would never give. She slumped.

'You are right,' she conceded. 'But if there is a way – any way – I must try. Please, Gilwyn Toms, for all that I have done for you, do this one thing for me. Tell me where to find his camp.'

'My lady . . .'

'I have not much time. If I do not return to the palace soon they will miss me.' Salina gave him her best, imploring pout. 'Please . . .'

Under her onslaught, the young man buckled. 'I'll regret this,' he sighed, flopping down on the bed. 'The camp isn't hard to find. It's two days ride from here. I can draw a map to make it easy for you.'

Salina went over to the bed and touched his clubbed hand, which was dangling off the edge of the bed. 'Thank you, Gilwyn Toms.'

The young man stared up at the ceiling. 'I am leaving in the morning,' he said.

'For your business in Liiria?'

'Yes. And if you don't mind, I'd like to keep that to myself, at least.'

He wasn't joking, and Salina didn't laugh. She knew she had forced him to betray a confidence. She squeezed his hand in thanks.

'Be well on your journey, Gilwyn Toms. If there is anything you need, tell Kamag and he will get it for you.'

Gilwyn sat up, smiling at Salina. 'My lady, you are very kind. If you do try to find Aztar, take care of yourself.' He laughed. 'I know now why Aztar cares for you so much. You really are beautiful.'

The young man's words made Salina blush. She had spent an entire night being admired by men, and was surprised by her reaction to Gilwyn's compliment.

'I hope we see each other again someday, Gilwyn Toms. And thank you for my message.'

'Good-bye, Princess Salina,' said Gilwyn. He rose and walked her to the beaded doorway. 'And good luck.'

Back out in hall, Salina let the beads shower closed behind her. Quickly she covered her face with the wraps, then scurried down the stairs to make her way home.

The next morning, Gilwyn breakfasted in the shrana house, sitting alone at a table near the back and enjoying his last bit of friendly comfort. Being close to dawn, the house itself was empty, allowing Gilwyn precious quiet in which to think and plan his long trip north. Now the Desert of Tears was behind him, he felt closer to Liiria than he had in years, but he knew that he still had weeks of travelling ahead of him. The black stallion that Aztar had given him waited for him outside. His few possessions had been packed and his pockets bulged with gold the desert prince had provided for his journey. It had already been weeks since he had left Jador, and Gilwyn had spent most of those in a ghastly, feverish slumber. Now, though, he was refreshed from his time in Aztar's camp and his brief sojourn in Ganjor, and he was anxious to at least be on his way. As he sipped at a hot cup of shrana, he wondered what had become of Baron Glass over the past weeks, and whether or not Kahldris had corrupted his old friend. Considering the possibilities made Gilwyn fearful.

Finishing his food, he left some coins on the table and headed for the beaded doorway. He had already said his good-byes to Kamag the night before. As he stepped outside, the desert air greeted him warmly. Gilwyn took a deep breath of it. In the cobblestone street outside the shrana house, the great black horse waited for him, easily shouldering the packs strapped along its flanks. With his clubbed hand and foot, it was difficult for Gilwyn to mount the stallion, but the intelligent beast had already grown accustomed to his handicaps and so stayed very still while his master mounted.

By the time Gilwyn had ridden an hour, he was already on the North Trail, the well-worn trade route connecting Ganjor to the rest of the continent. Ganjor itself fell away behind him, looking smaller and smaller as the vast Desert of Tears seemed to devour it. Gilwyn tossed a look over his shoulder to say farewell. He could see nothing of the shrana house where he had spent the night, and could not know that men from King Baralosus had come that morning – shortly after he'd departed – to arrest Kamag.

10

The next morning, Salina awoke later than usual, stretching out in her soft bed as if nothing had happened the night before. When her eyes fluttered open, she saw bright sunlight flooding through the numerous windows of her bedchamber. A basin of water and a steaming urn of tea had been laid at the table near her bedside. Nourah had already been here, she supposed. From the height of the sun, Salina could tell it was already mid-morning. But the night before had been Oradin, and she had already feigned the perfect excuse for remaining in bed. She sat up, coughed loudly and dramatically, and tried to look as sick as possible. It had been cramps that had supposedly driven her to bed. She rubbed her stomach and groaned in case anyone was listening.

No one came to check on her.

Salina relaxed. Her father and his many wives were still in bed themselves, no doubt. There seemed no reason at all to hurry. Salina listened to the quiet of her chambers, which consisted of many attached rooms and a fine bank of windows over-looking the palace grounds. Usually, Nourah came in to see her when she woke. She had a strange clairvoyance that always notified her of Salina's needs. Salina wondered how the rest of the night had gone. By the time she had returned to the palace, most of her father's guests had finally gone. She had managed to spirit her way into her wing of the palace without being seen, a small miracle that still made her sigh with relief.

'Nourah?' she called, careful to make her voice sound weak. When no reply came, she tried again. 'Anyone?'

Puzzled, Salina stepped out of bed onto the warm floor. The deep-piled rug tickled her bare feet. Still in her sleeping gown, she went out of her bedchamber into the main room. It too was filled with sunlight. Salina heard voices in the connecting hall. A man's brusk tone startled her, followed by the plea of Najat, her body servant. Startled, Salina hesitated before going forward. It was unheard of for a man to be in her chambers, unless it was her father. Salina listened closely. It was *not* her father.

'Najat?' she called.

The voices momentarily stopped. Salina went toward the hall and saw Najat there, arguing with Ghaith, one of her father's advisors. Ghaith's old eyes looked dark and troubled as he turned to Salina. Seeing her in her sleeping gown, he blushed.

'Najat, what is this?' Salina asked. 'What's wrong?'

Najat was no younger than Ghaith, but she fiestily stood in his way, blocking him from going further. She had been like a mother to Salina for years, and now protected her like one.

'Princess, your father wants you to come,' said Ghaith. 'He sent me here to bring you.'

'What?'

'Princess, go back and get yourself dressed,' Najat ordered. She glared at Ghaith. 'You – back into the hall.'

'What's wrong?' asked Salina. 'What's happened?'

'Your father wants to see you,' said Ghaith. 'Quickly.'

'Salina, get yourself dressed,' said Najat. She looked as troubled as Ghaith. 'Go.'

'There's no time,' said Ghaith. 'Princess, fetch yourself a robe.'

A horrible realization dawned on Salina. She looked around, but there were no other of her servants about. 'Where is Nourah?'

Najat's face tightened. 'Salina . . .' The old woman shook her head in defeat. 'Do as Ghaith asks. Go with him. I'll get your robe.'

Najat walked past Salina, avoiding her eyes as she disappeared into the bedchamber. Ghaith grimaced apologetically at the princess, who had suddenly lost the need to argue. She was in trouble and she knew it, and it terrified her to wonder how much her father had discovered. In moments Najat returned with her robe, a long gown of golden silk which the old woman draped over her as Salina absently held out her arms. Ghaith gestured down the hallway.

'Please come,' he said.

Not really sure what to do, Salina followed him out of the room, forgetting her bare feet.

'Wait,' said Najat. 'Sandals.'

She raced back into the bedchamber and returned with sandals for the girl's feet. Salina slid into them, looked hopelessly at Najat, then proceeded through the hallway with Ghaith. When they were out of Najat's earshot, the old man paused, leaning against a tapestry hung on the velvet wall.

'Princess,' he began in a whisper, 'forgive me for this. I had no wish to bring you this way. It is your father's order.'

Salina nodded, not really understanding. She knew only that Ghaith was a kind old man, too afraid of her father's wrath to do anything but his bidding.

'Where is he?' she asked.

'In his salon, waiting for you.'

'Is he very cross?' Salina touched Ghaith's arm. 'Did he tell you what is wrong?'

Ghaith's expression seemed heart-broken. 'Princess, talk to him. He will tell you himself.'

Ghaith then turned and went out of the hall, leading Salina close behind. The palace stood nearly deserted, with most of its residents still sleeping off the night's events. As they moved through the halls, servants stopped to see the princess coming toward them, quickly averting their eyes and scurrying in the opposite direction. It was unimaginable that she should walk about in such undress, even in the palace's vast apartments. Ghaith gruffly shooed them away as they approached, snapping at them to look away.

Salina remained quiet as the old man led her to the king's salon. Not far from her father's own vast rooms, the salon was Baralosus' favourite place to retire and read, a large but comfortable chamber furnished in a northern style, with upholstered chairs and rich wood panelling on the walls and ceiling. When Salina was a child, her father would read to her in the salon, telling her tales of northern barbarians or genies that lived in bottles. As they approached the salon, those fond memories came flooding over Salina. She had lost her innocence, and a sickening feeling of betrayal made her shudder. Ghaith stopped at the door of the salon, took a breath to steady himself, that knocked on the oiled portal. A moment later, King Baralosus' muffled voice sounded behind the door.

'Come.'

Ghaith slowly pushed the door opened, revealing the fabulous salon. There were no windows in the chamber, but a giant chandelier with a hundred burning candles lit the paneled walls like fire. Alabaster pillars veined with colour stood along the left side of the room, framing giant oil paintings of Ganjeese kings in battle. A mosaic archway tiled with countless bits of blue and amber glass glistened to the right, where a pair of throne-sized chairs sat imperiously near an unlit hearth. Stout beams of dark mahogony lined the ceiling, holding up the spidery chandelier. A collection of books stood like soldiers on a shelf above the hearth, preserved like heirlooms. As Ghaith enterered the salon, Salina followed meekly, spotting her father in one of the chairs. The other chair sat empty. King Baralosus did not look at his daughter. Instead his steely eyes impaled the girl slumped before him, weeping. Salina's breath caught when she realized it was Nourah.

'Great One, I have brought her,' said Ghaith softly.

King Baralosus nodded, but would not take his eyes from Nourah. Salina had never seen her father look so furious. His skin, normally dark and lovely, seemed to pulse an inhuman red. His fingers gripped the arms of his chair so tightly she could see the veins popping on his hands. He looked exhausted, no longer with the happy expression of a man enjoying Oradin. Instead his whole face clenched in an expression of bitter rage.

'This one has told me everything,' said Baralosus finally. 'Do you hear me, Salina? *Everything.*'

Nourah's weeping eyes turned painfully toward Salina. Her lips twisted as she tried to speak. 'I am sorry, Princess. Forgive me.'

Salina could not speak. Her hands froze at her sides. King Baralosus sat shaking in his chair.

'Ghaith, take her away,' he said, barely able to lift his hand. Ghaith rushed forward, took Nourah by the shoulders, and led the girl out the salon. As she passed Salina, Nourah shook her head as if there was no hope at all. Salina watched her go, then felt the heavy door close shut, sealing Salina alone with her father. An awful silence filled the salon. The paintings on the wall haunted the air. King Baralosus' laboured breathing made the only sound. He lifted his head to look at his daughter, his gaze full of wrath. Salina could not bring herself to approach him. The memories of the little girl she had once been – running to be with him – fled from her mind.

'What a terrible thing you've done,' said the king. 'What a horror.'

Salina's mouth dried like the desert. There was no way she could explain herself.

'I'm sorry, Father,' she managed, and that was all.

'You think so little of me?' the king asked. 'Is that what drove you to this madness? To embarrass your family this way? To ruin me?'

'No,' Salina gasped. 'No . . .'

'What, then?' Baralosus barked. 'Tell me!'

It was like standing in the wind, and Salina could hardly bear it. Under her father's withering gaze she groped for an explanation, but it all seemed ridiculous now.

'To help them,' she said. 'The way I always told you . . .'

'The northerners? Nourah has told me what you've done for them, Salina, giving them gold, directing them across the desert. That man Kamag – he helped you, too, that traitorous frog. You were seen in his shrana house last night.' Baralosus shuddered in disgust. 'How could you? Crawling through the streets like a harlot.'

'To save people, Father,' said Salina. 'Because you would not help them yourself.'

'It's my fault, then?' The king rose from his chair and stalked towards his daughter. 'I'm to blame for this disgrace? No, Salina. You are the one that gave the Seekers comfort. And I know how you warned the Jadori, too. You betrayed Prince Aztar. You betrayed us all. What I want to know is why.'

Salina could not help herself; she began to cry. 'Father, I didn't do any of this to hurt you. I only wanted to help those poor people.'

'But you knew of my plans for you, Salina. And you knew of my plans for Jador.'

'Yes,' Salina choked. 'To conquer them.'

'For our own good!' railed the king. 'Let Aztar bring them to their knees, that's what I told myself. Do you not see the value in any of this?'

Salina finally raised herself up. 'You always deal with the northerners. Look at this room!'

'Do not raise your voice to me,' seethed the king. 'Dare it not, Daughter. I am King! I decide how Ganjor deals with the north, not you. If you would once stop acting like a stupid child, you would see the truth in what I've done, the wisdom of it. The northerners come like a plague now, all because Jador has magic. And you try to help them! Madness!'

'It is not madness,' said Salina, trying very hard to temper her tone. 'It is kindness. And I never wanted to be bartered away like old bread, Father. You had no right to make that bargain with Aztar.'

'No right? You are my daughter. A *girl*. I decide these things for you, because that is the wish of heaven. Now, you will argue this no more, Salina. You are too old to make up such nonsense. You will not help the Seekers reach Jador, nor will you ever tell the Jadori of my plans again. I will kill all your doves, every last one of them.'

'Father!'

'And you will not talk back to me or harm my kingship. Gods and devils, all of Ganjor will be laughing at me when they learn of this.' King Baralosus looked sharply at his daughter. 'But you do not care, do you?'

'Of course I care, Father. Of course I care!'

'You do not. You would never have unleashed such a thing if you did. This is too big for me to keep secret, Salina. When the rest of Ganjor learns of it, I will be disgraced.' Baralosus looked heart-broken. 'Did you ever once consider that?'

Salina had to look away. The pain in her father's eyes humbled her. Perhaps she never really had considered him in all her plans, or how badly her actions might affect him. Perhaps she had never really thought she would be caught. About that, he was correct – she really was a child.

'What can I say to make this better, Father? There is nothing,' said Salina. 'Nor would I change things if I could. I am not ashamed of helping the Seekers. They are ill. If there is any magic in Jador, then they are in need of it.'

'And the Jadori? What will they think of me when they learn of my part in all of this? They think Aztar is their enemy. They think he is destroyed, the danger past. What will happen when they learn Ganjor helped in the attack on them?'

'I do not know,' Salina admitted.

'No, you do not,' said Baralosus, shaking with rage. 'Because you have not the mind for these things. Yet stupidly you played with fire, and now I am to be burned.' The king turned his back on her, thundering across the room. Seething, he came to stand beside the unlit hearth, staring vacuously at the empty pit. 'The worst part is, I should have seen this,' he sighed. 'I thought your defiance was something harmless, something you would soon outgrow. Instead of laughing as if it were a joke, I should have beaten it out of you.'

Salina said nothing. Her father had never laid a hand on her in anger.

'There will be troubles now,' her father continued. His tone quieted, as if he were merely thinking out loud. 'When the Jadori hear of this, they will come.'

'They will not,' said Salina. 'They are not strong enough to harm you, Father.'

Baralosus glared at his daughter. 'So now you are a diplomat? Or a military man, perhaps? Daughter, your advice is meaningless. It has caused me enough grief already. Without Aztar to fear, the Jadori will come.'

Salina bristled at her father's insults, and did not know how much to confess. He had said he already knew everything, but he clearly didn't know that Aztar was still alive. Then, like a magician, he asked the dreaded question.

'Tell me what happened last night,' he ordered.

'You know already.'

'Maybe. Now I want to hear it from you.'

'What happened to Kamag?'

Her father went back to his chair, sitting himself down wearily. 'He's been arrested. He's answered most of my questions.'

'What will you do with him?'

Baralosus ignored her query. 'He says that you met with a northerner, a young man who came from Jador. Who was he?'

'It doesn't matter,' said Salina. 'He has already left Ganjor.'

'Why did he want to meet with you? Kamag does not know everything. Was it something about Prince Aztar?'

'Father, you know already,' guessed Salina. She looked at her father curiously. 'Is that so?'

'Kamag says that Prince Aztar is alive. That's what this boy from Jador came to tell you. Do not deny it, Salina. I already know it is true. I have sent men out this morning to find Aztar.'

'Why?' asked Salina. Her father's decision made no sense to her. 'Aztar is hurt, Father. He can do nothing more for you.'

'I must know everything that happened to him. I want nothing more from him, Salina. Only his silence. And if he has needs, I want to help him if I can.'

Finally, there was a glimpse of kindness in him. Relieved to see it, Salina chanced going closer. She took a cautious step toward the hearth where he sat, trying to smile, to somehow ease his rampant anger.

'The northerner's name was Gilwyn Toms,' she told her father. 'He was heading back north to his homeland, Liiria. I do not know why.'

'Go on.'

'He told me that Prince Aztar is alive, Father. He told me that he was burned in the battle against Jador. He's given up his claim to the desert.' Salina took two more steps, then dropped to her knees before her father. 'He loves me, Father. That's what Gilwyn Toms told me.'

King Baralosus regarded his daughter coolly. 'Aztar has always loved you, Salina. From the first time he saw you, he wanted you. I am not surprised he wants you still. Does he know how you betrayed him?'

'Yes,' said Salina, though it pained her to admit it. 'And he still loves me. It amazes me, but it is so. Father . . .' She braced herself. 'I want to go to him.'

The king's expression was incredulous. 'Salina, you are not going anywhere. Most certainly, you are not going to Aztar.'

'Father, please, I must set things right with him,' Salina begged. From her place at his feet, she reached to touch his knee. 'If you are sending others to him, why not me?'

'Have I been talking to myself? Have you heard nothing? Salina, what you have done is a crime. You may not leave this palace. You will not even leave your chambers.'

'What? For how long?'

'For as long as it takes for me to clean the mess you've made. For a month, at least, while I decide what else to do with you. You are to be punished, Salina. What you did was betrayal, not just to Aztar but to me and all your family. If you were not my daughter you would be beaten for it.'

Salina reared back, shocked by her father's words. 'What will happen to Nourah? Will she be beaten?'

'Indeed she will,' said the king.

'No!' cried Salina, jumping to her feet.

'It is already happening,' said Baralosus. 'Or it is already over.'

Terror seized Salina then, not for herself but for her innocent friend. Nourah had always been innocent, blithely following Salina's orders, because she was the princess' handmaiden and could do nothing else. Now she would be beaten. And Kamag? The same or worse. Salina slumped on her knees, feeling the tears come again. First she had ruined

Aztar, and now her friends. To Salina, it seemed the world had simply ended.

'I didn't want this,' choked Salina. 'I didn't want any of this to happen.'

King Baralosus let his daughter sob, watching broken-hearted from his imperious chair.

11

The first thing Lukien noticed was the farmland. Lush and green, it spread out from the banks of the river all along its winding length. Beautiful, fragile, the farmland ended again where the desert took hold, but near the river it flourished, sending up sprouts of grass and hearty crops. Lukien let the vision wash over him, nourishing his depleted spirit. His eye scanned the horizon. From atop the rugged hill he could see for miles. The small village below beckoned him with its simple homes. Near the river, men and women toiled with chores while children played along the banks, their chatter barely perceptible above the stirring wind. Homes of mud and stone stood squat against the bright horizon, dozens of simple buildings with the same weathered exterior. A path ran from the village toward the mountains where Lukien waited, standing alone in the breeze. He had crested the mountain to see the horizon, wondering if he was at last getting close to Tharlara. When he saw the village, it had taken his breath away.

Lukien waited at the end of the high hill, looking down on the peaceful village, unnoticed. His horse waited for him at the base of the hill, exhausted from the long trek. For days they had followed the river the way Raivik had told them, leaving the dead Akari city to continue their lonely journey. And they had not encountered another soul along the way until now. Lukien listened, trying hard to hear the laughing children far below. They were beautiful to him, playing some imaginative game in the sweltering sun while their parents worked the soil and washed clothes in the river. A great sense of happiness welled up in Lukien, crushing his loneliness. It seemed like an eternity had passed since he'd said good-bye to Raivik, leaving Kaliatha to quest for Tharlara. In the days of endless riding that followed, he had missed his friends in Grimhold desperately. With only his horse and the river for company, he had watched the land slowly change from dead and rugged to the pretty valley now below him.

By now the river had widened into a remarkable body of water, slowly flowing eastward. Oxen lowered their huge heads to drink from its banks, while fishermen in little boats cast their nets, far from the village. Drying clothes waved like white flags, and barefoot women sat in happy circles, husking vegetables. Lukien carefully picked his way back down the hillside to where his horse waited, nibbling at the meagre grass.

'You'll be eating better than that soon,' he told the beast. 'We've found something at last.'

Lukien led his horse back the way they had come, then scooted around the hill to its northern face. The range of hills gave way to a great expanse of flat earth. Lukien looked around, then noticed the best place to cross. The weary horse perked up at the sight of the moderate terrain. Together they walked the grassy plain toward the path, which Lukien now noticed disappeared into the mountains toward the west. Eastward, though, the path was distinct, leading directly toward the village. He and his horse stepped onto the path and walked quietly along the river bank, toward the villagers and their modest homes.

With sunlight splaying across his face, Lukien cupped a hand over his brow. Cooking fires spiraled into the blue sky. The smell of the river and its loamy shore filled his nostrils. The river beside him moved sluggishly, like thick wine. Up ahead, a group of children played near the bank where the river had flooded the field, splashing in the mud. Lukien squinted for a better look. They were not dark-skinned like the Jadori, but fairer, like the Akari, but without that race's peculiar, pointed features. The eyes of the children were vaguely almond shaped, their skin the colour of honey. Both boys and girls played together, too busy with their games to notice Lukien.

'Hello?' he ventured, coming to a stop near the field. The boy nearest him, standing ankle-deep in mud, looked up from his playmates. Lukien quickly held up his hands. 'Don't be afraid,' he said. 'I'm a friend.'

The boy got the attention of the others, all of whom blinked up in confusion. They were a fair distance from the adults in the village. One young girl called helplessly to her far away parents.

'Haka!'

'No, don't,' Lukien repeated. He lowered himself as he met the girl's gaze. 'I'm just looking for a place to rest.' He stroked his unkempt beard. 'I must look frightening. I've been on the road a long time.'

Lukien looked at the children. Except for one tiny boy too preoccupied with the river to bother with him, they all stared in awe. Past them, back in the village, none of the adults had heard the girl's shout.

'I wish you could understand me,' he said.

The boy who had first sighted him cocked his head. 'We understand you.'

Lukien reared back. In his ears he heard the tongue, foreign and strange, but in his head he heard the words. At once he reached for the Eye of God, which had begun to burn against his chest.

'You do?' Lukien asked. 'You know what I'm saying?'

The boy looked at his playmates in confusion. The children all nodded.

'Who are you?' the boy asked. Again Lukien heard his voice vibrating in his skull, knowing it was magic that translated his language.

'My name is Lukien,' he said. He pressed down on the amulet hidden beneath his shirt, feeling its pulsing warmth and the ever-present Amaraz within it. He searched his brain for the presence of the great Akari, but felt only his own thoughts. 'I come from a place very far away,' he continued. 'Past the mountains and the dead city. I followed the river to get here.'

The children gathered closer, pulling themselves from the mud to get a better look. Their curious, dirty faces lit with amazement.

'The dead city? Where?' asked the girl who had first feared him.

Lukien pointed over the mountains. 'Back there, many miles. I came from there days ago.'

The boy spoke again. 'You walked?'

'And rode,' replied Lukien.

'What happened to your face?' asked another child, this one a girl slightly younger than the first. She frowned as she noticed Lukien's missing eye.

'I lost my eye in a fight. It was a long time ago. Can you take me into the village?'

The children looked at each other, unsure how to answer. Lukien gazed past them toward the smallest boy, still playing very close to the river bank. Something strange floated in the water. Like a log, it moved with ease through the still river, dark and barely visible, gliding toward the wading boy. While the children argued, Lukien puzzled over the thing, his smile fading . . .

'Fate above!' he cried. Exploding past the others, he raced toward the bank. 'Move!'

At the edge of the flooded bank, the boy heard Lukien's cry and slowly turned to see what was wrong. Seeing the Bronze Knight charging toward him, the boy startled and fell backward into the mud. The children shouted. The living log slithered quickly onto the bank, its jaws opening to snatch the fallen boy. Lukien sprang with a shout, launching himself against the crocodile. His hand flew to his dagger, unsheathing it and slashing it forward as he landed on the lizard. The boy shrieked in terror. The crocodile rolled its muscled body through the mud. Lukien felt the blade scratch across the lizard's armoured hide, then the sickening lurch as the beast spun him over. The great jaws hissed, clamping down on his arm. A dazzling pain ripped through his body. He heard the children shouting in the distance, their frenzied voices filling his ears. Through the muddy haze he saw the tiny boy still sitting helplessly nearby. Lukien wrenched his arm free of the crocodile's jaw, tearing off his sleeve and tatters of skin. With his other arm he went for the monster's belly.

This time, the dagger bit deep, ripping through the yellow flesh. A hot ooze soaked Lukien's hand. He peddled quickly backward, gasping to get away as the crocodile thrashed in hissing pain. The water around them blackened with gore. Lukien pulled himself desperately from the mud, his wounded arm burning with pain. When he reached the screaming child he scooped the boy up over the bank, struggling to reach safety. The crocodile snapped its great head upward, its eyes rolling beneath it's filmy lids. Lukien deposited the frantic boy on the bank and watched as the lizard's stubby legs thrashed and twitched, the dagger still in its belly. A great rent had opened in its flesh, spilling blood into the water.

'Mother whore,' gasped Lukien, falling to his knees. His arm throbbed in agony. Around him the other children began to rally, some shouting for the adults in the village, others comforting the muddied tot. Hunched in pain, Lukien fought to keep from fainting.

'You are hurt!' cried the boy who had first spoken. His eyes widened as he examined Lukien's arm, then flicked toward the dying crocodile. 'You killed it.'

Lukien nodded, grunting instead of speaking. He knew he was lucky his arm hadn't been lost. The pain was enormous, but the crocodile had only barely caught his flesh. He closed his eyes, steadying his breath. Already the Eye of God began to work its magic, filling his body with healing warmth.

'Help me, Amaraz,' he whispered. 'Help me . . .'

The spirit of the Eye awakened, and the red jewel spread its light across Lukien's chest. The pain in his arm began to ebb. Like a miracle, he felt the teeth marks knitting closed and the blood stop flowing from his wounds. As always, Amaraz remained mysteriously silent. Lukien didn't bother thanking the Akari. He began breathing normally, knowing he would be all right.

'We'll help you,' said the boy. He took Lukien's unhurt arm and tried lifting the knight to his feet. Lukien rose unsteadily, blinking to clear his one good eye, searching for the little boy. The boy was sobbing and talking at the same time, choking on his words. A team of children circled him. The boy helping Lukien glanced up at him, plainly awed by what he'd done. 'You killed the hooth. You saved him.'

Lukien looked back toward the dead crocodile. 'Hooth? Is that what you call them?'

'We should have watched for them,' said the boy. 'The hooth sometimes come here to feed.'

124

'My dagger . . .'

'I'll get it,' the boy volunteered.

Lukien quickly snagged his sleeve. 'Don't. Just leave it.'

By now adults were coming from the village, running to see what had happened. A young, attractive woman raced away from the rest of them, her eyes locked on the frantic little boy. He was no more than two years old, Lukien supposed, and the woman – most likely his mother – sprinted like an athlete to reach him. Not even noticing Lukien, she skidded to her knees in front of the boy, hugging and kissing him. The children around her began offering explanations. Remarkably, Lukien understood them all. As quickly as they spoke, the magic of the amulet deciphered their words. Within moments, a dozen more adults had arrived at the river bank, stopping to stare when they noticed Lukien. One of them, a large man with a troubled expression, called out to the woman, kneeling beside her and the child.

'Who's that?' Lukien asked.

'That's Jahan,' the boy answered. 'Naji's father.'

Once he realized his son was unhurt, Jahan stood to confront Lukien. His dark eyes surveyed the stranger, but Lukien could not read his expression. Jahan simply looked intrigued. He was about the age of his wife, a youngish thirty, and dressed like the others in his village, in loose-fitting clothes and a fabric belt cinched around his waist. A tightly pulled pony-tail of jet hair ran down his back.

'Who are you?' he asked. His almond-shaped eyes narrowed on Lukien.

'My name is Lukien,' said the knight. 'I'm a traveller, new to these parts.'

Jahan puzzled over the reply. 'You speak as we do? But not as we do. Where are you from?'

'From Liiria,' said Lukien. 'A place far away.' He didn't want to say more about the language or the magic that made their conversation possible. 'My home is east of here, past the mountains,' he said. 'Past the dead city and the desert.'

'What happened to my son?'

It was the boy who answered, speaking up to defend Lukien. 'A hooth, Jahan. Naji was playing too close to the water. We were watching him, Jahan. But then this man came . . .'

'You saved my boy from the hooth?' Jahan asked.

Lukien rubbed his still throbbing arm. 'I saw the crocodile in the water.'

'He killed it!' said one of the girls. 'We all saw.'

Jahan stepped closer, examining Lukien's arm. 'That needs tending.'

'I'll be all right,' said Lukien. 'But I could use a place to rest, and maybe some food. I'm no danger to anyone. As I said, I'm just a traveller.'

'You are not like anyone I have ever seen,' said Jahan. 'And no one comes from the east. I have questions.'

'I'll try to answer them if I can,' said Lukien. He gestured toward the man's son. 'Have you checked him? Is he hurt?'

Jahan looked back at his son, who had at last stopped sobbing. Jahan's wife still cradled the boy in her arms, holding his head against her breast. She told her husband that the boy was merely frightened. Relieved, Jahan looked back at Lukien.

'I am grateful for what you did,' he said. 'Every year the hooth take someone from us. If not for you, it would have been my son.'

'You are welcome,' said Lukien. 'And don't blame the children. It wasn't their fault. They would have watched your son, but I startled them when they saw me.'

'You have startled all of us,' Jahan laughed. 'A man from the east!' He glanced around at his fellow villagers, all of whom wore stunned expressions. Some had even gathered around Lukien's horse, studying the beast as if they'd never seen it's like before. 'You say your name is Lukien?'

'That's right,' Lukien replied.

'Well then, Lukien, you must come to my home. Rest and tell us your story.'

'I would like that,' said Lukien with a smile.

Having got Jahan's approval, Lukien let the children swarm around his legs, pulling at him as they guided him toward the village.

That night, Lukien found himself surrounded by Jahan's family, sitting near Jahan at the head of a plain table without chairs, sharing a good, basic meal.

For most of the afternoon, Lukien had slept. After being led to Jahan's modest house, Jahan's wife Kifuv had cleaned and dressed Lukien's wounded arm, then taken his muddied clothing out to the river for washing. The home was tiny, with only three rooms for the whole large family, but Jahan had given up the room that he shared with Kifuv so that Lukien could sleep. Exhausted, Lukien slept like a baby for hours, and when he awoke he found clean clothes for him to wear sitting next to the straw mattress. They were not the clothes he had dirtied, but rather traditional garb from Jahan's own supply – a comfortable white shirt with a large open collar and belt, and a pair of pants that Lukien had to cinch tightly with the cloth belt to keep from falling down. As he was dressing, Jahan came in and led him into the main room of the house, where the family took its meals. There, around the table, sat Kifuv and her six children, including little Naji. Led by Jahan, Lukien took a seat on a small pillow near the ground, thrilled by the sight of the food and humbled by the attention.

Although the village was small, it had provided an ample meal for them. The clay tableware was filled with bread, raisins, honey, and various types of dried fish that had been caught from the river. A brass platter – the only form of metal plate on the table – shone brightly in the torchlight, showcasing a roasted waterfowl that had been slaughtered for the occasion. There were utensils for serving the food, but none for eating, and Lukien had no trouble at all helping himself with his hands, which he could wash in a small, ceramic bowl filled with water when he was done. He still wore the Eye of God hidden beneath his shirt, and though Jahan and Kifuv had both noticed it when he undressed, neither had commented about the strange amulet. Mostly, they were simply convivial to him, as were their children, and Jahan spent the first part of the meal telling Lukien about the hooth, the great river, and their village.

'There were eleven of us who formed the village,' Jahan explained proudly. He dipped bread into honey as he talked, then broke off a bit to share with one of his daughters, seated beside him. 'That is the way the Simiheh do things. When we are growing up as boys we eat together, hunt together, learn together, everything. Then, when we are old enough, we leave together to form our own village. This village is twenty years old now.'

Lukien nodded, interested and full of questions. 'How did you choose this land? Did no one else have claim to it?'

'This is the territory of our people,' said Jahan. 'It is all Simiheh land.'

'Simiheh? That is what you call yourselves?'

'That is our name. My father was Simiheh, and his father before that, and all the fathers of the boys who came to build this village. We are three-hundred now, maybe more.' Jahan beamed at his wife. 'A strong village.'

Lukien felt happy for Jahan, and for the pride he took in his accomplishments. But for himself, Lukien felt disappointment. Clearly he was not in Tharlara. He took a drink from his cup, filled with a barley beer. He had taken an immediate liking to the beer.

'The Simiheh are all around this area,' Jahan continued. 'There are five more villages, all nearby. When my sons are old enough, they will go off with the other boys their age, and they will start a new village.'

'Then what will happen to this village?' asked Lukien. 'Who will defend it? Who will work the land?'

Jahan said casually, 'When the people are gone, the village will be gone.'

'But what about all you've built? What about the homes? I mean, what about the *village?*'

The question perplexed Jahan, who looked inquisitively at his wife.

'The village is the people,' said Kifuv.

127

Jahan nodded. 'Yes, that is it. The village is the people. The village is not the things we build. Do you see, Lukien?'

'I think so,' Lukien replied. It was very different from the way things were in his part of the world. 'But tell me again – this is the Simiheh land? Is that what this place is called?'

'It does not have a name, except that it is the village of Jahan, or the village of the men who began the village with me.'

'But what about this area? Does it have a name?'

Jahan shrugged. 'This is the land of the Simiheh. I have told you that already.'

'I know,' said Lukien. He slumped a little at the news. 'So this isn't Tharlara, then.'

Jahan regarded him oddly. 'Tharlara? How do you know that word?'

'It is the word I was told, the name given to the land I seek.'

'Tharlara is an ancient word. Who told you this word?'

'A friend,' said Lukien. 'His name was Raivik. He's . . . not from around here. He lives by the dead city I told you about.'

'The dead city of the Akari? You met a man who came from there?'

'Yes, but it is hard to explain,' said Lukien. He had already told Jahan about passing through Kaliatha, but not about Raivik, the Akari ghost. Jahan had known nothing of the Akari or their city. 'Jahan, I am looking for a land called the Serpent Kingdom. I was told that would be Tharlara.'

'Ah, then you are near the place you seek, Lukien. This is the land of the serpents.'

'It is?' Lukien looked around the table. All the children nodded. 'You mean this is Tharlara?'

'That is the word for the lands by the river,' said Jahan. 'All the villages, all the people, everyone who takes life from the river.'

'Yes,' said Lukien, growing excited. 'That's what Raivik called it – the riverland.'

'Wait, Lukien, let me explain. How do I say this? Tharlara is a big word. Does that make sense to you? Tharlara describes everything. It is not really a place, not the way you mean.'

'I understand,' said Lukien, 'but I am looking for a kingdom. A serpent kingdom. You say this is the land of the rass?'

'All of this land – everywhere that's called Tharlara – has rass, Lukien. They are part of the land. They are great and special creatures.'

'Where I come from, they are terrible creatures,' said Lukien. He had stopped eating, too enthralled by the conversation to have much appetite. 'Do you not fear them?'

'They are revered.' Jahan smiled at his young daughter as he spoke. 'We respect the rass. We love them because the great rass gives us life.'

'The great rass? What is that?'

128

'The great rass turns the river to blood,' said Jahan. 'To feed the land. Without the blooding, the land would die.'

This bit of news made Lukien reel. He leaned forward in earnest. 'Explain that to me, Jahan. I don't understand.'

Jahan said, 'Each year the river swells and floods the land. The waters bring life to the soil. Without the flooding, the land would be useless. And sometimes, the land grows weak, even with the floods. That is when the Great Rass comes. When she is killed, her blood flows into the river, and the river is born again. The river becomes strong, and when it floods the land, the land becomes strong.'

'And this happens every year?' asked Lukien.

'No. Only the flooding happens every year, when the rains are heaviest. But the Great Rass comes only once in a great while. And it is almost time for her to come again.'

It was a fine tale, but fantastic. Lukien tried looking convinced. 'And this is all true? It is not a myth?'

'Myth? No, Lukien, it is not a myth,' said Jahan. 'The Great Rass is real, just like the rass that live in the rocks beyond our village. Without the Great Rass, the people along the river would perish. What you call Tharlara would die.'

'What about the Great Rass, then? How does she die?'

'She is killed in her mountain home,' said Jahan. 'By the Red Eminence, he who rules in Torlis. When the time of the Great Rass comes, the Red Eminence battles her and kills her.'

'So where is Torlis? Is it very far?'

'Torlis is a long ride from here, Lukien. I do not know how far precisely. None of the Simiheh have ever gone there.'

'Jahan, I think your village is a wonderful place,' said Lukien carefully. There was no way he wanted to offend his gracious host. 'It is beautiful and peaceful, and I could probably be happy for the rest of my life in a place like this. But it is not a kingdom, and I was told to find the Serpent Kingdom. This place called Torlis – it sounds like the place I'm seeking.'

'It does,' Jahan admitted. Suddenly he seemed to have lost his appetite as well. He pushed his plate aside and looked at his wife, who smiled back at him, untroubled. 'The people of Torlis are not Simiheh, Lukien. They are like us, but they are not us. They have never warred with us, but they have never come here to offer friendship either. I do not know what it will be like for you there, or how you will be greeted. Must you really go to Torlis? Is it so important?'

'Yes,' said Lukien. 'It is.'

'Will you tell me why?'

'Maybe, but not tonight.' Lukien grinned. 'Tonight I want to rest and to eat.'

Jahan seemed satisfied. 'Then that is what we will do. And when we are done and the moon has come out, I will take you to the river, Lukien.'

'To the river? Why?'

Now it was Jahan who grinned. 'I will tell you later,' he said. 'Maybe.'

Night had long since fallen by the time the meal ended, and Lukien, full and well rested, waited outside the little clay home for his host to arrive and reveal his strange secret. Most of the villagers had gone inside their own homes; for the moment, Lukien had the world to himself. While he waited for Jahan to say good-night to his children, Lukien gazed around the torch-lit village, smelling the burning incense that filled the air. The odour was sweet and wholly unknown to Lukien, not quite a stink and not a perfume, either. The little homes gathered near the river twinkled with light as parents put their children to sleep and men and women finished their daily chores. Voices reached Lukien's ears, but they were too far away to understand. The Bronze Knight reached beneath the shirt his new friends had given him and pulled the Eye of God out by its golden chain. The red jewel in its centre continued pulsing with life, shining on Lukien's face. His wounded arm already felt remarkably better, but that was not the miracle that puzzled him. He rubbed at the jewel with his finger, hoping – wishing – for Amaraz to speak to him.

'No?' he whispered. 'Not tonight?'

Lukien smirked as he stared at the amulet. Only once had he spoken to Amaraz, when Minikin had brought him to the Akari's magical realm. Even then the great spirit had not spoken to him directly. Yet now, Amaraz was allowing him to speak to these foreign people, using his arcane strength to bend their minds to his eastern tongue. It was no great task for Amaraz, surely, yet he performed it the way he performed all his magics.

In secret.

'Why?' Lukien asked. 'Why won't you speak to me? Other Akari speak to their hosts. Why not you, Amaraz? Am I so unworthy?'

The silence seemed to confirm Lukien's question.

'Rot on you, then,' he hissed. 'You hear?'

If Amaraz heard, he refused to answer. As Lukien held the amulet before him, Jahan appeared from the house. He was all alone and smiling, and when he saw the Eye of God his almond eyes fixed on it curiously.

'What is that?' he asked. 'I have seen you touching it.'

Jahan had been full of questions since they'd met, and so far Lukien had managed to dodge them all, at least the important ones. He didn't like evading the man's queries, but he still knew so little about Jahan and his people, and he supposed the truth might frighten them. He tucked the amulet back into his shirt.

'Just a trinket. It was given to me by someone special.'

'That is hardly a trinket, my friend. It is precious to you. Is it a magical thing?'

Lukien laughed at his deduction. 'You see right through me, don't you? All right – yes, then. But it's hard to explain, and I'm not sure that I should. This amulet helps me.' Lukien thought for a moment. 'Jahan, when I talk to you, when we speak . . . what is it like for you?'

'It is strange,' said Jahan. 'Like I told you – your mouth moves, but the words are different. I do not understand how you do this thing.' He pointed at the amulet beneath Lukien's shirt. 'Is that what the jeweled thing does?'

Lukien nodded. 'I can't speak your words, yet you understand me. And I understand you, too, and everyone else here in your village.'

'Remarkable,' Jahan said, wide-eyed. 'Wherever you come from must be a glorious place. I want to know all about it, Lukien.'

'I wish I had the time to tell you everything,' said Lukien. 'But I have to keep on going. I have to get to Torlis, Jahan. It's important.'

It was obvious Jahan wanted to know more, but he was respectful to Lukien and asked no more questions. Instead, he said, 'I am grateful to you for what you did for my son. You know that, yes?'

'I know,' said Lukien. 'And I am grateful for your hospitality.' Then he laughed. 'And for the shirt!'

'Lukien, you have made all the village start to wonder. When I tell them you are seeking the Red Eminence, they will not believe me! No one has ever gone that far from our village.' A trace of wistfulness crept into Jahan's tone. 'They will envy you.'

'Jahan, why are we out here? What did you want to show me?'

'Ah, we are not without our own wonders here, Lukien. There is something you are ignorant of. Tonight you will learn.'

'I'm not sure I like the sound of that. Where are we going?'

The man with the pony-tail slapped Lukien's back. 'To the river,' he pronounced. 'Follow me.'

With only the moonlight to guide them, Jahan led Lukien out of the village, following the river bank westward. Lukien had seen the lush farmlands here earlier, when the sun lit the place, making it clearly visible from the village. Now, it glowed murkily on the moonlight, damp in places where the river had over-flowed its banks and shadowed by tall grasses that hissed when the wind blew. Lukien held out his hands and let the grasses tickle his palms. Behind them, the village disappeared beyond a hill. Jahan walked like a ghost, barely making a sound. He began to crouch a little, bidding Lukien to do the same. They were still near the river and could hear its gargling churn. The moonlight glistened on the water.

'How far are we going?' Lukien whispered.

Jahan pointed to an area of flattened grass up ahead. 'There.'

It looked like the kind of place where children played, where their eager feet had trampled the grass again and again until the grass at last surrendered. The ground was soft, though mostly dry, slightly elevated and affording a good view of the nearby river. Jahan knelt down in the clearing. He gestured for Lukien to come down next to him.

'What are we doing?' asked Lukien as he knelt beside Jahan.

The village man's voice was barely audible. 'Wait.'

'Wait? For what?'

'Lay down,' said Jahan. 'Like this.'

Jahan got down on his stomach, resting his elbows in the grass and his chin in his palms. Not knowing why, Lukien did the same, discovering that he still had an excellent little window through the grass in which to view the river bank.

'I'm going to show you something wondrous, Lukien,' Jahan promised. 'But we must stay very quiet. Do not move. If you must talk, whisper.'

Lukien nodded, though the position was uncomfortable and made his wounded arm ache. He remained completely silent, barely twitching, letting long minutes pass, wondering what he might see. Insects buzzed in the grass around them. An occasional bird took wing overhead. Jahan waited with endless patience, grinning secretly. By the time Lukien's own patience began to ebb, the villager finally spoke.

'Look there!'

He pointed a thin finger out for Lukien to follow, toward the river bank where a shadow slipped slowly into view. Lukien struggled to focus his vision. He saw the movement, yet heard nothing. He inched his head closer through the grass, then detected the flash of eyes and the quick lash of tongue. A great hood patterned with coils lifted slightly into the air. Lukien stopped breathing.

'Holy mother of fate,' he gasped. 'That's a rass.'

His first instinct was to flee, but Jahan grabbed his hand, holding it tight.

'Don't move,' Jahan ordered. 'It won't hurt us if it's not afraid.'

'I'm the one that's afraid, Jahan,' Lukien snapped. 'We have to go.'

'Fool, this is why I brought you here! Now hush yourself. Just watch.'

Lukien tried to steady himself, but could hear his own heart pounding in his temples. He had never felt such revulsion before, so helpless as he laid prone in the grass. Next to him, Jahan licked his lips in excitement, his eyes full of wonder. The rass dipped its giant head into the river and began to drink, using its enormous tongue – muscled like a man's arm – to slurp the water. As if all the other creatures in the world knew that a monster was around them, the river bank fell silent. The birds ceased to stir. The insects stopped their buzzing song.

'Isn't it beautiful?' Jahan eased back, finally sitting upright. 'It knows we're here.'

'Then we should leave.'

'You do not understand, Lukien. It will not harm us. It has only come to drink. The rass come every night to drink from the river.'

'This is what you wanted to show me?' asked Lukien. 'Why?'

'To make you understand. You cannot go through our lands without understanding the rass. What would the Red Eminence think of you? No, you must see the truth of them, how glorious they are.'

'Jahan, they are not glorious to me,' said Lukien. 'Where I come from, the rass are dangerous.'

'Dangerous?' said Jahan. 'Yes, of course. But that is their nature. They are hunters.'

Lukien sank down in the grass, studying the rass. The creature was immense, yet moved with grace along the river bank, deliberately slithering through the mud, its colourful skin glistening. 'All right,' Lukien admitted. 'It is beautiful. But dangerous. Why don't the rass attack your village?'

'The rass come to the river at night,' Jahan explained. 'We light the torches to keep them away.'

'Ah, you mean that smell?'

'That's right. There is a tree that grows nearby. When the leaves are dried and burned, they make a scent that keep the rass away.'

'So you fear them. Yet you love them?'

'It is the balance. Seeing the rass means that the Great Rass will come. Do you see?'

'I think so,' said Lukien, trying to understand. It made at least some sense. 'So the Red Eminence kills the Great Rass, and the land lives on.'

Jahan smiled, pleased with his pupil. 'Precisely so.'

'And when you see the rass, you know that the Great Rass will come and be killed.'

'Good.'

'I understand. But I still don't like them.'

Jahan sighed. 'You are hopeless.'

Together they continued to watch as the rass made its way along the bank, pausing occasionally before disappearing into the darkness. Jahan remained transfixed by the creature until the end, when at last he leaned back, his expression oddly satisfied. Lukien relaxed, glad to be rid of the beast. Tharlara might be the land of serpents, but that didn't mean he had to court them.

'Thank you, Jahan,' he said, not sure what else to say. 'Maybe you're right. Maybe they are special. They're special to you, at least.'

'They are sacred creatures, Lukien. You must respect that when you go to Torlis.'

'I'll try,' said Lukien. He got up from his knees, stretching his aching muscles. 'Can we go back now?'

Jahan looked disappointed. 'There will be others, but I suppose you do not care to see them. Yes, we can go back now, Lukien.'

The two men began the long walk back to the village. As they walked, Lukien spied the grasses warily. He felt safe with Jahan, though, and liked the village man's company. In the brief time he had spent with Jahan, he had learned a great deal. Finally, when they left the tall grasses and the village came into sight, Jahan stopped.

'Lukien,' he said, 'will you tell me now what you're looking for in Torlis?'

Lukien thought for a moment. 'Yes, Jahan, all right. A sword. I'm looking for a sword.'

Jahan considered the statement. 'This must be a very special sword. And you must have it?'

'Yes,' Lukien nodded. 'I must.'

'Then you cannot take the chance of failing.' The man's expression grew pensive. 'You have given me much today, Lukien. You have told me about the world beyond my village. You have saved my son. But what you're doing now . . .' Jahan grimaced. 'Dangerous.'

'I know. It's been a long journey for me already,' Lukien said wearily. 'But I have to go on. This sword is very important to me. If I don't find it, many will die. Friends.'

'I do not think you can find the way to Torlis on your own, Lukien. You do not even know that the rass are sacred! You need help on your journey.' Jahan folded his arms across his wide chest. 'I will come with you.'

'What? Jahan, no.'

'Yes,' Jahan insisted. 'It is my duty. You saved Naji from the hooth. If not for you, I would have been grieving tonight instead of learning from a new friend. I will go with you, Lukien. I will help you find this sword.'

The offer was more than generous – it was genuine. Lukien put his hand on Jahan's shoulder. 'You are the founder of this village, Jahan. I can't take you away from it. You're needed here.'

'You need me more,' said Jahan. 'When we have quested and found the sword, the village will still be here, and all its troubles, too. Remember, Lukien, the village is the people. All the people. They are strong. They do not need me the way you do.'

'Jahan, I saved your son because it was the right thing to do, and if it wasn't for me the other children wouldn't have been distracted. I'm just as much to blame for what almost happened as I am for saving Naji. There's nothing you need to repay.'

Jahan's face became stormy. 'Perhaps where you come from, men are different,' he said 'But the Simiheh know when a debt is owed. I cannot let you go to Torlis alone. I *cannot*, and that is the end of it. Now, we will go to the village and sleep, and tomorrow we will leave for Torlis.' Jahan took Lukien's hand and held it firm. 'Together.'

Seeing his argument lost, Lukien did not pull away from Jahan's grasp. 'All right,' he agreed. 'Come with me.'

Jahan beamed. 'Good.'

They walked back to the village together, and when they were almost at Jahan's house Lukien paused.

'I think you'll be a very good guide, Jahan,' he said. 'One thing, though – you've never been to Torlis, either.'

Jahan shrugged. 'Better for two men to be lost than one, yes?'

Lukien frowned. 'That makes no sense at all.'

Ignoring the jibe, Jahan headed eagerly for his little house. Completely unsure he had made the right choice, Lukien followed his odd new friend inside.

12

Jahan rode a donkey on his way to Torlis, a wide, floppy-eared beast with a coat the colour of rust and dark, disinterested eyes that only perked up when being bothered by a fly. Jahan bounced happily upon the donkey's back, his pony-tail swaying from side to side, his face perpetually smiling as he spoke. Lukien rode beside Jahan along the river. Upon his horse, he sat at least three feet higher than Jahan, occasionally glancing down at his companion, more interested in their surroundings than by anything Jahan was saying. The morning had been bright and clear, a good omen for their long trip, but the afternoon was turning hot. Lukien pulled at his shirt, pumping the fabric to blow a breeze down his chest. He still wore the clothes Jahan had given him the night before, leaving his own filthy garb in the village for Kifuv to burn. With his white skin and golden hair, Lukien still did not look like one of Jahan's people, but he supposed the native clothing would give him some cover. It had been at least five hours since they had left the village, following the river eastward, trotting casually along its muddy banks. So far, they had passed through two villages like Jahan's, both without incident, stopping only to give respect to the elders and not bothering to explain Lukien's odd appearance. Though the men and women of the villages eyed Lukien with surprise, they did not stare, keeping their conversation polite and blessedly brief. Later, Jahan explained how rude it would have been for them to do anything else.

'You are with me,' Jahan stated. 'That is enough.'

As they rode, Jahan told stories to Lukien, heartfelt tales about his village and his family, and about his place in the small world he inhabited. Lukien listened to the stories, rarely interrupting. Jahan's pleasant voice rose and fell with each adventure, babbling like the river while the sun burned their necks. They stopped occasionally to rest their mounts, letting the beasts sip from the river while they slacked their own thirst from waterskins and fed themselves from supplies Jahan's wife had packed for the trip.

Then, at last, Jahan ran out of stories. He simply fell silent, looking satisfied as he rode his donkey. He glanced at Lukien, who smiled back at him, grateful for the silence. Sometimes, it was better for men to ride in silence, thought Lukien, rather than gossip like women. Did Jahan ever think so? Lukien doubted it. He watched as Jahan reached into his goatskin bag, the repository of everything important to him. From the bag Jahan produced a wand of wood, which he showed to Lukien.

'A yuup,' he pronounced. 'For music.'

Lukien nodded at the simple instrument. 'A flute. That's what we call them.'

Jahan put the yuup to his lips and began to play. Not needing his hands to guide the donkey, he blew into the instrument and produced a lively tune. The tune he made soothed Lukien. Lukien looked into the river and saw a fish jump for a fly. A bird circled against the blue sky. Without another village in sight, the two travelers seemed alone in the world, and the world seemed at peace.

Jahan played his flute for almost an hour, rarely stopping to catch his breath. At last he lowered the instrument, returning it to his goatskin bag. He did not remain quiet for long. Instead, he looked searchingly at Lukien.

'You are very quiet,' he remarked.

'You were playing. I was listening.'

Jahan nodded, not quite satisfied with the answer. 'I have told you stories. I have played for you.'

'Yes,' said Lukien. 'Thank you.'

'Where you are from, do the people not tell stories?'

Lukien shrugged. 'Sometimes.' Then he realized what Jahan was saying. 'Oh, I see,' he sighed. 'There's a place I know called Ganjor, a great city near the desert. The people there tell stories. That's how they talk to each other.'

'Yes,' said Jahan brightly. 'This is how people speak. You see, Lukien?'

'So you want a story?'

'*Your* story. Tell me about the sword.'

'The sword? I don't know much about it.'

'But you are here, Lukien. You have come all this way to find it. Yet you will not tell me why. What is this sword? Why must you find it?'

The question irked Lukien, not because it wasn't genuine, but because it had come to define him. 'Is that my story? I suppose it is.'

Jahan noted his dark tone. 'It is something you must want very much. It is the desire of your heart?'

'No,' said Lukien. 'If I had a choice, I wouldn't be looking for it at all. I have to find it, that's all.'

'That cannot be all,' said Jahan. A peculiar expression crossed his face, not quite angry, not quite confused. 'Lukien, that thing you wear around your neck – it is a magic thing. You have told me so. You speak my language. You say that you cannot, yet I hear your words and understand them. You are remarkable! There is much to your story. Tell me what it is, please.'

'You're right – there is a lot to my story. A lot of it I don't understand. Like the sword. I don't even know what it is, or if it even exists.' Lukien grew anxious as he began to tell his tale. 'It's called the Sword of Angels. I think it's magical, but I don't know for certain. It must be, I suppose. All I know is that I have to find it. Someone told me to find it.'

'Who told you?'

The questions seemed impossible to answer. How could Lukien explain it all to Jahan, a man of such simple experience?

'A spirit told me,' he said. 'A spirit of someone who was important to me once. Do you believe in spirits, Jahan?'

'Of course,' said the village man. 'There are spirits all around us. Lukien, you must know that.'

Lukien smiled. 'Yes, I do. I didn't always believe it, but I do now. This spirit who came to me, she told me about the sword. She told me that it was hidden somewhere here in your land, Jahan. In the Serpent Kingdom.'

'This spirit was a woman?'

'Yes.'

'A lover, Lukien?'

Lukien laughed. 'Yes.'

Jahan grinned. 'Tell more.'

'Well, I have a friend named Thorin,' Lukien continued. 'Thorin Glass. He was a great man once. Everyone in Liiria – that's where I'm from – they all admired him once. He wears a suit of armour. Do you know what that is?' When Jahan shook his head, Lukien explained, 'It's like clothing made of metal, very strong. Where I come from, men wear armour into battle.'

'Men wear metal?' Jahan exclaimed. 'That is stupid. Metal is too heavy.'

'No, it's not. Not if it's made right,' said Lukien. 'My friend's armour has a spirit inside of it. Here, let me show you something . . .' Lukien took the Eye of God out from beneath his shirt. 'Remember what I told you last night? This amulet has magic, Jahan. There's a very powerful spirit inside it. He makes the magic so that you and I can speak.'

Jahan was wide-eyed, studying the amulet with child-like curiosity. 'It is very beautiful. How did you come by this thing?'

'There's a special place across the desert,' said Lukien. 'It's called Grimhold. That's where all this magic comes from.'

'Across the desert there are many things I have never heard of,' said Jahan with a trace of sadness. 'The Simiheh have none of these things.'

'Be grateful for that, Jahan. This magic has been like a curse to me. This amulet keeps me alive. The spirit inside of it will not let me die, though I have longed for it. I battle and I fight, and I am always healed, no matter how bad my wounds are. That is what it is like for my friend, too, the one with the armour. The spirit in his metal suit gives him power, but has made him do evil things. My friend cannot control himself or save himself from the spirit.'

'The spirit in the metal clothes – you cannot defeat it? You say you cannot die, Lukien. Then surely you can slay this spirit.'

'That's what I thought, too,' said Lukien. 'I did fight Thorin and he nearly killed me. And when I was near death the woman came to me. She told me to find the Sword of Angels, Jahan. She told me that it would be here.'

'And the sword – that is how you will defeat your friend in the metal clothing?'

'I think so. Amaraz told me there was a way. He's the spirit in my amulet. That's why I'm here looking for the sword.'

Jahan sat up tall and proud on his donkey. 'You see? Your story is very grand, Lukien. I am glad I came with you. I will teach you things and you will teach me, and together we will find this sword and save your friend.'

'I hope so,' said Lukien. 'I don't even know where to begin. It's all a mystery.' His neck began tightening with tension. 'I'm so far from home. Even if I find the sword, I have so far to go. And I've left so many people behind. I worry about them.'

'The spirit that protects you – can he not help you, Lukien? If he is so strong, then he will know what you should do.'

'Amaraz doesn't talk to me,' said Lukien sourly. 'I don't know why. He helps me, but he does so quietly.'

Jahan thought for a moment, his mouth twisting. 'Then we will ask the Red Eminence. He will know how to help you, Lukien.'

'Maybe. If he's as powerful as you think. Tell me more about the Red Eminence, Jahan. Tell me everything you know.'

'The Red Eminence is the life-bringer,' said Jahan. 'He has magic, like your spirit. When he fights the Great Rass, he summons his powers to defeat her. That is how he turns the river red.'

'What else?' probed Lukien. He has already heard that part of the story. 'Anything more you can tell me would be helpful.'

'There is not much else to tell. The Red Eminence rules Torlis. They are a great people. Do not worry, Lukien. The Red Eminence will have answers for you.'

Was it all just a myth, Lukien wondered? Some legend Jahan and his people went on believing? He refused to think too much about it. He had very little to grasp for hope, only Jahan and his incredible tale. And just like Jahan, Lukien needed to believe it.

By the end of their first day of travel, Jahan and his donkey were finally exhausted. Jahan had stopped talking and his donkey grew increasingly unwilling to go any further, and as the stars came out overhead the little party came to a halt. They found a clearing by the river, high and far enough from the bank so that the ground was firm and dry. A stand of trees stood like protective sentinels in the distance, but the clearing itself was mostly free of brush, providing a carpet of soft grass for the travellers. Lukien unmounted and began taking his bags off his horse, laying them in a semi-circle along the clearing. They had food enough for at least three days, but the waterskins they had filled were nearly all depleted now. Lukien unlatched a little metal shovel strapped to the side of his horse. They would need a fire as well as water, and so he began to dig, making a small hole in the hard dirt. Jahan, seeing what he was doing, collected nearby rocks and, once Lukien had dug his hole, surrounded it neatly with the stones.

'I will make the fire,' said Jahan. 'Unpack the food for us.'

While his friend set to work, Lukien started going through the things Kifuv had packed for them. Apparently, Jahan's people did not consume much meat, but Kifuv had filled her husband's bags with staples from their village, enough to delight Lukien. They would need water, though, so before darkness came fully he collected the waterskins and proceeded toward the river. Pushing his way past the tall grasses along the bank, Lukien's boots sank into the marshy earth. Squatting over the water, he lowered one skin into the river, watching as the water gurgled into it.

'Lukien!'

The shout made Lukien jump. He leapt to his feet, turning to see Jahan storming toward him, his arms flailing.

'Stop!' said Jahan. He looked at the waterskin in Lukien's hand. 'What are you doing?'

'What's it look like I'm doing? I'm filling the waterskins!'

'No!' Jahan hurried down the bank and snatched the skin from Lukien's hand. 'You cannot just take the water. Did you speak the prayer?'

'What prayer?' Annoyed, Lukien quickly took back the waterskin. 'I just want some water.'

'No, Lukien, you will disturb the Miins,' said Jahan. 'What is wrong with you? You cannot just take their water.'

'What are talking about? What are Miins?'

Jahan paused to collect himself. 'You know nothing, Lukien, truly.

That's what the spirits are called, the ones who live in the river.' He looked at Lukien as though he expected full understanding. When Lukien shrugged, Jahan said, '*Spirits*, Lukien. Like the ones you told me about.'

'Don't get cross,' said Lukien. 'We don't have Miins where I come from. Nothing lives in our water except fish.'

'Is that what you think?' Jahan scoffed. 'Please, give me that.'

Reluctantly, Lukien handed his friend the waterskin. 'It's not like I spit in the river, you know.'

'You must first tell the Miins of your intent,' said Jahan. 'They live in the river. It is their home. You must warn them first.'

'Warn them?' Lukien laughed. 'Can't they see me coming?'

'You do not believe?' Jahan pointed to Lukien's amulet. 'Is that not the home of the one you call Amaraz? I believed you, Lukien.'

'Yes, but . . .'

'The Miins live in the river,' repeated Jahan. 'You would not cut down a tree without first warning the forest spirits, would you?'

Lukien smirked. 'Maybe.'

'Oh, you know so little! Here, I will show you.' Jahan went down to the river, picking his way slowly through the grass. 'We must tell the Miins that we are here, and that we need some water.'

'But we've been taking water all day! Our horse and donkey have been drinking from the river.'

Jahan squatted near the water just as Lukien had done. 'But they are dumb animals, Lukien. They cannot ask permission. The Miins know this.'

'What about the children? They were playing in the river yesterday.'

'The children ask permission to play. Really, Lukien . . .'

Frustrated, Lukien looked at the water. 'So what do we do?'

'We tell the Miins of our need,' said Jahan. 'We warn them. Watch and listen.'

Jahan held the waterskin over the river, looking into the water at his own wavy reflection. Smiling, he told the Miins – or at least the water – of their great journey to Torlis, and how they had travelled the length of the day. They were tired, he explained, and without water of their own. Lukien listened sceptically.

'You have to tell them all that?'

'Shush!'

Jahan apologized for Lukien, telling the Miins that he was a stranger. 'He knows nothing of our ways, but I will teach him. So, I will take some water, just enough for our need.' He skimmed his free hand across the surface of the water, as if brushing the unseen Miins aside. 'Good. Thank you,' he said, then dipped the waterskin into the river to fill it. When he was done, he gestured for Lukien to bring the others, and these he filled as well. Lukien watched the entire ritual, shocked at the deference the man gave the river. Finally, Jahan capped the last waterskin and stood.

'Now they will not trouble us,' he pronounced.

Lukien grimaced. 'Good. I feel better.'

'We will be following the river all the way to Torlis, Lukien. Would you rather have the Miins angry with us?'

'I don't even believe in the Miins, Jahan.' Lukien followed his friend up the bank and back toward camp. 'But if you're right and they exist, then better to have them happy than mad.'

Jahan grunted at his answer. 'You have so much to learn, Lukien. It is well that I came with you. There are spirits everywhere, in every living thing. I thought you understood that already.'

'I'm a Liirian,' said Lukien. 'In Liiria men do not usually believe in such things.'

'They do not believe in life?' snorted Jahan. He laid the waterskins with the other bags and went back to starting his fire. 'What kind of people are they?'

'Maybe they're ignorant,' said Lukien. He sat down on the ground, watching Jahan work the flint. 'I didn't believe in anything until I found Jador. That's the place across the desert I told you about.'

'Where you found your spirit necklace?'

'That's right.' Lukien pulled the Eye of God out from beneath his shirt, letting it spin on its golden chain. Night was falling rapidly, but the red jewel in the amulet lit his face. 'I should not have laughed at you. I'm sorry. Maybe there are spirits in the water. I've seen enough in my life to make me believe.'

'A man must believe, Lukien. There is always more to learn.' Managing to ignite a dried out leaf, Jahan leaned down and began blowing gently on his fragile fire. As the other leaves and twigs caught, he smiled proudly. 'We should eat.'

As the stars twinkled to life overhead, Lukien and Jahan ate. Neither of them spoke much, but instead enjoyed the food and the simple peace of not moving. The sky grew ever darker as the sun slowly faded, birthing the stars one by one, until at last the heavens filled with them. Lukien ate slowly, savouring his food and staring up at the constellations, some of which he recognized from his time in Jador, when Gilwyn would point them out to him. He missed Gilwyn, as he always did when night fell, and wondered what his young friend was doing. He supposed he was safe in Jador, and that gave Lukien comfort. He leaned back on his elbow, suppressed a belch, and watched Jahan as he ate. Jahan had untied his pony-tail, letting his long hair fall loosely around his shoulders, giving him a different look entirely. He seemed deep in thought. Lukien picked up a small stone and tossed it over to him, breaking him from his trance.

'What are you thinking about?' Lukien asked.

Jahan smiled. 'I am thinking of my wife. I am thinking how much I miss her already.'

'Mmm, that's a good thing to think about.'

'Do you have a woman, Lukien?'

Lukien shook his head. 'Not anymore. It's been a lot of years.'

'The one you told me about, the one who came to you – she was your woman, yes?'

'Yes,' sighed Lukien, 'a long time ago.'

'If you were Simiheh, you would not be alone,' said Jahan. 'A woman would always be found for you. A man should never be without a woman.'

'I agree,' said Lukien, grinning like a wolf. 'So how does that work? You trade wives?'

'If a man needs a woman to marry, one is found for him. It is a very simple thing.'

'Everything is simple where you come from, Jahan.' Lukien decided to press his companion. 'Tell me what happens when your village is gone.'

Jahan tore himself a hunk of the flat bread and pushed it into his mouth. 'I have told you that story already.'

'I know. I like hearing it.'

'Ah, so you like stories now!'

Lukien laughed. 'All right, yes. Tell me again – when the people are gone, the village is gone, right?'

'Yes. The people are the village, Lukien.'

'And the boys all go off and start their own village when they're old enough, right?'

'Not all, but most.'

'And what happens to you? You just die?'

Jahan looked at Lukien strangely. 'Everyone dies, Lukien. Except for you.'

The joke surprised Lukien. He wasn't even sure it was a joke. 'You're an important man in the village. Will it always be that way?'

'No. My time will come. A man of influence should not live too long. When I am old enough, I will die before my mind is lost.'

'What if you don't?' Lukien asked. 'What if you just live on and on, like me? Will the others replace you?'

'I will not live so long,' said Jahan. 'Before then, the chilling breath will come, and I will die.'

Lukien sat up. 'What's the chilling breath?'

'That is what it is called. When I am old and the people lose faith in me, then I will die of the chilling breath.'

'You mean they'll just turn their back on you?' asked Lukien.

'They will help me make way for someone younger. It will be that way for all of us who formed the village, Lukien. The others will . . . help us to die.'

The admission left Lukien stunned. He looked at Jahan across the jumping fire, studying his face for any signs of regret. There were none.

'You mean they'll kill you,' said Lukien.

'No. I will die of the chilling breath.' Jahan returned Lukien's stare. 'Do you understand?'

Lukien shook his head. 'No, I don't think I do,' he said. 'I don't understand your ways at all, Jahan. First you tell me that the whole village will die when all of you have died, and then you tell me that you're going to rush that day by killing off your leaders. It's bizarre.'

'To you, perhaps. To us it is the best way. I am not afraid of my end days, Lukien. I will not be a burden to anyone. I will be allowed to die with great dignity, and let someone who is stronger and more able than me take my place. Is that not a good thing?'

'I don't think I could ever let people kill me,' said Lukien. 'I'm too much of a fighter for that.'

'And that is why you have no peace, my friend, and why you search endlessly for this sword, and why you have no woman to love. Because you fight. Always you fight.'

'Maybe,' Lukien muttered. He didn't like the way the conversation had turned. 'But I think I know why you came with me, Jahan.'

'Of course you do. I have told you why.'

'Because I saved your son. Yes, that's what you told me. But I think you want to live just as much as I do. I think you want to see something besides your village before you die.'

Jahan set his food aside. A flash of anger crossed his face, but it fled quickly. 'When we are done and have found your sword, I will return to my village, and I will be glad to do so.'

'I know,' said Lukien. 'But in the meantime you'll have a chance to learn and see things that no one else in your village will ever see. The truth now, Jahan – doesn't that make you a little bit happy?'

Jahan scoffed. 'You should be glad I am with you, Lukien. The way you stagger about, you should wear two eye patches. You need me.'

'You're not going to confess, are you?' asked Lukien. 'You just can't admit that you came with me to see Torlis and meet the Red Eminence.'

Looking up to the stars, Jahan smiled but stayed very quiet, ignoring Lukien's query. Finally he said, 'I will not live forever. There are things I wish to see before I, too, become a spirit.'

Lukien nodded. 'That's what I thought.'

The two companions finished their meal, staring up at the stars and wondering what lay ahead.

13

In the catacombs of Asher's prison, time had lost its meaning. The dreary lamplight and the never-ending din of distant, tear-choked voices twisted day into night and back again. Somewhere near Mirage's cell, a leak dripped water onto the stone floor. Through her bars, she saw spiders building webs in the corner of the murky corridor, the hallway terminating into unseen darkness. The occasional footfalls of a prison guard echoed through the complex, quickening Mirage, sometimes heralding the arrival of her tormentor. At any time of day or night, a whip would crack across bare flesh. Blood-curdling shrieks awoke her when she slept, never deeply, guardedly watching the corridor for shadows. Twice she had awakened to Asher's ghostly face grinning through the bars of her cell, ready to ply her with questions.

There were so many questions.

Mirage sat in the corner of her cell, her head down, her eyes sagging with exhaustion. Thoughts rattled around her skull, scrambled from hunger and lack of sleep. Bedraggled strands of hair fell across her soiled forehead. Her chin nodded upward at a distant sound, then down again against her chest. Her filthy clothes clung to her half-frozen body. Days in the cold prison had turned her skin an unhealthy blue. Her fingernails ached. The toes of her bare feet curled inward for warmth. Water had been supplied in drips, and now her mouth swelled like cotton. A painful knot tied itself in her empty stomach. Hearing the familiar noise of footfalls, her eyes fluttered open to stare outside her silent bars. Waiting had been the worst part of her torment. Not even her interrogations with Asher were as bad. With only fears to fill the endless hours, she imagined every sort of depraved torture, every small pain the gaoler might inflict on her. In front of her, the jeering wooden stool sat near the entrance to her cell, its seat still impaled with Asher's knife. The edge of the blade stood at attention, waiting for its master. So far, Asher had not used the knife, taunting her with it instead, twirling it between his digits like a baton during their long interrogations. In the days that she had been his captive,

Asher had come to her three times. Mirage remembered each episode vividly, but she could not recall how long she had been in the prison. Without a window to tell night from day, she was like a blind woman, completely lost to the passage of time. The lamp outside her barren cell shed the only light on her wretched home.

Asher had been remarkably patient with her. Over and over, he asked the same uncomplicated questions, making her repeat herself again and again. Though he had promised to harm her, he had so far declined to even touch her, using only his voice to wear her down. She had told him things she had never intended to, like how Baron Glass loved her and how much time they had spent together. Intrigued, Asher continued to press her on this, compelling stories out of her, circling her with his arguments until she surrendered shreds of dignity. Now, Asher knew almost everything, but she had yet to tell him the most important thing. No matter the time she spent with Asher, no matter the torture, she would not reveal her knowledge of Grimhold or the magic she possessed. She had promised herself that. She was proud of her resolve.

'You can burn in all the hells of eternity,' she sputtered. 'That I'll never tell you.'

Her voice rasped against her ears. Just using her voice made her throat ache. But hearing it strengthened her, too, and she knew that if only she could speak, she could keep herself sane. To keep her promise, she needed her wits with her.

'Kirsil?' she whispered. 'Are you here?'

The comforting flutter of her Akari entered her mind. Kirsil, the young spirit who had given her beauty again, dithered nervously just within her grasp. Mirage seized the sense of her, clinging to her hopefully. Kirsil had been precious little use to her, providing solace but no good ideas. They were both trapped, and the Akari seemed to know it. Mirage half expected the spirit to abandon her.

No, said Kirsil, appalled at the thought. *Never. We are together. We will always be together.*

Mirage closed her eyes, but somehow managed to keep from crying. 'Thank you, Kirsil. Thank you for everything you've given me.'

The Akari hesitated, reading her feelings as well as her thoughts. *Do you wish Sarlvarian was here?*

The question surprised Mirage. It was true that she had thought of Sarlvarian – her old Akari – many times since her capture. With his help, she might be able to escape Asher, burning her way past him and his many underlings with his magic fire. But she had traded Sarlvarian for Kirsil, and for beauty.

'No,' said Mirage, shaking her head. She kept her voice low so that no one else could hear. 'I've never been sorry you are my Akari, Kirsil.'

Then you must hold on, said the spirit. *You must stay strong, just as strong as you have been.*

Mirage leaned her head back against the unyielding wall. 'I don't know how much more I can last. My body hurts, Kirsil.'

You must protect Grimhold, Mirage.

'I'm trying.'

I will help you. Take strength from me.

The sentiment nearly broke Mirage's resolve. Drawing her legs closer to her body, she wrapped her hands around them for warmth, rubbing her knees. She studied the flame dancing on the wall outside her cell, willing it to warm her the way she could when Sarlvarian had been with her. It was not so long ago that she had power over flame. With only a thought, she could have made that lamplight explode.

'I'm so cold,' she said, then broke into a chorus of coughs. Without water to calm it, she coughed until the pain of it seared her lungs, then stopped abruptly. More footfalls sounded in the corridor, this time coming toward her. 'Oh, no . . .'

Mirage could barely bring herself to stand, but stand she did, determined to face Asher on her feet. Her captor had always been impressed by her strength, maybe even vexed by it. Mirage rose unsteadily, ignoring the icy floor as she squared her shoulders. Soon the sounds grew louder, then the shadows crept around the corner. Two men – both of whom she recognized – appeared outside her cell. She did not know their names, but the pair always accompanied Asher when he came to question her. This time, though, the inquisitor had not come. Puzzled, Mirage glared at the guards.

'Good, you're up,' grunted one of the men. Dressed in his dark uniform, he was the larger of the muscular pair, with eyes like burning coals that undressed Mirage when he stared. He fit the key into the stout lock and turned the tumbler, then pulled the iron door open with a screech. 'Come with us,' he commanded.

Mirage fought to control her terror. Short of breath, she gasped, 'Where?'

'Asher wants to see you,' said the other, slightly smaller man. In his hands dangled a chain with manacles on both ends. Stepping into the cell, he gestured for Mirage to turn around. 'Hands behind your back.'

With no way to resist, Mirage did as he asked, wondering if this – finally – meant the punishment Asher had promised her. The cold iron encircled her wrists, snapping shut. The man grabbed her hair and pushed her roughly toward the door. Her feet scraped across the jagged floor, stubbing her toe as she fell against the bigger man. Shutting the bars loudly behind her, the guard grabbed hold of her arm and dragged her down the corridor.

It was a long, wordless way through the hall. Mirage had only made the trip once before, when she been brought to her hole-like home. The dim light stabbed at her eyes, illuminating the rows of identical cells, most of them empty, others with huddled prisoners like herself. Mirage looked away, unable to face their vacant stares. At the end of the hall stood a spiral staircase. Vaguely, she remembered descending it, but to her numbed brain it seemed so long ago. She held on to Kirsil, frantically reaching for the Akari through her terror. The spirit coursed through her mind, calming her like a mother's touch.

'Up,' said her gaoler, lifting her by the armpit toward the first step. Nearly stumbling, Mirage leaned against his big frame as she struggled up the stairs. The guard dragged her impatiently along, bouncing her up each step, ignoring her cries of pain. The dizzying staircase spiraled endlessly upward, assailing her eyes with torchlight. Days in darkness had turned her vision to mush. She squinted at the growing light, her eyes watering, until at last she spilled out into another stone corridor, falling to her knees.

'Get up,' commanded the bigger man. Hovering over her, Mirage expected him to strike her, but he did not. Instead he hooked his hand beneath her arm and lifted her effortlessly to her feet. She looked around the giant hall, studying the high ceiling and bare, grey walls. She remembered this place, too, when she had first been taken into the prison. To her great relief, she saw windows at the far end of the hall, and daylight streaming inside. The sight of sunlight made her gasp. Where was Asher? Was she being freed?

'Where are you taking me?' she asked. 'Please tell me.'

But the guards ignored her question. Flanking her, they each grabbed an arm and guided her down the hall toward the sunlit windows. Mirage flailed against their grasp.

'I can walk!' she hissed, pulling free of their arms. 'I don't want your filthy hands on me!'

The big guard with the dark eyes pointed down the hall. 'Then walk. Or I will carry you.'

Mirage did as he commanded, shuffling across the floor, her pride wounded but intact. The men strode next to her, side by side, silently urging her onward. Mirage saw the windows growing ahead of her, looming large in a part of the prison she had not seen before, a place not nearly as dank as the rest of Asher's home. As they got closer, she rounded a corner to see a pair of open doors. Hardly believing it, she saw grass beyond the threshold. The scent of flowers – of freedom – filled her lungs. She paused, swallowing the fresh air. Looking at her captors in disbelief, they motioned toward the open doors.

'Move,' said one of them, taking her arm again and guiding her outside.

Her bare feet touched the carpet of grass. Soft and warm, it tickled her. Mirage looked around, spying the trees that lined the alcove. A ribbon of cobblestones had been preciously laid into the neatly trimmed grass, wandering around a stand of fruit trees. The sun beat down on the gardens, hurting Mirage's eyes, but she could not bring herself to look away. She squinted through painful tears, wondering where the guards had taken her. They guided her onto the stone path, careful not to let her fall, then stopped abruptly. The smaller one fumbled with her manacles and an unseen key, unlocking her binds.

'Go on,' he said, pulling off her chains.

Mirage rubbed her wrists. 'Where?'

'Follow the path,' said her gaoler.

Mirage looked at him in confusion. Were they freeing her? Listening, she heard gentle noises just beyond the trees, but could see nothing behind their blossom-laden limbs.

'Go,' said the larger man impatiently. 'We'll wait here.'

Not understanding, Mirage took a cautious step along the cobblestones, trying to focus her stinging eyes. To her surprise, the guards did not follow. In the shadow of the tall prison, she could not believe such a quiet place existed, and as she went deeper into the trees she saw a clearing set among the grasses, with a table and two chairs – one occupied by Asher. The table had been set with fine porcelain and silverware. An urn of tea steamed in the breeze. Asher sat with his back to a servant, a man at rapt attention dressed smartly in a kitchen uniform. Bread and fruit and dainty sandwiches dotted the table, and Mirage, who had not seen food in days, gaped at it. She froze on the pretty pathway, watching incredulously as Asher tried to smile with his malformed mouth.

'Sit,' said the man. It was more like a request than an order. Asher gestured to the empty chair opposite him. He had removed his blood-stained apron, donning a clean, silky shirt and combing back his wild hair. His swollen face twisted in delight. To Mirage, he looked like a child sitting at the table, playing tea party. When she did not come closer, he began to pout. 'Will you not sit?' he asked. 'I am sure you must be hungry.'

'What . . . what is this?' Mirage asked, massaging her frozen hands. She sneered at the man. 'Now you taunt me? Your knife wasn't enough?'

'Sit,' Asher repeated, losing his pleasant demeanour in an instant. 'Or I will not share any of this with you.'

'I don't want any,' spat Mirage.

'Then you can go back to your cell and rot.' Asher looked at her expectantly. 'What's that? You don't want to go back to your cell? You'd rather sit out here and have a nice meal?' His smirk grew intolerable. 'That's what I thought. Sit down, girl. Right now.'

Mirage inched closer to the table, terrified by Asher's tactics. She was not free; she knew that already. She took her seat at the table, feeling ridiculously out of place with her torn clothes and dirty face. A shining plate sat empty in front of her. The servant standing behind Asher twitched, as if waiting to act. Mirage looked at all the food and the hot, delicious smelling tea. She could not help herself. Her mouth and stomach screamed for it.

'Your eyes will adjust in a few minutes,' said Asher, sitting straight as an icicle in his chair. Mirage, however, could barely keep herself erect. She fought against her weakness, trying hard to be the butcher's equal.

'Tell me why I'm here,' she said, her voice scratchy.

'To talk,' replied Asher. 'Tea?'

'We have talked. We have done nothing but talk. If you mean to torture me, get on with it.'

Asher snapped his finger, bringing the servant to life. Soundlessly the man came to the table and poured tea into both their small cups. He selected an assortment of morsels from the platters, placing them on Mirage's plate before gracefully withdrawing. Mirage fought to keep her eyes off the food, locking them on Asher.

'Eat, please,' said Asher. 'I know you want to.'

'Of course I want to, you bastard.'

'There is no charge for it, girl. You may eat your fill and owe me nothing for it.'

Mirage laughed. 'You're so merciful.'

'This place is my solace, pretty Mirage. I come here to escape the filth of my prison. Even I need to see the sun and listen to the birds sometimes. Does that surprise you?'

'What do you want?'

'To talk.'

Mirage groaned, maddened by his answer. 'Tell me!'

Asher sipped at his tea, unperturbed by her outburst. During his interrogations, his patience had been boundless. When he worked, nothing shook his strange comportment. And he was working now, just as he worked when he sat on his stool in Mirage's cell, spinning the knife through his fingers. This time, though, his implements were tea cups.

'Mmm, that's good,' he sighed, smacking his lips as he set down his cup. 'Nice and warm. The prison gets so cold. Sometimes I can't stand being down in those cells. Mirage, have some tea. It will warm you.'

Mirage felt her body start to tremble.

'Eat,' said Asher. 'I can wait.'

Still Mirage did not touch her food. With some satisfaction, she watched annoyance cross Asher's face.

'Will you eat if I command it?' asked the prison lord. 'Perhaps that's the problem. Perhaps you have been in my charge too long already. You have lost every bit of yourself, is that it? In truth I do not care if you eat or starve. I will eat and be happy, and you will still be miserable. And hungry.'

'I am still my own, Asher,' gasped Mirage. 'I am not an animal. I can make my own decisions.'

Amused, Asher lifted his tea cup. 'Decide, then,' he said, and began to slowly sip, studying her.

It made no sense to Mirage, none of it. Why should she return to her hole with her stomach empty? To survive Asher's hellish prison, she needed strength, she decided. Her eyes lowered to her plate, spying a delicate tart. It had probably taken an artisan to create it, but Mirage picked it up and shoved it in her mouth with no more regard than she might have a grape. Its flavour exploded on her tongue. Instead of savouring it, she reached for another, swallowing the first without chewing and chasing it with its twin. Crumbs and bits of fruit fell from her chin as she devoured the treats. Unable to stop, she drowned in the tide of hunger and despair, looking up only briefly to see Asher's satisfied grin. Asher's peculiar face – scarred as hers had been – seemed almost lustful as he watched her. The tea cup in his hand shivered slightly, not going to his lips but rather hovering just beyond his mouth. Swallowing hard, Mirage picked up her own tea cup and drank, ignoring the heat of the liquid as she tried to quench her enormous thirst. Though most of it fell down her chin, she drained the cup and hurriedly reached for the urn, grunting for the servant to move off as he tried to pour it for her. The tea sloshed over the rim and onto the linen table cloth as she poured, then lifted the cup with both hands to her mouth. Gasping and drinking at the same time, Mirage finally set the cup down and fell back in her chair, covering her mouth. She stared at Asher, almost in tears.

'I want more,' she groaned.

'Eat,' crooned Asher. He seemed astonished by her hunger, even entertained. 'This is your chance now.'

Mirage took his meaning. Thinking of more endless hours of depravation, she filled her mouth with the breads and cheeses and beautifully made sandwiches, sating her hunger as quickly as she could, swallowing in chunks so big they hurt her throat going down. Ignoring Asher, she ate and ate, clearing her plate more than once until at last her bloated stomach could hold no more. A sickening gorged feeling swept over her, making her forehead break out in sweat. Asher noticed the change in her at once.

'If you're going to vomit, please, do so out of my sight.'

'I'm not,' said Mirage, taking deep breaths. She wondered if she should be grateful for the food, but the thought of thanking Asher turned her stomach even more. 'I'm done now,' she said, pushing aside her plate. Suddenly all she wanted was sleep.

'You have an appetite for such a petite girl,' Asher remarked. He had not touched a crumb of food himself, a fact that surprised Mirage.

'You didn't bring me out here for a meal,' she said. 'Why, then?'

'You are wrong, Mirage. I wanted you to see how things might be if you co-operated. There's no reason for you to live like a rat in that filthy cell. You can be clean and warm, and well fed. All you have to do is tell me what I want to know.'

'I've told you everything already.'

'No,' said Asher. 'Oh, I admit you've told me a great deal. It's all been fascinating, truly. But you're hiding something, pretty Mirage.'

'No,' Mirage insisted. 'There's nothing more. How many times are you going to ask me the same things?'

'I have not even begun to question you, girl.'

Mirage looked at him across the table. 'What, then?'

'Tell me more about Baron Glass,' said Asher. 'Tell me why he came to Liiria.'

It was the same, maddening line of inquiry. Mirage sighed, miserable to have to endure it once again. 'He came to protect Liiria against Jazana Carr. You know that already.'

'But then he went to her. He joined her.'

'That's right.'

'They were lovers. Tell me about that.'

'I don't know anything more.'

'Baron Glass must be a man of vast appetites. He cared for you as well as the Diamond Queen.'

'We had no relationship. Not beyond our friendship.'

'But he wanted more. Do you think that's why he turned back to Jazana Carr? Because you shunned him, pretty Mirage?'

Mirage looked down at her empty plate. She had never considered that possibility. 'I don't know.'

'Did you love him?'

'No.'

'Why are you protecting him? He left you for another woman. He betrayed you and your friends in Liiria, left you to die so that he could overrun you at the library with the Diamond Queen's hordes.'

'He didn't know I was there.' Mirage felt her neck tighten under Asher's barrage. 'Not until after the library fell.'

'But you went back to him. Corvalos Chane saw you with him.'

'Because I had nowhere else to go! I've told you this already.'

'Tell me,' said Asher, 'about the magic of Grimhold.'

Mirage looked up from her plate into Asher's laughing eyes, seized by a chill. 'What?'

Asher set down his tea cup. 'I wonder – did you really think we didn't know about it? You've been gone far too long, child. Everyone has heard about the Seekers and the magic of Mount Believer. And King Raxor has been thorough. He knows where to place his spies. And not just Corvalos Chane, though he was the first to tell us about the armour.'

Mirage fought to calm herself, to sort through her racing mind. 'I don't know what you mean.'

'You do, you do,' Asher assured her. 'The Devil's Armour. We know about it. Chane spent enough time in the library to hear about it and its power. We know that Baron Glass possesses it.'

He was baiting her. Mirage avoided his hooks. 'Yes. I heard the same.'

Asher chuckled. 'That's it? Nothing more?'

Mirage shrugged. 'The Devil's Armour. It came from Grimhold. That's all.'

'You know so much. I can see it all over your face. Do you think you've done a good job of hiding it from me, all your secrets? You are a child, Mirage. Every time you speak I can see the secrets struggling to get out. Tell me about the Devil's Armour.'

'I can't. I don't know anything.'

'You're protecting a man who crawled into the arms of another woman. A man who killed your friends at the library.'

'I'm not protecting him,' Mirage insisted. She felt hot suddenly, her cheeks blooming with colour. All she wanted was to flee. 'I swear, I don't know about the magic. Baron Glass has the armour. They say it's very powerful and ancient. I never saw it or saw him wear it. That's the truth.'

'I've had my whole life to cultivate patience, pretty Mirage.'

'So hurt me, then! Stop threatening me and do it.' Mirage stared at him, her lip curling up hatefully. 'You can make me scream with your little knife, Asher. But you haven't. Why not?'

Asher smiled his sick smile. 'I have enjoyed talking to you. You have been like a breath of fresh air in this putrid place. I've shown you courtesy, because it pleases me to do so. But believe me when I tell you this – I will burn out your eyeballs and skin you alive before I let you keep lying to me. I will hang your pelt over my hearth before I ever believe you know nothing about the Devil's Armour.'

The threat jolted Mirage. Her mind froze. Unable to speak, she simply stared at Asher.

'It's your choice, child. You may sit here and enjoy the sunlight and good food and tell me all you know, or you may go back to your cell and await me there. If you tell me what you're hiding, I promise you an easy time. If you do not, I promise you hell.'

Terror rose in Mirage. Her breathing quickened.

'You are right,' Asher went on. 'I have my knife, and I am not afraid to use it. Do not think for a moment that I would hesitate to do so.'

Mirage thought very hard, but all her options seemed dismal. There was so much she could confess, so much that would satisfy her captor. He would reward her for her information, surely. She would be spared his knife. And all for the simple cost of betraying Grimhold.

'The guards are waiting, Mirage,' said Asher. 'You want to be safe and happy.' He leaned across the table. 'Don't you?'

His tongue was almost out of his mouth as he spoke, waiting to lick her tears. But Mirage did not cry. Summoning the last of her courage, she rose from the chair and turned from Asher's table, walking back toward the cobblestone path and the waiting prison guards.

Hours passed, and day slipped slowly into night. Back inside her filthy cell, Mirage awaited Asher. She sat as she always did, with her back against the cold wall and her bare feet on the rough floor, her knees tucked like a child against her bosom, wrapping herself for warmth. In the hours since she had seen Asher, not a single guard had come to harass her. Instead, she had all the quiet she needed to think and wonder what Asher would do to her.

Why, she wondered, had he waited so long? She had expected her torture days ago. She stared at the little stool Asher used, sitting forlorn in the corner of her cell, the thin blade of his cherished knife sticking like an arrow from its seat. She could have used the weapon, she supposed, and tried to fight her way out of the prison, but she had always thought that a stupid idea. Asher had purposefully left his knife within her grasp to taunt her, abundantly confidant in her inability to use it. The guards, she knew, would have snapped her like a twig anyway.

'Why?' she seethed. 'Because he enjoys seeing me suffer.'

That was why he had waited so long, when he could have hung her in chains and skinned her days ago. Asher was just a cruel little boy, pulling the wings off butterflies. Not too quickly, or they would die and spoil his fun. But now he was ready. And Mirage was afraid.

She closed her eyes, listening to the distant noises in the dungeon. She had got very good at blocking out the screams, but she heard them now, moaning like wind that never died. Were they enemies of Reec, all of them? Was she? Perhaps. She had admitted her friendship with Baron Glass, and that was enough to condemn her.

'Then I will die,' she whispered. She searched her mind for her Akari. 'Kirsil, will I see you when I die?'

It was a question she had always wondered. All the Inhumans did. Minikin had never told then what would happen when they died, or if there would be life for them at all after death. It was simply too important a mystery, Minikin had explained, and not for any of them to know. Now, though, her sweet Akari Kirsil answered with sincerity.

'I think so.'

The answer satisfied Mirage. An accepting calm settled over her. She smiled.

Hours more went by unnoticed. Exhausted from fear, Mirage felt her head begin to totter downward. Her eyelids grew too heavy to keep open, shutting slowly in a flutter. She slept, though just on the surface of sleep, still faintly aware of every sound and the impending footfalls of her captor. Asher's deformed face twisted through her dreams. She realized with disgust that his would be the last fact she would see before she died. Not Lukien's or Minikin's or any other of the Inhumans she had left behind.

She did not realize how much time had gone by, but when she awoke it was to the sounds of boots scraping closer. Mirage awoke with a start, holding her breath and listening. The noise grew louder as the footsteps approached, unhurried. Bracing herself, Mirage got to her feet to meet Asher, determined not to weep or beg. Squaring her shoulders, she watched as a shadow swept across the threshold of her cell, followed by a large silhouette. Not Asher, Mirage realized. The figure stopped in front of the bars, blocking the meagre lamp behind him and holding a cloak and a pair of boots. Mirage squinted, thinking the figure vaguely familiar.

'You are awake,' said the man. 'Good.'

She recognized his voice at once. 'Chane . . .'

Corvalos Chane had a key in his hand which he expertly used to open her locked cell. As he moved to reveal the light behind him, his stony features came into relief. He looked at her as he unlocked the tumbler and pulled the bars open. There was no smile on his weathered face, only an expression of satisfaction. Stepping into the cell, he tossed the cloak and boots at her naked feet.

'Dress yourself,' he said. 'We're going.'

Hes the Serene, capital of Reec, spread out around Mirage like a sleeping dragon, twinkling with candlelight and still as a grave. Homes and businesses along the avenues had shut their doors hours ago, and the squat towers of the city brooded over the streets. Fading moonlight carpeted the cobblestones and brown, wooden structures, and the breeze stirred unlocked shutters as it tumbled down the lane. Mirage shivered in her cloak, burying her face in the fur lining. Corvalos Chane's broad chest pressed against her back as they rode, warming her. Their horse trotted slowly along the empty avenue, making lonely music as its hooves struck the paving stones. Up ahead, the two towers of Castle Hes beckoned, hanging over the city from their grassy green hill. In the silence of the city, time stretched like syrup. The lateness of the hour had put all of Hes to sleep, as though the capital had fallen under a peaceful spell.

From Asher's prison on the outskirts of Hes, it had not taken long for the pair to ride this far. Hes was not like Koth, Mirage realized. Instead the city was smaller and more compact, without Koth's towering spires and tangled alleys. In less than half an hour, Mirage and Chane had left the prison and made it almost to their destination. And in all that time, Chane had barely said a word to her, ignoring her pleas for an explanation. She knew they were going to the castle, and that was all. Mirage shifted on the horse's back, full of trepidation. She had been exhausted when Chane had come to her cell, and the big man had helped her out of the prison, almost carrying her up the winding stairs. Amazingly, neither Asher nor his guards had stopped them. The lord of the prison had not even come to see her go, a mystery that puzzled Mirage. Chane had helped her onto his horse, and they had simply ridden away from the prison. She was free.

Fighting the chill that had taken her, Mirage huddled the cloak around her shoulders as Castle Hes came clearer into view. 'I want answers,' she demanded. 'Why are we going there?'

'Sit still.'

Pinned between his arms, Mirage squirmed. 'Am I to be executed? Is that it? Or do you have some other torture waiting for me?'

'No torture,' Chane replied. 'Unless you prefer going back to Asher. That's still a possibility.'

'Chane, tell me what's going on!'

Corvalos Chane, who had been called the 'right hand' of King Raxor, thought for a moment before answering. Mirage twisted to glance over her shoulder. His white eyebrows knitted together.

'You are wondering why Asher did not harm you,' he said. 'Why do you think?'

'I don't know,' said Mirage. The question still vexed her. 'He could have tortured me. He told me he would.'

'He did not because I forbade it, when I brought you to him.'

Mirage craned to look at him again. 'What?'

'Asher likes his work too much. He was not lying to you, girl. He has a place where he takes his favourite women, and you were a favourite, I could tell.'

'You saved me? Why?'

'Because I have seen his handiwork. He is not a man at all. He is a crazed dog.'

Mirage still did not understand. Suddenly she wanted to be down from the horse, so that she could face Chane properly. 'Stop,' she said. 'Let me down and explain this to me.'

'You are expected at the castle.'

'Let me down!'

Chane heaved a groan and drew their horse to a halt in the middle of the avenue. Mirage knew she could not dismount until he did, and he did not. 'You're a harpy,' he said with frustration. 'That won't do at all. If you hear nothing else I tell you, at least listen to this – you are safe from Asher for now, but only for as long as you co-operate. When you get to the castle you can't act like this.'

Mirage grit her teeth. 'Chane, if you don't tell me what's going on . . .'

'What? What will you do?'

'Believe me, I can make enough of a scene to embarrass you.'

'I believe you.'

Dismounting, Chane slid down gracefully to the cobblestone street. 'Stay up there,' he ordered. 'We won't be stopping long.'

It was the first time that night Mirage got a good look at him. His weathered features crinkled in the moonlight. 'I'm ready for an answer,' she said. 'Why are you taking me to Castle Hes? Why did you save me from Asher?'

'I told you that already. Asher would have skinned you alive, just as he promised. It's what he does.'

'That's not all. It can't be. What do you care what happens to me?'

Corvalos Chane replied, 'There aren't many who could stop Asher. In his prison, he's the master. But being who I am, I have some authority over him.'

'The king's man,' said Mirage. 'Is that what you mean?'

Chane nodded. 'When I took you to him five days ago, I told him not to harm you. He resisted, of course. He took an immediate liking to you.'

'I noticed,' said Mirage, feeling cold again. 'But why? Why did you give that order? Not just to save me. That can't be it. You said yourself I'm an enemy of Reec.'

'Asher got a lot of good information out of you. I know because I get his reports. For the past two days he's been begging me to rescind my order. Tonight he sent me a letter. He said that he'd gone far enough, and that he was going to do what was necessary. He was going to disregard my order.'

'You mean torture me.'

'That's right. His lust finally got the better of him. I rode to stop him.'

'Just like that? He must have protested.'

'He did,' Chane admitted. 'I ignored him. Asher is very bold from a distance, but cowers like a schoolboy when confronted.'

'So, my interrogation isn't done, then,' said Mirage. She glanced away, unable to face Chane's probing eyes. 'That's why you're taking me to the castle. You'll be taking me for yourself.'

'You still have secrets,' said Chane. 'About Baron Glass. About his armour. Don't deny it, girl. Asher says that you know more, and he is never wrong about such things.'

'So, you'll take the pleasure of torturing me yourself, then?' Mirage glared at Chane, wanting to pepper him with curses. 'Do what you wish. I'll tell you nothing.'

'You would tell me everything I could ever want to know,' said Chane. 'An hour with me and you would be begging for death. Asher's not the only one who can use a knife.'

'So?' flared Mirage. 'Why did you take me away from him? If all you mean to do is kill me . . .'

'Quiet,' snapped Chane. 'You're not to be tortured. I didn't save you from that madman just to have you harmed. That's not why I'm taking you to Castle Hes. There's something else.'

'What?' asked Mirage, dreading his answer.

Chane took hold of the horse's reins. He looked up at her calmly and said, 'You're to be a gift for King Raxor.'

Mirage frowned as if she hadn't heard right. 'What do you mean?'

'You're to be one of the king's women,' said Chane, 'just as I am the king's man.'

'Those mean two different things, though,' said Mirage, groping for understanding. 'I'm no man's slave!'

'This isn't slavery, girl.'

'Yes, yes it is!' Mirage sputtered. 'You're talking about a concubine. What is that, if not a slave?'

'You are to be one of the king's women,' repeated Chane firmly. So that Mirage could not bolt, he kept his fist tight on the horse. 'It's been settled.'

'No!' Mirage railed. Her mind raced for a way to escape. 'You saved me for this? I won't do it.'

'You will, because you have no choice. King Raxor will love you. I knew it when I first saw you. That's why I made sure Asher did nothing to you.'

'So you let him torment me?'

'Why not?' Chane barked. 'I was right about you, girl. You have information.'

'I won't give it,' Mirage promised. 'Never. Is this your way of trying to make me talk? Another game like Asher played with me? Well his game didn't work and this won't either. You can enslave me, make me one of your king's whores. I won't tell you what I know. Not ever.'

'This is not a game,' Chane assured her. 'I have already told King Raxor about you. I promised him a woman of remarkable beauty, a women to make his heart sing.'

'But that's not me! And he's the king! Surely he can have his pick of women.'

'You.'

Chane began leading the horse along the avenue, resuming their trek toward Castle Hes. Mirage looked desperately around, searching for any way to escape. The quiet city might give ample places to hide, but if she ran Chane would simply mount the horse and stop her. So she tried pleading instead.

'Listen to me,' she begged. 'I won't be the kind of woman your king wants. If you do this, you'll just be hurting yourself, Chane. I won't please your king. I'll be the worst bitch he's ever seen.'

'Then you will be punished,' said Chane.

'Stop! Please . . .'

Chane halted, again turning to regard her. 'Girl, you're not understanding. You have no choice, except the obvious one. You can either agree to this or be sent back to Asher. Tonight. Asher keeps his knives sharp. He'll be ready for you.'

'Be skinned alive or be a whore to your king? That's no choice at all,' said Mirage bitterly.

Chane shrugged. 'But there it is . . .'

He resumed leading the horse down the street. And Mirage was out of answers. She slumped on the beast's back, all her arguments lost, the last of her hope snuffed out like a candle. Castle Hes loomed in the distance, growing ever closer. She could see its spiked portcullis glowing in torch-light. Her courage withered, and for the first time she cursed her new-found beauty. Even covered in grime, her hair matted with filth, men still lusted for her, men like Asher with their twisted appetites and men like Raxor, always eager to bed some new harlot. For a moment, she had thought that Chane, too, had lusted for her, assuming that to be his motive for saving her. But Chane wasn't like other men. He was cruel like them, certainly, but he had not heart at all, just the clockworks of a machine spinning in his chest.

'You've told your king about me?' she asked.

Chane did not turn to look at her, but kept on walking. 'That's right. And you'll be good to him, girl, or you'll be sorry.'

'I had thought you meant to rape me when you caught me. I thought you saw me in that bar and meant to take me for yourself. But you're not even man enough to do that, are you? You're just a blind dog, doing whatever your master bids.'

'I have my duty,' said Chane, barely bristling.

'Yes, no mind of your own,' spat Mirage. 'And nothing between your legs. If you were a man – a real man – you'd let me go. You'd see the wrongness in all of this.'

'You're reaching, girl.'

Mirage didn't care. 'This is my chance to tell you what I think of you, Corvalos Chane. You're as much a slave as I am, only you're too stupid to know it. Is this what it means to be the right hand of Raxor? To find him poor girls? I can't wait to see what a monster he must be, to have to send you out to get women for him. What a bastard he must be . . .'

'Enough!' roared Chane. With a face like thunder, he turned on her and jerked the reins until she almost tumbled. 'You may speak of me as you wish, but if you ever speak so of the king again I swear I will kill you. Do you understand? Beautiful or not, I will kill you.'

Mirage met his wild gaze, refusing to back down. 'That's your duty too, I suppose. To kill innocent people. No women for Corvalos Chane, the mindless eunuch.'

'You know nothing,' said Chane. 'I cannot have a woman. I am devoted to King Raxor. He is my life, my only reason for existing. So close your mouth or when we get to the castle I will have one of the seamstresses sew it closed.'

Chane continued his march toward Castle Hes, this time more quickly. Mirage shrank in the saddle. No amount of jeering could deter him, she knew, and the bitterness in his words had surprised her. There was, she supposed, something human in him after all.

'You may lie to me, even to yourself,' she said. 'But I know why you saved me. Because you didn't want to see me harmed.'

'I already told you that. Now be quiet.'

'I'll give you myself if you let me go, Corvalos Chane.'

Chane slowed but did not turn to face her. 'Stop now.'

'Just one night,' said Mirage. 'You can have me.'

'Please, stop talking.' Chane came to a halt. He turned around slowly. 'Don't do this to yourself, girl. However much I may crave you, I can never have a woman. So do not bargain yourself. You have pride. You're not a whore, and King Raxor will not make you one.'

Finally, Mirage surrendered. Her façade dissolved, leaving her unable to argue or even believe the things she was saying. She nodded, stifling tears that threatened to burst from her eyes. 'Take me to the castle, then,' she said. 'But know this – I will not give up my secrets.'

Something like pity crossed Chane's face. 'You will, girl. You just don't know it yet. In time, whatever you know about Baron Glass and his armour will come falling out of your mouth, and you won't be able to stop it.'

'You're wrong,' said Mirage.

Chane smiled, not victoriously. 'You'll never leave Reec. Your life in

Liiria is over, and once you realize that you'll see there's no value at all in your keeping secrets.'

Then, without another word between them, Chane led Mirage the rest of the way to Castle Hes.

14

Mirage had thought she would never be warm again, but in the perfumed water of the luxurious tub, Asher's frozen prison became just a distant, terrifying memory. Mirage opened her eyes, feeling trails of water drip from her forehead and watching wisps of steam thread through her toes. With a deep, satisfied breath, she smelled the lavender from the exotic salts that had been sprinkled into her bath. Her naked body floated in the clean, warm water, her chin hovering just above the surface. Her wet hair, now brushed free of its tangles and filth, splayed out around her shoulders, dancing on the water. For the first time in days, her skin felt soft. Oil in the water had tinged the bath pink, turning it to silk. Mirage could taste it on her lips. The steam untied the knots in her muscles, and though she had already slept the day away, her eyelids fluttered with exhaustion.

The day had passed in a remarkable blur. It was almost night again, but Mirage had spent the daylight hours in a soft bed with clean sheets and a pillow that cradled her head like a cloud. In a beautiful room with huge, soaring windows, she had eaten fine food brought to her by servants, watching the busy city from her perch in one of the castle's towers. Though it had been just before dawn when Chane had brought her to Castle Hes, the servants had already been waiting for her. Eager to pamper her, the women had shooed Corvalos Chane away, caring for Mirage as though she were a favourite pet. They brushed her hair and made her bed, and gave her quiet so that she could sleep. The maids watched her anxiously, jumping to please her but never answering her questions. Finally, Mirage had given up, surrendering to them and all their temptations. After eating she slept, and her sleep was dreamless and pleasant, so deep that when she awoke she could not remember where she was until a happy faced girl appeared over her bed. Announcing it was bath time, the girl led Mirage to an adjacent room in the tower, where the steaming bath had already been drawn and a young maid – who could have been a twin of the first – stood ready with a brush. And just as she had surrendered to the food and soft bed, Mirage slipped out of her dressing robe into the warm, silky water.

Now, once again on the verge of sleep, Mirage considered all that had happened. A gilded window at the far side of the chamber told her that the sun was setting. She could see it sending up its dying, purple rays, dipping slowly behind the city's silhouette. For the moment, her maids had left her, allowing her to relax and enjoy the bath. They were full of questions, Mirage could tell, but they held their tongues and spoke only of the work at hand, marveling at how beautiful Mirage looked and how lovely her hair was once washed. It was all simple, girlish talk, pleasant and diverting, and Mirage was no longer afraid. Surely being in Raxor's bed would be better than being in Asher's chains. Would she be his slave, she wondered? They were making her pretty for him, that much she had guessed. Was he a kind man? Would he beat her?

Mirage sank in the tub. She knew almost nothing about King Raxor, only that he was an old man now and that he had ascended to Reec's throne upon his brother's death. He had been a war hero once, a long time ago when Reec and Liiria were enemies. Lukien had faced him in battle many times. But Lukien was never one to talk about old battles, and Mirage cursed herself for not listening to him more intently when he did.

'Has he no wife?' Mirage asked herself. Kings could have as many wives as they wished, she supposed, and as many harlots to satisfy their lust. The notion made her pensive. She missed home desperately. She missed Minikin more than she ever thought possible.

Soon, though, she heard footsteps approaching. Mirage sat up, ignoring modesty as she peered to see who had come. An older woman appeared, simply garbed in a grey maid's dress, her hair pinned back in an unflattering bun. Mirage had seen her before, directing the other maids. She held a fresh white robe in her wrinkled hands. A brittle smile cracked her face.

'It's time to get you ready,' she announced.

Mirage looked up uncertainly. 'For the king?'

'You're clean and rested. And King Raxor is expecting you. Come out of the bath. We'll brush your hair and dress you.'

Even naked, no one could see through Mirage's magic. Not a hint of her burned skin made it through Kirsil's mask. It still amazed Mirage, who smiled at the old woman.

'What's your name?' she asked.

'My name is Laurella,' said the woman, holding out the robe. 'Come on – out with you now.'

'Are you one of Raxor's women?'

Laurella faintly blushed. 'I'm one of the king's maids, child. I've been employed at the castle all my life, just like my mother and father before me.'

'He has other women, the king?'

'Too many questions,' Laurella sighed. She lowered the robe, looking sympathetically at Mirage. 'Child, do not worry. King Raxor is a gentle man.' Then, glancing over her shoulder, she lowered her voice to a whisper. 'And probably too old to do much with you. If you're a virgin, I shouldn't be worrying about losing your prize to him.'

Laurella's faded blue eyes smiled down at her, encouraging Mirage out of the bathtub. At last, it seemed she had found an ally. Trusting the old woman, Mirage lifted herself up, dripping wet, letting Laurella help her out and into the robe, a garment of such thick fabric Mirage felt lost in it. The whole experience had made her feel small, in fact, like a little girl. Laurella toweled dry her hair until it fell limply across her eyes. She produced a pair of waiting slippers for her feet, then led Mirage out of the bath chamber and into an adjoining dressing room. There, the two younger maids who had tended her earlier urged Mirage into a chair set before a magnificent mirror. Brushes and all colours of waxy rouge and lip polish had been arranged on the vanity table. The girls chirped excitedly as Mirage took her seat.

'You're so beautiful!' said one of them.

'Beautiful,' the other quickly agreed. Together they touched her dripping hair, playing with the strands.

'Child, look here,' said Laurella. She had walked to the other side of the room, near a small bed beneath a window. She picked up a dress from the bed and showed it to Mirage. 'This is for you.'

The twins cooed at the garment. It was unlike anything Mirage had ever worn, the kind of dress only princesses put on, with a skirt of emerald ruffles and white silk ties for her waist meant to accentuate her womanhood.

'You'll be the prettiest thing in the castle,' said Laurella. 'Like it?'

'It's very nice,' said Mirage modestly. She had never been the prettiest thing anywhere.

'Your skin is so lovely,' said one of the girls, studying Mirage's face with envy. 'Like cream.'

'Your hair, too,' said the other, still twirling it between her fingers. They were both younger than Mirage, though not by much. Even so close, it was easy for Kirsil to work her magic on them, and Mirage had no fear at all that they might see through to her burned skin. Laurella came closer, studying Mirage in the mirror.

'Two hours, then I'll be back for you,' said Laurella. 'Sela and Meleni will take care of you.' She put her hand on Mirage's shoulder, gave it a reassuring squeeze, then turned and left the chamber. Mirage looked blankly at the twin maids.

'What now?'

'Sit and be at ease,' the girl on her left directed. 'We'll make you ready for the king.'

By the time two hours had passed, Mirage could not believe her transformation. The two vapid girls had made her into a beautiful lady. In her dress of emerald silk, Mirage twirled along the floor, studying herself in the mirror with amazement. Sela and Meleni nodded, pleased with themselves. Starting with a raw canvas, they had made Mirage into a masterpiece. Mirage stuck her face close to the mirror, studying the exactitude of her makeup and the way it made her shine. She was, in fact, the prettiest thing she had ever seen, reminiscent of her long dead mother. Pleased with their handiwork, the two maids beamed. They had brushed and curled Mirage's hair, painted her face like artists, and dressed her in the expensive gown. Now the twins looked weary and satisfied. Leaning over the vanity table, Mirage stared down into her cleavage in disbelief. In Grimhold, she had always felt like a child. Now, with her own womanhood staring back at her, her girlish façade fell away.

Then in the mirror Laurella appeared, pushing open the door to the chamber and peering inside hopefully. When she saw Mirage, she brightened at once.

'Splendid,' she declared. The compliment made Mirage soar. 'How do you feel, child?'

She wanted to say that she felt beautiful. Instead Mirage replied, 'Afraid.'

'Of course you're afraid.' Laurella came to stand before her, taking her hands. 'But I promise you, no harm will come to you. You must believe me. King Raxor is not a brute. Forget what you might have heard about him.'

'I've heard nothing of him,' said Mirage. 'Nor has anyone told me anything.'

Sela and Meleni quickly agreed. 'See Laurella? We told her nothing.'

'It's time for her to find out, then,' said Laurella. 'Are you ready to go? It's time.'

Mirage took a breath. 'Then I'm ready.' She turned back to the two girls. 'Thank you for what you've done. Will I see you again?'

'Of course,' laughed Sela. She added, 'We're not going anywhere,' implying that Mirage wasn't going anywhere either. Mirage acknowledged her with a little wave, then followed Laurella out of the chamber.

They were in the eastern tower of Castle Hes. According to Sela and Meleni, it was the tower of the king himself, where the royal family

165

resided. Despite their claim that they had told Mirage nothing, the gabby maids had talked incessantly, explaining proudly how they were 'east tower' maids, and obviously thought themselves the betters of their west tower sisters. Mirage had seen very little of the eastern tower, but as she stepped out of the dressing chamber she got her first good look at the stunning place. Following Laurella down a wide hall, she marvelled at the paintings hung along the walls, great portraits of dead kings and their ladies, and of violent battles fought on bloodied landscapes. The walls themselves had been papered in velvet, textured gold and scarlet. Brightly polished sconces tossed dancing light across the amber floor. Maids and servants Mirage had yet to meet passed them as they walked, smiling politely or entirely averting their eyes. Self-conscious in her expensive gown, Mirage felt a blush of embarrassment at their deference.

'Where are we going?' she asked in a whisper.

Laurella, walking quickly, replied, 'To the drawing room.'

'Drawing room? What's that?'

'The *withdrawing* room,' Laurella explained. 'Where guests go after a meal. You'll learn all this in time.'

Mirage wanted to protest, because she had no intention of staying Raxor's woman that long. 'Will there be others?' she asked.

'Just you, child. Tonight it's all about you. Come. It's not much further.'

They passed more of the same elaborate paintings, turning down labyrinthine halls. Luckily, none of Raxor's family seemed to be at home, or if they were they were otherwise engaged. Mirage put the daunting prospect of meeting them out of her mind. First, she had to meet Raxor, and if he wasn't pleased with her . . .

What? Back to Asher?

'Here.'

Laurella stopped in front of a pair of lacquered wooden doors. They had passed through a huge dining room to reach the portal, the table set but empty of food. Mirage felt a swell of nervousness.

'The drawing room?' she asked. 'Is he inside?'

'Child, the king doesn't wait. You wait for him.'

Opening the doors, Laurella revealed the dark and spacious chamber. Like the halls of the tower, it was decorated with oil paintings and bright tapestries. A fire had been lit in the hearth, and near the hearth two chairs sat, looking like miniature thrones. A small table with finely-turned legs sat beside one of the chairs, sporting a decanter of wine and two pear-shaped, crystal goblets. A musty collection of books lined the wall opposite the hearth, the shelves burdened with trinkets. The chamber smelled of age.

'Should I sit?' Mirage asked, stepping inside.

'There,' said Laurella, pointing toward one of the chairs. Near it stood a wooden veil painted with vines and roses. Like a signpost, the veil sat atop a pole. Mirage went to the chair and studied the veil.

'What is it?'

'To block you from the fire while you sit,' said Laurella. 'It will keep your makeup from running.'

Mirage thought the contraption remarkably silly. 'You mean it will melt?'

'It's what fine ladies do, child,' said Laurella, guiding Mirage into the chair and arranging the veil. 'You'll learn these things. I'll help to teach you.'

'Laurella, you've been kind and I'm grateful. But I don't intend to be here that long.'

Laurella blanched. 'Ease your tongue. You mustn't let the master hear you talk that way.'

'I can't be his woman,' Mirage protested. 'I'm no slave.'

'Nor am I,' said Laurella. 'Now hush yourself. Behave and all will go well. I'll see you when the king is done.'

'Wait . . .'

Too late. Laurella was already gone, closing the great doors behind her and sealing Mirage into the chamber. Mirage shifted in her plush chair, looking around. There were a thousand mementos to interest her, keepsakes from a long lifetime of battles and politics. Over the hearth stood a portrait of a handsome warrior – perhaps Raxor himself in long ago days. Mirage admired the painting, featuring the soldier on a broad white horse and holding an axe in his hand. A green flag with a snarling lion – the symbol of Reec – unfurled behind him. He was, Mirage admitted, a fetching figure. Her eyes shifted to the books on the shelves, then the carefully preserved trinkets. A golden goblet encrusted with sapphires twinkled by the firelight. Porcelain statues of deities watched her lifelessly from the shelves. Mirage looked away, then glimpsed something interesting on a table near her chair, opposite the wine decanter and glasses. Leaning closer, she noticed it was jewelry, a long necklace with a cameo and a matching silver bracelet. The carefully made cameo featured the profile of a striking young woman, with long hair and graceful curves to her nose and chin.

Curious, she got out of her chair to better inspect the cameo. She picked it up, cradling it carefully in her hands, noticing its lightness and delicacy. The figure of the woman had been expertly carved into some milky, translucent stone, like alabaster.

'Lovely, isn't it?'

Startled, Mirage nearly dropped the piece. She hurried to put it back on the table as she turned toward the doors. A man stood blocking the threshold, staring back at her. Tall and barrel-chested, his nearly bald head sprouted stubs of wiry grey hair. A finely tailored jacket fitted his wide frame over a white, ruffled shirt that looked as though it had never been worn before, so crisp were its lines. His eyes, icy green and faded like Laurella's, fixed on her, unblinking.

'I'm sorry,' she stammered. 'I didn't harm it.'

The man cocked his head to study her. He was old, certainly, but hardly enfeebled, with powerful arms that flexed beneath his jacket and a thickly muscled neck. Years of sunlight had roughed his skin. His expression brightened as he watched her, full of wonder. Mirage licked her lips and searched for something to say.

'Are you King Raxor?'

The man took his time replying, stepping into the room. 'Remarkable,' he whispered. Whatever had entranced him escaped Mirage. In his overwhelming presence, she felt unbearably small.

'I am waiting for King Raxor,' she said timidly. 'Are you he?'

'I am Raxor,' said the man. 'And I am pleased to meet you – Mirage.'

Mirage shrank back. 'You know my name. But then, you know a great deal about me, I'm sure. Your man Corvalos Chane must have told you everything.'

As if finally catching himself, King Raxor shook off his spell. 'What I know of you I learned from Asher. Everything you told him has been reported to me.' He smiled. 'Corvalos Chane was right about you. You are staggeringly lovely.'

The compliment unnerved Mirage. 'Your maids have been generous to me, my lord. Thank you for that, and for releasing me from Asher. It was your word that got me out of there, no doubt.'

'And it was my word that put you there in the first place,' said Raxor.

Mirage nodded, unsure what he meant. 'Yes, I suppose that's so.'

'Please, sit down,' the king directed. 'I want to look at you. I was warned, but you are more than I expected.'

Confused, Mirage took her chair again. 'My lord?'

'No, nothing,' said Raxor, waving off his comment. He grinned, admiring her. 'You've gladdened this old man's heart by coming here.'

His big, royal shadow fell over Mirage as he loomed by her chair. Because he was a king, Mirage held her questions, though he could tell they were on the tip of her tongue.

'Do not worry,' he told her. 'You are thinking I might send you back to Asher. Never mind that. You have already been spared his talents. I would be a beast indeed to send you back there.' King Raxor went to the decanter of wine on the table near his vacant chair. 'I want you to be comfortable. My promise is as good as gold. You have nothing to worry about.'

'I want to believe you, my lord,' said Mirage carefully. She watched as he poured her some wine, than handed her the heavy crystal glass.

'You will be well taken care of here for as long as you stay,' replied the king. He poured himself a glass then lifted his goblet to toast her. Mirage touched his glass reluctantly with her own, watching him sip but not tasting the wine herself.

'And how long will that be, my lord?' she asked. 'I'm confused, you see. I was captured by your man Corvalos Chane. Then I was imprisoned and mistreated. And now . . .' She shrugged. 'Now, my lord, I don't know what I'm doing or why I'm here with you. No one has explained it to me, except to say that I am to be yours.'

Raxor put down his glass. She expected her words to anger him, but his expression remained gentle, as though she were a little bird he didn't want to frighten off.

'Corvalos Chane isn't the same as Asher,' he said. 'I trust Chane and always have. I do not trust Asher. There was no way you could have been left in his care and lived. I know that he frightened you, and I am sorry for that. In time, perhaps, you will see the necessity of what happened to you. Do you know why Chane was in Liiria?'

'I think so,' said Mirage. 'He's a spy. He was watching to see what happened there.'

'I have many spies in Liiria, girl. Not all all of them are as good as Chane, however. He was watching to see what your friend, Baron Glass, did in Liiria, and what he might be planning for Reec. Don't pretend not to know what I'm talking about. You are an old friend of Baron Glass. Asher told me that much already. He also told me that you have more knowledge of the baron and his armour than you've yet been willing to reveal.'

Mirage looked down into her wine. 'I have my secrets, my lord. Things have passed between us that I cannot reveal, not even to you.'

'Glass is called the Black Baron here. Did you know that?'

'I have heard that, yes,' said Mirage. Asher had called Glass that many times.

The king dragged the chair away from the heath so that it faced Mirage, then sat down with his glass of wine. 'You are a gift to me, Mirage. I know you don't understand that yet, but that is why you were spared from Asher's prison. Corvalos Chane saw something in you.'

'Something that his king would enjoy, you mean,' bristled Mirage. 'Am I your *type*, my lord? Is that why I'm to be your concubine?'

'Corvalos looks out for my needs. And you are very lovely, Mirage, a great prize. No doubt he thought you would fill an emptiness in my life.'

'My lord, you are the King of Reec. Surely you can have any woman you desire. What is special about me?'

The king nodded toward the jewelry on the table. 'That cameo – pick it up.'

Mirage did as he asked. The piece felt heavy in her small hand. 'It's very lovely. Who is this woman? Someone special to you?'

'Special? Yes indeed, pretty Mirage. That was made for my wife, Helea, when she was about your age. That's her image in the stone.' Raxor chuckled. 'Haven't you guessed yet? When you turn sideways, you look just like that cameo.'

Mirage looked hard at the image. 'You mean I look like your wife?'

'My dead wife,' Raxor corrected. 'And you are the perfect picture of her, almost her twin. There are paintings of her all over this castle. That's how Corvalos Chane knew how much you look like her. It's why he brought you to me.' The king relaxed in his tall chair. 'I am an old man. I've lived a very long time, and Helea was the love of my life. When she died I died with her. But I'm still alive, and that is the hell of it, you see.'

'No, my lord, I don't see,' argued Mirage, alarmed by the turn of the conversation. 'I am not your wife, and I am sure I could never replace her.'

'Corvalos Chane thinks otherwise. You're a gift to mend my broken heart, Mirage, so that I can be strong again, a leader. Reec needs a leader. The world around us is caving in, and I can't do anything to stop it. Your friend, Baron Glass – he has yet to threaten Reec directly, but he will in time. No doubt he and his bitch-queen Jazana Carr have already laid designs on my country.'

'No,' said Mirage. 'That's not true. I know Thorin Glass, my lord. All he ever wanted was to go back to Liiria.'

'As a conqueror? You were at the great library. You saw what Baron Glass and his armies did to it, and to the rest of Koth. And Jazana Carr has an appetite like a dragon. To think she is satisfied is foolish. She has her greedy eyes on Reec, have no doubt of it.'

'That's why you have your armies stationed on the border,' Mirage surmised. 'I saw them when Chane brought me across.'

'Sooner or later they will come, and we must be ready for them. *I* must be ready for them. But I am old and weak and my heart is broken. I have spent my life in war, and I haven't the stomach or steel for it any longer. That is what my advisors fear, Mirage – that I will not be ready to defend Reec when the time comes. Corvalos Chane most of all fears this, for he knows my heart like no one else.'

'And that's why he brought me to you,' said Mirage, finally understanding. 'To replace your wife.'

'To make an old man feel young again, yes.' King Raxor slumped, forgetting his wine, ignoring everything but his comely guest. 'You do make me feel . . . something. Memories, perhaps. Better days. My wife was much like you, Mirage. Even your voice reminds me of her. Do you sing?'

'No, my lord,' replied Mirage. All she wanted was to leave.

'That is a pity. Helea had a nightingale's voice.'

'I have a voice like a rusty hinge, my lord. I could never replace your wife.'

She expected Raxor to agree with her. He did not.

'Baron Glass was an enemy of mine for many years. Do you know your history, Mirage, of the days before the peace?'

'When the river Kryss divided the nations. I know of it.'

'I was War Minister in those days, when Baron Glass was powerful in Liiria. He was a great fighter before losing his arm. I faced him many times, and the Bronze Knight as well.'

Mirage grimaced at Lukien's name. 'Yes, my lord. Those must have been difficult days.'

'You told nothing of the Bronze Knight to Asher.'

'He did not ask me, King Raxor.'

'No.' Raxor steepled his fingers beneath his chin. 'But the stories go that Lukien went to Jador, and that he came back with you to Liiria. Chane saw Lukien at the library. Many thought you were his woman. Were you?'

The question broke Mirage's heart. She had wanted so badly to be Lukien's woman. She shook her head. 'No.'

'And Baron Glass – he has no claim to you either?'

'No, my lord.'

'Then you have no man?'

Seeing where the talk was heading, Mirage said, 'I have no man, but I cannot be your woman, my lord, whatever that might mean. Your wife is dead, and I'm sorry for that. But I can't replace her.'

'I will not make you my concubine, Mirage, if that's what you fear. I won't force myself into your bed. But I do desire you to stay.'

'Desire, my lord? Or do you order it?'

'It's too dangerous for you in Liiria. War is coming, and Hes might be the safest place in the world for you. You say Baron Glass has no claim on you?'

Mirage hesitated, careful with her answer. 'He has . . . feelings for me.'

Raxor frowned. 'Oh.' He looked away thoughtfully. 'But he does not know you're here.'

'But if he learned I was your prisoner . . .' Mirage let the implication hang there. 'He has a temper like thunder.'

'I should not be surprised,' mused the king. 'You are too lovely for men to ignore. But I will not send you off to him.'

'Because I remind you of your wife? My lord, please . . . that is no reason at all to keep me.'

'I will keep you here because I wish it, because it gives me joy to look at you. And because you have secrets yet to tell me, girl. Asher is right about you – you have too much knowledge in your pretty head to simply let you leave.' Raxor got out of his chair, then dropped to one knee before Mirage. He took her hand, stroking it and smiling. 'Let me be kind to you. Maybe then you will trust me, and you will see that you are only protecting a madman.'

'My lord, I cannot love you, not ever, not the way you want.' Mirage pulled back her hand. 'If you truly want to be kind to me, then let me go.'

The old king looked at her, rebuffed and saddened. He got slowly to his feet.

'War is coming,' he said softly. 'I will be ready for it. And you will help me be ready. You will make a man of me, Mirage. You can keep your body from me, I don't need it. Just your beauty is enough for me.'

'No, my lord,' Mirage protested. She rose to face him. 'I won't have it. I won't be your slave or your salvation. I'm a free woman and not the chattel of any man, even a king.'

'You are my guest, Mirage,' said Raxor evenly. 'For as long as I wish it.'

The king turned to go. Helpless, Mirage chased after him.

'No, King Raxor,' she pleaded, grabbing hold of his arm. 'You must know this is wrong. Your wife is dead. Would she want you to do this?'

'My wife loved Reec, and she knew my duty to it. If it meant helping me protect our country, she would understand.'

'Well then,' said Mirage indignantly, 'she was as mad as you are.'

Raxor smiled, reaching out to brush her check. 'Even when you're angry you look like her. Rest now, child. I will see you soon.'

Then, as quickly as he'd come to her, King Raxor left Mirage. Stunned, unsure where to go, she simply stared.

'Madness! Is all of Reec filled with madman?'

Mirage went back to her chair, first taking the cameo from the table. As she sat she held the image of Raxor's dead wife. She saw the resemblance between them now and it frightened her.

'Kirsil,' she whispered, summoning her Akari. 'I think we're in trouble.'

Not far from the drawing room, in a hallway separate from the dining area, Corvalos Chane stood alone, waiting for his master to return. He remained very still, ignoring the servants who had long ago learned to ignore him in kind. As the king's man, he was accustomed to being in the east tower, though not a drop of noble blood flowed through his veins. In his worn leather trousers and soldier's jerkin, he looked completely out of place among the castle's art and finery, keeping mostly to a shadowed corner.

Corvalos Chane had much on his mind. More than anything, he wanted his master to be pleased. He had taken on the impossible task of resurrecting Raxor's broken spirit, trying to heal his king and make him ready for battle. Reec needed Raxor, and all the history and glory he represented. When the Diamond Queen at last marched her armies across their border, it would be Raxor that would turn them back. No one else was up to the task.

In the quiet of the hallway, Corvalos Chane thought about the girl, too, and how frightened she had looked when he'd rescued her. She was a jewel, that one, worthy of his king, but she had also set the spy's heart fluttering. Chane had not been with a women since he could remember. Until now, their allure held little temptation for him. Mirage was different, though. She was beautiful in a way that other women were not. She was a mystery, and that intrigued him.

Chane straightened when he heard the familiar sound of Raxor approaching, the distinct din of his heavy boots clicking on the polished floor. Raxor appeared quickly, his face shining in the hall's candlelight. He was a big man still, as tall as Chane himself and almost twice as wide, and when he grinned he lit the room. Corvalos Chane smiled back at his beloved king.

'My lord is pleased,' said the spy.

King Raxor put his giant hand on Chane's cheek, patting it. 'I'm grateful, Corvalos. I didn't believe you at first, but she is everything you promised. She is so beautiful it takes my breath away.'

'She is Lady Helea's spitting image, my lord, is she not?'

'Aye, she could be her daughter. And fiery!'

Chane shrugged. 'I did warn you.'

'Ah, she is afraid, that's all.' Raxor twisted a stout golden ring on his finger, the way he always did when worried. 'She won't be harmed. I promised her that, though I don't know if she believes me.'

'Give her time, my lord,' Chane advised. 'She will learn to love you.'

Raxor looked at his trusted friend. 'That is too much to hope. Her heart belongs to another, I can tell. Perhaps Baron Glass himself.'

'It doesn't matter. She is here with you, and not with Baron Glass.'

'Indeed,' said Raxor. 'And I will keep her for myself, no matter what storms the Black Baron might bring us.'

15

'You can get off here,' said the boatman. 'It's not far to the centre of the city. You can walk the way easily.'

Lukien looked out over the edge of the dock, to the sprawling city on the riverbank. The spires of Torlis shadowed his face. He smelled the briny scent of salt drying along the rocks at low tide and the pungent odours of crowded humanity. While black flies swarmed their boat, the boatman, Akhir, guided his tiny vessel toward the dock, scraping it alongside and tossing ropes to dark-skinned workers. A hundred other boats were tied there, and a hundred more choked the river, fishing boats and barges filled with cargo. Men and boys waded in the shallow parts of the river, tossing nets. Along the bank, homes of mud brick baked in the sun, erected on pylons to keep from flooding when the river rose. Beyond the homes, the centre of Torlis beckoned with its densely built temples and minarets. Somewhere in the distance a bell rang.

The workers with the ropes jerked the boat to the dock. Lukien held to the rail as the vessel jolted to a stop. Akhir hurried to secure the moorings, his gnarled hands quickly tying knots. Beside him stood Jahan, looking moonstruck as he gazed upon Torlis. For three days they had been aboard Akhir's boat, hiring him out of a busy fishing village, the only man willing to ferry them to Torlis. For the price of their worn-out horse and donkey, Akhir had navigated them up the wide river, expertly avoiding the treacherous spots. Years of piloting his ancient boat had given Akhir a confident hand, and while he captained Lukien and Jahan could relax and rest themselves. It had been a pleasant, unremarkable journey, and the two men had deepened their friendship, getting to know one another and swapping tales. Under the starry nights, Torlis seemed a thousand miles away.

But now the great city towered all around them, and Jahan did not speak at all. He simply gazed, his eyes wide with breathless awe. His ponytail of hair pendulated to the rocking surf. Lukien sidled closer. For both of them, their arrival was a victory. As Akhir secured the vessel,

Lukien and Jahan pondered the city and its people. To Lukien, they were very much like the villagers he had already encountered in Tharlara, but their city was much more advanced. Monuments were everywhere, sprouting like reeds among the paved roads cut between the grand buildings. In the centre of the city rose an elaborate palace of shimmering limestone. A trio of graceful spires turned upward from the palace, capped with golden domes that showered sunlight into the streets. The palace was easily the largest building in Torlis, dwarfing everything around it and surrounded by greenery and pools of blue water. Lukien nudged Jahan.

'The Red Eminence?'

Jahan nodded. 'It must be.'

Torlis itself went on for miles, but beyond the city rose a mountain range, and from that range grew a single giant of a mountain, its broad shoulders packed with snow, its peak puncturing the clouds. The river they had followed for so long snaked around the city and disappeared into the mountains. The glorious mountain drew Lukien's gaze. He had never seen its like before, and despite the grandness of Torlis it was the mountain that made him feel small.

The boatman finished tying off his moors and came to stand beside his passengers. Akhir was a lean man, long of bone, with thoughtful eyes that gave him an air of wisdom.

'That's where the river comes from,' he said, noticing the way Lukien spied the mountain. 'When the snows melt, the river swells. It will soon happen again.'

'And make the land strong,' said Lukien.

Akhir smiled. 'Yes. You are learning, foreigner.'

'And what about that big mountain?' Lukien asked. 'Does it have a name?'

'That's a holy mountain,' said Akhir. 'The people of Torlis call it the House of Sercin.'

'Who is Sercin? A ruler?'

'Sercin is the god of this land. Look, you will see his image everywhere,' said Akhir. He pointed toward the city and its spires. 'You see that temple? That is a temple of Sercin.'

Lukien and Jahan both peered through the daylight. From out of the mud and limestone buildings jutted a tower topped with the image of what looked like a snake, its fanged maw opened wide.

'You mean that one?' asked Lukien. 'With the serpent's head?'

'That is Sercin,' Akhir explained. 'That is how the people of Torlis say he appears. He is the patron of the city, the one who looks over them.'

'And he lives in the mountain?'

Akhir shrugged. 'So they say. I do not believe or disbelieve. The people

175

of Torlis turn the river to blood when the time comes, and that is all I care about.'

Lukien was careful not to ask too many questions. So far, they had managed to avoid telling Akhir much about their journey, and the wily boatman seemed not to care. When they had requested passage to Torlis, Akhir had not asked why, but had merely taken their animals and given them to his family for safe keeping. Now, with his cargo safely delivered, he was eager to return home.

'I have to stock my boat,' he said. 'And then I will leave.'

'How long will you remain?' asked Jahan.

'An hour. Maybe two.' Akhir frowned. 'You do not want to go?'

Apprehension made Jahan's lips curl. 'No. We will go.'

But he didn't move.

'Jahan?' probed Lukien. 'What's wrong?'

Jahan looked uncomfortable. 'All of this. It is more than I expected. It is so big! It is nothing like my village. And all these people. I have never seen so many.'

'Jahan, this is what you wanted – to see Torlis.'

'Yes,' Jahan agreed.

Still he did not disembark. Akhir made a face of displeasure.

'I can take you back with me if that's what you wish,' he said. 'Those were good animals you gave me. But tell me now. If you are riding back with me, I will buy enough food for us all.'

'I'm going,' said Lukien. 'I have to. Jahan, go back with Akhir if that's what you want.'

Jahan shook off his apprehension with a laugh. 'Go back? No, Lukien. How would you find your way without me?'

'I don't think I could,' said Lukien with a grin. 'Come on, then.'

They said good-bye to Akhir, wishing the boatman a safe journey home, then stepped off his shaky vessel onto the dock. The wooden structure gave a groan beneath them, directing them toward the beach where dozens of fishermen and boys waded into the water or stayed ashore mending nets. Not far ahead of them, the crude homes of mud brick glowed orange in the sunlight. Stepping off the muddy bank and onto a crowded street, Lukien pointed with his chin toward the palace in the centre of the city.

'There,' he said softly. 'That's where we'll find him.'

Jahan's nervousness grew. He licked his wind-chapped lips as he surveyed the looming palace. Around it stood scores of lesser buildings, all beautifully constructed of gleaming stone and precious metals. It would be a long walk, but Lukien could tell it was not the distance daunting his friend.

Swallowing his emotions, Jahan squared his shoulders and proceeded toward the gates. Lukien walked beside him, imitating his friend's fearlessness. He had travelled for months and endless miles to reach this place. The hope that his journey had neared its end was overwhelming. Not wanting to hide himself, he lowered his hood to present his white face and golden hair. Inside the gates, a contingent of guards dressed in their perfect uniforms gathered to confront them, clearly surprised by the visitors. The guards held long, spear-like weapons of ebony topped with hooked blades. In their sashes were short, curved swords. Each wore a jewel in his headdress, all of them rubies except for one, who pinned his head gear with a diamond. A man of rank among his peers, the one with the diamond broke from the others to peek through the gate. He looked perplexed rather than angry.

'Who are you?' he asked. For a moment, Lukien did not understand his words. Then, as had happened with all those he'd met in Tharlara, the words became clear to him, magically translated in his mind. Lukien glanced at Jahan and saw that he too understood the guard, though their dialects were markedly different.

'My name is Lukien. This is my friend, Jahan, a Simiheh from a village a long way from here.'

The leader of the guardians regarded Lukien curiously. A young man, there was innocence in his eyes. 'You are strange looking. And your words . . .' He looked at his comrades, who all had the same reaction. 'They're different, but we understand!'

'Please don't be afraid,' Lukien cautioned. 'I'm from a land far away, a land called Liiria. I speak differently from you. But I have a way to make people understand me.'

The guard turned to Jahan. 'You are from the river lands beyond the city.'

'I am Simiheh,' said Jahan proudly. 'My village is far from here. I took this man up the river so that he could see the Red Eminence.'

'A peasant and a foreigner?' The guard shook his head. 'The Eminence will not see you.'

'Please listen,' implored Lukien. 'I've come a long way, many miles. I must see the Red Eminence.'

'It is not possible,' said the guard. 'You are not expected, you are not of important families, you do not even bring gifts with you. The Eminence will not see you.'

'But it's important,' Lukien argued. 'Have you ever seen my kind before?'

'No,' the guardian admitted.

Lukien raised his voice just enough. 'Then how do you know I am not important? I have business with the Red Eminence, probably something you cannot understand. I have come a long way to bring something from my land, something of great value. Now, open the gate and let us pass.'

Lukien's bravado caught the attention of others on the grounds, guards and holy men who came to gape at the strangers. One man in particular, far older than the rest, came to stand beside the man with the diamond headdress. Surrounded by young acolytes in flowing robes, the old man stared inquisitively.

'What have your brought the Red Eminence?' asked the guard, growing annoyed.

Lukien reached beneath his clothing and pulled out the Eye of God. 'This.'

The gathered men gave a collective gasp of interest, instantly bewitched by the amulet. Lukien let it dangle before them, twirling it on its chain. As if on cue, the ruby jewel in its centre flared to life.

'This is an artifact of powerful magic,' said Lukien, unsure of the wisdom of his gambit. 'It is from my land across the desert, a mighty land with great sorcerers. The magic of this amulet lets you understand my words.'

The guard stepped back, bewildered. Before he could speak, the old holy man came forth.

'You are from across the desert?' he asked.

'I am,' Lukien declared.

The holy man watched the Eye of God as it spun on its chain. Sunlight danced off the amulet and the old man's shaved head. A tattooed serpent slithered on his neck, its head almost biting his ear, where a single earring dangled. His young acolytes bore earrings as well, but no tattoo.

'That is a magic thing, you say? From your people?'

Lukien nodded. 'Yes.'

'And who are your people? What are they called?'

'I'm from Liiria. That's what my people are called – Liirians.'

'Liirians.' The old man chewed on the word, looking disappointed. 'That's not right.'

'What do you mean?'

The holy man shook his head. 'If you were the one, you would know.'

The old man turned and shuffled back toward the palace.

'Wait!' Lukien called. 'What is it you want me to say? What answer are you looking for?'

'If I told you that, then you would have the answer,' laughed the man.

'This amulet isn't Liirian,' Lukien rushed to add. 'It was made by others, by Akari.'

The old holy man stopped walking. 'Akari, you say?'

'Akari, yes,' said Lukien. 'Does that mean something to you?'

'Something, yes.' The man looked at the guardian with the diamond in his headdress. 'Let them enter.'

'Karoshin?'

'It is all right,' said the holy man. 'Open the gate.'

At the old man's order the guards opened the gates for Lukien and Jahan, then stood aside for them to enter. Lukien went to the holy man at once.

'Thank you,' he said, still holding the Eye of God. 'This amulet – do you know of it?'

'No.'

'But then how can you know the word Akari?'

'My name is Karoshin,' replied the old man. 'I am a priest of Sercin. You have come seeking the Red Eminence?'

'Yes. Will he see us?'

'I will take you,' said the priest. 'You have many questions. The Red Eminence will have answers. Come.'

The acolytes were quick to surround their venerable leader as he headed toward the palace. Lukien and Jahan hurried after him. Behind them, the guards closed the gate but did not follow, and Karoshin did not turn to face them as he led them up the lane. The palace soared overhead, spreading its giant shadow across the gardens. Pools filled with colourful fish lined the way, reflecting the high, golden domes of the spires. The palace itself had a hundred different entrances, all of them arched beneath a roof that shaded the strolling priests. Vibrant tiles lined the archways, giving way to busy halls filled with busy servants. Karoshin led them beneath the roof and past a dozen arches until at last entering one, a splendid portal of shimmering bronze. Walking beneath it, Lukien marvelled at the way it reflected the light.

Inside, the palace was no less dazzling, as the archway led into an immense hall of vaulted limestone, painted in a thousand hues of blue. Reliefs of vines and flowers stood out from the carved stone, tangling into a remarkable mosaic that writhed with life along the ceiling. The tiles echoed musically with their footfalls, delicately painted with complex patterns of gold and crimson. Light from small, bronze-fretted windows filled the hall, setting it ablaze with colour, while statues bathed in the sunlight, arching their naked bodies. Lukien took it all in, his heart racing with anticipation. He glanced triumphantly at Jahan, but the village man was too awestruck to notice.

'Jahan,' Lukien whispered. 'How do you feel?'

Jahan's reply was soft and shallow. 'Lukien, I am blessed. That is how I feel.'

The hallway terminated into another vast archway. Without doors, the arch revealed an effusive chamber beyond, where guardians stood watch and priests milled about in quiet conversation. As Karoshin approached the chamber, the priests turned and bowed. Karoshin raised his hand in a gesture of thanks. Lukien looked over his shoulder and saw the grand chamber for the first time, an enormous throne room with stout pillars and tiled mosaics and wooden chests along the walls. The chamber of the Red Eminence was filled with people, many of them priests like Karoshin, others dressed more formally, chatting or studying scrolls. And though he tried to locate the Red Eminence himself, Lukien could not see past the pillars.

'You will wait here,' Karoshin directed. He told his young acolytes to watch over the visitors, than disappeared into the throne room. The priests and others gathered by the arch watched them curiously, clearly surprised by their presence. Lukien smiled disarmingly.

'Hello,' he offered.

The men did not reply. Jahan took hold of Lukien's sleeve.

'Say nothing,' he whispered. 'They do not trust us.'

'They don't know us, Jahan.'

Jahan was like a child suddenly, giddy and frightened at the same time. 'Tell me again, Lukien – what will you say to the Red Eminence?'

'The truth. It got us this far.'

But Karoshin's reaction had puzzled Lukien, and he wondered how the old man had known about the Akari. He should have asked him about the sword, he supposed, but soon he would have his audience with the Eminence. Soon, all his questions would be answered. He tried to ignore the onlookers as he waited, studying the palace and marvelling at its architecture. Jahan stood beside him, fidgeting under the glare of the white-robed priests.

After what felt like a very long time, Karoshin finally returned. Standing in the threshold of the arch, he held out his hand for Lukien, bidding him to come.

'And my friend?' Lukien asked.

'And your friend,' replied Karoshin gently. To his acolytes he said, 'Remain out here, all of you.'

Bracing himself, Lukien followed Karoshin beneath the arch and into the splendid throne room, dazzled by what he saw. The pillars supporting the cavernous roof rose up like giants, painted in bright depictions of serpents and gods, spiraling toward a magnificent ceiling of sweeping constellations. Twinkling bits of glass had been set into the plaster, mimicking a thousand stars, while a gigantic sun of bronze and moon of pearly stone rose from opposite sides of the ceiling, battling for the heavens. Along the ornate floor tiles had been arranged in complex patterns, spiraling like red roses along a sandy beach. Instead of tapestries, the walls were hung with golden lanterns, each one lit with leaping flames.

The chamber was simply enormous, dwarfing all those within it, and Lukien still could not see a throne behind the pillars and priests milling about. Beside him, Jahan remained uncharacteristically quiet, as spell-bound as Lukien by the fantastic chamber. His soft shoes made no sound as he padded across the ornate tiles.

At last they worked their way past the gathered men, toward an area of the throne room that abruptly thinned of people. There, across the floor, Lukien saw the throne itself, an enormous chair of gold that swallowed its occupant. At the edge of this quiet area Karoshin paused, dropping to his knees. The person on the throne turned her gaze toward him.

Lukien blinked in disbelief. On the golden throne sat a girl.

Until now, the priests and advisors in the chamber had talked without end. But silence suddenly gripped the throne room. On her magnificent throne, the girl looked at Lukien, perplexed. She wore a gown of silk with a pleated skirt, cinched around her waist with a belt of turquoise. Chains of gold and obsidian hung around her wrists and neck. Heavy makeup lined her dark eyes, giving her the air of age, but her underdeveloped body told Lukien she was less than fifteen. Short, shimmering hair had been cut straight along her ears, revealing dangling jewels and feathers. Her hands clasped the arms of her throne, which were cast into the likeness of serpents. Behind her, the back of her throne formed the hood of a rass, and she, in its folds, seemed lost.

'Eminence, these are the ones I told you about,' said Karoshin. Still on his knees, he kept his eyes to the floor as he spoke. 'They have come many miles to see you.'

The girl on the throne appeared stunned, as if Lukien's arrival was like a falling star crashing through her throne room. Her ruby-coloured lips parted in disbelief. She watched her visitors carefully, searching for words. Jahan quickly grabbed hold of Lukien's arm.

'Lukien, this can't be,' he whispered.

'Easy,' Lukien urged.

Karoshin turned from his knees to glare at them. 'Kneel.'

Taking hold of Jahan, Lukien guided himself and his companion down to the ground, copying Karoshin exactly.

'Karoshin, send the others away,' said the girl. 'Everyone.'

The old priest rose at once, turning toward the gallery of onlookers and ordering them to go. Without hesitation the advisors and holy men retreated, departing the chamber through the great arch until it echoed with unnerving silence. Lukien remained still, not daring to look up or offend the young ruler. When all the others had gone, even the girl's guardians, Karoshin spoke again.

'This one is Lukien,' said Karoshin, pointing down at the knight. 'It is he who bears the magic amulet.'

'And the other?' The girl assessed Jahan. 'He *looks* like one of us.'

'I am Simiheh,' Jahan pronounced. 'My village is far from here, but I am of the river lands, like you.'

Lukien chanced a glance at the girl. She did not look displeased.

'You may rise,' she told them.

Karoshin urged the pair to their feet, then stood between them and the girl. Now that all the others had gone, he seemed at greater ease. 'Lahkali, he knows of the Akari. He's not one of them, but the amulet he has was made by Akari.'

'Show me,' the girl told Lukien.

Without hesitation Lukien took the Eye of God from beneath his shirt, holding it out for her to see. 'It is Akari, Eminence,' he assured her. 'They made it many years ago, ages before it came to me. It was given to me across the desert, by a people I came to live among.'

'Give it to me,' said the girl. 'I wish to see it clearly.'

Lukien hesitated. 'I cannot. The amulet's power keeps me alive, Eminence. If I part with it, I will die.'

'A powerful item,' Karoshin remarked, though Lukien's claim did not seem to startle him. 'Go closer then.'

'Yes, come closer,' said the girl, leaning over her throne. 'Let me look at it.'

Lukien did as the young ruler asked, stepping up to her throne and holding the amulet out for her. Her expression deepened as she inspected it, nodding without really understanding.

'Karoshin, I cannot tell if it's genuine,' she said. 'How can I know?'

'I am not certain, Lahkali.' The holy man stuck his face out, almost touching the amulet with his nose. 'It's old, certainly. And it gives him the power to speak our tongue, and for us to understand his own. That is remarkable, surely. And I did not tell him the word Akari – he knew it on his own.'

'It is genuine, Eminence, I promise,' said Lukien. 'It's true that I don't know everything about the Akari. But I do know how you might have heard of them. Do you know of an Akari named Malator?'

The Red Eminence looked mindfully at her holy man. 'Yes,' she said after a moment. 'We have heard of him.'

Lukien's heart leapt at the news. 'That is a great relief to me, Eminence. What can you tell me about him?'

'No,' said the girl. 'What can you tell us of him?'

'Me? I don't understand?'

'You have come for a reason. You have come seeking something, perhaps?'

'Yes,' said Lukien. 'A sword. The Sword of Angels, it's called. Do you know of it?'

Lahkali the Red Eminence grew circumspect. 'What do you know of the Akari called Malator?'

'Not very much, I'm sorry to say. I was told about him in a dead city across the desert. A spirit told me about him.'

'A spirit?' Karoshin perked up at this. 'You can speak with spirits? Lahkali, do you hear?'

'I hear,' said Lahkali. There was a measure of excitement in her tone. 'Go on, Lukien of Liiria. Tell us more.'

'I don't actually speak to spirits,' Lukien explained. 'Rather they have spoken to me. I know it's hard to believe, but it's true. This city I mentioned – it was once called Kaliatha. It was the city of the Akari before they all died. They were slaughtered by a race called the Jadori, many years ago. This spirit that spoke to me was an Akari. He told me that Malator came here to Tharlara, looking for help against the Jadori.' Lukien looked hopefully at the girl. 'Is that how you know about the Akari, Eminence? Because Malator came to your land?'

Again the girl looked to Karoshin for guidance. The old man nodded his approval.

'You are right,' said the girl. 'Mostly it is a story to us, handed down through the years. And it is just as you have said. The Akari called Malator came to Torlis seeking our help in his war.'

'But he never returned home to his people,' said Lukien. 'That's what the spirit told me. Is that so?'

'Karoshin?'

'Tell him what you must, Lahkali,' advised Karoshin. 'I see no danger in it.'

'Then I will tell you that Malator did not return to his people,' said the girl. 'He remained here in Torlis until he died.'

Jahan, who had so far stayed quiet, now came forward. 'May I speak?' he asked.

His interruption perturbed the girl. 'You have a question?'

'Yes, Eminence. Are you the one who turns the river to blood?'

The girl turned to her priest. 'Karoshin . . .'

'Your questions are an insult,' hissed the holy man. 'She is the lord of Torlis.'

'Jahan meant no insult,' said Lukien quickly, surprised at the offense the girl had taken. 'His village is far from here. They're simple people, and he came to help me.'

'And to see you, Eminence,' said Jahan. 'Forgive me. But where I came from you are special to us.'

The ruler's face twisted. 'And you did not expect a girl to be on Torlis' throne.'

Seeing the situation worsening, Lukien said, 'Eminence, he is my friend. Without him I would not have made it here. He simply wanted to see you and your city. It has overwhelmed him.'

'I think he is overwhelmed because he thinks me a child,' said the girl. 'But you, Lukien – you have not explained yourself. You say you have come here for a sword.'

'Yes, Eminence, the Sword of Angels. Do you know of it?'

'We know of it.' She looked expectantly at Lukien. 'You've come to claim it?'

'Yes, please, Eminence. It's important that I find the sword and bring it back with me across the desert. I will offer anything I can for it.'

'You need not offer anything,' said the girl. 'Just tell us where it is and it will be yours.'

'But I don't know where it is,' said Lukien. 'That's why I've come, to ask your help in finding it.'

'You don't know . . . ?' Once again Lahkali turned toward Karoshin. 'Karoshin, this is not correct . . .'

Karoshin said, 'Lukien, what do you know of the sword?'

'Almost nothing,' Lukien admitted. 'I was told about it by another spirit, a woman. She said I would find it here in the Serpent Kingdom. In Tharlara.'

'But you don't know where? You don't know it's location?'

'No.' Lukien felt stupid suddenly, as if he'd missed something obvious. 'I'm sorry, I don't. But if you tell me . . .'

'We cannot tell you,' said the Red Eminence. 'You are supposed to know where the sword is hidden.'

'But I don't, Eminence. That's why I came to you.'

'You do not understand,' said Karoshin. 'Only Lahkali knows where the sword of the Akari is hidden, and she may not reveal it to anyone.'

'The story of the sword is sacred to us,' said the Eminence. 'It has been passed to me through all of the rulers of Torlis. Someday, the seeker of the sword is to come, and he is to know where it is hidden. You have surprised us by coming at all. I can barely believe it. You know of the Akari and of Malator, and how his race was at war with the Jadori. All of these things are part of the story, but they are not the secret part. The secret hiding place of the Akari sword is known only to me – and to he who seeks the sword.'

'That's me. I'm the one seeking the sword,' said Lukien, exasperated. He searched his memory for anything else Cassandra might have told him, any helpful bit. He had been near death when she came to him, hanging on to life by his fingernails. But he remembered the encounter vividly, and he knew he had not forgotten a single word. 'The spirit who came to me said nothing about this,' he said. 'She told me I would find the sword here in the Serpent Kingdom. And I have come to claim it.'

'But that is not enough,' said Lahkali. 'The story is clear. The seeker of the sword will know where it is hidden.'

'But how can I? I've already told you all that I know.'

'Perhaps the seeker is supposed to be an Akari,' Jahan suggested. 'Lukien, remember what you told me about them. They are powerful with magic. An Akari would know where the sword is hidden.'

The theory made sense. Lukien took hold of his amulet, concentrating. Inside the Eye of God he could sense the awesome presence of Amaraz. Surely the great Akari could help him. Helpless, Lukien tried to channel the spirit. With sweat beading on his forehead, he stared hard at the amulet, trying to penetrate its arcane world.

'What are you doing, Lukien?' asked Jahan.

Lukien did not answer, fighting instead to summon Amaraz. But the spirit of the Eye did not answer, leaving Lukien desperate and frustrated.

'I don't know,' groaned Lukien. He looked up from the amulet. 'Eminence, I don't know where the sword is hidden. I only know that it's somewhere here in your kingdom, and that if I don't find it people are going to die. People who are important to me.'

The girl on the throne sounded powerless. 'I am sorry.'

'No, I know you're sorry. But Eminence, I cannot go home without the sword. I cannot!'

'If you can prove to me that you are the rightful seeker, than the sword will be yours. I do not play games with you. I would gladly let you claim the sword, but you must tell me where in Torlis it lies.'

'What else can I tell you?' Lukien asked desperately. 'You know about Malator. He came from Kaliatha when his people were at war. He had a brother named Kahldris, who made a suit of armour called the Devil's Armour.'

Lahkali shook her head. 'That's not what I need to hear. Only where the sword lies.'

'But this armour has claimed a friend of mine! It's like this amulet – it has the spirit of Malator's brother inside it, controlling it. I've tried to fight him but I can't. I need the sword to beat him!'

Still, nothing convinced her. The Eminence looked forlornly at the knight. 'I may not release the sword to anyone save he who knows its hiding place.'

'Who then? If not me, who?'

'For countless ages my ancestors have kept the secret of the sword. You're the first to ever come to find it. I admit, you tempt me with your knowledge, but no, I cannot give it to you.'

'Then I have come here for nothing,' said Lukien bitterly. 'It doesn't matter to you that I have spoken to spirits or that I know every bit of your precious puzzle save one. That sword should be mine! Please, Eminence, I do not ask this for myself. I will bring it back to you once my task is done. If—'

'No and no,' said the girl. 'If you cannot tell me where the sword is hidden, then you may not claim it.' She rose from her throne, stepping off the dais to stand before Lukien. 'Do not beg me. What you ask is not possible.'

Lukien's bravado collapsed. He stared at the girl. Unsure what to do, he placed the Eye of God back beneath his shirt.

'So this means nothing to you,' he said. 'Not the Eye of God or its magic, nor anything I have said to you.'

'Speak to the spirits again,' said Karoshin.

'Again? I don't pull them out of my pocket, holy man.'

Karoshin poked him hard in the chest. 'Command them to speak to you! The one inside your amulet – make him tell you where the sword is hidden.'

'I can't! He has his own mind, and he's made it up against me. He never speaks to me, no matter how much I beg him.'

'Until you learn the location of the sword, I cannot let you claim it,' said Lahkali. She offered him a sympathetic smile. 'I regret it is this way.'

'So do I,' said Lukien. 'So do I.'

Jahan searched Lukien's face. 'What should we do now? Go back home?'

'That may be the only sane thing to do,' Lukien supposed. 'But I can't go home without the sword. I have to find out where it's hidden, Jahan. Somehow.'

'Yes, but how?'

'I don't know,' said Lukien. 'We'll find a way. Eminence, is there anything more you can tell me? Anything that will help me figure out this riddle?'

'You know much of it already,' said the girl. 'And you may take us much time as you wish to figure out the rest. Stay here among us if you like. There is more than enough room for you, as you can see.'

'Thank you, Eminence. We would like that, both of us. We've come so far . . .'

'And you are so weary, I can tell.' To Lukien's astonishment, Lahkali reached up and touched his face, the wounded side with the patched eye. 'Stay here and rest. And when you are ready, tell me about your world and these friends of yours. I want to know what makes them special enough to take you so far from home.'

Lukien took her hand, feeling its small, caring fingers. 'I will do that. Thank you.'

'But it is not a bargain,' Karoshin warned. 'Tell her whatever you wish, but exact no price. You will not be able to cajole the sword's secret from her.'

'I understand,' said Lukien, unsure if the holy man believed him.

'Karoshin will give you rooms. I have servants to feed you and look after your needs. Whatever you want, you have only to ask.'

Lukien bowed and thanked the young ruler, urging Jahan to do the same, then followed Karoshin away. Out of Lahkali's earshot, Karoshin began explaining things to them, where they would be sleeping and when they could expect meals to be served. Lukien pretended to listen, but his thoughts were a hundred miles away.

Lahkali had been kind, and he appreciated her charity. But she was also young and distracted, and he was sure he could win her trust in time. Time was all he needed. In time, she would tell him where to find the Sword of Angels.

16

King Lorn the Wicked looked at the bridge, silently considering his plan. In the dark light of the stars, he could barely see its outline fording the pretty river, but he had come this way countless times and he knew the way perfectly. On the outskirts of Jador there were few homes and no marketplaces or businesses. Here, on the south side of the city, fruit trees sprouted from the sand, spreading their fronds over ancient streets and fountains. In daylight, this part of Jador teemed with children, playing along the man-made waterways while their parents drank shrana beneath shady canopies. In the time of great Kahan Kadar, the area had thrived, built by his generosity for the enjoyment of the populace. Kadar had spared no expense in this part of Jador, and Lorn loved coming here with Eirian and Poppy. In the long weeks since Gilwyn had left him in charge of the city, he had stolen every moment he could to take them to this place, to stroll the avenues and pick lemons from the trees while Poppy bumbled blindly in the sand, laughing as she made her unseen castles.

Tonight, the sun had long since slipped below the horizon and the people of Jador slept. They were a good people, stronger than Lorn had imagined, and with his help they had worked hard to rebuild their city, rolling up their sleeves just like the foreigners beyond the white wall. Lorn admired the Jadori and the way they spoke about their dead Kahan. But he could not imagine how Kadar's blood could possibly flow through White-Eye's veins.

As they did most nights, Lorn and White-Eye rode together through the outskirts of Jador, checking on the security of the city. To White-Eye, the nightly task seemed a colossal waste of time. There were still enough men to patrol Jador's borders, she had argued, and because she could not see she made a very poor lookout. But Lorn had ignored the obvious logic in her argument, wanting instead for her to take action, and to forget that she was blind. To Lorn, it did not matter that the young Kahana could not see. She was Jador's rightful ruler. Nearly a month had passed since he had taken White-Eye from Grimhold. At first, it had seemed a fair challenge. He had promised Gilwyn he would look after Jador, and he had realized that Minikin was right about the city's needs. Jador needed its Kahana.

Now, though, Lorn regretted his promise to Gilwyn. At Minikin's bidding, he had taken White-Eye from Grimhold's safety, sure that time would ease her the pain of her blindness. But in the weeks gone by, White-Eye hadn't warmed to him at all and still had servants doing everything for her. She simply refused to help herself.

Lorn rode slowly toward the bridge, careful to balance White-Eye in front of him. She did not seem to realize it, but she was comfortable on horseback now, and barely looked to him for support as they rode, not speaking as the midnight moon arced across the sky. Lorn had once again taken to wearing northern clothing, having found willing donors of the garb among the Seekers beyond the city's wall. With White-Eye back in Jador, Lorn no longer wished to look like his dark-skinned hosts, but rather to encourage the Jadori to look to White-Eye for leadership. His long, leather riding coat scraped his black boots as he rode, his arms wrapped around the blind girl's waist. She was a tiny thing, completely engulfed by his broad chest, and the horse they rode hardly noticed her added weight. Tonight, White-Eye had been her usual self, quiet and polite and completely distracted by her blindness. But when Lorn slowed the gait of their horse, she noticed.

'Where are we now?' she asked with little interest.

'Where do you think? Can you tell?'

'Where you always take me,' sighed White-Eye. 'Near the bridge.'

'That's right,' said Lorn brightly. 'That's very good.'

'It's not. You are predictable, that's all.'

Lorn ignored her sullen response. With a light wrist he brought the horse to a gentle walk. 'The night is lovely.'

'Yes.'

'Can you tell that?'

White-Eye shook her head. 'No.' Then, 'Yes. In a way.'

'Tell me what you sense.'

'Why does it matter?'

'I'm in the mood to talk tonight. Tell me.'

'How is the city?' White-Eye asked instead. 'It's quiet, I know, but how does it look?'

'No trouble,' said Lorn. 'If there was I would tell you.'

'No trouble, because there is never any trouble. This is a waste of time.'

Lorn smiled, perturbed by her petulance but not wanting to show it. Even though she was blind, she had learned to detect his many moods.

'A ruler needs to see her city, even if she cannot see.'

White-Eye's black hair brushed against his chin. 'Others look after the city. My father never rode through the city like this, especially not at night.'

When she argued, she was like a little girl to Lorn, making the same silly points again and again, forcing him always to explain himself. Lorn felt his stomach knot with aggravation.

'When your father lived, Jador was strong,' he told her. 'That's not so anymore. But it will be again. In time.'

'I believe you,' said White-Eye. 'You have worked hard for Jador.'

'A compliment? Well, my lady, thank you!'

White-Eye endured his sarcasm with a shrug. She turned her blind eyes toward the sky, blinking, looking frightfully small in the arms of the old king. They had spent many hours together in the last month, but White-Eye had never confided anything in him. Instead, she resented him, and Minikin too, who she blamed for leaving her. Tonight, White-Eye seemed uniquely vulnerable, as if all their long rides were finally wearing her down.

'Faralok used to tell me about the stars.'

'Your Akari?'

'He knew everything about the stars, all the names of the constellations and all their stories.' White-Eye craned her neck as if to see better. 'How do the stars look tonight?'

Lorn followed her gaze. In the desert, the night sky teemed with stars. 'Beautiful, my lady.'

He trotted them toward the stream and the little stone bridge. In the daylight, children fished over the edge of the bridge, rarely catching anything but always trying. For Lorn and his new love, Eirian, the bridge had become a magical place, but for White-Eye it was a challenge, and as they neared the stream the blind girl bristled.

'I hear the water,' she remarked.

'That's right.'

For some reason she feared the bridge. In their first week together, Lorn had brought her to it, asking her to cross it without his help. He had thought it the easiest of tasks, designed to boost her shattered confidence. White-Eye had refused. She had refused ever since.

'Let's sit,' she suggested. 'Near the water.'

Surprised by her request, Lorn guided his horse to the edge of the stream where a week earlier he had sat with Eirian. Then, they had brought a blanket to spread across the sand. Lorn dismounted, then helped White-Eye down from the horse, loosely tying the beast to a nearby tree. In the darkness it was difficult to see, but his eyes had adjusted, mostly, and the moonlight on the water made things easier. Hoping White-Eye had decided to try the bridge again, he decided not to rush her, guiding her down to the warm sand where she sat, cross-legged.

He dropped down next to her, his old joints groaning at the effort. The nearby bridge looked serene, empty and dark, but White-Eye had turned her face from it. Because of her great sensitivity to light, she wore a long scarf around her head that she could quickly wrap around her milky eyes, but in the darkness of midnight she had no need of it. Still, she never left the palace without the scarf, a reminder to Lorn of the painful ordeal she had endured just weeks before, when she had lost her Akari.

They sat together in silence, leaving Lorn puzzled but pleased. Whenever they went scouting, White-Eye was in a hurry to return to the palace, but tonight she was thoughtful and governed her tongue. Lorn glanced at her, not staring even though she could not see him. Before them, the desert city rose up, its towers and homes dark and peaceful. On the west side of Jador, Lorn could see the shadows of the palace stark against the distant mountains. He yawned, feeling the day's activities at last catching up to him. White-Eye heard his yawn and grinned.

'We can go back now, if you wish.'

'No,' said Lorn. 'I want to stay. We need to talk, you and I.'

White-Eye nodded. 'I could tell there are things on your mind,' she said. 'And I have things to say as well.'

'Oh?'

'Yes.' The girl collected herself, pursing her lips as she thought. She was a beautiful young woman, and it was easy to see why Gilwyn adored her. With her long fingers clasped in her lap, she said, 'I have noticed what you have done for Jador. You think I do not care, but I do. Everyone is grateful to you, King Lorn. They speak about it to me, how you have helped them rebuild. You have helped them feel strong.'

'Kahana, that is what I am trying to do for you. But you must let me.'

'I understand your intentions. I didn't always, but I do now. When Minikin let you take me from Grimhold . . .'

'You were furious,' said Lorn.

'I was terrified. I still am. You do not know what this is like for me. It is more than just blindness. When I had Faralok, I was never alone. He was more than just my sight. He was my wise teacher. You should know that you could never replace him.'

'Faralok is gone,' said Lorn. 'He took your sight with him, and neither of them are ever coming back.'

'I know that,' said White-Eye sharply.

'Do you? Sometimes I wonder. You have spent the month feeling sorry for yourself. I've given you that time to grieve because Minikin wished it. But no more. Now I must do what she charged me to do. I must make a ruler out of you, my lady.'

White-Eye smirked. 'You made a bold promise to her. Maybe I am not my father's daughter.'

193

'If you believe that, then you are doomed to fail. And I am wasting my time.' Lorn gazed at the city, his thinking cagey. 'And if that is so, then Jador is doomed with you. I have seen the way your people look at you, Kahana. They adore you. They are even part of the problem! They won't let you do anything for yourself, and so with them around you will never learn. But they need you. Will you let them down?'

'That is a strange question coming from you,' said White-Eye. 'The Seekers tell stories about you.'

'They call me King Lorn the Wicked. I know this already.'

'They say you abandoned your country and let Jazana Carr take the throne. They say you ran away.'

'My country was taken from me,' Lorn insisted. 'And you are trying to change the subject by aggravating me.'

'No,' said White-Eye. 'I know you love your daughter Poppy. I may be blind, but I can see that, at least. You are a good father. You did the right thing by taking her away from the war in Norvor. But I am wondering why you agreed to this task of Minikin's, King Lorn.'

'I made a promise to your favoured, my lady. That is why I do this thing.'

White-Eye turned to him. 'Let's speak plainly. I think you are doing this to find favour with Minikin, so that she will make a place for Poppy in Grimhold. It's what you've always wanted, why you came here in the first place.'

Lorn sneered, offended by the notion. 'You are a suspicious child. Minikin has already made this clear to me.'

'But do you believe her? Do you truly? I think you are a schemer, my lord, and you will have to prove yourself to me, just as you are making me prove my own worth.'

'You are audacious!' Lorn laughed. 'Ah, but you are honest. I am a schemer, Kahana, because fate has made me one. Sometimes a ruler must scheme to survive. In time you will learn that for yourself. There is much for you to learn. Much of it I can teach you, if you'll let me.'

'So that I'll someday be called White-Eye the Wicked?' The girl shook her head. 'No. But thank you for the offer.'

'If you think all I have to offer you is trickery, than you are a fool, child. I was a great king! I was loved when times were good and feared when times were bad, and the only reason the Diamond Queen defeated me was because her coffers knew no end. Men follow Jazana Carr because she pays them to do so. She makes slaves of them. Men followed me because they chose to.'

'Some men, my lord. Not all.'

Lorn considered her argument. 'No,' he agreed. 'Not all. But sides must be chosen, and ruling a country is not for the timid. You have been far too timid, Kahana. It it time for some courage.'

White-Eye seemed to look toward the bridge. 'Gilwyn trusted you. I do not know why, and I have thought about almost nothing else these weeks. What is it about you that made him give you my city?'

'Jador is not mine, Kahana,' said Lorn. 'Do not make the mistake of thinking you must wrest it from me. Jador belongs to you. But it is yours in name only, because you are the daughter of Kadar. If you truly want to make the city yours, you must claim it.'

White-Eye groaned. 'You do not understand what I am saying. I do not want to be your pupil, King Lorn. You will make me as ruthless and unloved a ruler as you were in Norvor. And Minikin is away in Grimhold. She has not even come to see me! She has left me in your hands, to do what you want with me. It frightens me.'

Lorn felt the sting of her words. He studied her sightless eyes, and knew that even her confession had taken courage.

'You are right,' he said. 'I will have to prove myself to you. I did not think of that until now.'

'It will take a great deal,' said White-Eye. 'More than promises.'

'Tonight all I have are promises, Kahana. I admit all my past indiscretions. And I apologize for none of them. But my promise to Gilwyn Toms was true. I have lost everything else but for my daughter and my word. Both those things are priceless to me.'

'And you will not make me in your image? Promise me that tonight, King Lorn. I need to believe it.'

Lorn reached across the sand and seized her small hand. 'Do you remember what I told you when we met in Grimhold?'

White-Eye smiled, the first genuine smile she had ever given him. 'You said that I had dragons to slay.'

'And what else?'

'That we would slay them together.'

'That's right,' said Lorn, glad she had remembered. 'Now it is time for you to trust me.'

White-Eye turned her head. 'The bridge?'

Lorn stood, pulling her up. 'It's a small step. But for you, it could be a first victory.'

The young Kahana took her time before speaking. Though she could not see the bridge, she knew exactly where it stood, staring at it blankly. 'I'm not sure why it frightens me so much. It is only a bridge.'

'It is a place from here to there,' said Lorn. 'Perhaps that is what frightens you.'

'And falling in the water.'

'That won't happen,' Lorn assured her. Slowly he guided her to the foot of the bridge. 'When you reach the other side, just turn around. I will be here.'

'It's so dark.' White-Eye bit her bottom lip. 'Everything is so dark.'

'Hold on to the rail,' Lorn directed, then let go of her hand.

White-Eye wobbled, then caught herself. But she did not move toward the bridge.

'They call me King Lorn the Wicked,' said Lorn, not rushing her. 'But do you know what they call you?'

'What?'

'I have heard the Seekers beyond the wall talking about you. They know you cannot go out in daylight. They're calling you the Midnight Queen.'

White-Eye's brows knitted. 'The Midnight Queen . . .'

'I think it's a fine name,' said Lorn. 'A strong name.'

'Strong,' whispered White-Eye. 'Yes . . .'

Lorn said nothing more. He simply waited, confident. White-Eye shuffled forward. Putting her hand on the thick stone rail, she eased herself onto the deck. Then, without turning back, she walked across it.

The king and queen rode back to the palace in silence. White-Eye, pleased with herself, leaned against Lorn as he guided her back to her fabulous home, safely nestled in his arms. It had been a remarkable night. Lorn wanted to savour it. He rode unhurried back to the palace, but he was anxious to return and tell Eirian of his breakthrough with White-Eye. She would be asleep, he knew, unless Poppy was restless, but she always awoke when he returned, eager to see the man she loved. As Lorn approached the palace, he smiled at its graceful towers, so at peace in the dark night. For the first time, he had actually *reached* White-Eye. It was a night to celebrate.

Against his chest, it seemed the young Kahana had fallen asleep, but Lorn knew she was as charged as he was by what had happened. To recount the story would sound like such a minor thing. What would he tell Eirian and the others? That White-Eye had walked across a bridge? They might never understand the triumph of the moment, but Lorn didn't really care. In that instant, he had watched her become the Midnight Queen, full of grace as she confidently strode the bridge and back again.

'Tired?' he asked her. 'You are very quiet, my lady.'

White-Eye shook her head. 'Just thinking.'

It was enough of an answer to satisfy Lorn, and he said nothing more as they rode onto the palace grounds, passing Jadori guards atop wild-eyed kreels. The men greeted their Kahana in their own language, then nodded at Lorn, who suddenly seemed little more than a chaperone. Lorn trotted his horse through the perfumed gardens, guided by the light of torches and huge braziers of burning coal. When they reached the main entrance, however, he noticed more of the Jadori guards around the great arch, and a handful of northern men looking grossly out of place. Amarl, the Jadori whom Lorn had most come to trust, waved at him as he stood beside his massive kreel. Lorn peered through the darkness at the foreigners. There were four of them, but Lorn recognized three of them at once. With their stooped postures and wavy dark hair, they were unmistakable.

'My lady,' he said, riding into the courtyard. 'We have company.'

White-Eye cocked her head to listen. 'Who?'

'Men from the village beyond the wall, friends of mine,' said Lorn. He waved back at Amarl, then at his three comrades from Marn, the bone-diseased brothers who had helped him rebuild Jador's ruined defenses. Their names were Tarlan, Harliz and Garmin, and to those who barely knew them they looked nearly identical, their clothes old and worn, their posture painfully stooped from disease. Tarlan and his brothers gave Lorn a smile as he rode up to them and dismounted. The fourth man who had come with them – a stranger – did nothing but stare down at the dirt.

'Tarlan?' Lorn asked. 'What's wrong? Why are you here?'

Amarl the Jadori interrupted Tarlan before he could speak. 'They have news, King Lorn,' said the warrior. At once he went to Lorn's horse, helping down his queen. White-Eye fell into his large hands, letting him guide her to the ground.

'What news, Amarl?' White-Eye asked. Her blank eyes searched the voices. 'Who are they?'

Tarlan and his brothers had never seen White-Eye, and now they watched her nervously. Harliz stepped forward and gave her a bow, barely inclining his already bent back.

'We're from Marn, Kahana,' he said haltingly. 'We are friends of King Lorn. We've been waiting for him to return.'

'They are friends, Amarl,' confirmed Lorn, a bit angered the warrior had kept them waiting outside in the darkness instead of inviting them into the palace. He turned to the stranger. 'But I don't know you.'

'This one has the news,' said Amarl. The warrior had removed the wrappings of his gaka from his face, focusing his fierce eyes on the stranger. 'He came with the others.'

'We brought him here, Lorn,' said Garmin. 'He came across the desert two days ago.'

'My name is Jaton,' said the man nervously. He crushed a cap in both his hands, his eyes darting between Lorn and White-Eye. 'I'm from Nith, my lord. I brought my family across the desert to find Mount Believer.'

Both Lorn and White-Eye let out a little groan.

'Garmin, why did you bring him here?' Lorn asked. 'We can't do anything for them, you know that.'

'No, you don't understand,' said Tarlan, coming to his brother's rescue. He grew serious. 'Lorn, remember when you told us about Aztar? How everyone thinks he is dead?'

Lorn felt his insides seize. 'Yes . . .'

'He's not dead,' said Harliz. 'Not according to this fellow.'

'Not dead?' White-Eye exclaimed. Amazingly, her gaze found the stranger. 'How do you know that?'

'I was in Ganjor before crossing the desert. My family spent days there trying to find someone to take us across. We heard things about Aztar. He is alive, my lady. Everyone in Ganjor thinks so.'

'That's why we brought him here,' said Garmin. 'We met him just a few hours ago, in a shrana house. We started talking, and that's when he told us about Aztar.'

'How could Aztar be alive?' White-Eye asked. 'How could he have survived?'

'They say he is burned, my lady,' explained Jaton from Nith. 'He has a camp, hidden somewhere in the desert.'

'There are still men with him?' Lorn asked.

Jaton nodded. 'So they say. I heard at least two hundred have remained with him. My lord, I heard about his battle with you when I was in Ganjor. Before just a few weeks ago, the Ganjeese thought he was dead, too.'

'Then how did they find out he's alive?' asked White-Eye.

'Because he is in bed with them,' Lorn grumbled. 'That fat bastard Baralosus – he still has designs on Jador no doubt!'

'I don't think so, Lorn,' said Tarlan. He looked urgingly at Jaton. 'Tell them the rest.'

'I'm unsure of the rest,' Jaton explained, 'but they say King Baralosus' daughter is imprisoned.'

'Salina?' Lorn gasped. 'Why?'

'For helping you here in Jador, my lord. They say she was discovered in treachery, that she warned you about Prince Aztar. Mind you, I never heard of any of these people before going to Ganjor. I only wanted to come across the desert. But the whole city is talking about this, my lord.'

The awful news staggered Lorn. He had only met Salina once, but she had been a great help to him, and to all of Jador. He looked at White-Eye and saw dread on her face. The Kahana stood stoically by his side.

'Gilwyn . . .'

Lorn considered the possibilities. Had Gilwyn been discovered, too?

'What else did you hear?' Lorn asked. 'Tell us everything.'

'Did you hear about a boy, a northerner with a clubbed foot and hand?' asked White-Eye.

Jaton grimaced. 'No, I don't think so,' he said, clutching his cap. 'Just about the princess.'

'But how did Baralosus discover her?' Lorn asked. He felt panicked suddenly. 'Come now, remember everything you heard.'

'That's all of it, my lord, I swear,' insisted Jaton. 'King Baralosus found out his daughter was helping you. I don't know how he discovered her treachery. Maybe no one knows. I didn't ask.'

'And you never heard the name Gilwyn Toms? That doesn't sound familiar to you?'

'No,' said Jaton anxiously. 'No, I'm sorry.'

'We thought you should hear all of this quickly, Lorn,' said Tarlan. 'That's why we brought him here tonight. We've been waiting for you for hours.'

'You did the right thing, Tarlan,' sighed Lorn. 'Thank you. Jaton, I want you to stay here, at least for the night. I want you to think very hard, and to remember anything else that you can. Amarl, will you take these men inside? Give them food and a place to sleep.'

Amarl agreed, looking unhappy. But before he could lead the northerners inside Jaton stepped forward to confront White-Eye.

'Kahana, my family has travelled a long way . . .'

'No.' Lorn put up his hand. 'Don't ask it, Jaton.'

Jaton looked at him, heart-broken. 'But my wife is very ill. If—'

'Stop. I know the story, Jaton. I brought my own daughter here thinking the same thing as you, but there's no magic here to heal your wife. Now, just go inside and rest.'

Jaton began stuttering, but Amarl's broad hand turned him away from the Kahana. The warrior led Jaton into the palace, bidding Tarlan and his brothers to follow. The stooped trio glanced at Lorn.

'It's all right,' Lorn assured them. 'He'll take care of you. I'll be in soon to talk with you.'

When they were gone, White-Eye ordered the other guards out of the courtyard, leaving herself alone with Lorn. The two said nothing for a long moment, contemplating all they had heard. Finally, White-Eye asked the pertinent question.

'What do we do?'

Lorn's simmering anger threatened to overwhelm him. 'That snake Baralosus – he plots against Jador, I swear. I told you, Kahana – your city is under threat.'

'I should tell Minikin,' said White-Eye.

'Minikin is too weak to help us,' said Lorn. 'You said so yourself.'

'She needs to know about this.'

'Indeed. And we will tell her. But what about you? You're the Kahana. You must prepare the city for whatever is to come.'

The order made White-Eye shudder. 'I wish Gilwyn were here.' She turned toward Lorn. 'Do you think he is all right?'

'I don't know,' said Lorn dismally. 'Maybe he got out of Ganjor. Jaton didn't say anything about him.'

'That one? He is a stranger. He doesn't seem to know anything.'

'I know,' Lorn growled, 'but what are we to do? We're weak. If Gilwyn has been captured . . .'

'Then we must help him!'

'No.'

White-Eye frowned at him. 'No?'

'This is a night of important lessons for you, Kahan. Now here is another for you – if Gilwyn has been captured, then he knew the risks. Your duty is to Jador now.' Lorn fixed her in his stare. 'You see? You see how right I was? A ruler may never rest.'

White-Eye put her hand out for Lorn. He took it, steadying her. To his surprise, he saw steel in her expression.

'We do not know if Jaton is correct,' she said. 'We are . . . blind.'

'Correct. Go on.'

White-Eye thought hard. 'If Aztar is alive, we do not know his intentions.'

'His intentions are what they've always been,' said Lorn. 'To harm us.'

'But we cannot attack him.'

'No,' Lorn agreed. 'We cannot.'

'So we shall wait,' White-Eye decided. 'We will make ourselves strong again.' Leaning against Lorn, she let the old king guide her into the palace. 'And you will make me strong, too. And I will learn from you.'

17

Mirage picked her way through the narrow lane, marvelling at the diminutive, pastel-coloured homes. Sunlight streamed in between the closely spaced buildings, brightening the avenue, while street vendors sold treats and admired the pretty lady who had come to visit. Overhead, the sky glowed a perfect blue. Birds walked the wooden gutters, warbling their morning songs. Along the lane children kicked stones as they played beneath the shade of shingled roofs, their mothers and fathers busy with work. The doors to the tiny homes sported plaques with Reecian names, all of them small and jammed together in the winding avenue. Enchanted by the storybook setting, Mirage wandered unafraid past the homes and the men and women tending them. She had been told by Laurella that it was called the Rainbow Lane, a source of pride among the people of Hes. With its tiny, colourful homes and charming iron lamp posts, it gave the city its name – Hes the Serene.

Mirage walked alone through the Rainbow Lane. She had been in the castle for almost a week, and though Raxor had given her complete freedom – provided she stayed within the complex walls – she had not yet ventured outside.

Until today.

Today, she had no chaperone and no curfew of any kind. She had awoken early to one of Laurella's fine breakfasts, and the bright rising sun through her chamber windows told her that today she should free herself of the castle and explore the city that Raxor so adored. Her decision to finally venture outside had pleased Laurella, for the old maid had urged her for days to explore the city, highly recommending a walk down the Rainbow Lane. It was where Laurella had been born, the old woman had explained, and where she still had cousins who were cobblers. Mirage noticed a man with tacks in his mouth, cursing under his breath as he worked outside, mending shoes. She passed the man with a smile, wondering if he were Laurella's kin. The smile made the grizzled man's eyebrows shoot up in pleasure. He stopped his hammering just long enough to return the pretty girl's grin.

The castle complex was not what Mirage had expected. In all her time with Lukien, who had spent years battling Raxor and the Reecians, the knight had never once commented on the city's splendour. Hes had charmed Mirage at once, and the vast complex of Castle Hes was like a great and fabulous maze to explore, with alluring homes for the armies of servants and countless courtyards surrounded by manicured gardens. The tower of a cathedral rose up in the distance, its copper roof showering sunlight across the pastel homes. Nearby, a belvedere with marble columns stood like an ancient titan, its grounds criss-crossed with perfectly angled sidewalks. Mirage stopped to admire the structure, noticing a fountain gurgling in its yard. She left the narrow lane and moved toward the belvedere, staring up at the magnificent structure and counting its many arches. There were pines around the fountain, dwarfs of their giant siblings, and lovers sitting on the grass, listening to the fountains ringing music. Mirage went to the fountain and dipped her hand into the cool water. She watched in awe as spouts of water jetted up to strike the bowls of brass, each one singing a different note. Here she was away from the crowds, invited by the fountain and flower beds to relax and think.

Choosing a patch of comfortable grass, Mirage laid herself down in the sunlight. Wrapping her arms around her knees, she closed her eyes and let the warmth caress her face. The last week had passed in a blur, and now she took the time to catch her breath. From Asher's ghastly prison, she had been delivered into the hands of a demented, kindly king, who could not do enough to please her but could not bring himself to free her. Mirage had seen very little of Raxor since their first meeting. He had come to her twice since then, only to see to her needs, and he had not touched her the way she had feared or ordered her to his bed. That surprised Mirage. She was his woman now. Yet she still didn't know what that meant.

Kirsil, what am I doing? she asked silently. *I should run from him.*

Her unseen Akari blossomed in her mind. Like her host, Kirsil was calm now, much better than she had been during those days in Asher's prison. Kirsil's voice appeared like a brook through her mind, gently lapping at the shores of her thoughts.

If you go past the wall, he will find you, Kirsil warned.

How do we know that? He trusts me, Kirsil. He is so damned faithful.

He loves you, the spirit tittered.

Mirage frowned. *It's not funny. We are prisoners.*

Raxor says otherwise. In time he will trust you too much, and then you can simply leave him.

She wasn't sure why, but the prospect of leaving Raxor troubled Mirage. In his day, Raxor had been a brutal war hero, and Mirage had not forgotten the things Lukien had said about him. In battle he had been a beast, mercilessly taking heads with his axe, but he had also been a fair man, Mirage remembered, and now she could see that in him, struggling.

He means me no harm, said Mirage. She opened her eyes and looked across the lanes toward the castle tower where he and his family resided. It was her home now, too. 'He's just old and lonely,' she whispered.

Kirsil's tremor of displeasure told Mirage the spirit did not agree. *No more joking, now. You were right – you should leave. But be smart about it. Wait until you are sure.*

'Yes,' Mirage agreed. 'When I'm sure . . .'

Mirage settled into the grass for a spell, pushing aside her concerns. It was a glorious day and she was free, at least partially, to walk where she wanted and explore the fair city. She rested near the fountain for a leisurely time, then stood and brushed the grass from her backside, looking around. Now that morning was well underway the avenues began to fill with people. Again noticing the awesome tower of the cathedral peaking up above the tiled roofs, she chose her direction, using the tower as a landmark. Supposing the cathedral looked deceptively close, she did not fully intend to reach it, but rather to use it as a guide by which to navigate. On her way back she would use the castle itself, and if she happened to wander past the wall of the castle complex . . .

What would happen to her, she wondered? She looked furtively over her shoulder, wondering if Raxor had sent unseen chaperones with her, but all she saw were workmen and children in the streets and lovers too occupied to pay her much attention. Satisfied, she went back to the lane with the tiny houses and made her way south, until the lane widened and the pastel homes gave way to grand buildings of stone and darkly painted wood. Here the avenue curved into a circle hidden with tall, official looking structures and crowds of people and animals, all shuffling through the street with carts of wool, fruit and timber. Mirage avoided the crowd, picking her way to the other side of the street where a sidewalk guided her further toward the cathedral's tower, still visible over the crenulated tops of the buildings. On a corner she paused to get her bearings, then heard a noise in the distance. Like cheering, or the roar of a river, the sound leapt over the buildings and into the street. Curious, Mirage followed the noise. Rounding the corner, she came suddenly to a flat, gigantic parade ground. And on the ground were horsemen – hundreds of them – drilling on their proud mounts to the precise music of trumpeters. Under the shadow of the lofty cathedral, the field waved with flags and shook with pageantry, burdened with rows of carts piled high with supplies and stable boys shoeing horses, ordered about by men in armour and elegant uniforms. Among the teams of horses marched throngs of foot soldiers, while others practiced with pikes or fenced with swords under the critical gaze of officers. Not knowing what she had stumbled upon, Mirage scooted back around the corner, peering out her head for a better view. Pleased that none of the Reecian soldiers had noticed her, she watched in awe as they drilled, preparing for some unknown war.

'Kirsil, do you see?' she whispered.

Her Akari replied with alarm. *What is this?*

'I don't know . . .'

Mirage tried counting up the troops. There were at least five hundred of them, most on horseback but all similarly garbed in the armour of Reecian fighting men. Like the ones she had seen when she'd crossed the border into Reec, the soldiers seemed to be making ready.

But for what? asked Kirsil, reading her thoughts. *Is Reec in trouble?*

Mirage thought for a moment, wondering about the warning Raxor had given her. He had said that Baron Glass was plotting against Reec; he'd been so sure of it. Unable to see clearly, Mirage stepped out from behind the corner, sure that she was in no danger from the troops. She was Raxor's woman, after all. The parade ground enthralled her, its soldiers beautiful. Their frenzied noise filled the field. Sunlight from the blue sky played off their shining, armoured bodies and polished weapons. Galloping past her came a team of thundering horsemen, their heads bowed as they circled the enormous field. Mirage stepped back from the field as the horses blew by, awestruck by their power. At the head of the team rode a man in silver armour with a crimson plume sprouting from his helmet. A sword slapped against his leggings. He had led his team past Mirage and for a moment kept on riding, but fifty yards later he reined his horse to an abrupt halt, wheeling about to face her. The dozen horsemen he led fell into place behind him, but the man – his face hidden behind his helmet – ordered them to go. His metal face leered at Mirage. Then, he snapped the reins of his chestnut steed and stalked toward her.

Mirage pressed herself against the corner. She thought of running but couldn't make her feet obey. Instead she watched as the grand horseman trotted closer, coming to a stop a few feet away. Atop his snorting beast he towered over Mirage, looking down on her through the eyeslits in his metal mask. Gripping his reins, he leaned back comfortably, nodding.

'You're the one,' he said. The young voice echoed beneath his helmet. Finally he raised a gauntlet to lift his faceplate, revealing his sharp nose and piercing green eyes. A red goatee covered his chin, partially hidden by a veil of chainmail. 'You're my father's new plaything.'

The accusation stunned Mirage. 'I am no one's toy, sir,' she spat at the knight, but she already knew the man's name. So far she had avoided meeting Raxor's children, the two daughters and one grown son who lived in Castle Hes. According to Laurella they were a selfish lot, accustomed to taking from their father and giving little back. The knight laughed at Mirage's tartness.

'I recognize you,' he said. 'I have seen you at the castle. My father spoke of you to me when you came.'

'You're Roland,' said Mirage, not backing down. 'I see you do not have your father's manners.'

'Or his luck with women,' laughed the knight. 'To have such a pretty young thing to share his bed with! I do envy my father sometimes.'

Roland the Red was a major in Reec's army, an accomplished cavalry-man with a streak of arrogance that made his men dislike him. Mirage only knew what Laurella had told her about Roland.

'Is that why you came? To accuse me? I should think a prince would know better how to introduce himself.'

'You *are* fiery,' said Roland. 'And you do look like my mother.' He waved his gauntlet at her. 'Step out. Let me look at you.'

'Shall I open my mouth for you, too? Let you check my teeth? I'm not a horse for you to inspect.'

'No,' said Roland, his smile greasy. 'You're hardly a horse. But my father has bridled you.'

'I'm his prisoner,' Mirage shot back. 'I don't wish to be here at all.'

Roland spun his horse to the other side, keeping it expertly in check. 'I know that,' he said. 'And believe it or not I am sorry for you. In case you haven't figured it out yet my father is demented. He mourns for my mother like a little boy.'

'He loved her,' said Mirage, unsure why she was defending Raxor. 'And if you loved your father you would not speak of him so.'

'I loved the man he used to be,' said Roland, 'the man Corvalos Chane thinks you can make him again. Oh, yes, we've all heard the story! I admit you could have been my mother's twin, but you can't replace her, woman, and you can't make a sick old man whole again.'

'I don't intend to,' said Mirage icily. 'As soon as your father realizes that, he will send me on my way.'

'He won't,' laughed Roland. 'You are here to stay. You should know that. Don't make yourself mad with thoughts of escaping. My father is already obsessed with you. He will never let you go.'

Mirage cursed herself for blundering into this argument. 'What is all this?' she asked, hoping to change the subject. 'You're preparing for war?'

'Indeed, pretty lady, for war is upon us! Your man, the Black Baron – he has forced us to the march. I'm leading these men to the Liirian border, along the Kryss river. We leave in a few days.'

'Baron Glass has attacked?'

Roland shook his armoured head. 'Not yet, no. But he will, and when he does we will be ready for him.' With his icy eyes, Roland glared at Mirage. 'You haven't told my father anything about Glass yet, have you?'

'But you have secrets. Asher has said so, and he is never wrong about such things.' Roland sighed, sounding almost pitying. 'You should tell the truth, woman, and spare yourself the agony. I tell you the truth when I say Asher isn't done with you.'

'I speak to your father, and what I tell him is between he and I,' said Mirage. 'I am not afraid of Asher. And you are wrong about Baron Glass – he has no interest in Reec. I've already said that a hundred times.'

'Ah, and do you speak for the Diamond Queen as well, lady? That insatiable bitch?' Roland waited for Mirage to answer. 'Eh?'

'No,' Mirage admitted.

'No. So please, do not pretend to know the threats we face. We have burdens enough.' Roland hoisted a thumb over his shoulder toward the parade ground. 'These men are riding into battle, but the battle cannot come until my father joins it. They won't follow me, not without the king. So you see? You have a difficult task.'

Mirage was puzzled by him. 'What task?'

'Take care of my father. Will you do that? No one else can make a man of him again.'

'I am no whore, Sir!'

Roland held up his hands. 'And I am not calling you one. I'm just saying the obvious. You're a beautiful woman and you were brought here to service him. If you haven't figured that out yet . . .'

'You're a disgusting troll,' sneered Mirage. 'I'm not a prostitute your father hired out of the gutter, and I'm not surprised these men won't follow you. Better to follow a crazy old man than an arrogant young bastard.'

Roland smiled at her from his high perch. 'Good luck to you, Mirage. For the sake of Reec I hope you are happy with my father. You have no choice but to stay with him. The sooner you understand that the better your time here will be.'

He didn't wait for her to reply. Roland the Red simply spun his horse away and rode off toward his waiting cavalry, leaving Mirage stunned and speechless. With just a few words he had shredded her meagre peace. The bright day felt suddenly cold, and all she wanted was to run back to Castle Hes and lock herself in her chambers. Turning slowly from the field, she went back around the corner and started walking the long way home. But before she took even five steps a figure startled her.

'You've met Roland.'

Mirage jumped at the sound of the voice. Blocking the sidewalk stood Corvalos Chane, tall and lean in his leather armour, his arms folded over his chest. The sight of him made Mirage instantly angry.

'You've been following me!' she railed, emotion flooding her voice. 'How long?'

'All day.'

She felt like a fool, doubly so now. She shook her head and thought she might cry from frustration. 'I thought he trusted me.'

'He does. I don't,' said Chane. He stepped closer, putting his long hand on her shoulder and leading her away from the parade ground. 'You shouldn't have come here,' he told her.

'Then you should have stopped me!'

Chane hurried her away so that none of the soldiers could see her. When they were safely hidden from the field by the stone wall of a soaring building, Corvalos Chane faced her with a scowl.

'You're right,' he said. 'But Laurella warned you about Roland. He is a whelp, and not accustomed to holding his tongue. Don't take his words to heart. I'm the one his father trusts, not him.'

'He's going to the border,' said Mirage. 'He's going to war.'

'Aye, to be with the others. But he'll do nothing until his father joins him.'

'Joins him? You mean Raxor is going too?'

'In time,' said Chane. 'But not now, not until he is ready. You must make him ready, Mirage. The men will not follow Roland. He is too ambitious and they know it. They'll follow only Raxor, because he was great once and because they love him. Especially the officers. Roland knows this.'

'I don't know what to think,' Mirage lamented. 'The way Roland spoke of his father – does he hate the man or love him?'

'He is jealous of him, I think. Even Roland knows what a great man his father once was.'

'And I must make him great again,' sighed Mirage. 'You're all mad.'

'Just give him confidence,' said Chane. 'Let him feel like a man again. Once he does, he will ride to the border to defend us.'

Mirage laughed at the order. 'That's all? Just make a man out of him? Fate above, listen to yourself.' She began walking away. 'I'll tell you what I told Roland, Corvalos Chane – I may be a prisoner, but I am no whore. Now, take me back to the castle.'

With Chane hurrying after her, Mirage began walking the long way back. In her mind she heard Roland's hateful words again and again, taunting her. She was not a slave or a harlot, and they would never make her one. But she pitied Raxor and worried about what he was to do, for there was no way the old man could ever stand against Thorin Glass in battle. With his Devil's Armour, Thorin would tear Raxor to shreds.

And for that she was truly, deeply sorry.

*

Late the next afternoon, Corvalos Chane surprised Mirage again.

She had spent the morning and the whole day before alone in her chambers, miserable over the things Roland had said to her and unwilling to rekindle her curiosity about the city. Laurella had spent some time with her, mostly ranting about Roland, and then had sent the young maids Sela and Meleni to cheer her up. With their effervescent smiles, the girls managed to pull Mirage from the worst of her doldrums, but like Laurella they could not convince her to ignore Raxor's son or the cruel things he had said to her. Mirage told the maids about what she had seen on the parade ground. When she did, Laurella simply nodded as if she already knew.

'It's why you're here,' the old woman had said gently.

But Laurella did not try to make her see the logic in her imprisonment the way Corvalos Chane had, and she did not condone what her beloved king had done to her. Laurella was becoming a friend, and Mirage cherished her counsel. She brought Mirage her meals, told her the idle gossip around the castle, and generally comforted her when she was morose, cheering her with simple talk about her family and what it was like to get old. It was strange for Mirage to be growing so attached to the maids, because she was a royal woman now in the eyes of the castle and she had noticed how the others of rank within the castle treated the servants. To Roland and his siblings, Laurella and her ilk were far less than equals. As she spoke to the maids, Mirage remembered her childhood with her parents, and how they had once been wealthy.

Before the fire.

By late afternoon the next day, however, Mirage had tired of talking and wanted only to be alone. She sat in a hard wooden chair near the window, looking out over the city and wondering if Roland the Red had left yet for Liiria. From her place in the tower Mirage could not see the parade ground or the steeple of the grand cathedral, but she could see the border of Hes and the rolling hills of farmland beyond. She smiled mournfully at the pretty sight. Would she ever go into the hills again, or ride through forests the way she had with Lukien? Would she ever see Lukien again.

'No,' she muttered. Roland's words came back to haunt her. 'I'm here forever.'

As she stared out the window, she hardly noticed the shadow creep into the room over her shoulder. Thinking it was Laurella, she did not turn around.

'Yes?' she asked, staring out the window. When Laurella didn't answer, Mirage turned to see Corvalos Chane standing in the room. 'What are you doing here?' she asked sourly.

Chane wore his usual expression, both arrogant and inscrutable. It amazed Mirage that she had not heard his heavy boots against the floor. He had shaved the stubble from his rugged face, looking almost handsome in the sunlight through the window.

'The king has sent me to collect you,' he said.

'To collect . . . ? No, not today,' said Mirage.

Chane laughed. 'You're mistaken if you think you have a choice. The king has summoned you, girl.'

'Summoned me where?'

'I cannot say,' Chane replied. 'It is to be a surprise.'

The statement puzzled Mirage. She got out of her chair, looking past Chane toward the adjacent room. There she saw Laurella, waiting dutifully and quietly. She had obviously been unable to stop the intrusion.

'If Raxor wishes to see me why didn't he come himself? Why did he send you?' Mirage scowled at the man. 'Why are you always popping up?'

Chane shifted. 'Because I'm supposed to protect you,' he sighed. 'The king has ordered it, and so I am here. Now please, will you come?'

'Protect me?' Mirage found the notion delicious. 'From what?'

'From anything. From a hangnail. Enough questions, girl. Now come along!'

She loved getting under Chane's skin, and was finding it easier all the time. He didn't like being her chaperone, she could tell.

'All right,' she relented. 'Are we going outside? If so I'll need a coat.'

'Then bring one,' drawled the spy. 'There's a carriage waiting for you.'

Inside the splendid carriage, Mirage watched as the city rolled by through her gilded window. With no one inside the conveyance to accompany her, Mirage had no distractions, and could not even see Corvalos Chane as he led the carriage through the streets on horseback. She had asked the spy why he did not accompany her inside the carriage, but Chane had not answered, not even with a shrug. He had simply helped her into the vehicle, ordered the coachman to follow him, then mounted his tall stallion and led them away. Mirage's mind raced with possibilities, not all of them pleasant. She feared the worst from Raxor's surprise, wondering if at last he would demand more from her than just conversation. She had learned that the old war hero had a sweet side, but he was also suffering some kind of depression that made him unpredictable, and fighting him off would not be an option.

What would Chane do if Raxor came at her? What if she screamed for his help? She supposed Chane was too loyal to Raxor to lift a finger to help her, and that sickened her. If she was to be raped, she certainly didn't want an audience.

The carriage moved slowly through the streets, rocking gently back and forth. At last it came to a stop. Mirage peered expectantly out the window and saw they had parked in front of a large edifice of stone with a pair of rounded wooden doors, already opened wide like a mouth. The street in front of the building seemed empty. The utilitarian building frightened Mirage, who knew at once that it was not a residence at all but more like a concert hall, vast and echoing. She waited for the coachman to open her door. He did so silently, bidding her to step out then taking her hand and guiding her down the carriage's two steps. She stood gaping at the giant building as Corvalos Chane dismounted. The spy handed the reins of his horse to the young coachman.

'Remain,' he ordered the driver, then smiled teasingly at Mirage. 'Come along, girl. The king is waiting.'

'What is this place?' asked Mirage, refusing to walk through the rounded doorway. She noticed now that there were many such doorways, though the rest of them were closed, lining the round façade of the building.

'A forum,' said Chane. He shooed her toward the entrance.

'I'm supposed to be some sort of entertainment?' Mirage protested.

'You are so tiresome,' groaned Chane. 'Nothing is going to happen to you. Will you believe me for once and just go inside?'

'Fine, let's just get this over with,' said Mirage, walking past him into the doorway, at once entering a dark hall with a low ceiling and a worn-out floor of gravel. There was light at the other end of the hall. Mirage could see a vast area there, open to the sky. She was indeed in some huge arena, and didn't know why. With Chane keeping back a few paces, she walked warily forward.

'Go on,' urged Chane.

Mirage continued, finally reaching the end of the hall, stepping out onto the circular field. The sky spread out overhead, dwarfing her. Her breath caught at the sensation, and the noise of her gasp echoed through the arena. Above the walls of the arena she saw endless rows of empty seats. Not a single spectator was there to greet her entrance. Yet she was not alone within the arena. Far off to her right she saw Raxor. He wasn't alone, either.

'Fate above,' Mirage exclaimed. Quickly she looked at Chane for an explanation. The spy smiled in amusement.

'I'll wait here,' he said, then slunk back into the dark recesses of the hall. 'Go ahead. I told you, you won't be harmed.'

Mirage could not bring herself to move, for with Raxor were a pair of enormous bears, huge and black, one standing on its hind legs, the other rolling playfully onto its back while Raxor coaxed them both with treats. The king wore no armour, no protection of any kind, just a child-like grin on his face that widened when he saw Mirage. He snapped his fingers, ordering the bears to attention, and at his command both beasts stopped their tricks.

'We have company!' sang the king. The beasts turned to regard Mirage, and all she wanted was to run.

'Oh no . . .'

'Don't be afraid,' said Raxor. 'I know they look frightening but they won't hurt you.' He waved her closer. 'Come over here. I promise, it's all right.'

'I'd rather stay here, my lord, if it's all the same.'

'No, it isn't all the same,' said Raxor. He knelt down between the two bruins, resting his hands on their necks. 'They want to meet you.'

Madness, thought Mirage. She had suspected it before, but now she was certain.

'My lord, you should come out of there,' she suggested. 'I don't think it's safe for you.'

'Nonsense! They're like big children.' To prove his point, Raxor nuzzled the neck of one of the bears, burying his nose in its thick coat. 'See?'

Speechless, Mirage could only imagine what sickness of the brain had driven the old king to such actions. Though he was a big man and obviously strong, the bears were many times his weight and could easily have killed him.

But they didn't, and to Mirage they seemed remarkably tame. Even gentle. She inched closer, keeping an eye on the beasts.

'My lord, is this what you wanted to show me? These two monsters?'

'Not monsters, Mirage. Friends.' Raxor stood up between the bears, who opened their mouths and let their tongues loll out. 'I've had these two since they were cubs. They were born right here in this forum.'

'Here?' Mirage looked around. 'It doesn't seem the place for them.'

'They have other areas where they spend most of their time. There's a whole team of men who look after them and the other animals.'

Mirage stopped moving. 'What other animals?'

'Birds mostly, from all over the continent. I collect them.' Raxor patted the bears' heads. 'But these two are special. I bring them out here to play when I visit.'

'Is that what all those things are for?' asked Mirage, noting the balls and other toys scattered on the ground. 'For play?'

'That's right,' said the king. From his pocket he produced some treats, giving one to each of his pets. Their big tongues licked them out of his hands. Still a safe distance from the bears, Mirage watched them in awe.

'What was that you gave them?'

'Just bread balls. But they'll eat almost anything. Butter, scraps of fat, fish heads . . .'

'Sounds delightful.'

Raxor smiled brightly at Mirage. 'I thought you'd like to see them. Aren't they beautiful?'

'Yes, my lord, they are,' Mirage agreed. Slowly she felt herself relax. 'But why do you have them? I don't understand.'

'All the kings of Reec have kept bears, since the founding of Hes. Bears are the symbol of the city. If you look you can see them everywhere in the architecture.'

'Yes,' realized Mirage suddenly. 'Yesterday when I was walking. I did see bears.'

Raxor continued scratching the heads of the beasts, careful not to neglect one for the other. 'They say a bear was with the first king of Hes when he founded the city. That was almost five hundred years ago, but you can still find bears in the hills around Hes.'

'And these two live here all year round?'

'They have to,' said Raxor. 'They couldn't live out in the wild. Look at them! They wouldn't last a day out there.'

'They do *seem* gentle,' said Mirage. Curious, she went closer, studying the bears who watched her in kind, their dark eyes following her every move. 'Do they have names?'

'Broud and Varsha,' Raxor answered. He patted the slightly larger one. 'This is Broud, the male. They're brother and sister.'

'How old are they?'

'Almost three years. They won't get much larger than this.'

Charmed by the beasts, Mirage could not stop herself from going closer. Their furry faces seemed to smile at her. And Raxor looked like a boy between them, innocent and happy, without all the trappings of kingship dragging him down. He even looked younger.

'Would you like to touch them?' asked Raxor.

He was giving her a gift, Mirage knew. This whole spectacle was for her benefit.

'I'm afraid . . .'

'Do not be,' said the king. 'I promise you, they won't harm you. Here, I will prove it to you.'

Kneeling down again near the big male, Raxor put his head beside Broud's mouth. 'Open,' he commanded, and when the bear opened wide its great jaws Raxor placed his neck between them.

'My lord, stop!' cried Mirage.

Raxor laughed but did not pull free. 'You see? I raised these two myself. I'm like their mother!'

'Just stop, please!'

At last Raxor removed himself from Broud's mouth. 'Now it's your turn.'

'I'm not sticking my neck in there.'

'Of course not. Just touch them.' King Raxor waved her forward. 'Come easy. Don't be frightened.'

Mirage reached out her hand but only moved a few inches nearer.

'Closer than that.'

'I know,' said Mirage. 'I'm coming.'

Finally in range, she let her fingers brush the crown of the Varsha, the female. The sensation thrilled her.

'It's so soft, like a blanket!'

Confident the bear wouldn't harm her, she buried her hand in Varsha's coat, rubbing hard and eliciting a happy groan from the beast. Varsha's big brow knitted together in pleasure at Mirage's touch.

'You see? Like children,' said Raxor.

'My lord, children have tempers. Haven't they ever harmed you, even in play?'

'Never. They never could do such a thing.'

'Let's see them play, then,' Mirage suggested. 'Let's see some of their tricks.'

King Raxor looked at her lovingly. His expression frightenened her more than the bears did. 'If that's what you wish,' he told her. 'They'll perform for you all night.'

'Just something simple,' said Mirage.

Just as she was drawn to the bears, she was drawn now to Raxor. The affection in his eyes was startling, and for a moment Mirage forgot that it was not truly for her, but rather for a dead wife. She stood aside while Raxor ordered the bears through tricks, delighted by their antics. Under his careful hand the bears stood up tall, rolled, and made sounds that were almost human, rewarded after each trick by a treat from Raxor's pocket.

'You have to give them something for each trick,' he explained. 'And you can't eat sweets around them. Anything sugary drives them mad.'

He lifted his hand high into the air, bringing both bears to their feet. The bears walked in a circle around him. Mirage laughed, enchanted by the beasts, who suddenly seemed more like house cats to her than wild animals. Throughout their performance Broud and Varsha growled playfully, never threatening either of the humans. And they never tired or grew bored, but rather continued to entertain their new guest, showing her every trick they knew. The way Raxor handled them was remarkable. As big as he was, he was like one of the bears, brusque on the outside but calm and gentle within.

For almost an hour Mirage watched the bears play, sometimes involving herself by tossing bread balls into the air or rubbing the beasts' broad backs. She forgot that she was with a king, her captor, or that Corvalos Chane was somewhere in the shadows, watching her. Finally, when Raxor's pocket of treats was exhausted, he gave the order for the bears to sit, laying them down on the ground at his feet. The old king beamed, pleased with himself and his pets. And Mirage, exhilarated by the experience, finally felt her breath return.

She looked at Raxor, not knowing what to say. The king smiled awkwardly.

'Thank you,' said Mirage. 'This was so unexpected. But why?'

'Because Corvalos told me what happened to you yesterday, and the things my son said to you. I am sorry for that, Mirage. Roland has always talked too much.'

'I have thought about this,' said Mirage. 'It was I who wandered off and uncovered his secret. Some of the things he said to me . . . well, they don't really matter. It's his army that concerns me.'

'Roland has much on his mind,' said Raxor. 'If he offended you I'm sorry. He speaks without thinking.'

Mirage didn't care about Roland, and no longer wanted to talk about him. 'But the army, my lord – they're making ready to march for the border. And you're going to join them.'

'Yes,' said Raxor, looking away from her. He knelt down beside Varsha to scratch her ear. 'Things have been happening in Liiria, things no one has told you. Baron Glass has crowned himself king. My people in Koth have told me so. A week ago, he called his troops around him in Chancellory Square. He declared himself Liiria's ruler. All of Jazana Carr's lieutenants were there. He called them from Norvor to witness his declaration.'

'All right,' said Mirage. 'But that doesn't mean there's war coming. Thorin doesn't want war, my lord. He only wants Liiria.'

'I wish that were true,' said the old king. His rheumy eyes looked up from his quiet pets. 'The word from Koth says otherwise, Mirage. My people tell me that Baron Glass has become paranoid, that he worries about all the enemies he's made. He's seen my armies on his border and he thinks we mean to invade.'

'Then you should pull them back, my lord.'

'And leave the border unprotected? You're asking me to trust the Black Baron, and I can't do that.'

'But you're provoking him,' said Mirage. Trying not to reveal too much, she added, 'Thorin only wants Liiria, but if you chase him into a corner he'll be like one of these bears. You have to treat him prudently, my lord.'

Her candour intrigued Raxor, who grinned at her. 'You have so many secrets.'

Mirage tread carefully. 'I just know him, that's all.'

'No, Mirage, you know so much more than that. But you may keep your secrets. I told you already – I won't harm you. When you are ready you will tell me what you know about the Black Baron.'

But it may be too late by then, thought Mirage. She asked, 'When will you leave, my lord?'

'In a week perhaps. Let Roland command the men for a time. They don't need me yet, and I don't want to provoke Glass more than I must. If he learns that I have come to be with my troops, he will either talk to me or fight me. I hope he chooses talk.'

'Talk,' said Mirage, 'Yes.' But she knew Thorin would not talk to Raxor, any more than he had talked to Lukien when the knight had tried to stop him. 'My lord . . .'

Raxor glanced up at her. 'Yes?'

Mirage hesitated. 'You must be careful. This armour Thorin wears . . .' She stopped herself, not knowing if she should continue. 'Please don't ask me to explain it all. There are things I can't reveal to you, not ever.'

The old king rose and stood before her. 'Your secrets are safe. But please, tell me what you must.'

Not wanting to betray Grimhold, Mirage kept her words particular. 'The Devil's Armour is everything you've heard it is,' she whispered. 'It cannot be destroyed, and while Thorin wears the armour he cannot be defeated. Please, King Raxor, don't ride into this battle.'

Raxor reached out and traced his finger along her cheek. 'I don't seek battle, Mirage. I will talk with Baron Glass first.'

'He won't listen to you,' said Mirage. 'What your men have told you about him is the truth – he is suspicious. He fears anything that might take Liiria away from him. The Devil's Armour has possessed him.'

'Possessed? What do you mean?'

Mirage shook her head. 'I can't explain to you. It's magic, just like you were told. It's a powerful magic and it has corrupted Baron Glass. It has maddened him, my lord, and he will not listen to your reason.'

'Then what shall I do? Be a coward? I cannot let him come to Reec to spread Jazana Carr's empire. No. No matter what weapon he wields against us, we will confront him. That is the way it must be, Mirage.'

There was no arguing with the old king. Mirage saw his logic immediately. But in her mind she also saw his broken body, savaged by Thorin and his armour, and the image brought a surprising tear to her eyes.

'I know,' she said, nodding quickly. 'I know. Just . . . be careful.'

King Raxor puffed out his broad chest. 'Ah, have confidence in me, girl. Ask Corvalos to tell you some stories about me. I was a great solider in my day, more than a match for Thorin Glass.'

'Yes,' Mirage agreed, collected herself. 'I've heard. And I don't think you're too old, and I don't think you're crazy, my lord. I think you're just a kind and lonely man.'

'And strong,' said Raxor. 'Don't forget that one.'

Mirage smiled. 'Yes, strong,' she told him.

But in her heart she knew she was lying, and that he had no chance at all against Thorin.

18

Lukien spent his first days in Torlis trying to fathom the city's grandness. Though he had lived his entire life in Koth, a place renowned for its science and accomplishments, he had never seen anything like the land of the Red Eminence or the magnificent palace she called home. To his surprise, Lahkali's holy man Karoshin gave him and Jahan full run of the palace, not forbidding them from any area, inviting them to explore the palace and its elaborate grounds. Under orders from his young queen to give them anything they required, Karoshin had assigned them a fabulous set of chambers in one of the palace's vast wings, complete with maids and body servants to attend their needs. Jahan, who had grown up in his simple village, remained awestruck by the palace and its abundance. Food came to them on silver trays, and baths were not taken in the river but rather showered over them with perfumed water. Beautiful girls were made available to massage their backs and soothe their feet, and talented musicians came with their meals to entertain them with their strange instruments. For Lukien, exhausted from his long journey to the Serpent Kingdom, Torlis and its palace were heavenly. For the first time in countless weeks, he was comfortable.

Still, his mind did not relax, plagued as it was by the riddle Lahkali had laid at his feet. He spent endless hours in discussion with Jahan, pondering the location of the Sword of Angels and wondering if he had forgotten some important tidbit from his encounter with his dead beloved, Cassandra. He questioned each new servant sent to their chambers, asking them all they knew about the outside world and the legend of Malator, but each time he got the same friendly, useless answers.

Even in the great comfort of the palace, Lukien despaired. He had come so far and proven the existence of the sword, and it was so close to his grasp now that his hand trembled when he thought of it. Yet it was kept from him, its location locked in the mind of a single person, and young Lahkali had no intention of divulging her secret.

On his fourth day in Torlis, Lukien found himself wandering the grounds of the palace, admiring its flawlessly formed trees and considering his dismal options. Alone, he made sure to stay well away from the praying holy men who peppered the grounds, kneeling in their white robes among the flowered lawn. In Torlis, the weather always seemed perfect, as if the god Sercin had forbidden clouds or wind from disturbing the contemplation of his monks. Today was like the previous days, warm and glorious, enjoyed as much by the larks in the trees as by the people strolling the ground. Lukien avoided the others, finding a spot away from the busy lanes, where a large rock waited by a trickling stream, a tiny tributary of the great river that raged down from the mountain. He could see the holy mountain in the distance, like a titan overlooking the city. Akhir had called it the home of Sercin.

'Sercin, if I prayed to you would you help me find the sword?'

Lukien waited for an answer, gazing at the mammoth mountain. He sat himself down on the rock, smoothed by countless backsides over the years.

'No?'

The mountain and its god did not reply. Lukien took the Eye of God from beneath his shirt, holding the precious thing in his palm and staring into its scarlet jewel. During his time in Torlis, he had begged Amaraz to speak to him, to help him unlock the riddle of the sword. Amaraz, who knew so much, could surely help him with Lahkali's secret. But as he always did, the great Akari ignored Lukien's pleas, keeping silent in his golden home.

'Amaraz, you came to me once,' said Lukien. 'I need you. Do you hear? I *need* you.'

The red jewel in the Eye's centre pulsed at its usual tempo. Lukien touched it with his finger, feeling its living warmth. He had never understood why Amaraz ignored him, when all other Akari spoke freely with their hosts. Only once had the spirit appeared to him, and even then he had ignored Lukien, speaking directly to Minikin as if Lukien were not even there. The insult had hardened Lukien's heart.

'You're a great, powerful being,' said Lukien. 'But you're also unspeakably cruel. You sent me on this mission, Amaraz. You told me there was a way to defeat Kahldris and his armour, and all I'd have to do is find it. Well I have found it! It's here, and all I have to do is lay my hands on it. Now speak to me, you wretched imp.'

Still the amulet gave no change, no signal at all that Amaraz was listening. Lukien laughed bitterly.

'Don't talk, then. Just listen. The life you've given me is a curse, you know. You and your mission are just keeping me from Cassandra. I should rip you from my throat and toss you in the ocean, and I will once I'm done with the Sword of Angels. I will, Amaraz, and you won't be able to stop me.'

He had made the same threat to the Akari before, many times. It felt good to threaten a god.

'So I'll die. Do you think I'm afraid of that? I welcome it. I think every day of it, of being free of you. And what will become of you then? Perhaps a whale will swim by and swallow you, and then you can give the whale immortality. Would you like that?'

His taunts were useless. Nothing he could say would shame Amaraz into breaking his silence. Placing the amulet back beneath his shirt, Lukien left the solitary rock behind, heading west toward the sun, where earlier he had noticed a large, walled area attached to the palace but not nearly as well maintained. The wall was barely six feet high and built of stones laid one atop the other. It looked like it had been there forever, long before the rest of the palace. To Lukien, the area hinted at a stable. Drawn by curiosity, he made his way toward the wall, which had no entrance that he could see but simply continued on around the back of the palace. Reaching it, he put his hands to the wall to feel its construction, then heard a commotion on the other side. A man's voice, shouting. And angry.

Unable to find a way in, Lukien settled on peering over the wall instead. Not wanting to be seen, he tiptoed to an area of the wall shrouded by trees. Being just over six feet tall, he could barely see across the top of the wall, into the field beyond. Like the flowery grounds of the garden, the area hidden by the wall had trees that blocked his view. Beyond the trees, he saw figures moving, but only barely.

'Damn . . .'

Lukien repositioned himself and, straining atop his toes, hoisted himself up with his arms and elbows, dangling on the wall as carefully as he could. Still hidden by the trees, he was confident the figures could not see him. But he could see them now, and what he saw intrigued him, for there was young Lahkali, dressed like a warrior of Torlis in a black flowing robe with a golden rope cinched around her waist. In her hands was a giant, spear-like weapon, two-pronged like the tongue of a snake, just like the ones Lukien had seen the palace guards carrying. She was on her knees, desperately holding the spear before her, trying sloppily to ward off blows from a man Lukien had never seen before, a thin-boned dagger of a man with two curved swords that wheeled against Lahkali, driving her further to the ground. Lahkali cried with effort as she fought to hold back the onslaught, but it was obvious to Lukien that she was in no danger. Not far from her stood her trusted holy man Karoshin, stroking his chin unhappily as he watched the girl defend herself.

Lukien watched the fight intently. The muscles in his arm began to burn with the effort of holding himself on the wall. Lahkali tried gamely to rise to her feet, but each attempt brought harder blows from the man with the swords, driving her down again. Finally, with tears spouting down her cheeks, Lahkali cried out for the mêlée to stop.

The field grew quiet. Lukien held his breath. The man with the swords stopped his attack but did not help the Red Eminence to her feet. Instead he tossed his weapons into the dirt, a look of disgust on his bony face. Angry words poured out of him, but he was too far away for Lukien to comprehend. Still, his meaning was plain, and while he berated her, Lahkali simply stood and took his abuse, looking at her feet in shame.

'Son of a bitch,' Lukien whispered. She was only a girl, but her brutish teacher railed at her like she was an officer in his command. He picked up Lahkali's weapon, demonstrating how poorly she was holding it, as if he had already given her this same lesson a hundred times. Karoshin did nothing to come to the girl's rescue. The tattooed priest merely chewed his lip unhappily.

At last the warrior collected himself, taking a deep breath before speaking softly to the Eminence. He set aside the forked spear, speaking directly, never taking his hard gaze off his pupil. Lahkali tried to listen but Lukien could tell her mind was elsewhere, struggling with the shame of her performance. She nodded at everything the warrior told her, yet the tears continued. Then, like a little girl she wiped the sleeve of her garment across her face.

The warrior bowed and left her, turning almost in Lukien's direction before departing for the palace. Lukien lowered himself until he was sure the man had gone, then peered again over the wall. By now his arms were on fire, and he knew he could not hold on much longer. Grunting under his breath, he watched as Lahkali sunk to her knees again, weeping. This time Karoshin rushed to comfort her, putting both hands on the girl's shaking shoulders. Lahkali turned her face from him, shooing him away. The priest lingered a few moments, ignoring the girl's request, until Lahkali angrily ordered him to go. Long-faced, Karoshin followed the warrior out of the training field.

Lukien slunk back down the wall, leaning against it. If he listened carefully, he could just make out Lahkali's sobs. The sound of it broke his heart, and he did not know why. He remained there, hidden from the girl, waiting for her crying to subside. When it didn't, he hoisted himself all the way up the wall, tossing one leg over it and then the other before dropping down on the other side. The noise of his descent startled Lahkali, who looked up with a gasp. Lukien paused at the wall, waiting before coming closer. Lahkali stared at him through her tears, shaking her head miserably.

'You saw?' she asked.

'Yes.' Lukien offered her a kind smile. 'I didn't mean to spy. I'm just tall, you see.'

The joke fell flat with Lahkali. 'You should not have watched. This is a private place.'

'You're right, but I'm here now,' said Lukien, going to her. He glanced around, pleased to notice they were alone. 'Really, I am sorry. I don't mean to embarrass you. I wouldn't have watched if I wasn't concerned.'

Lahkali let Lukien help her to her feet. She was amazingly light, as though her little frame was filled with feathers. Her whole hand disappeared in Lukien's fist. She brushed the tears from her eyes, trying to look like Torlis' ruler.

'You can go,' she said. 'I'm fine.'

But Lukien didn't go. Instead he looked at the weapons strewn across the ground, the two curved swords the warrior had used and the long, twin-forked spear. He picked the spear off the ground, feeling the heft of its ebony shaft. It was a well made weapon, but heavy and much too large for Lahkali.

'I've seen these around the palace. The guards carry them. What are they called?'

'That is a katath,' said Lahkali. She eyed the thing angrily. 'All the warriors of Torlis know how to use them, and the swords.'

'All the warriors. So why are you training with it, Eminence?'

'Because I must. Because I have no choice.'

Lahkali turned and sat back down on the ground, folding her arms around her legs and resting her chin atop her knees. Lukien looked down at her, not sure what to say. Surprisingly, she did not order him away.

'I am the Red Eminence. Do you know what that means, Lukien?'

'Not really,' Lukien admitted. 'Jahan told me some, about how you turn the river to blood by slaying the Great Rass.'

'Your friend Jahan does not think much of me,' Lahkali grumbled. 'I saw it in his face when he met me. Others come from closer villagers to see me, and they always have that same look about them.'

'What look, Eminence?'

'Disappointment. I'm not the man they expect to find on the throne of Torlis. I'm not a man at all. I'm just a girl.'

Lukien knew she was right about Jahan's reaction. Jahan still had not stopped talking about it. 'You're the ruler of Torlis. Why should it matter that you are a girl? Someday you will grow into a full woman, and I have known some powerful women, Eminence.'

Lahkali's eyes flicked up at him. 'Have you?'

'Oh, yes! For years I was in the employ of a woman called Jazana Carr. They call her the Diamond Queen. Trust me when I tell you that she lets no man push her around.'

'I wish it were that way in Torlis,' said Lahkali dreamily.

Lukien stuck one end of the katath into the ground, leaning against it.

'Why are you training with this, Eminence? To kill the Great Rass? The boatman who brought me here said it was almost time for the Great Rass to appear again.'

'That's right,' said Lahkali. 'And it's my task to kill it. Only I cannot.'

'Because you can't wield this weapon? There are other ways, surely.'

'No, you don't understand. The weapon is not the problem. The problem is me.'

'Being female isn't a problem,' said Lukien. 'With time you can learn techniques—'

'Lukien, no.' Lahkali put up her hand to silence him. 'No. The problem is not the katath. The problem is me, inside me. I do not have the abilities I need to battle the Great Rass, the ability all my line had before me.'

Lukien lowered himself to one knee beside her. 'Anyone can learn to fight. It isn't in the blood.'

'Perhaps not. But not everyone can learn to control the rass. Only my line has that power, all the ones that came before me. My family, Lukien. That is why I am the Red Eminence.'

'Because you can control the rass? How do you mean?'

'I don't really know,' said Lahkali. 'I've never been able to do it. They told me that it would come when I was older, but it never did. My father could control the rass, right up until he died. Not just the Great Rass, either, but any rass. With his mind he could calm them.'

'I see,' said Lukien, at last understanding. 'Where I come from, there is a boy who can read the thoughts of other creatures, make them do things. His name is Gilwyn.'

Lahkali seemed amazed. 'An outsider could do this? Could he control the rass?'

'I don't know,' said Lukien, feeling melancholy. 'It's been a long time since I've seen him. It was a new ability for him, but I'm sure he's growing into it.'

'For him it is magic? Like that amulet you wear?'

'That's right.'

'Then it is different, because for us it is not magic. It cannot be learned, either. It is just part of us.' Lahkali lowered her eyes. 'But not me. And there is no way I can fight and win against the Great Rass if I cannot control it.'

'But that man I saw training you – he's trying to teach you how to use this spear.' Lukien still held the katath as he kneeled, propping himself up. 'He must think you have a chance.'

'That man you saw is Niharn, the fencing master. He teaches me because he must, but he does not believe in me, Lukien. You saw the way he spoke to me. He is frustrated and I do not blame him, because he knows I will not be able to kill the Great Rass.'

222

Lukien rose, studying the spear in his hand. It was a lithe weapon, heavy, flexible but far too weighty for Lahkali to wield. He was sure that was part of her difficulty.

'Eminence, what would happen if you did not kill the Great Rass?'

'What would happen? Everything would die! When the river turns to blood it feeds the land. We live off the land, Lukien. It gives us fish and waters our crops. We would not survive without the blood water.'

'And there is no one else that can slay this creature?' Lukien asked. 'Why must it be you? Why not Niharn or some other warrior? Why not an army of warriors, make sure it gets done right?'

'Because that it is not how it is done, Lukien. Only my bloodline may slay the Great Rass. That is the pact we have made with Sercin.'

'Sercin. Your god?'

'He is the one that sends us the Great Rass. He becomes the rass, but of course he cannot be killed. When the rass is slain it is only the body that dies. Sercin's soul returns to the sky.'

It was a fanciful, frustrating story, and Lukien didn't know if he should believe it. Clearly Lahkali believed it, though, and that was all that mattered. He turned to look out over the wall, toward the range of hills in the distance and the single, fabulous mountain rising above the rest.

'The home of Sercin,' he whispered. 'Eminence, how will you know when the Great Rass comes?'

Lahkali grew suspicious. 'Why?'

'Curiosity. Is there a certain date? How do you know how much time you have?'

'In a few more weeks the rains will come,' replied the girl. 'Then the river will start to swell. That's the time the Great Rass comes to the mountain. There is always light in the clouds around the mountain when the rass is there.'

'That's it? That's how you tell?'

'It has been seven years since the clouds around the mountain glowed, Lukien. They do not glow any other time. And it has been seven years since my father killed the last Great Rass. It is time for it to come again.'

With his thumb, Lukien tested the two points of the katath's forked head. 'Why are there two blades like this?'

'A rass has two hearts, Lukien. Side by side.'

'Ah! So to kill it with one blow . . .'

'One blow is all that should be used. To butcher the rass would be an insult to Sercin.'

'And one blow is probably all you'll get,' mused Lukien. He considered the task ahead of the girl, realizing it seemed hopeless. 'Once a rass strikes you it would be deadly. How can anyone survive it?'

'They do, Lukien,' Lahkali assured him. 'Even if they are wounded.

When the rass is dead the Eminence drinks the blood of the rass. That heals him.'

'Not him,' said Lukien with a grin. 'You, Eminence. So if you are hurt you drink the blood – what else?'

'There is nothing else. Once the rass is dead the river turns to blood. That is all.'

'I see.' Lukien studied the blades of the weapon, reminded of the serpent skins he had seen in Kadar's palace. 'Lahkali, do you remember that place I told you about across the desert? The one called Jador?'

'I remember,' said the girl. With her arms wrapped around her legs, she looked up inquisitively. 'Why?'

'Well, this might appall you, but in Jador the rass are not worshipped the way they are here. In Jador the rass are vicious. Maybe they're different from the ones you have here, I don't know, but they're not welcome in Jador. They're hunted.'

'Hunted? You mean killed?'

'That's right. They attack people where I come from. But I know a man named Kadar who knew how to kill them. He was the Kahan of Jador, the leader, like you are in Torlis. He had rass skulls and skins that he collected like trophies. Some of them were giant! I couldn't believe a single man could kill a something like that.'

'I can't believe a man *would* kill a rass like that,' said Lahkali.

'That's not the point. He was *able* to kill them. He had help from a creature called a kreel, a big lizard the Jadori ride like horses. The rass and kreel are mortal enemies.'

'So that made the difference,' Lahkali pointed out. 'Without this creature's help he would not have been able to kill a rass. Just like me, Lukien. Without my family's ability to control the rass, how can I kill one?'

'I don't know yet,' Lukien admitted. 'But if it's as important as you say, you have to find a way.'

'I have tried, Lukien! I practice every day with the katath . . .'

'Forget the katath. Or at least forget this one.' Lukien tossed the weapon aside. 'It's too large for you. Niharn should have told you that. You need a weapon built just for you, something light and quick.'

'Like the swords?'

'Maybe. I'm not sure yet, Eminence, but I've trained men all my life, and I know that anyone can learn to fight. They just need the right weapon. And confidence.'

'Confidence,' Lahkali groaned. 'No one has confidence in me, Lukien. Not even Karoshin, but he's too kind to show it. The other priests know I am powerless, and the warriors like Niharn think I'm too young and weak to face the Great Rass.'

'But you're planning on fighting the rass anyway,' said Lukien. 'I can see it in your eyes.'

'I don't care if I die,' said the young ruler. 'If that is what Sercin wishes, then so be it. I will not run from this. Niharn and all the others think that I will, but I will not.' Lahkali rested her chin back on her knees. 'I have been the Red Eminence since my father died a year ago. He had no other children, and no one knows why. I have no mother and I have almost no support in Torlis. All that I have is Karoshin. I trust him. He protects me.'

Lukien could not help but pity the girl. 'You're too young to bear so many burdens.'

'I'm young, yes,' said Lahkali. 'And alone.'

And lonely, thought Lukien. For a moment she reminded him of White-Eye. He thought of his promise to the blind kahan, and how he had pledged to protect her. It was why he had gone on this dangerous quest, to find the means to defend her and her people. Now, though, another young ruler needed his help.

'I'll teach you.'

She glanced up at him. 'What?'

'Lahkali, I'll teach you how to kill the Great Rass. That man Niharn has no faith in you. He can't teach you if he doesn't believe in you.'

Lahkali stared in disbelief. 'You? Why would you . . .' Her question trailed off. 'No. I know why. Lukien, Karoshin told you there could be no bargain. I cannot tell you where to find the Sword of Angels.'

'I know that,' said Lukien. 'I honestly do. But I'm here anyway, and while I'm here I can learn from you and your people. Maybe something will happen. Maybe I'll discover something about the sword that will help me find it. And even if nothing happens, I can repay you for your kindness.'

'Lukien, you are a foreigner. You have one eye . . .'

'I may not look like much but I know how to fight, Eminence. I didn't always have this amulet to keep me alive. I survived battles because of my skill, and I learned a lot of things that I can teach you.'

The girl got slowly to her feet, doubting his offer. 'I still have Niharn. He is a great fighter, too.'

'I saw his methods, Eminence. I'm not impressed. Anyone can flail at you with swords. I'm talking about changing your heart. If you let me, I can turn you into a warrior.'

His promise touched something in the girl. Hearing his bold words lit a fire in her eyes.

'What makes you want to help me, Lukien? I do not understand.'

For Lukien, the question had no answer. 'It's what I do, Eminence. Call it a curse.'

PART TWO

THE RIDDLE OF
THE SWORD

19

Alone on his weary horse, the last Royal Charger of Liiria rode into Nith. His name was Aric Glass, and like that long line of soldiers from his homeland he dressed in the uniform of a cavalryman, with black boots riding up his calves and a hat pulled down across his brow. The dirt of a thousand miles clung to his cape. Wind and rain had weathered young skin. Beneath his hat, dark, cow-licked hair hung in tendrils down his neck, but he kept his face clean-shaven, the way a good soldier should. Plagued with hunger, his body looked older than his twenty years. His eyes searched the valley warily, but he was not afraid. Like a vagabond with a begging bowl, he had been to the kings of the nations surrounding Liiria, asking for their aid and always being turned away. Finally, he had come to knock on Daralor's door.

Aric Glass stopped his horse on top of a small hill. Below him lay a village, quaint and pretty, and beyond the village stood a castle, the modest home of Prince Daralor. Daralor Eight Fingers they called him now, though Aric supposed he loathed that nickname. In the Principality of Nith, Daralor was the only man that really mattered, the lord of a small but fanatical army who guarded their land jealously. Having just come from Marn days ago, Aric knew why the Nithins shunned their neighbours. Like all the other rulers, the Marnan king had sent him away empty handed. Even Sithris of Farduke, a man with no love at all for Baron Glass, had refused to pledge support, choosing instead to wait and see what plans the Black Baron might have.

Aric spied the prince's castle, so small compared with all the others. In Marn, he had seen a palace with spires that reached into heaven, with so many rooms a man could lose himself in its labyrinthine halls. Yet still King Deborba had refused him, too fearful of Aric's father to even hint at support. Like Sithris in Farduke, King Deborba had been watching the goings-on in Reec, waiting for the bloodshed to begin.

Aric Glass knew the Reecians were fighters, but he had seen what his father and the Devil's Armour had done to Lukien, and he knew that

Raxor's men had little chance. In all the days since the library had fallen, Aric had spent his time wandering the lands around Liiria, begging kings to join his cause. And all the while rumours reached his ears about Liiria and Norvor, and about the great army his father had built to secure his kingdom. Aric missed his father. He missed that brief moment they had enjoyed together in Koth, before the armour had taken him. After years of estrangement, he had finally rediscovered the man who had bounced him on his knee.

But it had all ended too quickly.

As he sat upon his horse, Aric thought about his father, feeling like a little boy again. Once the library had fallen, he and the other survivors had fled, promising Lukien they would wait for him. That had been months ago, and but Aric had not lost faith in Lukien. Sure the Bronze Knight would someday return, he had kept his promise to Lukien, patiently waiting, always believing. When the night grew dark and cold, Aric believed, and when he was all alone in strange lands, penniless and hungry, Aric believed. He had believed in Lukien all through his father's mad rise to kingship, tracking the rumours that followed him from place to place, listening helplessly as Liiria fell ever more under the thumb of the demon in the armour.

In all those months, Aric had never once returned home to Koth. He had considered it, when he was desperate, wondering if perhaps he could reach his father and talk sense to the man he had once loved. But then he remembered Lukien, and how the knight had tried that same folly. They had battled, his father and Lukien, and Lukien had so effort-lessly been defeated, left to die in the middle of a muddy road. That's when Aric knew his father was lost, and that the old man needed to be defeated.

Somehow.

A breeze strirred along the hill, carrying to Aric the scent of lilacs. He had seen lilacs all through the valley of Nith, and the smell brought a forlorn smile to his face. Nith was certainly the most peaceful place Aric had seen in years, like a pleasant memory from his boyhood. He breathed deeply, reminded of the days when he was a child and Koth was strong and whole and all the worries of a little boy could be dispersed with just a word from a well-loved father. Those days were gone now, like the glory of Koth, and Aric Glass could only hold on to the memory of them. He was more than just a stranger in Nith. He was like a ghost from the past, the last man alive willing to wear the uniform of a Royal Charger.

Aric straightened his hat and brushed the dust from his sleeves. Prince Daralor might hang him for invading his tiny nation, but the thought of the gallows did not dissuade Aric. He had grown accustomed to threats. They had only hardened him. Past the pretty village with its taverns and flower boxes, the castle of Prince Daralor rose up from the green earth, blocking the sun with its single, stout tower. Shepperds guided their flocks along the tiered hillsides, and somewhere in a distant farm a cowbell rang. Aric imagined bread baking in the homesteads and the taste of fresh milk. Hunger made his stomach clench. He put a hand to his belly to silence the rumbling.

'Maybe later,' he told himself. If Prince Daralor was generous and didn't kill him on sight, he might at last have a decent meal. Then, down the hillside he rode, not quickly nor slowly, and not hiding from those in the village who might see him. At the bottom of the hill he found the road again, a winding dirt path that led toward the village, then forked. Guiding his horse onto the road, Aric ignored the village to his left and took the fork that led toward Daralor's castle. Children in the village spotted him and pointed. A handful of men gathered at the edge of the street to watch him. Aric ignored them, not turning to make eye contact. In Nith, strangers were a rare and troubling thing, and Daralor's people were not known for hospitality. Yet Aric did not flinch as he rode past the village, but rather sat tall atop his wearied mount, trotting undeterred toward the castle. Behind him, he heard the curious murmurs growing as the Nithins in the village gaped, forgetting their work. Ahead, Daralor's home rose up on its green tor, surrounded by a meadow of wild flowers instead of iron gates. At the entrance to the meadow the road widened considerably, paved with cobblestones. A lone sentry patrolled the road, stationed at the mouth of the meadow. Spear in hand, the sentry wore an emerald cape around his slight shoulders. His eyes blinked in disbelief as he saw Aric riding toward him.

'Halt,' said the young man, sounding as if he'd never issued the order before. His tongue darted out to nervously lick his lips. Crossing the spear over his person, he asked, 'Who are you?'

Aric Glass drew his horse to a stop in front of the soldier. 'A stranger,' he said. 'Here to see your prince.'

The throne room was immaculate. And empty. Aric Glass stared at the seat of Prince Daralor, standing vacant in the spartan chamber. Tall windows flooded the room with afternoon light. A pair of emerald-draped guards stood at the entrance. Standing alone before the throne, Aric felt his legs slowly growing numb. The throne before him was a simple thing, not at all like King Deborba's grand chair. Made of smooth white stone, the throne rested on a modest dais, shining dully in the dusty light. Twin lions had been carved into the armrests; the feet looked like bird claws. Behind the throne hung a tapestry. For nearly an hour Aric had stared at the tapestry and the battle it depicted. He recognized the flag of Marn, shown falling as a band of bloodied Nithins brought it down. The giant tapestry was the only remarkable thing in the chamber, and it seized Aric's attention while he waited for the prince.

His feet throbbing in his boots, Aric took off his hat, holding it respectfully in both hands before him. The guards who had escorted him into the throne room had said almost nothing, ordering him to wait before disappearing. He had told them his name and his business with Prince Daralor, and he had expected the tiny castle to fly into activity. Yet the castle remained quiet. Prince Daralor had not come to confront him, nor had anyone else of importance. Only the lowly guards in the emerald capes watched over him. Aric began to twitch uncomfortably. Though he was young, he was quickly learning the games that men of power liked to play. This one, he knew, was meant to unbalance him.

So Aric calmed himself, waiting patiently, studying the tapestry and doing his best to ignore his own exhaustion. Finally, after another half hour had past, he heard the sound of people approaching through the connecting hall, then turned to see the guards parting at the rounded entrance. A splendid looking man paused at the threshold for a moment, spied Aric with his brilliant blue eyes, then entered the chamber with an entourage of stoic advisors, heading purposefully for the throne. Aric felt his mouth go dry as Prince Daralor glided up the dais in his flowing garb of sapphire silk. A black leather belt wrapped his waist, buckled with a golden lion's head. Around his shoulders he wore the same emerald cape as his soldiers, though his was trimmed with fur and gold embroidery. Prince Daralor sat gracefully on his throne, flanked at once by his gaggle of advisors, all sharp-eyed men who fixed Aric with suspicious glares. The prince made himself comfortable, placing his hands on the armrests of his throne. At once Aric noticed the missing fingers of his right hand. The little pinky and ring finger were gone, terminating in stumps. The three remaining fingers drummed the lion's head of the armrest as Daralor took his measure of Aric.

Aric cleared his throat, then gave a little bow. 'Prince Daralor. Thank you for seeing me.'

The prince's youthful face remained unreadable. An advisor approached the throne to whisper in his ear. Daralor nodded. His good hand went to his chin thoughtfully, as if he had no idea what to make of the man who had dared to interrupt him.

'You have your father's brass,' he said finally. 'Every time a Liirian comes to Nith, there is trouble.'

'Your Grace—'

'No,' Daralor interrupted. 'Don't speak. Let me look at you.'

Aric straightened, allowing the prince to study him. Daralor's expression seemed distant, as if lost in thought.

'Your father has been a great menace,' said the prince at last. 'Not just to Liiria, but to us in Nith as well. Did you know he came through here? He was wearing his accursed armour.'

'No, Your Grace, I did not know that. I—'

'He's a single-minded man, your father. He could have easily gone around Nith but he must have been in a great hurry to reach Liiria. He killed one of my men in a tavern in the village. It was unprovoked murder.'

Aric didn't know what to say, or even if he should speak at all.

'Your Grace, I spent very little time with my father. We were defending Koth against Jazana Carr. My father came to join us.'

'And then betrayed you.'

Aric nodded. 'Yes.'

Prince Daralor looked quietly puzzled. 'I am wondering, Aric Glass, why in the world you have come here. Speak now. Tell me your story.'

'Your Grace, I have come for your help. Since the fall of Koth I have been to all the kings of the countries surrounding Liiria, asking them to aid us.'

'Us? Who are you referring to, Aric Glass?'

'The defenders of Koth, Your Grace. The ones who survived.'

Daralor held back a chuckle. 'But you've come here alone. Where are these others?'

'They are scattered,' Aric admitted. 'There were maybe three-hundred of us who survived the battle at Koth. None of us could remain in the city, so we left to find safety before Jazana Carr's mercenaries could hunt us down.'

'But only you have come here,' Daralor pointed out. 'Aric Glass, you are all alone. That tells me that the others are lost to you, that they want no part in your crusade. I'll ask you again – what are you doing here?'

'Your Grace, you must see the danger you're in. My father has made himself the King of Liiria, but he is not a man any more. He is possessed by a demon that knows no rest, and he is backed up by a woman with more gold then you can possibly imagine. I have told this to all the kings, but they all sent me away. They refuse to see the truth in what I'm saying.'

'So you're here to warn me, then?' asked Daralor with a smirk. 'Thank you for that.'

Aric felt the wind going out of his sails. 'Prince Daralor, I have come to beg your aid. I'm here to make you see the danger that's growing and to ask you to help fight it. Do you think that Nith is too small to interest my father? That he'll overlook you? He won't, because the demon that controls him will never let him rest. The demon thirsts for blood, and he doesn't care if it's Nithin blood or Liirian blood.'

'You've come a long way just to try and frighten me,' said Daralor. 'But I already know these things you've told me. I have kept my eye on your father, believe me, and I no more trust him or that whore that shares his bed than I would any devil. You've told me nothing new. And if Baron Glass and his armour should come to Nith, then we will fight him.'

'And you will lose, Your Grace, because you will not be enough. Your army is great, but small. If you wait for all the others to fall first, then there will be nothing to stand in my father's way. All of the kings, one by one, will be picked off, because none of you will stand together.'

'We are waiting,' said Daralor. 'We are cautious.'

'Yes,' said Aric with disgust. 'Waiting to see what happens with Reec. That's what all the kings have told me. They're all waiting. They're just going to sit back and watch the Reecians be slaughtered. And then what? Will you sit by and watch Marn fall?'

'Watch your tongue,' hissed one of the advisors. A fat man, he stepped forward and touched the throne. 'Prince Daralor, let us be done with this boy. His father is a butcher. Let's not waste our time.'

'You're wasting my time,' Aric answered back. He was fearless suddenly, possessed of a desperate strength. 'Maybe I'm the fool here. All of you are the same, everyone of you power mad kings. You don't care what happens to your neighbours, just so long as you're left alone. Well, Baron Glass and Jazana Carr won't leave you alone. Not any of you. That's my message, Prince Daralor. Mark it well.'

Aric turned and stormed toward the archway, to the gasps of Daralor's advisors. Before he reached the exit, however, the prince clapped his hands and the guards at the threshold crossed their halberds to stop him. Aric paused, then angrily turned back to the prince.

'You can kill the messenger but it won't change the truth.'

Prince Daralor laughed. 'You are an absurd boy. But Fate above you're spirited! Come here. We have not concluded.'

Surprised, Aric went back to his place before the throne, looking up at Prince Daralor in confusion. Daralor lost his humour quickly, his face growing serious.

'You are in Nith. Do you realize what that means? We do not make alliances. And we never allow foreign soldiers on our soil.' The Prince lifted his three-fingered hand, holding it out for Aric to see. 'Look at my hand. Do you know how this happened?'

'Yes,' said Aric, because everyone knew the story. 'King Akeela did that to you.'

'More precisely it was his henchman, Trager. But you are mostly right. We fought Akeela and his army because we would not allow them through our territory. That day, they butchered hundreds of my men. So forgive me if I don't seem overjoyed to see you, Aric Glass. Nithins are never happy to see Liirians.'

'It doesn't change what I've told you, Prince Daralor.'

'No,' agreed the prince. 'Everything you've spoken has been the truth. I'm not a fool, despite what you might think. I know what a danger your father is. But they say the Devil's Armour cannot be defeated. They say your father is indestructible. You cannot blame us for wanting to see how the Reecians fare against him in battle, for if these rumours are true . . .'

'They are true, Your Grace,' said Aric. 'I won't lie to you. It may be that men have no chance at all against the armour. But there is a way.'

Daralor leaned forward. 'What way?'

'A sword. A magical sword, I think. It's called the Sword of Angels, and it's said to be the only way to defeat the Devil's Armour.'

'I have never heard of such a sword.'

'Nor had I until just a few months ago. But the Bronze Knight Lukien has gone to quest for it. It's said to lie beyond the desert somewhere, in a kingdom of serpents.'

'A fanciful tale,' Daralor snorted.

'I believe it's more than that, Your Grace. I believe the Sword of Angels exists and that Lukien will find it. That's why all the others have disbanded. They're waiting for Lukien to return.'

'Or they've lost faith,' Daralor suggested. He waited for Aric's reaction. 'Hmm?'

'No,' said Aric. Then he shrugged. 'Or maybe.' Admitting the truth to Daralor was difficult. 'Some of them have lost faith, but it doesn't matter. I'll wait until Lukien returns with the sword, and if only the two of us have the courage to fight my father then so be it.'

'And what will you do? Kill your father? This is your *father*, Aric Glass. Am I to believe you hate him so much?'

'I loved my father once, Your Grace. But that thing on the throne of Liiria isn't my father. I'm doing this to save my father.'

Prince Daralor leaned back in his throne, considering Aric's words. The fat advisor who had asked for Aric's dismissal came forward again, but before he could speak the prince waved him off.

'You are a boy of great faith, to have undertaken this mission,' sighed Daralor. 'I am moved by you, Aric Glass.'

'Thank you, Your Grace,' said Aric, astonished.

'Tell me again – what did King Deborba say to you?'

'Very little,' Aric replied, recalling the arrogance of the Marnan king. 'He granted me an audience once he knew who I was, but mostly he just wanted to gloat. I think he likes what's happened to Liiria.'

'Of course he does. Deborba is a pig. That is why we have no use for Marnans. But Reecians are another story entirely. They are good people. Tell me what you've heard on that front.'

'The Reecians?' Aric shrugged. 'Not very much. They've placed an army on their border with Liiria, near the river Kryss. They're determined to defend themselves.'

Daralor nodded. 'We hear the same. But old King Raxor is not well. They say he is demented. I wonder if he is sharp enough still to avoid a war with Liiria and Norvor.' The prince put his head back against his throne and sighed. 'A brave man.' He looked at Aric. 'Have you gone to Reec yet?'

'No, Your Grace. It was easier for me to head southeast. I thought I would find more friends this way, but even Farduke turned me down.'

'Farduke,' Daralor scoffed. 'More fops and cowards. You should have gone to Reec. They would have listened to you.'

Aric smiled hopefully. 'I came to Nith instead, Your Grace.'

'But these others you've gone to – they will never join in this alliance you seek, not until they are threatened directly. Until Baron Glass and his mercenaries are at their doorstep, they won't lift a finger to help you, or to help Reec.'

'And you? What will you do, Your Grace?'

'We are Nithins. We are not afraid of anything. But we're not fools, Aric Glass. Even if the Bronze Knight finds this magic sword, we haven't the men to charge against Liiria. Not alone.'

'But if no one joins us . . .'

'The Reecians,' said Daralor. 'They are the only ones. They are the first ones to feel the threat of your father, and so they will accept our help if offered.'

Aric brightened. 'So you'll fight with them?'

'Not yet. Not until they need us. And they must ask for our help first. If you want to make this alliance, you must ask them.'

'You mean go to Reec?'

'Of course. Or you may wait here for the Bronze Knight to return. The choice is yours.'

'But Your Grace, you could march men to Reec now. Perhaps the show of force—'

'No. Any show of force will only provoke your father. We have heard that the armour has maddened him. He is suspicious and afraid.'

'Yes,' said Aric, knowing it was so. 'Then what?'

'Go to Reec, Aric Glass. Tell them that we of Nith are ready to stand with them. When the Bronze Knight returns, we will march with him into Liiria, and together we will battle Baron Glass and his Diamond Queen.'

Aric stood staring at Prince Daralor. 'Your Grace? You're really going to help?'

'You're young,' Daralor said with a laugh. 'It's not your fault you went to cowards first. But you're not in Deborba's throne room this time, boy. There are no cowards in Nith.' He put his hands together, rubbing the stumps of his missing fingers. 'Whenever my hand aches, I think about my unfinished business with Liiria.' He gave a sardonic smile. 'Do you understand me?'

Aric smiled. 'I think so, Your Grace.'

'Good. It's not vengeance, boy. Just a need to right some old wrongs, and do the world a favour at the same time. Now, you look hungry. Are you?'

'Starving, Your Grace.'

'Then eat, Aric Glass. Eat your fill and rest. You have a long road ahead of you to Reec.'

Aric went to the dais, then knelt before Prince Daralor. 'Thank you, Your Grace.' His voice crackled with relief. 'Thank you.'

Prince Daralor rose from his throne and stepped down off the dais, putting his maimed hand atop Aric's head. 'Liirians are brave, too,' he said, then walked slowly out of the chamber.

20

Jazana Carr looked into the freckled face of the child on her lap and smiled. Like all the children, she sat cross-legged on the grass of the yard, enjoying the sunlight of the long awaited Spring. In one hand Jazana balanced a storybook full of pictures she had salvaged from the ruins of the library. In the other hand she kept the little girl from bowing over. The girl with the red scraggly hair listened intently as Jazana read, as if she was the only child in the world and the twenty others in the yard had simply disappeared, leaving her alone to enjoy the Diamond Queen's attention. Wide-eyed, the girl rubbed her runny nose, staring at the hand-painted picture in the book, a fabulous, page-filling illustration of a dragon. Her sticky finger reached out to trace the creature, laughing in delight.

'Monster,' she declared.

The children in the yard waited for Jazana Carr to show them the page.

'That's right,' said Jazana. She held the book up for all the children to see. 'And what do we do with monsters?'

'Kill them!' chorused the children.

Jazana Carr proudly beamed. 'Good.'

She went on with her story, dramatically turning the pages, slowly telling of the dragon and the band of heroes sent to slay it. It was one of Jazana's favourite stories and she read it often to the orphans of Koth, reading it always in the same theatric voice. From the corner of her eye she watched the children, rapt with attention. Their bellies full from a meal in Lionkeep's kitchen, it was their minds and hearts that hungered now. There were hundreds of children like them in Koth, orphaned by the civil strife or abandoned by parents too desperate to keep them. Living in burnt-out husks of homes or in the city's elaborate sewers, Jazana had rescued them from the horrors of the streets, housing them in orphanages she built and staffed with her own great fortune. Too numerous to count, the orphans of Koth had gradually come to trust her, the queen who had conquered their country, and had been brought to Lionkeep in small groups like this one to feel Jazana's love.

'Then Barkin the Black snuck up on the sleeping dragon,' said Jazana. She held up the new page. 'Look!'

The children stared, barely breathing.

'And Barkin took out his sword and ran the dragon through!'

A boy in front shrieked, 'No!'

'Yes!' said Jazana. 'The dragon roared and roared, and Barkin the Black fell back against the cavern wall, frightened by what he had done.'

Jazana turned the page, and the red-haired girl in her lap began to cry. She pointed at the new picture, this one of a dead dragon.

'Poor monster,' said the little girl.

Jazana laughed. 'No, Anala, not poor monster. Bad monster! Don't you remember? He killed people.'

Little Anala chose not to be consoled, but rather turned her head away. 'Good dragon. Bad people.'

The boy in the front also lamented the dragon's death. At only five years old, he was full of questions. Raising his hand, he asked, 'Is there more?'

Jazana closed the book. 'No. That's how it ends.'

'Can you read another?' asked a dark-haired girl named Vivia. Jazana remembered her because of her contused face, abuse she had taken from a man who had put the six year-old to work. He was dead now, that man, dealt with by Jazana's swift justice.

'No more today,' said the queen, shooing Anala off her lap. 'It's a sunny day. Go and play now.'

Reluctantly the children got up from the grass, then quickly ran off across the lawn, playing under the watchful eyes of Jazana's guards. Jazana rose and stretched her aching back, smiling at the scene of the children against the backdrop of the apple orchard. The day was lovely, one of the best since Spring had come, and Jazana thrilled at the warm sun on her face. Slowly, she and Thorin had been rebuilding Koth. One at a time, merchants were returning and the old, ruined constructs were being repaired, returned to the glory they had enjoyed in Koth's heyday. It had taken enormous resources to make the city whole again and lure people back, but the diamonds from her Norvan mines had paid for the reconstruction, and Thorin's powerful glamour assured the populace that they were safe. For Jazana, she could not remember a time when she was happier. Thorin had been the perfect lover, attentive and kind to her even though troubles plagued him. And though Jazana suspected the demon in his armour of triggering his rages, he was always gentle with her, always forgetting his worries when he laid in her arms. She chose not to see the things others saw in Thorin, the way he obsessed over the library's reconstruction and the fabulous thinking machine. When she looked at him, she saw only the man she loved, imperfect but worthy of her loyalty.

Jazana watched as the children made teams and kicked a ball between each other, happily shouting on the sun-drenched lawn. She had become their saviour and they adored her, nuzzling in her lap as though she were their mother. Jazana had never produced her own children, a fact that had long plagued her, but now she no longer felt the need for offspring. The orphans of Koth were her children, just like the orphans of Norvor had been. Just as Thorin had promised her, they were bringing good to the world. She was glad she had stayed with him.

'My lady?'

Jazana turned from her day-dreaming, finding her man Garen approaching. The mercenary's look told her something good had happened.

'Garen?'

'My lady, I have news. Rodrik Varl has returned.'

'Rodrik?' Jazana's smile widened. 'When?'

'Just now, my lady, a few minutes ago. He's taking a meal inside. I told him I'd come find you.'

Jazana Carr nodded quickly. 'Look after them, will you?' she asked, gesturing to the children.

Garen blanched at her request. 'Uhm, I'm not really the one for this . . .'

'Oh, they're just children, Garen. Fate above!'

'Yes, my lady.' Garen sighed. 'Varl's in the kitchen.'

Famished from his long ride from Norvor, Rodrik Varl had gone straight for food upon arriving in Lionkeep. He had been gone from Koth for almost a month, and Jazana was anxious to see him. She was not surprised at all that her red-headed bodyguard had chosen food first over her, because he had an appetite like a horse and very little patience for children. Jazana hurried toward the kitchen, nearly gliding in her good mood. She had sent Rodrik to their homeland to find out about Elgan's rebellion, and she expected good news from him.

When she arrived in the kitchen, she found Rodrik still in his dusty riding coat, seated at the wooden cooking table hunched over a plate of chicken. His greasy hands and mouth picked at the bones, his tongue eager for every morsel. A pitcher of beer stood next to his plate without a tankard. As Jazana walked into view, Rodrik Varl sat up quickly, wiping chicken bits from his face with his sleeve.

'Jazana . . .'

Longing shined on his bearded face. His smile broke like a gentle wave. Jazana paused before stepping closer, admiring her handsome bodyguard. They had been too long apart and the emotion of their reunion charged them both.

'Were you so hungry you couldn't come to greet me first?'

Rodrik nodded. 'Yes.'

'I forgive you.' Jazana went to the soldier and kissed his ruddy cheek. 'I'm glad you're back.'

Varl nodded, offering his queen one of the uncomfortable chairs. 'Will you sit?'

With no staff around to bother them, Jazana took a chair opposite Varl, eager to hear his news. He offered her some of the beer from the pitcher.

'I can get you a tankard . . .'

'No,' said Jazana. 'Just talk to me.'

Varl pushed his plate away and sighed. 'All right.'

'I don't like your face, Rodrik. If you have something bad to tell me, say it quickly.'

'You haven't heard anything from Norvor, my lady?'

Jazana felt a flutter of panic. 'Not for weeks.'

'Not about Carlion?'

'Rodrik, tell me, damn you.'

Varl had to force himself to look at her. 'I can hardly say it. It's gone, Jazana. It's fallen.'

It took a moment for his words to reach her. Jazana stared at him. Her voice dropped to a gasp.

'What's fallen?'

'Carlion. Jazana, it's fallen to Elgan.'

Jazana opened her mouth to speak, not knowing what to say. 'No . . .'

'It's true. Elgan and his men killed Gondoir. They took the old castle three weeks ago.'

'And you had to eat before telling me this?' Jazana took his plate and flung it against the wall. 'You had to fill your big stomach first?' The queen stood up and slapped Varl hard across the mouth. 'How dare you.'

Varl sat very still, but his temples pulsed with rage. 'What could I have done? Garen told me you were with those children . . .'

'You could have told me you lost my capital!' Jazana railed. 'I sent you there to protect things!'

'I didn't lose it, it was lost when I got there. Three weeks ago, Jazana. That's how long Lord Gondoir's been dead.'

'And what about Manjek? That useless toad – couldn't he have helped?'

'Manjek and the others didn't move against Elgan because they don't have the men.' Varl finally got out of his chair, facing his irate queen. 'I told you that already, but you wouldn't listen.'

'But you could have helped . . .'

'I'm only one man!' Frustrated, Varl backed off. 'Jazana . . .' He put up his hands. 'I don't want this. I'm telling you what's been happening.

There are more loyalists around Carlion then any of us realized. They've heard that Lorn is still alive and they're waiting for him to return. They follow Elgan because he's one of them. He's the old rule. I don't think Gondoir even knew what was happening.'

'And what about the other cities? What about Rolga? What about Vicvar?'

'They're secure. For now. I don't think Elgan has any plans to move against them. He doesn't have that kind of reach, and he doesn't have the men to mount any kind of attack.'

'But the capital,' Jazana sputtered. 'He has the capital?' She put her hand on the table to steady herself against the unbelievable news. Not even a year ago, she had marched into Carlion, driving Lorn out of the city. The people had welcomed her as a saviour then. 'Why?' She looked at Varl desperately. 'Rodrik, why?'

'You know why, Jazana. I told you why months ago.' Varl pulled out a chair and guided his queen into it, hovering over her. 'I told you Norvor needed you. They needed to see you, to believe you haven't forgotten them.'

'I haven't forgotten them!'

'But you've taken all your fortune and spent it here in Liiria! Not in Norvor where the people need it. They think you've abandoned them, Jazana. And sometimes . . .'

The bodyguard stopped himself.

'What?' Jazana asked. 'Whatever you're thinking, say it.'

'Sometimes I think so, too.'

Varl's confession crushed Jazana. 'How can you say that? You! You of all people know my heart.'

'I know, my lady. I do,' said Varl. He pulled his chair close to Jazana's and sat down, leaning forward to confront her. 'But you've fallen under Thorin's spell. You don't see the truth about him.'

'What truth?' spat Jazana. 'You've been gone, Rodrik. You haven't seen all the good that Thorin's done.'

'I know that he's declared himself King. I heard about it in Norvor.'

'And the people follow him. They love him!'

'They're terrified of him! He's a—' Varl quickly stopped himself, glancing around. 'He's a madman, Jazana,' he whispered. 'The people all know it. Garen knows it, or haven't you asked him?'

'You're jealous,' Jazana sniffed. 'You've always been jealous of Thorin.'

'And you're blind. Because you love him you refuse to see the truth about him. He's bleeding Norvor to death, Jazana, just to protect Liiria. Just to rebuild that library of his. That's where he is right now, isn't he? I bet he's hardly left that place since I left here.'

Jazana had to look away. Everything he'd said was true, and too stinging for her to face. 'There are threats against Liiria. Thorin has to protect it.'

'You mean the Reecians?'

'That's right.'

'The ones on the border? The ones who haven't made a single move against Liiria for weeks?'

'How do you know they're not planning an invasion?' asked Jazana.

'Is that what Thorin believes?'

Jazana refused to look at him. 'It could be.'

'Or it could be that they're afraid of *us*. They're just protecting themselves, Jazana. It's the right thing to do.'

'Exactly,' said Jazana. 'It's the right thing to do. We have to protect ourselves, too. We didn't fight for Liiria to have it taken away from us.'

'And to hell with Norvor, is that it?' barked Varl.

'No! I haven't forgotten about Norvor. I never could.'

'Then prove it, Jazana,' Varl implored. 'Tell Thorin to send troops back with me to Norvor. Tell him to stop spending so much Norvan treasure in Liiria.'

'He will,' Jazana insisted. 'He's already told me that. Once he's dealt with Reec he'll go to Norvor himself and take care of Elgan. He's promised me that.'

'You're willing to wait?' Varl looked disgusted. 'You're afraid of him. You're afraid he'll leave you again.'

'That's enough,' said Jazana, getting out of her chair. 'I won't listen any more.'

'You won't listen? I just told you the capital fell! How can you ignore that?'

'I've heard you!' railed Jazana. 'But there's nothing I can do, not yet. First Reec, then Norvor. Thorin has promised me!'

'And you believe him?' Rodrik Varl looked at his queen in disbelief. 'Jazana, I never thought you could be this way. I never thought a man could make you so weak.'

Jazana had to stop herself from leaving. She closed her eyes, wondering what she could say to explain herself.

'Rodrik,' she sighed, 'I'm happy. For the first time in my life. Thorin loves me. He takes care of me. I've been taking care of myself for so long, I've forgotten what it's like to just be like a child.'

'I love you too, Jazana. You know that.'

Jazana nodded. 'Yes.'

'And I wouldn't lie to you just to get my way. Norvor needs its queen. Someone has to explain that to Thorin.'

'He won't listen to you,' warned Jazana. 'He listens only to the armour.'

'He would listen to you if you made him listen,' said Varl. 'But you won't do that, will you?'

Jazana thought for a moment, not wanting to admit the answer that came so quickly. Finally she said, 'No. I won't.'

Rodrik Varl, her loyal man, seemed profoundly hurt. He took his beret off the table, slapping it onto his head. 'Is Thorin at the library?'

'Don't . . .'

'Excuse me,' said Varl, pushing past his queen. 'I have business to attend.'

Jazana watched him impotently as he left. She sat herself down again in the empty kitchen, her good day ruined.

Baron Glass stared up at the painted ceiling, mesmerized. For nearly an hour he had studied it, loving its colours and intricacies, marvelling at the talent of the man who had created it. The scene Lucio had painted stretched across the vaulted ceiling, jumping the beams to continue unbroken on a series of panels, each one effortlessly blending with the others. Amid the torchlight of the giant chamber, Baron Glass could see the hundreds of tiny figures the artist had brought to life, some on horseback, others laying dead on the bloodied field while the racing river threaded through the landscape. The opposing armies of Liiria and Reec appeared as they had that long ago day, repeating the way that had clashed for ages, charging each others mounded defenses with snorting horses and wind tearing at the banners. On the furthest panel, the Reecian King sat atop a golden maned stallion, peering across the river as his soldiers stormed the Kryss. King Karis had been bold that day; Thorin remembered him perfectly, young and confident, prepared to prove himself through the blood of others. He had come to the river with two-thousand men, determined to seize the waterway. Thorin heard the shouts of the soldiers as they battered the defenders, his own Liirians, outnumbered but unafraid, waiting for reinforcements with their swords drawn.

It had been a great and bloody day. Thorin felt its memory stirring though his body. The distant sounds of workmen fell away as he stared up at the magnificent ceiling, lost in its complexity. He was like a shadow suddenly, barely moving in the darkened room, his armoured arm tingling with excitement. Through his eyes, the demon Kahldris studied the ceiling too. Thorin could feel the spirit's impression. Amid the noise of hammers ringing through the library, the man and his Akari were silent. Baron Glass let his gaze slip once again to a middle panel, where he himself had been painted on horseback. Like Karis of Reec, he was young again, with both arms made of flesh and thick hair sprouting from his head. His mouth opened wide with a shout, rallying his men. His sword pointed high and skyward.

Baron Glass smiled, pleased with the depiction of himself. Lucio had captured him perfectly. In one of the library's only undamaged chambers, Lucio had worked tirelessly for months, creating a gift for all of Liiria. He was an old man now but he had worked with vigour, speeding through the panels miraculously, helped by a team of talented youths who had come to the library with the master to rebuild its glory. Like other artisans, Lucio and his acolytes had heeded Thorin's call, eager to remake the library they had all so beloved. Now, seeing Lucio's masterwork, Thorin knew his efforts had not been wasted.

'It will be better than it ever was,' whispered Thorin. Pride swelled his chest. 'Just as I promised.'

So far, he had spent a large part of Jazana's fortune rebuilding the library, with still much left to do. It would take years to make the place over and repair the damage his own men had wrought, but Baron Glass was determined. Liiria needed the library. If she was ever to be great again, the symbol of Koth had to rise again. Some said he was obsessed, and Thorin supposed there was truth to their claims. But he knew that only obsessed men accomplished great things, and that men like Lucio shared his obsession. Seeing the ceiling, Thorin thrilled at what he had so far accomplished.

'We are great,' he said, his smile growing. His voice echoed in the giant room. Long ago emptied of its scrolls and manuscripts, the chamber magnified every tiny sound, even his own breath. Soon, the workmen could return the books to the chamber. And one day the library would once again call scholars from across the world.

You are proud? asked Kahldris.

Thorin nodded. 'I am.'

He was one with the Akari now. He flexed his fleshless, armoured arm to feel the connection. The rest of the Devil's Armour lay safely locked away in Lionkeep, but Baron Glass never removed the enchanted parts that made up his left arm. With them he was whole again, able to move the digits of his gauntlet as if real fingers filled the metal.

Then, Kahldris came to life beside him, shimmering in the dim chamber. Sometimes he came in armour, like the soldier he was in life. Most often though he came in the wizard he had been, the summoner who could commune with the dead, and that was how he appeared to Thorin now, in a simple shirt with flowing sleeves and breeches of silken fabric that made no sound when he moved. His translucent form glowed with unholy light, but the smile on his face comforted Thorin. His eyes burned with dark fire as he spied the ceiling. An ancient finger raised to trace the painted battle.

'I am reminded of my own days of war,' said the Akari. 'And how it was against the Jadori. These Reecians – they have plagued your people like the Jadori plagued my own. Now they come again to plague you.'

There was empathy in the demon's tone. Thorin considered his words, finding truth in them. He did not fear Kahldris the way he had once, and the spirit's presence in the room no longer made him stare in awe. Their alliance calmed Thorin.

'You should be proud,' said Kahldris. 'You have done much. You are king now. Men like Lucio have gathered to your flag. There are no rebellions inside Liiria. No one starves here.'

'Yes,' agreed Thorin.

'But remember – it can yet be taken from us,' the spirit reminded him. 'Not by the Reecians – they can never harm you.'

'I have not forgotten your brother, Kahldris.'

'When the boy comes . . .'

'When he comes he will help us,' said Thorin sharply. 'He will.'

So far, they had waited months for Gilwyn to come, and while they waited the catalogue machine lay dormant, collecting dust along its armatures and miles of metal rods. Even Kahldris with all his ancient knowledge had been unable to work the intricate tool, baffled by its arcane design. Still, the Akari brooded constantly about the thing he called 'the thinking machine,' sure that somehow it could tell him where his brother hid.

'Time is not our friend,' said Kahldris. His ghostly face grew drawn. 'The boy takes too long in coming here.'

'At least he is alive,' Thorin pointed out, relieved that Kahldris had once again been able to feel Gilwyn's presence in the world. For a time, the Akari had been unable to sense Gilwyn, even with all his strength. Now, though, Kahldris was sure Gilwyn was alive. Very faintly, he could feel the boy growing closer. 'And he's crippled, remember. He cannot travel quickly.'

Kahldris grinned at his host. 'Look at you. Your face changes when you speak of him. Like a proud father.'

'Why shouldn't I be proud of him? He comes to save me from you, demon.'

'That is what you think?'

Baron Glass regarded the image of Kahldris, wondering at his meaning. 'Is there another reason?'

'Do you think you should be saved from me?'

'I am strong enough to deal with you,' said Thorin confidently. 'Gilwyn worries because he loves me.'

The shimmering face of Kahldris darkened in disappointment. 'When the boy arrives he will tell you something. It is something you should have figured out yourself by now. He is not coming merely to help you resist me, but to have his vengeance on me.'

'Vengeance? For what?' Thorin looked demandingly at Kahldris. 'What have you done?'

'I have put the wheels in motion.'

'Tell me what you've done,' growled Thorin.

'I have struck at him,' said Kahldris, 'in the only way to make him move. At the girl he cares for.'

'What are you saying?' Thorin asked. 'Be clear, damn you!'

'The kahana, Baron Glass. The girl that Gilwyn loves.'

'White-Eye . . .' Thorin braced himself. 'What have you done to her?'

'I have taken her Akari,' said Kahldris. He did not flinch as he spoke. 'She is blind again.'

The words unbalanced Thorin. He stared mutely at the spirit, horrified. 'You what?'

'Be strong, Baron Glass,' Kahldris commanded. 'We have need of the boy and his skills. It was the only way to lure him here.'

'By attacking a girl?' Thorin hissed. 'When she's done nothing to you?'

'She is Jadori,' retorted Kahldris, folding his arms across his chest. 'That should be enough reason to harm her. But I did so for far better reasons, Baron Glass, and you must see the truth of that. I warned you not to be weak.'

'But to harm White-Eye . . .'

Thorin fell back, staggered by the news. For the first time in weeks, he felt a pang of regret.

'You are weakening, Baron . . .'

'No,' said Thorin. 'I am stronger than you think, demon. And a man who is strong does not blind little girls.' He looked away, disgusted with Kahldris and with himself for what the spirit had done. 'There could have been another way to get Gilwyn to help us. There must have been.'

Kahldris glided closer to him. 'You still don't understand, do you? To the world you left behind, I am a monster. Why? Because I do the ruthless things that must be done. In Kaliatha I was a madman because I wanted to save my people. Now your friends say I am evil, but I am the only one willing to help you rescue your country. Where were your friends when Liiria was suffering? Did they come to help you defend her?'

'No,' Thorin admitted. 'They did not.'

Kahldris' glowing face nodded. 'To rule is hard, Baron Glass, but it is what you wanted. I will teach you these things you need to know.'

Thorin gazed up at the ceiling. High above, he saw his past glories depicted in brilliant colours, but his heart sank at the news of White-Eye's maiming. Suddenly it was obvious to him why Gilwyn was heading north. Kahldris' brutality had lured him, not love.

'You've given me much already,' said Thorin. 'I am grateful to you, Kahldris.'

'I can give you much more,' said the Akari. 'But I hunger, Baron Glass.'

Thorin turned to him. He looked straight into the spirit's burning eyes and saw the bloodlust there.

'No.'

'I must feed to be strong,' Kahldris argued. 'To keep you strong.'

'I have seen you feed, Kahldris. It is nothing that I wish to see again.'

'Blood is life, Baron Glass, and life is what I have given you. I cannot go on without blood.'

'Why not? The Akari in the Eyes of God do not crave blood. Why are you so different?'

'Because my armour is a thing of war,' Kahldris thundered. 'And the Eyes of God are not indestructible. Why do you think no blade may nick you? You have wakened me from a great sleep, and now I must feed!'

'Quiet,' grumbled Thorin. 'We're not alone, remember.'

'The workmen cannot hear me because I do not wish for them to hear me,' said Kahldris. 'Hear me, Baron – the armour must drink if you wish to stay strong. It has been much too long since Nith.'

'Don't.' Thorin turned away, not wanting to be reminded of the man they'd murdered. 'You have told me too many things already today. Don't speak to me more. I don't want to hear your bad news.'

But Kahldris would not be ignored. He floated over to Thorin, wrapping his ethereal arm around the baron and putting his dead lips to his ear.

'Feed me, Baron,' he warned. 'Or watch your nation fall again.'

There was no escaping the demon. Everywhere Thorin turned, Kahldris moved to face him. At last Thorin put up his hands.

'Stop!'

Kahldris retreated, then smiled. 'Listen.' He cocked his ear toward the entrance. 'Someone nears.'

A moment later Kahldris vanished, leaving Thorin alone beneath the vaulted ceiling.

Rodrik Varl walked through the darkened corridors of the library, guided by the light of distant torches. It was an enormous structure, unsafe now due to the bombardment, but the workmen were busy in another wing entirely, leaving Varl to search for Glass alone. The smell of paint filled the air, making him light-headed. Up ahead, he saw the entrance to the great, round reading chamber glowing with orange light. His boots scraped quietly across the tiled floor, not wanting to alarm Glass but not wanting to surprise him, either. Along the walls of the corridor, haunting reminders of the library's glory stuck him by their absence, for where once grand portraits had hung there were now only faded spots of brick. The defenders of the library had sold almost everything of value in the place, all but the books which still lay everywhere in mammoth, unloved piles.

Varl had come to the library alone, without Jazana's blessing. He had waited until nightfall, unsure what he would say to the Black Baron. The library had been mostly deserted, but a few intrepid craftsmen still worked on the front façade, where the bombardment Varl himself had unleashed had been the hardest. Their progress had impressed Varl, who had stopped within the library's enormous entry hall to tell them so. With weary eyes the workmen nodded, not saying a word, then returned to work. Varl left them, sure of where he would find Baron Glass.

It had not been a secret that the great artist Lucio had come to Koth to paint a masterpiece. By the time Varl had left the city for Norvor, Lucio and his team had just arrived, eager to meet the challenge Baron Glass had laid before them. Though the carpenters and bricklayers worked out of fear, the great Lucio saw only the chance to create something grand, and that was why he had heeded Glass' call. The ancient artist had seen the turmoil of the last twenty years bring his beloved country to its knees. And had no love for Baron Glass, whom he had openly called a tyrant. Yet his love for Liiria empowered him enough to overcome his prejudices, and give one last gift to his homeland.

Varl was eager to see what Lucio had created, and he knew that Baron Glass would be there still, admiring Lucio's handiwork. As he neared the round chamber, Varl listened for any sound of Thorin, but the chamber up ahead was silent. He paused, noting the flickering torchlight. An ugly sense of fear twisted through him. Each time he saw Glass, the baron was different. Slowly, the Devil's Armour corroded more and more of the good man he had once been. Gathering his courage, Varl went to threshold of the chamber, swallowed instantly by its dark enormity. Overhead, the fresco created by Lucio and his novices came breathtakingly to life, animated by the light and smoke from the torches. Directly below the masterpiece, in the dead centre of the chamber, stood Glass. He had his back to Varl, but he slowly turned to face him, his armoured left arm glowing unnaturally with black light. The baron's appearance startled Varl. He seemed younger, full of vigour, his jaw strong and squared, his shoulders broader. The skin of his face stretched tight across his cheekbones, pulling out the wrinkles Varl knew had been there months before. Glass' eyes shone like gemstones. His hair looked lustrous. He reached out with his enchanted arms, using the magic fingers to beckon Varl inside.

'Come in and look,' said Glass. 'Isn't it marvelous?'

Varl let his eyes scan the ceiling as he stepped inside. It was indeed marvelous, depicting one of Liiria's many battles against Reec. Not a student of Liirian history, Varl could not determine the particulars, but he easily recognized the river Kryss and the flags of the opposing armies.

'That is me,' said Glass, pointing toward a panel directly overhead. 'At the Battle of Sandy Ridge. See me? With the sword?'

Varl squinted to better see the painted figure. 'You don't look much different these days, Baron.'

Glass smiled as if it had been meant as a compliment. 'Lucio has a miraculous talent. It's not done yet, but mostly. Some details to work on or some such nonsense. But I will unveil it soon so that the people can see.'

'The library is hardly safe enough for that,' argued Varl.

'And whose fault is that, eh?'

It was the old argument. Varl had never been sorry he'd attacked the library. His action had saved lives.

'Thorin, I have been to see Jazana,' Varl said, changing the subject. 'I have brought her news from Norvor.'

'Good news, I take it.'

'No, Thorin, not good news. Not at all.'

Thorin grunted and turned away. 'Bad news? I have had my fill of that today, Varl. I don't want to hear it.'

'But you must hear it,' said Varl, stalking after him. 'Norvor is in peril. Thorin, Carlion has fallen.'

Baron Glass stopped pacing. He lowered his head to his chest, muttered a curse, then looked up again.

'When?'

'Three weeks ago.'

'Elgan?'

Varl nodded. 'He and his men took the castle. Gondoir is dead.'

'And the others?'

'The others are safe. Elgan's men have not moved beyond Carlion. They're digging in, waiting for an attack. Manjek hasn't moved against him, and neither has Demortris. Rolga looks safe.'

'So it's quiet?'

'For now.' Varl looked sharply at the baron. 'But maybe not for long. Elgan and his men are waiting for Lorn to return. They know he's alive, Thorin. There are a lot more people loyal to Lorn the Wicked then we thought. And they think Jazana has abandoned them.'

Thorin turned his face away. 'Do they?'

'Yes. Because you've kept her here, in Liiria. And because you've taken all the diamonds, too, to rebuild Koth and the library.'

'I'm protecting Koth.' Glass looked up at the ceiling and sighed. 'Haven't you noticed? We have enemies.'

'The Reecians? They're on your border because they fear you, Thorin. They're the ones protecting themselves.'

'You're an idiot for thinking that, Varl. Look at this painting! Do you know how long we battled the Reecians for the river Kryss? It was ours! It was always ours until Akeela gave it away.'

'And made peace with Reec,' Varl argued.

'There is no peace with wolves,' said Thorin. 'Wolves are always hungry. The Reecians have the Kryss by right of treaty, yet still they mount on our borders? And you say that is because they are afraid?' The baron flexed his metal arm. 'Well, they should be afraid. Soon I will deal with them, and take the Kryss back for Liiria.'

Varl's jaw fell open. 'Another war? After all that's happened?'

'Yes!' barked Thorin. 'What would you have me do? Let them spit in my face? The Reecians are coming to fight us. There's no other reason for their buildup. But they do not know that Baron Glass is not an old man any more! And I have all the resources of Norvor to help me.'

'Yes, *our* resources,' said Varl. 'Norvan diamonds and Norvan blood. Didn't you hear what I said, Thorin? Carlion is gone!'

'It will be ours again,' said Thorin. 'Once I have taken apart Raxor and his pathetic son. Once the river Kryss is taken back for Liiria.'

'Jazana told me you'd say that,' said Varl. 'She believes you, Thorin. She loves you.'

Slowly Baron Glass turned his frightening face toward Varl. 'And you? Do you believe in me, Varl?'

'No.' Rodrik Varl stared into Thorin's fiery face. 'I think you're demented. And I don't think you care at all about Norvor. Oh, you love Jazana, I'm not denying that. But what you really want is her gold and diamonds, so you can feed your vanities.'

'Rodrik Varl, you have stones of steel to speak to me that way!' laughed Thorin. 'Good, I say. Be honest with me, I don't mind.' Thorin took a step closer, smiled, then quickly brought up his gauntlet, seizing Varl by the throat. 'And let me be honest with you.'

Varl felt the metal fingers closing off his windpipe. His hands went up to pry loose the grip. At once his face began to swell as the pressure built in his skull.

'I won't have you questioning me,' said Thorin softly. 'Do you hear? I won't have it.'

Varl worked desperately to pull off Thorin's grasp. The steely hand kept clamped around his throat. Speaking was impossible; only a wheeze issued from his throat.

'Stay out of my way, Rodrik,' Thorin warned. 'Liiria is mine, and so is Jazana. If you ever speak against me again I swear I will kill you.'

Thorin held Varl by the throat until the mercenary could no longer breathe. Then, with Varl's eyes rolling backward, he at last let go, watching as the man fell gasping to his knees. Varl coughed as he found his breath, coughing up spittle and massaging his aching neck. He looked up into Thorin's angry face and saw the mask of a madman.

'Go to Norvor and fight if you wish,' said Thorin. 'I have no use for you here. I keep you around only because Jazana cares for you. But take no one else with you. They're needed here.'

It took effort for Varl to rise to his feet. Checking his rage, he held back the insults dangling on his tongue, looking hatefully at Thorin. Killing him was impossible. He knew that even as his hand went to his dagger. Thorin saw his hand and shook his head.

'Don't,' he suggested.

Varl let his hand fall away. His breathing steadied. 'I can't stop you. I can't kill you and I can't stop you from ruining Norvor.'

'I don't intend to let Norvor fall to ruin, Rodrik. But I will save her in my own time.'

Varl hesitated, then slowly backed away. Thorin quickly turned his attention back to the ceiling. Instantly mesmerized, the baron seemed to quickly forget his row with Varl. Seeing this, Varl moved to the door, more certain than ever that Glass was insane.

Worse, Jazana was in danger. Her love for Glass had made her blind, and though he claimed to love her too, Varl could easily imagine his mood changing. Violently.

As he left the chamber, Varl decided he would not go back to Norvor. Jazana needed him, more than ever. He would stay with her, and if he could, protect her from her mad lover.

21

Princess Salina entered the garden and took a breath of the precious air. She had not been out of the palace in over five weeks, and she had counted each of the arduous days on a calendar made from beads. The day was perfect, full of sunlight and the scent of flowers. A gentle breeze stirred the palms along the cobblestone path. Behind her, her two ubiquitous bodyguards kept two paces back, watching her without saying a word. They had been with her constantly since her imprisonment began, escorting her everywhere she went within the palace, even standing outside the doors of her bedchamber when she slept. Her father had taken every precaution to keep her inside. Salina walked slowly along the path, relishing the light and sweet-smelling air. Around the bend, she could see the servants in their white jackets standing dutifully around her father's table. King Baralosus sat with his back toward the path, waiting for his daughter to arrive. They had not seen each other since her treachery had been discovered, and her father's summons surprised Salina. She supposed she should have been delighted by it, but she was not. Instead, Salina felt afraid.

Her weeks imprisoned in the palace had been interminable. At first, her father had not even allowed her to leave her chambers. Eventually he had softened on this, letting her move throughout the palace, but only with her bodyguards, and her contact with others was severely curtailed. She had learned quickly that her trusted handmaiden Nourah had been beaten and sent away for her part in Salina's deception, and Kamag the tavern owner had been publicly hung. Hearing this, Salina had sent word to her father, begging him to come to her, but Baralosus had ignored her pleas. At last, Salina had given up the idea of making amends with her father.

Until today.

Nervous, she padded along the walkway until she reached the bend, where she paused to see her father seated at the table. Tea and confections had been laid on the table and King Baralosus had already begun consuming them, sipping absently from an alabaster tea cup. Salina knew her father had heard her approach. She waited for him to greet her. At last he put down his tea cup.

'Come, Salina,' he ordered, not turning around.

Salina steadied herself, then stepped into his view. His eyes finally flicked toward her. He seemed older than he had just weeks ago. Thinner, too. His troubled expression filled with tension when he saw her.

'Sit down.'

A servant pulled out a chair for her, opposite her father. Another filled her cup with tea. When they were done Baralosus shooed them away.

'Go now,' he told them all.

The servants quietly dismissed themselves, leaving Salina and her father alone with her bodyguards. The king dismissed the soldiers as well, sending them back along the cobblestone path. An uneasy quiet filled the garden. Salina found it hard to look directly at her father. Baralosus remained silent, studying his daughter. His silence pained her.

'You sent for me,' she reminded him.

The king nodded. 'Are you angry?'

'No,' said Salina. Emotion took hold of her, making it hard to speak. 'I'm afraid.'

'You've had time to think now on what you did.'

'Yes,' said Salina.

'And?'

'I'm sorry, Father. I've always been sorry. I told you that.'

King Baralosus looked neither satisfied nor assured. 'It's time we spoke again, Salina. I can't keep you imprisoned forever. You're not a pet. But you need to understand things. Do you understand?'

'Why you're angry with me? Yes, Father, I understand. But I don't understand what you did to Nourah and Kamag. Nourah was innocent. And Kamag didn't deserve to die.'

'You are wrong on both accounts,' said Baralosus. 'Nourah knew that she was helping you, and what Kamag did was nothing less than treason. I cannot have that in my kingdom, Salina. Not ever.'

'Kamag was a good man. All he ever wanted was to help people. That's all I ever wanted, too.'

The king groaned. 'Then you don't understand, Salina. What you did was too big to keep secret. The whole kingdom knows about it. Not everyone is like you, you know. Many honour the old ways.'

'The dark ways, you mean,' said Salina bitterly. 'Is helping people so wrong?'

'You went behind my back, girl. You deceived me, and made me look a fool. You have no idea how much trouble you caused me. And yourself.' Leaning forward, Baralosus said, 'You were in danger, Salina. Even some of my advisors wanted you beaten in public.'

'What advisors?' Salina asked indignantly. 'Kailyr?'

'Yes, Kailyr. And others. You may think they're just foolish old men, but they know the heart of the people. It was not easy to quiet them, but I did.'

Her father's words shocked Salina. 'Would you ever do such a thing? Have me beaten in public like a dog?'

'Salina, you are but a girl,' said the king. Frustration reddened his face. 'And whether you honour our ways or not, this is a holy land. Girls do not disobey their fathers. Especially not my girls. Now, you have been trouble to me most of your life, but I overlooked it because I love you.' He smiled. 'You are my favourite. You've always known that, and you task me because of it.'

'Yes,' sulked Salina. 'Your favourite dog.'

'My favourite child,' corrected the king harshly. 'But that doesn't mean you may do whatever you wish. Being a girl child means you have a place that must be kept. When you step out of that place it is I who must defend what you've done. You went too far by helping those foreigners, Salina. You must understand that. I cannot go on protecting you.'

'No? You're my father. It is a father's job to protect his children, no matter what they do.'

'You are wrong, Salina. When you break the law, when you embarrass me or do things that threaten my rule, it is my place to punish you, not protect you.'

'So my imprisonment is to continue, then,' said Salina, looking down at her empty plate. 'You do not trust me.'

'You've given me no reason to trust you. That's what pains me most of all. I brought you here to discuss these things, but after five weeks you still don't see the wrongness of what you did.'

Salina said nothing. Her father saw her clearly – she didn't think her actions wrong. This time, though, she had sense enough not to argue. There were other plans being laid in her mind, plans she had not given up. And everything her father said convinced her of her rightness.

'Kailyr wanted me flogged?' she asked.

The king nodded. 'Yes. Publicly.'

'Just for helping those wretched northerners?'

'And for betraying Aztar. Or have you forgotten that?'

His words stung. 'No,' said Salina. 'I haven't forgotten.' She carefully steered the conversation. 'A month ago you told me you'd send men to Aztar. Did you, Father?'

Baralosus picked up his tea cup. 'I did.'

Salina tried to curb her excitement. 'He is well, then?'

'No.' Her father seemed distracted. He began toying with the confections on his plate. 'What you heard from the northern boy was true. Aztar was burned. The men I sent to see him say he suffers greatly.'

'Oh . . .'

The king picked up a tiny cake, looked at it, then put it down. She could tell he was mulling things over.

'Prince Aztar wants nothing to do with us,' he said. 'I offered him help, but he claims he has all that he needs. His camp is in the Eastern Skein, a day or so from here.' The king shrugged. 'He's close enough to come to Ganjor for food and supplies, but his people are content, or so he says.'

'His people?' Salina remembered what Gilwyn had told her. 'His followers are still with him?'

'Some. Aztar was always a remarkable man. People follow him because they love him, because he makes them believe. Whatever you think of the way I used him, I always respected him, Salina. I made a good bargain for you with him. Even you might have learned to love him.'

Salina glanced away. Her feelings for Aztar were a great mass of confusion. 'Has he asked about me, Father?'

'What Aztar wants from you no longer matters,' said the king sternly.

'But Father—'

'I won't have you speaking about him. Don't even think about him. You betrayed him, and that's all you need to remember.'

For Salina, it was impossible to forget.

'You're being unfair,' she told her father. 'I know what I did to Aztar. I know I was wrong. All I want now is to know if he asked about me.'

'There is no point to it,' said Baralosus. 'And that is the end.' His eyes narrowed. 'Do you understand?'

With great effort, Salina nodded.

'Good. Now, I have news for you.' The king brightened. 'You're not the only one who had time to think, daughter. I have considered what you've done and how well behaved you've been these past weeks, and since I have quieted the ones who want you punished, I think it's time you were freed from your curfew.'

'No more bodyguards?'

'No more guards. Let's make things the way they were, and forget about all the bad. Would you like that?'

'Yes,' said Salina, meaning it sincerely. 'I would.'

She wanted desperately to have her father's love again. Lying to him broke her heart.

'And you'll remember what we talked about today? About your place?'

'I won't forget, Father.' Salina smiled at him sadly. 'I know how important it is to you.'

Satisfied, King Baralosus called the servants back to the table, inviting his daughter to enjoy the confections. Salina chose a berry tart. Her father quickly launched into a story. Like they had throughout her girlhood,

Salina and her father shared private time in the garden, Baralosus telling unimportant tales, his daughter laughing politely at his jokes.

But Baralosus didn't know that things had changed, or how deeply he had hurt his daughter. She was grateful for his love, but Salina realized it had limits, mostly born of politics and pride. He was not the man of boundless protection she had imagined as a child.

Now, more than ever, she wanted to see Aztar.

22

Four days later, Salina left Ganjor with tears in her eyes.

In the days since making peace with her father, Salina very carefully laid her plans, going to the market and attending meals with a smile on her face, building her father's trust. She never spoke again of Aztar or her imprisonment within the palace, but instead kept her conversations girlish, speaking of things that pleased her father, like wearing the ceremonial mejkith and spinning silk the way her sisters did. By the time four days had past, Salina was sure she had convinced the king of her sincerity. Still, she had not expected her escape to go so easily, and as she rode her drowa though the burning Desert of Tears, she continually looked over her shoulder for pursuers.

Amazingly, none came after her.

For more than a day Salina had ridden alone, leaving behind Ganjor in the middle of the night after a clandestine meeting with Dahj. Unlike Kamag, the other player in their conspiracy to smuggle northerners to safety, Dahj had gone unnoticed by her father's spies. A man of the streets, Dahj had easily gone underground when he'd heard of Kamag's capture, blending into the populace the same as any peasant. And true to his word, Dahj had waited for Salina, just the way they had arranged should they ever be discovered. In a little hidden home on the poor side of the city, Dahj had hidden himself, loyally waiting for his princess to return.

Salina took the gaka Dahj had given her, wiping her perspiring face with a handful of the cloth. She looked like any other traveller now, her womanhood hidden by the folds of fabric. Dahj had given her everything she needed to cross the desert, even the enormous drowa, but he had so badly wanted her to stay.

'Come with me to Dreel,' he had pleaded with her. 'We'll be safe there.'

His words echoed in Salina's mind. The hot sun made her see mirages. It was noon now, the worst part of the day, and Dahj's plea seemed better than it had in the cool of the morning. For the first time since leaving

Ganjor, Salina felt afraid. Glancing over her shoulder, she saw the nothingness of sand, endless and forever. Her city had long since disappeared. Up ahead, the dunes of the desert shifted in the winds, blasting her face with sand. The drowa lopped across the desert, blinking against blowing dust. Overhead she watched the condors wheel.

'Soon,' she told herself.

The oasis Dahj had promised her was close. It had to be, because she had done just as he had advised, following the sun until it rose for three hours, then heading north toward the mountains that never seemed to grow closer. She knew the location of the Eastern Skein where Aztar and his camp waited, but she also knew that her father would send men after her, and they would head directly for Aztar. With twelve hours or more to beat them there, Dahj and worked out an alternate route for the princess. Hoping that the winds had buried her tracks, Salina followed Dahj's instructions perfectly, timing her progress with an hourglass. She could still see the distant mountains on the horizon. The stabbing sunlight forced her eyes into slivers. She had no map to guide her, only Dahj's instructions and his promise that the oasis did indeed await her.

'Soon.'

Leaving Ganjor had broken Salina's heart. Afraid but determined, she had stolen out of the city like a thief, looking back with tears in her eyes as Ganjor slowly faded away, the giant desert swallowing her whole. She knew her father would come after her, but strangely she no longer cared. He, too, had broken her heart. In his world, the world of men, she was nothing but a girl. All her life Salina had seen girls stoned to death in public for incomprehensible crimes, but she had never imagined she might be one of them someday.

'Why?' she asked herself. Remembering she was alone, she raised her face to the sky and shouted, 'For what?'

This time there were no tears, only a crushing frustration. Hearing her cry, the condors flew away. Confused, Salina licked her dry lips and squinted at the mountains. She had been awake for almost a day, and her body ached for rest. There would be water at the oasis, she knew, and shade for herself and the drowa. The enormous beast could go days without water, but not without rest. Already the drowa's pace seemed to be slower, weary from the long day in the sun. Salina fixed the gaka around her face, alarmed by the growing wind. The sand struck her face, forcing her to turn away. She fought to see past the blowing dust, desperate now to locate the oasis. The hour glass that hung from her belt was nearly empty again, a sign that – according to Dahj – she was very close.

'Hold on,' she told her drowa. 'Just hold on.'

Looking south, she saw the wind whip the dunes into a rolling cloud of dust. The cloud spiraled closer as the wind intensified. The sight startled Salina. Frightened, she urged her drowa on more quickly, wondering how best to avoid the coming storm. When she was younger, she had ridden with her father and his men through the desert many times, but they were always close enough to home to avoid the witch winds. Now she recalled the stories the men told, of how the winds could blind a man for hours or blast the skin from his bones. Panicked, Salina looked for a place – any place – to shield her. Suddenly, she wished she had gone north with Dahj.

'No!' she hissed, gritting her teeth. She had come this far, risking everything to reach Aztar. She would not be silenced by the wind. Determined, she took hold of the drowa's reins, tucked herself behind its hairy neck, and kicked her heels against its flanks. With a load shout, she drove the beast forward. Urged on by her cries, the drowa galloped across the sands. Salina kept her eyes as open as she could, searching desperately for shelter, a rock or stand of trees that could stave off the winds, but only the distant mountains were visible, too far away to be any help at all.

Then, through the swirling sand, Salina saw an apparition, blurred by the dust. The tops of trees peered up above tall rocks, bending as the wind pulled at their broad leaves. This time, Salina knew it was no mirage. Like a saviour from the storm, the oasis beckoned her.

'Thank Vala!'

Renewed, she raced toward the oasis, watching as it grew out of the storm, filling her vision with its rugged outline. Just as Dahj had described, the oasis was more than a mere watering hole. As Salina entered its outskirts, she at once noticed its scale, with looming rocks that could shield her from the wind and swaying palms erupting defiantly from the cracked earth. Salina quickly led her drowa toward the largest rock near the centre of the oasis, then paused the beast to look around. Behind her, the witch wind rolled inward, threatening her. She could hear its eerie shriek tearing at the dune. She studied the rocks and the trees, trying to determine the best place to hide. Nearby, a spring bubbled up from the stones, soaking the ground with muddy water. Spears of flowering plants blanketed the soil, but the birds that remained quickly fled as they sensed the coming storm.

Salina had little time to choose a refuge, settling on an outcropping of rock on the other side of the spring. She hurried her drowa toward it, not stopping for the beast to drink, then dismounting to guide the drowa by hand. With its reins tight in her fist, Salina examined the narrow gorge cut between the rock. It was dark but could accommodate them both, so she dragged the drowa toward it. The drowa, however, reared back in protest.

'Come on!' Salina urged, pulling on the reins. This time the drowa snapped back its powerful neck, wrenching free of her grasp and peddling backward out of the gorge. Cursing, Salina lunged for the reins again. 'No, you have to come!' she told the beast. 'Please!'

Ignoring the winds, the drowa wanted no part of the dark niche. Again it reared back, dragging Salina with it with an angry snort. Salina did her best to hold on, but the frightened animal shook off her efforts, bolting away toward the spring.

Salina tossed her hands in the air. 'You stupid . . .'

Once more, she went after the beast, trying to speak softly to it, cooing as she begged it to come. The drowa rolled its dark eyes at her, chewed its flabby cud, and turned away. Behind it, Salina watched as the witch wind churned closer. The leaves of the palms began snapping off in the breeze.

'You have to come!' she shouted. 'If you don't you'll die out here!'

Worse, all of her supplies were belted around the beast, most preciously her food and water. She took another step toward the drowa, inching closer, but when she was finally in reach and held out her hand, the drowa again bolted.

'You stubborn monster! You've got my food!'

Ignoring the princess, the drowa stayed out of reach, until at last Salina knew she had to give up. The wind began tearing at her hair and face, blinding her with the driving sand. Her ears rang with its fury. Hunching over, she tried one more run at the drowa, but the animal again sprinted off, this time all the way toward the edge of the oasis. Salina watched dreadfully as the wind grew over the drowa, darkening the sky. Panicked, the beast ran off, straight into the mouth of the storm. Instantly the witch wind caught the flailing drowa, lifting it and spinning it like a doll. Horrified, Salina fell back against the rocks, shocked by the wind's power. She heard the drowa's horrible cries as the wind, like a tidal wave, broke over the oasis, sweeping toward Salina. Instantly she lost sight of the drowa as the blackness of sand swallowed it. Salina dashed toward the narrow gorge. As the wind came alive at her back, she squeezed herself deeply into the niche, burrowing like a badger to escape the storm. Just beyond her sanctuary, the witch wind clawed at the rocks, screaming as it wound through the gorge. Salina put her hands to her ears and shut her eyes.

All around her, the earth shook, dropping bits of rock onto her head and driving her to her knees. She chanced to open her eyes, and saw beyond the niche the terrible darkness of a world without sun. Though she could go no deeper into the gorge, she pressed herself against the rocks, feeling the wind grab at her clothing. Bracing herself, Salina imagined that she was safe, back at home in Ganjor. Remarkably, it was the image of her father that calmed her.

'Father!' she cried over the wind. 'Why did you do this to me?' She felt a terrifying urge to cry, but refused the tears, biting down hard. 'I'm just a girl! It's not a crime!'

The wind answered with an irate howl. Salina stuck her face out into the tugging storm and cursed it.

'You won't stop me! You won't!'

Again the witch wind replied with a maddening shriek. Salina buried herself against the rocks. All she could do was wait, she knew, and determine to hold tight. She forgot about her drowa and the food she had packed and stopped wondering how she would ever make it to Aztar now. All she could do was grit her teeth and wait for the storm to pass.

Salina endured a dark eternity inside the gorge. And then, the winds abated.

Cautiously, she moved away from the rocks and saw sunlight returning to the oasis. Creeping out from her hiding spot, she surveyed the damage the storm had occasioned. All around her lay scattered leaves and broken fruit. The wind had tumbled rocks and flattened trees. Salina stepped out from the protection of the gorge and saw that the little spring still bubbled up fresh water, a sight that gladdened her heart until she saw her drowa.

It lay at the edge of the oasis, its body twisted and unmoving. The packs had been ripped from its back, taken by the wind. There was no chance it had survived, and Salina knew it. She stared at its battered carcass, trying to comprehend what it all really meant.

'Gone,' she whispered.

Her food, her blankets, even her transportation. Now she was stuck in the little oasis, her tracks erased, with no chance of rescue. The stupidity of what she had done struck her like a second storm.

'I'm trapped.'

The word terrified her. She glanced around, at once wondering what she might be able to salvage, but could find nothing of the things she had packed. Alone, defenseless, Salina slumped to her knees.

That night, Salina slept within the crack of the gorge, continually awoken by the sensation of insects on her skin. She had spent the rest of the daylight hours scouring the area around the oasis for bits of her belongings, lucky enough to find two of her food packs and a blanket that had miraculously been blown into a tree. With the blanket rolled like a pillow beneath her head, Salina waited for the morning to come, unsure how she would escape the oasis. Sleep came to her in brief little fits, ruined by worrisome dreams and the terrible realities she faced. With her drowa dead, she had only her legs to carry her to Aztar's camp in the Skein. Because she had taken a circuitous route to avoid any pursuers, she was further from Aztar's camp than she should have been, at least a full day's ride by drowa, and she had never heard of anyone successfully walking such a distance through the desert. The oasis provided water and some food, and these were good things, but Salina knew she could not remain forever in the little refuge. Sooner or later, she would have to leave.

She awoke the next morning to a sun already burning hot. As she emerged from her dark niche in the rocks, a salamander skittered past her hand. After a night spent with bugs, the lizard barely startled her. Driven by thirst, Salina went at once to the spring, kneeling down in the warm mud surrounding it. She saw her reflection in the cool water bubbling up from some miraculous source, and realizing how horrible she looked, gasped at the sight of herself. The storm had teased her hair in every direction and lines of dirt smudged her face. To Salina, she looked old, as if she'd been wandering the desert for decades. She spread her hands through the water to clear it of debris, then cupped a drink for herself, dribbling the water into her mouth. This she did again and again until the burning left her throat. Then, satisfied, she leaned back on her haunches and looked around. There was fruit to eat and the things she had managed to salvage from her packs, but fear had mostly banished her hunger, and all she really wanted was a drowa to take her home.

'Home.'

Could she go home any more? Or would her father hang her the way he had Kamag? It was her father's sternness that had driven her away, his absolute unwillingness to see the goodness in what she'd done. He had imprisoned her, but that wound had already healed. Rather, it was the deep cut of his willingness to side against her that hurt the most. And though Salina longed for the safety of the palace, she knew she could never return there. She had cast her lot with the desert, knowing all its many risks.

'I have to go on,' she told herself. 'Somehow.'

She looked south, the way the storm had come. There were no roads in the desert, but there were established passes that the kreel riders of Jador used in the days when they frequented Ganjor. The passes were mostly abandoned now, because the Jadori no longer came to Ganjor and because Aztar's war on the northerners had frightened others off. But to Salina, the southern routes seemed her only hope. If she could come across a caravan . . .

Her odds were nearly hopeless, but Princess Salina of Ganjor refused to cower. She could die in the oasis, long and slow, or take her chances in the Desert of Tears, where the condors might feast on her by nightfall. With only a sliver of hope to bolster her, Salina made her decision. She rose from the spring and made her preparations, first using the blanket as a sling to gather all the fruits she could. The fruits were full of water, she knew, enough to keep her alive. When she had filled the blanket full, she tied it like a sack. She then took the bags she had salvaged from her drowa, wondering if either of them could hold water. Emptying them both of their food, she dipped the first into the spring, filling it with water before lifting it up. The test failed at once as the leather bag quickly leaked its contents. The second bag, more sturdy then the first, fared better. The water held – mostly. Salina watched as it soaked the dark leather, saturating it then starting to drip slowly from the bottom.

'Good enough,' she determined, and cinched the bag closed. Finally, she gathered her things, tying them around the belt of her robes and closing the gaka around her face. Because it was still morning the sand remained cool. Salina knew she could travel three or four hours before the heat turned unbearable. How far could she get in that time? She grimaced at the question, for she knew that on foot she would not get far before the sun slowly roasted her.

'No fear,' she told herself. 'No fear . . .'

She took one last look at the oasis, then proceeded southwest across the sand, confidently walking away from the only refuge she would see for miles. She walked south because that's where the passes lay, and west because Aztar's camp was west, somewhere in the Skein. According to Dahj, the Skein was a full day's ride from the oasis, and there was no way of knowing where in that scrubby patch of tangled trees and rocky earth Aztar's camp was hidden. With her packs and blanket full of fruit wearing her down, Salina conserved her energy as she walked, avoiding soft spots in the sand as best she could to keep from getting bogged down. Luckily, she found the sand beneath her feet firm in places, enough to keep her going. And as she walked she scanned the horizon for witch winds, knowing that if another came she would not survive it.

After nearly an hour of walking, though, Salina was already exhausted. Her back ached from carrying her supplies. Her feet burned with blisters. The oasis had long ago disappeared amidst the dunes, and the mountains on the western horizon – the ones that never seemed to get closer – remained hopelessly out of reach. Salina paused to catch her breath, taking a fruit from her pack and biting into the sour citrus. The juice made her mouth pucker but quenched her thirst, and she quickly devoured the fruit before again setting off, tossing the rind over her shoulder. Up in the sky, the condors that had accompanied her the day before returned, eyeing her hungrily. Salina raised her hand in an obscene gesture.

'You won't eat me today,' she spat. 'Maybe tomorrow.'

She went on for an hour more, not stopping again, blindly ignoring the pain growing in her body. Beneath her gaka her face began to sweat, soaking the fabric of her wraps while the sunlight grew intensely on her back. The sand shimmered with the mirage-making light, dazzling her eyes. Salina kept her head down as she slogged through the sand. The minutes passed with tortuous silence, slowly slipping from one to another. Her unchanging surroundings began to madden her. Fear kept constantly at her heels, nipping at her, driving her on, and though she did her best to banish it she could not help but feel its grip tightening around her throat. When an hour more had passed and the sunshine became unbearable, she wished she had never left the oasis.

Exhausted, she dropped to her knees for a rest. From her knees she fell onto her back. The relentless light stuck her covered face, steaming through her closed eyelids and making her see spots. She licked her lips and felt how dry they were, already cracked, and with effort took the pack from her belt that had all along been dripping water. She had drunk from it slowly but continuously, and now she opened it fully, letting the water flood her mouth.

Don't, she told herself. *Not too much . . .*

But she could not stop herself. The delicious water felt so good, and she was so thirsty. Convincing herself it would leak out anyway, she finished the water in a glorious lapse of judgement. When it was empty, she left the leather bag at the side of her head, using it to cool her cheek.

'I won't make it,' she whispered.

She opened her eyes and saw the condors circling, spiraling closer. The horrible sight snapped her dread.

'No!'

With all her strength she rose from the sand and stood, steadied herself, and proceeded on again with renewed vigour. Her skin burned but it did not matter. Her feet screamed but she ignored them. Only the horizon kept her focus, and she nailed her eyes to it firmly, refusing to look away.

And then, amazingly, she saw something.

Salina kept walking, but slowly now. What looked like drowas moved across the vista. When she was sure there were people atop them, she stopped.

'Here!' she cried, her voice painful and hoarse. 'Look here!'

If they heard her, the distant riders paid no heed. Forgetting her exhaustion, Salina dropped her blanket full of fruit and ran toward them.

23

Their names were Fahlan and Rakaar, and in their dark gakas Salina had quickly realized what they were. She had seen Aztar's Voruni men come to the palace many times, and because they dressed so unmistakably Salina had not been surprised by their accents. When she had run to them, they took care of her. But when she questioned them, Fahlan and Rakaar were silent.

The two Voruni men – who the folks of Jador called Raiders – rode silently back toward Aztar's camp. They had given Salina food and water, invited her to rest before going on, then hoisted Salina onto the back of Fahlan's drowa for the long ride to the Skein. Still reeling from her good luck, Salina leaned against Fahlan's chest as they rode, her head wrapped carefully in her own white gaka. The two riders had somehow happened upon her, seemingly unsurprised when they found the princess, and when she told them her name and identity they had simply nodded, doing their best to avoid her queries. In their thick Voruni tongue – a language similar to Salina's own – they told her that they were indeed men of Aztar, loyalists to the wounded Tiger of the Desert, and that they would take her to see him.

Now, her body rested and a full waterskin at her side, Salina whiled away the hours as the bouncing motion of the drowa lulled her to sleep. After her agonizing ordeal in the desert she could hardly keep her eyes open, and was glad when she noticed the sun going down. Not much earlier, Rakaar, the more quiet of the silent duo, had commented that they would have to bed down in the desert for the night, but would arrive at the camp sometime the next morning. Perhaps it was her glee over being rescued, but Salina trusted the two riders implicitly, and the thought of sleeping near them barely made her anxious. She was safe now, on her way to Aztar by some unexplained miracle, and that was all that mattered.

As promised, the riders found a suitable place for them to spend the night, near one of the desert's occasional hillsides of rock. Scraggly brush and cacti sprouted from the sun-baked earth, the kind of hiding places adored by rass. As they dismounted, Salina looked around suspiciously, voicing her fears to the men. Both Fahlan and Rakaar laughed and patted their scimitars. Fahlan smiled at Salina as he stroked his oiled beard, bragging about how easy it would be for him to protect her.

'You are Salina of Ganjor,' said the desert man. 'If harm comes to you, what do you think Aztar would do to us?'

Salina saw her opening. So far, she had avoided discussing Aztar with her rescuers. 'It's been months since I have seen Aztar. How is he?'

Fahlan shrugged and began unpacking his things from the drowa's back. 'Well enough,' he said.

Salina looked to Rakaar, who had his back to her. He too seemed eager to avoid the subject.

'He was burned in the battle with Jador,' said Salina. 'I know. I heard of this in Ganjor. Please, I only want to know what's been happening with him.'

'You will see him soon, Princess,' said Rakaar without turning around. 'We should rest now.'

Frustrated, Salina asked no more questions, and her tight-lipped companions continued their silence as they made camp for the night. Rakaar made a fire to stave off the coming chill while Fahlan rolled out their bed blankets beneath a sky already popping with stars. Her body aching for sleep, Salina declined the food the men offered and went straight for her blanket, closing her eyes as dusk disappeared and the moon came out to light the sand. She awoke periodically, worried about rass or some other desert calamity, but mostly she slept, replenishing the strength she had lost through the day. By the time the first slivers of morning light crept over the dunes, Salina felt as through she had been gone for days. Groggy, she sat up and saw Fahlan already breaking camp.

'Good, you're awake,' he said with a smile that creased his bearded face. 'We should go.'

Leaving their comfortable camp behind, the trio once again mounted their drowas for the trip to the Skein. According to Fahlan, they were only hours away now, and Salina could see the landscape changing, becoming more like the Skein she had always imagined. Dried bushes curled up from the earth, spreading their dead tendrils toward the sun, and now there were creatures skittering across the rocks, mostly rodents chasing bugs and scorpions. Towering rocks studded the dunes, shaped by the wind into fearsome reliefs. Salina settled back against Fahlan to study them. While he drove the drowa, she relaxed and watched the world go from an endless sea of sand to a brooding hulk of stones and scrub.

They did not break at all that morning, instead eating and drinking from the backs of their mounts. Fahlan and Rakaar exchanged occasional conversations, mostly commenting how close they were coming to home. Salina began running her fingers through her hair to untangle it, wishing she could bathe or at least see a mirror. They were very near Aztar's camp now. The drowa picked up their pace, almost imperceptibly. The ground flattened and the dunes disappeared, and suddenly on the horizon Salina saw pavilions twinkling in the light, their red and white canopies like brightly coloured flags against the dreary backdrop.

'That is it, Princess,' declared Fahlan. 'That is home.'

Home for Fahlan was a collection of tents and wells dug into the ground. A handful of fires blazed in the camp, spiraling smoke into the air, and stunted olive trees poked up between the pavilions. Livestock roamed the areas surrounded the camp, and Salina could see women working at long tables and children playing around them. It was larger than she had thought, stretching a good distance between the rocks and groves of twisted flora. As they neared it, the drowas sensed the end of their long journey and guided them into camp. At once the women and children gathered to see them, calling to their men, and soon Salina was surrounded by excited Voruni. Fahlan and Rakaar spoke quickly to them, telling them that they had found the Princess walking in the desert. The speech between them rifled so quickly that Salina could barely understand, but it seemed to her that somehow they were expecting her. Before she could ask, a woman came out of the crowd and took hold of their drowa.

'Princess, welcome,' she said, smiling up at Salina. Her voice had a Ganjeese quality to it, like one who had spent a good deal of time the city. 'Come down, please.'

'I will help,' said Fahlan, who dismounted and then offered Salina a hand. Salina slid carefully off the drowa's back, standing in the centre of the growing throng. Rakaar dismounted as well, telling the people to give the princess some space. The woman with the Ganjeese tone took hold of Salina's hand.

'Look at you,' she said with a grin. 'You have been through so much!'

'Yes,' Salina agreed. She looked around for Aztar. Confused, she frowned. 'Why so many people?'

The woman smiled. 'My name is Harani. I will take care of you. Come, please . . .'

She tugged at Salina's hand, urging her to follow. Salina glanced at Fahlan.

'Go with her,' said Fahlan. 'She will look after you.'

'But Aztar . . .'

'The Master will see you, Princess. But you must rest first. Go with Harani. I promise, you will be safe.'

Before Salina could protest Fahlan and Rakaar both turned away from her, speaking quickly to the crowd as a group of boys hurriedly took away their tired drowas. Some of the group tried to follow Salina as Harani guided her away, but Harani hissed at them to keep back. A pretty child with dark hair began to cry. The girl's mother knelt to comfort her. Eager to be away from the crowd, Salina let Harani take her through the rows of pavilions, past the cooking fires and the livestock grazing on the scrub. Her mind reeled with questions, but the suddenness of everything had muted her.

'Here,' said Harani, approaching a small but pleasant looking pavilion near the edge of the camp. 'This is a quiet place for you.'

A flap of greyish fabric covered the entrance to the tent. Harani, who Salina guessed to be only slightly older than herself, pulled aside the flap and bid the princess to enter. Crossing the threshold, Salina noted the comfortable interior, which looked a good deal larger than the deceptive outline of the pavilion. A low bed with coloured pillows lay in one corner. Beside it sat a basin and golden pitcher. Incense burned in a tiny urn, and a low table rested in the centre of the tent, the kind desert people used for meals. The table reminded Salina how hungry she was. She drifted into the chamber, loving the cool darkness.

'Harani?'

The woman was quickly at her side. 'Yes, Princess?'

'I'm confused.'

Harani nodded. 'You are tired. And you must be hungry.' She gestured toward the bed. 'Rest. I will bring you food and clean clothes.'

'And a brush for my hair?'

'Yes,' laughed Harani. 'And a brush for your beautiful hair.'

Too tired to pursue the woman, Salina simply let her leave, then collapsed into the bed of silk pillows.

By the time Salina awoke, the sun had already gone down. Throughout her sleep she heard Harani enter the pavilion, speaking to her softly as she laid food on the table and fresh, clean clothing near her bedside. Salina vaguely remembered thanking the woman before falling back asleep, and Harani did not come again to disturb her. The bed and pillows cradled Salina as though she were an infant, and her battered body surrendered to its plush caress, drifting easily into unconsciousness. When at last her eyes fluttered open, Salina could see that the sunlight had gone. Outside the flap of the pavilion, there was only darkness. Unafraid, Salina walked slowly to the table and sat herself down. By this time she was ravenous, and did not wait for anyone to join her. She tore into the meat and bread and dates Harani had provided, washing it down with liberal cups of sweet-tasting wine and the best tasting water she'd ever had.

When she had finished her meal, Salina turned to the clothes Harani had provided. They were simple desert woman clothes, a white shirt with a vest and a long pleated skirt of wool to keep off the sand. Plain and unadorned, they were nevertheless clean and Salina was grateful to have them. Confident she would not be interrupted, Salina stripped off her own filthy garments, discarding them in a heap, and washed herself in the water from the pitcher, watching the filth of the road collect in the basin. After that she slipped on the fresh clothes. The transformation was immediate; she felt like a woman again. Just as Harani had promised, she had also left a brush for Salina, and a silver, hand-held mirror. Salina picked up the mirror, grimacing when she saw her reflection. The ordeal in the desert had sapped her face of moisture. Desperate to regain her looks, she started brushing her long black hair, pulling roughly through its tangles. Gradually, her unruly hair yielded to the brush, at last bringing a smile back to Salina's face. Relaxing, she sat back on her feet as she worked the brush, luxuriating in the simple pleasure. She barely noticed the sound of the tent flap opening.

'Harani, thank you,' she sighed, not turning around. 'I feel much better now.'

When the woman did not reply, Salina turned around to greet her. But what she saw in the threshold made the smile fall from her face. She knew who he was, though he said not a word. Though his face was scarred, she saw the familiar glint in his eyes. Prince Aztar had come a single pace inside and moved no further. His body had lost its lean, powerful look, ravaged by the fire that had seared his face and hands. His drab brown cloak hung down to his saddled feet, hiding the worst of his scars, and his dark hair curtained his face, falling into his penetrating eyes. His lips curled back unnaturally, his maimed skin tugging them backward. One missing eyebrow had been replaced by a knotted wound. He watched her, trying to smile, his gaze brightening as their eyes met. Salina let the brush and mirror drop from her hands. Slowly, she got to her feet.

'I can hardly believe it is you,' he said. 'That you would come here.'

His voice remained unmistakable. Untouched by the fire, it reminded Salina of music.

'I had to come,' she offered. She studied his face. 'Are you displeased?'

'No.'

They had never known each other well, yet every time they were together the same connection quickly ensued. Salina felt drawn to him, and the love she had always seen in his eyes was still there, fighting to come out. Aztar resisted it, however, and did not move.

'I wondered when you would come,' said Salina. 'I thought maybe in the morning.' She shrugged, not sure what to say. 'Your woman Harani, she looked after me. I've slept most of the day.'

Aztar looked at her as if in disbelief. 'What you did was beyond stupid, Salina. If my men had not found you—'

'I would have died. I know that. It was my chance to take.'

'But why? Why did you come here?'

'To see you,' Salina argued. 'To speak to you.' She felt her resolve shaking. 'Because I had to see you.'

'Because the boy came to you,' said Aztar. 'Gilwyn Toms. He made it safely?'

'And delivered your message, yes,' said Salina. 'He told me that you were still alive. And that you love me.'

Aztar did not look away. He nodded. 'I am glad. He was a remarkable boy. We tended to him, right here in this pavilion. Harani looked after him just as she has you. You sent him on his way?'

'He was heading north, back to Liiria,' said Salina. 'I don't really know why. I gave him all that I could to help him. I have not heard from him again.'

'And because you helped him, you were discovered,' said Aztar. 'I am sorry, Salina. I have worried about you.'

His apology surprised Salina. Like a knife through her heart, she remembered what had drawn her here.

'*You* are sorry? Aztar, I betrayed you. I know that Gilwyn told you what I did, helping the Jadori. How can you stand there and apologize to me? Look at—' Salina choked on her words, shattered by the sight of him. 'Look at you, Aztar. Look what I did to you.' She began to cry, and to hate herself for doing so. Even lost in the desert she hadn't cried. 'I did this to you. I ruined you. And I'm sorry . . .'

Prince Aztar at last inched closer. 'That is why you came here? To tell me this?'

'Yes,' Salina said, holding her hand to her face.

'Salina, you did not do this to me,' said Aztar. 'It was the will of Vala.'

'No, Aztar . . .'

'Yes. I'm the betrayer, not you. It was my love for you that made me betray Vala and fight against Jador. I prayed mightily, but I never confessed the truth to Vala. I made a deal with your father for you, Salina. I wanted to cleanse the desert but I wanted you even more. That's why Vala punished me.'

'No,' Salina argued. 'I know you believe this but it is not so.'

'It is!' Aztar thundered. 'The little woman of Jador – she made the fire come! She is Vala's favoured, not I. How can anyone command the sky without the help of Vala? She is blessed by him, and I tried to destroy her.'

'And that's why Vala burned you? Why he makes you suffer? Because you loved me?'

'Because my love for you led me to betray him,' said Aztar. He held up his burnt hands, hands that had once been beautiful. 'I will always have these to remind me of what I did, Salina. To you, it may look like a curse.

271

But it has opened my eyes to the truth, and for that I thank Vala every day.'

'Your burning was the magic of Jador, Aztar, nothing else. Gilwyn Toms explained this to me . . .'

'The boy said the same to me,' Aztar snorted dismissively. 'But he is not one of us. He doesn't know our ways, our beliefs. I have never seen the hand of Vala so clearly in anything before, Salina. And I accept what Vala has done to me – and why.'

Salina tried to argue, but her words began to fail. There was serenity in Aztar's eyes, the one thing she had never expected to find there. And there was love as well, just as plain as it had been before his maiming, when they had walked through her father's gardens and he had read his love poems to her. Had she loved him then? Did she love him now?

'I don't know what drew me here,' she told him softly. 'I just knew I had to come. I had to see you and tell you what I did. My father said you will not speak to him any longer. He said he sent men to you to help you, but you sent them away.'

'Your father is part of my sins,' said Aztar. 'I cannot see him any more, or take aid from him.'

'He told me you would not speak of me, either,' said Salina. She looked at him hopefully. 'And now I know why. You think I have corrupted you.'

'No,' said Aztar. He sighed and went to stand beside the table, still littered with Salina's supper. 'How can I make you understand this? Only I am to blame for what happened to me, Salina. I made the deal with your father. I attacked Jador. I thought the Jadori were filth polluting my desert. And I was pleased to make my bargain with your father.'

'Because you love me,' said Salina. 'You love me still. You told Gilwyn that you do.'

'I am not embarrassed by my love for you. It is what we do with our love that matters. I used mine to betray Vala and to attack those he protects.'

'But you're wrong, Aztar,' pleaded Salina. 'You have to see that. The Jadori are not chosen by Vala, and you were not condemned by him.'

'You say this? After protecting them?' Aztar turned away in frustration. 'Even you saw the worth of the Jadori, Salina. When I was harming and killing them, you protected them. And you were right to do so. Vala favours them.'

'He doesn't.'

'He must!' said Aztar, whirling to face her. 'You were not there, Salina. If you had felt the fire as I did, you would believe.'

The serenity on his face fled, replaced by a grieving pain. Salina went to him. Taking his hand, she guided him down onto the pillows by the table. Aztar relaxed at her touch, yielding to her, and together they sat staring at each other. Neither spoke for a time, and suddenly the insects buzzing outside the pavilion seemed the only sound. Both kept a determined eye on the other, sure of their positions. At last Aztar looked away, picking up a pomegranate from the table and rolling it in his palm.

'I am glad you came,' he said softly. 'Whatever else you might think of me, I want you to know that.'

Salina smiled. 'Thank you. And thank you for saving me.' She laughed at her good fortune. 'I could not have gone on much more without Fahlan and Rakaar. If they hadn't found me when they did, I think I would have died within the hour.'

'You would have gone on as far as you could,' said Aztar. He shook his head with a dark chuckle. 'All this to reach me. I'm honoured, Princess.'

'When my drowa died I thought I'd never reach you, Aztar. I tell you, I cannot believe my fortune! To be found in the desert . . .' She shrugged. 'The odds of it stagger me.'

Aztar's red lips tightened. He glanced away. 'Not so staggering.'

'Yes! I didn't even know where I was!'

'Salina, we must talk.'

Salina lost her smile. 'We are talking, Aztar.'

'No. We must talk about your father.' Aztar put the pomegranate down on the table, then flicked it away. Facing her, he said, 'What did you think your father would do? Just let you leave Ganjor?'

'My father? He will send men to come after me,' Salina admitted.

'He *has*, Salina. They arrived here yesterday.'

Salina reared back. Suddenly she understood. 'That's why Fahlan and Rakaar were in the desert. They were looking for me.'

'You should have made it here before your father's soldiers,' Aztar explained. 'When you didn't, I sent my own men out looking for you. Not just Fahlan and Rakaar but dozens of them. Fahlan and Rakaar went to the oasis because it seemed the sensible place to look.'

Salina grew alarmed. 'And where are these soldiers now?' she asked. 'Still here?'

'Still here and waiting for you.'

Like a noose tightening around her neck, Salina felt her breath catch. She studied Aztar's face, hoping for a clue to his intentions. His burned expression simply seemed troubled.

'I won't go back with them,' said Salina. 'Don't try to make me.'

'I want you to think about all of this, please. You need to be reasonable.'

'I can't be reasonable, and I can't go back,' Salina insisted. 'I knew what I was doing when I left Ganjor. It wasn't just to see you, but to escape my father.'

'Your father? Why? Because he made you stay in your rooms?'

'Because he killed the man who helped me,' said Salina. 'And a girl who knew almost nothing – my handmaiden – was flogged. He's of the old ways, Aztar.'

'Like me?'

Salina nodded, hating to admit it. 'Yes. Like you. His advisors have all spoken against me. Some of them wanted me flogged like my maiden. And my father agrees with them. He only stayed his hand because I'm his daughter. What kind of life is that for me, Aztar? I can't go back to it. I won't.'

'Salina, you are not thinking. It was madness for you to come here, and it would be madness for you to stay. You are your father's daughter. You—'

'Don't tell me that I'm being a silly girl, Aztar. I know I'm a girl. Does that mean I don't have rights? That I can be beaten like an animal whenever a man chooses?' Salina gave the prince a withering glare. 'Is that what you believe?'

'The old ways have served Ganjor well,' said Aztar.

'Maybe, but you're not Ganjeese. You're a Voruni. Do the Voruni beat their women?' Salina took his hand. 'Do you see what I'm asking you, Aztar? If you send me back, you send me to be beaten or worse.'

'Your father loves you. You are his favourite. He would not do such a thing.'

'He would, because he listens to his advisors and because it's what the people demand,' said Salina. 'I won't have it.'

'You cannot remain here,' argued Aztar. 'I have told you already – you are the cause of my betrayal. Vala does not want us to be together.'

Salina tried to stay calm. 'No, Aztar.'

'Yes! Damn you, yes!' Aztar got quickly to his feet and pointed toward the tent flap. 'Those men are in my camp. They know you're here and they're waiting for me to bring you to them, Salina. What shall I tell them? That the Princess of Ganjor won't go home because she's afraid of her father?'

'You may tell them anything you wish,' said Salina acidly. She got to her feet and faced Aztar's fury. 'If they take me, they'll do so by force, because I will not go willingly.'

'Then they will carry you! Not like a child, either, but like a trussed up chicken! Is that what you want?'

Salina felt her legs go weak. 'I want to stay here,' she said. 'With you.'

The anger fled from Aztar's face. 'I know,' he said wearily. 'But you cannot.'

'Because you believe in some mad curse? I know Vala too, Aztar. It was he who gave love to the world. If you love me, why would he condemn it?'

'I do not know,' said Aztar. 'But he has chosen the Jadori and given them his might. The little woman who leads them – she is his favoured, not me. And you are the reason I fought them, Salina. Not just to claim the desert but to claim you for my wife. My love for you is a corruption.'

'How can that be? How could love be such an evil?'

'I tell you again, I do not know,' said Aztar. He shuffled toward the exit, stopping short of it. 'I don't have all the answers, Salina. I'm not even sure why you came here. Was it just to escape your father? Or to apologize to me?' He paused, then stole a glance at her. 'Or was it love that brought you here?'

'Love,' said Salina, surprising herself. 'It must be.' She drifted closer and stood in his warmth. 'I didn't know it when I left. I only knew it when I was walking across the desert so I could see you again.'

The answer twisted his face with pain. 'Come with me,' he said, then went to the flap and held it aside for her.

Salina didn't have to ask where he was taking her. At first she hesitated. She made to speak but he held up a hand to silence her, urging her outside. The princess relented, stepping out into the cool night air. As she did, the woman Harani appeared. She had been sitting on a barrel near the tent, waiting attentively, and now rushed forward.

'Master?'

'Bring them, Harani,' ordered Aztar.

Harani blanched. 'They are waiting in their tent,' she said. 'A moment, Master.'

The young woman sped off, disappearing around one of the many pavilions. A handful of Aztar's men stood nearby, waiting for any order the prince might give. Among them were Fahlan and Rakaar. Salina's rescuers both gave her a mannered nod. The princess acknowledged them with a wan smile. It had been a long ride from Ganjor. Now it would be a long ride back.

Aztar said nothing as they waited, his eyes occasionally looking skyward at the stars, doing his best to avoid Salina. It was unthinkable to her that she should leave Aztar and return to her father to face his wrath, but now that the soldiers were coming she decided not to fight them. They would win easily, after all, and she was still a princess. Determined to keep her dignity, Salina waited solemnly for them to arrive.

It did not take long, for when Harani returned she led the soldiers into the moonlight. Salina recognized the pair at once. Jashien, the taller of the two, had been one of her chaperones during her month in the palace. The other, a young soldier named Zasif, often watched her from the shadows, admiring her the way many of the palace's young men did. Jashien sighed with relief when he saw his princess.

'Princess Salina, thank the heavens you are well! Your father has been insane with worry.' Jashien looked her up and down, smiling at her appearance. 'And you are well, just as they told us. Thank Vala.'

Salina was not at all surprised that her father had sent the smooth Jashien after her. He was a lean, quick-witted man, easy to like. And the young Zasif looked unthreatening, the kind of man you might send for a favour.

'Jashien, my father wants me back? You heard him say that?'

'Of course, my lady!' In his button down shirt and red silk sash, Jashien looked splendid, a true herald of the king. 'I thought I had done with the duty of protecting you. Too soon, I see. You can rest tonight, Princess. We'll set out in the morning. Your father must have news of you.'

'No,' said Aztar.

Salina looked at him, confused. So did Jashien.

'Prince Aztar?'

'You may go in the morning, but not with the princess. She is staying.'

'Aztar?' probed Salina.

'My lady, let Vala damn me for this, but I won't have you taken back to Ganjor to be paraded through the streets just to ease your father's politics.'

'What?' Jashien sputtered. He looked at his princess. 'My lady . . .'

'Aztar, I can stay with you?'

Aztar put up his hand, ignoring her question. He looked at the soldiers squarely. 'Go back to your king,' he ordered. 'Tell them that his daughter is safe and well, but that I will not be the one to return her to him. You may stay the night or longer, but when you return home it will just be the two of you.'

'Prince Aztar, I cannot accept that,' said Jashien. 'I was sent to bring back the king's daughter. And now . . . what? A ransom?'

'Nothing so despicable,' said Aztar. 'She has asked for sanctuary here, and I am granting it.'

'But you cannot! She belongs to the king!'

'I belong to no one, Jashien,' Salina fired back. 'I am my own woman. I make my own choices. You may tell *that* to my father.'

Jashien laughed. 'And you condone this? Really, Prince Aztar, think on what you're saying. This girl has no right to ask your aid. If you give it, you'll only invite the king's anger.'

Aztar nodded darkly. 'I know this.'

His answer vexed them all. Jashien frowned and looked at Salina. 'Princess . . .'

'You have my reply,' said Salina. She straightened, liberated by Aztar's protection. 'Go and tell my father what I've told you. Tell him that I am a free woman, with my own free will. Tell him that exactly.'

'You're making a mistake, Princess,' Jashien advised. 'Please don't do this.'

But Salina had already made up her mind. It was a decision she'd made weeks ago. She ordered her countrymen to go, and did not wait for them to respond. Instead she took Prince Aztar's scarred hand and led him back into the tent.

24

On the river, Lukien's troubles seemed a thousand miles away, and the towns and farms on the banks lulled him, calling to him to stay. Overhead, the sun was perfect, the way it always was in this part of the world, glistening off the blue water as the barge skimmed quietly across the river's placid surface. Past the rocky shore where a fishing village clung to the shoals, a range of blue-green mountains reached skyward, crowned with mist. Children gathered on the shore, wading into the river as the barge passed, announcing the Red Eminence of Torlis with a snapping scarlet flag. Wind tugged at the cloud-white sails, filling them with gentle strength. Below deck, unseen by Lukien and Lahkali's royal entourage, a team of oarsmen waited to paddle the barge when the wind failed. Lukien looked across the shore and waved at the shouting children. They had been at sail for most of the morning and the saline air invigorated him. The children waved back excitedly.

It was called a feruka, this royal boat they sailed, and though the river around Torlis teemed with them none were so grand as Lahkali's own. She was bigger than the others, a barge of royal bearing, her blonde wood oiled and shining, her stout masts groaning as the wind met the sails. On its top deck sat Lahkali's entourage, serious-looking men and their gilded wives, shielded from the sun by silk canopies. At the bow, a handful of sailors piloted the ship while most of their comrades remained below, out of sight.

Lahkali herself sat on a throne in the centre of the deck, raised above all the others. To Lukien, she looked radiant, dressed in a white gown that fell only to her knees, her neck and wrists decorated with gold jewelry. The old priest Karoshin sat at her right with a smile on his face, pointing out the landmarks on the bank while Lahkali nodded politely. To Lukien's great surprise she had reserved the seat at her left for him, a comfortable chair of tawny leather that was shorter than her own but still a good bit grander than those occupied by the others on deck. Among those others was Niharn, the fencing master. Seated near the stern of the barge, Niharn turned around just as Lukien thought of him. The two shared an insincere smile before the soldier looked away.

It had been nearly two weeks since Lukien had taken over Lahkali's training. In that time he had worked the girl to near exhaustion, always without Niharn's help. Lukien had asked nothing of Niharn, and he supposed the old master had taken umbrage at the slight, though he never dared show it. In truth, none of Lahkali's underlings had been impolite, allowing Lukien full reign over their young ruler to train her as he wished. So far, the process had been difficult, yielding mixed results. Lahkali had not yet worked with the katath, the forked weapon so favoured by her people. She had neither the size nor strength for the one she had been trying to use, and while the smiths of the palace made her one more suited to her stature, Lukien had trained her to fight using sticks instead.

Lukien stole a glance at Lahkali. The Eminence, distracted by Karoshin, did not notice. He smiled, pleased with her. Beneath the lines of her gown he could see the leanness of muscle taking shape, and he knew that behind her white gown, purple bruises had risen. Lahkali had taken some powerful blows during her training, but she had never once cried or broken down in defeat. More importantly, she had done everything he had asked of her, refusing to capitulate even when her body screamed for rest. And that was why he had granted her this day on the river. She had earned it.

Lukien turned fully around to see the bow of the vessel. There, among the sailors in their knotted-button shirts stood Jahan. His friend looked pensive, staring out toward the misty mountains, alone and ignored by the busy sailors. It had taken some convincing before Jahan had agreed to come along. Unlike Lukien, his simple friend from the village had yet to grow accustomed to Torlis or its fabulous palace. Lukien tried to get Jahan's attention, but the man with the ponytail remained lost in thought, his eyes locked on the riverbank. At last one of the sailors saw Lukien's gesture. Nudging Jahan, he pointed toward Lukien.

'*Come here,*' Lukien mouthed, waving his friend over. Jahan smiled and shook his head. Lukien frowned then waved more insistently. To this, Jahan simply turned away.

'He is welcome to sit here,' said Lahkali suddenly. She too had turned to see Jahan. 'He knows that, Lukien, yes?'

Lukien nodded. Except for Karoshin, the others on deck were mostly out of earshot, a blessing for which Lukien was grateful.

'He keeps to himself, your friend,' Karoshin commented. The old priest seemed perturbed. 'He does not like it here, I think.'

'We have tried to welcome him,' Lahkali reminded Karoshin. 'I do not know what else to do.'

'Let him be,' said Lukien. Jahan's behavior had troubled him for weeks, but he had already decided there was nothing to be done. He had asked Jahan, to help him train the young Eminence because Jahan was more like them and Lukien wanted the company. Jahan, however, had taken poorly to the city and its inhabitants.

'It is us,' said Lahkali. 'He fears us.'

'It is *you*, Lahkali,' said Karoshin. 'Forgive me for being so precise, but you saw his face when he met you.'

'Because I am a girl,' sighed Lahkali. 'It is always the same. Lukien, are you listening?'

'I am, Lahkali, but there is nothing I can do about it,' said Lukien tartly. He continued watching the shore, though by now they had passed the fishing village.

'You have spoken to him about this?' asked Karoshin.

Lukien tried to change the subject. 'Forget about it. It doesn't matter.'

'But it troubles you,' said Karoshin. 'And if you are troubled than you cannot do your best. And you must do your best to teach Lahkali. That is what troubles *me*, Lukien.'

Lukien avoided the priest's glare. 'I understand, Karoshin. I will do my best. You have my promise.'

'We trust you, Lukien,' said Lahkali.

Karoshin turned his probing attention back toward Jahan. 'He stays with you. He wants to go, that much is plain. Yet he remains.'

'He stays because he's loyal,' said Lukien.

'Loyal to you?'

'Yes.'

'For what reason? He's not your servant.'

'He is a friend,' said Lukien. 'Don't you have friends, Karoshin?'

'Very few! When I was younger I had friends. But now it takes much to make a friend of me. Come now, Lukien, the truth – why does Jahan stay with you?'

Annoyed, Lukien said, 'Because he thinks he owes me a debt. Because I saved his son from a crocodile, in the river near his home. A hooth, I think he called it.'

'Ah!' Karoshin exclaimed. 'I see.'

'No you don't, and don't look so smug about it.'

'A hooth?' Lahkali raised her eyebrows, impressed. 'Then what you did deserves his loyalty. A hooth could have killed you, Lukien.'

'No, my lady, it could not have, for I am cursed, you see.'

Lahkali nodded. 'Your amulet.'

'And the spirit that keeps me alive, yes. Tell me something – you have never asked me about my amulet, not since that first day. Why not?'

'Because it does not surprise us,' said Karoshin.

'It does not surprise you? A man that cannot die?' Lukien laughed. 'Now who needs to be truthful, Karoshin?'

'Karoshin means that we have our own thoughts on these things, Lukien. We have our own magics that we believe in.'

'Oh?'

Karoshin spoke before the girl could reply. 'There are always mysteries, Lukien. As a priest I can tell you that. Like the power of Sercin – to you, that is magic. To you, it is hard to believe that a god can become a snake.'

'I would believe anything after the things I've seen,' said Lukien.

The conversation wearied him. He returned to studying the shore. The feruka had drifted well past the villages now, entering a quiet part of the waterway where the shore was marked by broad-leafed trees and dense grass. Dark hills rambled among the groves and tangled vines. The water licked laconically at the muddy bank. Intrigued, Lukien decided to ask where they had drifted. Pointing toward the hills, he asked, 'What is this place? It looks different from the rest of the bank.'

'This is Amchan,' said Lahkali. 'A wild place.'

The crowd on deck came to a hush, enchanted by the calls of wild things issuing from the shore. The women sidled closer to their men.

'Amchan. Does that have a meaning?'

'Amchan is an ancient place,'said Lahkali. 'No men live here. That is what the word means to us – the wild place.'

Lukien leaned forward in his chair. 'I can hear them, the wild things. What lives there? Birds?'

'Birds and everything else,' said Karoshin. 'When I was a boy, I came here to hunt and to see the rass. They are all through these woods.'

'Rass? Like the Great Rass?' asked Lukien.

'No, the Great Rass is special,' said the priest. 'The Great Rass is unlike any other. But yes, there are rass here of every kind and colour. They thrive here because there are not men to frighten them.'

Lukien laughed. 'Frighten them!'

'Oh yes, that's right,' said Karoshin foxily. 'I had forgotten that men where you come from fear the rass. But here the rass are revered and keep to themselves, mostly. They are wise enough to avoid people.'

'Not like the dumb ones back home, eh? Thanks, but I'll go on fearing them if you don't mind.'

'Should you fear them? Is that what you want to teach Lahkali?'

'Call it respect, then,' said Lukien.

'She must slay the Great Rass, not run from it.'

Lukien rolled his eyes. 'You know what I mean. You know what she's up against.'

Lahkali, who was in the middle of their argument, held up both hands. 'Enough now. Karoshin, Lukien knows what he must do to teach me.'

'That's right,' said Lukien, though truthfully he was not quite sure. Fighting a rass wasn't like fighting a man or even an army. He watched Amchan thoughtfully as its groves drifted by, wondering just how he could ever teach Lahkali to slay such a monster.

'When will you teach me the katath, Lukien?'

Lukien looked up at the girl. 'What's that?'

'The katath! You haven't even started teaching me to use it. You won't even let me touch it.'

'Oh, the katath.' Lukien smiled to taunt her. 'There's time for the katath.'

'Yes, but when?'

'Soon, my lady.'

'How soon?'

Lukien shrugged. 'The katath Niharn was using to teach you was too large.'

'So? We can make another! I am tired of training with sticks, Lukien.'

'Sticks are weapons, too, Eminence. The katath is just a stick with a knife tied to it.'

Lahkali grew flustered by his evasiveness. She said sternly, 'The clouds around the mountains will thunder soon, Lukien. When they do the Great Rass will come.'

Karoshin added, 'She needs to be ready, Lukien.'

'She will be,' said Lukien. 'Soon.'

By late afternoon, the feruka had berthed near a muddy beach of palm trees and sun-baked rocks. Far from the villages they had passed on their way, the beach contained a small, pretty harbour off-limits to fishermen and the other peasants of the riverland. Instead of modest homes, a plain but impressive home had been built near the shore, a sort of retreat for the Red Eminence and her royal family, springing up out of the green grasses and surrounded by swaying trees. Tonight, according to Lahkali, they would all spend the evening at the tiny palace, where servants had spent the day preparing for their arrival.

Lahkali exalted in the sight of the retreat. Far from the rigours of Torlis, here she could escape most of the advisors who plagued her, enjoying the quiet of the river and its shore. As usual, she was first to depart the feruka, excusing herself from Lukien and telling him that the staff of the palace would see to his needs. Lahkali was anxious to get away, and after greeting her servants she escaped from Karoshin and Lukien, heading toward the back of the grand home where few ever ventured. Here, a tributary of the river diverted into a sandy stand of trees and rocky outcroppings, where newborn fish gathered in a shallow pond. Whenever she came to the palace on the river, Lahkali always went to the pond to see the fish and tadpoles. This time, though, she discovered something else.

Jahan did not hear the Eminence approach. Instead he stared into Lahkali's pond, oblivious to her. Lahkali paused behind a palm tree, her footfalls hidden by the sand beneath her feet. Jahan looked contemplative, and grossly out of place. While the others had gone to feast, he stood alone. For a moment Lahkali considered leaving him, sure that he would prefer the solitude. But then she remembered her conversation earlier with Lukien, and the things the knight had said about Jahan. She watched him, intrigued by him, wondering what had drawn him to the pond, away from everyone else, even Lukien, his friend. He was an enigma to Lahkali, this simple man from an unnamed village, with peasant ways that delighted some and invited scorn from others. The way the sunlight dappled his face flattered his kind features. In his long, tied-up tail of hair, Lahkali decided he was handsome.

Jahan knelt down next to the pond and began speaking, not loudly or clearly enough for her to hear. Was he addressing the fish, she wondered? She inched closer, revealing herself from her hiding place, trying better to discern his words. So far, Lahkali had led a sheltered life. Despite being the great 'Red Eminence,' she was but a youngster and well aware of her short-comings, and she had never ventured far enough from home to get to know the many villages like Jahan's that dotted the countryside. Jahan continued speaking, then finally dipped a hand into the water, cupping a single tadpole. The creature wringled out of his watery palm and splashed back into the pond. Jahan laughed with delight.

'Hello?' Lahkali ventured.

Startled, Jahan jumped to his feet. He blanched when he saw the Eminence.

'Jahan, it is all right,' she told him, careful to speak softly and slowly. Their dialects were nearly the same, but without Lukien's odd magic to translate she was unsure they would understand each other. 'Do you hear, Jahan? It is all right.'

'Yes, Eminence,' Jahan replied. He wiped his wet hands on his pants. 'I will leave . . .'

'No, it's fine,' said Lahkali quickly. 'This is a good place to come and think.' She went to him, smiling to put him at ease. 'You can eat with the others, you know. You do not have to stay here alone.'

'Thank you, yes, I know this,' said Jahan. 'Later, maybe, I will eat.' His eyes shifted uncertainly.

'So you came to be alone,' Lahkali ventured. 'Like me.'

Jahan nodded. 'Yes.'

His silence made her awkward. 'They are safe here,' she said, looking down into the pool where the tadpoles played. 'That's why they come, too, to get away from the big fish. You and I are not big fish, either. Maybe that is why we both found this place.'

'No, Eminence, you are a great fish. The greatest fish.'

'But I am a girl,' she reminded him. 'How can a girl be a great fish?'

Jahan puzzled over the question. 'I do not know. But you are the Red Eminence.'

'But not what you expected?'

'No,' Jahan admitted. His brow wrinkled as he worked the problem. 'None of this is what I expected. You are all just . . . *people.*'

Lahkali laughed. 'Yes.' She dipped her hand into the water the way she had seen him do. It felt cool on her painted fingers. 'And I can't control the rass the way my father could or his father before him. Maybe that's what it means to be a girl. To be weak.'

'No, Eminence, do not say so. If my wife heard those words she would scold you!'

'You are married?' asked the girl.

'To Kifuv. To the greatest wife in my village.' Jahan flushed with pride. 'Kifuv let me come to Torlis to meet you. She made me promise to tell her about everything I see here.'

'This is a great journey for you, isn't it?' asked Lahkali. She stood to face him. 'Lukien told me this about you, that you came to meet the Red Eminence and to see Torlis for yourself.'

Jahan seemed embarrassed. 'This is true, Eminence.'

'And you came to protect Lukien, because you owe him a debt.'

'Also true.'

Lahkali manoeuvreed toward a palm tree, where she leaned against its peeling bark. They were alone, the two of them, presenting the perfect chance to get her questions answered. As though waiting to be dismissed, Jahan kept his eyes to the ground.

'You are welcome here,' said Lahkali. 'You must know that by now. Even if I am not what you wanted to find in Torlis.'

'Yes, Eminence. Thank you.'

'And Lukien needs you. You trouble him with your silence. He is a stranger here, just like yourself.'

'He needs my help to find the sword. I have promised him that.'

'That is good,' said Lahkali gently. 'But it is too much for him to have to worry about both of us, Jahan. You must be strong for him. Can you do that?'

Jahan finally straightened. 'I can. But sometimes I hear my village calling. Sometimes I want to go back to them.'

His loneliness struck Lahkali. 'I understand. I miss my family, too. My father mostly. But we both have things that we must do, yes?'

Jahan nodded. 'Yes.'

He turned from her and went back to staring into the water. The still pond replied with a wavy reflection. Curious, Lahkali followed him. She knelt down next to the pond and looked at her own reflection. The two of them stared. He was not so different from her, Lahkali supposed. They were both outsiders, surrounded by people who thought little of them.

'Look at our faces,' she said. 'See how alike we are? Is that what surprises you so much, Jahan?'

Jahan studied his reflection in the water, then shifted his gaze toward the girl's. Lahkali watched his brow knit.

'In my village, we talk about Torlis like it is a place of gods,' said Jahan. 'We believe the Red Eminence can do anything. I told Lukien to come and speak to you. I told him you would know where to find his sword. And you do know. You just won't tell him.'

'I'm sorry,' said Lahkali. 'I cannot. That's why you're here, Jahan – to help him.'

'Yes,' said Jahan. His tone grew determined. 'You are right.'

'He is a quiet one, Lukien. It is hard to know his heart. But he speaks to you, Jahan. You must be a friend to him.'

Jahan nodded. 'Lukien needs a friend, yes. He mourns.'

'Mourns?'

'For a woman. A beloved.'

Lahkali leaned back on her heels. 'Tell me about this.'

Jahan shrugged. 'I do not know much of it. She was his woman, and now she is gone.'

'Dead?'

'Dead, yes. She has gone to the next world.' Jahan retreated a little. 'Do you have another world, Eminence? Is that what you believe?'

'Of course,' said Lahkali. 'It is only Lukien and his kind that do not seem to believe.'

'Lukien believes. He did not always believe, but now he does. He has spoken to his beloved. She has come to him.'

'Really? How?'

'Like a spirit,' said Jahan. 'That is what he told me.'

Lahkali rose. She had not known that anyone beyond Torlis could speak to the dead. She puzzled over this, wondering how much more Jahan knew.

'That is why Lukien is so dark?' she probed. 'Because he mourns?'

'Yes, Eminence. I have thought about it, and I think he hates the amulet that keeps him alive. He would rather die, I think, and be with his beloved.'

A frown crossed the girl's face. At last, things were making sense. 'That's why he saved your child from the hooth . . .'

'No, Eminence,' Jahan insisted. 'Lukien is brave. He was not afraid of the hooth.'

'You're right, Jahan,' said Lahkali darkly. 'He's not afraid of anything.'

A man who wished for death wouldn't be, Lahkali supposed. Saddened, she knelt again in the damp sand, watching as the tiny fish darted through the water. Jahan had been more enlightening than she'd intended. How had Lukien spoken to his beloved? She was dead, and only the people of Torlis could speak to the dead.

That was the one great gift Malator had given them.

25

Aliz Nok lived on a busy street, but he was mostly forgotten by the people of Torlis. For five decades he had remained in the tiny house with the shop at the back, even after the death of his wife. He worked in solitude, without helpers of any kind, seeing only those few customers who came to his shop to sharpen their knives or reminisce about the old days. At nearly seventy, Aliz Nok was the oldest blade maker in Torlis, a skill that had long ago given way to quicker, modern methods, leaving Aliz Nok's quaint shop quiet, the hearth and hammers rarely used.

In his youth, Aliz Nok had been renowned, forging blades for the royal family and its many generals, patiently working long nights in his smoky shop while wide-eyed apprentices watched and learned. The apprentices were gone now, as were his customers, but Aliz Nok had never forgotten his skills or let them decay from disuse. Though no one seemed interested in his fine blades any longer, the old man continued to refine his ancient methods, finding better ways to harden steel and sharpen the edge of the blades he made. He did not stamp out blades the way the modern makers did, with their dies and machines, producing inferior blades in such great numbers that the rulers of Torlis forgot the slower, better ways. Instead he worked patiently with fire and forge, making the metal bend to his will.

Aliz Nok's bald head glistened with sweat. The stinging heat of his firepit spat sparks and embers into the air, lighting his shop like fireflies. A hammer trembled in his hands, its soiled handle worn to a perfect fit by his strong fingers. Slowly, slowly, he folded the metal over itself, hammering it smooth. Already he had completed one of the blades for the katath, and now its twin took shape on his anvil. He had worked tirelessly on the weapon, honoured by the commission. The one-eyed stranger would soon come to claim it. Aliz Nok did not let his deadline hurry him. Precisely, he hammered out a paper-thin fold of the metal, and when it was perfect bent it back over the countless other folds. Soon, he would encase the blade in clay, leaving only the edge exposed to the air while the blade tempered in his firepit. From there the core would slowly cool, hardening it, making it unbreakable. Aliz Nok smiled, pleased with himself and the tricks he had learned. He had seen the brittle blades his competitors made, so useless, so easily snapped. Not so with his kataths. His kataths never shattered, and this one would be the greatest of them all.

'It will be perfect,' said Aliz Nok as he hammered down the fold. He could see its perfection taking shape. His white robe soaked with perspiration, he licked his lips to wet them. So thirsty, yet to rest now would ruin his work. He needed to be disciplined, always, for perfection to take shape. His shop had no windows, and Aliz Nok knew not the time. It had been daybreak when he'd begun, and now it was long past sunset. His stomach screamed for food, but he had already eaten once today and that was enough. Lost in his work, the old katath maker ignored the needs of his body, thinking only of the blade.

Would the one-eyed man come, he wondered? He would bring gold for the commission, but that did not matter to Aliz Nok. He would not accept payment for such an honour. Just being remembered was enough for the old man. The stranger had come from Niharn, he'd said, the great fencing master himself. To think of this made Aliz Nok swell with pride. Niharn had remembered him and his craft. The world was not hopeless after all.

'Work,' he told himself. 'It is for *her.*'

Because she was a girl and only slight of build, the katath had been a challenge. It could not be tall, nor uselessly short. It needed weight, but could not be heavy. But most of all, her katath needed blades that could pierce the hide of the Great Rass and puncture its twin hearts.

And that was why Niharn had sent the one-eyed man to Aliz Nok.

The old man worked tirelessly that night, forging the blade until morning, then carefully encasing it in the clay he had made, leaving the edge exposed so that it would heat and cool quickly. If not tempered this way, the core would cool too quickly, making it brittle. Not so with the edge. To hold its sharpness, it needed to cool fast. Aliz Nok worked hunched over his filthy table, laying the clay lovingly across the curved blade. Already he had made the shaft for the blade and its twin, drying and splitting the bamboo so that it whistled when twirled through the air. He had spun the shaft on one finger to test its balance. Soon he would tan the leather to attach the blades, then carve the shaft with powerful runes. He looked forward to this, for he had long ago mastered the runes of Sercin and was sure that the God would appreciate his handiwork.

When at last he had covered the blade with clay, Aliz Nok went to his firepit to stoke the flames. The hearth roared as he fed it air and coals, lusting for the blade. Patiently he waited for the heat to build, feeling the skin of his face tighten with pain. Then, when the fire was right, he slid the blade off its paddle and into the burning coals, sending up a shower of sparks.

The katath maker waited.

He watched the flames engulf the blade, searing and hardening the clay around its core. This was the time that always made him anxious. He found his stool nearby and sat down, and his thoughts drifted like smoke toward his dead wife in heaven. He was ready to join her, he decided. Thinking of her made him smile. She was proud of him, he was sure, looking down on him from the realm of the dead, watching as he made his last great blade.

'It is a blessing to do this work,' Aliz Nok whispered to himself. 'Thank you, Sercin. Thank you for sending the stranger to me.'

At last the blade had fired, and the old man took it from the flames with pincers, placing it directly into the urn of waiting water. The water hissed and bubbled, sending steam into his eyes. He turned his face from the spitting urn, counting to himself as the blade cooled. Soon the boiling subsided. Aliz Nok stopped counting. He withdrew the blade from the bath and set it down on his work table, studying the edge and the clay-covered core. The clay had hardened perfectly, without a single crack or blemish. He knew without opening it that he had succeeded. Smiling, he took his hammer and gently smashed away the clay, brushing the dust away to reveal the blade beneath.

Aliz Nok nodded, pleased with himself. Like its twin, the blade was perfect. Exhausted, he left the blade on the table, still half-encased in its clay. The hardest part was done, he decided. He had earned some sleep.

Three days later, Lukien arrived at the home of Aliz Nok. He had not seen the katath maker since giving him the commission, granting the old man the full month he needed to make Lahkali's weapon. The narrow street was filled with noise when Lukien arrived as mid-day crowds shopped among the many market stalls and bargained with merchants behind pushcarts. Aliz Nok's humble house sat behind a new, larger home, which cast a sad shadow over the old man's door. Surprisingly, the door was open when Lukien arrived. He pushed it open to peer inside, noting at once the smell of sulphur and sweat. The windows all remained closed, letting dusty sunlight into the living chamber. The home had not been cleaned since the last time Lukien had been there, and he noted the same bits of debris scattered right where they'd been a month ago. Without a wife to help him, the old master had let his house decay to a depressing sight, and Lukien held his breath against the strong smell of smoke that had polluted it.

'Aliz Nok?' he called.

No answer came. Lukien stepped inside and looked around, shutting the door behind him. Across the dismal living area lay the door to the shop. It, too, stood open. Lukien hesitated. He had been surprised by Niharn's insistence that the old man could help him, and when he'd first seen the home he had almost turned around. But Niharn had assured him with sincerity, promising Lukien that he would find no better smith to make Lahkali's weapon. Now, surrounded by Aliz Nok's depressing home, Lukien's doubts returned.

'Hello? Aliz Nok, are you here?'

Again the old man did not respond, prompting Lukien forward. He went across the living area to the shop, sticking his head over the threshold. The room stunk of oils and metal and burnt out coals. The firepit stood at the far side of the chamber, cold. Bent bits of iron blanketed the floor around the workbench, where scattered tools lay. Lukien cleared his throat against the smell, looking for a window to open but not finding one. Instead he found Aliz Nok, sprawled on the floor, his body partially covered by a blanket. An old, soiled pillow cradled his head. His mouth stood open, but no sound came from him. Concerned, Lukien went to stand over him, watching for any sign of breathing. When the old man's eyes opened it startled them both. Aliz Nok bolted up with a shout, making Lukien jump.

'I'm sorry!' Lukien cried, catching his breath. 'It's just me – Lukien.'

'Lukien?' The old man shook the sleep from his head. 'Yes . . .'

'Fate Almighty, I thought you were dead! You gave me a scare, Aliz Nok.' Lukien put out his hand and helped the man to his feet. 'This is where you sleep?'

'Sometimes,' said Aliz Nok. 'When I am busy. I have been very busy for you.'

Just as it had for everyone else in Torlis, Lukien's amulet translated the man's words. The remarkable feat had stunned Aliz Nok at their first meeting, convincing him Lukien was something special.

'It's been a month,' said Lukien cautiously. 'Have you had enough time?'

'I have,' replied the old man. A strange smile crossed his wrinkled face. 'You will be pleased.'

'It came out well, then?'

'No, not well. Perfectly.'

Aliz Nok let go of Lukien's hand and went to his silent workbench. Beneath it lay a long box of polished wood, perhaps four feet in length. He held it out before him, beaming. A proud twinkle lit his ancient eyes.

'Is that it?' asked Lukien excitedly. 'You made that box as well?'

'It is a special weapon, Lukien. It deserves a special place to rest. Come.'

As Lukien approached, Aliz Nok noisily cleared the debris from his workbench with his forearm, then set the box down. Carved into the top of the box was a symbol Lukien had seen before in Torlis, a rune that twisted like a snake – the mark of Sercin. With Lukien hovering over his shoulder, Aliz Nok began undoing the box's tiny golden latches. A long, gleaming hinge ran along the back of the top, and when the old man had finished with the latches he lifted the top on its silent hinge, revealing the weapon gently cradled in a cushion of velvet.

'Here it is,' said the old man. 'A katath unmatched.'

What he saw in the box made Lukien's eyes widen with delight. Inside were two separate shafts of split bamboo, each one lovingly carved with exotic symbols and both fitted with metal collars to lock them together. Separate from these was the head of the katath, two precisely matched blades, each curved and forged together in a V-shaped hook. Lukien could see the edge on them, gleaming dangerously in the dim light. A collar similar to the ones on the shafts lay at the base of the head, ready to fit it to its body. To Lukien's admittedly untrained eye, the katath looked exactly as Aliz Nok claimed.

'Perfect.' Lukien reached out to touch it, then pulled back his hand. 'May I?'

'Of course. It is yours now, to give to the Red Eminence.'

Its beauty amazed Lukien. He could easily tell how the thing went together, but instead asked the old man to do the honour for him. Aliz Nok nodded proudly and began assembling the katath, first fitting the two shafts together, then snapping the bladed head in place. When it was done he held the weapon out before him, showing its balance by holding it only by a fingertip.

'You see? Just as you asked. Not big, not heavy.'

'And the blade?' Lukien asked. 'Is it sharp enough?'

'My friend, you will not find a blade sharper, not anywhere. I have worked until my hands bled to make these blades. They are the finest I have ever made, sharper than the teeth of the Great Rass itself.'

'They need to be, Aliz Nok,' Lukien reminded him. 'They have to get through the hide of that beast.'

'They will, I promise. If you can train the Eminence to get close enough, my katath will do the rest.' The old man turned the weapon upright, showing off its two-bladed head. 'Look, you see how hard these blades are? They will not break, never. And the edge is soft enough to hold its sharpness. She may train with it, but it must be sharpened before she fights the Great Rass. Do not let it dull, Lukien.'

'I won't,' said Lukien. Finally he took the weapon from its maker, at once loving its weight and balance. It seemed to have no weight at all, yet there was heft in its ornate shaft, enough for easy thrusting. He rolled it carefully in his hands, admiring its entire length. 'Aliz Nok, it is remarkable,' he said. 'Niharn was right about you.'

The old man bowed his head. 'I am honoured to be remembered by Master Niharn.'

'You are, I can tell,' said Lukien with a smile. 'Niharn and I aren't friends. When he suggested you I did not know what to think. It is his job to train the Eminence, after all, not mine.'

'No,' said Aliz Nok. 'You have been chosen by Sercin for this.'

'No,' said Lukien, shaking his head.

The old man was insistent. 'Yes. Sercin has touched you, guided you here with his own hand. And then he guided you to me.' He gazed at the ceiling, but Lukien could tell he was really looking toward heaven. 'Thank you, Sercin,' he said with joy. 'Thank you for not forgetting me.'

Lukien watched silently as the katath maker said his prayer. Perhaps he was right. Perhaps it was Sercin guiding him. His own Liirian gods, that fickle bunch of misfits, had never done anything Lukien could comprehend, and so he had never believed in them. But in these desert realms the gods had power. Lukien had seen it. Beneath his shirt he felt the Eye of God and knew its power was real.

'Maybe your god has guided me,' said Lukien. 'I don't know. Whatever is true, you've done me a service, Aliz Nok. I'm grateful to you.'

'You will do well,' said Aliz Nok. 'You have talents; I see them in you. Sercin would not have chosen you otherwise. The Eminence is fortunate to have you for a teacher.'

His praise embarrassed Lukien. 'I hope so,' he said. 'You've made the weapon. Now I must teach her how to use it.'

26

King Baralosus looked across the table at Minister Kailyr, exhausted and wanting to quit. They had been stuck in the squalid chamber most of the morning, going over ledgers and papers that burdened the table and spilled over onto the floor. Empty tea cups and half-eaten morsels lay scattered among the papers, the remnants of meals meant to keep them going. Kailyr, who always enjoyed this time of the season, smiled despite the drudgery, looking invigorated by the amount of work still ahead of them. It was accounting work, the kind of thing Kailyr excelled at, and the Ganjeese Minister of Treasure always insisted that his king be present at least once a season while the ledgers were balanced. It was an unnecessary formality, a way for Kailyr to prove that his vast department was without corruption. More importantly, it gave the king a true impression of how his treasury was faring. Kailyr worked with his usual aplomb, tabulating every important transaction and making notes in his ledgers with his favourite quill, a dandy pen with a white ostrich feather. He was Baralosus' most trusted advisor and had been with the king since their boyhoods, and because he was so loyal Baralosus indulged him like this four times a year, pretending to take interest in the dull work of accounting.

'We have more orders with Marn still coming,' said Kailyr, referring to their fruit trade with their northern neighbour. The Marnans had always adored Ganjeese dates and pomegranates, and the past season had yielded fine crops of both. Kailyr grinned in delight as he noted the order in his ledger. The accounting of the crops had taken longer than usual, but the Minister seemed in no hurry to finish.

'Good,' said Baralosus. 'That's good news.'

He knew what his old friend was trying to do, and in an odd way Baralosus appreciated it. It had been days since he'd learned of Salina's disappearance, and so far he'd heard nothing of her welfare or location. The entire palace had been mourning her loss, sure that she'd perished somewhere in the desert. Baralosus own wife was shunning him, blaming him for driving their daughter away. The pall over the palace had driven

Baralosus to depression, yet he was grateful for Kailyr's attempt to distract him.

When will they come? he wondered to himself, not even hearing Kailyr as the Minister counted aloud. Four days ago, Jashien and Zasif had left for Aztar's camp, and so far neither man had returned. *Are they dead? Has Aztar killed them?*

He had tried to stop asking these questions, but they came anyway, flooding his fevered mind. He spent long hours staring out the palace windows, waiting for Salina – or anyone with news of her – to return. Kailyr had seen the senselessness of this and insisted that the king join him in the counting chamber. For a man who'd spent his entire life with numbers, Kailyr was surprisingly wise.

Kailyr licked the tip of his ostrich pen, then dipped it into his ink well. 'Look, Majesty – I have found an error! Those merchants who came from Dreel last year – did they pay all they owed?'

'How should I know, Kailyr? I'm the king, remember? Counting coins is your job.'

'Of course, Majesty. But I have an imbalance here.' The Minister wrinkled his beakish nose. He loved puzzles, and always took glee in finding mistakes. 'Let me see . . .'

As Kailyr worked, Baralosus poured himself some wine. He had already drank more than he should for so early an hour, but boredom had got the best of him and the wine helped to loosen his knotted shoulders. Part of him worried that he would never see Salina again. Part of him believed his wife's accusations, that his cruelty to their daughter had driven her away. But another part of him – the part that knew Salina best – believed in her. She had always been a wily girl, and not at all stupid. She had planned her escape from the city well, and if anyone could survive the desert alone, it was she. Baralosus tried to convince himself of this, using the wine as a balm.

The afternoon wore on like the morning had, with the two men talking about things that didn't really matter, things that a king should not trouble himself with but which Kailyr insisted was important. Eventually, Baralosus succumbed to his friend's peculiar charms, so blunted by the wine that he no longer cared how many hours they wasted. They broke for a proper meal at midday, a great respite for Baralosus, but at the Minister's insistence they went back to work exactly one hour later. Baralosus returned just as the last sands drained from Kailyr's hourglass. The Minister looked up from his papers at the king.

'I didn't think you'd come back,' he said, gently grinning.

Baralosus took his chair. 'You would have found me if I didn't.' A young serving girl offered him a drink from a collection of northern liquors. The king looked at the girl askance. 'I didn't order these.'

'I did, Majesty,' said Kailyr. 'I thought they'd help us pass the time.'

The king smiled at his Minister, told the girl to set her tray down, then dismissed her. He sighed across the table at Kailyr.

'Much more?'

The Minister shrugged. 'We could go on for days.'

'Please, let's not do that.'

'No,' agreed Kailyr. 'Really, it's just something to do. While you wait, I mean.'

Baralosus nodded. 'I know.'

There was silence between them, awkward and tense. The door behind Baralosus opened. He assumed another servant had come in, but then saw Kailyr push his work aside. The king hesitated, then quickly turned around. In the threshold stood one of his grooms, a man named Goval. The groom's taut face told the king something had happened.

'Majesty, forgive me . . .'

'Goval? What is it?' asked the king. He heard the dread in his voice and tried to tame it. 'Is there news?'

'Majesty, Jashien and Zasif have returned,' said Goval.

'Well?' barked Kailyr. 'Do they have the princess with them?'

'No,' said Goval nervously. 'I'm sorry, Majesty. They are alone.'

The news sent Baralosus crashing. He leaned back in his chair, unable to speak.

'Where are they?' asked Kailyr.

'They've only just arrived,' said Goval. 'They've barely got off their horses. I heard the news and ran up here to tell you.' The groom looked at his stricken king. 'Shall I bring them, Majesty?'

It took effort for Baralosus to speak. 'Yes,' he groaned. Then, 'No. Just Jashien, I mean. Just bring Jashien.'

'Quickly, man,' urged Kailyr. 'Bring him here and don't talk to anyone else.'

As Goval left the chamber, Baralosus felt himself go numb. It was bad news at least that his scouts had returned alone, and all he could think of was his daughter – his precious Salina – dead somewhere in the desert. The thought made his mind reel, forcing him to grip the arms of his chair. Kailyr, seeing his indisposition, went to stand beside him.

'It is Vala's will, whatever has happened,' he said softly.

The notion did little to comfort the king. 'She's my daughter . . .'

The Minister nodded and leaned against the table. A few interminable minutes went by until they heard Goval's footsteps returning down the hall. Baralosus hurried out of his chair and stuck his head outside the door, at once seeing his groom leading Jashien toward the chamber. The soldier looked weary beyond words, his hair matted, his clothing caked with filth. He hadn't shaved in days and his eyes had a wild, sunken appearance. When Jashien saw his king he mustered up a strong façade.

'Jashien?' probed Baralosus. 'What news?'

Minister Kailyr took his friend's arm and guided him back into the chamber. 'Inside, Majesty. Jashien, come inside.'

Baralosus let Kailyr sit him back in his chair. He looked up expectantly at Jashien. 'Have you news?' he asked. 'Have you found her?'

'I have, Majesty, and she is well,' said the soldier. 'Don't fear for her. She is unharmed.'

The king let out the breath he'd been holding. 'She's unharmed,' he whispered. 'Thank Vala, she's unharmed. Where is she?'

'We found her in Aztar's camp in the Skein, Majesty. That's where she remains. Aztar had men rescue her from the desert. She was lost, on foot when they found her. She would have died if not for him.'

'Aztar saved her?' Baralosus couldn't believe the luck of it. 'He actually found her?'

'She was on his way to him, just as you thought,' said Jashien. He licked his lips, which were so dry they looked bloody. He cleared his hoarse voice. 'She wasn't in camp yet when Zasif and I got there. She didn't come till the next day.'

'Jashien, sit,' bid Kailyr, holding out his own chair for the soldier. 'You look about to drop. Goval, you may go now.'

The groom gave his king a glance to make sure he was no longer needed. Baralosus quickly waved him away. Kailyr handed his own wine glass to Jashien, who thanked the Minister and drank. Baralosus waited impatiently for the soldier to finish.

'Majesty,' said Jashien, 'there's more.' He steadied himself. 'The princess is well, have no fear of that. I spoke to her myself and saw no harm in her. But she would not come back with us to Ganjor. She refused, Majesty.'

'What do you mean, she refused?' asked the king. 'You had orders to return her.'

'I know, Majesty, and we tried. But she wanted only to stay with Aztar, and Aztar would not release her to us.'

'That girl!' Kailyr erupted. 'She has worked her wiles on him again!'

Baralosus put up a hand to silence the Minister. 'Jashien,' he said evenly, 'explain this to me. You were sent to bring my daughter back. Are you telling me you left her there? With Aztar?'

The young soldier swallowed nervously. 'Yes, Majesty.'

'Why?' thundered Baralosus. 'In the name of Vala tell me why! She's just a girl – was she too much for you?'

'She is under Aztar's protection, Majesty,' Jashien argued. 'You sent two men after me – me and Zasif. Aztar has many men, and all of them are willing to die for him. We tried to reason with him, but he refused to let us take her against her will, and there was no way we could force him.'

'We'll force him,' Kailyr argued. 'We'll send an army after Salina if we must!'

'That would be better, I think, then sending just two men against him,' suggested Jashien. 'I am sorry, Majesty, but I returned without her because I knew you were worried and wanted news. I'll go back for her, right now if that's what you wish, but please give me something to threaten Aztar.'

'He's a fox, that one,' said Kailyr. 'He's always wanted the Princess and power both. Now he means to ransom her.'

'He says not,' said Jashien. 'When I asked him that same thing he was insulted.'

'Of course he was! He's not going to admit it.' Kailyr turned toward his king. 'Majesty, you cannot let this stand. Once the people hear what Aztar's done, they will demand action. You must send men after her, as many men as needed.'

'And I will lead them gladly,' Jashien added. 'Give me the enough men, and I'll bring the Princess back to you, Majesty.'

Baralosus' head ached with confusion. Jashien's news had stunned him, and he was still overwhelmed at Salina's welfare. Part of him rejoiced that she was well. But another, darker part began to scheme. Prince Aztar had always been an ambitious man, a player of games. That political muscle that Baralosus used to detect deceit told him that Salina had become one of Aztar's pawns.

'Jashien, thank you,' said the king. 'I'm grateful to you. We'll talk again tonight.'

The soldier grimaced. 'Majesty?'

'You're dismissed,' said Baralosus. 'Go and rest now.'

Minister Kailyr raised an eyebrow, but had the good sense not to speak until Jashien left the room. He and the king watched Jashien go. Kailyr closed the door behind him.

'You're thinking something,' said Kailyr. 'Tell me what it is.'

King Baralosus took his time. He leaned back, he cracked his knuckles, he sorted through his confusion. Aztar was playing a bold game this time, but he had the most important game piece. He had Salina. The king doubted very much that the Tiger of the Desert would harm her. He loved her, after all, and Baralosus knew his love was genuine. Surely, that could be a lever.

'He wants something from us,' said the king finally. 'Salina, certainly. Power, probably. A place at the table.'

'We can't bargain with him, Majesty,' said Kailyr. 'By refusing to return

Salina he has spat in your face. If you let that stand there will be trouble, not just with your ministers but with the people.'

'The people adore Aztar, Kailyr. Not all of them, but enough of them. He's a hero. If we harm him, we'll undercut ourselves.'

'If you let him blackmail you, you do yourself the same damage,' said Kailyr. He hovered over the king like a shadow. 'Listen to me, Baralosus. Aztar has been a problem long enough. It's time to deal with him.'

'Deal with him. You mean kill him.'

'Yes, I mean kill him. Right now.'

Baralosus considered his friend's counsel. It was not without appeal. Inside, he raged at the insult Aztar had delivered, taking his daughter from him, the sheer gall of standing up to the king. But that was what the Ganjeese loved about him. It was what had drawn so many Voruni tribesmen to his banner. There was a glamour about Aztar, a magic cloak that made people adore him. He was dangerous alive, surely. But dead?

'If we kill him, he'll be an unspeakable menace,' said Baralosus. 'The Voruni will blame us, and so will some of our own people. It would be a bloodbath.'

'He's not as strong as he was,' Kailyr reminded him. 'He lost most of his men at Jador.'

'He has enough still to harm us, and he still has my daughter, remember. What would he do to her if he saw our army marching toward him?'

'He would let her go without a scratch,' said the Minister confidently. 'You know he'd never harm her.'

'And should I chance that? We need another answer, Kailyr, something that gets us all out of this mess.'

'A bargain, you mean.' Kailyr looked disgusted. 'Mark my words, Majesty, this is a mistake.'

Baralosus turned away from his Minister, looking at all the ledgers strewn across the table. His family had more wealth than any other in the city. He could pay a hefty ransom for Salina and never miss the gold. But he knew that Aztar wanted something more than gold, something that only he, the king, could legally grant.

'I have bargained with devils before,' said Baralosus, 'and so have you, old friend. It's politics, always.'

Kailyr's expression went from disgust to a kind of grudging understanding. He was an old fox, just like his king, and understood the ways of politics.

'I see your meaning, Majesty,' he said.

He was quiet for a time, and then went back to his books.

27

Night draped its dark arm across the Novo Valley. From a hillside by the river Kryss, Aric Glass watched the distant campfires wink to life. He had ridden hard by the last light of the sun, trotting quickly through the valley as dusk descended, but when at last he saw the camp of Raxor's men he paused, reining back his lathered mount to marvel at the army. It had grown, the rumours had claimed, and Aric could see the veracity of those claims now, for the Reecian army stretched like the tail of a dragon across the Novo Valley, that great weary expanse of grassland that rested between Liiria and Reec. Divided by the river Kryss, the Novo Valley had long been the sight of numerous battles between the two nations, its trees fed by the blood of both sides. Now, with Raxor's brooding army bedding down, Aric could see another feast of blood festering.

The road from Nith had been long and hard, and Aric Glass had not slept for days, not since he'd heard the news of Raxor's growing force. In Norvor he had followed the Kryss north, occasionally crossing the river at its periodic bridges to enter Liiria. Without a genuinely safe route north, Aric had lived on his wits to avoid being discovered, stopping along the way at small villages to rest himself and hear the gossip of peasants, all of whom repeated the same ominous tale. The Reecian army was growing, they had said, waiting on the border for the battle with Liiria. Aric Glass let his eyes linger on the sight. In the gathering darkness he saw men and horses moving through the camp and fires coughing up sparks. He saw the armoured wagons lined up in long rows, their metal-covered hides studded with rivets, their sides cut with arrow loops for the soldiers inside. A company of horsemen drilled upon their splendid mounts, bearing spears with feathers and sporting gleaming Reecian armour. Stableboys and squires darted through the dirty lanes. Aric tried to number them, supposing at least a thousand men had come to face his father. Impressed, he rolled his head along his soldiers, stretching his tired muscles and hearing them pop. To the west lay Liiria, his homeland, shrouded in the coming night, hiding his father and his dark designs. Aric

Glass peered closely through the valley and could not see any army gathering to oppose the Reecians.

The silence made him uneasy.

'Father, what is your game?'

In Koth, miles away, his father Baron Glass brewed a poison potion for the Reecians. Aric knew this with certainty. Yet he could see no evidence of it in the quiet Novo Valley, only the Reecians and their army and the rolling river Kryss that divided the two lands. Unnerved, Aric hesitated. He had come so far to meet King Raxor and deliver the message of Prince Daralor, and only fate had steered him here, to this unexpected army. In the villages they had said that Raxor himself was coming to join the battle, and now that he could see the king's army Aric no longer doubted this. Still, he had expected to ride to Hes to find the King, a prospect that would have added days to his journey.

Am I ready? he wondered.

Along the way he had rehearsed his words many times. He had practiced and was pleased with himself, but now his mouth dried up and his stomach pitched with nerves. How could he convince anyone to join with Daralor? The man was shunned by the rest of the world, a pariah among kings. For years he had kept his little principality safe from the storms on the continent, avoiding contact with outsiders and sending away foreign emissaries. But Daralor had courage, like the Reecians, and it was that lone similarity that had convinced Aric to take up his mission.

He's there, Aric told himself, staring at the Reecian camp. *Raxor.*

The air around the camp seemed charged. Only a king could make the air tremble. Aric considered the danger, the very real possibility of his imprisonment. He was the son of Reec's greatest enemy. Surely that might earn him a rope at the gallows.

'It doesn't matter,' he whispered.

It was a lie, but it made him feel better. Taking a breath, he took hold of the reins again and steered his horse onward, toward the Reecian camp. Quickly the gelding picked up speed as it hurried down the slope, and Aric Glass did nothing to slow it. Determined, he let the horse take him straight toward the heart of the camp, until at last he approached the outer perimeter where men on guard duty patrolled with spears. Aric could smell the powerful smoke and the dung of horses. The distant guards, bored and talking among themselves, seemed not to notice him as just one more horseman trotted toward camp. Wearing armour and red capes against the chill, the men ignored the cavalrymen drilling nearby as the sounds of Aric's own horse were drowned by the pounding hooves of the parading teams. Aric sat up tall in his saddle, trying to look unthreatening, and trotted up to a pair of weary-looking guards, who at last turned to regard him.

'Hello,' Aric called to them, putting up his hand. He slowed his horse just a bit. 'May I come forward?'

The guards blinked in confusion. 'Who are you?'

'A messenger,' Aric replied. 'I have business with your king.' From the corner of his eye, Aric watched as a pair of cavalrymen quickly broke ranks with their team, spinning their horses toward him. For the moment he tried to ignore them. 'This is the camp of Raxor, yes? I would speak to him.'

The guards looked stunned. One of them stepped forward, spear in hand. 'Stay where you are,' he warned, 'and tell us what this business is.'

Aric eased back on his horse, bringing it to a stop. The two horsemen were coming forward now, one a furious looking man with shocking red hair, the other older and more seasoned looking. The younger, red-haired man quickly took the lead, galloping forward then jerking his horse to a stop between Aric and the guards.

'Who are you?' he barked.

He stared demandingly at Aric. Tall and thin, his cape was grand, trimmed with gold and silver threads. His horse wore armour over its flanks and face, snorting with the same anger as its master. Just his presence made Aric pale.

'I'm a messenger,' Aric repeated, not sure how much to reveal or how long he could keep up the pretense. 'I have come to speak to King Raxor.'

'No one speaks to the king, especially not a boy,' said the red-head. He peered through the darkness, at last noticing Aric's battered uniform. 'And a Liirian!' The man glanced at his older comrade, who seemed equally confused. 'You're a Liirian?'

'Yes,' Aric admitted. 'A Royal Charger.'

'There are no Royal Chargers,' said the older man. From his place atop his horse he looked Aric up and down. 'They're all gone now.'

'No, not all of them are gone,' said Aric. 'I am a Royal Charger, Sir. And I'm not one of Baron Glass' men. I've come from someplace else.'

'Are you one who fought at the library?' the old soldier asked. There was a measure of respect in the question.

'Aye, Sir, I am,' Aric replied. 'I fought under Breck at the battle of Koth.'

'And now you're here to see my father?' the red-haired man burbled. 'Why?'

'As I said, I bear a message,' said Aric. Immediately he knew who he was addressing. Like most Liirians, he had heard the name Roland the Red. 'Prince Roland, what I have to say to your father is greatly important. If he is here . . .'

'You know who I am,' said Roland, puffing a little. 'Whatever you have to tell the king you can tell to me.'

Aric avoided his traps. 'I should tell it to both of you, I think.'

Roland grinned. 'You task me, boy. Give me your name.'

It was the question Aric dreaded. 'Aric Glass,' he said, then waited for the storm to come.

'Aric . . . ?' Roland looked again at his comrade, this time in disbelief. 'Aric Glass?' he sputtered. 'Aric *Glass?*'

'The son of Thorin Glass, yes,' said Aric. He watched as the faces of the men twitched. 'Prince Roland, I'm here because I have important news for your father, news about my own father that might help all of us. Please, I've ridden for weeks looking for help. If I can have an audience with the king—'

'For what reason?' asked Roland sharply. 'You're the son of Baron Glass.'

'It's not a ploy,' said Aric, bracing himself. 'Sir, I've come from Nith. I've come with a message from Prince Daralor to your father. I'm on your side in this, believe me.'

Roland put his hand to the pommel of his sword. 'And I'd be a fool to let a snake into camp, boy.'

'Prince Roland, please listen to me. I need to see your father.'

'You are seeing *me*,' said Roland, his ire growing. 'Tell me what your business is. What is this message from Nith?'

There was enough steel in his words to make Aric ease back. He had seen men like Roland before – quick to anger, needing to prove himself. He had given himself away with every poorly chosen word. Risking Roland's wrath, Aric shook his head.

'I can only give my message to the king,' he said. 'It's just by good fortune that I find him here. I was on my way to Hes to speak to him.'

Prince Roland turned an apple shade of scarlet. He started to speak, then caught himself as he noticed his men looking at him. Finally, the older man spoke again.

'Your father will want to speak to him,' he said to Roland easily. His tone was practiced. 'Let the boy deliver his message.'

Roland smiled crookedly at the older man. 'Is that what he would want, Craiglen? Then my father should have what he wants, shouldn't he? He's the king, after all.'

The man called Craiglen turned from the prince and ordered the guards to stand aside. To Aric he said, 'Dismount. My men will take your horse.'

Aric did as ordered, and the guards came forward to take his mount. The older soldier then dismounted himself, handing off his own horse, and called to other guards who had gathered nearby to listen. These men surrounded Aric at his order. Prince Roland, still upon his horse, gazed down imperiously at Aric, yet nevertheless looked out of place.

'Are you coming?' Craiglen asked him.

Roland grimaced, then finally got down off his own horse. It shocked Aric how much things were out of his hands. Even the low ranking guards looked to Craiglen for direction.

'Follow me,' Roland said, then led the way into the heart of camp.

Surrounded by armed men, Aric followed the prince, stepping into the perimeter to the stares of dumbstruck soldiers. The men who had first greeted him led away their horses, and soon Aric was engulfed by the camp. He studied the war machines the Reecians had brought with them, the armoured wagons and carts laden with weapons. A few burly, bare-chest men sweated with an enormous catapult, cursing as they refitted its splines. Horse dung littered the ground, though gaggles of stableboys worked gamely to clean it, and men in armour and scarlet capes gathered around campfires to talk and laugh, falling quiet as Prince Roland passed. It took long minutes to cross the camp, and every step impressed Aric. King Raxor was taking no chances. Whatever his motives, he intended to win against the Liirians.

But Aric knew how impossible that was. Raxor might be brave and have an army with him, but he didn't know what he was up against, or the sheer power of the Devil's Armour. To think of it made Aric forlorn.

At last they came to the far end of the camp, where a pavilion stood alone and the camp fires had thinned. Here, more of the guards greeted them, though these were more alert than the ones who'd greeted Aric. Standing at attention, their uniforms crisp and clean, they glared at Aric as he approached, at once sensing the stranger in their midst. Prince Roland exchanged a few words with them, mostly ordering them to step aside. Backing up the prince's order was Craiglen, who nodded at the guards. The guards parted reluctantly, letting all of them pass. Aric looked around and saw that more soldiers milled near the grand tent. Huge dogs – mastiffs by the looks of them – were chained to posts near the fire. Soldiers tossed them meat. Others groomed the howling beasts. Aric noticed another campfire, this one apart from all the others. A single man enjoyed the fire, surrounded by unleashed dogs. The dogs knelt dutifully by him as he went from one to the other, giving each of them treats and patting their heads. He was an old man, older than Craiglen, dressed in a long coat with a collar of wolf fur. Though he stooped to tend his pets, Aric could tell he was enormous. Except for his head, his entire body was draped by the dark coat, his hands and feet shielded in black leather as well. Enamoured of his dogs, he seemed not to notice the approaching men. The group paused just outside the light of his fire. Prince Roland stepped forward.

'Father,' he said, 'someone is here for you.'

King Raxor didn't bother lifting his head. 'Who?'

'A messenger. A boy named Aric Glass.'

The distracted king took a moment before he realized what had been said. He turned to look at Roland, then straight at Aric. Their eyes met, making Aric shrivel. Raxor had been legend once, a warrior of great renown, and had lost little of his ability to intimidate.

'Glass?' said the king.

Craiglen stepped forward. 'My lord, this is Baron Glass' son. He has come with a message from Prince Daralor of Nith.'

'I am more amazed each time someone speaks! Nith, you say?' The old king examined Aric. 'And this is the Black Baron's son?' He laughed. 'It's a day of miracles.'

'This isn't a joke, Father,' said Roland. 'He claims he's the son of Thorin Glass.'

'I have never seen a son of Thorin Glass and would not know him if I did,' said Raxor. He took a bit of meat from the bag at his belt and tossed it to one of his mastiffs, then frowned at Aric. 'A trick? Because I expect tricks from you Liirians, boy.'

'No,' Aric assured him. 'It's no trick, my lord. I am who I claim.'

'You're wearing the uniform of a Royal Charger,' Raxor commented. 'The Royal Chargers are dead.'

'He says he fought with Breck at the library,' said Craiglen.

'It's true,' said Aric. 'I am not an ally of my father, my lord.'

'Why were you in Nith?' asked Roland. 'No one goes to Nith.'

'I went to ask their help against my father,' Aric said. 'I went to all the kings of the southern lands, and everyone turned me down. Except Prince Daralor.' He looked at Raxor earnestly. 'My lord, he's the only one besides you who understands the danger. I went to Marn and Farduke and even the Viscount of Lonril, and all of them sent me away.'

Raxor looked intrigued. 'But not Daralor?'

'How do we even know you are who you claim?' argued Roland.

Raxor nodded. 'My son makes a point, boy. You say you went to Nith to ask aid against your father? Why would you do such a thing?'

'Unless he's just a traitor,' sneered Roland. 'Maybe you want gold to sell out your own flesh? I would believe that of a Glass.'

The insult riled Aric, but he let it pass. 'I'm not a traitor,' he said evenly. 'I loved my father once. I still do. But he's not my father anymore. He's been corrupted by the armour he wears.'

Raxor's eyebrows shot up at once. 'You know about his armour?'

'Yes,' said Aric. 'Not much, but enough to know what a danger it is. It's a magical thing, my lord, a weapon made by an ancient magician.'

'We know this,' said Roland. 'Tell us something useful.'

'I can tell you that I've seen my father in battle,' Aric shot back. 'I've seen what the armour has done to him, and what it can do to an army like yours. That's why I went to Nith and the others. None of you alone are strong enough to stand against him.'

'An alliance? Is that what Daralor proposes?' asked Raxor.

'Yes,' said Aric. 'My lord, Prince Daralor knows of this army you've massed on the border. He honours what you're doing here. He told me that you're the only brave king left on the continent, and to be true I think he's right. All the others want to wait and see. They're not willing to join up and face down my father.'

Roland grimaced at this. 'They want others to do their work for them.'

'That's right,' admitted Aric. 'But Daralor is ready to fight with you, if you'll have him.'

One of Raxor's mastiffs came to stand beside him then. The old king patted the dog's head, commanding it to sit. He stared pensively at the beast for a moment, his lower lips disappearing.

'Can you imagine how this sounds to me, boy?' he sighed. 'How do I know that anything you've said is true? You come into my camp, you make fantastic claims and ask me to trust you. But what proof have you brought with you?'

Aric patted his pockets remembering the note Daralor had penned for him. He looked sheepishly at the king.

'In my saddlebags there is a letter from Daralor,' he said. 'To you, my lord, written in his own hand and sealed with his own seal. Your soldiers have my horse.' He looked around frantically. 'If I could get it . . .'

Raxor held up his hand. 'I'll see your letter in time, boy. What else have you brought?'

Aric shrugged. 'Nothing. Just my own tired self.'

Roland was unmoved, but Craiglen looked sympathetically at his king. Aric hurried to explain himself.

'My lord, I have been on the road since the fall of Koth, knocking on doors like a beggar, trying to get people to listen to me. I've explained myself a thousand times. I can show you my blisters, but that's about all. I *am* Aric Glass, son of Thorin. And believe it or not, I'm here to help you.'

'Look around, boy,' directed Roland. 'We have an army of our own.'

'I have seen it,' said Aric. 'It won't be enough.'

Roland turned to his father. 'He tricks us. Send him to Asher to see what he knows and let's be done with him.'

'Asher?' Aric probed.

'Our interrogator,' said Roland with an ugly grin. 'At least then we'll get the truth from you.'

'But I have told you the truth!'

'And I believe you,' said King Raxor. 'I do, boy. Be at ease.'

'Father . . .'

'Quiet,' Raxor ordered his son. He knelt down next to his heeling dog, running his wrinkled fingers over its black scalp. 'You've been honest with us, Aric Glass. I can tell that about you, at least. I don't know what motivates you to betray your father. It doesn't matter I suppose. So let me be honest with you – we have already sent word to your father to talk. We don't want war, and we're only here to protect ourselves. Somehow I have to convince your father of that.'

'It won't be easy, my lord,' said Aric. 'As I said, the armour has changed him. He doesn't reason the way a normal man does. There's a demon in the armour that possess him.'

'A demon?' said Raxor with disgust. 'Black magic from the desert lands.'

'Has he replied to you yet, my lord?'

'No.' Raxor stood. 'It's been three days and still no word. He plays games with us.'

'He means to intimidate us,' said Roland. 'Every day his army grows. Our spies have seen it.'

'But he hasn't moved troops to the border,' Craiglen pointed out. 'Perhaps that is hopeful.'

Raxor looked at Aric. 'Is it hopeful, boy?'

Aric thought for a moment, unsure how to answer. Growing up, his father had been a gentle man. A taskmaster at times, but kind enough to his sons. What happened to that kindness, Aric wondered? Had Kahldris devoured it all?

'My father cannot be trusted,' said Aric. 'The demon that controls him will not let him rest. I have seen the things my father has done. The man who raised me would never have done those things, like betray his friends at the library or join with Norvor.' The dark seemed to settle over Aric as he spoke. 'There were hundreds of men at the library, and they all thought my father would help them. He came with promises and made us all believe in him. And then he betrayed us to side with Jazana Carr. He and his men killed Breck. He tried to kill Lukien, his best friend. No, my lord, I don't trust my father. And neither should you.'

Prince Roland seemed stunned by Aric's admission. Like Raxor and Craiglen, he was quiet. The guards kept their eyes to the ground. Even the dogs fell silent. Aric waited for someone to speak.

'Roland, Craiglen, leave me with the boy,' ordered Raxor.

Roland turned to him. 'Father?'

'Let me talk to him alone. Please, all of you go.'

Craiglen hesitated, then carefully touched Prince Roland's arm. Roland hesitated, but a glare from his father changed his mind. Craiglen ordered the guards to step back, out of earshot, but to keep on eye on the Liirian. When they all had gone, leaving only Raxor and Aric in the light of the campfire, Raxor went back to his dogs. The old king smiled forlornly as he fed the beasts treats from his pockets. Confused, Aric watched silently as the mastiffs ate.

For a long time King Raxor ignored Aric, but Aric could tell the old man was thinking. Tonight, a lot had landed in his lap. He fed his mastiffs one by one, sometimes scratching them or checking their ears. And when at last he had run out of treats he stood and faced Aric. The king shrugged.

'So, your father has trapped me,' he said. 'You have seen that, yes?'

'My lord? I'm sorry, I don't take your meaning.'

'I had to come here, Aric Glass. I had to defend what is ours, what we fought for over too many years. Your father knows that. He has trapped me. He wants this war, I fear.'

'I think you're right,' said Aric. 'But you don't have to accommodate him.'

'I do. That's something I have to do, you see. I don't want to be here, but I must because honour demands it. I cannot let your father take the Kryss from us, if that is his design. I cannot yield an inch of Reecian land. My son – he's anxious for this battle. I'm sure you've already seen what a fool he can be.'

Aric smiled at the king. 'I'd rather not say, my lord.'

Raxor answered him with a grin. 'These men who've come here – they came because of me. They'll fight because they're loyal to me, no matter what your father and his whore-queen throw at us. But Roland . . .' The king grimaced. 'He doesn't inspire them. And so I'm here, an old man in the cold, fighting a battle he's desperate to avoid.'

'Maybe you can avoid it, my lord.' Aric went closer, sensing his need. 'If you join with Prince Daralor, others might join as well. And then my father might be convinced to stop with Liiria and leave Reec alone.'

Raxor shook his head. 'It's too late for that. I've sent my message to your father. It's time to talk. Or to fight.'

'And what if he chooses to fight? What then? He has the Devil's Armour, and the fortune of Jazana Carr. '

'We'll defend what is ours,' Raxor assured him.

'My lord, you mustn't fight,' Aric warned. 'No matter what my father says or doesn't say, no matter what he replies to your message, you can't fight him because you can't win.'

'Can't?' Raxor gave a sceptical laugh. 'I have enough men here to defend the border, boy. I may not win, but I don't plan on losing, either.'

'My lord is mistaken,' said Aric. 'My father is invincible in his armour. You won't be able to stop him.'

'Boy, he is but one man! An army cannot stop him? You think too much of this armour he wears.' The king eyed him shrewdly. 'If you have secrets you're not telling me, I can get them out of you. Roland was right about Asher – he can make you talk.'

The threat came impotently from Raxor's mouth. Aric could tell he didn't mean it.

'I'll tell you anything I can about the armour, my lord. What little I know is yours.'

'I've heard things about it,' said Raxor. 'From . . . people.' He shrugged. 'Rumours, mostly. No one seems to know much about it.'

'It's a mystery, even to me. Even to my father, I think,' said Aric. 'We talked about it once, before he went over to Jazana Carr. He said it made him strong, made him whole again. He said it was magic.'

Raxor nodded. 'Yes. I have heard this.' His eyes grew distant and he looked away, surveying his camp but not really seeing. 'I have a woman back in Hes,' he said.

Surprised, Aric replied, 'Yes, my lord?'

'She's young and more beautiful than you can imagine, Aric Glass. She makes me feel like a whole man when I am with her. That is how your father feels in his armour. I know it. I know what it is like to get old.'

The sadness in his voice struck Aric. 'Yes. That is how my father feels. You're lucky, my lord, to have such a woman.'

'Not luck. I have made her care about me. But I want to go back to her.' Catching himself, Raxor straightened abruptly. 'What you're asking is impossible, Aric Glass. I cannot run from this fight.'

'But you can wait, surely. Unless my father crosses the Kryss, you can wait. And you can join with Prince Daralor and give me some time. Maybe others will join if they see that you have joined, my lord.'

'Who will join us? The cowards of Marn? They have already sent you away, boy.' Raxor set his jaw. 'This is our fight, a Reecian fight. We will settle old scores with Baron Glass, if that's what he wishes.'

Aric felt the hope drain out of him. 'I beg you not to do this, my lord. Don't fight my father unless you have a death wish.'

'I should be insulted by that,' Raxor warned. 'But I assure you, I want to live and go back to Hes to see my woman again. I've brought an army to secure that future, and I don't think any man – demon driven or not – can stand against an army.'

'My father can,' said Aric. 'The Devil's Armour can.'

'Tantalizing hints,' growled Raxor. 'That's all I hear about this armour. I will find out for myself if that's what it takes.'

'I wish I could tell you more. All I know is what I've seen.' Aric held his breath a moment. 'Except for one more thing, my lord.'

Raxor stopped fidgeting. 'What?'

'There is something else I haven't yet told you, another reason for you to wait. There may be a way to defeat my father and his armour.'

'Then tell me what it is!'

'It's nothing you can do, my lord. It's a sword. A special sword called the Sword of Angels.'

Raxor rolled his eyes. 'More magic?'

'Lukien is questing for it, my lord. It is said to be the only way of defeating the Devil's Armour.'

'I know Lukien,' drawled Raxor. 'Too well. You're asking me to trust another enemy.'

'I'm asking you to wait, my lord. Just wait. If Lukien finds the sword—'

'It's nonsense, Aric Glass! There is not a suit of armour in the world that can save a man from a thousand knives. The Bronze Knight wastes his time. He should find himself an army instead of searching for a sword.'

'He had an army, my lord,' Aric reminded him. 'I was part of it.'

'And you lost. I know. But I cannot wait. It won't be magic that saves us from Baron Glass, young Aric. It will be Reecian blood.'

The king was done talking. Aric could hear his finality.

'So I've come this way for nothing,' said Aric wearily.

'You did what you were supposed to do. You have delivered your message.'

'To no good at all,' keened Aric. He shook his head in defeat. 'I'm sorry for you, my lord. Prince Daralor was right – you are a brave man. The Chargers at the library were brave too.'

'You mean to frighten me, boy? I am already frightened.' Raxor eyed his quiet pavilion. 'I'm tired. I want to sleep now. You have a decision to make, Aric Glass. What will you do now?'

'I can't go back to Liiria, my lord. If you will have me, I would rather stay and wait for my father's reply to you.'

'And then?'

'That's up to you,' Aric told him. 'It's all up to you, my lord.'

Alone in the firelight, the two men fell silent. A mastiff snuffled its fleshy jowls, looking questioningly at its master. King Raxor searched his pocket for a treat, forgetting it was empty. The dog barked unhappily. Raxor snapped at it to be quiet and tugged his coat around his neck. He told Aric to have the guards find him shelter for the night, then turned and walked toward his lonely pavilion.

28

In the years they had spent together in Norvor, Thorin had made love to Jazana hundreds of times. But in those days she had always exhausted him, because she had the appetite of a woman many years younger and because Thorin had no magic to keep his manhood at attention. They had been well-matched lovers, though, and had enjoyed each other, and seldom spoke of their growing age.

For Thorin, those days were gone now. In the influence of his Devil's Armour, he was so much younger than he'd ever been, and never tired of love making. With the spirit of Kahldris firing his loins, he could bed the beautiful Jazana over and over without tiring, proving his prowess to her each night in their grand bed. Tonight, Thorin listened to her moans, watching her breasts in the moonlight as her eyes rolled backward into her head. Cradled in his armoured arm, her neck pulsing with breath, she had yielded like a flower to his yearnings. Outside, a storm had rolled southward, rattling the windows with rain. Thorin listened to the thunder. In his mind he felt the pleasure of the demon Kahldris, like a good friend sharing his conquest. Through his eyes the demon watched the woman in the bed, adoring her. From the first time he had seen her, Kahldris had lusted for Jazana. And unknown to her, two lovers put their flesh against her.

Thorin held his passion, governing it, savouring it. His rigid body moved like a instrument over Jazana. His hand took her head, lifting it from the torn pillow, and her whole body came off the bed. She cried out, not in pain, and let his kisses pelt her neck. She was naked, twisted in the sheets, her hair wildly splayed, her fingers clawing his back. Kahldris trembled at the sensation, loving the way her nails bit Thorin's flesh. Dawn was coming quickly, but tonight the lovers barely slept. On the eve of battle, Thorin's hungers knew no end. Soon his armies would march. Soon the Kryss would be his again. The memories of former glories charged his body, exciting him.

'Look at me,' he groaned. He grasped Jazana's hair. 'Jazana, look at me.'

Her eyes fluttered open. Panting, she could barely speak. She smiled, her voice shaking. 'I love you, Thorin. I *love* you.'

'Jazana, I love you. You belong to me.'

'Yes . . .'

'You're mine.'

'Yes!'

Hearing her laments broke the dam of his control. Kahldris loosed a silent scream as the passion convulsed Thorin's body. He cried out just as thunder shook the tower. Slowly, slowly, his muscled tensed and then relaxed. The burning in his loins subsided. Still cradling Jazana, he lowered her to the mattress. Her body rose and fell with heavy breaths. Her eyes filled with him. Kneeling, Baron Glass leaned back and put his armoured arm across his chest, feeling the burning metal. Kahldris spoke to him. His words came like a syrupy dream.

Thank you.

Thorin nodded, catching his breath. It had been Kahldris that had pushed him, Kahldris who had wanted one more go before the sun rose. The demon laughed the way a comrade might patting Thorin's back. Together they looked down at the woman, pleased with themselves.

'Sleep now,' moaned Jazana.

To Thorin, it sounded like a plea. She always did so much for him, never arguing, never refusing him. To others, she was made of steel. But sometimes, Thorin thought her weak.

'Yes,' he agreed, and lowered himself down next to her, draping his arm of flesh across her chest and putting his nose close to her cheek. As Jazana stared up at the dark ceiling, exhausted, Thorin eyed the window and the dark night beyond. At once his thoughts turned to battle.

In the city and the hills around it, his army waited, bivouacked in tents or housed in the old barracks of the Royal Chargers, enduring the rain and the long wait to fight. They were mercenaries mostly, seasoned troops who had long been part of Jazana's world, but there were Norvan regulars as well, those who had not marched back to Norvor after Koth fell. Baron Glass supposed he had three-thousand men in the city ready to fight. A goodly number, surely, though not all he had hoped. The troubles in Norvor had prevented Demortris and Manjek and the others from sending troops, leaving Thorin to make do with his mercenaries. He knew that Raxor had come with almost as many men, and that the Reecians were all regulars, with not a single mercenary in their ranks. He was sure that his old enemy had brought only the best with him, and his scouts had confirmed the Reecian war machines and mastiffs. They would not be easy to defeat, but Baron Glass felt confident. In his fabulous armour, he alone could slay an army. He was convinced of that now. It would be no harder than taking a woman.

'Your eyes are open,' Jazana whispered. 'Close your eyes.'

Thorin took a breath, smelling Jazana's perfume and musk. He had not lied to her during their love-making – he loved her truly. She was more faithful than anyone had ever been to him.

'I don't deserve you,' he told her.

Jazana laughed. 'No more sweet talk. I'm tired. Go to sleep.'

'I cannot sleep.'

'You're thinking too much. Close your eyes and relax.'

But Thorin was like a little child, too excited to sleep. He had still not answered Raxor's letter, and enjoyed the thought of the old king twisting and afraid. Like the marvelous painting in the library, he had battled Raxor many times in his youth, when they both were virile. Raxor was old now, but Thorin was young again. He wondered what Raxor would think when at last they met.

'He's afraid of me,' said Thorin. 'That's why he wants to talk.'

Jazana said nothing, for she did not like speaking of the matter. For too long she had lived with war. Now she wanted only peace.

'I am thinking of speaking to him,' Thorin went on, 'in a day or so. When the weather clears.'

Jazana opened her eyes. 'Are you? That's good.'

'We should speak. I want to see him. I want him to see me.'

'Oh.'

Jazana rolled over.

Thorin admired her naked back. He traced a finger over her smooth skin. She was like a sculpture, beautifully timeless. Age had given her experience without robbing her looks. It was easy to tell when she was troubled, and Thorin knew she was troubled now.

'They come to harm us, Jazana. I did not invite them here.'

'You said you would talk to them. I misunderstood.'

'To make him see what he is up against!'

'To make yourself feel like a man. Now I understand. Go to sleep, Thorin.'

'You try me sometimes, Jazana, do you know that? I have explained this to you.'

'And I have accepted it.'

Still she gave him her back. Thorin grimaced.

'I had a fine time tonight. Thank you, my love.'

The Diamond Queen chuckled. 'Good.'

'You have to understand, Raxor tasks me. He has brought his army here to challenge me. To challenge *us*, Jazana.'

'So why talk to him? You've already made up your mind, Thorin. You're going to take back the Kryss. I know you well enough, Thorin Glass. You want this war, so please don't tell me you don't.'

'The Kryss is ours,' muttered Thorin. He glared at the ceiling. 'It was ours until Akeela gave it away.'

Jazana's back rose with a sigh. 'Promise me one thing, Thorin. Promise me that you'll keep your promise to me.'

'Eh?'

'About Norvor!' Jazana swiveled to face him. 'Remember?'

'Of course I do! When I have dealt with Raxor I will deal with Norvor,' Thorin assured her. 'Just as I promised.'

'Norvor needs us, Thorin. It can't wait forever.'

'Have I not promised?'

She looked sceptical. Her lips twisted. 'I worry, that's all. We've lost Carlion . . .'

'I have told you, I will deal with it. When this business with Raxor is done, I'll ride to Carlion myself to kill Elgan. You will have his head, my lady, and any other part of him you wish for your shelf.'

Jazana closed her eyes and was quiet for a moment. 'War. I am sick of it. You should talk with Raxor.'

'I will.'

'No, I mean really speak to him. See what he wants.'

Before Thorin could reply, he felt Kahldris push his way forward, to the front of Thorin's mind.

She speaks like a woman, the demon jeered. *Raxor has come to test you, Baron.*

Thorin tried ignoring the Akari. 'Jazana, do not worry. We are stronger, stronger than Elgan. Stronger than anyone. Elgan's days in Carlion are numbered. Soon you will return. But not yet. Please, not while I need you.'

Do not beg her! said the demon with disgust.

'You should talk to him, Thorin.' Jazana finally turned to look at him again. 'Will you talk?'

No.

Thorin put the demon from his mind. 'We have enough men to defeat them. I do not need to talk, Jazana. It will only make us look weak.'

'That's not what Rodrik says. He says the Reecians have come to defend themselves, because they're scared of us. Scared of you, Thorin.'

'Varl's council clouds your mind, my love. Why is he here anyway? He should be back in Norvor.'

'He is a good soldier, Thorin. Won't you use him in your battle?'

'No.' Thorin grinned. 'He stays to protect you from me, Jazana. He loves you.'

The accusation made Jazana uncomfortable. She draped her arm across his chest and, as usual, changed the subject. 'We have Liiria, my love.' She kissed his cheek. 'That's all you ever wanted. And I have Norvor, and that's all I ever dreamed of having. Let the Reecians have their river. Talk to them and send them away.'

'Jazana . . .'

'Talk to them for me. Show your love for me, will you? Have I not done much for you?'

Thorin had to nod. 'You have. And I am grateful.'

Kahldris began to seethe. *No, Baron.*

'Will you at least answer Raxor's message?' asked Jazana. She watched her lover carefully. 'Say you will, Thorin.'

He could not say no to her. Because he loved her, because she had given so much to him, he relented.

'All right,' he grunted, pulling away from her lips. 'For you, I will talk. *Just* talk.'

'My big bear,' Jazana purred. 'I'm happy.'

'Wonderful,' drawled Thorin. He closed his eyes. 'Now let me sleep.'

But Thorin could not sleep, for the promise he made haunted him, and the demon Kahldris screamed angrily in his mind. He felt betrayed, the Akari told Thorin, and refused to let his hope escape into slumber. Thorin lay naked in the bed with his eyes open, listening to Jazana's soft breaths as he argued with Kahldris, finally tossing his feet over the side. There was a robe on a peg near the bed. Thorin grabbed it quietly, hurried it around his shoulders, then left his sleeping lover, going into the adjoining dressing room. He turned the key on a oil lamp along the wall, lighting the room gently and squinting against its brightness. Rain continued pelting the window and tower walls. The wind tore at the bricks. It would be an ugly day when dawn finally came.

Dress yourself, Kahldris commanded.

'What?'

Walk with me, Baron Glass.

'I'm tired, demon, and in no mood to fence with you.'

To Kahldris, there was no room for discussion. In a voice like ice he repeated his order.

Get dressed.

Instead of arguing, Thorin relented to the spirit's command. In the room he found clothes for himself, quickly dressing in trousers and a wrinkled shirt. The shirt had only a right sleeve. The left one had been torn off to accommodate his armoured arm. He pulled boots onto his feet, found his leather cloak draped over a chair, and left the room by gently closing the door behind him. Out in the hall he heard only silence. Lionkeep and its servants slept. Thorin waited for Kahldris' direction. Like a leash he felt the tug, dragging him onward, dragging him toward the stairs descending the tower. Man and demon were silent as they walked the halls, finally coming to a door leading out toward the stable. Thorin paused here, standing in the threshold and looking at the teeming sky.

'I'm not going out there,' he declared.

Sometimes he could see Kahldris' face. Other times, like now, he could not, yet he could still feel the Akari's sinister smile.

I have something to show you, Baron.

'Something out there?'

Come with me.

Thorin hesitated a moment, then cinched the collar of his cloak tight around his neck before stepping into the night. At once the mud of the grassy earth sucked at his boots. Cold rain pelted his face. Unable to see clearly without the aid of his helmet, he looked around at the shadowed trees and buildings, wondering what possible lesson could be found in such a dismal place. Like the library, Lionkeep had been brought back to life after the battle of Koth. At least mostly. With him and Jazana Carr calling it home, the former palace of Liirian kings had been rebuilt, staffed with Liirians and Norvans alike and guarded by Jazana's ubiquitous mercenaries. But in this part of the keep there were no guards, only empty stables and dilapidated buildings begging for repair. The wind made the broken hinges of the buildings sing. Leaves tumbled down from the trees, striking Thorin's face.

'So? Why are we here?' he asked.

As he finished the question, he watched the air before him start to shimmer. Out of it stepped Kahldris, his body glowing, his face drawn with anger. This time, he wore the garb of the general he'd been in life, with a gleaming black breast plate and bare, muscular arms. A ghostly sword hung at his side. His eyes glimmered with unnatural light, turning to slivers when they locked on Glass.

'Just walk,' he told the baron, then turned and proceeded through the rain.

Thorin followed, confused by his appearance. Kahldris walked like a living man, but his feet made no impression in the muddy earth. His long hair trailed down his back, untouched by the rain, and there was no sound when he moved, only the noise of the breeze passing through him. He led Thorin past the old buildings and the broken corrals, into a field dotted with twisted trees. Shadows crawled across the rolling ground. In the east, the first blush of sunlight struggled up the horizon.

'Where are you taking me?' Thorin asked.

Kahldris extended his arm. 'Come,' he bade. 'Walk beside me.'

'I'm wet and cold, Kahldris. Tell me where we're going.'

'To a place far away, Baron Glass. A place long ago.' Kahldris put his arm around Thorin. 'Keep watch, and listen to my story.'

'Story?'

'A lesson, Baron Glass.' Kahldris let his arm slide off Thorin as he walked. 'Listen.'

'Be quick, please,' Thorin quipped. 'I—'

He stopped, not just talking but walking, too. From out of the darkened trees he saw a rider approach, thundering toward him. Dressed like Kahldris, the man was clearly Akari, garbed in the same elaborate armour and bearing a long spear. His horse snorted as it tore up the ground. Thorin drew back as the beast bore down, dodging its gallop. Without regard the rider hurried past them. Thorin watched as he disappeared behind the curtain of rain. The wind swallowed the hoof-beats.

'What was that?' he asked. He turned to Kahldris. 'Where are we?'

'This place – it's like a place I remember,' said Kahldris. He continued walking, ignoring the Akari rider. 'I have been watching Liiria, noticing it, how you adore it. And then tonight when you spoke to Jazana I remembered.'

'No riddles,' Thorin demanded. 'Tell me what you remember.'

'This,' said Kahldris.

With a wave of his arm he thickened the clouds. The sun sank backward and the sky darkened. The wind retreated but the rain grew, as did the trees which pulled themselves up from the muddy earth. The world stretched in all directions, and soon the corrals and buildings were gone, replaced by foreign hills. Thorin wheeled, stunned by the enchanted world, and knew he was no longer in Koth.

'This is one of your magics,' he declared. 'Take me back, Kahldris. I don't wish to see this.'

'I was a young man here,' said Kahldris casually, completely ignoring Thorin's plea. His gait was unhurried as he walked the strange world. Another of the Akari riders appeared ahead of them, but Kahldris paid the man no mind. 'I was like the rest of them, so sure of myself. We were strong in those days. We thought we could beat anyone.'

The wind picked up again. Thorin clamped his cloak around him, unsure what he was seeing. He was used to Kahldris's lessons, but this one's vividness alarmed him. Ahead, he watched as a troop of riders joined the one horseman. Together they reined back their horses, pointing and shouting among themselves. Thorin looked about, wondering what they were seeing, or if they could even see him.

'Three-hundred of us went to Maluja that day,' Kahldris went on. 'Three-hundred! More than enough, we thought.' He continued walking with Thorin in tow, still oblivious to the gathering soldiers. 'I was a minor commander in those days. Maybe I had fifty men under my command, I don't remember.'

'Kahldris, tell me what this is!'

'Just walk with me, Baron Glass. Listen to my story. We had got a message from a Jadori named Dahlgen. He had built an outpost near our city Kaliatha. It was a forward position, the furthest the Jadori had pushed into our territory. But Maluja was close to our land, so we agreed to meet him there.'

Now there were dozens of Akari soldiers, not only gathered up ahead but galloping past them toward some unseen goal. Noise began to fill the field. Thorin heard shouts and the distant din of battle. He craned to see past the rain and darkness, and saw for the first time the outlines of Jadori. All around them, the glowing eyes of kreels blinked in the murk. Like a noose, the outlines took shape and converged.

'By the Fate, speak to me, Kahldris! Tell me what this is!'

'This is what comes of talk, Baron Glass!' Kahldris spun to face him. 'Look! Watch!'

The earth began to shake. The Akari riders stormed around them. The kreels came down from the hills, crashing likes waves over the unsuspecting men. With their spears and slashing sword, the Akari defended themselves from the flashing claws of kreels. Thorin stood frozen as the battle raged around them, never touching them. Kahldris grinned.

'Closely now,' he advised. 'Watch.'

With nowhere to run, Thorin girded himself against the onslaught, barely able to stand. Around him the Akari warriors were falling like grass, easily cut down by the kreels and their screaming riders. The black-skinned Jadori worked their beasts effortlessly, darting under the Akari defenses and bringing up their snapping jaws. The hills around them filled with Jadori, pouring down mercilessly on the Akari. Thorin saw the faces of the men, their desperate eyes and open mouths screaming.

How long it took for the massacre to end, Thorin was unsure. The minutes stretched magically, making time intangible. One by one the Akari fell, or fled back into the hills. The bodies of them piled atop each other, until Thorin and Kahldris were knee-deep in corpses. Around them, the Jadori had stopped their attack. Amazingly, their enemies were gone, and the dark-skinned victors let their mounts pick at the bodies, stripping the meat from the bones with their reptilian tongues. It was daybreak suddenly, and the rain had stopped. The hills fell quiet as the Jadori rummaged through the dead.

'I escaped,' said Kahldris. 'I don't know how. I can't remember.'

Thorin's eyes darted wildly about the carnage. The conversations of the Jadori went on around him, yet they remained oblivious to the strangers in their midst. Looking down, Thorin saw a man clawing at the ground, dragging himself with his one good arm away from the battlefield. Like an insect he crawled over Thorin's foot.

317

'Fate save me,' Thorin gasped, shaking the apparition of his boot. 'Kahldris, I want to go. I want to go.'

A Jadori saw the crawling man. Curious, he got down from his kreel and went to him. He spoke some words Thorin could not understand, then raised his spear and put it through the man's back, pinning him to the mud. Seeing this, Thorin cried out.

'Get me out of here!'

Kahldris shook his head. 'I'm not done with my story.'

'What story? What is your point, monster?'

'Can't you tell?' Kahldris seem perturbed. 'This is Maluja, Baron Glass. The meeting place. This is what happened when we answered Dahlgen's request to talk.'

'All right,' Thorin growled. 'I understand.'

'Do you? I wonder. You frighten me, Baron Glass. You've called an army to you, yet now you promise your woman to talk. But talk is not for men like us. Talk is for the weak, Baron. The losers.'

'End this,' Thorin commanded. 'I have seen all I need to.'

Kahldris folded his arms across his chest, staring at Thorin. Then, with a sign he said, 'It is over.'

And it was. A strong wind blew and wiped the world clean. They were back in Koth again, in the shadow of Lionkeep with the sun rising on the field. The corpses vanished, the hills flattened, and the Jadori ghosts returned to their realm. Thorin remained very still, listening to the rain. He didn't know how long he'd been gone, but the clouds were parting overhead and the rain was more a drizzle now.

Kahldris was gone.

Thorin looked down at the ground where the Akari man had been. He could still feel the warmth of blood on his boot.

29

King Raxor of Reec watched in silence from the bridge as the messenger from Koth trotted out from the army. Riding a white horse and flanked by a dozen soldiers, the messenger sat tall as he approached, looking unafraid as he neared the Reecian king. Behind him, the gathering army of Baron Glass readied for the coming clash, positioned a good distance from the river yet close enough to smell their fires. It had taken nearly a week for Glass' army to arrive, and Raxor had watched it with dread, sure that his request to talk had fallen deafly on the Baron. While his own army rested and prepared, the forces of Liiria slowly took form on the west side of the river, rumbling into place beneath the banner of Liiria.

Raxor waited and did not say a word. With him were his son and a handful of bodyguards, all of them mounted on armoured horses. Ten days had passed since Raxor had made his offer to talk, and ten days were all he had given for his offer to be considered. After so long a time, he had not expected any reply. Like the others, he had been shocked to see the riders coming toward them in the morning light. Behind them, their encampment buzzed with excitement. Old King Raxor licked his lips. He was not a man who panicked, but the sight of the arrogant rider made his courage wane.

'Look,' said Roland. 'He comes with Norvans.'

Roland spoke with disgust in his voice, a sentiment shared by most of the Reecians, for although the messenger rode under the banner of Liiria, the men who accompanied him were clearly mercenaries, brought and paid for by the Norvan queen. In fact, there seemed to be very few Liirians in Glass' army, a hodge-podge of different uniforms and colours. Though they had come at Glass' order, Raxor could tell that the rag-tag army consisted mostly of Norvans from various regions of that fractured land, with only a sprinkling of Liirian regulars among them.

'You see, Father?' Roland commented. 'Baron Glass has not the love of his people. Not even the messenger rides with Liirians!'

'He goes with those he trusts,' said Craiglen, Raxor's old friend. 'You underestimate them, I think, Prince Roland.'

Roland snorted, 'Look at them, Craiglen. They are a bunch of hoodlums, not an army.'

'And they broke the will of Breck's Chargers at the library,' said Raxor angrily.

'They're a horde,' said Roland.

'They're a plague,' said Craiglen. 'And only a stupid man is unafraid of plague.'

Roland smouldered at the insult. 'But they come to talk, you see? Baron Glass plays games with us. It is brinksmanship, but I for one would rather fight.'

'Quiet,' Raxor rumbled, never taking his eyes off the approaching messenger. He could see the man more clearly now, a seasoned looking soldier in the distinct garb of Carlion, the Norvan capital. A scarlet cape blew from his shoulders. His silver breastplate gleamed. A dozen mercenaries rode behind him, some with bows on their backs, others with daggers lined in bandoliers across their chests. A dark-skinned man rode closest to the Norvan. Like a Ganjeese man or some other desert ilk, he wore no armour at all over his person, just a loose-fitting tunic. A jumble of black hair sprouted from his head. Raxor regarded him curiously. He knew from Aric Glass that men of every colour served Jazana Carr, made loyal by her endless wealth. He wished suddenly that Aric was with him now, but he had kept the boy far from the river so that he wouldn't be seen, leaving him anxiously waiting in camp.

On the bridge, the Reecians waited, counting the lines of their enemy. There were three such bridges within sight of the armies, but neither side had yet to claim them, keeping safely distant so as not to provoke the battle. It surprised Raxor how cautious Baron Glass was being, and he took it as a hopeful sign. At least a thousand men had made camp in the past week, but they had not moved within half a mile of the Kryss. Nor had they brought heavy weapons with them the way Raxor had, with his siege wagons and catapults. The old man held tight to this glimmer of hope.

And yet the messenger was fast approaching, and might quickly dash the old king's fragile hope. Raxor barely moved upon his horse, refusing to look afraid or betray the turmoil roiling inside him. When the messenger and his gang were only twenty yards away, he turned to the trusted Craiglen.

'Roan-Si. Do you remember, Craiglen?'

As if Craiglen shared his thoughts, the soldier nodded. 'When we fought with Akeela. I remember, my lord.'

It had been so long ago, yet Raxor remembered the day with perfect clarity. They had been allies with the Liirians then. They had met on the bridge at Roan-Si.

'It was before you were born,' said Raxor to his son. 'In better days.'

Now at last the messenger was upon them. The man in his shining breastplate raised his hand and brought his group to a halt. Raxor, who had not so many men with him, returned his steely gaze. An air of arrogance hung around the mercenaries, making Roland bristle. Raxor cleared his throat, a warning to his son.

'My name is Thayus,' said the messenger. 'I serve Baron Glass, ruler of Liiria. He has received your message, King Raxor.'

'Thayus? You are from Carlion.'

The messenger frowned. 'Yes.'

'Why doesn't the Ruler of Liiria send a Liirian to deliver his message?' Raxor asked. 'Please help me with this mystery. I am an old man and easily confused.'

Roland laughed, but the man named Thayus had a grin more of contempt than humour.

'Norvor and Liiria are allies now, my lord,' said Thayus. 'They are like a giant with two big fists.'

'Giants are clumsy,' said Raxor. 'And a two-headed giant is clumsiest of all. Tell your master to be careful, good Thayus, or he may trip and hurt himself.'

'My lord surprises me!' Thayus chirped. 'But you need not pretend bravery, I have good news for you. Baron Glass will speak with you.'

There was silence among the Reecians.

'Good,' said Raxor quickly, pretending he wasn't stunned. 'He made the right choice.'

'You or your representative may come across, King Raxor, at a time of your choosing no later than sundown,' said Thayus. 'I am prepared to escort you now if you wish.'

'Not now,' said Craiglen, 'and not the king. If we decide to talk, I will speak for Raxor.'

'Or I will,' said Roland quickly. 'You may tell your master that the King of Reec will not step lightly into a snare. You will have your answer by sunfall.'

Thayus, clearly a man of breeding, inclined his head politely. 'I will tell Baron Glass your wishes,' he said. 'Is there anything else you require?'

'We will bring men with us for safety,' said Roland. 'If they are turned away there will be no talk.'

'Of course,' said Thayus with a nod.

'Return to your master, Norvan,' said Raxor. 'By sundown you will know our minds in full.'

Thayus thanked Raxor, and for a moment the contempt fled from his eyes. He was playing a part, Raxor knew, but this man who carried Glass' messages was more than he seemed. Unafraid, surely, but not because of arrogance. It was clear that Thayus had been a soldier for a very long time.

Raxor waited on the bridge until the man from Carlion had turned his men around and began trotting back toward their camp. Roland began to speak, but the king snapped at him to hold his tongue.

'Not now,' he said. 'I won't sit here talking in the wind.'

When he was satisfied that Thayus and his men were far enough away, King Raxor turned his own horse about and headed back toward camp.

Aric Glass had been waiting impatiently near Raxor's pavilion for the king to return. At Raxor's orders he had remained behind, far out of sight of any Liirians or Norvans who might come to the bridge. He had been given a cot in a tent not far from Raxor's, bedding down with soldiers who were among Raxor's personal bodyguards. Just as they were charged with protecting the king himself, the soldiers had been given orders to see that no harm befell Aric, and that he did not wander away. He was, in a sense, still a prisoner of the Reecians, though he was treated more like a guest by the kindly old king. In the days since he had arrived in the Reecian camp, neither Raxor nor his underlings spent any time interrogating him, and the threat to send him to their infamous interrogator had ebbed. A tenuous trust had taken hold between Aric and the king, and Aric appreciated it. More, he worried now for the good man's safety.

As Raxor spoke to Roland and the others, Aric watched and listened carefully. The invitation to the meeting had surprised him, though he was glad for it and planned to offer any guidance he could. Besides Raxor's son, the stone-faced Craiglen was there as well, sitting to the king's left. Other men of rank – about half a dozen of them – had come too, listening as Raxor explained what had happened at the bridge. It was barely past daybreak and many of the Reecians still had sleep in their eyes. Most, like Aric, sat cross-legged on the ground, arranged in a semi-circle around the king, who, like Roland, had a proper chair for himself. A slobbering mastiff sat between Raxor and Roland, snuffling with disinterest as Raxor told his story. It was not much of a tale, and was over quickly. When he was done with its telling, Raxor sat back and scratched the head of his pet, waiting for advice.

'You have to go,' said one of the men, a young looking lieutenant whom Aric had seen in camp many times.

'He can't go, Jakane,' said Roland flatly. 'He's the king.'

'But he has to talk, see what the baron is offering,' said Craiglen. 'Though I agree, my lord, that it can't be you. Send me. I will speak for you.'

'No, Craiglen, I'm going,' Roland insisted. 'And don't argue, Father. I've made up my mind.'

Surprisingly, Raxor did not argue with his son. He barely even acknowledged him.

'This is no more than we asked for,' said the king. 'And more than I expected, frankly. If Baron Glass is willing to talk, then we must talk. But I won't go myself because that is what he wants, to preen and puff around me like a rooster.'

'He's not expecting you, my lord,' said Jakane. 'He can't be. He would never expect you to accept his terms. The meeting is on his side of the Kryss.'

'It has to be somewhere,' said Roland. 'I'm not afraid to go.'

Raxor grimaced at his son's bravado. He turned to Aric. 'What say you, boy? Is it a trick? Or is your father sincere?'

'I don't know, my lord,' answered Aric honestly. 'But he's not afraid of you, that I can promise. I don't know why he's agreed to talk, but it's not because of fear.'

'Something else?' Raxor probed.

Aric nodded. 'It must be.'

'A trap?' Craiglen suggested.

'He has no reason to trap us,' said Raxor. 'Aric Glass?'

'No, I agree,' said Aric. 'If my father is willing to talk, there's a reason.' He shrugged. 'But why I can't say.'

'He didn't bring his army here to talk,' said Roland. The prince looked at each of the men seriously. 'He could have talked from Koth, sent his messenger to us days ago. No, he wants this battle. He wants the Kryss.'

'Aye,' agreed Jakane, and was quickly echoed by some others.

'We're talking in circles,' said Raxor with a sigh. He looked exhausted suddenly. 'If he's spoiling for a fight, we're ready. We won't give back the Kryss, and he needs to know that. That's what we're going to tell him.'

'Who, then?' Roland asked. 'Let it be me, Father.'

Raxor hesitated. 'Roland, we need tact now.'

Roland looked offended. 'Tact? We need to face the storm, Father. We need to show the Black Baron our resolve.'

'You need to make him listen,' said Aric. All eyes turned to him. 'I'm sorry, but it's true. There's only one person in this camp that my father will really listen to, my lord.'

Raxor smiled. 'No, boy. Forget what you're thinking.'

'My lord—'

'No.' Raxor shook his head. 'No.'

Aric tried to stay circumspect. Seeing his father again was not something he relished, but the logic of the choice seemed obvious. Aric was sure he could get his father to listen.

'My lord is trying to protect me, but it's not necessary,' he said. 'I know the risks, but I also know my father will listen to me.'

'You have a mission,' said Raxor. 'Do you think I have forgotten? You have an alliance to make. You're more important than a messenger. You will stay here, Aric Glass, safe and out of sight. And if battle comes you will not join it. You will stay safe and you will live. Do you understand?'

Reluctantly, Aric nodded. 'Yes, my lord.'

'Then it will be me,' said Roland. He looked sanguine. Glancing at his father, he watched the old man agree.

'Very well,' said Raxor. 'Choose who will go with you and make ready.'

'No one needs to go with me,' said Roland. 'If it is a trap, a handful of men aren't going to help. They'll only die along with me.'

'Prince Roland, that's stupid,' said Craiglen. 'I'm going with you, like it or not.'

'You're not,' Roland boiled. 'I'm going alone to speak with Baron Glass. Much as I hate to admit it, you're needed here, Craiglen.'

Aric expected Raxor to protest, but instead saw a flash of pride in his eyes. The king looked at his hot-headed son and smiled.

'My son means to prove himself,' he said. 'I say it is time.'

Baron Glass took a seat at the edge of his encampment, sipping on a sherry from crystal glass as the sun fell behind him. Though there were other chairs arranged around his fire, the baron sat alone, staring pensively into the distance. Thorin's mind stretched in a hundred different directions. He heard Kahldris in his skull, talking to him, berating him for agreeing to meet. He thought of Jazana, too, and of her beautiful body laying next to him, and how much he owed her. And then he thought of Raxor, his old enemy. Surely Raxor was afraid. That was why he wanted to talk, why he had agreed to send his son across the river. The baron tasted his sherry, swirling it in his mouth, patiently waiting for Roland to arrive. According to his scouts the prince had already crossed the bridge. In just a few minutes they would be face to face.

Just a few minutes.

No time to think. There was never enough time these days. There was only work to be done. Thorin leaned back in his canvas chair and tried getting comfortable. Nearby, Colonel Thayus stood beside a tree, waiting for Prince Roland. The colonel from Carlion craned his neck to see over the camp. He had told Thorin what an impressive man Raxor was, still, and how the old man had baited him. He was not backing down easily. Thorin respected that. He swallowed his sherry and looked down into his glass.

Talk, he told himself. It's just talk.

Kahldris had said Jazana had gelded him, that he was not a man any more, but the puppet of a woman. Jazana's lapdog. Thorin knew the demon was wrong. He simply did not understand.

'Kahldris,' he whispered, 'you live because of me, because I am a man and you are nothing but smoke. Without me you cannot taste the wine. Remember that.'

He felt the Akari squirm through his brain, twisting angrily at his statement. Since deciding on this meeting, Kahldris had been in a bitter mood.

I hunger, Baron Glass, he reminded Thorin. *It is time to feast.*

Thorin shook his head. 'I'll not be controlled.'

His arm began to burn, his armoured arm, the one that no longer existed.

'I feel you,' he grumbled loudly.

Then take my meaning, Kahldris warned. *Don't forget what I have given you.*

Colonel Thayus, who was used to Thorin's seemingly one-way conversations, turned to regard the baron, then quickly looked away.

So? We need each other, Thorin told the spirit.

Then give me what I need. Give me blood.

Thorin set his sherry down on the little table next to him. 'First we talk.'

In his mind, Kahldris screamed. But Thorin had become deaf in shunting the demon away, and so ignored him as he looked out over his army. Many had come, though many were mercenaries and few were Liirian. It stung him to realize how right Rodrik Varl was, how the Liirians still feared him. But Rodrik Varl was back in Koth, and Thorin knew that he was in charge now. The mercenaries would not question him. They, too, feared the Black Baron.

The minutes passed and the sun finally disappeared. Thorin waited by his fire, growing impatient, until finally he heard Thayus give a shout.

'He's coming,' said the colonel, then went to stand beside the baron.

'Sit, Thayus,' Thorin told him, gesturing to the chair beside him.

Thayus took his seat reluctantly, looking uncharacteristically nervous. He was a man who'd been through many campaigns, and had even been a loyalist to King Lorn. He was not afraid of the coming battle, yet seemed disturbed by the turn of events.

'What will you say to him?' asked the colonel.

'We're just talking.'

Thayus shrugged. 'I don't understand any of this.'

A moment later Thorin saw his men approaching. The dark-skinned man was in the lead, looking pleased with himself as he escorted Roland through the camp. Like Thayus, Kaj had been key to winning Koth. A free-lancer from Ganjor, he was one of Jazana's best commanders, and his men, the Crusaders, had almost single-handedly taken the north side of the city. Kaj nodded as his eyes met Thorin's, then stepped aside for Prince Roland. The mercenaries halted, and Roland the Red grimaced.

'Come ahead,' Thorin called to him.

Prince Roland was a tall, well-dressed young man, with a handsome, cocky face. Thorin at once saw the shadow of his father in him, though Raxor was certainly more muscular. In contrast, Roland was lean and wiry and walked with a long, bouncing gait. The prince had come empty-handed into the camp of his enemies, without even an arming sword at his side. Around his neck hung a chain of gold with a diamond dangling from it, the kind of thing a woman might wear. He fixed his jaw when he saw the baron, summoning his courage.

'I'm Baron Glass,' Thorin thundered, letting his armoured arm rest in his lap. 'Welcome, Prince Roland.'

Roland at once tried claiming the high ground. He said curtly, 'I am here to talk for my father, Baron Glass, the King of Reec. He wishes to know your mind.'

He was a child. Thorin realized it at once. Like a dog, Thorin could smell the fear on him.

'Will you sit?' he asked the prince.

Roland thought for a moment, then stepped forward. Despite his awkwardness, Thorin admired his courage. While Kaj and the others kept back, Roland went to sit before the baron and his colonel. As he settled down, Thorin grabbed another glass and filled it with sherry.

'Here,' he offered. 'A drink will steady you, I think.'

Roland's hand paused in mid-air. His temples began to pulse. 'Let us talk, Baron Glass, about why you are here. About your designs.'

'We'll talk. Just take the drink, boy.'

The prince took the drink, and without smiling tipped the glass over, spilling the wine into the dirt. His long fingers opened, dropped the glass, and sent it shattering downward.

'Why no feast, Baron Glass? Why no dancing girls or musicians? I haven't come to make merry. So let us speak our minds.'

Next to him, Thorin felt Thayus tense. Inside him, he heard Kahldris gasp.

Insolence.

Thorin steadied them both. He said easily, 'Your father is the one that should explain himself, youngster. Why has he moved so close against the Kryss?'

'To defend what is ours,' said Roland.

'You mean what was given to you,' Thorin corrected.

Roland snorted in disgust. 'I knew that was why you came here, Baron Glass. To take back the Kryss. If you expect us to capitulate . . .'

'The Kryss is ours,' said Thorin. 'It was given to Reec in a time of weakness by King Akeela who was brainsick. But you're wrong, Prince Roland – I don't expect you to give it back to us. You've come ready to fight, haven't you?'

'We have,' said Roland confidently.

Thorin smiled. 'And that's what you want, isn't it?'

'We are not afraid to fight, Baron Glass.'

'No, boy, I'm talking about *you.* You have no idea how obvious you are, do you? Your father wants peace. That much is obvious. He'll fight for the Kryss because he must, but you'll fight because you want to fight. You're a whelp. And like all whelps, you have something to prove.'

The prince bristled. 'You talk big, old man.' He looked down at Thorin's gleaming arm. 'That armour of yours – you think it will save you from a whole army? Have you seen what we've brought with us?'

'I've seen,' said Thorin confidently. 'A goodly force, to be sure.' He shrugged with nonchalance. 'If you think it's enough, then make your move. That's why you came alone, so no one else would hear your bargain. Please don't insult me by denying it.'

Sweat began erupting on Roland's upper lip. Outwardly, though, he controlled himself. 'I'm here at my father's request, to tell you there is no bargaining about the river Kryss. It was given to Reec by the King of Liiria. It belongs to us now.' A flash of hatred ran through his eyes. 'And Baron Glass, if you're so good at reading my mind, then you know I'm not afraid of you. Nor is my father. So do not try to cow us. We are Reecians. We are not afraid of anything.'

'You are your father's son,' laughed Thorin. 'If he were here, those would be his words exactly.'

Why do you play with him? He insults you!

Thorin paid the spirit no mind, but Kahldris quickly erupted with such force it jolted Thorin forward.

Do not ignore me!

Struck like a hammer, Thorin put his hand to his head and closed his eyes, willing Kahldris to be silent. But the Akari's anger pushed forward, demanding to be loosed.

I need blood! Blood to live!

Thorin got to his feet, fighting for control. Prince Roland looked at him, plainly confused. Colonel Thayus jumped up and stood before the baron.

'Baron Glass? What is it?'

The world began to spin. Thorin opened his eyes and saw a red haze. His head began to pound. His armoured arm twitched. He tried to speak but could not, and realized too late that he had pushed Kahldris too far.

'Don't,' he managed to sputter. 'No . . .'

Kahldris was on him, suffocating him. Thorin tried to move backward, to run, but the demon held him firm. Prince Roland got to his feet and stared, his mouth agape as Thorin's face began to twist. Inside Thorin's head, he heard Kahldris' voice, calm and lilting.

It is time.

Thorin jerked forward and shoved Thayus aside. Unable to stop himself, his enchanted arm shot out and grabbed Roland by the throat. As if watching a dream, Thorin saw the gauntlet close about the prince's neck. The prince writhed as the arm lifted him to his toes. He gave a stunted, gasping scream. Thorin watched as the gauntlet tightened. He wanted to turn away, but no part of him would obey, not even his horror-stricken eyes. Roland's throat became smaller and smaller, until it was just an impossible reed. Colonel Thayus was shouting, roaring for Thorin to stop.

'Fate above, enough!' Thorin cried.

Crushed in Thorin's vice-like fist, Roland's neck ruptured. The veins bulged and exploded, spraying blood against Thorin's face. The head lolled back with a death rattle. Like a snake the armoured arm coiled around Roland, soaking up the blood. Nausea swam through Thorin's brain. Thayus and the others began to wretch. As it had before, the Devil's Armour began to feed. Thorin's armoured arm writhed with life, glowing as the figures embossed in its metal danced with animation. Thorin shook the dead prince, wringing every drop of blood from his neck, carefully smearing it along the gauntlet and mail. And then, when he was done, he dropped the wizened corpse to the ground.

Power flooded Thorin's body. Inside him, Kahldris let out a sigh of ecstasy.

Glorious!

Thorin's will buckled. He looked down at Roland's violated body, wanting to vomit but then succumbing to the demon.

'The Kryss is ours,' he said in a voice not quite his own. 'It is time.'

By now Kaj and the others had joined Thayus, circling Thorin in shock. Thorin looked at them in challenge.

'Do you hear? Kaj, to your men! Thayus, my friend, it is time!'

Baron Glass did not wait for his men to follow. Locked away in his private tent, the rest of the Devil's Armour called to him.

30

Aric was napping when the commotion awoke him. He had been dreaming of a woman he had once met in Calon, a town in southeren Liiria known for its prostitutes. When he heard the shouts of men around him, he opened his eyes with a groan. Around him, the soldiers with whom he shared the tent were pulling on boots and hurriedly dressing themselves. The pleasant memory of Aric's harlot quickly fled as he sat up, looking around in dazed confusion. The Reecian soldiers were talking loudly but he could not understand their words. Most were fleeing the tent. Aric tossed his naked feet over the side of his cot and tried to get their attention.

'What is it?' he asked.

A young man who Aric recognized looked over at him as he was buttoning up his jacket. His eyes were wild as he said, 'They're coming!'

'Coming? Who . . .'

But then Aric understood. His mind wrapped slowly around the happenings. Prince Roland had gone to his father to talk. Was is it over? Aric wondered how long he'd been asleep.

'Don't just sit there. Get your boots on!' cried the young soldier. And then he was out of the tent, following his brethren in to the night.

Aric jumped to his feet. Outside he heard the crescendo of men making ready for battle. He found his boots beneath his cot, pulling them on to his feet, then grabbed his coat from the edge of his mattress and ran outside. As he pulled his arms through his coat's leather sleeves, he looked about in disbelief. The camp had erupted into activity. All around him men were shouting, galloping past on horses or running in aimless directions. Officers called out orders over the din, directing the chaos while dogs barked and squires stumbled past with arm-loads of arrows. A full moon lit the camp, and through its silvery haze Aric could see men marching toward the Kryss. Colonel Craiglen sat atop a grey charger, his face red with effort as he yelled to his officers. Overwhelmed by the scene, Aric stumbled forward, unsure what to do or even what was happening. Craiglen saw his confusion and galloped toward him.

'Aric Glass!' he called. He jerked his grey horse to a halt. 'Protect yourself, boy.'

'Protect myself?' Aric sputtered. 'What's happening?'

'Your father is attacking,' sneered Craiglen. 'Under the very truce of peace! His men are making for the bridges. We have to form our lines. Find yourself cover!'

'No!' Aric cried. 'I'm not going to hide!'

'Look at you! You're not ready for this. You—' Craiglen stopped himself with a growl. 'Oh, fine!' He stretched down his hand. 'Come on.'

Aric took his hand and let the old soldier pull him onto horseback. Wrapping his arm about Craiglen's chest, he held tight as the colonel galloped away.

'Where are we going?' Aric asked.

'To Raxor,' said Craiglen over his shoulder, and soon the two were darting through the camp, dodging men and machinery as they headed toward the front. Aric strained to see the distant river. In the moonlight and glow of torches he could see the horizon swarming with movement as his father's forces gathered into position. Flags and flashing spears punctured the night sky. Barely visible, the main bridge stood over the river, still abandoned by either side, though Aric's father's mercenaries were nearer to it and quickly closing the gap.

'What happened to the talks?' Aric asked in Craiglen's ear. 'What about Prince Roland?'

'I don't know,' snapped Craiglen. 'Dead I think.'

'Dead? How?'

'Stop talking to me, boy!'

As Craiglen raced through the crowds Aric pondered his words. Roland was dead? It made no sense, but he asked no more questions of the busy colonel, instead holding on as the horse bounded across the camp. At last they spotted Raxor through the disorder, atop his charger and surrounded by men. The king had fixed his crown to his head and wore a full regalia of battle garb. The most disquieting look suffused his face. He turned toward them as he noticed Craiglen coming forward. The old colonel skidded to a stop and took measure of the horizon.

'They've sent men toward the north and south bridges,' Raxor informed him. 'Looks like the bulk of them are coming straight for the main bridge.'

Craiglen nodded, but even Aric knew the news was grave. There were three bridges nearby, and his father planned to overwhelm them all. The main bridge, as Raxor called it, was the largest of the three. And the nearest. Days earlier, he had met on that bridge with the Norvan colonel.

'Darltin took a troop north,' Raxor continued. 'Craiglen, you join them. Take Karik's company with you. I'll send Jakel to the south bridge.'

330

'And the main bridge, my lord?' asked Craiglen with dread. 'What of it?'

'I have the dogs, Craiglen, don't worry,' said Raxor.

'This is where Baron Glass will come through,' said Craiglen. 'Let me stay with you.'

'Do as I ask, and hurry,' ordered Raxor. His eyes met Aric's. 'And you. Get down.'

Aric hurried off the back of Craiglen's horse. He looked up expectantly at Raxor. 'My lord, tell me what to do.'

'Just keep yourself safe. Stay with me.'

'But I can fight!'

'I'm sure you can,' agreed Raxor. He turned toward a group of squires, calling for a horse. 'You'll ride,' he told Aric. 'And you'll keep back with me. Your father's a snake, boy. I want to know what other tricks he might have for us.'

'I'm sure I don't know, my lord,' said Aric. 'Just let me fight—'

But Raxor was already ignoring him, berating Craiglen for still being there. He ordered his old friend away, and with a reluctant nod Colonel Craiglen galloped off, toward the northern bridge. Raxor shot orders to the other officers, sending most of them scurrying. Around them the catapults screamed like twisting metal as the crews began getting them into position.

'There wasn't time,' Raxor growled. His eyes grew distant. Aric could tell he was thinking of his son. 'They come like wolves.'

'My lord?' Aric probed. 'Prince Roland?'

Raxor shook his head. 'They just started coming, Aric.' The old man looked lost. 'There was nothing. No word, no warning.'

The words were horrible, made more so from a father's lips. Aric stood frozen even as a squire hurried up to him with a horse.

'My lord, I'm sorry,' he offered. 'But maybe—'

'He's dead,' said Raxor, cutting him off. 'Get on your horse, boy.'

The horse that had appeared was not Aric's own but a larger, brown gelding already outfitted for battle, with iron plating along its flanks and hammered metal covering its snout. It chewed anxiously on its bit as Aric mounted then wheeled it about, wondering where they were headed.

'What now?' he asked the king.

Raxor was already on the move. Flanked by lieutenants, the old man was quickly giving orders, pointing out different regions of the battle-ground as he rode. They were woefully unprepared for the attack, that much was plain. Aric could see the trepidation on Raxor's face.

'The dogs,' the king called back to him. 'They'll be first.'

Up ahead, the dog handlers waited, each of them holding a leash of ten snarling mastiffs. At least two-hundred of the beasts barked at the horizon, eager to race toward the bridge. The handlers looked at Raxor anxiously. Cavalry men still gathered near the line. Aric imagined Raxor's strategy. The dogs, he knew, would buy them time.

'Let them go,' Raxor ordered.

The handlers released the beasts. One by one they twisted the chains from their stout collars, sending the mastiffs snarling into the night. The air filled with their angry barks. Soon the field was flooded with them, their powerful bodies bounding toward the bridge.

Aric watched them go, sure that on the other side of the river, his father awaited them.

Baron Glass charged for the bridge, his body encased in his magical armour. Through the eyeslits of his helmet, night had become day, and he did not need the feeble moon to light his way. Like his enchanted, missing arm, his entire frame became one with the armour, animated by Kahldris and his powerful magic, and Baron Glass did not feel the weight of its metal or the constriction of its binds. As light as a robe, the Devil's Armour danced on him, forming to him like a second skin. His fingers articulated perfectly in his spiked gauntlets, and the Akari sword he carried into battle felt like a twig, feather light as it whistled through the wind. Behind him, an army followed, straining to keep up with the baron as he hurried toward the river. Among them were the only Liirians in the battle, a company of loyalists to Thorin led by a man named Siagan. Siagan had answered Thorin's call to arms, gathering Kothans to his banner with the promise of gold. Unlike Liiria's Royal Chargers, they were outlaws and farmers, mostly, but they were Liirians still and so rode with their new king into battle.

Beside Thorin, the mercenary Rase fought to keep up with the baron. Like Siagan, he too had soldiers with him, nearly a thousand Norvan mercenaries. Rase, a friend of Rodrik Varl, had replaced Varl as Thorin's top mercenary. Rase kept low in the saddle as he rode, his eyes fixed on the coming river and the men beyond. They had surprised their enemies, clearly. Across the Kryss the Reecian soldiers hurried to arrange their defenses. Thorin watched as the catapults screeched into place and the horsemen circled in confusion. In the centre of the Reecian army, the banner of King Raxor wavered in the breeze, lit by smoky torchlight. His army of ten-thousand moved like a wave on the horizon, undulating into action. They were more numerous than Thorin's forces and better equipped, and yet Thorin had no fear at all.

No fear, Kahldris whispered in his ear.

And Thorin knew the truth of Kahldris' words, and did not fear the giant army on the river's other side. He could not be nicked by a Reecian sword or felled by a Reecian arrow or overwhelmed by their great numbers. And when he saw the Reecian dogs, he simply nodded.

'Look at that!' cried Rase.

Swarming over the bridge came the mastiffs, spreading out like a screaming tide. Racing across the field, their necks encircled with steel collars, their bodies mailed and thickly muscled, the war dogs darted through the darkness, their open jaws snapping toward Thorin's army. Siagan called back to his men, ordering them to ready themselves. Rase and his mercenaries tucked down on their mounts. Mastiffs choked the bridge as they fought to reach the field. Those already on the field made ready to pounce.

Baron Glass saw the dark eyes of the dogs and braced himself. At the point of his army, he raised his sword and commanded his men into the fray.

'To the bridge!' he cried.

Then like a hammer the first mastiff struck him. Leaping through the air, the great dog launched himself up and over Thorin's horse, catching the baron square in the chest. Thorin's ears rang with the scraping of nails and the slobbering snarl of a snapping jaw. Surprised, he caught the beast by the throat and hurled it aside, only to have two more swarm him. His armoured legs easily parried their insistent jaws as the beasts tried vainly to take hold. Thorin yelled out in anger, used his sword to dislodge the first, then wheeled his horse to face the second. Instantly other mastiffs joined the mêlée. Thorin found himself surrounded. Already Rase and Siagan were in battles of their own. The field filled with cries.

'Come!' Thorin taunted, waving his sword.

The mastiffs stalked closer, then leapt. Thorin felt their blows as the armour deflected them all. He had but to turn to and they were off him, sliding like water off his black metal skin. Around him, Rase and his mercenaries fought off the worst of them, their advance cut down by the wall of dog flesh. The monstrous dogs easily pulled the mercenaries down from their horses, dragging them screaming through the night. Siagan and his Liirians hurried to aid them, slashing a path through the mastiffs.

Thorin turned, then felt another of the dogs tearing at his boot. The fangs should have easily pierced the leather, but the magic of the Devil's Armour surrounded every bit of Thorin, and as the dog hopelessly tried getting hold of him Thorin reached down and took hold of the mastiff's metal collar. The dog growled and thrashed its huge body, fighting like a fish as Thorin lifted it from the ground. It snapped its jaws in Thorin's face, trying to reach him. Bringing down his helmeted head, Thorin crushed its skull. As the mastiff went limp, Thorin tossed it aside, determined to make for the bridge.

There, he saw a hundred more mastiffs waiting to fight him. Undaunted, he slogged his way across the bloodied field.

Colonel Craiglen arrived at the north bridge just as the mercenaries reached the river. His own forces, led by a young officer named Darltin, had arrived only minutes earlier, and were gathering to meet the mercenaries in battle. Craiglen found Darltin in the chaos and quickly took command, ordering his own company to the bridge. He could see the wave of Norvans cresting on the other side, disappointed that they had not reached their destination sooner. Amazingly, Baron Glass had sent a larger part of his army to the north bridge than he had the main one, where Raxor was battling. Counting up their numbers in the darkness made Craiglen blanche. Along with the companies of Darltin and Tom, he had perhaps a thousand men under his command, but it seemed to Craiglen that the Norvans had at least that many, a ragtag army of enraged mercenaries without any cause to fight for save their own enrichment.

Craiglen had no dogs or war machines to stem the tide. The catapults, which weren't ready anyway, had all been stationed further south to hold the central bridge. It would be man to man here, Craiglen knew.

'The way things ought to be,' he muttered.

Colonel Craiglen could remember his every battle. He had been charmed since birth at the art of fighting, gifted with a sword and touched by heaven so that he'd never once been wounded. And yet, seeing the mercenary army made him afraid. At the bridge, he watched as the first of Darltin's men forded the river, the Norvan mercenaries quick to meet them. On the other side of the Kryss waited the rest of the motley force, some trying to come across on horseback and being swept away by the fast-moving tide. The Reecians picked at them with arrows. Others sent volleys skyward, reaching across the Kryss to strike the enemy. Craiglen thought for a moment, wondering how best to direct his forces. It was simply a fight for the bridge, he determined quickly. On the bridge, the battle would be won. Or lost.

Craiglen took out his sword and thundered forward. At the top of his voice he called his men to follow, rallying them to war. With his company in tow, he raced for the bridge, and when he reached it fought his way to the front of the mêlée, slashing past the Norvan blades, face to face with his foes. Yards away he saw the dark-skinned man. Craiglen recognized him at once. He had come with the Norvan colonel that day to talk peace at the bridge. Enraged, Craiglen brandished his blade high.

'You, desert man!' he cried. 'Scum!'

They were fine fighters, all of them, these men who the dark man commanded. Like their leader, many of them had the same sun-baked skin and wild, colourful garb. With their curved swords and leather-wrapped spears, they clashed against Craiglen's armoured cavalry, smashing together with a thunderous din. Craiglen muscled his horse across the bridge, step by agonizing step toward the dark-skinned leader. One by one he fought through the mercenaries, bringing up his sword against the attacks. His soldiers bolstered him, surrounding him as men and horses tumbled from the bridge. Craiglen fought for every inch, screaming at his quarry, who at last caught a glimpse of him through the battle. Craiglen spat in his direction.

The desert man spun off from his fellows and headed for Craiglen. The old Reecian colonel obliged, using his shield like a battering ram to pass the throng of fighters. With his sword at the ready, Craiglen brought it windmilling overhead just as his foe came in range. Instantly the dark man had up his defense. The two circled, exchanging blows, Craiglen blocking with his shield while the other used only his expert sword arm. Ignoring everything around them the men were like dancers locked in a deadly waltz. Craiglen renewed his attack, driving the mercenary to the edge of the bridge.

'Is this how you talk peace?' he raged. 'By murdering the prince?'

The desert man grunted, fighting off the big man's blows. Nearby, his men saw his predicament and cried out to him.

'Kaj! The edge!'

Too late, the desert man saw the stone rail. Forced into it by Craiglen's horse, he leaned back too far to avoid the Reecian sword. Craiglen pressed his attack, but the other mercenaries had charged forward now, pushing and unbalancing him. Now both close to tumbling, the two men grabbed for each other. The desert man was going over. Craiglen could see it in his eyes. Too close for swords, they grappled with each other until the pressure from the battle drove them over the edge.

Only blackness filled Craiglen's eyes. He felt the sensation of the world whipping by, then the stunning cold of the river.

King Raxor ordered his cavalry to the bridge.

It had taken almost an hour for Baron Glass' forces to deal with the mastiffs, more than enough time for his men to make ready. Lines of archers had filled the air with arrows, softening up the mercenaries and the complicit Liirians while the dogs slowed their advance. Behind Raxor, the catapults were finally ready to launch. Each one had a brazier filled with hot coals, burning wood and flammable liquid, ready to send the potent mixture skyward. Along the river, handfuls of Norvans had fought their way onto Reecian soil, making human chains and using ropes to pull themselves though the Kryss. Skirmishes had broken out all along the bank, but on the bridge, barely visible to Raxor, a small number of mastiffs still held back the bulk of Glass' forces. Reports were coming in from the north and south. Raxor listened to them all keenly. Craiglen's men had so far held the bridge, but in the south the mercenaries had already broken through.

'How the hell can that be?' Raxor shouted, glaring at his young lieutenant.

'They have more men, my lord, and they reached the bridge before us.'

'Darltin?'

'Still alive,' the officer reported. 'He requests more troops.'

Raxor quickly dispatched another company, this one a reserve unit he'd hoped to use himself against the baron. The young lieutenant thanked his king and galloped off, guiding the new troops south. But Raxor knew that the south was already lost. Once the bridge was breached, stemming the tide would be impossible.

'My lord, let me go with them,' pleaded Aric Glass. So far, he stayed true to the king's order, never wandering far. Together they had watched the battle unfolding in the moonlight.

'Stay,' the king commanded.

'My lord, I'm useless to you here. Let me fight, please!'

'Useless? You are useless?' King Raxor at last took the time to look at Aric. Despite the battle raging around them, he spoke in a soft, kindly voice. 'When this over, you might be the most important person in the world to my kingdom.'

Aric shook his head. 'I have to see my father. At least let me do this.'

'Rubbish. You'll stay here, boy. Stay safe. You have a mission to accomplish.'

Aric smouldered as Raxor turned aside. At the bridge the Reecian cavalry met the first of Glass' men.

Overhead, Thorin heard the roar of fire. Streaking skyward came the hot missiles from the Reecian catapults, firing one by one in rapid succession, lowering their deadly payload among his troops. Behind him he saw the impact as the first load of coals and liquid exploded, splaying out like a fiery hand amidst the unprepared Liirians. Siagan had fallen back, his men pushed to the rear by the onslaught of the mastiffs. Among his men he still fought the last of the dogs, but when the payload crashed around him his horse reared up with a cry. For a moment the night turned to daylight as the flames engulfed the soldiers, dazzling Thorin with its terrible light. He wheeled on the bridge to see the result as another missile crashed, this time closer than the first. By the time the third one hit Thorin could not see Siagan at all.

The baron spun around to face the coming cavalry. A rain of arrows continued to fall, heralding their arrival. Rase and a few dozen of his men had reached the bridge, ducking the deadly shafts. Thorin raised his sword to rally his mercenaries.

'No retreat!' he cried. 'The bridge is ours! Don't give it up!'

But as the Reecian horsemen thundered closer, the baron's boast seemed hollow. Thorin braced himself as the lead riders lowered their lances. More of his men were fast approaching, but the Reecians made a tidal wave as they approached, shaking the bridge with their attack. The first of the horsemen galloped across, aiming straight for Baron Glass. Without a shield to parry the lances, Thorin let his armour take the blow. The horseman aimed his weapon. Thorin steeled himself, then felt the lance smash against his breastplate. Splinters flew as the weapon buckled. Stunned, the rider kept on going, straight ahead toward Thorin's blade. The sword whistled and the head tumbled, and the Devil's Armour drank the blood that fell like rain.

Now the Reecians swarmed the bridge. Thorin felt the madness descend. His blade was everywhere, finding every mark, shattering his enemies as his magic armour glowed with life. It writhed on him, its metal hot with blood, its black spikes moving like snakes. Against the hurricane of Reecian lances Baron Glass withstood the storm, not giving back an inch as the Reecians came to challenge him. His sword arm swung without tiring, cutting down the cavalry and littering the bridge with corpses. Amazed, Race and his mercenaries pressed onward, shielded by the miraculous killing machine.

'Let them come all night!' bellowed Baron Glass, sure that somewhere across the bridge Raxor watched with dread. He ignored the arrows pelting his hide, and paid no heed to the sky filled with fire. He forged on, meeting every lance and sword, easily besting the Reecian barrage.

You see! Kahldris laughed. *How beautiful you are! How indestructible!*

'Yes!' Thorin cried, loving the sweet madness. 'I'm alive again!'

Undaunted, the Reecians came across the bridge, and one by one Baron Glass slaughtered them. And while he fought his Devil's Armour fused to him, taking every blow like a gentle kiss.

Colonel Craiglen exploded up out of the water. Around him he heard the roar of the river and the screams of men. He gulped for breath, groping for anything that would get him to shore. Next to him, the mercenary who'd tumbled with him over the bridge was swimming for shore. The dark-skinned man had survived.

Exhausted, Craiglen went after him. His aching arms stroked quickly through the river, fighting the current to reach the rocky bank. The mercenary glanced over his shoulder.

'Don't follow me!' he cried.

Determined to catch him, Craiglen kicked and pinwheeled his arms, forcing himself to breathe. His body ached from the concussion of the fall. His head pounded with agony. Still he swam, and just as the mercenary clawed his way ashore he caught hold of the man's boot.

'No way you live!' he growled, pulling him back into the river. The man kicked out, catching Craiglen's jaw and sending teeth and blood flying. But the old colonel kept hold, and with his other hand freed the dagger from his belt.

'Dog!' he spat. 'Dog for hire! That's what you are!'

Colonel Craiglen raised his dagger, and in that moment saw the stranger on the bank, lowering a crossbow. With an awful, split-second calculation he realized he was dead. He cried out, leaping from the river like a shark, plunging his dagger into the dark man's back. The man called Kaj cried out, his head falling hard against the rocks. Then came the twang of the crossbow.

As the bolt struck his neck, Colonel Craiglen released his dagger. He felt his legs go slack and the current take him. His eyes fluttered, but for an instant he watched his enemy on the rock, sagging with death.

Unable to stay alive, Craiglen stopped trying. He let the river carry him away.

Aric waited helplessly at Raxor's side. While the moon swept overhead, he counted the hours going by as the battle continued. King Raxor had refused to fall back, even as the mercenaries forded the river and the battle for the central bridge raged on. Wave after wave of cavalrymen had been sent to the bridge, but so far they had been unable to secure it or beat back their outnumbered enemy. Aric chaffed atop his horse, eager to get into the fight. Mostly ignored by Raxor, he listened as the king took council from his lieutenants and listened gravely to reports from the north and south, where the fighting continued. Raxor had already sent most of his reserves to the main bridge. He had come to the Kryss with nearly ten-thousand men, but throughout the night that number had dwindled. Raxor's face glistened with sweat and twisted with a kind of disbelief. Aric, however, was stoic, and could easily believe the carnage his father was causing.

Reports from the main bridge told of the slaughter. Baron Glass and his mercenaries had somehow held out against the Reecian onslaught. A handful of men had so far returned, running messages to and from the bridge. Each of them told of Baron Glass in his armour and how he was holding the bridge nearly single-handedly. Raxor scoffed at the reports, refusing to look at Aric. Instead he sent more of his men into the fight, even as the Norvan free-lances forded the river and threatened their southern flank.

The catapults had fallen silent. The only light came from the torches and the waning moon. In the darkness, the noise of battle seemed louder, deafening Aric, driving him to ride in impatient circles. Despite the king's bravado, he knew that only retreat could save the day. Dreadfully he watched as the reserves dwindled, slowly drained by his father's ragtag army.

'My lord,' he said at last. 'Will you listen to me now? Is it not as I have told you?'

Old King Raxor refused to hear him. 'I have lieutenants, Aric Glass.'

'And what do they tell you? They're being slaughtered! Craiglen's dead, my lord. The north bridge is already lost.'

'We can retake it,' said Raxor foolishly.

'They're coming across the river!'

'They are out-numbered!' Raxor raged. He looked possessed suddenly, staring blankly at Aric through the torchlight. 'This can't be.'

'My lord, it is,' said Aric, his heart breaking for this old man. 'If—'

A soldier galloped up between them, jerking back his horse to face the king. Like most of Raxor's army he was young, and the fight had given him a wild, untamed look. Dirt and blood soiled his armour. Lather flowed from the mouth of his depleted horse. He got the king's attention at once.

Through laboured breath, he said, 'Word from the north. The line has broken. The baron's men have regrouped and overrun us. Jakel asks for your orders.'

Jakel, who had taken over for the dead Craiglen, had been a tent-mate of Aric's, a surly major with a chest-full of medals. To hear him asking for permission to retreat chilled Aric.

'Hold the line,' Raxor ordered. He glanced at Aric, then added, 'As long as you can.'

'My lord, Major Jakel says it won't be much longer.'

'As long as you can!' Raxor railed, dismissing the soldier with a wave.

Aric watched the trooper ride off, back toward the carnage up north. It would not be long now until the battle was over. Unbelievably, it had only taken hours. He looked toward the main bridge, toward his father. Shrouded in darkness, he could barely see the outskirts of the battle.

'I have to go,' he said suddenly. He looked at King Raxor. 'My lord, I have to go.'

Raxor took his meaning and frowned. 'Stay,' he ordered.

'I have to see my father, my lord. I have to try and talk to him.'

'Stay!'

'No! If you won't call retreat, it's the only way!'

Ignoring Raxor's calls to stop, Aric bolted off, driving through the darkness toward the bridge. He passed the catapults and the frightened page boys, and then the archers dug into their makeshift trenches, most of whom had already stopped firing. The battle was thick for both sides now, too close for arrows or catapults now. As he galloped toward the mêlée,

Aric wondered what he would find at the bridge and what possible thing he could say to his father. There was a man inside the Devil's Armour still, he was sure of it. If he could reach him . . .

The bridge came into view. Aric slowed his horse. Along the river bank men clashed with swords and axes as the chain of mercenaries continued pulling themselves ashore. Bodies and fallen horses polluted the field. The maddening sound of screams and clanging metal boomed in Aric's skull. He drew his sword and forced his horse into the thick of it, muscling past the Reecians gathered near the bridge. Some had yet to find an enemy, though hordes of Norvans and handfuls of Liirians had come across the river. To Aric, it seemed that the bridge was already lost, for the Reecians had been shattered into pockets, their discipline destroyed as they vainly fought to hold their line. Confused, Aric craned his neck to see the bridge, to find his father in all the chaos. Bit by bit he drew closer to the bridge, taking cover behind the Reecian cavalry. At last the crown of the bridge came into view. Choked with fighting men, one man in particular stood out from the rest.

Aric froze. He stared at the man, aghast but unable to look away. There was his father, giant and fierce, with dark armour glowing and writhing on his body, slick with gore and madly wielding his massive sword. Around him lay the dead, piled high, oozing blood that flowed down the bridge like water. There was no face to the man, just the deathmask of a helmet, jeering as its two horns jutted up like knives. The spikes of his armour moved with life, as did the tiny figures carved within its breastplate. Joyously the armoured man cut down those who came against him, effortlessly slaughtering them as their weapons slid harmlessly off his person.

Not a man, thought Aric in horror. *A monster.*

The bridge had become a slaughterhouse. His father, the butcher. And suddenly Aric's mission seemed the worst of folly. There could be no talking to his father now. His father was gone.

'Fall back!' he cried. 'Retreat! Retreat, now!'

But the soldiers ignored him. Frustrated, Aric hurried his horse about and galloped back the way he'd come, toward King Raxor and the safety of the reserves. In his mind burned the image of his father on the bridge, and as he rode hot tears stung his eyes. He had seen war before, but this was different. This was hell itself.

He found Raxor where he'd left him, still huddled with advisors beneath his royal banner. The king looked up anxiously as Aric rode toward him. An air of defeat hung over them all. Aric brought his horse to a stop and flung himself off its back and strode quickly to Raxor. Wiping the tears from his face he dropped to his knees.

'Retreat, my lord,' he pleaded. 'Retreat before it's too late.'

Raxor lost his steely expression. His advisors gaped.

'What of your father, boy?' the king queried.

'My father's dead,' Aric spat. 'There's a monster that calls himself my father and that's all.' He pointed toward the bridge. 'Go and see for yourself!'

'Get on your feet,' Raxor told him. His face began to collapse. 'Please . . .'

Aric was nearly sobbing now. He rose unsteadily, never taking his eyes off the king.

'My lord, please,' he begged. 'There's no chance. My father is a horror. Let him have the bloody bridges! Give him the whole damn river. Just go!'

Raxor's aides watched in silence, but their faces told the old king their feelings. The north bridge was already lost, and word from the south was little better. The truth slowly dawned on Raxor's face.

'My lord? Will you call retreat? For the sake of everything, will you?'

King Raxor looked vacantly at the horizon. His son had died today, and his closest friend, too. To Aric, he looked far older than he ever had before.

'Give the order,' he told his aides. 'Baron Glass has won.'

31

Princess Salina had never been happier than during her days with Aztar. Despite the sun and dust, despite the chores she had been given to help in camp, she had found an oasis in the burning desert, a place not at all like her plush existence back in Ganjor. Each day she awoke to a simple meal, spending time tending to the animals or helping with the children. Though she could not cook the way other women could, Salina helped with the bread or stirred pots, learning things she had never learned at the knee of her royal mother. Then, when her chores were done, she would spend time with Aztar, and they would walk together through the outskirts of the camp. And sometimes, when the mood struck him, he would read love poems to her by moonlight.

As the days passed, Salina learned that the 'Tiger of the Desert' was more – and less – than the fierce warrior he portrayed. Surrounded by his loyal Voruni, he did not feed off their adoration in the way Salina had expected. Rather, he was contemplative and private, yet willing to let her into his little world to see the man behind the legend and his burned, ruined face. In his camp, Salina quickly forgot about her father and the life she had left behind, revelling in the simplicity of washing her own clothes and the brilliance of a sunset.

On the night of her tenth day in camp, Salina went to sleep dreaming of surprises, for Aztar had told her that a surprise awaited her the next morning. As always, she went to sleep in her bed next to Harani, the Voruni woman who had greeted her that first day in camp. It had not taken long for Salina and Harani to become friends, and Salina was grateful for all the young woman's kindnesses. What little Salina had learned so far about cooking and mending clothes she had learned from Harani.

That night, Salina succumbed quickly to sleep, tired from her long day in the desert. When morning dawned, however, she was awake to greet it, bathing quickly from the rose water jug always ready near her bedside. She brushed her hair, put on one of Harani's prettiest dresses, then shared a quick meal with the other women while she waited for Aztar's surprise. The Voruni prince did not keep her waiting long. Once she had finished breaking her fast, Aztar appeared outside her tent, riding a strapping black drowa. He had dressed for the unknown occasion too, wearing a splendid white gaka with flowing scarlet leggings, cinched around his waist by a braided belt of gold. His face, which was not hidden behind his gaka, looked refreshed and coy as he smiled down at Salina.

'Have you eaten?' he asked.

Salina stepped away from Harani and the others. 'I have.'

'Good, because it is a long ride.'

'To where?'

'You shall see.' He stretched down his hand for her. 'Come.'

In their brief time together they had yet to ride on the same drowa. Salina felt a thrill at the prospect as she took his hand. With one powerful yank he pulled her up, helping her onto the drowa's back. Quickly she wrapped her arms around his waist as she settled in behind him.

'This is your surprise?' she asked.

'Yes. No more questions, now. Enjoy the ride.'

Curious, Salina waved good-bye to Harani and the other women as Aztar spun the beast around and headed out of camp. There were bags hanging from the drowa's tack, which Salina supposed held food and other supplies. If they were going far they would need water, but she decided not to worry about that. Aztar would have everything covered, she was certain. So she tried to relax as the drowa loped forward, leaving behind the camp and heading south toward the distant mountains. Aztar said nothing to her as they rode, keeping up his coyness as the camp disappeared behind them and the dunes took over, obscuring the horizon in places with their undulating humps. Because it was still morning the sun was not yet hot, and the breeze felt cold as it caressed Salina's face. She smiled, loving the mystery of being taken away, and placed her cheek against Aztar's back.

They were in love. They had already confessed it to each other. Soon – be it a day from now or a month – her father would come looking for her, and though Salina dreaded that day it did nothing to lessen her love for the man who had rescued her. Aztar had risked everything to keep her safe. It was hard not to love a man like that.

'Tell me where we are going,' she said into his ear. Playfully she kissed him. 'To have your way with me?'

'Hush, girl.' Aztar brushed aside her advance. 'I do not have to carry you away for that.'

'No,' purred Salina, 'you don't.'

She put her hand to his chest and felt his heartbeat. She imagined it racing the way her own did when they spoke of such things. Aztar took her hand and brought it to his mouth, kissing it.

'You'll see soon,' he told her. 'Be patient.'

Patience had never been a virtue of Salina's, but she settled in as best she could and watched as the landscape began to change around them. They had gone from the hard earth of the camp to the soft, blowing sands of the desert, but now the world was changing again, becoming jagged and studded with stones. Salina looked over Aztar's shoulder and saw a stand of hills in the distance covered with shrubbery, the kind of hearty plants that thrived in the dry desert. Beyond the shrubs were a few taller trees, and beneath the shade of these trees some flowers bloomed, bursting with colour against the desolation.

An oasis, thought Salina happily, like the one she had taken refuge in. And like that one in the north, this oasis must have had water. Salina could tell by the way the trees had grown in circles, taller at the centre of the oasis and thinning out along its outskirts. The place was small, yet lovely and welcoming, and seeing it made the princess smile. She glanced over her shoulder and realized that their camp was miles away, and that she and her lover were truly all alone.

'It's beautiful,' she said with a sigh.

'It is,' Aztar agreed. 'It is a place I come to sometimes, to be alone and think. But the oasis is not the surprise, Salina. There's something else.'

'What else?'

'Wait,' directed Aztar.

He slowed the drowa as they entered the oasis. Wide-eyed, Salina took in its beauty. The fronds of a tiny palm brushed her shoulder as they rode past. Salina reached out for it and grabbed a handful of its delicate leaves, letting them tumble like sand from her fingers. Beneath them, the ground was sugary-white. Trickles of water from a bubbling spring meandered through the glassy stones. Salina took a breath, filling her nose with the sweetness of flowers. The palms overhead knitted a canopy to shade them.

'This is a special place,' said Aztar. 'There is something very rare here that I want to show you. It should be the time.'

He had piqued Salina's interest now. She urged him to stop the drowa so they could get down. He did so, then followed her down off the back of the beast, dropping into the soft sand. Salina put out her hands and felt the glorious breeze on her face and the sunlight dappling through the palms. The gentle music of the spring plied through the oasis. She knelt and took up a handful of the water snaking between her feet, tasting it.

'Sweet,' she said with a smile. 'It's so clear!'

'Like a diamond it sparkles,' said Aztar, squatting beside her. He too tasted the water, cupping up a man-sized handful. When he was done he ran his wet hands through his dark hair. To Salina he looked fabulous, just as striking as their surroundings. She never saw his burns when she looked at him, only his eyes, which were always filled with love. She nudged him with her elbow.

'So? What is this surprise, then? Not the oasis.'

'No, not the oasis.' Aztar glanced to his left where a hill rose up to border the greenery. 'Over there,' he said, and took her hand.

Salina let him guide her deeper into the oasis, and when they reached the hill they rounded it, stepping out into a tiny meadow of grass and flowers. Thorn stuck her legs as they entered the grass. She cried out in protest, but Aztar urged her on.

'No, come with me,' he told her gently. 'It's not far.'

'What are we looking for?'

He took her a few more steps into the grass, then paused. With a great smile on his face he said, 'That.'

Salina followed his finger to what looked like a rose bush sprouting out of the hillside. It stood alone, defiantly breaking through the rock, full of thorns and twisted shoots. Its leaves were tear-shaped and spiky, a waxy, deep green that sparkled in the sunlight. Its roots pulled out of the earth in spots, holding fast to the difficult ground. There were no buds along its limbs, nothing at all to make it remarkable.

Except for its single, fabulous flower.

Proudly bursting from its crown sat a perfectly formed bloom with bright, multi-coloured petals and two fuzzy stamen that seemed to move with life in the breeze. Mostly orange, the flower sported reds and yellows as well, blushing its petals like gentle brushstrokes. Big as a hand, the flower somehow balanced on the delicate limb, held up like a prize by the bush. Salina stopped breathing when she saw it.

'That's it,' Aztar whispered. 'That's why I brought you here.'

Salina took a step toward it, forgetting the thorns that clawed at her legs. 'I've never seen such a thing! What is it, Aztar? A rose?'

'We call it a rainbow kiss,' said Aztar. 'It's a Voruni flower. I don't think it grows anywhere but this part of the desert.'

He was still whispering, as if to talk too loud would somehow damage the fragile bloom. Salina stopped edging toward it, but could not pull her eyes away.

'A rainbow kiss.' She smiled. 'Yes.'

'It's more special than you think, Salina. A rainbow kiss only blooms once every five years, and only then for a day or so.'

She looked at him askance. 'Then how did you know . . .'

'Because this is my desert,' said Aztar with a grin. 'Or it was, once. I come here to think, remember. I have come to this spot for years. And I have waited for it to bloom again. Yesterday I came here and saw it starting to come out. Today I brought you here to see it.'

Just a small kindness, but to Salina it was a great gift indeed. She melted at the sight of the flower.

'Once every five years. Remarkable.'

'You see how beautiful the desert is, Salina?' Aztar gave a look of utter satisfaction. 'This is all I ever wanted. It's all a man could ever need.' Then he took her hand. 'That and a woman.'

She looked away, surprised to feel herself blushing. 'It can't always be like this, Aztar. There is a real world outside the desert. Soon it will come for us.'

'Perhaps,' Aztar replied. 'But not today.'

He let go of her hand and picked his way toward the magnificent flower, and when he reached it he hovered over it for a moment, sticking his nose into the bloom and grinning at its scent. Then, to Salina's horror, he cupped the flower in his hand and pulled it loose of its stem.

'No!' Salina shrieked. 'Aztar, why'd you do that?'

He held the bloom carefully in his hand as he returned to her. 'Because it only lasts a day. Because nothing lasts, Salina, and while it's still alive I want you to have it.'

'But you've killed it!'

'No, it will not die until tomorrow. Even if it were on its stem it would still die tomorrow. So until then, it is for you to enjoy.'

His logic was maddening, yet she took the flower when he handed it to her, gently cradling it with both hands. Its breathtaking scent climbed up her nose, something like the orchids her father grew back home but a hundred times more pungent.

'It's like perfume!' She sniffed again. 'Expensive perfume.'

'Priceless,' Aztar said. 'And only a handful of people know where to find them.'

Salina smiled at him. 'Thank you, Aztar.'

He took her hand again. 'Come. Let's sit by the water.'

Happy to be free of the thorns, Salina hopped her way out of the prickly grass and followed Aztar back around the hillside, still cradling the flower in her palm. He guided her toward the spring bubbling up from the earth, spreading its clear water like fingers in all directions. Near the spring was a patch of flattened grass, obviously pushed down by Aztar's many trips to the oasis. They sat upon the grass, cooled by the shade of a nearby palm and calmed by the sound of the spring. Aztar leaned back, inviting Salina to lay next to him. Salina took the invitation but placed her head on his chest instead. Both of them stared up into the blue sky.

For a long time, neither of them spoke.

Salina let her mind trip through happy memories, enchanted by the days she had spent with Aztar. Like the rainbow kiss, their love had bloomed. She was not a princess anymore. With Aztar and his people, she was just a woman, young and plain, ready to get her hands dirty tending sheep or cooking meals. It was idyllic, the world that Aztar had created, far from the turmoil of city life or the thousand pressures of being a king's daughter.

'I'm right, you know,' she said finally. 'It can't last. They'll come for me.'

Aztar took his time responding. He continued looking up into the sky. At last he nodded. 'Yes.'

'And all this will end.'

'No.'

'No?'

He hesitated. 'I won't let it.'

'Even you can't defeat my father, Aztar.'

'Can I not? If there were an army, I would defeat them for you, Salina.'

Salina laughed. 'You would try, my love.'

'All right, yes. I would try. Speak no more of it. Not today.'

But there were things on Salina's mind that would not go away. She said softly, 'This is what you wanted, isn't it? The peace of the desert.'

'Mmm, yes,' Aztar sighed. 'Glorious. The desert is full of magic.'

'We can have peace. We can go somewhere where my father will never find us. What do you think of that, Aztar?'

She felt him shake his head.

'We cannot.'

'No? Why not?'

'Because we are not alone, Salina. Because I am not alone. I'm not free to leave. My people need me.'

'But surely they would understand . . .'

'No, Salina. Maybe it is you who doesn't understand.' Aztar began to stroke her hair. 'These people who follow me – they aren't just friends. They're even more than family. They came to me because they believed in the same things I did – a free desert, unpolluted by northerners or politics. They could have left me when I led them to defeat at Jador, but they did not. They don't have anywhere else to go, and I would never leave them. Never. Do you see?'

'Yes,' said Salina, though it pained her to admit it. 'I do see.'

'I don't want power, Salina. I did once, but no more. And I don't pretend that the desert is mine anymore. Vala has taught me all about folly! Now I know what is important. You're important. And my people are important.'

Salina closed her eyes. His words were beautiful to her.

'Salina? Tell me what you're thinking.'

'I'm thinking that the sky is very blue today, Aztar.' Salina took a breath, concealing her emotions. 'I'm thinking that it doesn't matter what happens. Today is perfect.'

Salina and Aztar spent the rest of the day at the oasis, finally leaving in the late afternoon. It was a race to return to camp before the sun went down. Her belly full from the food and wine Aztar had packed for them, Salina settled onto the drowa, this time sitting in front of Aztar and resting her head against his chest. They spoke very little on the ride back, for there seemed little to say. Salina felt marvelously contented and didn't want to spoil her mood with words.

By the time they reached the encampment, the sun was sinking below the horizon. A fiery aura lit the western sky. Torches and campfires had come alive in camp and a lull had settled over the Voruni as they made ready for the evening. Salina could smell the cooking fires and the savoury odour of rendering sheep fat. To her, it smelled like home. Voruni men and women came out to greet them, waving casually as they passed. A boy in a ragged desert tunic hurried forward to offer help, taking hold of the drowa's bridle. Aztar gently shooed the boy away as the drowa sauntered toward Aztar's pavilion. Then, as they neared the grand tent, Salina noticed a group of men seated around a campfire. Many of them were Voruni, people familiar to Salina. Many of them were not. Aztar slowed his drowa, tensing at the sight of them. Salina felt her heart skip.

'Jashien . . .'

Her bodyguard had returned, and this time had brought soldiers with him. At least a dozen Ganjeese guardsmen waited with Jashien, looking impatient as they sat near Aztar's tent. As the prince and princess approached, the Voruni men got to their feet. Jashien turned to face them and immediately rose. Out of the crowd came Harani, looking perplexed.

'Harani,' Aztar began carefully. 'When did they arrive?'

'This morning,' said Harani. 'Not long after you left.'

Salina looked toward Aztar. 'They're here for me.'

Aztar nodded. 'I know.'

'Aztar—'

'Don't worry.'

The prince rode up to the gathered men, greeting his Voruni and barely glancing at his Ganjeese visitors. Jashien was careful not to talk too soon. Aztar got down from the drowa, then helped Salina off its back.

'Harani,' he said, 'take Salina with you.'

'No!' Salina insisted. 'I want to stay.'

Aztar grimaced, but relented quickly. He glared at Jashien. Beside the bodyguard lay a chest, sitting closed near the campfire. Salina spied the chest, wondering what kind of bribe lay inside. She stood beside Aztar.

'I'm not going back,' she told Jashien. 'No matter what's inside that chest.'

Jashien was not a villain, at least Salina had never thought him one. His face filled with concern at her defiance.

'Princess, your father worries about you. He cares for you deeply and wants you to come home. That's why I'm here.'

'Is that why you brought soldiers with you?' Aztar asked pointedly.

The guardsmen were all on their feet and looking at Aztar. Though they were surrounded by Voruni men, they seemed unafraid. Salina knew they were seasoned fighters, all of them, meant to intimidate Aztar. Jashien smiled diplomatically.

'Last time I came here I was alone, with only one other man to help me,' said Jashien. 'You're right, Prince Aztar – these men are here to make a point. King Baralosus wants you to know he is serious.'

'Serious?'

'About getting his daughter back.'

Aztar gestured toward the chest. 'And that?'

'The same thing,' said Jashien. 'To show you how serious the king is.'

'A bribe,' Aztar sneered.

'An offering, Prince Aztar. A gesture of goodwill and friendship.' Jashien shrugged. 'A gift, if you like.'

'What is it?' Salina asked crossly.

Jashien turned to his one of his men, a soldier close to his own age. Producing a key from his pocket, he tossed it to the soldier and said, 'Open it.'

The guardsman worked the key in the lock, took the bolt from the clasp and slowly opened the lid of the chest. What Salina saw dazzled her. Every imaginable treasure sparkled inside the chest, gleaming in firelight. Twinkling golden jewelry, ruby encrusted goblets, chains of silver and ropes of pearls lay atop each other, piled high inside the chest. Coins of every size slipped between them like sand.

'A fortune,' said Jashien. 'Enough to start your own small kingdom, I would say.'

Salina was speechless, as was Aztar. She looked at him for any sign of weakness. The prince stared at the riches in the chest, but his expression was unreadable. She could not tell if he was enamoured or offended by the offering.

'This isn't all, Prince Aztar,' Jashien continued. 'There's more.'

Aztar finally pulled his eyes from the chest. 'What more?'

'King Baralosus knows of your love for his daughter. He honours it. He also knows the cravings of your heart, Prince Aztar.'

'What? No man knows my heart.'

Jashien shrugged. 'Call in a sense, then. Once you sought recognition from the king. You wanted the desert to be yours, to set up a kingdom of your own here. That can happen now. If you'll do as the king requests.'

Salina tightened her grasp of Aztar. 'My father wants me back. That's it, Jashien, isn't it?'

Jashien nodded. 'Yes, Princess.'

'No,' said Aztar quickly. 'That will not be.'

'Prince Aztar, please,' cautioned Jashien. 'Think on what the king is offering. A place at his table. A voice in decisions! And your own kingdom, recognized by Ganjor.'

Aztar gave a bitter laugh. 'The desert is no man's to grant,' he said. 'Or to claim. I have learned that the hard way.'

'King Baralosus can grant it,' Jashien argued. 'He has the power and the riches to make it happen. You know that, Prince Aztar. If the king says you too are a king, than it shall be. And those treasures in the chest can all be yours.'

'And Salina? What of her?'

Jashien hesitated a moment. 'Prince Aztar, there are realities, things to consider. As I have said, King Baralosus honours your love for his daughter.'

'Yes?'

'But what you have done has harmed him. It is kidnapping.'

'No,' Salina protested. 'I came to Aztar. He did not take me against my will.'

'Some don't see it that way, Princess. Some say that Aztar has stolen you, and that your father is weak. Not all the people think this, but enough. And after what you did . . .'

Salina felt herself shrink. 'Yes.' She nodded. 'I'm the one who harmed my father. Not Aztar.'

'So?' Aztar pressed. 'What does he offer us?'

'You may marry Princess Salina, but not quickly. Time, Prince Aztar. That's what the king is asking of you. Time to let things relax, time to let his enemies forget.'

'Enemies? You're talking politics.'

'That's right. We're both men, Prince Aztar. We understand these things. You do, certainly. You knew the risks when you let the princess stay with you. And now you have a chance for all the things you ever wanted! You just have to be patient.'

'And return me to my father,' said Salina. She considered the possibility of it, and it filled her with dread. 'Aztar?'

'You're afraid, Salina,' said Aztar. 'Do not be. Jashien, go back to Ganjor. Take the chest home with you.'

Jashien looked stunned. 'Prince Aztar . . .'

'Go and tell King Baralosus what I've already said. Salina is staying here with me because that is what she wishes. She's not a slave or property. She is a woman grown and has her own will, and her will is to remain here.'

Salina steeled herself for Jashien's reaction. He had brought soldiers with him for a reason.

'If that's what you want, I will give the king your message,' said Jashien. 'But I must warn you, Prince Aztar. There is more that the king wishes you to know.'

Aztar remained cool. 'Tell me.'

'These men aren't here to fight you,' said Jashien. 'They're only here to protect the treasure. But if I don't return to Ganjor with the princess, more soldiers will come. This is King Baralosus' promise to you. This is his threat.' He looked at Salina. 'Please tell him, Princess. Tell him that your father is not lying.'

Wrenched by what Jashien was saying, Salina looked at Aztar. On his wounded face she saw determination, and not a hint of fear.

'Aztar, he means what he says. My father—'

'I mean what I say, too,' Aztar insisted. 'I will not give you over to your father, Salina. Let him come. Let him bring his armies!'

'He will, Prince Aztar,' said Jashien. 'He *will*. This is your chance. Take it, for your own sake.'

But Aztar was as a deaf man, hearing none of Jashien's pleas. He told the bodyguard, 'I have all that I need now, Jashien. I have no use for golden goblets; all the wine tastes the same to me. Go and tell your king that his daughter is safe. And that she will not be coming back to him.'

Jashien knew his argument was lost. Salina saw resolve on his face. He nodded solemnly, then went to the chest and closed it with a thud. 'I admire you, Prince Aztar,' he said. 'You're a brave man. But bravery is dangerous. And sometimes stupid.'

Aztar merely smiled. 'Stay the night and rest. Eat. But in the morning be gone from here.'

Keeping hold of Salina's arm, he led her past the gathering and into his tent. There, he closed the flaps behind them, shutting out the rest of the world. Salina felt unsteady, her stomach pitching with nervousness. She sat herself down on the pillows near the low table, reaching for a pitcher of wine but not pouring any. Her eyes darted around the room. Her thoughts came in staccato waves.

'What will happen now?' she asked.

'Your father will come for you,' said Aztar. He sat down before her on the pillows. 'He won't give up until he has you back.'

'Then I must go to him. I can't let him harm you.'

Aztar shook his head. 'No, you won't do that. It's not what either of us want, Salina. We have taken this stand. We cannot surrender now.'

'Then what?' Salina looked hard at him. 'He is powerful, Aztar. He has the men and weapons to get what he wants.'

'He may come,' said Aztar, 'but he won't get what he wants. He wants you, Salina. And when he comes for you, you won't be here.'

32

Far from the palace of the Red Eminence, past the holy river and the hills that lined the valley, stood a thick forest of trees and rocks where no one farmed or bothered to explore. According to Lahkali, the forest was called the Skees, a word that no had no real meaning in Lukien's tongue except for 'dark.' Because of its densely woven canopy and ubiquitous moss, the forest lay in perpetual dimness, shielding out the powerful sun that baked the rest of Torlis.

Within the forest, Lukien had found the perfect venue in which to train his young pupil. Away from the prying eyes of the palace, he spent hours with Lahkali among the trees and hidden caverns, showing her how to use the katath and – to the best of his ability – to fight the Great Rass. The vines from the trees hid Lukien's face as he stared down the tunnel of limbs. Hanging from the limbs were a dozen small targets made of straw, swaying gently on ropes. At the other end of the tunnel stood Lahkali, her special katath held in both hands, her face resolute. Even so far away from her, Lukien sensed her trepidation. Between them, hidden somewhere in the trees, waited Jahan.

'Remember, every target,' Lukien called out.

Lahkali nodded. Her pretty mouth twisted with worry.

'When you reach me – if you reach me – it has to be quick. Don't waste time. Hit the targets and evade Jahan. Don't think too much.'

Young Lahkali tightened her fingers around her weapon. She had done remarkably well with it so far, treating it like the great prize it was and training with it tirelessly. Her body had hardened over the past weeks, becoming lithe. She moved with grace now, no longer like a gangly teenager but like an athlete. Devoted to her training, she had yet to disappoint Lukien.

Yet Lukien still worried.

'When you fight the rass you may not be able to see it,' said Lukien. 'It'll be much faster than you, so always be moving. Don't keep your eyes locked in one place. Don't get stuck like that.'

Lahkali nodded. They had talked about that many times. 'I understand, Lukien.'

She was twenty yards away. Not a long distance to run, but with Jahan after her it would be difficult. He was armed. Lukien couldn't help being a little afraid for her. She had taken blows before, but this time was different. This time, he had told Jahan to attack her for real.

'When you're ready, then,' he said.

Lahkali took a breath, steadying herself as if she were entering the cave of the Great Rass itself. She peered down the tunnel made by the trees, spying the swinging targets, sizing them up. Her eyes grew alert; her ears listened sharply. She knew that somewhere in the trees Jahan waited, ready to spring.

Then, like a leopard, she sprung herself, leaping into the tunnel with her katath outstretched before her. With a quick sweep of the weapon she took the first target, slicing it easily from its rope. She spun, ducking low, then took out another target with equal ease. Confident, she leapt ahead. As she spied the next swinging target, Jahan sprang. Bursting from the trees, he had his bamboo stick swinging for his prey. Lahkali dodged the first blow easily, jumping over the whistling weapon. Jahan pursued, righting himself and bringing the stick around. It rushed for the girl's back, yet Lahkali sensed it in time. Twisting away, she lopped off the third target. Lukien watched, pleased and impressed as the girl hopped away from every attack, expertly using the katath for balance. She moved like a dancer through the swinging targets, inch by inch closing the gap between them.

'Faster, Jahan!' Lukien called. 'It's too easy for her!'

Hearing this, Jahan sped his attack. Long days on his farm had muscled his body and given him speed. Racing ahead of Lahkali, he feinted with his bamboo stick to force her sideways, blocking her way. Focused on the next target, Lahkali saw his strategy too late. His stick sliced the air, catching her leg and knocking her down. For a split second Jahan looked horrified – enough for Lahkali to spin away.

'Get after her, Jahan,' Lukien called. 'She's faster than you think!'

Jahan's face twisted angrily as once again he went after her. With more than a yard separating them, Lahkali took out two more targets, then centred on a third. In a blur the twin blades of her katath cut the air, ripping into the target and sending straw flying. She turned just in time to dodge Jahan's attack. The bamboo stick came down, and the sharp blades of the katath easily sliced it.

'Ha!' Lahkali boasted, then turned away from her opponent. Lukien smirked. Jahan was not without surprises.

From out of his deep pocket he pulled a weighted rope, quickly unspooling it as Lahkali ignored him. It was called a garok, a hunting weapon of Jahan's people, and just as he had practiced all his life he swung it twice overhead before launching it at Lahkali. It struck the unsuspecting girl, catching her waist and pulling her backward. Stunned, she began to fall, but as she fell she worked her weapon, trying hard to cut the rope. Failing, she let out a cry as her back smacked the ground. This time Jahan didn't retreat. He jerked the rope, pulling Lahkali off balance as she tried to regain her footing.

'Evade!' cried Lukien.

'I'm trying!' yelled Lahkali.

She worked the katath, reversing it and coming up under the rope. The two blades caught the garok, severing it. Jahan stumbled back in surprise as Lahkali leapt to her feet. Covered in dirt, she went after the target just above her head, crying out in frustration as her blades ripped it to shreds. Angrily she glared at Lukien, who stood with arms crossed at the end of her ordeal. The Bronze Knight stuck out a hand and waved her forward.

'Keep on coming.'

Lahkali was panting now. As quickly as she could she danced past the remaining targets, her katath darting in and out of them. Now weapon-less, Jahan nevertheless continued his attack, roaring as he leapt for her. Bigger and stronger than Lahkali, he should have reached her easily.

But he did not.

Lukien watched with pride as the girl side-stepped his every move, sending him sprawling or tumbling to the dirt while she pirouetted her way through the swinging targets. She was only feet away now. Victory shone on her face. Lukien readied him. She had been too far away to see the bamboo staff behind him, and while she worked he reached back and grabbed it.

'Too slow, Jahan,' he jibed.

Finally, Jahan gave up. With a big smile on his face he watched as Lahkali finished the final targets, tearing through them with glee. When the last one exploded with straw, she landed at Lukien's feet . . .

And fell like a rock to his unsuspecting blow.

The staff had hit her square in the chest. Not hard, and not enough to hurt her, but enough to make her tumble. Lahkali dropped her prize katath. On her back, she lay staring up at Lukien. Disbelief gripped her face. So did anger.

'Why?' she cried. 'I made it through!'

Lukien tossed away his staff. 'What did you think would happen when you reached me?'

'Nothing!'

The knight nodded. 'Right. That's the problem.'

He offered down his hand. Lahkali angrily rebuffed it. 'I can get up on my own!' she grumbled.

Lukien shrugged. 'All right. Then stand up.'

The girl did so, and for a moment stared hard at her teacher. She was more than mad. She was hurt by what he'd done, and not physically.

'You did well,' said Lukien. 'But not well enough. Rest now.'

Walking past her, he left Lahkali standing alone in stunned silence. Ahead of Lukien lay Jahan, looking equally aghast. Lukien avoided his friend's gaze, but as he passed the village man followed him.

'What was that?' Jahan asked.

'What?'

'Why did you hit her, Lukien? She made it through your test.'

'No, she didn't,' said Lukien, and kept on walking.

Jahan followed him. 'She did, Lukien. You said nothing about that trick.'

'Trick? She has to fight a rass, Jahan.'

'So?'

'So she has to be better! She has to think faster, use her imagination!'

Jahan grabbed his shoulder. 'Stop.'

Lukien turned to face Jahan. 'I'm too harsh. Is that what you want to say?'

'She's just a girl, Lukien. She is trying.'

Past Jahan, Lukien could see Lahkali brooding, staring down at the ground where her katath lay.

'It's not enough,' he said. 'She has to fight a rass, Jahan, and I don't know what that means.'

'What? Lukien, I don't understand.'

Lukien pulled Jahan closer, turning him around so that Lahkali could not hear. He said, 'I'm her teacher, right?'

Jahan nodded. 'Yes.'

'I'm to teach her how to kill a rass, yes?'

'Yes.'

'Don't you see? That's the problem, Jahan. I have no idea how to kill a rass.'

The home of fencing master Niharn lay along a quiet, twisting avenue, more than a mile from the palace of the Eminence. On a street lined with many such houses, Niharn's home was neither plain nor grand. With little open space to divide it from the other homes, it rose up three stories high, a structure of clay and stone that shone a peculiar orange in the heat of the day. Long ago the home had been white-washed, but the sun had bleached away the wash so that the brick shone through easily. Over the door hung a limestone lintel. The door itself had been made of wood, a strange wood of black that had been lacquered so many times that Lukien could see his reflection in it.

Because he was a man of rank in the city's military, Niharn had servants to cook his meals, look after his large brood of children, and to greet visitors who came to his home. Lukien only needed to knock once to bring one of the servants running. This time, as last, an old man named Tagna answered the door. Lukien recognized him at once.

'Hello again,' he said sheepishly.

Old Tagna did not smile. He simply nodded. 'Greetings.'

'Is your master at home?' Lukien asked.

'He is,' replied Tagna, and the magic of Lukien's amulet translated his words. The servant glanced down at the gift Lukien had brought along, a bottle of a kind of wine Niharn had mentioned a fondness for last time they'd met. Lukien had found the liquor in a marketplace not far from Niharn's house. He'd been shocked by the cost of it.

'Will you tell him I'm here, Tagna? I'd like to speak to him.'

Tagna stepped aside so that Lukien could enter the home. Typical of the architecture he'd seen in Torlis, the first floor of the house had been given over to rooms for receiving guests and conducting Niharn's military business. A number of comfortable looking chairs had been arranged near the room's hearth, but the hearth itself was cold. Laticed windows let sunlight into the room. The walls were appointed with military things, like an old katath and some worn-out ribbons, perhaps accommodations the fencing master had earned. As Lukien entered the room, a young girl seated near the hearth stood. She smiled at the visitor.

'Lukien,' she said. 'You're back.'

Her name was Shalra, and she was Niharn's youngest daughter. A precocious girl, she was five years old and loved to say Lukien's name.

'Hello Shalra,' said Lukien. 'I'm here to see your father again.'

'He's upstairs,' said the girl. 'With mother.'

'Oh,' said Lukien sheepishly. He looked at Tagna. 'I could come back . . .'

'I will tell the master you're here,' said the servant. 'Sit.'

Tagna disappeared into another room. Soon after, Lukien heard him ascend the unseen staircase. He looked at young Shalra and grinned.

'I didn't think I'd see you again,' he said.

Shalra jumped out of the chair which was too big for her anyway and came to stand before Lukien. 'My father said you'd be back.'

'Did he?'

'He said you would need his help.'

'You're father's very smart,' said Lukien sourly.

The girl looked at the bottle in his hand. 'What's that?'

'A gift for your father. It's vaf.'

Shalra made a face. 'Vaf? My mother says that tastes like—'

'Shalra!'

The girl froze at her father's voice. In the threshold between rooms stood Niharn, scowling at his daughter.

356

'What were you going to say, child?' he asked with a tone of false threat.

'Nothing,' said Shalra. Her little grin quickly defused her father's ire.

'Go and play with your sisters. Let your father talk to his guest.'

Shalra excused herself, saying a polite good-bye to Lukien before leaving the room. Niharn watched her go. A hint of fatherly pride glinted in his eyes. Tagna entered the room again, waiting for his master's orders. Lukien heard other voices in the adjoining chambers, but no one entered to disturb them. When Niharn turned back to Lukien, a trace of smugness crossed his dark face.

'Welcome, Lukien,' he said. 'You found your way back here.'

'Yes.' Lukien handed him the bottle of vaf. 'This is for you.'

Impressed, Niharn's eyebrows went up. 'You brought this from Toors in the market near here, yes?'

'That's right.'

'Toors is a thief but he finds the best vaf. Expensive. Thank you.'

'You're welcome.'

Niharn handed the bottle off to Tagna. The air charged with awkwardness. Niharn gestured to the chairs, all of them upholstered with colourful silk.

'Sit,' he offered. 'I sometimes take guests out to the garden, but it's too hot today.'

'I remember,' said Lukien, taking a seat. 'Thank you.'

Niharn took a chair opposite him, leaning back and steepling his fingers. He smiled at Lukien. 'Aliz Nok has made the katath for the Eminence. I have seen her practicing with it. How has that been for her, the katath?'

'Very good, Master Niharn. You were right about Aliz Nok. The weapon he made for Lahkali is peerless.'

'He's the best,' said Niharn. 'And she is happy with it? It is the right weight for her?'

'Yes,' Lukien replied. When he had first come to Niharn for help, they had argued over the heft of the weapon. They had argued over just about everything. Still, Niharn had offered his advice.

'I am glad,' said Niharn. 'The Eminence has been doing her best for you. I have seen the change in her. She speaks of you often, Lukien.' The master laughed. 'You are all she speaks about in court! It is good that she has someone like you to train her. A foreigner. I see now that her own people were not enough.'

'No, I wouldn't say that.'

'You did say that.'

'No, not precisely, Master Niharn . . .'

'Let's not argue.' Niharn at last waved Tagna away, not so much as offering Lukien a drink. 'The Eminence is doing well. That's all that matters.' He looked expectantly at Lukien. 'So . . . ?'

'So, you want to know why I've come back.'

'That would be nice, yes.'

'Because I need your advice, Master Niharn.'

The admission made the warrior's face light up. 'Oh? Tell me, please.'

'Enough, please. I know I offended you. I never meant to. You helped me find a man that could make a katath for Lahkali. Now I need your help again.'

Niharn grew serious. 'I am listening.'

Staring at Niharn made Lukien feel small. He had rebuffed the master's offers of help, replacing him as Lahkali's teacher. For Niharn, the insult had been great. Still, Lukien found himself liking the smug man. Despite Niharn's feelings of betrayal, he was loyal to Lahkali and willing to help.

'There's a problem with her training,' Lukien began. 'Not with her, mind you. She's a fine student. If you had given her the chance you would have learned that, I think.'

'Really? You say that even though you know what she is up against? You're not even one of us, Lukien. You can't even speak our tongue without that . . . *thing* around your neck.'

'All right,' said Lukien. He held up his hand. 'All right. Let me start again.'

'No, Lukien, let me start,' said Niharn. 'You tell me that you mean no offense to me, yet every time you open your mouth you offend me. I am a fencing master! Do you know what that means?'

Lukien grimaced. 'I have to admit that I don't.'

'It means that I have trained the greatest fighters in Torlis. The best men in our armies have come to me to learn the katath. I know what a person can do. And I know what the Eminence cannot do. She cannot fight the Great Rass and win.'

'So she's wasting her time?'

'And she's wasting *your* time. You should go back to wherever you came from, Lukien. Ah, but you can't, can you? Because you're looking for the Sword of Angels.' Niharn leaned forward curiously. 'How is that going for you, Lukien?'

'It's not,' Lukien admitted.

'No? Have you not found out anything useful?'

'You know I haven't, Niharn.'

Niharn sat back again. 'You think that if you help the Eminence defeat the Great Rass that she will tell you where the sword is hidden.'

Lukien shook his head. 'You're wrong.'

'I don't think I am. But I will tell you this, my friend, from my heart – Lahkali cannot beat the Great Rass, because she does not have the gift of her blood. No one can kill the rass if they can't control it.'

It was the same tired argument Niharn – and everyone – had made before. Lukien could only ignore it.

'I believe in her,' he said. 'So does Karoshin.'

'Karoshin!' Niharn laughed. 'That old man believes because he must, because he loves Lahkali like a daughter and can't see anything through his blindness. Karoshin does not train warriors, Lukien. He believes because he knows no better. But you are a warrior like me. Tell me the truth – do you truly believe? I see fear in your eyes.'

'I'm afraid for her, yes,' Lukien admitted. 'But she has to try. You know she has to.'

Niharn looked circumspect. 'Yes,' he sighed. 'Touching on this other matter of the sword – you have not been looking for it?'

The question made Lukien shift. 'No.'

'Why not?'

'I don't know where to look, Niharn. I have thought and thought, but where to start? Only Lahkali knows where the sword is hidden.'

'And she will never tell you.' A trace of sympathy passed over Niharn's face. 'You have all this magic, Lukien. So much power. You are a mystery to all the people in court! But this sword is a curse to you. Why must you find it? Why not just go home?'

Lukien grinned. 'You would like that, I know. But I have business here. I'll go when I'm ready, Niharn.'

'All right, then, business.' Niharn opened his hands. 'So? Why are you here?'

'I need your help.'

'Again?' Niharn looked pleased. 'Continue.'

'Have you ever fought a rass?'

'Why would I do that? The rass are—'

'Revered. Yes, I know. But not where I come from. Where I come from men have fought the rass. Is there no one in Torlis who has ever fought one?'

Niharn shook his head. 'No one.'

'Then how do you train for it?' Lukien asked, frustrated. 'How can anyone fight a rass?'

'You forget – it is the gift of the blood! No one fights the rass, not the way you have been thinking, Lukien. The Red Eminence *controls* the rass, brings it to him.' Niharn smirked. 'Or her. That is the only way.'

'That can't be the only way,' said Lukien. 'I can't accept that. I need to learn. I need to find the way.'

Niharn looked intrigued. 'How?'

'I need transport,' said Lukien. He lowered his voice to a whisper. 'To Amchan.'

33

From the deck of the feruka, the forest of Amchan seemed primeval, an endless soup of tangled vines and steaming, dew-dropped trees. Shadowed by the mountains that towered like overlords in the distance, the arms of the river surrounded Amchan, holding it tightly and squeezing up the trees until they touched the grey sky. Lukien watched through his one good eye as a flock of dark birds winged over the forest, calling to the creatures far below. A million angry insects answered, filling the land with their buzzing.

It had taken Niharn's feruka most of the morning to reach Amchan. The vessel skidded to a stop along its flat keel, resting in the mud of the riverbank. A dozen burly sailors waited on deck with long poles, ready to free the feruka from the mud once Lukien and Jahan had departed. The captain of the vessel, a long-trusted friend of Niharn, stood nearby, stone-faced, not rushing his passengers off his boat. He had said very little throughout the journey, staying close to Niharn and following the old Fencing Master's orders. Niharn did his best to keep his friend informed, but it was a secret mission after all, and Lukien trusted that Niharn had mostly kept his mouth shut.

A sprinkle of rain touched Lukien's nose. He studied the sky and the gathering clouds. He had not counted on rain, but it made no difference. He only had a day before Lahkali would miss him, perhaps two, but soon after that she would wonder why he and Jahan had left the palace. He had not spoken much to Lahkali since training her in the woods near the palace, and because she still resented him she had not sought him out, preferring to be by herself while she sorted out her troubles. Lukien thought about Lahkali as he gazed out over Amchan, and suddenly he was melancholy again. She had worked so hard to please him.

But realities were hard, and so were the challenges she faced. Like it or not, she was the Red Eminence, and that meant killing the Great Rass. Now, the time had come for her teacher to learn how – if possible – such a thing could be done.

Next to Lukien, Jahan stood silently watching the forbidding forest, his tail of hair swaying gently to the lapping waves. He had come willingly on the journey because Lukien had requested it, and because he knew far more about rass than Lukien could ever hope to know. Like Lukien, Jahan had come prepared for the trek, carrying a long, curved sword called a culther to cut through the vines and tree limbs. The blade dangled from Jahan's belt, naked, while over his shoulder was slung a pack of food and supplies. His face was stoic while he awaited Lukien's orders.

Around Lukien's neck, the Eye of God gave its quiet assurance. Lukien fingered the amulet, wondering if at last its power might be challenged. He had been at the door of death before, but the amulet and its mighty spirit had snatched him back to life. In a way, he hated Amaraz for that.

'Give us a day,' said Lukien finally, speaking softly to Niharn. 'If we are not back by the morning, leave without us.'

'If you're not back by the morning, you'll be dead,' said Niharn without a trace of humour. The old master took measure of Lukien. 'And if that happens, I will explain to the Eminence what has become of you.'

'Thank you,' replied Lukien. He smiled faintly. 'Thank you for what you've done for me, Niharn.'

Niharn shrugged. 'I have helped to kill you. That is all.'

'Then I'll be out of your way at last,' Lukien joked.

'Yes.'

An unspoken understanding passed between them. Despite their differences, Niharn was an honest man, so loyal to Lahkali that he had risked his reputation to bring Lukien to Amchan. It would not go easily for him when he returned to Torlis but it was necessary, and Niharn seemed to understand that now.

'How will you find a rass to slay, Lukien?'

Lukien gestured toward Jahan. 'Him.'

Jahan nodded. 'I will find a rass, do not worry.'

He spoke with such confidence that Niharn asked no more of him. Instead he reached out for the katath Lukien held in his hand, pinging the blade with his fingernail. The weapon was one of Niharn's own, given to Lukien by the fencing master.

'Take care of her and she won't fail you,' said Niharn. Then he added with a grin, 'You should have let me give you some lessons.'

Lukien laughed to break the tension. He turned to Jahan. 'Ready?'

'I have been ready.'

Lukien turned to Niharn and said good-bye, then watched as the captain's men dropped a gang plank from the deck into the muddy bank. The long wooden walkway hit the earth with an unpleasant sound. Anxious to leave the feruka, Jahan was the first down the plank, bouncing across the ungainly strip with all his gear unbalancing him. He moved like a cat, though, and jumped down into the mud with a smile on his face. Lukien followed with equal success, using the long katath to balance himself. When both men were safely ashore, Lukien turned one more time to Niharn and the sailors.

'We will see you by morning!' he called to them confidently.

Then, with katath in hand, he trudged up the river bank toward the waiting unknown of Amchan. The wall of trees and rocky hills cast its dark shadow at his feet. Behind him, the noise of the river disappeared amidst the insistent chirping of birds and cries of hidden wildlife. Jahan took a deep breath, smiling at the sweetness of the air. Amchan was very unlike his village, yet he seemed at home. He spared no look for the men aboard the feruka, quickly stepping toward the trees.

'This way, Lukien.'

Unsure where he was going, Lukien let Jahan guide him, and soon the two were engulfed in the trees, leaving behind the river and the safety of the barge. Jahan had his culther up at once, using its sharp edge to whack away the vines that hung thickly from the gnarled trees. A heavy wetness hung in the air, clinging instantly to their clothes and forming streams of perspiration on Lukien's forehead. The stinging water blinded him as he followed Jahan through the forest, using the katath like a walking stick. The ground beneath him gave way easily, a soft, loamy soil that sound-lessly absorbed his movements. Staring up into the knitted canopy of leaves, he saw a family of hairy, monkey-like creatures leap from limb to limb. As they moved a shower of raindrops fell from the trees.

'Jahan?' he asked softly. 'What are we looking for?'

Jahan slowed a little, letting Lukien catch up. He looked back the way they had come with a look of satisfaction. 'We can't see or hear the others. Good.'

'Good?'

'Yes, Lukien. We need to get far from them if we are to find a rass. They will not come so close to so many people.'

'Oh, I forgot,' Lukien drawled. 'They're shy.'

'You laugh? They have enough sense to be afraid of people. And they can smell very far with their tongues. When we get near them, we must make sure to stay downwind of them.'

'How will we know when we're close?'

'I will know,' said Jahan. 'But first we must find the river again.'

'The river? Jahan, we just left it.'

'No, Lukien we must be well away from the others. I saw from the boat how the river bends. That's where we will go. At night the rass will come to the river. There will be marks in the mud where they have been.'

Lukien nodded, understanding. 'So if we find the marks we'll find the rass.'

'Just so. But first we need to find a place in the river far enough away from the boat so that the rass can't smell it.'

'How far is that?'

Jahan grinned. 'We have all day, do we not?'

Just before dusk, Jahan found that special place by the river.

It had taken all of the day to reach it, a sandy beach where the forest receded and water birds came to stand in the stream and peck at fish with their long beaks. A ridge of hills stood in the distance, blocking the falling sun. Near the trees, long openings had been flattened among the tall grasses, a sign to Jahan that something big had passed this way before, many times. Lukien, exhausted from the day in the forest, rested at the edge of the beach as he watched the sun go down. They had reached the serene place hours ago, taking a meal and napping while they waited for night to arrive. Confident that this was a place of rass, Jahan had shown their tracks to Lukien, a collection of fat grooves carved into the soft earth by the giant bodies of the serpents. The sight of the tracks had given Lukien a chill.

As the darkness came, he and Jahan had spoken less and less, and their voices dimmed to whispers. Jahan ignored the sunset, staring instead in the other direction, toward the tree line and the glistening beach. His eyes shone with excitement. An expectant smile stretched across his lips. He had been an expert guide and Lukien was glad to have him, yet he could hardly understand his enthusiasm. His love for the serpents was uncanny.

'I'm going to have to kill it, you know,' Lukien whispered.

Broken from his spell, Jahan's smile disappeared. 'Yes.'

They were downwind of the beach, just as Jahan had planned. Hours ago they had buried their food and washed themselves in the river. It was hard for Lukien to imagine a rass being afraid of anything, but he had done everything that Jahan had asked of him. Keeping behind the rocks, Jahan raised his head a little to peer out toward the tree line.

'Soon.'

'It was darker than this when we saw them in your village,' Lukien pointed out.

'They will come,' said Jahan.

Lukien grimaced. 'How big do you think?'

'Oh, big,' Jahan assured him. He turned and looked at his companion. 'That's what you wanted, Lukien. That's what you said.'

'Yes. Still . . .'

'You are afraid.'

'I'd be stupid not to be.'

Jahan thought for a moment. 'Your idea is good,' he pronounced. 'I have been thinking about it. There is no way for Lahkali to kill the Great

Rass if she does not know how. So you will learn how, and then teach her. Yes, it is a good idea.'

Lukien wondered about that now. 'You don't mind?'

'No,' Jahan sighed. 'It is a shame, but it is for Lahkali. It is for the good of her village.'

Lukien smiled at his quaintness. 'I have done my best for her, you know. You think I am hard on her, but—'

'You are hard on her, Lukien. But I understand.' Jahan spied the beach again. 'She cares for you.'

'Does she?'

'It is plain to see, Lukien.'

'Yes,' said Lukien, nodding. 'She has done everything I've asked. I can't fail her.'

'And that's why you're here?'

The question surprised Lukien. 'Of course.'

'The only reason?'

'Jahan, I don't take your meaning.'

Jahan did not turn his attention from the tree line. 'No more talk. Watch now.'

Lukien stiffened. 'You see something?'

'It is the rass that we don't see that I am afraid of, Lukien. Keep your eyes open for me.'

They both became still as the night settled over the beach. Darkness crept over the sand as the waves curled back. Lukien began readying himself. They would come to the water; Jahan had assured him of that. After that? Lukien considered his strategy. It would be best to confront the beast on the openness of the sand, he decided. His fingers tightened around his katath.

An hour passed and the moon appeared, bathing the sand in its silvery light. Overhead, the sky cleared of rain clouds, popping with stars. The buzzing of the insects intensified. Lukien felt sweat gathering on his chest. He scratched at it, pushing aside the Eye of God as he did so. The warmth of the amulet touched his fingers. Inside, he felt the ever-present Amaraz, mutely waiting with him for the rass to arrive.

Will you keep me safe?

Lukien's question went unanswered, and for a moment he wondered if he really wanted to be kept safe at all. Niharn's words to him came back suddenly, like an unpleasant itch. He hadn't found the Sword of Angels yet, or even any clue to it. And he had promised Cassandra he would see her again. He looked at Jahan, at last realizing what his friend had meant.

'What?' asked Jahan, feeling Lukien's eyes on him.

'I'm not here to die, Jahan.'

A long silence ensued. Jahan sighed. 'As you say.'

Lukien was about to speak again, but Jahan quickly held up his hand. The village man leaned forward, peering through the darkness. Excitement tensed his body.

'Lukien, look . . .'

Lukien looked but saw nothing. 'Where?'

'There, all the way down the beach.' Jahan pointed. 'By the fallen trees. Do you see?'

The trees had collapsed and rotted into the sand. Lukien had seen them earlier, when they'd first arrived. He focused on them now, struggling to see. A movement caught his eye, a slow undulating of flesh. Colourful hides caught the moonlight. Then, a single great hood emerged, raising up from the dead trees as the rass wound toward the river.

'Fate almighty,' Lukien gasped. 'Look at the size of it.'

Jahan's face was all beaming glee. He raised his head for a better look, almost completely coming out of his hiding place. 'He's far away. He won't smell us from here.'

Following his lead, Lukien emerged out of the rocks, clutching his katath and wetting his lips with his tongue. The rass moved silently, oblivious to them, its stout body pushing aside the sand. Its giant head came up, reflecting the moonlight in its glassy eyes. The tongue flicked out to taste the moist air. The coiled designs along its hood glistened blood-red against its greenish hide. And just as it lowered its head, another appeared. Lukien held his breath. Jahan let out a sound of exaltation.

'Beautiful . . .'

To Lukien, the rass were monstrous. He froze, not with fear but with revulsion, awed as the big rass led its cousin to the river.

'Two of them,' he whispered. 'I can't fight two.'

Jahan lifted himself out of the hiding place. Like a little boy chasing butterflies he inched along the sand. Lukien followed without knowing why, but then reached out to slow Jahan's approach.

'Wait,' he snapped. 'Not too close.'

'They want water, Lukien, not us. Probably a male and female. Mates.'

'Oh, gods, I don't need to see *that*.'

The larger rass – the male – reached the river first, surveying the bank in protection of its female, whose colourful body was only slightly smaller but speckled with spots of black and yellow. The enormous serpents at last settled to drink, slipping into the river and almost disappearing in the mud. Doubts overtook Lukien as he watched them. There was no way he could take on two of them, even with the amulet to keep him alive. And they were mates . . .

'Jahan,' he whispered. 'Wait.'

But Jahan still moved toward them, tip-toeing quietly along the sand.

Infatuated by the creatures, he paid no heed to Lukien's cautions, finally coming to a stop ten feet away. He turned with a smile to urge Lukien out.

'It's safe, Lukien,' he assured with a wave. 'Come.'

Shadows danced along the beach, blackening the sand. Lukien's one eye barely saw the darkness gathering to Jahan's side. At first he thought it merely one more tree, rising up unnaturally from the others. Lukien turned casually toward it and saw its spreading hood. He gaped, staring at it, confused even as the maw opened and the sabre-like fangs filled its reptilian face. It's eyes seized on Jahan.

'Lukien?' Jahan was smiling. 'Come with me.'

Time snapped forward. Jahan was speaking as the fangs appeared. Lukien opened his mouth to shout a warning as the rass came down, striking Jahan like a hammer with its enormous head and sending him sprawling. Lukien screamed, jumping toward him, but the rass had seen him now, using its tail to whip him back. The blow blackened Lukien's vision. He was falling, spinning backward, dropping the katath and scrambling for footing. He looked up from the sand and saw Jahan's frozen body, paralyzed by the poisonous strike. Dazed, Lukien staggered to his feet, ready to rush the snake. The rass ignored him, and with inhuman speed took Jahan in its mouth and slithered back into the trees.

'No!'

Lukien sped after it, dodging tree limbs as he fought to follow the racing rass. Already he had lost it. It simply disappeared, swallowed by the darkness. Lukien kept on, screaming as he bumbled past the branches, his face struck by the sharp limbs. Moonlight sifted through the canopy, and for a moment he thought he caught a glimpse of the beast, but it was only a vine swinging in the wind. He looked around desperately, unsure which way to go. Suddenly everything looked like a serpent.

'Jahan!'

His cry tore through the forest, unanswered.

Sick with grief, Lukien dropped slowly to his knees. Jahan was gone.

34

True to his promise, Master Niharn waited the day for Lukien and Jahan to return. Aboard the feruka, he whiled away the time talking to his old friend, Thaget, the captain of the vessel and playing card games in the hot sun. When night fell, the two old comrades spent the evening drinking and swapping tales, and by morning they were ready to sail home.

But Lukien did not return that first morning. And Niharn continued to wait. Thaget set his sailors to the many tasks of the boat, and as they day wore on the sun baked the deck and turned the beach where they were moored the colour of burnt glass. Master Niharn spied the forest, hopeful that Lukien and the quiet villager would emerge at any moment.

But they did not.

Finally, as night fell on the second day, Niharn knew he had a decision to make. Rumblings among the sailors reached his ears, but Thaget kept them in line with his sharp tongue. Still, they were right to be concerned, and when at last Thaget came to Niharn the captain looked troubled. Niharn was still at the edge of the deck, leaning contemplatively over the shallow railing as he watched the forest for movement. Except for the lizards and crabs that crept along the bank, he saw nothing. Over his shoulder, he saw Thaget's concerned face in the lamplight. The two hadn't talked in hours, and now there seemed little to say. Niharn struggled against his own disbelief and the enormity of what he had done, bringing Lukien to Amchan.

'He said he couldn't die,' the master whispered. He realized dreadfully how silly that sounded now. 'I believed him.'

'He has magic,' said Thaget optimistically. 'We've all heard of it.'

'He could not be this late. Something has happened.'

Thaget didn't argue, because the facts were so plain. Instead the feruka captain waited for his friend's orders.

'We have supplies for days, and fresh water from the river. We can stay, Niharn, if that's what you want.'

'The Eminence will know we are gone. She will guess that we have taken Lukien away.'

'She won't know we've come here, though.'

Niharn considered this. 'No.'

There was so much to think about, and so little that made sense. He had agreed to take Lukien to Amchan to kill a rass, and that alone seemed like madness. Lukien was a stranger, and in many ways a rival. Why then did his heart ache now?

'Your men want to leave,' said Niharn. 'They are afraid.'

'I'm their captain,' said Thaget. 'They will stay.'

'And you? Do you want to leave, Thaget?'

The captain of the boat reared back indignantly. 'I'm not afraid, Niharn. I would not have come if I were.'

'No,' said Niharn with a grin. 'I know. But they are very late, and they are strangers here. They do not know the things they should to survive out here.'

'The man from the village – he seems to know.'

'Yes,' Niharn agreed. 'He's part savage, that one. And he has not come to fight a rass. But Lukien . . .' The old man shook his head and sighed. 'I do not think he can survive it.'

On the third night in Amchan, the rain returned.

Lukien, stripped to the waist and smeared with mud, stood outside the den of the rass, waiting with his katath, his Eye of God dangling at his naked chest. In the blackness he was invisible, smeared with earth so that his skin and hair were hidden. His eye glistened like an angry pearl. His toes dug into the loamy ground, bootless. His trousers, soaked with river water, clung to his muscled legs. Behind a single, broad-leafed fruit tree he stood, statue-still, his breathing calmly matching the wind. In the moonless night he could barely see the yawning cavern the rass called home, a craggy opening covered with slime and lichens. Lukien concentrated, summoning the power of the amulet, using its ruby light to warm himself. Though the rain fell cold, he did not shiver. His mud-caked body stood rigid.

For a day and a night he had tracked the rass, following the tell-tale drops of Jahan's blood and studying every leaf and broken twig. The rass had moved like lightning, stealing away the dead Jahan, but its giant mass had left clues to trace. Slowly, painstakingly, Lukien had found its lair. After a dozen false starts, he came at last to the object of his vengeance.

And then he waited.

For more than a day he had gone without food, refusing to leave the lair of the beast to hunt for sustenance. Everything he had brought with him – save the katath – he had left at the beach where Jahan had been killed, not wanting anything to slow or distract him. Refusing to reveal himself, he had stripped away most of his clothes and washed away his scent in the river, doing just as Jahan had taught him to avoid the snake's sharp senses. His coat of mud kept the insects at bay. For food, he used thoughts of vengeance. Endlessly patient, Lukien watched the lair of the rass.

The night grew deeper. The rain slackened. Inside its home of rock the serpent did not stir. Satisfied from its human meal, it had no use to hunt. But did it need water? Lukien could only guess.

I am here for you, ugly one. Soon you will have to come out, and I will be waiting.

He had seen snakes in Liiria, little ones, swallowing whole eggs without ever stopping to chew as their mouths grotesquely dislocated. He imagined that's how Jahan had been eaten, all at once and slowly.

You will not die so horribly. It will be quick for you, but you don't deserve such mercy.

Jahan had always tried to convince him that the rass were noble. But to Lukien, they remained the most evil of creatures.

Jahan was noble.

Would he want such revenge? To Lukien the question hardly mattered. Revenge was for the living to decide.

Near dawn the rain finally ended. Lukien fought to keep awake. Looking up into the sky he saw the twilight stars struggling through the moving clouds. The leaves and grass began to glow beneath their light. He steeled himself, disappointed that the night had fled. It would be another day at least before his quarry emerged. The strength that had kept him erect so long began to ebb, making his eyelids heavy.

They come out at night . . .

His gaze dropped, and for a moment sleep edged across his mind.

No! Stay awake!

He took a breath.

But sit. Rest . . .

And then at last he heard a sound. It was unlike any other he had heard during his vigil near the cavern, a small, almost imperceptible scraping that tickled his ear. His heart began to race. His gaze widened and his jaw began to tighten. Crouching, he spied the hole of the serpent, and saw to his amazement the shadowy beast start to emerge. The head appeared, big and black, its dark eyes looking lifeless as they narrowed in the starlight. The cautious tongue came out to sniff the air, hissing as its forked muscles shook. The hood spread wide and the great beast rose up, surveying its domain.

Lukien slowly released his breath. In his hand the katath trembled. He rose, stretching himself tall to confront the creature.

'Look here,' he commanded.

The black eyes of the serpent snapped forward, fixing on him. Half naked and muddy, his hair slicked back against his head, Lukien raised the katath over his head.

'You're the one,' he said. He had only seen the rass for an instant, yet now he recognized it immediately. 'I have come for you, monster.'

What might have been disbelief flashed across the serpent's features. It's huge head bobbed backward and forward as it watched Lukien, searching for him with its terrible tongue. The amulet around Lukien's neck flared to life, flooding his features with a rush of crimson. He stood fearlessly before the rass, staring into its hypnotic gaze.

'A friend of mine is in your belly. I have come to avenge him. Don't think me another easy meal, beast. I am damned. Nothing can kill me, not even you.'

His words echoed through the night. The creature swayed in confusion. It pulled the rest of its bulk from its lair, coiling its tail around itself like a spring. The hood pulsed with breath, spreading and contracting in easy movements. The lidless eyes kept watch on Lukien as it opened up its red, pulpy mouth. A great hiss issued forth.

'You mean to scare me?' Lukien sneered.

The rass reared back. Lukien knew a strike was imminent.

It came like a bolt, swift and silent. The coiled spring of the serpent's body exploded forth, its head dashing for Lukien. Lukien dove. He hit the ground, somersaulting away as the mouth snapped closed. Surprised, the rass rose quickly, searching frantically as Lukien leapt to his feet. Seeing his chance, Lukien spun the katath overhead, slicing through the air and catching the beast just below its head. The blades of the weapon went through its hide, ripping through the scales. The rass hissed and jerked back. Lukien danced away. Coming around, he jabbed at the beast just as it tried to strike, this time smashing the twin blades into the creatures snout. The rass thrashed its head, dislodging the blades easily and tossing Lukien backward. It's tree-trunk body shot skyward, towering over Lukien.

For a moment the two locked eyes. Lukien waited for the coming blow. The rass flexed its hood and opened its maw, showing its gleaming fangs. Dazzled by its fearsome face, Lukien saw the coiling tail too late. It stuck like a whip, smashing into his back and knocking him to the ground. He tried to desperately to avoid the rest of the body, but the snake worked itself around him, moving with such speed that Lukien lost sight of it. A moment later he felt the strong muscles suffocating him.

'Gods!'

The tail lifted him bodily from the ground, bringing him face to face with the rass. Every fibre in him fought for breath, and remarkably he held tightly to his katath, refusing to loose the weapon even as his hands went numb.

'Amaraz, help me!'

A single blast of the serpent's venom would paralyze him. But the spitting fangs were a second weapon for the beast, which instead used its powerful body to crush the life from Lukien. Lukien felt the pressure building in his chest and head, threatening to pop his skull. His fingers clawed around the katath.

'Amaraz!' he cried.

At once he felt the power of the Eye coursing through him. Amaraz answered his summons with a flood of raw strength. The pain ebbed, and soon Lukien could breathe again. To the great astonishment of the rass he looked into its black eyes and cursed.

'Kill me!' he cursed. 'You stupid beast, kill me!'

The mouth opened, ready to spit. Lukien readied his katath. With all the strength Amaraz had given him, he jammed the katath into the soft flesh, cutting through the snout and severing the flicking tongue. A spurt of liquid struck his face, the venom from ruptured poison sacks. Lukien cried out, fighting the burning pain as he felt the muscles in his face go slack. His one eye blinked away the filth, holding firm to the katath as the rass uncoiled its massive body. With one last twist Lukien ripped apart its mouth before he hit the ground.

The earth struck him, blasting the air from his lungs. Looking up, he saw the bloodied rass thrashing in pain. Nearby he found the katath, reaching for it with his outstretched fingers. His face screamed with pain and his crushed ribs felt as though they were coming through his flesh. Lukien staggered to his feet, beating back the pain as he rushed against the rass. Katath in hand, he drove the blades into the monster's gut, bringing it up with a shout and ripping open its hide. A flood of fluid erupted from its wound, splashing Lukien's naked skin and soaking the ground. The rass rose up in one great cry, shooting skyward and stretching out its long body. Then it fell with a shudder to the ground, writhing and whipping Lukien backward. Dodging the beast, Lukien fell away and watched the creature die. The rass crept toward its lair, almost unable to move. With agonizing progress it reached the hole, about to hide its head within its safe recesses. Seeing this, Lukien stepped forward, looking straight into the snake's shining eye.

'Time to die,' he whispered.

Raising the katath overhead, he brought it down hard against the serpent's skull, driving it through the skin and skull. The creature tensed, opened its bleeding mouth, and collapsed.

Lukien staggered back, leaving his weapon inside the beast's head. For a long moment he was silent. His face twitching with pain, he dropped to his knees and wrapped his arms around his broken ribs. He would heal, he knew. Already the amulet worked its magic.

Laying down on the gory earth, Lukien slept.

The afternoon sun bore down on Niharn as he sat on the deck of the feruka, sipping from a cup of wine from Thaget's private bottle and feeling the heat cook the back of his neck. Steam rose up from the river bank, disappearing like ghosts into the breezeless air. Niharn's shirt clung to him, wet with perspiration. An insistent fly buzzed around his ears. The men of the feruka sat on the other side of the boat, mostly doing nothing because there was nothing much to do. Others waited below deck, out of the sun. They had been beached in Amchan for over three days and their restlessness showed on their bitter faces. Some had taken to splashing in the water or laying on the beach, liberated from their duties by Captain Thaget, who had the good sense to try and defuse their anxiety. Niharn sipped languidly from his cup, feeling the wine work its way over his brain. He was more than bored now, and past the point of worry. He had already told Thaget that they would be leaving in the morning, and Niharn had given up hope of ever seeing Lukien or Jahan again.

We should leave now, he told himself blackly. His eyes lingered on the woods in which his charges had disappeared. *They're gone. They must be.*

He felt a fool for waiting as long as he had, and he dreaded the look Lahkali would give him when he returned – without Lukien.

The Katath Master lowered his cup to the rickety table and stood, stretching his tight back. Peripherally, he glimpsed something on the beach. Thinking it one of Thaget's men, he momentarily ignored it. A second later his head snapped around again.

'Lukien . . .'

In disbelief he ran to the gangplank, pausing there to see the man trudging toward the bank. Lukien, half naked and starved, still held the katath Niharn had given him. His golden amulet swung from his neck. But he was alone. And his face had the look of tragedy to it.

Niharn called to Thaget as he bounced down the gangplank then splashed into the muddy waters. Behind him, sailors gathered on the deck of the feruka. He heard Thaget's gasp of surprise.

'Lukien!' Niharn called. He stopped with his ankles still in the water. 'What has happened?'

The knight from across the desert turned his single, hollow eye to the master. A filthy beard covered his sunken cheeks. The trousers he wore had been torn and stained with blood, and his hair was matted back against his head, caked with mud. He spoke in a rasp.

'Jahan is dead,' he pronounced. 'And so is the rass that killed him.'

Niharn fell speechless. All he could do was stutter a feckless reply. 'I am sorry.'

Lukien held out the katath. 'Take this,' he said. 'And take us home.'

Handing off the weapon, Lukien staggered up the gangway and onto the waiting barge.

35

The Walled Garden of Castle Hes contained more roses than Mirage had seen in her whole life. They bloomed in every variety, climbing trestles and smothering ancient statues while they filled the garden with perfume. Mirage worked diligently among the flowers, clipping back the sprouts the way Laurella had taught her, careful to watch the thorns that had already pricked her fingers, teaching her the hard way to use the gloves Laurella had provided. The morning sun blanketed the garden, threatening a hot day. Mirage glanced up at the blue sky, noting its perfection. The last week had passed in a day-dream of perfect weather, and she had been glad to get out of the castle and help Laurella with the chores. With Raxor gone, she had more than enough time to pitch in, and while the royal women of the castle ignored her and called her whore behind her back, Mirage was content to work as the servants did, tending to the garden or shadowing the maids while they cleaned the enormous home. She had been in Castle Hes for more than two months now, and the only friends she had made in the city were servants like Laurella. Laurella had taken Mirage under her tutelage, teaching her the fineries of court gossip and pointing out the best ways to avoid King Raxor's arrogant family. She had cared for Mirage like a mother, and Mirage was grateful to the old woman. She had made Mirage's confinement in Hes bearable. Amazingly, it was starting to feel like home for Mirage.

Home had never been a word Mirage was comfortable with. For her, home was her burnt-out house in Jerikor, where her parents had died and where she had been scarred to the point where pity shone in every eye that looked at her. And like the little girl she had been on that awful night, she carried that memory of home throughout her years in Grimhold, where she had struggled to find her place among the Inhumans and to be the daughter Minikin had always wanted her to be. She had chaffed in those years, never really feeling at home, and then when Lukien had come . . .

Mirage paused, staring at the bright red rose just in front of her nose, her shears poised to clip back its dead leaves. It struck her as beautiful suddenly, and she realized that she had not thought of Lukien in weeks. Her time in Castle Hes had gone that quickly, and instead of pining for Lukien she spent her days worrying about Raxor. Now, though, the memory of Lukien came flooding over her like the scent of the rose, so strong it forced her to remember. Her heart twisted with a tiny pang, and she lowered her shears long enough to sigh.

Where was he these days, Mirage wondered? Had he found the sword? Was he even still alive?

'And does he think of me?'

From the other side of the row of roses, young Sela glanced at her. The girl was on her knees in the dirt, sweating but happy-faced, enjoying her work. She peered through the blooms inquisitively.

'Mirage? Are you talking to me?'

'No,' said Mirage, quickly shaking her head. 'I was just . . . thinking.'

Laurella, dressed in a long brown work gown, sat on a stool at the other end of the garden, filling a basket with the most perfect of the roses. Overhearing the conversation of the girl's, the old woman glanced over, nodding with a smile at Mirage. Mirage nodded back, embarrassed.

'Take a break if you're tired,' Laurella suggested. 'Take some water.'

'I'm fine,' said Mirage.

'You don't have to be here, you know,' said Laurella gently. 'You can go inside.'

'No, I want to be here,' Mirage insisted.

There were four entrances to the Walled Garden, each one an archway built into one of the four high walls. At the northern entrance stood Corvalos Chane, keeping his watchful visage over Mirage as she worked. Mirage stole a look at him, spotting a hint of humour on his hard face. He smiled, one of his wry grins, forcing Mirage to roll her eyes. Next to him was a barrel full of cool water that he had been helping himself to while the women worked. He patted it tauntingly with his hand. And all of a sudden Mirage was thirsty.

'All right,' she relented, getting off her knees and wiping the dirt from her work gown. She pulled off her gloves and dropped them to the ground, then sauntered over to where Chane was standing. Wherever she went in the castle or its grounds, Chane went with her, hovering like a vulture. At King Raxor's orders he had been assigned to protect Mirage while the king was gone, and Chane had never once faltered in that duty. He was always nearby, waiting when she took her meals or went down to sleep at night, even when she bathed. He had become such a part of her life now that Mirage hardly noticed him any more, and that was why he occasionally taunted her. Like a spoiled brat, he wanted her attention.

'Hot,' he commented when she came up to him. He took a tin cup from the side of the barrel and dipped it into the water for her, offering her the drink.

'How would you know?' she jibed. 'You're just standing here.'

'Looking after you is work, girl, believe me. Do you want a drink or not?'

'Yes,' said Mirage, taking the cup out of his hand. 'Thank you.'

He grinned. 'Will you be much longer? It is going to get hotter, and Laurella is right – you don't have to be out here working like a slave. You are the king's woman.'

'I choose to work, Corvalos Chane,' said Mirage tartly. 'And you can do more than just stand around making faces. Gardening is man's work, too, you know.'

'It may be that, but it is not my work, girl. My work is to see no harm comes to you. So be careful with those shears, will you?'

'You are in a mood today,' Mirage snorted, then at last took a pull of the cool water. From the corner of her eye she could see the boyish satisfaction on his face. 'Of course if standing around is too much for you . . .'

'I am fine.'

She handed him back the cup. 'Tonight Laurella is going to teach me to sew. What do you think of that?'

'It sounds like great fun.'

Mirage nodded. 'After supper then. You'll be there?'

'Of course,' said Chane, but a small knitting of his brow betrayed his displeasure. 'I serve at the pleasure of my king.'

'And you've done such a good job, Corvalos Chane, really,' sighed Mirage. 'Protecting me from all these flowers. If not for you I might be stung by a bee!'

Laurella and Sela heard her joke and laughed. Mirage studied Chane's face, watching cracks develop in his stony façade. He was a handsome man, her bodyguard, or he might have been if he wasn't so thin. His face, like the rest of his body, held no fat at all, just taught skin stretched over his strong bones. The hot sun and her constant sarcasm made his scalp turn red.

'The king cares for you, girl,' he said. 'He would not have anything happen to you, or I would be the one to answer for it. So beware of the bees, please. The thorns, too.'

Was it a sweet thing to say? Mirage wasn't sure. So many of Chane's statements were couched in mystery. Despite their tension, they had become close during the month of Raxor's absence, a fact that amazed Mirage. He was the one who had captured her, after all, and taken her to Raxor. But he had also saved her from Asher, and since then there was an unspoken attraction between them. He had told her once that he could never have a woman of his own. Still, he was a man, and his eyes revealed his desires.

'I'll be only an hour or so more,' she told him. 'We'll break for a meal then.'

Chane nodded as though disinterested, letting her return to her work. Mirage went back to her place in the garden, quietly trimming back the rose bushes. Occasionally she felt his eyes on her, admiring her, but when she looked up he glanced away, without the slightest trace of guilt to give him away. The hour passed slowly, and by the end of it Mirage and Sela were both exhausted and hungry. They looked hopefully at Laurella, who nodded as she rose from her bench.

'Yes, all right,' she said. 'We can stop now.'

Happily Mirage laid down her shears and began to stand, and then noticed a man hurry into the garden, running up to where Corvalos Chane stood. He was a soldier, one of the guardians Mirage often saw around the castle, and his face was drawn with worry. Mirage and the others stopped, instantly alarmed as the man began talking, struggling to catch his breath. Chane listened, though Mirage could not hear what was being said. She watched as Chane's expression lost its usual apathy, collapsing suddenly with disbelief. His mouth dropped open as the man spoke. Mirage stopped breathing, sure something terrible had happened.

Corvalos Chane looked stricken. His eyes moved purposelessly around the garden, as if lost. The soldier stopped talking. He stared at Chane. Mirage froze.

'What is it?' she called from across the garden.

Chane ignored her. He dismissed the soldier, then turned and slowly left the garden. Shocked, Mirage looked at Laurella, but the old house-maid simply shrugged. Young Sela went to stand beside Mirage.

'What happened?' she asked. 'Where's he going?'

Mirage was determined to get answers. 'Wait here,' she told Sela, then hurried out of the garden after Chane. She caught up to him quickly just outside the garden wall. He did not turn to look at her, but kept walking toward the castle, his face emotionless.

'Chane?' she queried. She grabbed hold of his sleeve to stop him. 'Wait!'

Corvalos Chane stopped walking, and very carefully took her hand off his arm. 'Don't touch me. I have to go.'

'Go where?' Mirage insisted. She looked ahead, toward the soldier scurrying back toward the castle. 'Who was that?'

'No one. He's no one.'

'What did he tell you?'

Chane fought to control himself. He looked at her, then quickly looked away. 'Prince Roland is dead,' he said. 'King Raxor is on his way home.'

Mirage stepped back. 'What?'

'The king . . .' Chane could barely speak. 'His army – they were defeated.'

'Defeated?' It seemed unbelievable. 'Raxor?'

Chane looked disgusted. 'Did you not hear what I said? The king's son is dead.'

'I heard you,' said Mirage. 'I . . .' She caught herself. 'I am sorry.'

Chane shook his head. 'His only son . . .'

Once again he turned away, walking slowly as if through a haze. Mirage took a step after him, then stopped herself. Her own shock tied her tongue into a knot. The heartbreak on Chane's face frightened her. Behind her, she heard Laurella and Sela approaching. What would she tell them?

Under the perfect blue sky, Mirage watched Corvalos Chane leave.

As she always did since Raxor's departure, Mirage ate her supper with Laurella and the other maids, late at night after the royals had all gone to sleep. Tonight, however, the usual bawdy conversation around the table was stunted by the terrible news of Prince Roland's death and the even more unbelievable fact that the king's great army had been defeated. Because she was an outsider still, Mirage heard very little about what had actually happened, and though all the servants listened earnestly to the talk among their masters, they still had almost no idea of what had actually happened. Mirage ate sparingly, saying little as she contemplated the awful truth about what Baron Glass had done. The rumours that reached her and her servant friends were filled with tales about the 'Black Baron' and his evil armour, and how he had been the one to murder Prince Roland. The thought curdled Mirage's appetite so that she pushed her potatoes around her plate without tasting them.

Corvalos Chane had not come to her, either. Mirage supposed he was somewhere in the Castle, mourning the loss of his king's son. Like many in Hes, Chane had no real love for the prince, but his love for King Raxor was boundless and Mirage was sure he shared the old ruler's pain. She imagined what Raxor might look like now, broken and defeated, his only son slain in the most horrible fashion. He had been kind to her and Mirage had been looking forward to his homecoming, but now she dreaded it. The news of his defeat fell over Castle Hes like a blight.

That evening, she did not go to her rooms as usual, but instead walked the corridors of Castle Hes in search of Corvalos Chane. The king's relatives had all gone to the parlours to discuss the bad news of the day, leaving the castle ghostly and quiet. What had been a long day ended in a blood-red sunset, visible from the castle's many windows. Mirage paused to watch the crimson dusk disappear into darkness, wondering

378

where Corvalos Chane was hiding. He would not be pleased to see her, she was sure, but she was drawn to him tonight. She needed his quiet strength.

She inquired about him to servants she passed in the halls, and when they claimed to know nothing she left the castle to survey the grounds, where a sharp-eyed page boy told her he had seen Chane a few hours earlier, taking a horse from the stable. Mirage cursed her bad luck, sure that Chane would not be back before the morning. She stood in the courtyard, alone with the page, unsure if she should wait or simply go to bed.

'Did he say where he was going?' Mirage asked the boy.

'Master Chane doesn't speak to me,' laughed the boy. 'Sorry, Ma'am.'

He excused himself and then was gone, leaving Mirage confused. She was angry too, because King Raxor had ordered Chane to look after her and in the whole past month he had barely left her side. Now that she needed him . . .

'No,' she said, stopping herself and feeling bad for cursing him. She wasn't a Reecian, after all, and could not really know the depth of his pain. Suddenly she found herself wandering, not wanting to go back to her rooms. She felt like a foreigner again, unwelcome.

He'll come back eventually, she told herself.

He just needed to be alone, just for a while, to deal with the terrible news. So Mirage went to the stable where she was sure Chane would reappear. Like everything in Castle Hes, the stables were enormous, and manned day and night by rough-looking hands who eyed her suspiciously when she stepped through the wooden gates. The ground, pitted with horseshoe marks, smelled of horse manure. A few lanterns hung in the stalls. The boys who had finished their hard day of work squatted in a circle in one of the stalls, playing a dice game. They all stopped when they saw Mirage. The look on their faces spoke of desire, the kind Mirage was still unaccustomed to. She glanced away, gazing at the stalls and the resting horses until a man – a soldier – called to her from across the way.

'My lady? Have you need of anything?'

He had a brush in his hand and was grooming a horse, a big, chestnut coloured beast that whinnied at his loving attention. Mirage paused, taking a moment to remember him. She had only seen him briefly when he'd come into the garden to deliver the terrible news.

'No,' she said. Then, 'Yes. I'm . . . looking for someone.'

Did he know who she was? Most in the castle did, but never took the time to speak to her.

'There's only me here, my lady,' he said, 'and the boys who work here. Who are you looking for?'

'My name is Mirage,' she offered.

He nodded. 'I know who you are, my lady.' He surprised her with a smile. 'You are the king's woman.'

'Yes,' she replied. She had been called that so often it no longer offended her. 'Sir, I am looking for Corvalos Chane. Have you seen him tonight?'

'You were with him in the garden, when I told him the news.' The soldier looked inquisitive. 'You heard by now, then?'

'Everyone has heard, but I don't know the details,' said Mirage. 'That's why I am looking for Corvalos Chane. Where is he? Do you know?'

'He has gone,' said the man. 'He rode out hours ago but didn't say where he was going.'

'Just like that? He just left?'

'Just like that, my lady,' said the soldier. He let the hand with the brush drop to his side. 'I was unlucky enough to give him the news. I've never seen his face like that, not in all my life. And I have known him a long time.'

'He's supposed to protect me,' said Mirage impotently. She laughed at the notion. 'That must sound silly to you, but he surprises me. To leave without a word to me . . .'

'He has much on his mind, my lady. The king will be return in less than a week. I am sure Chane does not relish seeing him.' The soldier set down his brush and stepped away from his horse. 'My name is Donil,' he said.

Mirage returned his smile. He had that rare quality among the people of Castle Hes, a genuine kindness. 'The folk of the castle have kept me in the dark all day, Donil,' she said. 'Will you tell me what has happened?'

'To Prince Roland, you mean?'

'To the prince, yes. And to the king.'

Donil shook his head. 'It's not for a woman to hear, my lady.'

'But I must,' said Mirage. 'I have waited all day to hear the truth of what happened, and I cannot sleep at all until I know. Please, Sir Donil – if Corvalos Chane is not here to tell me, then won't you?'

The soldier studied her face, considering her request. 'You're a Liirian, I've heard,' he said. 'I suppose you have a right to know what your countrymen did.'

'Then you have heard wrong, Sir Donil, for I am not a Liirian and the men that did this deed are not my countrymen. Forget what you've heard about me, please. I'm neither a Liirian nor the king's whore.'

'My lady, your pardon,' said Donil without offense. 'But you were a consort of Baron Glass. I have heard that correctly, at least.'

'A consort? No,' Mirage corrected. She thought of going further but stopped herself. 'It doesn't matter anyway. Please . . . tell me what happened at the river.'

'I know only what the king's riders told us,' said Donil. 'They came ahead of his army.'

'They arrived this morning?'

Donil nodded. 'Just before I saw you and Chane in the garden, my lady. It was decided I would tell Chane what had happened. A bitter duty, believe me, but he is well with me.'

'You are friends?'

Donil laughed. 'No, madam. Corvalos Chane counts no one as his friend. He serves only his master. But we talk, and if anyone in Castle Hes knows his mind then it is I, I suppose.'

'I have never seen him the way I did this morning,' said Mirage. The memory of his face rattled her. 'And it isn't just because of Prince Roland. Tell me – how bad was the defeat?'

'The defeat was total, my lady. The king was lucky to escape alive, I think. I don't know how many men died. Hundreds at least. But they say your man Glass—' Donil corrected himself. 'Baron Glass. They say he was unstoppable, my lady, like a thing from hell.'

The description made Mirage freeze. 'They say that?'

'Those who survived, yes. The rumours of him are true, then. Do you see now why the whole castle trembles tonight? If Baron Glass comes, there will be no way to stop him.' Donil looked at her strangely. 'Unless you know of a way, my lady.'

'Me? Why would you ask me such a thing?'

'As I said, I hear things,' said Donil. He glanced around, lowering his voice. 'My lady, you need to be careful.'

'Why?' Unable to help herself, Mirage looked over her shoulder. 'What are you telling me?'

'Just keep yourself safe until Chane returns, is all. There are people talking.'

'Donil, what people?' Mirage demanded. 'What are you talking about?'

Donil smiled, determined to say no more, and turned back to his waiting horse. 'Chane should be back by the morning,' he told her. 'Until then, do yourself the favour of staying out of sight.'

His words frightened her. And perplexed her. She had a thousand questions for the enigmatic soldier, but his manner told her not to ask them. Mirage looked suspiciously around the stable. Nothing seemed out of order. The stable hands continued with their dice game. The horses rested happily. It felt late suddenly, and oddly cold.

'I'll go now then,' said Mirage awkwardly.

She watched Donil. The soldier didn't turn around, but gave her a cheery farewell.

'Sleep well, my lady.'

Mirage had got used to Corvalos Chane around her, and without him to protect her she found sleep almost impossible. With only her Akari to keep her company, Mirage lay beneath the expensive sheets, staring at the copper ceiling and wondering about the riddle Donil had set at her feet. Kirsil wandered in and out of her mind, as perplexed as her master as to the meaning of the soldier's words. Were they in danger? Laurella didn't think so, nor did any of the other maids. Castle Hes was in mourning, and the thought of anyone doing harm to Mirage in Raxor's absence seemed unthinkable to Laurella, who insisted that Mirage go to bed after her wanderings through the courtyard. Mirage sighed and turned her head to glance out the open window. She had pulled the wooden shutters wide apart to let in the meagre breeze. Moonlight spilled into her opulent chamber. The world was remarkably quiet, and Mirage could clearly hear her own heartbeat, thumping uneasily in her chest.

Kirsil? Are you there?

The young Akari replied, *I am always here, Mirage. You know that.*

'Yes,' Mirage whispered. She did know Kirsil was always with her, though sometimes she needed reassurance.

You should sleep now, said Kirsil. *Try, at least.*

'Where's Chane, do you think?' Mirage asked. 'Do you think he'll return?'

Of course. He must return. He is pledged to the king. And to you now, Mirage.

'Yes . . .'

The spirit's words did little to comfort Mirage. But she was tired and it was very late, and soon her eyelids grew heavy. Half fighting it, she began to slip toward slumber, at first restlessly, then more deeply as her exhaustion won out. The gentle noises outside her window lulled her, and she began to dream.

Mostly, she dreamed of Thorin. She dreamed of how he had once been, when he was kind. He had loved her and comforted her. Even before she had changed her appearance, he had showed her kindness. In her dream she longed for him, as though her dream had unlocked a passion she had long kept suppressed. She missed the old man.

The dream faded, and Mirage slept. An hour passed without her notice and then another, and in her mind she heard the sound of scraping. She ignored it, but when it came again her eyes fluttered open. She felt Kirsil jolt through her mind.

Wake up! said the Akari.

Mirage bolted upright with a gasp. 'What?' Her pulsed raced and her eyes scanned the room. Through the dark and silvery moonlight, she could barely see at all. 'Kirsil? Was that you?'

Mirage, look!

'What?'

And then she saw him. He sat at the edge of her bed, one leg casually crossed over the other, staring at her with his manic gaze. His hands were clasped over his knee. The whiff of a demented smile curled his lips. His scarred face twitched when their eyes met.

Mirage went numb. The door to her chamber was closed. He was alone, though she couldn't tell for certain. She raised the sheet over her bosom, unable to speak.

'Good evening,' Asher drawled.

He waited politely for her reply. Mirage could barely find her voice.

'What are you doing here?' she gasped.

'It's been quite a day for me, pretty Mirage. You can imagine my surprise at the news of King Raxor's defeat.' Asher leaned forward. 'What do you think I am doing here?'

'I don't know,' spat Mirage. 'But if you don't leave I will scream.'

'You may scream as long and as loudly as you like. My men are right outside that door, and no one is going to come to help you. You're mine, finally, the way you always should have been.'

Mirage sat up quickly. 'Laurella! Sela! Help!'

'The maids have been excused for the night,' said Asher. He grinned, pleased with himself. 'And good King Raxor is not here to come to your rescue this time. No one is going to rescue you, child. They blame you for the death of Prince Roland. And rightly so, I might add.'

'That's madness!' cried Mirage.

'I told you I would find out your secrets. I always knew you were hiding something. I should have pulled off your pretty fingernails the moment I met you, but I was soft and you . . .' Asher sighed as though he'd just finished a great meal. 'You were so beautiful.' He looked pained suddenly. And completely mad. 'I was tempted by you. You weakened me. But now I'm going to find out your secrets, pretty Mirage.'

'What secrets?'

Anger flashed across Asher's face. 'The armour, you whore!'

Mirage leaned back against the headboard. 'You're insane.'

'And you are hiding the very thing that could have saved Prince Roland and the rest of the army. But never mind – you may tell all the lies you wish for now. I'll get the truth out of you.'

Asher got to his feet and went to the door. Opening it, he revealed a team of burly prison guards, all dressed in the same frightening grey tunics. The men leered at her, enjoying the sight of her in her nightdress. One stepped forward quickly with a pair of manacles.

'Take her,' Asher ordered.

'No!'

Mirage sprang to her feet, desperate to escape. The men rushed at her, grabbing her arms and twisting her around. She tried to fight them, but they were like a straight-jacket suddenly, suffocating her and pinning back her arms. She screamed, but a giant hand fell over her mouth to silence her. Angrily she bit it, tasting blood. The guard howled. Violently he yanked back her head, preparing to strike her.

'Don't you dare,' said Asher quickly. He stepped forward as his men put the manacles around her wrists. His spidery fingers came up to brush her chin. 'She's perfect, Garl. That's how I want her – a perfect canvas for me to paint on.'

Garl, the prison guard, grunted and stepped away, favouring his bleeding hand. Two of the others took Mirage by the elbows.

'Maybe I should muzzle you,' Asher suggested. 'Like any wild bitch.'

Mirage replied by spitting in his face. The saliva running into this drooping eye made her smile.

'When King Raxor finds out about this he's going to skin you alive, Asher. He's going to gut you and hang your ugly pelt over his throne.'

Asher wiped his face on his sleeve. 'When his Majesty returns you will be dead, child, and I will have the means to defeat Baron Glass. I think that will ease his mind a bit.' He nodded to his men. 'Let's go.'

As Asher left the room his burly guards dragged Mirage after him, lifting her by her bound arms toward the door. Fighting them was impossible – they were far too strong, and all Mirage could do was scream. Out in the hall, she let out the loudest cry she could, begging someone – anyone – to help her. But the halls were empty, and only silence met her echoing voice.

'Where's Laurella?' Mirage demanded. 'What have you done with her?'

'Don't worry, child. The old woman is fine.' Asher laughed as he sauntered down the corridor. 'She's been subdued, though I must say she's a tiger!'

'If you've hurt her—'

'Yes, yes. Save your strength, girl,' said Asher. 'It's going to be a long night!'

The anticipation in his voice told Mirage of the awful danger. He meant what he said – he would torture her, then he would kill her. With a renewed vigour she struggled against the guards, but they were unmovable to the slight girl, who could only allow herself to be dragged through the corridors and down the long, curving stairs. Her mind filled with images of horror, of Asher's ghastly prison and the cell there she had so narrowly escaped. She had thought she had left it behind forever, but like a recurring nightmare Asher had returned.

Down the in castle's main hall, porters and stable boys and a few of Laurella's own maids had gathered, looking stricken as Asher's men dragged Mirage along. A handful of Raxor's large, mostly nameless family were there as well, along with the caste's own guardians, none of whom moved an inch to stop the determined Asher. Mirage shouted at them, begging them to help her, but all they did was look shamefully away, too afraid or too filled with hate to come to her aid. She stumbled out of the hall and through the huge oak doors of the castle, spilling out into the courtyard where Asher's carriage waited, surrounded by more of his men on horseback. The crowd that had gathered in the hall did not follow them outside. The wardens stared down at her from atop their horses, looking pityingly at her, knowing her plight.

'Get her inside,' Asher ordered, climbing the steps of the beat-up carriage and opening the door for himself. He sat himself down inside and watched with satisfaction as his men stuffed Mirage through the small portal, seating her on a hard bench opposite the prison master. The door closed noisily behind her, and Mirage found herself staring into Asher's monstrous face.

'Don't do this,' she told him, trying one more time to convince him. 'I don't know anything more. And King Raxor will be back soon. He will, Asher, and if you harm me he'll kill you.'

'I'm willing to gamble on that,' replied Asher. Because it was a warm night, both windows on the sides of the carriage were open. Asher stuck his head outside one of them and called out to the driver. 'Get going!'

The carriage lurched forward, pinning Mirage back against her seat. The stout metal cuffs bit into her flesh as she squirmed to get free. Asher watched her struggling, licking his lips.

'Look at you. You're as limber as a cat.'

Mirage groaned, 'You're sick. You don't know what you're doing.'

Asher waved off her comment and settled back for the ride to his prison. He looked smug, like a boy who had captured a firefly, beaming with excitement to get his new pet home. Mirage raced through the possibilities, trying to think of anyway to free herself. She needed Raxor, and he wouldn't be back for days yet. By then she would be dead.

The carriage moved quickly out of the courtyard. Through its left-hand window Mirage could see the gates of Castle Hes, open wide and waiting for them. She heard the clip-clop of the horsemen accompanying them, precisely guiding them. Her breath quickened as hopelessness closed like a noose around her neck. The carriage bumped along the rocky path, picking up speed. Castle Hes fell away behind them as they neared the looming gates. Mirage watched as the lead horseman approached the gate, and then saw another man riding past them, paying no heed to the carriage or Asher's entourage. For a moment Mirage did not recognize him. Her thoughts clouded with fear, it took long seconds for her to realize the man was Corvalos Chane.

'Oh, gods,' she whispered. Then, exploding off the bench, she stuck her head out the little window and cried, 'Chane! It's me! Help me!'

Asher was on her instantly, cursing and pulling her back. Mirage continued to scream. Corvalos Chane paused for a moment, looking toward her, and just before Mirage lost view of him she saw recognition flash across his face.

'Drive on!' Asher yelled, his head out the window. He looked back toward Chane, then hollered at his driver, 'Faster!'

The carriage bolted, knocking Mirage to the floor. Rolling to her feet, she fought to reach the window, but Asher fell on her, pulling her away. A small man, he had trouble with his own footing and stumbled badly, and when Mirage glimpsed his open thighs she fired her knee up into him. Asher writhed in agony, doubling over and falling against the opposite wall. His nimble hands clawed the air, reaching for her as she made it to the window. Chane was pursuing.

'Chane!' she called. 'It's Asher!'

'I know!' the bodyguard growled. His whole face reddened with rage. 'Hold on!'

He caught up quickly to the last, lagging horseman, drawing his sword even before the man knew he was there. Chane's blade moved like lightning, puncturing the man's back. As the warden fell from his horse the others drew their weapons. Chane sneered and rode them down. Mirage fit herself further out the window, then felt Asher's hand on her nightgown, pulling her backward.

'You wretched whore!' He spun her around and struck her face hard. The blow stunned her and she collapsed. Wavering on his feet, Asher leered down at her, his face twisted with pain. 'He won't save you,' he grunted. 'I won't let him.'

'You can't stop him!' spat Mirage. 'You're a weak little toad.'

Enraged, Asher reached down and grabbed hold of her hair, pulling her screaming to her feet. He shoved her face out of the window and called out to Corvalos Chane.

'Is that what you want, Chane? This whore? This traitor? Is that what you think the king wants?'

But Chane was too involved to answer or even look at them. He had run down another of the guards, leaving his corpse in the road. Two more of the wardens were battling him back. Chane's sword was up and parrying their assaults. He moved more quickly than any man Mirage had ever seen. Asher noticed this, too, and grunted out a string of curses.

'Why save her?' he roared. 'She's an enemy, Chane! A slut of Baron Glass!'

But his taunts only enraged Chane, who drove his horse ever faster and put his blade through the eye of a warden. The carriage went over a rut in the road, tossing Mirage back from the window. She landed on her rump and kicked out to avoid Asher who fell next. Together they squirmed on the floor of the cab as the carriage careened along. The noise of the battle outside reached Mirage, and she knew that Chane was getting closer.

'You hear that?' she trumpeted. 'He's coming Asher!'

Asher looked stunned as he managed to find his footing. He went back to the window and peered outside. And what he saw – or didn't see – made his face go blank. Mirage was on her feet again and threw herself against him, knocking him aside. Still weak from the blow to his groin, the prison lord collapsed. Mirage fought to locate Chane, but saw only his empty horse quickly falling back. The wardens were gone.

'Chane!' she called. 'Chane!'

But the bodyguard didn't answer. She thought of him laying dead in the road, wondering if one of the distant corpses was his. Up ahead she saw the remaining riders, looking perplexed as they pointed backward and shouted. The driver looked over his shoulder and screamed.

Corvalos Chane descended out of the darkness, running along the roof of the cab and falling on the driver with his sword. Blood splashed against Mirage's face and she cried out, clearing her vision to see the driver dumped aside and Chane taking the reins of the racing horses. He jerked the steeds to a halt, bringing the carriage to a sudden stop. Asher's wardens wheeled their mounts around to face him. When the carriage halted, Chane jumped to his feet, sword in hand. Standing on the driver's seat, he bid the wardens to come.

'Fight me and die,' he said, ready to spring. 'Or lower your weapons and live.'

The wardens – perhaps eight of them – waited cautiously, none of them moving to attack. From inside the carriage Mirage could see them eyeing Chane, sizing him up. Asher muscled his way past her, quickly opening up the carriage door. With one hand he grabbed hold of Mirage and pulled her down the steps and onto the road.

'I have her, Chane,' he warned, dragging her toward the front of the vehicle. With his hand in her hair he violently shook her head. 'Look at her. She's the reason the army was defeated. She's the reason the prince is dead!'

'She's mine to protect, Asher,' said Chane. Slowly, he got down from the carriage and stood before Mirage and her captor, careful to keep his distance. 'I can't let you have her. You know that.'

'She has secrets! She knows about Glass' armour.'

Chane nodded. There was reluctance in his eyes. 'It's not up to you to decide what happens to her. Only the king can release her.' The bodyguard lowered his sword. 'Undo her binds.'

Asher glanced at his wardens. Mirage felt his fingers tighten against her head. He was calculating, she could tell, wondering about his chances.

'I'll kill them all if I have to, Asher,' said Chane. 'And then I'll kill you.'

Asher's hand began to tremble against Mirage's scalp. She tried to pull away, but his grip tightened instantly.

'Don't you move until I say so,' he rumbled in her ear. 'You should be *mine.*'

'In hell,' cursed Mirage. With only a moment to act, she snapped back her head and smashed it against Asher's nose. He let go instantly, screaming, letting her bolt toward Chane, who quickly grabbed hold of her and pulled her behind him. Asher came up hissing. He ran for her, but Chane's quick sword halted him, coming up to catch his chin.

Asher stopped, raising his hands in surrender, the tip of the sword pricking his skin. His bruised nose dribbled blood.

'Corvalos Chane, you are an idiot,' he sneered. 'All of this – what will it get you? When the king returns she'll be mine again.'

'When the king returns, then,' said Chane with a nod. 'Unlock her chains.'

Asher stepped back, then ordered one of the wardens off his horse. The man came forward with his jangling keys, quickly loosing Mirage's manacles. When she was free Mirage rubbed at her wrists, glaring at Asher, who returned her gaze with a perverse leer.

'Be on you way now, Asher,' ordered Chane. 'And don't come to the castle again. If I see you again I will kill you. I swear it. To whatever devil you worship I swear.'

Asher's face sank, for he knew he was defeated. He gathered his wardens around, looking back along the road at the litter of bodies. His driver was dead. So were at least four of his men.

'You'll hang for this, Chane. You will. And it will be on my very own gallows.'

Chane laughed. 'A grand dream, little man.'

Asher ordered one of his men to drive the carriage, then limped back up the steps and closed the door of the vehicle. Chane and Mirage waited until Asher and his party were on their way before turning back toward Castle Hes. The darkness had thickened, and they had no horse to ride back.

'We'll have to walk,' Chane told her. He looked at her, his expression concerned. 'Can you walk?'

'I'm fine,' said Mirage. 'Just shaken a bit.'

It was a lie and Chane realized it. He put his arm around her. 'Lean against me. We'll go slow.'

Mirage did as he asked, sinking into his strong embrace. 'I'm not safe,' she said. 'Chane . . .' She looked at him. 'I'm afraid.'

'No one will harm you now,' he assured her.

'But the others, Raxor's family . . .'

'Mirage, no one is going to hurt you. Not while I'm with you.'

36

Gilorin Court came into view past the hedgrows as the barge slipped along the river. Bordered by a tall green forest and acres of hunting grounds, the small estate rested comfortably on the sandy bank of the river, looking squat and ancient in the afternoon sun. A long path of cobblestones meandered from the castle to the shore of the river, flanked by rolling lawns dotted with cherry trees. Horses cantered across the grass, moving with unhurried grace. A small band of men and women gathered at the bank, standing clear of the mud as they watched King Raxor's barge float toward them. They had dressed for his arrival, the women all in expensive gowns while the men looked smart in tailored jackets and polished shoes. Behind them stood a row of servants. And behind the servants stood the castle, peacefully mute among the cherries.

Aric Glass sat near the king's dais to Raxor's left, close enough to enjoy the shade of His Majesty's awning. It had been a leisurely trip, taking up most of the morning, but Aric had welcomed the change from horseback to boat, surprised by the calmness of the river and lulled by the untouched surroundings. Gilorin Court, King Raxor's estate, was miles away from Hes, in the wooded north of the same Reecian province. Throughout their long march back, Aric had expected to arrive in the capital, but Raxor had changed his mind just days earlier. Gilorin, he had said, was a place to think. And Raxor had much to think about these days.

It had taken weeks for the defeated army to slog its way home. Aric had passed the time by getting close to the old king. At first Raxor's grief over Roland's death had been overwhelming, and he had spoken to no one. But as the days and tedium wore on the king eventually opened up, surprising Aric once more by taking him into his confidence. They had left a good many of the Reecian troops behind to guard the eastern provinces, and by the time they reached the river there were only one hundred of them left. Raxor had spread the word across his territory that Baron Glass and his army of mad Norvans had taken the Kryss. Invasion seemed imminent. Worse, there seemed to be no way of stopping the baron or his enchanted armour, and as they rode Raxor picked at Aric's knowledge, questioning him about his father and all he knew about the Devil's Armour.

Aric watched the gathering on the bank of the river. He had expected there to be servants at the estate, but the sight of so many Reecian royals made him uneasy. Not all of Raxor's men had greeted him warmly, and even those who had got to know him didn't trust him. He was Thorin Glass' son, and to many that made him a blood enemy. He settled back in his seat, forcing himself to relax as the crew guided the vessel toward shore. Raxor's lovely estate beckoned, easing the creases in the old king's face. Noting the crowd with satisfaction, Raxor spoke to the advisors who had come aboard with them earlier in the day, talking in whispers Aric could not overhear.

None of them pitied Raxor, and to Aric that was good. He was still their king, still their hero. And while he was with them he gave them a strength Aric could see on their troubled faces.

'Aric,' said Raxor suddenly. 'Come here.'

Surprised, Aric stood. 'My lord?'

King Raxor patted the empty spot beside him. 'Sit with me. We must talk.'

Alarmed, Aric took his seat next to the king and looked at him quizzically. 'My lord? Is there trouble?'

Raxor gestured to the men and women who had gathered on the shore. 'You see them? I want you to stay clear of them while you're here in Gilorin. Don't talk too much to anyone, all right?'

'Yes, my lord,' Aric agreed. 'But who are they?'

'They have names you'll need to remember. That one, in the red jacket . . .' Raxor pointed at the man with his chin. He was only a speck but his scarlet clothes stood out among the crowd. 'Duke Joric of Glain. That man next to him is Duke Redhorn.'

'And next to him, my lord? Another duke?'

'You see my meaning?'

'I think so. Men with armies.'

Raxor nodded. 'I have explaining to do, Aric Glass. And better to do it here in Gilorin than in Hes with so many ears around. I have family in Hes, and I don't care to face them. But I'm still in need of these men. They came because I asked them to come. They need to know what we're up against, and they have to hear it from me.'

'Is that why you brought me here, my lord?'

'No,' said Raxor. 'Not precisely.'

'No? Why, then, my lord?'

Raxor smiled. 'You have told me so much. But I still have questions.'

'I have tried to answer everything.'

Aric waited, but Raxor grew quiet, leaving Aric to wonder at his meaning. They said nothing more to each other as the boat came to shore and the royals smiled with wide greetings. Among them were sprinkled a handful of soldiers. One in particular caught Aric's eye. A long, lanky man, he looked oddly familiar, and his clothes were unlike anyone else's. Instead of the usual Reecian uniform, he wore tight leather armour over his body, accentuating his muscular physique. He was older than the others too, though not at all feeble looking. He stood apart from the nobles and their wives, his hands at his sides, his taut face stoic. While the others spoke among themselves, the man in leather remained silent.

'That one, my lord,' said Aric, pointing at the stranger on the bank. 'Who is he? Not a duke, surely.'

'No, not a duke,' replied Raxor. He leaned back and let the breeze strike his face. 'Aric, I should tell you something. There are people who will have questions for you, people who will want to know all about the things you've told me already.'

Aric nodded. 'I understand, my lord. I don't expect anyone to trust me. That man – is he one of them I should be worried about?'

'No,' said Raxor flatly. 'That's one of the only men in the world you can trust. And that's why I brought you here. For your own protection.'

Before Aric could speak again, one of the king's men reappeared, whispering in his ear. Raxor nodded and ordered the man to make the others ready. The man called to the rest of the passengers, telling them to make ready to disembark. Raxor remained seated, straightening imperiously while oarsmen guided the barge to shore, finally lifting their oars when the boat's flat bottom hit shore. He gestured for Aric to stay beside him while the servants waded into the mud, pulling the vessel further ashore. A great commotion ensued while Raxor's underlings eagerly made ready for him. The royals on the shore quieted. Aric heard the old man sigh beside him.

A man with a small trumpet called the king from his seat. Raxor's advisors lined up behind him as the crew of the barge lined the starboard side of the vessel to help him down. Aric kept close to Raxor as the king stepped off the boat and into the mud, landing with a sucking noise. Aric and the advisors piled out after him, all trudging through the mud toward shore. The man in leathers came forward, striding to the king's side. Raxor paused to greet the many nobles who'd come.

'No ceremony,' he called to them. 'Be at ease.'

Relieved smiles broke out among the crowd. Servants hurried at Raxor, filling his ears with reports. Raxor nodded impatiently, gesturing for Aric to stay close. Enduring the confused stares of the nobles, Aric remained at the king's side while he and the leather-clad soldier inspected the nobles. Raxor's ringed hand came out, bidding each of the nobles to kiss it. The women curtsied, averting their eyes, their painted lips curled with polite smiles. A few of the dukes embraced the king, telling him solemnly how much they felt his loss. Raxor kissed their cheeks, thanking them for coming.

'We must talk, old friend,' he told Duke Redhorn. 'Later, after I've rested.'

Duke Redhorn was a long-necked, elegant man, reminiscent of a swan. He curled himself around Raxor, embracing the king and nodding. 'You have my loyalty, Majesty. Always.'

Raxor thanked the man before moving on to the next duke, the shorter, serious-looking Joric. Joric took Raxor's hand in both of his own as he dropped to one knee. 'We'll avenge your son,' he promised. 'May Baron Glass rot forever for what he has done.'

At that Aric grimaced, trying not to look at Joric directly. Glad to move on, he followed the king the rest of the way toward the end of the line, where Raxor turned to his loyal subjects and thanked them richly for making the trip to Gilorin.

'Stay and be comfortable,' he told them. He smiled. 'Forgive me, but I need rest now.'

The dukes and their wives all gave accommodating nods, appreciating the king's needs. As they dispersed, Raxor strode up the lawn toward the estate, pulling the man in leather close to him.

'Corvalos,' he sighed, 'I am awake? Or is this nightmare still continuing?'

'I grieve for you, my lord,' said the lanky man. 'I feel your loss so sharply it is though it were my own.'

'I cannot tell you what happened, Corvalos. It was beyond words. I have never seen the like of Baron Glass before. He is not a man any more.' Raxor paused, satisfied that they were out of earshot of the nobles. 'Tell me what has happened. My woman – she is well?'

The man called Corvalos had so far barely glanced at Aric. 'She is well, my lord. And good that you called us here. I needed to get her away from Hes.'

Raxor's raised an eyebrow. 'Tell me.'

'My lord, you will hear things among the servants.'

'True things?'

The man grew sheepish. 'Yes, my lord.'

'But she is well?'

'She is, my lord. I have protected her.'

Raxor looked unbearably weary. He turned to Aric and waved him closer. 'Aric Glass, this man is going to protect you while you are here. His name is Corvalos Chane and I trust him more than any man alive. You're to do the same. You're do to everything he asks of you. Do you understand?'

'I understand,' said Aric. 'But why? If I am in danger—'

'Your name puts you in danger, boy,' the king interrupted. 'Corvalos, this is Aric Glass, son of Thorin Glass.'

Corvalos Chane blinked. 'I'm to protect him as well, my lord? This will be a lot of work.'

'I will meet with the dukes later. But now I want to see her. Bring her to the gallery, Corvalos. Go now.'

The soldier bowed and left quickly, hurrying back toward the estate. Aric watched him go, confused by what was happening. 'My lord?' he asked. 'Should I not go with him?'

'He'll be back for you,' said Raxor. 'For now you'll come with me. There's someone I need you to meet.'

'I listened very carefully to the things you told me on our ride home,' said Raxor as he guided Aric through the halls of Gilorin. They were alone, having passed through the king's guard chamber and left the throngs of nobles and servants behind. An enthralling mural covered the ceiling of the hall, replete with creamy, textured roses and singing birds. Aric craned his neck to marvel at the art, then quickly turned his attention to the king.

'My lord? I'm sorry, you're meaning escapes me.'

'Everything you said to me about your father and your time in Koth at the library – I listened carefully. I tried to find a flaw in your stories, some kind of inconsistencies, but there weren't any.'

'No, there wouldn't be. I haven't lied to you, King Raxor.'

Raxor nodded as he led Aric through the hall. He had not yet explained where they were going or why, and the solitude made Aric curious.

'Remember when I told you there would be questions?' Raxor asked. 'Don't be afraid, but it's time for some answers.'

He pushed aside a large oak door, revealing another of the court's splendid chambers. This one, called the gallery, held more of the fine paintings Aric had seen in the hall, all lined up perfectly on the paneled walls. A huge marble hearth stood at the opposite end of the long room, and above the hearth stretched a gigantic, framed portrait of men on horseback. A handful of chairs were arranged near the heath, in one of which sat a young woman. Next to her stood Corvalos Chane. The woman's eyes widened when she saw Raxor enter.

'My lord,' she exclaimed, rising from her chair, her pretty face lit with relief. Aric looked at her, sure that she was familiar to him. He paused a few steps behind Raxor.

'Mirage?'

The woman shifted her gaze at once, locking eyes with him. Her face fell in surprise. 'Aric . . . Aric?'

Both Aric and the girl looked at Raxor, who frowned. 'I thought as much,' the old king grumbled. He said to Aric, 'Mirage is from the library at Koth. Yes?'

Aric stared in amazement. 'Yes. But how . . . ?' He looked at the woman, who he had never known well. Together they had seen Lukien off on that last day in Liiria. 'Mirage, what are you doing here?'

Mirage groped for answers. 'I . . .' She shrugged. 'I'm the king's woman.'

'What?' Aric erupted. 'King Raxor, what is this? How did she get here?'

Raxor lost none of his sternness. 'She was brought to me by Corvalos Chane. It's as she says, Aric Glass. She is my woman.'

'You mean a slave?' Aric gasped. He went to Mirage. 'Is that so, Mirage? Is he keeping you here? Did he kidnap you?'

Mirage seemed unwilling to talk. Her eyes shifted nervously between Aric and the king. 'Aric, it's difficult to explain.'

'Someone do explain, please,' begged Aric, looking to Raxor for any scrap of knowledge. 'My lord, tell me what's going on here. You brought me here to see Mirage. Why?'

'Because of what happened at the Kryss,' said Raxor. 'And because of the things you told me. Mirage is trying to spare my feelings, but it's all true. She was captured and brought to me. She was meant to mend this old fool's heart.' The king smiled at Mirage, then sighed. 'But she has kept secrets. I know that now. Others tried to tell me. But now I must have answers.'

Mirage swallowed nervously at the accusation, but it was Corvalos Chane who spoke up.

'My lord, Asher came for her while you were away. When he heard what had happened to Prince Roland and the others he took her from the castle. There was a fight. Men died. But I got her back.'

The news sent the last bit of strength from Raxor's face. He went pale suddenly, licking his dry lips and going slowly to one of the chairs. Mirage and Chane stood over him, both with surprising concern. The scene made Aric shake his head.

'I don't understand any of this,' he grumbled. 'Mirage, are you here because you want to be? Because that's what it looks like and it makes no sense at all!'

'I was taken here Aric, against my will,' said Mirage. She sank down next to Raxor's chair, falling to her knees and taking his hand. 'My lord, I'm sorry for what happened to your son. I am. I hope you believe me.'

Raxor took her hand in his much larger fingers, gently squeezing it. 'You're safe? Asher didn't harm you?'

'No, my lord,' Mirage answered. 'He meant to, though. If not for Chane . . .' She smiled, reassuring the old man. 'But no. I'm fine.'

Aric watched, dumbfounded by what he was seeing. What was it about Raxor that made people love him, even his enemies? Corvalos Chane hovered over them, offering no words as the young girl and ancient king enjoyed their strange reunion. The memories of his last days in Koth flooded over Aric, brought to life by the revelation of Mirage. What did she mean, the king's woman? She had loved Lukien once. Did she now love Raxor?

'This is impossible,' said Aric. 'Mirage, you don't belong here. What happened? I thought you were with my father.'

Mirage rose hesitantly to her feet. 'I know,' she said. To Raxor she added, 'My lord, it's true. I was on my way to him. I had nowhere else to go. And if Chane hadn't captured me that night I would have gone to him.'

'So you knew him better than you ever admitted,' sighed Raxor. 'Were you lovers?'

'No,' answered Mirage.

'No,' Aric added, 'but they would have been if my father had his way. He loves her, King Raxor, or at least he did once.' Aric glared at Mirage. 'What have you told him?'

'As little as I could,' Mirage shot back. 'I had to protect myself.'

'She has secrets, my lord,' said Chane. 'About that, at least, Asher was right.'

Raxor kept hold of Mirage's hand. 'Aric Glass, you haven't lied to me yet. Tell me now – what do you know about this girl?'

'Not much,' Aric confessed. 'She came to the library with Lukien in the last days before it fell. She came from Grimhold, and she was a friend to my father back before the armour claimed him. I know that she loved Lukien and that my father loved her. I know because that's what Lukien told me and he never lied, my lord.'

His words stung Mirage, who glanced away sheepishly. 'I couldn't tell any of this,' she said. 'It was nobody's business.'

'But it is my business, don't you see?' insisted Raxor. 'You knew what Baron Glass would do to us, Mirage. You knew and you kept it from me.'

'I didn't!' Mirage pulled her hand free. 'I told you all that I could about the Devil's Armour. I tried to make you listen, to keep you from the battle. But you had to go because of your precious honour! Don't blame me for what happened, my lord. Roland's blood is on Thorin's hands, not mine.'

The pain in Raxor's face was stifling. 'What else haven't you told me? You have so many secrets. What were you doing in Grimhold?'

Mirage stiffened. 'I cannot tell you.'

Raxor looked at Aric. 'Do you know?'

Aric shook his head. 'No. But she's right, King Raxor. She didn't know what the Devil's Armour could do. No one knew until we all saw it used at the Kryss.'

'Mirage,' said Raxor, looking straight at the girl and sounding like a parent, 'I need to know everything. You were not at the Kryss; you have no idea what happened. Your man Glass—'

'He is not 'my man,'' Mirage said angrily. 'You insult me when you say that, my lord. I have told you all I can about him. I would have gone to him because I was alone in Koth and had no one else to turn to. Aric told you about Lukien, yes? He left me in Koth, just like everyone else to hunt for a riddle. What was I to do? Starve?'

'You're better off for coming here,' said Aric. 'Mirage, you do not know the man my father has become. He's nothing like he was. He's become a monster now.'

'An unstoppable monster,' said Raxor. 'Unless you know a means to beat him, child.'

Mirage shrank from the question, turning to Aric instead. 'And you, Aric? Why have you come?'

'I came to offer the help of Nith,' said Aric. There seemed a great deal to explain, but he told her simply of his time with Prince Daralor and how he'd been sent back north to make a truce between the prince and Reec. 'I thought to help King Raxor at the Kryss, but all I could do was stand around and watch the slaughter,' he said, and admitting it pained him. 'I believe you, Mirage. You couldn't possibly know how to beat my father's armour. Lukien knew it, too. That's why he left us.'

'To find the sword you spoke of,' said Raxor wearily. 'Mirage, do you know of this sword?'

'Only what Lukien told me, which is nothing at all,' said Mirage bitterly. Arching defiantly, she told the king, 'You may send me back to Asher if you wish. I'll not tell you any more about myself. You've had my loyalty, my lord. I don't know why, but I gave it freely. I can give you nothing else.'

She waited for his reply, as did Aric who wasn't even sure what she meant. He had heard the name of Asher bandied about like a threat. No matter who he was, he wouldn't stand for Mirage being harmed.

'You think that little of me?' said Raxor, his chin sinking to his chest. 'You are safe here, child. And I will deal with Asher for what he did to you.'

His answer relieved Mirage, who smiled sadly at the old king. But Aric wasn't satisfied. Mirage was no slave, even if she had come to believe it.

'My lord, she's not a bird to be kept in your cage,' he protested. 'She's a free woman. I cannot let you lay this claim to her.'

Raxor looked at him with thunder in his face. 'You heard her, Aric Glass. She has nowhere else to go.'

'Be that true or not true, she was kidnapped by your man here. She pleases you, I don't doubt it. But she is a free woman.' Aric braced himself for the king's wrath. 'You must release her.'

Corvalos Chane took a step from the shadows, eyeing Aric angrily. Raxor flicked his hand to steady the soldier.

'I brought you here to help me understand things,' he said. 'And now I do, mostly. You may stay as long as you please, Aric Glass, and then you may go back to Nith and await the Bronze Knight. And while you're gone we shall all pray for a miracle.'

The dismissal made Aric bristle. 'Yes, my lord, I'll go to Nith and make the peace between you. But you must promise me in return that you will let Mirage go.'

'You're talking to the king,' rumbled Corvalos Chane. 'Mind your tone, boy.'

'You have your father's arrogance, Aric Glass,' said Raxor. 'You'll have to do better to persuade me.'

Aric pushed past his fear, using the only weapon he could. 'I can't make you give her up. I know that, King Raxor. But my father loves this woman. If he knew you were holding her he would come for her.' He waited for his words to take hold. 'He would, and you would not be able to stop him.'

Raxor rose a bit from his chair, then stopped himself with a monumental effort. 'You threaten me?'

'I tell you only the truth. Give her up, my lord, or she will be your doom.'

'After all I've done for you . . .'

'My lord knows I take no joy in this,' said Aric. He pointed at Mirage. 'She fought alongside us at the library. She deserves better than to be your concubine.'

'Aric, he has not harmed me,' Mirage explained. 'He has never once touched me.'

'And that's enough for you?' Aric railed. 'We fought for freedom at the library! And now you surrender yourself for the sake of a warm bed and some food?'

'Where else will I go? I have no one and nothing!'

'Enough,' ordered Raxor. He put up both his hands, begging for silence. 'Enough.' The old man finally stood finally. Again he took the girl's hand. 'Child, Aric speaks the truth. If Baron Glass learns you are here, he will come to find you, and I cannot have his vengeance fall on Hes.'

Mirage reared back. 'My lord, are you releasing me?'

'If that's what you wish,' said Raxor. It was plain he regretted his choice, and Aric regretted making him choose it. There was real tenderness in Raxor's eyes as he held Mirage's hand. 'If you stay, I will defend you. Not only against Asher and the others, but against Baron Glass, too. But if you wish to go, I can't keep you. Not anymore.'

It was not what Mirage expected to hear. For a long moment she was silent. Then she nodded and backed away. 'But nothing has changed. I still have nowhere to go.'

'Then stay,' said Raxor. 'You've never been my slave. You know that.'

'Go, Mirage,' Aric urged. 'Lukien wouldn't want this for you.'

'Wouldn't he?' asked Mirage bitterly. 'Lukien would not care, Aric. He never cared for me. He wanted me out of his hair. Nothing more.'

'You're infuriating,' Aric seethed. 'You let Lukien go without a good-bye. You threatened to go to my father, even after you saw what he did. And now this? You'd rather stay here than be free? You learned nothing at Koth. Not from Lukien or Breck or anyone. This whole thing is demented.'

'Aric, you don't understand . . .'

'I don't. You're right. And I don't care. Keep your secrets, woman. You've been no help to anyone ever. All you care about is yourself.'

'Watch yourself now,' Raxor warned.

But Aric did not back down. 'My lord, keep her. Do what you want with her. But be warned – she is a selfish harpy who will bring no good to you. She could have told you about the armour – she still can! But she refuses.' He scowled disgustedly at all of them. 'I'm going back to Nith. I'll leave in a day or so. I'll tell Prince Daralor that you're making ready to join him, and when Lukien returns we'll come back, King Raxor. I've done my part. I'm done with all of you.'

Then, to the shocked faces of them all, Aric turned and left the gallery. Not even sure where he was going, he let his anger carry him away, back down the hall and into the meandering unknown of Gilorin Court.

37

Just as he had promised, Aric Glass left Gilorin Court two days after his arrival, leaving Mirage alone again, with no one from her past life to remind her of the things she had left behind. Aric had made a terrible impression on her, however, and in the days since his leaving his accusations haunted Mirage, preventing her from enjoying the serenity of Raxor's estate. By the time five more days passed, all the nobles had left Gilorin Court, but King Raxor had remained, keeping to himself and taking his meals privately, never again asking Mirage about the secrets she harboured.

For the first time in weeks, Mirage felt safe. Without Raxor's family and all their suspicious glares, she felt at home and at ease amid the genteel court. More importantly, Asher was miles away, and no one threatened her with prison or even spoke the madman's name. They were good days, or at least there should have been, but Mirage could not escape the things Aric had said to her, and soon she realized how right he had been. The time had come for her to make a bold decision.

As usual, Corvalos Chane kept watch over Mirage, shadowing her through Gilorin's gardens and hovering nearby during meals. Though the danger was far less now that she'd left Hes, Chane continued taking his charge to protect her seriously, a duty that Raxor had yet to relieve him of. Raxor himself saw very little of Mirage, passing by her politely in the halls or along the flowered lanes but never once coming to her rooms to check on her or to have one of their long, pleasant conversations. Surprisingly, Mirage missed the old man. He was in mourning still, and the cloud that followed him everywhere never seemed to lift from his face. Mirage waited patiently for him to come, but the old king never did, and by the afternoon of their eighth day together, she decided to go to him herself.

Raxor was in a woodlot about half a mile from the main house, alone among the trees with an axe in his hands and sweat pouring from his wrinkled face. At Mirage's request, Corvalos Chane had ridden her out to the lot to speak to Raxor. The ground around his booted feet rose high with wood chips and poorly stacked lumber. Lost in thought and the noise from his swinging axe, he did not hear Chane's horse arrive or Mirage's light footfalls as she approached. Corvalos Chane dismounted but kept back from the king, hidden behind a stout sycamore tree. He kept a watchful eye on Mirage as she made her way toward Raxor, her feet crunching on the dead leaves. Ahead of her, Raxor swung his axe, oblivious. Shards of wood flew from the timbers. Each time one gave way beneath his axe, he stooped to place another on the stump he used like an anvil. Mirage paused a few paces away, sure now that the king had seen her. Raxor glanced at her, but only for a moment, then went back to working his axe.

'My lord . . .'

'Wait,' he ordered.

The chips continued to fly. Mirage's anxiety crested. What she had decided would upset him, she was sure. He might not even allow it. She thought of turning back yet managed to remain, watching as Raxor avoided her eyes, pretending that all the wood he chopped was so much more important.

At last King Raxor lowered his axe, breathing hard as he rested the blade on the massive tree stump. A peculiar looked crossed his sweaty face. He stared at Mirage.

'My son . . .' The king shrugged. 'He died and I couldn't save him. They butchered him.'

Mirage shuddered. 'You couldn't save him, my lord.'

'I didn't try. I didn't even know what was happening.' Raxor tossed his axe aside. 'Do you hear? I didn't know! I'm so old and stupid I couldn't see the obvious trap!'

'No,' said Mirage, hurrying toward him. 'Prince Roland died like all the others. In battle.'

'And where was I?' the king railed. 'I didn't see battle. I was hiding like a woman behind my troops.'

'You were commanding them.'

Raxor slumped. Slowly he dragged his weary body down to sit upon the tree stump. 'That's why you were brought to me, Mirage. To be kind to a useless old man. Years ago I would never have fallen for a ruse like that. Baron Glass played me and I let him. And now . . .'

His voice choked off as emotion strangled his words. Mirage stood before him, pitying him. Finally he looked up at her.

'You are leaving.'

Mirage nodded. 'Yes.'

Raxor smiled sadly. 'I have thought on what Aric Glass said to me. He was right. You are a free woman, and all I've done is make a pretty cage for you. But I tried, you see. I wanted you to be happy here.'

'And I have been, my lord. At times.' Mirage looked at him fondly. 'You have been kind to me. I did not expect such tenderness from you. You are not what the rest of the world says you are, King Raxor. In Liiria they remember you the way you were.'

Raxor scoffed. 'When I was young and strong, you mean.'

'When you were cruel in battle. That's what they say and that's why I feared you. I found instead a good man who tries very hard to do what's right.'

King Raxor grinned at this. 'You know, you look very much like my wife, but she would never have spoken the way you do, Mirage. You are really not like her. Oh, she was saintly. There was no better woman alive. But she was simple and unworldly. Not like you. You are wise. I will miss your counsel.'

'Will you?' asked Mirage, surprised. 'Thank you, my lord.'

'It is good that you leave,' sighed Raxor. 'There are terrible days ahead. Go north, far from Reec and Liiria. Or go home to Jerikor. Anywhere is better than Reec now.'

Mirage hesitated. She could lie, she supposed, but she still needed a bit of help from the king. 'My lord,' she began, 'I'm not going north. I'm going back to Koth.'

Raxor looked up, his self-loathing flying from his face. 'What?'

'I'm going back to Koth. I'm going back to Thorin.'

'What?' sputtered Raxor again. He rose in disbelief. 'You can't do such a thing!'

'I must, my lord. You're not the only one who has thought about the things Aric Glass said. He was right about me. I have been nothing but selfish for years. You don't even know the woman that I am, not really.'

'I have tried,' said Raxor. 'But you're a mystery still. Now tell me more about this madness. Why must you go to Glass?'

'To reach him, my lord. To try and get him to stop his madness. He loved me once. He might still love me. He'll listen to me.'

Raxor shook his head. 'He won't. That's what Aric thought, Mirage, but when he saw what a demon his father had become he rode back to the line. He knew he couldn't reach Glass, and neither can you.'

'I'm a woman, don't forget,' Mirage reminded him. 'Love is powerful, my lord.'

'You're a beauty, true,' Raxor laughed. 'But no, I cannot allow this. If you go to Koth there is no telling what will happen to you, and I could not bear you being harmed. Not now, not after what happened to Roland.'

'I'm a free woman,' Mirage told him. 'You said so yourself. Unless you go back on your word to me, I may go where I wish.' She looked at him harshly. 'Are you going back on your word, King Raxor?'

Frustrated, Raxor towered over her. 'Don't play games with me, child. You have no idea of the danger you'd face. You did not see Baron Glass or the carnage he occasioned.'

'How can I make you understand?' Mirage wondered aloud. She thought for a moment before seizing on Roland. 'It is like your son, my lord. You grieve because he is dead, but you also grieve for the things you thought you could have done differently. You think you could have saved him, and no matter how I argue otherwise you will always think that.'

'I should have tried,' said Raxor. 'That's all.'

'That's right,' countered Mirage. 'That's what you think. It is the same for me. I must try, King Raxor. I *must.*'

'But why? I do not understand.'

How could she explain it to him? She had kept such secrets from him already, and there was still no way for her to reveal the truth. The magic of Grimhold was not to be shared, and he might not believe her anyway.

'There are things I cannot tell you, my lord,' Mirage said gently. 'Things about myself and where I came from. Secret things.'

'Things about Baron Glass?' asked Raxor.

'In a way. We share the same secrets, my lord.'

'That's why you think you can make him listen?'

Mirage sighed. 'Maybe. At least I have to try. Will you let me? I will need passage to Koth.'

King Raxor considered her words, looking around at the trees and the blue sky. The pretty day shined on his face but did not hide his melancholy. He licked his lips as if stalling, not wanting her to go.

'You are not the selfish girl you think, Mirage,' he said finally. 'You have helped me more than I can tell you. For a while I felt young again when I was with you.'

'You can thank me, then, by letting me go.'

'If that's the only way,' said Raxor regretfully, 'then you may go to Koth. But not alone. Corvalos Chane will go with you. He will see that you make it safely, at least.'

Mirage at last relaxed, letting out a long breath. 'I would like that. It's a long way to Koth and Chane would be welcome.'

'He'll protect you, Mirage. But once you are with Baron Glass . . .'

'I know,' said Mirage. 'I'll be on my own.'

'That's right,' said the king. 'But you will always have a place here, if ever you want to return.'

His words comforted Mirage. She had never felt at home anywhere, not even in Grimhold. It was good to think she had a place in the real world that would welcome her. 'You mean like home, my lord?' she asked.

'Home is the best place, Mirage,' he said. 'Everyone needs a place to call home.'

38

A flash of distant lightning lit the open doors to the library, bringing the murky interior to light. Jazana Carr, wet from rain, stared down the maw of the corridor, noting the vast emptiness. A clap of thunder rang in her ears, spooking her horse. Somewhere far away an owl hooted. Library Hill stood starkly in the moonless night, cluttered with abandoned equipment and the tools of workmen. The long, meandering road up the hill coursed with muddy rainwater. Jazana Carr shook the rain from her face and stared into the library. Thorin had not lied to her about the progress. An enormous amount of work had already been done. The grand interior, once collapsed by Norvan catapults, was gradually returning to life.

'Let me come with you, Jazana,' said Rodrik Varl. 'It's dark and unsafe. You don't even know where he is.'

'I know where he is,' Jazana replied. There could only be one place. 'Just wait for me. I don't know how long I'll be.'

Rodrik looked up into the threatening sky. So far the worst of the storm had missed them, but the clouds were rolling south toward the hill. Rodrik pulled up his collar, soured by her decision. He had argued against coming so late, but Jazana had insisted.

'Come back in the morning,' Rodrik suggested. 'If Thorin hasn't returned by then, I'll take you back.'

'How long should I wait?' Jazana retorted. 'I want to see him. Tonight.'

'When there's a monster in the wardrobe, a wise man waits till morning, Jazana. He won't take well to this intrusion.'

Jazana stiffened, trying to look brave. She wasn't afraid of Thorin, at least not completely, but she didn't blame the others for being so. Since the fall of the Kryss she had seen him only sparingly, but he had been shocking to behold. Drenched in blood, he had returned to Lionkeep like a madman, followed by tales of his unbelievable carnage. Two days later, Jazana had ridden out herself to the river to see the stacks of corpses. Some said the Kryss would never be clean again.

'He's avoiding me,' Jazana confessed. 'And he made me a promise.'

Varl smirked. 'A promise from a devil is no promise at all.'

'He's not a devil,' Jazana shot back. 'You should all know better than to talk that way of him.'

'I know what I know, Jazana. And I know what I saw with you at the Kryss.' Varl scoffed. 'Ah, but what use is it? You see none of it, only your love for him.'

'Stop now,' Jazana urged. 'I have to go.'

'Then go.'

'He needs me,' Jazana tried explaining.

'Norvor needs you, Jazana. But go on . . . go to him. I'll wait.'

They had endured this argument a hundred times. Jazana surrendered, slipping down from her horse and standing at the library's threshold. Through the twin oak doors she saw a handful of candles along the walls, lighting a path. Listening, she heard nothing. The workmen reconstructing the library had all quit for the day, long ago. So had the painters and sculptors and all the other artisans Thorin had brought to Koth for his grand obsession. His projects and passions had bled Jazana's coffers nearly dry. And still he dwelt here, slipping day by day deeper into the grip of his magical armour.

Jazana hesitated.

'Are you going?' Varl asked.

'Yes.'

'Then go.'

'Shut up,' Jazana snapped, then crossed the threshold without looking back. The vast hallway swallowed her down its inky throat. The walls swam with shadows. Overhead, a mural of intense looking scholars spied Jazana as she followed the candles down the hall. Most had burned down to nubs, providing only enough light for her to grope her way along, helped by an occasional blast of lightning through the stained glass windows. Jazana glanced over her shoulder and barely saw the outline of Rodrik Varl and the horses standing in the rain. She took a breath to steady herself. The catalogue room was a the other end of the library. A long walk, especially in the dark, but as she continued through the halls Jazana noticed that the candles continued guiding her along, perfectly placed to lead her to the hidden chamber. She moved quietly, listening to her shallow breathing, noting the rows and rows of empty book shelves and the small, lonely reading rooms.

'The Cathedral of Knowledge.'

Her whispered voice carried through the dusty hall. She smiled, enchanted by the memory of what the place had once been. It would be like that again, Thorin had promised, but his vow had taken on ominous proportions. Jazana's smile quickly faded. So many dreams . . . what had gone wrong?

She continued through the maze of chambers, amazed to find each one lit for her and realizing that Thorin had no need for any of the other rooms. He was only interested in one, and needed only one route to it. Her pace quickened, spurred on by the terrible silence. Her feet padded eagerly across the dusty floor. She turned down a corridor lit like all the others, and finally saw her quarry at the other end of the hall.

Jazana paused. The catalogue room was always locked, but tonight its metal door stood open. A strong glow of candlelight flooded its threshold. Jazana held her breath a moment, not wanting to be overheard. Inching forward, she leaned ahead to listen, surprised to hear Thorin's voice. His tone was gravely, almost strained, and she knew he was talking to himself. Again she hesitated. Coming here suddenly seemed like the worst of ideas, but she knew she could not turn back. Thorin needed her. Whatever had happened to him at the Kryss had changed him.

'I can't,' said his distant voice, reaching her across the hall. 'I can't make it work.'

His voice sounded desperate. Jazana had never heard such weakness in him. She tiptoed closer, careful not to make a sound as she approached. The light wavered in the catalogue room as Thorin spoke, disturbing the candles. A clap of thunder shook the hall. 'I have tried everything,' came Thorin's angry voice. 'Do not tell me to try again! The boy will make the machine work. We must wait for the boy!'

Jazana paused. Was he alone? She heard no one else reply to him, yet his words seemed two-sided. She went ahead, finally coming to the threshold of the chamber. Peering inside, she saw the vast room lit by the candles on the walls and on the tables, filling the place with a reddish glow. Along the floor stretched the machine, the arcane invention of the dead genius Figgis. Jazana had never seen it lit so well, with every rod and armature exposed. Its sprockets glistened with oil. Its unmoving wheels rose to the ceiling. At the front of the machine sat Thorin, slumped over the simple wooden desk, his face buried in his armoured arm, his chest rising and falling with laboured breaths. His clothes hung limply from his powerful body, drenched in filthy sweat. The stench of him reached Jazana like a hot wind. He muttered to himself incomprehensibly, shaking his head. The machine – his obsession – sat mutely before him.

Jazana trembled, forcing herself to speak. 'Thorin,' she whispered. 'Look at me.'

Startled, Thorin bolted up in his chair. He turned his wild eyes on her, wide with dread. Jazana stepped back, shocked by his face. The bones of his cheeks stood out from his swollen eye sockets, flushed an unhealthy red. His lips drew back, thin and purple. His burning gaze fixed on her, bloodshot. When his dried tongue moved to speak, she could hear his thirst.

'What are you doing here?' he rasped.

Though his visage stunned her, Jazana tried to stay calm. 'Thorin? Are you all right?'

'Why are you here?' he asked again, his voice rising. 'I am working!'

Jazana looked around the room. 'Who were you talking to?'

Thorin reared back. His face twisted. 'You were listening to me?' He chuckled, covering himself. 'Have you come to spy on me, Jazana?'

'Thorin, I was worried about you.' Jazana chanced a step toward him, studying his bizarre face. 'You've been here for days. You haven't come to Lionkeep or spoken to anyone in almost a week. Look at you! You haven't even eaten.'

The baron turned away as if nothing were wrong. 'I . . . have work to do, Jazana. And you should not have come. Go, please. You're disturbing me.'

'Thorin, no,' Jazana insisted. 'I won't go, not until I know you're all right. Why are you working so hard with this contraption? Why don't you come home?'

'I don't need a wife,' Thorin grumbled. 'Or a mother.'

The insult riled the Diamond Queen. She went to him, grabbing his shoulder and forcing him to face her.

'Talk to me,' she insisted. 'Something is wrong with you. Something has happened to you, Thorin.'

'Rubbish,' he laughed, removing her hand.

'It's the armour, Thorin,' said Jazana. 'It's changing you. Since the battle at the Kryss—'

'No, no,' Thorin warned, holding up a finger. He shook his head as though speaking to a child. 'There'll be no talk of that. Don't speak of the armour, Jazana.'

'Why? Why are you afraid to talk about it, Thorin? What's it done to you?'

'It's made me strong! Gods, woman, isn't that enough for you?'

'No, it's not enough! If it keeps you from me, no.'

Thorin steadied himself. He smiled. 'You are right,' he sighed. 'I am sorry. I have neglected you. I should spend more time with you, Jazana. And I will, I promise.'

Jazana moaned in frustration. 'Thorin, no! You're not understanding at all. I'm not here because I miss you. I'm here because something has happened to you. The armour, Thorin . . . it's killing you!'

'It is not,' said Thorin. He struggled to contain his fury. 'It gives me power.'

'It takes power! Have you seen yourself? You look like a shadow!'

'Jazana, enough,' Thorin warned her. 'I have work to do.'

'What work? This thing?' Jazana waved her arm toward the machine. 'Why, Thorin? What's so important about this thing?'

'It is a thinking machine, Jazana.'

'I know what it is! I don't care any more. You're obsessed with it, Thorin. Why?'

'I . . .' Thorin stopped himself, looking away. 'I cannot tell you.'

Jazana checked her growing rage. The urge to shake him felt over-whelming. 'You're lying to me,' she said. 'You're keeping secrets from me. And you're ruining us, Thorin. You've spent almost all our gold rebuilding this library. All your people are terrified of you. They do nothing but talk about you and the things you did to the Reecians. That's what going on outside these walls!'

Thorin leaned back his head. 'You exhaust me, woman. Let me be.'

Jazana glared at him. 'You're becoming demented. The armour has maddened you.'

'Has it?' Thorin lifted his left arm, flexing the armour covering it. It moved perfectly, like flesh. He moved his missing fingers in the enchanted gauntlet. 'With this arm I can tear down the whole place, brick by brick.'

'Yes,' said Jazana. 'You're like a storm now, Thorin. Strong. And mindless.'

Thorin slammed his fist onto the table. 'Go!'

'No,' hissed Jazana. 'You made a promise to me. Or have you forgotten?'

'I have not forgotten.'

'Well then? The news from Norvor is worse everyday. When will we go?'

'We will not,' said Thorin. He turned his gaze back toward the machine. 'I cannot leave now.'

'What? Thorin, you told me we would go when you had done with the Reecians. They are beaten now.'

'I cannot go, Jazana,' said Thorin calmly.

'You have to go! You have to help me get Carlion back!' Jazana kicked at his chair, insisted he look at her. 'Haven't you heard anything? Carlion is gone and Vicvar will be next. I've had reports, Thorin. Everyday I hear more and more about Elgan. He's not afraid of us at all! Doesn't that mean anything to you?'

With a shake of his head, Thorin said, 'I am sorry.'

'We're losing Norvor!' screamed Jazana. 'I'm losing it! You have to help me!'

'I will,' promised Thorin, 'when I can. But not now.'

'Why not now? Tell me why!'

Thorin gestured toward the machine. 'Gilwyn Toms is on his way. He knows how to work the catalogue. I must be here when he arrives.'

Jazana felt hot blood rushing to her cheeks. 'Thorin, Norvor is falling to our enemies! Liiria is falling apart around you and you're worried about this cursed machine?'

'You don't understand, my love,' sighed Thorin. 'And I can't explain it to you.'

'You can! But you have to try. You're shutting out everyone, Thorin, even me. You have to trust me. Tell me, please – what is wrong with you?'

Thorin tried to smile, but she could see the struggle in him. 'I am well. I am better than I've ever been.'

'That's a lie,' said Jazana. Suddenly the rage blew out of her, replaced by a crushing sadness. 'You're becoming demented, Thorin. You have to see that. You have to see what your armour is doing to you.'

'Jazana . . .' Thorin looked pleadingly into her eyes. 'You don't know. You can't know. Just leave me to my work. When I have the way to work the machine it will all be good again. I promise, my love. Do you hear? I promise.'

'You have promised so much already,' said Jazana. 'If you won't go to Norvor with me now . . .'

'I can't!' Thorin cried. 'Not now! Not until Gilwyn gets here.'

It was madness, arguing with him. Jazana knew that now. Determined to wait for the boy Gilwyn to arrive, Thorin would not relent. Jazana resigned herself in disgust.

'Fine,' she snapped. 'To your work, then.'

Turning, she heard his groaning lament, begging her to understand, but Jazana ignored it. Driven by hurt, she hurried back through the halls of the library. This time, he had truly betrayed her. Day by day, Norvor continued to slip from her fingers, and only Thorin could save it for her. But Thorin was gone now. A ghost had replaced him, a shell of a man puppetered by some unseen demon. Jazana knew very little about Grimhold and its magic, but she had heard the rumours. The Devil's Armour was possessed. And in its possession was her lover.

She stopped, the tears finally overwhelming her. Her knees buckled and she dropped to the marble floor.

'I love you,' she moaned. Her body shook with angry sobs. 'I've given you everything and you take and take!'

Her words echoed down the corridor. Her hands felt the stone beneath her. Jazana Carr put her cheek to the cold marble and wept like a child.

Thorin waited in the catalogue room, listening to Jazana's sobs carry through the corridors. An hour later they finally subsided. He closed his eyes, unable to concentrate. His exhausted body screamed for sleep. Kahldris hovered insistently in his mind. He had hurt Jazana, and the pain of it broke his heart. He loved her, though he doubted she believed that now. The machine, Gilwyn Toms, his aching desire to rebuild the library – it was all too much to explain to her. Even trying seemed a waste.

She is gone, said Kahldris. *We must work now.*

Thorin groaned. 'I cannot.'

You are thinking of her. Forget her. She no longer matters. Only the machine matters. Only my brother can stop us.

'I can't work the machine,' Thorin again told the demon. 'I have tried. It's impossible. Only Gilwyn can make it work.'

Frustrated, Kahldris roared in his mind. He had no body, so he did not kick and shout the way a man might. But Kahldris still could throw his tantrums, tearing at the fibres of Thorin's brain until the pain was unbearable. Thorin lowered his head to the desk and held his skull with both hands. Kahldris had driven him mercilessly the past week, insisting they find the way to work the machine. It was his obsession, not Thorin's, and the demon filled the baron's mind with all the terrible things that might happen to him.

Do you want to lose it all? he railed. *Not just your arm. Not just your manhood. Your kingdom. Everything!*

'Get out of my mind!'

Kahldris shook with ire. *I have lost it all, Baron. I know what it is like. Shall I show you more?*

'No more,' Thorin begged. 'No more . . .'

I should remind you.

'No.' Thorin lifted his head with effort. 'We waste our time.'

He braced himself for the spirit's attack. This time, there was none. Thorin felt the anger ebb.

Yes. Kahldris seemed to sigh. *We need the boy.*

'He's coming,' Thorin reminded him.

Too slowly.

'He's a cripple.'

He waits.

'He's resting,' said Thorin angrily.

For weeks now Kahldris had been able to sense Gilwyn, sure the boy was drawing near. He had long ago crossed the Desert of Tears, making his way slowly north to Liiria. Thorin had been glad for the boy's progress, not only because he needed his help but because he simply missed Gilwyn. But lately Gilwyn's progress had slowed. And it irked Kahldris.

I will make him hurry, said Kahldris. *He must come now. There is no more time.*

'What do you feel?' Thorin asked the spirit. 'Where is he now?'

Kahldris stretched himself, partially leaving Thorin's mind, making the baron light-headed. For a long moment he swam the invisible sea between Koth and Gilwyn, searching for the boy.

I can see him. The boy sleeps.

Thorin smiled, thrilled by the image. 'He is well?'

He sleeps in hay.

'He is still at that homestead.'

It was where Gilwyn had been for days now, though Kahldris did not know why. But he was safe, and that was all that Thorin really cared about. Despite the changes that had wracked his body – changes he knew had happened – he still loved Gilwyn like a son. Just as he still loved Jazana.

Baron, go to your woman, said Kahldris.

'What?'

Go to Jazana Carr. Make love to her. Rest. You are right. We have tried. Only the boy can work the machine.

Thorin grew suspicious. 'What will you do?'

A smile bloomed on the demon's invisible face. *Gilwyn Toms has lost his way. It is time for me to guide him.*

'Don't you harm him!'

I will not, Kahldris assured, mildly annoyed. *Now go to your woman. Make amends, Baron.*

'Yes,' said Thorin with a nod.

He still needed Jazana. And all she ever needed were some well-placed kisses to bring her around. Summoning the last of his strength, he rose from his chair and headed out of the catalogue room, staggering into the candlelit hall. Behind him he felt Kahldris lingering, slowly separating from his mind.

Go, the Akari urged gently. *And do not worry. I will not harm the boy.*

39

Gilwyn Toms settled down into the warm straw, his body aching from a day of chores, his belly filled with good home cooking. As his head nestled in the hay he belched. Then, like a teenager, he grinned at the sound of it. Overhead he heard the patter of rain on the red wooden roof, soft like a cat on a midnight walk. In the distance he heard thunder rumble, but it was far enough away not to concern him. Tucked between the two grey mountains, the little valley always seemed safe from the worst of the rain. Gilwyn listened to the breeze blowing through the planks of the barn. On the roof he heard the weathervane spin, fickle about the wind's direction. The noise reassured him, and as he settled into his bed of straw he knew that all was right with his new little world.

You'll sleep well tonight. You ate enough for three boys your size.

The voice was Ruana's, sarcastic but playful. Gilwyn saw her in his mind's eye, smiling at him with her pretty lips.

'I worked hard today,' he reminded her. 'Besides, Marna doesn't mind.'

She loves to watch you eat.

Gilwyn chuckled. 'She doesn't know I'm eating for two. You were very quiet today, Ruana. Are you all right?'

As soon as he asked the question Gilwyn realized how odd it sounded. Could a spirit be anything but all right?

You were with Kelan most of the day, Ruana pointed out. *How could I talk to you?*

Gilwyn nodded, not wanting to think too hard. He was tired from his day with Kelan. The kindly old man had let the porch of his home fall to ruin over the years, and was grateful for Gilwyn's help repairing it. Between the two of them, they had two good hands. And, just like Gilwyn, Kelan had a limp, an injury he had picked up as a young man in King Jarlo's army. That was almost forty years ago, but Kelan still liked telling tales about his time as a soldier. He wasn't much of a farmer, after all, and used his memories to cushion his difficult old age.

'It took longer than I thought it would,' Gilwyn remarked. He closed his eyes and tried to ignore the ache in his back. Most of the morning had been wasted getting the wood they needed. The ride had taken five hours, an uncomfortable journey on the old couple's rickety buckboard. 'I don't mind, though. I like listening to Kelan. He's interesting.'

Ruana said nothing, which surprised Gilwyn. He was sure the Akari had something on her mind.

'We'll be finished tomorrow,' he told her. 'Then I'll work on fixing this roof. Look . . .' He pointed up at the gap in the planks. 'It's leaking again.'

Everything about the homestead needed work. Kelan had built it himself with the help of his long-dead neighbours, but now the farmer and his wife were too old and feeble to do much of anything on their own. It was why they had welcomed Gilwyn into their lives, feeding and housing him for the past three weeks. What had started as a request for one night's rest had stretched into something of a holiday for Gilwyn, who loved being part of the farm and of the lives of the two old folks. He had become like an adopted son to Kelan and Marna. And now, he did not want to leave.

It had taken Gilwyn months to make it this far north. He was in the land of Roall now, a tiny kingdom south of Marn known for its rocky terrain and very little else. He had come to Roall exhausted, ill from relapse of the rass sickness he had endured in the desert. The venom that had put him to sleep for days in Aztar's camp had stayed in his blood the entire trip north, forcing him to take frequent rests in the towns and forests along the way. After his sojourn in Ganjor, he had headed north along the merchant roads, riding straight for Dreel where a run-in with highwaymen nearly cost him all the gold Princess Salina had given him for the ride. From there he headed to Nith, avoiding that principality by going around it the long way, a journey that should have taken days but rather took him weeks. His strength spent, Gilwyn rested a spell by the Agora river, making a camp for himself away from any towns or farmlands. That was when the loneliness really took hold.

'Ruana,' said Gilwyn dreamily. 'My mother died when I was young. Sometimes I can't remember what she looked like. I try, but sometimes . . .' He shrugged. 'She was kind, though, like Marna. I was thinking today how much she reminds me of her.'

Ruana was careful with her words. *That is a nice thought, Gilwyn. You should sleep now.*

'Yes,' agreed Gilwyn. Again he closed his eyes, but although he was tired sleep evaded him, and his eyes reopened a moment later. He could hear the cows at the other end of the barn, already asleep. Each morning he milked the pair of beasts, glad to help Marna with the task. Her gnarled fingers just didn't do the job any more. Gilwyn thought for a moment, wondering what would happen to the sweet old couple once he left them. They were always grateful for his help and said nothing to encourage him to stay, but he could tell they enjoyed having him around. For the first time in a long time, Gilwyn felt useful.

'Did you see the sunset tonight, Ruana?'

Yes, Gilwyn.

'They're beautiful here, aren't they? It's the mountains. The way they block the clouds makes the sunlight shine that way. Figgis told me that, a long time ago.'

Figgis, his old mentor at the library, had taught him many things. Some, like the bit about the mountains, were only useful in trivial ways. Other things, like how to deal with people, came in handy more and more as Gilwyn matured. It was Figgis who had raised him, not his mother. Still, the lonely journey north made Gilwyn miss his mother more than ever.

Are you eager to see Koth again? asked Ruana.

'Of course,' Gilwyn answered. 'What a strange question.'

Is it? You don't speak of home much lately.

Gilwyn frowned. 'I've been busy, Ruana.'

Yes, you have.

'What's that supposed to mean?'

You have spent a lot of time here with Kelan and Marna. You are rested now. Your illness passed, long ago.

Her meaning was obvious. Gilwyn shifted in his bed of hay.

'I know. I know we have to go soon.'

You don't speak of Thorin at all any more. You don't even speak of White-Eye.

'Ah, now that's not fair,' Gilwyn protested. 'I think of her all the time. I don't tell you everything, you know.'

Your thoughts are my thoughts, Gilwyn, and now they turn to sunrises and milking cows. But you have a mission.

'I haven't forgotten,' said Gilwyn. 'It's just . . . I don't know. I'm happy here.'

Ruana touched him with warmth. *It pleases me to see you happy.*

'But I need to go now. Is that what you're saying?'

Of course.

'Hmmm.'

Kelan and Marna have done fine without you. They will survive when you leave.

'They've been so kind to me. These have been good days.'

And you deserved them. You were exhausted. But now you are strong again. Strong enough to go on, at least.

Gilwyn stared blankly at the dark roof of the barn. 'I suppose.'

So?

'So I will think on what you've said,' Gilwyn told the Akari. Once more he closed his eyes, hoping to silence her. 'I'm tired now. Good-night, Ruana.'

Good-night, Gilwyn.

Gilwyn felt light on his eyes, surprised that morning had come so quickly. He turned to his side crankily, not wanting to wake up, but as the light grew more intense his eyes finally creaked open. He yawned, expecting to get a mouthful of straw, but tasted sand on his tongue instead. The odd sensation startled him.

'What . . . ?'

He raised himself onto an elbow, suddenly fully awake. A breeze struck his face. Wet sand clung to his body. Overhead stretched a misty sky. A lake lapped at a nearby shore. Gilwyn sat up, his heart bursting in his chest, fighting the disorientation quickly taking over. He had seen this place before, but could not remember when. The haze on the lake skidded like ghosts upon the water. Crickets buzzed in the trees. Gilwyn stared at the horizon, blinking in disbelief.

'Where am I?' he asked himself, then noticed another figure next to him. Ruana, looking just as alive as he was, came awake next to him. The pretty lady rose from the sand, looking sleeping and confused. She put a hand to her face, looked at Gilwyn, and wondered aloud what had happened.

'Gilwyn?'

'Ruana, what is this?'

Ruana seemed alarmed. She got to her feet and observed their strange surroundings. 'This is my death place,' she said.

'Yes,' said Gilwyn, remembering. She had brought him here before, the first time they had met. Then it had been Minikin who had brought them together, and Ruana had showed him the lake and how she had perished. But that had been the only time, and Ruana had never frightened Gilwyn before, or taken him into her world without his knowledge. Gilwyn rose, brushing the sticky sand from his trousers.

'What are we doing here?' he asked. 'Ruana, I was sleeping . . .'

'I didn't take us here, Gilwyn,' said Ruana. There was no glow around her, no hint at all that she was a spirit. She studied her hands, turning them in surprise, then listened to the birds and insects in the trees. 'I don't understand.'

Then, turning toward the lake, Ruana bit her lip.

'What is it?' probed Gilwyn.

Ruana hesitated, her face twisting. 'Something is coming.'

Gilwyn went to stand beside her, following her gaze across the lake. 'Something bad?'

The stricken look on Ruana's face gave her answer. She waited, her eyes narrowing, her lips curling in anticipation. 'We shouldn't be here,' she whispered.

'Then get us out of here.'

'I can't,' said Ruana. 'This isn't my magic, Gilwyn.'

'No? Who's then?'

Ruana kept her eyes on the lake. 'The one who is coming.'

The sound of oars moving through water broke the spell of the placid shore. The prow of a rowboat peaked through the curtain of mist. Slowly the boat glided toward them, moving easily across the water as the hooded figure gently rowed. With his back to the shore, Gilwyn could not make out his features at all, just his thin frame draped in a drab grey robe.

'Ruana, what's going on?' he asked nervously. 'Who is that?'

'Stand your ground, Gilwyn,' Ruana ordered. 'Don't let him know that you're afraid.'

'Who?' Gilwyn demanded.

'Kahldris.'

Gilwyn's jaw fell open. His pulse began to gallop. Across the lake the little boat drew nearer, bearing the grey figure of the creature who'd caused him so much pain. Kahldris, the spirit of the armour, had somehow made this magic world, reaching into his mind and forcing Ruana to join him.

'How?' asked Gilwyn. 'He's miles away.'

'He is here, Gilwyn,' said Ruana ruefully. 'Just as he touched White-Eye. I can feel him. He's so strong.'

'But why? What does he want with us?'

'Calm yourself,' said Ruana. 'There's nowhere to run. Wait and see.'

Free now of the mist, the rowboat turned as it skidded to shore, beaching noisily on the wet sand. The grey figure casually retracted the oars. Then, a hand came up to pull away his cowl. Kahldris sighed and shook out his long white hair, turning a smile on Gilwyn and Ruana. He remained seated in his little vessel as he clasped his hands on his lap.

'You see? I can be everywhere,' he said. 'Listen to your Akari, boy. There is no place to run from me.'

His sugary voiced carried easily over the shore. His dark eyes sparked with light. He was old yet timeless, thin but powerful. His body resonated a kind of fearlessness. To Gilwyn, he was impossible to look away from, a horribly compelling figure more like a dream than a man.

'This is my world,' hissed Ruana. 'You have no right to come here, demon.'

'Your death place, Ruana,' said Kahldris with a grin. He glanced around. 'A pretty place to die. You were luckier than me.'

Ruana refused to retreat. 'What do you want here?'

'Thorin Glass talks of you often, Gilwyn Toms. He is fond of you.'

Gilwyn battled to control his fear. 'He is a good man. You've corrupted him.'

'Yes, a good man. Good at doing the things I need him to do. I am here to bring you a message, Gilwyn Toms – the baron belongs to me. You have come all this way, but you have wasted your time.'

Ruana stepped between Gilwyn and the demon in the boat. 'You're already growing weaker, Kahldris. I can feel it. How much will it exhaust you to construct this charade?'

'I will sleep for a week, but it will be worth it,' laughed Kahldris. 'Little girl, do you really think you can protect him? I am so much stronger than you. I was a summoner! What are you but a pretty face?'

'Go,' commanded Ruana. 'Your words are meaningless. We do not hear them.'

'Oh, I think young Gilwyn is listening,' said Kahldris, peeking past Ruana. 'Aren't you, boy? You're afraid. That's good. Embrace your fears! They will keep you safe.'

'Gilwyn, don't listen to him,' said Ruana. 'He's trying to make you doubt yourself. But he can't harm you.'

'Ruana, child, why would you lie to him like that?' asked Kahldris. He rose, stretching to his full height without rocking the boat at all. 'I can reach out my fingers and reach you wherever he goes. I can haunt his dreams and make his life an unending nightmare.' Kahldris turned his mad eyes on Gilwyn. 'I can hurt him just like I hurt his precious White-Eye.'

'You stinking piece of filth,' raged Gilwyn. 'White-Eye is still alive. You can't hurt her anymore!'

'Alive, yes,' crooned Kahldris. 'And bumbling around in the dark like an animal, like all the rest of you wretched Inhumans. You may call that a life if you wish, but what does White-Eye think of it?'

His words tore at Gilwyn, shaking his will. Ruana sensed this and pushed Gilwyn backward.

'You don't like to be challenged, do you Kahldris?' she crowed. 'You can't stand the thought of Gilwyn breaking your hold over Glass.' She laughed straight in Kahldris' face. 'Don't be afraid of him, Gilwyn. He can't do anything to you! He would have done it already if he could.'

'I can ruin you, Gilwyn,' warned the Akari.

'But you won't,' challenged Ruana. 'Because Baron Glass would know if you did, and he would never stand for that. That's it, isn't it, Kahldris? That's why you're here to frighten us off.'

Kahldris' face contorted horribly. 'You arrogant little bitch . . .'

'We're coming, demon,' said Ruana. 'We're going to avenge what you've done. And you can't stop us.'

'White-Eye never did a thing to you,' sneered Gilwyn. 'She was kind and good and you hurt her. Why? To get to me?'

Kahldris lifted his eyebrows. 'Are you clever enough to figure this out? Don't listen to Ruana, Gilwyn. I am not afraid of you. Nothing can break my hold over Baron Glass, certainly not a whelp like you. When you come to Koth, you will see what I have done to Baron Glass, the control I have over him.'

'Why then? You attacked White-Eye to get to me, to lure me north. That's right, isn't it?'

'That can't be it,' said Ruana. 'He's afraid of you. He's just trying to scare you off.'

'Kahldris, tell me what you want of me.'

'Gilwyn, no!' snapped Ruana. She turned and grabbed his arm. 'Don't bargain with him.'

Kahldris laughed in delight. 'Such a riddle! Are you smart enough for it, Gilwyn? Can you unravel this great mystery?'

'I don't know.' Gilwyn staggered back. 'Ruana . . .'

Ruana angrily kicked a boot full of sand at Kahldris. 'Go! Go back to whatever slime spawned you, Kahldris! Get out of our minds!'

'Think about it, Gilwyn,' said Kahldris calmly. 'If you help me, you may save the baron.'

'What is it?' pleaded Gilwyn. 'Tell me.'

Kahldris tapped his ghostly head. 'Think.' Then he smiled again. 'You have time, boy. Too much time. The way you limp to Koth is appalling.'

'Don't listen to him, Gilwyn,' said Ruana. 'He's just taunting you.'

'But why?' Gilwyn asked. 'Kahldris, tell me what you want.'

'That's for you to figure out, Gilwyn Toms,' said the demon. 'I will be in Koth, waiting for you.'

Kahldris sat down again and picked up the oars of his boat. With one great pull of the oars the little vessel left the shore, floating swiftly back into the mist. Gilwyn watched it disappear, bearing away all his answers. His hands trembled. Ruana stood mutely beside him, her face troubled and afraid. Neither of them spoke until they were sure Kahldris was gone.

'That was very stupid of you, Gilwyn. You let Kahldris in to your thoughts.'

'I know,' said Gilwyn. 'I'm sorry. But he wants something of me. He wants me to come north.'

'He's afraid of you, Gilwyn. I could sense it.'

Gilwyn let the mists collect around him. It was just as Kahldris had said – a great mystery.

40

Eight men and a woman gazed at the city, mantled by dusk, rising from the desert and shimmering with heat. A soaring white wall rose up from its centre, protecting the pretty minarets and the golden towers of the palace that looked down like a sentinel across the flowered lanes. Beyond the white barrier sprawled a shanty town, crowded and mismatched, its ugly homes like discarded bones tossed over the wall. The spires of the city blinked with candlelight, while in the town at its feet oily campfires burned and sputtered up smoke. The travelers, who had come from many miles away, looked exhaustedly at the city. For none of them did the place meet their expectations. Looking hard, they saw people huddled in the avenues of the broken homes outside the wall. Children played with filthy dogs. In the towers, music called the faithful to prayer, but the folk of the shanty town ignored the call, for they were not of this place at all but rather foreigners of hard luck who had come across the desert to find only disappointment.

Princess Salina had been warned about all of these things. Yet some-how, her expectations had been grander. She had heard from Gilwyn Toms about the foreigners camped outside of Jador, how they had come from the northern world for the magic of Grimhold and how there had been no room for them within the walls. Once, Jador had easily absorbed the northerners, back in the days when they had all been merchants and well-off enough to pay for their homes. But in the days since Grimhold's discovery, the exodus across the desert had swelled the foreigners ranks, breaking Jador's finances and forcing the ugly situation Salina now witnessed. The princess looked at the city without saying a word. She had traveled for three days through the Desert of Tears, leaving Aztar's camp and the man she loved. Her gaka clung to her unbathed body, caked in dust and heavy with sweat. Her drowa, like all of the beasts, drooped from the long ride. And the men of her party, all Voruni men assigned by Aztar to protect her, stared quizzically at the city they had once battled, remembering the great fire that had killed so many of their brethren.

Adnah pulled his drowa to a stop, holding up his arm so that the others did the same. Salina rode up next to him and paused. She had become expert in guiding the huge beast, a latent talent that surprised her. She was quiet as she let Adnah have his moment of reflection, noting her guide's troubled expression. Adnah had returned to Jador because it was what his master Aztar wished, but he had no love for the place, and like so many of the Voruni he feared the city's magical population. It was the Jadori wizards who had summoned the fire that had burned Aztar, an event that still haunted the boldest of his warriors.

'You see?' said Adnah with a grimace. 'The northerners – they live like pigs outside the white wall. They are like slaves to the Jadori. They have no pride at all.'

'They are forced to live like that,' said Salina, though she knew her argument would do no good. Adnah was loyal to Aztar and did everything his master ordered, but he had made up his mind about northerners a long time ago. 'They came here for a better life,' Salina continued.

'That's why you helped them?' asked Adnah. 'Because you think they deserve such a life? You are a kind girl, Princess. Misguided, though.' The Voruni man smirked. 'Northerners have no soul. See how they ignore the prayer calls?'

Salina refused to be baited. 'If you're afraid to go further, I can make the rest of the way myself.'

'Afraid?' Adnah looked over his shoulder to his men, laughing. 'No, Princess, I am not afraid. I merely meant to educate you. Aztar has sent you here for your protection. He is wise and knows what he is doing. But you should be wary of this place and its people.'

'Thank you for warning me, Adnah,' said Salina dryly. 'I'll remember your counsel.'

At every turn, Adnah reminded her why they had come, but Salina had never wanted to leave Aztar. He had insisted, because he knew that her father would soon return with an army to reclaim her, and he was sure that the powerful people of Jador could protect her. Salina had protested – pleaded, in fact – but Aztar had made up his mind and sent her away. It had broken her heart to leave him at the camp, but Salina relented for only one reason – the people of Jador owed her a favour. Now, it was time to collect.

'Let's hurry,' she told Adnah and the others. 'Before the sun is gone completely.'

'How will we get beyond the wall?' asked Adnah. 'Have you thought of that, Princess?'

'Adnah, I am a Princess of Ganjor,' she pointed out proudly. 'I have only to ask and the doors will open.'

White-Eye put her hands to Minikin's elfish face, a form of greeting she had learned in the darkness of her blindness. She felt the sharp ridges over Minikin's eyes, the smooth, knowing brow, the turn of the lips curled in a cool smile, and the knowledge of the Mistress' face came to her like sight itself. White-Eye grinned, perfectly happy. She had not spoken with Minikin in months, not since the little woman had given her over to King Lorn. It had been an a difficult situation, but a necessary one, and it had pained both of them to be apart.

'I have missed you so much,' said White-Eye, barely able to contain her emotions. Her fingertips paused on Minikin's cheeks. 'I wondered every-day when you would come.'

Minikin reached up and stroked her hair. White-Eye could feel the sensation of her small fingers, soft and familiar, as gentle as a mother's. The mistress pulled White-Eye's hand to her mouth and kissed it.

'I came when I thought I should come,' she said. 'When I thought you would understand.' A paused. 'You do understand now, yes?'

'Yes,' said White-Eye, fine with the explanation. 'I know you did what you had to do.'

Through her fingertips she felt relief on the ancient lady's face. Minikin had worried, that was plain. White-Eye had heard it in her voice that day, when she had turned her over to Lorn. For a brief time afterward, White-Eye had wandered in the deepest pain, asking again and again why Minikin had abandoned her, leaving her in the hands of the northerner. But she had never hated Minikin for it, because her love for the mistress was unshakeable. Then, gradually, she began to understand.

Minikin had come unannounced to Jador, catching White-Eye alone in the garden outside the private wing where her chambers were located. Evening had come, releasing White-Eye from the confines of the palace. With the sun gone, she could at last enjoy the fresh air and honey scents of the garden, sitting beneath the gentle light of the stars while a fountain gurgled nearby. Lorn had left her for the day, eager to spend time with his daughter, and White-Eye had dismissed her servants, confident now in her ability to find her way around. But she had heard Minikin's light footfalls on the garden path, a sound that struck a chord deep inside her.

'Trog?' she asked, facing the direction where she heard the big man breathing. 'You're here, yes?'

'He's here,' said Minikin.

White-Eye smiled. 'I can hear him. I can hear everything, Minikin. It's like a whole new world! Trog, come and let me touch you.'

The giant gave a reluctant grunt, then shuffled toward the Kahana's outstretched hands. White-Eye reached high to touch his face. Rough and rock hard, it was so much different from touching Minikin's sweet face.

Finding his mute lips, she kissed her own fingertip and delivered the kiss to the bodyguard. Trog nodded affectionately.

'Trog, it's good to see you, too,' said White-Eye, knowing the greeting the big man would deliver if he could speak. He had always been kind to the slight White-Eye, towering over her like the shelf of a mountain. When Trog was around, White-Eye never felt afraid. She released him, then turned her smile toward Minikin. 'But I wasn't expecting you! Why didn't you tell me you were coming? I could have had a meal ready for you, something special.'

'We haven't come for food, child, but to see you,' Minikin said cheerfully. 'We'll eat later. For now, it's just good to look at you.' Another pause. 'You look well, daughter. So like a grown woman! Ah, but you are Kahana now. Truly.'

'I've worked hard, Minikin,' said White-Eye. 'Lorn has taught me many things. And the others, too. They have all taught me things. You see? I am not afraid to be alone anymore.'

'I did see that,' said Minikin proudly. 'When they told me you were alone here . . . well . . .' A crinkling sound revealed her shrugging shoulders. 'You have changed, White-Eye.'

White-Eye felt her face flush with pride. 'Come inside,' she said. 'Let's talk.'

'Yes, we should talk,' agreed the mistress. 'But not inside. You love the night, I know. Let's walk, White-Eye. You can guide me.'

Along the lanes around the palace, White-Eye and Minikin strolled amid the fruit trees and burgeoning flowers. Trog kept pace with them, but kept back a comfortable distance, giving both women a sense of privacy. Because of the lateness of the hour, the palace's gardeners and grounds keepers had all disappeared, leaving the many patches of grasses and winding lanes alone for them to enjoy. Minikin held White-Eye's hand as they walked, but White-Eye did not guide her through the lanes as Minikin had requested. Instead, White-Eye quickly fell back into old habits, so comfortable with Minikin that she let the tiny woman act like a parent, directing her along. The talk between them was casual, mostly trivial topics like the heat of the day or how well the hibiscus had bloomed this year, but White-Eye knew the conversation would soon turn. She could sense trepidation in Minikin's tone, a kind of cautiousness just waiting for the proper time.

'There's a bench near here, I think,' said White-Eye. 'Do you see it?'

Her father, Kadar, had made the palace grounds a sanctuary for the people of the city, a place where all could enjoy the trees and fragrant greenery carefully coaxed out of the dry desert. He had spent a fortune building shaded knolls where lovers could sit and talk and families could play with their children. He was a remarkable man, and like all of Jador, White-Eye missed him. So did Minikin, who spoke often of her old friend.

'There,' said Minikin, spying the bench. 'We'll sit a while.'

White-Eye remembered the bench from the time she could see, a pretty slab of stone big enough for three, situated beneath an over-hanging willow. When she was a girl, the bench had been her favourite, a place to sit and people-watch or to lean back and stare into the myriad limbs of the great tree. Letting Minikin guide her to it, she reached down and felt its smooth stone before setting herself down upon it. Minikin hopped onto the bench next to her. Trog came to a halt a few paces away. White-Eye heard his big feet stop in the gravel. Minikin sat quietly, her own feet barely reaching the ground. White-Eye waited patiently for her to begin. After a few moments more, the mistress spoke.

'Quiet,' she remarked.

White-Eye nodded. 'Yes.'

'Things could have been chaos here,' said Minikin. 'But you have done a good job, White-Eye. The people love you and respect you. So many troubles, but even the northerners outside the wall are well.'

'It is Lorn,' White-Eye explained, giving the northern king his due. 'He is like a bull drowa, Minikin. He never rests. And the others from the north know this. They trust him, because he is one of them.'

'And he has been good to you? Not too unkind?'

White-Eye's grin widened. 'Ah. Now I think I see. Is that why you have come? To make sure I am unharmed?'

She felt Minikin's small hand slip onto her thigh. 'Am I so obvious?' She laughed. 'All right, yes. I'm just an old woman, full of worries! When I sent him to you I was unsure what to expect. Put me at ease, daughter – tell me he has treated you well.'

'He has, Minikin,' White-Eye assured her. 'It was hard at first. He has a will of iron, and no one can make him bend. I did try!'

'I can't imagine tears getting to him.'

'They did not. But he was gentle in his own way. He has pushed me, Minikin, but he has made me change.' White-Eye turned to the mistress hopefully. 'Can you tell?'

'Yes,' said Minikin. 'You have grown so much. You are your father's daughter! He would be proud of you.'

Thinking of her father again made White-Eye wistful. It was a generous compliment, but she knew she was really nothing like her father. Kahan Kadar had built everything around them. He was a man of great vision, something the blind Kahana could never be, and not just because she couldn't see. Men like her father were rare, both lion-hearted and deeply kind. She might try to be like him – did, in fact, try with all her might – but she was sure she would always fall short of his mark.

'No can replace my father, Minikin, but I've done my best. I have, and I'm glad you see that in me.'

'No grudges, then?'

'None,' said White-Eye sincerely. She hesitated, having a subject of her own she was afraid to broach. It had been many weeks since she had seen the mistress, but she heard little improvement in the lady's mood. It was true what she had said – she was old and probably tired, but more than that she had exhausted herself fighting Aztar's army, inflicting a wound on her soul that had yet to heal. 'Tell me about Grimhold,' she said brightly. 'I miss it.'

'Things are the same,' said Minikin. 'Things there never change. You know that.'

'How is Monster?' White-Eye asked, eager for news of her old friend. 'He should come to Jador soon. Tell him that for me, will you?'

'Monster knows he is welcome here,' said Minikin. White-Eye detected a certain slyness. 'Now, tell me what you really want to know. We keep secrets from each other. Not good.'

'You're so worried about me,' sighed White-Eye, 'but I have done almost nothing but worry about you, Minikin. You say you're old, but you have the Eye of God. You can never be old, not really.'

'Magic is one thing,' said Minikin, 'but time still passes.'

'But you are the Mistress of Grimhold! You did not have to give me over to Lorn. You could have taught me these things yourself.'

'I could not,' said Minikin adamantly. 'I have never been a king, never a true leader. And never when so much is at stake. Lorn will teach you the difficult things, daughter. As you said, he is made of iron. He has done things in his life that none of us would do in our nightmares.'

'And that's the man you left me with?' White-Eye chuckled, but she too had heard the stories, mostly from her beloved Gilwyn. 'He's more than all of that, though. He is a good man, really. They call him 'the Wicked', but that's not the side he has shown here in Jador. He cares about Jador and the promise he made to Gilwyn.'

'I believe you,' said Minikin. 'I did not at first when Gilwyn told me the same, but now . . .'

She hesitated.

'What?'

Minikin patted the girl's leg. 'Still, be on guard. Will you do that for me?'

'On guard? For what?'

'Don't lose yourself, that's all. Lorn will teach you things you must know to be Kahana. Good; let him tutor you. But don't forget who you are.'

White-Eye took her hand and squeezed. 'I am the daughter of Kahan Kadar. I will never forget what that means, Minikin.'

At peace, Minikin spoke no more. Together the two women – one young and unproven, the other as ancient as the trees – sat in the starlight and listened to the tunes of unseen insects. White-Eye took a breath of the sweet evening air, satisfied that Minikin was well. She revelled in the little woman's presence, thrilled that she had come after so long an absence. Minikin, too, seemed satisfied, pleased to just be with the girl she had always called a daughter. For a moment, White-Eye thought that nothing could spoil her mood.

Then, she heard his footfalls.

Heavy and deliberate, leaden by boots of northern design, his steps were unmistakable, and White-Eye did not need the sighted Minikin to tell her that Lorn had come. He moved quickly, breathing hard, as if he'd been looking for them for quite some time.

'Kahana,' he called to her. He halted in front of them. 'Mistress Minikin.' His voice sounded unsurprised, even pleased to see her.

Minikin stood. 'King Lorn.'

'Your pardon, Mistress, but I have news for both of you,' said Lorn. 'White-Eye, you need to come.'

'What is it?' asked White-Eye, suddenly alarmed.

'Another visitor has come,' Lorn explained. 'Someone I don't think any of us was expecting.'

Lorn had not seen Princess Salina since he had left her in Ganjor, months earlier. He had heard of the princess' arrival from Fouro, one of the palace's many grooms, who had come rushing into his chambers while Eirian – Lorn's woman – was feeding his daughter Poppy. The news of Salina's arrival stunned Lorn, who went at once to fetch White-Eye and Minikin. Now, as the three of them walked the empty corridor, Lorn wondered why Salina had come and how she had managed to make it unscathed across the desert. She was a remarkable girl, this desert princess, and Lorn grinned like a wolf when he thought of her. She had likely come to them with bad news, but to Lorn that hardly mattered. She had already impressed him, because she had helped him and the other Seekers and because she had beliefs, something Lorn found sorely lacking in the world he'd left behind.

At Lorn's orders, Princess Salina had been taken to one of the palace's antechambers. He had directed Fouro to bring food and drink for her, but to separate her from the warriors who accompanied her. They were, Fouro explained, Voruni men, another part of the mystery Lorn meant to unravel. He explained this to the others while they walked.

'Fouro says there are eight of them, all of them dressed like Aztar's brood. She didn't say why she had come, only that she needed to speak to you, White-Eye.'

White-Eye moved cautiously through the hall, holding Minikin's hand. Although she had progressed amazingly over the past few weeks, the news of Salina's arrival had unbalanced her.

'Is that all?' she asked. 'No word about Aztar?'

'Not as yet,' Lorn warned. 'But the Voruni . . .'

'The Voruni are Aztar's people,' said Minikin. 'They would not have come with her unless she has spoken to him. Prepare yourself, White-Eye – she bears a message for you.'

Lorn concurred, then guided the women to the antechamber where Salina waited, seated at a long table beneath a frescoed ceiling. The food and wine that had been arranged for her lay untouched. She sat alone, wide-eyed as she studied her impressive surroundings, but when she heard Lorn and the others approaching she stood at once. Fouro, who had been waiting nearby, fled the antechamber at Lorn's brusque order. Salina looked at all of them in turn, but her gaze rested comfortably on Lorn. An expression of utter relief washed over her and she smiled.

'Lorn,' she sighed. 'The people outside the wall told me I would find you here. Do you remember me?'

Lorn was careful not to overstep his authority, but could not help being enthused about her arrival. 'Would I ever forget someone who helped me so much? Welcome, Princess Salina.' He stepped aside to introduce the others. 'Kahana White-Eye,' he pronounced, carefully taking her hand.

Salina, looking all the more like the child she was, licked her lips nervously, stepping forward and bowing. 'Kahana,' she said reverently. 'Thank you for seeing me.'

'I wish I could see you,' said White-Eye softly. 'I have heard from King Lorn what a lovely young woman you are.'

Salina blushed. 'The king is kind.' Her eyes went to Minikin, filling with wonder. 'The lady of Grimhold.' Again she bowed, but this time more slowly. 'I am in awe of you, lady.'

Minikin floated closer on her tiny feet. Behind her towered Trog, though the big man kept respectfully distant. The mistress inspected Salina with a smile, then reached out and took her chin, lifting the girl's eyes to face her.

'Don't look away, child,' she said gently. 'I want to see the brave girl who has done so much for us.'

The princess coloured. Like White-Eye, she was dark-skinned, yet her girlish embarrassment was plain. She managed to hold her gaze on Minikin, but only slightly.

'My lady, all my life I have heard the stories about you. And now I

426

know they are true! To see you now is like . . .' Lost for words, she faltered. 'I am amazed.'

'As am I, child,' chirped Minikin. 'None of us expected you to be here. Please, sit. Tell us why you've come all this way.'

With no servants around, it was up to Lorn to pull out the chair for her. He did so quickly, then did the same for White-Eye and Minikin, at last choosing a seat for himself at the Kahana's right hand. Together they looked at Salina expectantly, none of them really knowing how to begin. Salina seemed on the verge of bursting. Her eyes jumped between the three, finally resting on Lorn, the only one of the trio she knew.

'Where do I start?' she lamented. 'So much has happened.' She pushed aside the plate that had been set before her. 'You know I came here with others, yes? Voruni men?'

'We know,' said Lorn. 'They are Aztar's men.'

'We know that he's still alive,' said White-Eye. 'Have you been with him?'

'Yes,' said Salina softly. Lorn picked up the dreamy quality of her tone. 'I have left my father and gone to him.' She looked earnestly at White-Eye. 'We are in love, Kahana. My father has forbidden it but it is so, and he has protected me so far from my father's anger.'

'Forbidden it?' White-Eye cocked her head. 'It was your father that sent Aztar against us! You were to be the prize for him. Why would he forbid it now?'

'For politics, that is why,' said Salina. 'He still bargains me like a gaming chip, but now he does so to move the conscience of the people. They think he is weak, that Aztar has made a fool of him, and so he still bargains with Aztar for me.'

'And Aztar?' asked White-Eye. 'What about him? What does he want from your father?'

'To be left alone and nothing else,' claimed the princess. 'My father has offered him land and a title if he returns me, but he's refused.' She puffed a bit at this. 'Aztar is a changed man, and that's what I'm here to tell you. Lady Minikin, you most of all must hear this – Aztar isn't the man he was when he attacked Jador. He's not my father's puppet or a zealot. He's a good man who's heart has suffered.'

Lorn ached to jump in with questions, but he controlled himself, leaving the battlefield for White-Eye. To his pleasure the Kahana did not retreat.

'Prince Aztar killed hundreds of people. All of them were innocent.' White-Eye's voice was steady and cool. 'Forgive us, Princess Salina. We are not ungrateful. None of us have forgotten what you've done for us. But to speak of Aztar this way . . .'

'Let me convince you,' Salina told them. 'Kahana White-Eye, Lady

Minikin – I have spoken with the one called Gilwyn Toms. He was with Aztar at his camp. He knows of what I speak.'

White-Eye leaned forward. 'Gilwyn? What do you know of him?'

'He came to Ganjor. He sought me out – at your insistence, King Lorn.'

Lorn nodded. 'That is so.'

'He told me of his mission to save your friend, the one named Baron Glass. I gave him gold and direction for him to be on his way.'

'He was well when you saw him?' asked White-Eye. 'What else did he tell you?'

'He was well, Kahana, but only because of Aztar.'

Salina told them her story about Gilwyn, how he had come to her in Ganjor after his time recuperating in Aztar's camp. A rass had attacked him, she claimed, and Aztar's people had nursed him back to help. He had spent time with Aztar, speaking to him, learning about the events that had changed him.

'Aztar wanted him to return here,' claimed Salina. 'He wanted Gilwyn to tell all of you that he's not your enemy, that he knows now that Vala did not choose him to destroy you.'

'But Gilwyn could not return,' Minikin guessed. 'Because of his mission.'

'That is right, lady,' said Salina. 'But everything I've said is true. If not for Aztar, Gilwyn would not have survived.'

White-Eye drew back, contemplative. Lorn read her expression, knowing the questions running through her mind. If Salina spoke the truth, their worries about Aztar were over. With no reason for him to attack, they were safe from him at last.

'This news is welcome,' said the kahana. 'Until recently we thought Aztar was dead. And after all he has given us reason to fear him.'

Lorn added, 'Indeed. Tell me, Princess – how can a man like Aztar change so much?'

Salina raised an eyebrow. '*You* ask me this? Where you come from you are called King Lorn the Wicked.'

Lorn smirked. 'An apt name, where I come from.'

'And would you have us all believe that all your wickedness follows you wherever you go, and that the evil things you've done are all that your life amounts to?'

'No,' Lorn admitted, 'I would not.'

'It is the same with Aztar,' argued Salina. 'He *has* changed. And now he is in danger.' The princess looked pleadingly at Lorn. 'He needs help, my lord.'

'Help?' Lorn guessed at her meaning at once. 'You mean the threat of Jadori force.'

Salina nodded. 'If my father knew that the Jadori were in league with

Aztar – if you were willing to protect him – he would think again before sending his army to rescue me.' She turned to Minikin. 'He knows that happened to Aztar's army when they attacked you, Lady. He fears your magics.'

'Protect Prince Aztar? The Jadori?' scoffed White-Eye. 'Why would we ever do such a thing, after all that he's done to us?'

Salina drew back. 'Kahana, my father imprisoned me for helping your people. I warned you about Aztar's attack. I gave you time to prepare and because of that you defeated him.'

'And now you think we owe you a debt,' White-Eye surmised sourly. 'And maybe we do. But what you ask is impossible.'

Lorn tried to hide his budding smile. With no coaxing at all, White-Eye had risen to her station.

'Is that why you're here, child?' queried Minikin. 'Aztar sent you all this way to ask our help?'

'No, Lady,' replied the princess carefully. 'Aztar has no idea that I'm asking this of you. He sent me here for protection. He asks only that you give me sanctuary.' Her face clouded with sadness. 'He wants me to be safe.'

'And you may stay, of course,' said Minikin gently. 'We are grateful to you, Princess Salina. Please believe that.'

Salina gave a grudging smile. 'I do believe you, Lady. And what I did for you was not meant to be a lever. I did it because I believed in it, and I'd do it again. I have no regrets at all.' Her face darkened deeper. 'It revealed things to me, about my father and the kind of world he wants. I love my father, but he would make me a prisoner simply because I am a woman! I'll not live that way.'

Lorn nodded, at last understanding. This wasn't just the struggle of two lovers. It was a tussle between a father and a daughter.

'I'm a father, too,' he told the girl. 'Imagine just for a moment what it is like for him, Princess. You are young. Maybe you do not yet realize that the world doesn't change simply because you wish it.'

Salina bristled in offense. 'You have not lived in Ganjor, King Lorn. You have no idea what it is like to a woman there.'

'Women have their place,' Lorn countered. 'Just as men do.'

'Is it there place to be slaves?' Salina asked sharply. 'Yes, perhaps it is that way in Norvor, too.'

'Stop now,' said Minikin, wrapping on the table to get their attention. 'Princess Salina, it doesn't matter why you are here. Whatever your reasons you are welcome.'

'Is she?' Lorn questioned. 'Mistress Minikin, you do not speak for Jador.'

Minikin's face creased. 'Don't I?'

'Your pardon, but no,' said Lorn. 'White-Eye is Kahana. It is for her to

429

decide whether or not Jador grants this sanctuary.' He turned to his charge with all seriousness. 'And think hard before you decide, White-Eye. What will you do if her father comes with an army to claim her?'

White-Eye blanched at the question. 'I do not know.'

'My father will come for me,' said Salina dreadfully. 'And his army will crush Aztar.' She looked at her three benefactors helplessly. 'Are all of you just going to let that happen?'

'We can do nothing to help Aztar,' said White-Eye. She had already made up her mind on this, a point that Lorn applauded. 'Even if we wanted to help him we could not. Jador is devastated, Princess Salina. We endured two wars in two years, one of them with your beloved Aztar. How many men and kreels do you think it would take to defeat your father?'

'But you would not have to fight him,' insisted Salina. 'My father fears you. If you would just stand with Aztar . . .'

White-Eye shook her head. 'We don't have the strength for it.' She stiffened. 'Or the will.'

Salina shrank against her chair. Her eyes wandered from White-Eye to Minikin, hoping for sympathy. Minikin smiled warmly but echoed White-Eye's words.

'I am sorry, child, but the Kahana is right,' she said. 'Jador doesn't have the power to stand against your father. If Aztar chooses to fight him, he will do so alone.'

'But he has changed,' Salina maintained. 'If you could just see him, speak to him, you would believe me.'

'You're not hearing us,' said Minikin. 'It does not matter if Aztar has changed. I believe you when you say this, and I wish no harm to him. But Jador is weak. Another war would ruin us.'

'It's true, Princess,' said Lorn. 'Believe me, I know.'

Princess Salina relented at last, her hopes dashed. 'If I cannot change your mind . . .'

'You may stay in Jador as long as you wish,' offered White-Eye, trying to console the girl. 'We will keep you safe as long as you can.'

'At least until your father comes,' said Lorn.

Silence. Minikin grimaced at the prospect.

'Thank you,' said Salina. She stood, then looked around in confusion. 'The men that came with me . . . I should talk to them now.'

Minikin volunteered to take the girl away, noting Lorn's sudden anxiousness. He nodded gratefully to the mistress, bid White-Eye to remain, then said a quick farewell to the Princess from Ganjor. Together they listened to the footsteps disappearing down the corridor, the ante-chamber returning to its previous silence. White-Eye stared blankly into

430

space, her face a mask of disquiet. What had started as a fine night had quickly dampened to dismay.

'You want me to say something,' she sighed. 'What is it?'

'I need you to think on what just happened,' said Lorn. 'There is a lesson here.'

'Tell me what it is. Please don't make me guess.'

'Will you really let Salina remain here?'

White-Eye turned to him. 'Shouldn't I?'

'What do you think?' pressed Lorn. 'What do you think might happen?'

'You mean with her father,' groaned White-Eye. 'I don't know. If she's right and he's afraid of us . . .'

Lorn nodded. 'Then you are off the hook, Kahana. But I'm a father, too, and I know what it means to love a daughter. If Salina were mine I would not be swayed so easily.'

'So?'

'So a ruler must think clearly, White-Eye. A kingdom is a giant game board, and it's up to you to move all the pieces. If her father's army comes here, what will you do?'

'I won't give her up,' White-Eye resolved. 'I won't.' She pinioned Lorn with her sightless gaze. 'Is that what you want me to do? Turn her over to her father after all she's done for us?'

Lorn laughed and clapped his hands together. 'You have come so far. You've delighted me tonight, Kahana!'

'What?'

'Of course you shouldn't turn her over.' Lorn got out of his chair and stood over the stunned girl. 'Sometimes, White-Eye, a ruler simply must do what's right.'

41

Mirage sat on her horse in the middle of the deserted avenue, staring at the far-off hill and the gaunt gargoyle of the library perched at its peak. Splayed in moonlight, the sad and lonely place seized her weary gaze. Outlined darkly against the night sky, the library hovered silently over the city of Koth, broken but undefeated. An empty lane meandered up the hill, littered with equipment, the remnants of the workmen who had toiled to bring the structure back to life. A cloud floated past the library's tower. At the foot of the hill, the capital slept. Mirage felt her eyes blurring from the long day on the road. She stiffened, keeping herself erect in the saddle of her worn out horse. In the bowels of Asher's prison, she had never thought to look on Koth again or to see its vaunted library climbing skyward once more. A hundred memories crashed against her.

She thought of Lukien, beautiful and bronze, riding out to battle, and of Vanlandinghale, kind and generous, dead under a slab of fallen granite. She thought of Thorin, too, and how he had come to her that last day, looking like a madman, sending her off to rescue Lukien as he lay near death in the street beyond the city. To Mirage, who had spent months in the gentle care of Raxor, these memories seemed a lifetime ago, but now they thrust themselves against her demandingly. Mirage quivered under the force of them, groping for words but unable to speak. Next to her, Corvalos Chane sat brooding on his stallion, scanning the avenue for trouble. Strangling voices reached them along the twisting lanes, but the city slept now and except for a few Norvan soldiers on patrol, the streets were empty. Corvalos Chane slipped his gaze toward the library on its hill.

'They've made progress,' he commented.

To anyone who had been there during the bombardment, the progress was obvious. Thorin and his Norvan catapults had collapsed huge portions of the library's roof, but the damage was all repaired now. The improvement heartened Mirage, yet the sight of the library haunted her.

'It's strange to be back,' she whispered.

'I thought you would be glad,' said Chane.

Mirage looked around. It was a street very much like this one where Chane had captured her. The little tavern where they'd 'met' was nearby, just around the corner, she recalled. He had frightened her very nearly to death that night, and changed her life forever.

'I was on my way to Thorin,' she said.

'Eh?'

'When you captured me. I was on my way to Thorin that night.' Mirage scowled. 'And now I am again.'

Corvalos Chane kept his eyes on her. He had observed her like this throughout the day, knowing they were reaching Koth. It was not a cruel or questioning look, but rather a peculiar gaze that made Mirage uneasy. Never a man of words, Chane had been even more quiet than usual. He merely watched.

'I was right about you, though,' he said finally. 'You made the king happy, at least for a time.'

'Happy enough for him to ride into battle and see his son slain,' replied Mirage. 'Yes, that was a brilliant move you made.'

'It was enough. I'm satisfied.'

They hadn't spoken of it since they'd left Hes. During the whole nine-day ride, they hadn't spoken of anything of consequence. Now that the barrier was down, however, Mirage turned on her companion.

'None of you had any right to do what you did,' she said harshly. 'To treat me like an animal, snag me from the streets . . .'

'It was war, girl.'

'Ah, but not me! I wasn't a spy. I was just a plaything.' Mirage shook her head, not really clear on what she meant and not really caring. 'You have no idea how afraid I was of you. And then Asher . . .'

'Asher is gone,' said Chane. 'Forget Asher. Concentrate on what you must do next.'

What was that exactly? Mirage was completely unsure. Back in Hes, returning to Koth had seemed like a good idea. But how could she change Thorin's heart, really? Did he even have a heart to change anymore? Some said no. Of the people they had met on the long road to Liiria, none of the stories about Baron Glass were hopeful. He was being called a butcher and a demon. At best, he was demented. Could she reach that maddened mind?

'Lionkeep is far from here,' said Mirage at last. 'That's where Thorin will be.'

Chane nodded. 'In the morning, then.'

'What? No . . .'

'Not tonight, girl,' argued Chane. 'You're tired, and so am I. I mean to get a room for us and leave you in the morning.' He glanced ahead. 'That tavern isn't far from here.'

'No.' Mirage shook her head. 'No.'

Chane looked at her askance. They had taken rooms before, most recently the night before last, in a little town called Jorio on the Reecian border. 'Why not?' he asked. 'You can't go to him tonight, it's too late.'

She knew he was right, but something about his manners made her skittish. 'Take a room if you want. I'm going on.'

'Mirage, you're being silly. You must rest. Can you go to Glass stinking of the road? How will that help your plans?'

It wouldn't, and she knew it. Mirage's only hope was to appeal to Thorin as a woman, and that meant looking her best. Seeing Chane's logic, she surrendered.

'All right,' she agreed. 'There's a tavern called the Red Stallion.' She gestured with her chin toward the corner. 'That way.'

A gleam lit Chane's eyes, but he said nothing. Together they steered their horses toward the corner, rounding it and entering the street where the Red Stallion waited, its windows lit with oil lamps. Beyond the greasy glass Mirage could see the silhouettes of patrons seated at tables. Outside the inn, a boy who tended the customer's horses looked toward them hopefully. As they rode closer, Chane leaned in toward Mirage.

'They'll be soldiers inside,' he whispered. 'Norvans, probably. Don't say anything and don't look at any of them directly. You're with me, and that should be enough.'

Chane wasn't afraid of anything, a comfort to Mirage in this rough city. Because neither of them had dressed in anything that would give them away as Reecians, she was confident that no one would ask many questions, yet she remained guarded. Drunken mercenaries were notorious for putting their noses where they weren't wanted. She kept close to Chane as they reached the inn, dismounting and telling the boy to look after their horses. Chane dug deep into the leather pouch at his belt, producing three coins for the boy.

'Listen to me closely,' he said, locking eyes with the child. 'I swear to heaven that if anything happens to these horses I will skin you alive.' Then he smiled and added. 'You can try to run from me, but you'll only die tired. Right?'

The boy's jaw dropped and he nodded.

'Good fellow,' said Chane, handing him the coins. He stepped aside for Mirage. 'Let's go.'

Pushing open the tavern door, Mirage felt immediately swept back in time. Just like that night, months ago, the place was nearly empty. And just like that night, the chubby faced proprietor rushed up to greet her. He began to give his usual welcome, then paused.

'I've seen you before,' he said with a grin, his eyes narrowing. 'You've been here, yes?'

Mirage glanced at Chane, then nodded politely. 'Yes. A while ago.'

'I remember,' said the man, beaming. 'I never forget a beautiful woman.' Then he looked at Chane and his smile diminished. 'Are you together?'

'Of course,' boomed Chane. He feigned hurt. 'Don't you remember me, too?'

The chubby man nodded. 'Yes,' he replied, not looking pleased. 'A table, then?'

'Near the fire,' directed Chane wearily, and didn't wait for the proprietor to agree. Guiding Mirage by the shoulder, he went to the little vacant table near the hearth and sat himself down. Mirage, uncomfortable, sat down beside him. 'Bring us food and drink. Any drink you have that's cold and any food that's hot. And a room.'

Mirage bristled at this. Taking two rooms would have caused too much attention, and although Chane had always been a gentleman she had a bad feeling about tonight. The inn-keeper rushed off to bring them their orders, leaving them alone to survey the room. Only a handful of patrons occasioned the Stallion, all of them military men from the looks of them. Mirage couldn't really tell the difference between a Norvan or Liirian, but she knew that none of them wore the garb of a Royal Charger. From their unkempt, unalike 'uniforms,' she supposed them all to be mercenaries.

'Don't stare,' Chane cautioned her softly.

Mirage turned her eyes to the hearth instead. 'Norvans?' she whispered.

'That's right.'

They didn't speak again until the proprietor returned with their drinks, two large tankards of beer overflowing with foam. 'The food will be just a few minutes,' he said with a smile. When he put down the beers he waited for their approval. Chane nodded.

'Very good. Thank you.'

The proprietor cocked his head curiously. 'You're not from around here.'

Chane looked up. 'What?'

'That's what you told me last time,' said the man, grinning at Mirage. 'I don't forget a pretty face like yours. I remember you said you were here in Koth looking for someone. Did you ever find him?'

Mirage wasn't sure how to answer. 'No,' she tried.

The man sighed. 'I'm sorry. The war?'

'Yes, the war,' Mirage feigned, not really remembering her old conversation with the man.

'You have family here?'

'What's with the questions?' Chane barked.

The proprietor backed off. 'Sorry,' he offered, then left them alone again. Chane picked up his tankard and began to drink, not taking a breath until the mug was halfway done. Mirage watched in awe of his capacity, sure that something irritated him. Across the room, a pair of prostitutes were laughing as they sat on a patrons lap, his hands around their waists. Chane stared at the trio, simmering.

When the inn-keeper returned, he had two plates with him, both piled high with steaming food. He set them down with a proud smile, setting off a memory in Mirage about how good the cooking was at this little tavern. Her mouth began to water at the sight of it.

'Another beer,' croaked Chane, pushing out his tankard. 'And when you see me empty, don't make me wait.'

His bad mood curbed Mirage's appetite. With all that she already had on her mind, trying to figure out her brooding companion was an unwanted chore. Chane didn't help her unravel the riddle, either, stabbing at his food with his fork and filling his mouth with beef and potatoes so that he could barely grunt, much less carry on a conversation. And each time he swallowed he washed it all down with mouthfuls of beer, keeping the surprised inn-keeper busy with refills. Mirage ate slowly, picking lady-like at her meal, watching Chane suspiciously. He would be drunk tonight, and that unnerved her. In all their time together she had never seen him drink.

'What's wrong with you?' she finally asked. 'Why are you drinking so much?'

He didn't answer her, but shrugged as if the question was of no importance. Mirage returned to her meal, eating more quickly now, eager to be away from him. When she had her fill she pushed aside her plate and rose from her chair. Chane looked up at her, surprised.

'Where you going?'

'Up to the room,' she replied.

'Already?'

The proprietor, seeing her rise, hurried over to the table. 'Is everything all right?' he asked.

'Fine,' said Mirage. 'I'm just tired. Could you take me upstairs now?'

Eager to please, the little man pulled out her chair. 'This way,' he directed, then took her by the arm and led her from the table. Mirage looked over her shoulder at Chane's sour face, refusing to explain herself.

Mirage was asleep by the time Chane came upstairs. She had no idea how much time had passed, but her head was thick with slumber and her eyes struggled to open when she heard the door open. Corvalos Chane stood in the threshold, wavering, watching her. Mirage sat up slowly, remembering her worries.

'Close the door,' she directed softly.

Chane's mouth was open a little. He stepped inside and closed the door clumsily. He was more than just a little drunk, confirming her worst fears. Mirage prepared herself, unsure what he was like when he'd been drinking. With that in mind, she hadn't even taken off her boots.

'Lay down,' she told him. 'You need sleep.'

There were two beds in the room, and very little else. Chane eyed his own bed miserably, but did not move toward it. In the flickering light of the oil lamp, he looked ghostly and sad.

'I was downstairs, watching the girls,' he told her. His voice slurred badly.

Mirage braced herself. 'Who? The prostitutes?'

'The harlots, yes.' He stepped closer to her bed, his expression shifting in the meagre light. 'You were wrong about what you said. You weren't a plaything, Mirage. You were special to the king. You were special . . .'

'All right, yes,' said Mirage easily. 'There's your bed . . . go to sleep now.'

Chane hovered, not moving. He stared, his eyes bloodshot. 'I can't have any of them, do you know that? I can't have a woman. I'm the king's man.' He laughed. 'Do you know what that means?'

'Yes, I think so.' Mirage smiled, not encouragingly but calmly. 'But you can have a woman if you want. I won't tell anyone.'

'I don't want one of those whores,' he growled. 'I want a special woman. Someone like you.'

Mirage put up her hands. 'Uh, no, that's not what you want,' she warned. 'Remember Raxor.'

'I remember Raxor. I think of him all the time. I think of what your precious Baron Glass did to him.' Chane's face twisted. 'What are you going to do when you go to him? Will you be his lover?'

'You're drunk,' said Mirage. 'You need to sleep.'

'You're afraid of me,' slurred Chane. His breathing grew heavy, as though he had climbed a mountain. 'Everyone's afraid of me . . .'

He staggered closer to her bed. Mirage jumped out of it. They faced each other, the stench of beer striking her face. Somehow, she was not afraid of him now. Standing drunk before her, shoulders slumped, he simply looked pitiful.

'I always cared for you,' he whispered. Then he put a finger to his lips. 'But hush . . . don't tell anyone. Don't tell Raxor, right? I love him. I do.'

'I know you do,' said Mirage gently. And suddenly she understood. She reached out and took his hand. Amazingly, he succumbed to her touch, walking like a small boy to his waiting bed. 'Go to sleep now, Corvalos.'

Sitting down on the edge of the mattress, he looked up at her and chuckled. 'You don't call me that. You don't call me Corvalos.'

'Yes, well tonight is different. Go to sleep now.'

'No . . . you won't be here when I wake up.'

Mirage smiled sadly at him. 'That's right.'

'Don't be afraid of me,' he sighed. 'I never wanted you to be afraid of me.'

'All right,' she said gently, and with a light push sent him falling into the mattress. He collapsed, staring up at the ceiling, letting her pull off his big boots. Mirage placed the boots near the bedside, then gazed down at him. His eyes were already closed. 'Good-night, Corvalos,' she said sweetly.

Then, grabbing up her things from the room, she left the tiny chamber to go in search of Baron Glass.

42

Of all the damage that had been done to the great library, Baron Glass had never considered the loss of the books until now. Sitting on the floor with stacks of books surrounding him, he poked through the volumes one by one, blowing the dust from the texts and mourning the scars that had savaged them. The thorough bombardment from the Norvan catapults had collapsed whole sections of the library's roof, bringing rock raining down on thousands of precious manuscripts. Baron Glass, alone in the light of a single torch, paged through the books with regret.

In the days of King Akeela, while the baron himself endured exile in Norvor, scholars from across the world had come to Koth, filling the shelves of the library with significant works. The place groaned with them, fat, dusty tomes teeming with forgotten knowledge, the kind of books only learned men could understand. Figgis, the head librarian, had done a remarkable job with the collection, making it the envy of kings, and Akeela himself had opened the library to all, his great gift to the ignorant masses. Baron Glass had never understood Akeela's obsession with the library, but now, as he sat among the countless piles, he glimpsed an insight into his foe's strange passion.

Thorin had been at it for hours now, letting the sun set and all the workmen return to their families. The deep of night was always the best time for Thorin, when he could come and be alone in the library, undisturbed by the noise of hammers and chisels. Most nights Thorin toiled over the machine. Tonight, however, his mission was different. He had reasoned that the machine was nothing more than a catalogue, listing all the books – and all the knowledge – the library held. And if he could not get the machine to work – which he could not – then perhaps the books themselves would hold the answer.

And yet, Thorin had been sidetracked in his quest. For the first two hours he has diligently looked for references to the Akari, any small bit that might help him find the location of Kahldris' hated brother. The search had been fruitless, but then Thorin had stumbled upon this sad little reading room. Overhead, the collapsed roof had been repaired, but all the books had been shaken from the shelves, strewn lovelessly across the dirty floor. Hundreds of them.

Such was the sin of Rodrik Varl, who had ordered the library attacked. An act of mercy, Varl had claimed, a way of convincing the defenders inside that they would never stand against the army arrayed against them. True, Varl had acted selflessly. The Black Baron accepted that now. But in so doing he had damaged so much, taking away the very thing that made Koth great. Thorin had spent months and more than a fortune rebuilding the library, but he had neglected the one thing for which people came for miles – the books.

Kahldris was quiet as Thorin read, skimming the pages of a book about warfare, an ironic choice amid all the destruction. Amazing, it was a book that Thorin had read before, many long years ago in his war college days. He still remembered the odd writing, the big, bold strokes of the monks who had toiled to copy them, each of them nearly identical. Over the years, Thorin had thought about the book, putting its tactics to use many times. As though he were just a friend looking over Thorin's shoulder, Kahldris whispered invisibly in Thorin's ear.

You won't find what you're looking for here.

Thorin shrugged the comment off. 'Look at this – I was a boy when I last saw this!'

Useless.

'Why?'

We are both Generals, Baron. We both know you cannot learn war from a book.

'Oh, but the basics never change . . .'

Thorin continued thumbing through the manuscript, oblivious to the darkness swimming around him and the tug of sleep. Since merging with Kahldris, sleep was almost a thing of the past, but not completely. He marveled at how much he could do without the interruption of sleep, but he still got tired after long days, and the last week had been a miserable one. Jazana had left, riding off against his wishes to the Norvan border. She would return, she promised, and Thorin knew that she would. But he missed his emotional queen. In his zeal to unlock the secrets of the machine he had ignored his lover, and the damage he had done between them seemed irreparable sometimes. Still, Thorin kept on with his work, never explaining himself to Jazana or revealing the true reasons for his obsession. Jazana Carr was not a stupid woman, but matters of the spirit evaded her, and Thorin was sure she could never understand the intricacies of the Akari.

'Your brother,' Thorin started. 'He was your younger, yes?'

Yes. We have been over this.

440

'I forget. And after he left for the Serpent Kingdom . . . no one heard from him again?'

No.

There was a trace of sorrow in Kahldris' tone, a stitch that had never been there before. Surprised, Thorin let it go, knowing how Kahldris hated prying. The Akari was free with information always. He had told Thorin everything he knew about his brother Malator, all the details of his betrayal. But when it came to his heart – if indeed the demon had a heart – he sealed it tight like a vault, hissing with anger when questioned about it.

'It will take a year to find what we're looking for in all this rubble,' Thorin grumbled. 'But until Gilwyn gets here we will try.'

Kahldris acknowledged this with a wave of gratitude, a warm feeling that blanketed Thorin's mind. Thorin closed the book and set it aside, surveying the stacks of other manuscripts waiting for him. The history of the Akari – was it anywhere in the library? Had it ever been written? He had found books about the Jadori already – most of them filled with inaccuracies – but so far not one mention about Kahldris' odd race. To Thorin, the task looked hopeless.

He stood, stretching like a lion, thinking of returning to his bed at the keep. He had lost track of time but knew that dusk had come hours ago. Outside the big glass windows, moonlight trickled through the sky. He turned toward the chamber door, then felt a stab of surprise from Kahldris.

Baron, said the demon suddenly. *Someone is coming.*

Thorin listened but heard no one. 'Who?'

An Akari!

'Akari? Gilwyn?' asked Thorin hopefully.

Kahldris waited a moment. *No.* Thorin felt the spirit's surprise. *A woman.* Surprise turned to pleasure. *A very beautiful woman.*

Mirage had made it as far as the old Chancellery Square before being stopped by Thorin's soldiers. There, a trio of Norvan mercenaries on patrol spotted her on her horse trotting slowly toward Lionkeep. Unafraid, she declared herself a friend of Baron Glass, a woman with secrets from his past days in Jador, someone of importance who demanded to see him at once.

Impressed enough to listen, the Norvans who had captured her decided not to take any chances. Knowing their new king's obsession with the library, they confiscated Mirage's horse, allowing her to ride it to Library Hill while they controlled the reins, making their way slowly through the empty streets of Koth and finally up the winding road to the library. At first the Novans had been full of questions, but Mirage kept up her mysterious, demanding air, refusing to answer their many queries and threatening them with Thorin's wrath if they did not take her to see him at once. Suitably afraid, the mercenaries did as she requested. As they crested the hill, the library loomed up darkly before them, its huge doors open like the mouth of a dragon. Two of the soldiers carried lamps as they rode, lighting he stony path. The library itself stood mostly dark, expect for a meagre string of candles illuminating its grand interior. Mirage peered through the fantastic portals as she dismounted, glimpsing the place she had heard too much about, weak-kneed as her feet touched the ground.

'He's inside?' she asked. 'You are sure?'

The only man without a lamp had been the one guiding her horse. His name was Gogin. He wore a golden tunic, taut over his ample chest, and green leggings of the kind the archers of Reec wore. If he was a Reecian, he didn't say, but Mirage knew that Norvan mercenaries came from everywhere. Gogin got off his own horse, looking unhappy at the prospect of disturbing Baron Glass. She had promised him that the baron would be far less pleased with him if he had her wait until morning, but now he appeared to be struggling with that decision. His companions each dismounted, then stood looking at each other for direction. Surprisingly, they had all been polite to her, which pleased Mirage immensely after her awkward night with Corvalos Chane. In a way, she even pitied the trio. The stories she had heard about Thorin suddenly seemed all the more true.

'All right, wait here, then,' said Gogin, volunteering himself. 'I'll take her in myself.'

Relief shone on the faces of the others, both of whom nodded and said they would look after the horses, an act of kindness that impressed Gogin not at all. The mercenary in gold and green turned to Mirage and scowled.

'He's in here most every night, all by himself, and he doesn't like to be disturbed, so if you're not who you say you are be prepared. It won't be me who kills you, lady, but the baron himself.'

Mirage scoffed. 'I'm not afraid.'

Gogin frowned. 'Because you're one of them? A sorcerer?'

'Believe it,' Mirage threatened. 'Take me to Thorin.'

Thorin's name tripped off her tongue so easily she had no trouble convincing the soldiers of her friendship with the baron. Gogin shook off his trepidation as he headed for the entrance, waving Mirage to follow him. She had not given her name to the men, nor told them anything at all about herself. Amazingly, just her claim of friendship with Thorin had been enough. She followed Gogin through the giant doors, and all at once the soaring magnificence of the place dwarfed her.

'Oh . . .'

She was a little girl again, looking up at everything because she was so small. Above her head reigned the cathedral, all vaults and frescoes, alive with the dancing lights of the candles on the wall. Ahead loomed the hall, wide and fabulous, pulsing with the echoes of her own rapt breath. Stately and wise looked the eyes of the scholars, depicted in paint and gazing down from their heavenly perch, watching the intruder who had awakened them. Like a pool of shimmering fire, the marble floor guided her forward, beckoning her down the puzzling hall.

'Come on,' whispered Gogin, annoyed. 'He'll be in the catalogue room.'

Mirage snapped back to reality. 'What's that?'

'It doesn't matter. Just follow me.'

He continued on as Mirage followed, deeper through the hall, the entrance falling back behind them. The columns along the way shrouded them with shadows, creating a maze of dimly lit alcoves and unseen hazards. Gogin, who clearly knew the way, ignored the frightful visages, walking quickly through the giant corridor. Then, like he'd hit a wall, he stopped. Mirage stopped behind him, focusing her eyes on the darkness ahead. She gasped when she saw the figure. Gogin stuttered a feckless greeting.

'My lord, I'm sorry,' he said quickly. 'I've brought this woman here. She says she knows you . . .'

The man in shadows held up a silencing hand. His eyes, the only thing truly visible, fell on Mirage like glowing jewels. Mirage felt all her bravado slip away under his withering gaze. Of all the tales she had heard of him, none had prepared her for the truth.

'Thorin . . .'

Thorin Glass stood like a statue in the corridor, a terrible shadow of the man he had been. His left arm glistened, the living metal of the armour making flesh out of the air. His thin face, boney now and ripped with lines, grimaced like a mask, twisting when he saw her. His brow raised over his troubled eyes, filling with surprise. His mouth opened, but he did not speak. He simply watched her in amazement.

Mirage took a step toward him, trying to smile. Like a cancer, the Devil's Armour had savaged him, but she warned off her pity, knowing he would read her in an instant.

'Thorin, it's me,' she said gently. 'Mir—' She stopped herself. 'Meriel.'

'My lord, this woman insisted she be brought to you,' Gogin explained. 'She says she is from Jador.'

'Go,' Thorin ordered, not looking at the soldier.

The simple command was enough to send him scurrying. Without a good-bye or wish of luck, Gogin left Mirage, fleeing back down the gloomy corridor. Silence swarmed in after him. Thorin stood, unmoving, blinking in disbelief. Instead of anger or glee, pain filled his countenance.

'Meriel . . . why?'

'I've come to see you, Thorin,' said Mirage. Throughout the long ride to Koth, she had rehearsed what she would say to him, but her practiced words fled her mind.

'But why?' he asked again. 'Where's Lukien?'

'I don't know,' she lied with a shrug. 'He left me. I've been on my own ever since.' She took another step toward him. 'That's why I'm here, Thorin. I have nowhere to go.'

'You're alone?' Thorin leaned closer. 'And still with your new Akari. I had forgotten how beautiful you are now.'

Mirage couldn't help herself. His tenderness struck her hard. 'Thorin, what's happened to you?' she sighed. 'You've changed. You look so different, so much older.'

Embarrassed, he turned his face away. 'I'm ugly now. Please – don't speak of it.'

'It's the armour,' she said flatly. 'It's devoured you, just like Minikin said it would.'

He put up his hands. 'Stop.'

Undeterred, Mirage stepped closer. As the light struck his face she could see the deepness of the damage, the almost demented look of his eyes, the thin curl of his lips. 'Thorin . . .' She shook her head, unable to hide her pity. 'Look at you.'

She reached out to touch him, but his armoured arm rose up, clenching around her wrist with its ice cold gauntlet.

'No,' he hissed. 'I'm not a wounded dog, Meriel. And you had your chance to love me once.'

'I came to help you.' She did not pull free of his iron grip, but instead very calmly said, 'You're hurting me, Thorin.'

He released her at once.

'You're here to talk me free of the armour,' he chuckled. 'You forget yourself, girl. The armour's made me invincible.'

'Thorin, no. It's made you a monster. I can see it in you!'

Thorin reared back, but it was a new voice this time that shook the hall.

'She lies!' came the cry, with so much force it staggered Mirage backward. She looked at Thorin, then at the air beside him, shimmering. Pulling itself free of Thorin came another figure, shrouded and wavering, more like a ghost than a man. Its fierce face snarled hatefully at Mirage as it separated from its host, ripping free with a wail from Thorin. 'You're an imp,' accused the figure. 'A sniveling little slut here to blind him.'

Mirage steadied herself, stunned by the sight of the spirit. Instantly she knew it was Kahldris. The Akari pinioned her with his fiery eyes, pointing a bony finger.

'She has an Akari, Baron,' he spoke. 'She comes in disguise!'

'She is a friend,' Thorin gasped, clearly weakened. 'Her Akari keeps her well.'

Kahldris smiled in discovery. 'Her Akari is a mask.' He drifted closer. 'I can see the ugly truth behind it.'

'Keep away from her,' ordered Thorin. 'I already know the truth.'

Kahldris paused. 'I want to see for myself.'

'Get away,' hissed Mirage, backing off from the demon. Inside she could feel Kirsil's terror. Kahldris lifted his hands, reaching out for her. 'No!'

He was on her before she could move, dropping over her, smothering her, his immutable hands cupping her face, pulling Kirsil from her like the way he himself had torn free of Thorin. Mirage heard herself scream, heard too the awful cry of Kirsil as their bodies ripped apart. The Akari – *her* Akari – faltered, losing grip on the hold between them. Past Kahldris she should could see Thorin, his mouth hung in shock, and above her the struggling form of Kirsil writhing toward the ceiling. Kahldris stood triumphant in his rape, holding a handful of Mirage's hair and dragging her toward Thorin.

'Look and see the *true* Mirage,' he demanded. 'Look at this hideous creature.'

Mirage buried her face in her hands, crying out for Kirsil. She could feel the spirit's battle to reach her through the powerful wall Kahldris erected between them. She struggled against Kahldris' grip, but it was Thorin who rescued her, bounding forward and pulling her free of the demon.

'Leave her!' he bellowed, shielding her in his arms.

'Kirsil!' cried Mirage. Overhead, the girl Akari floated helplessly.

'Why don't you look at her, Baron Glass?' goaded Kahldris jealously. 'Before you fall for her charms, look at her ugliness.'

'I have seen her,' spat Thorin. 'Bring back her Akari – now!'

Kahldris shook with rage. 'She's not here to help you!'

'Do it, beast!'

Kahldris looked disgusted as his eyes met Mirage's. Then, just as quickly as he had appeared, he vanished from the dark hall, leaving Mirage shuddering in Thorin's arms.

'Don't look at me,' she pleaded, hiding her face.

'It's over,' said Thorin. 'Your Akari has returned.'

It *was* over. Mirage could feel Kirsil again, part of her once more. Yet somehow she could not bring herself to face Thorin or show her lovely mask to him. The ordeal, over in mere moments, had shaken her. How easily Kahldris had torn away her magic!

'He's gone,' Thorin assured her. 'Meriel, look at me . . .'

Finally, Mirage brought up her eyes. Thorin was smiling at her. He looked exhausted, like a beaten dog, but he had saved her.

'You're the only one who can understand,' he told her. 'I'm glad you've come. I need you . . . Mirage.'

43

Lukien rode his horse along the narrow road. Karoshin rode a donkey. The old priest led the way without saying a word, fully expecting Lukien to follow him. The day was hot and Lukien was irritated, and as he rode he cursed himself for agreeing to the journey. With no one else for company, the pair had ridden most of the afternoon, and Lukien could tell by the lengthening shadows that dusk would soon be falling. They would not make it back to the palace before sundown, but Karoshin seemed unconcerned. Up ahead, the mountains loomed high and fore-boding. Snow capped the tallest peak, a colossal tyrant of a mountain rising up among its brothers. It was called the House of Sercin, and it was the first thing Lukien had noticed about Torlis when he had first seen the city from Akhiir's little boat. It had captivated him then, and in the months since he had thought about the mountain often. It was where the Great Rass was said to dwell. Still, he had no idea why Karoshin had insisted on taking him there today.

For Lukien, the last few weeks had passed in a fugue. Since the death of Jahan, he stopped training Lahkali entirely, keeping to himself in the chamber they had once shared, venturing out only at night to walk the grounds of the palace alone. It was he who was responsible for Jahan's death, and though he had avenged his friend by slaying the rass, there was nothing he could do to turn back the clock and return the gentle villager to life. His entire mission in Torlis seemed pointless now, because he had found no clues to the Sword of Angels and because he knew – knew – that Lahkali had no chance at all against the Great Rass.

The young Eminence had given Lukien time to grieve. She had scolded him severely upon his return from Amchan, but that was all. Master Niharn made his apologies, convincing Lahkali that he and Lukien were only doing what was necessary. Surprisingly, Lahkali had cried upon the news of Jahan's death. Though the two of them rarely spoke, they had formed a strange understanding.

'All right, Karoshin, enough now,' Lukien grumbled. 'We've gone far enough. Tell me why.'

'We are not there yet,' called the priest over his shoulder.

'Then we should have left earlier! Karoshin, it'll be dark soon.'

'Dark? Yes,' said Karoshin. 'Do not be afraid, Lukien.'

'You stubborn old fool, I'm not afraid. Just tell me where we're going.'

'To the mountains. That should be obvious.'

Convinced the old man was vexing him on purpose, Lukien bit back his insults. Karoshin had not told Lukien to bring anything but himself on the trip, but the priest's own mount was laden with saddle bags, a sign that Lukien took as trouble. He had resisted the journey but Karoshin had been determined, and in the end Lukien didn't really think he could refuse. He was still a guest in Torlis, after all, and priests like Karoshin held the power.

The road to the mountains snaked alongside the holy river. Here, the river rushed in a torrent, pouring down from the snow-laden peaks. In the lore of Torlis, the blood of the Great Rass would turn the river red, feeding the land for years to come. But that would mean killing the rass . . .

Lukien shook this thought from his mind. He had done his best, hadn't he? And all his efforts had only made for a muscular Lahkali. The girl queen had continued her training without him, practicing every day in the courtyard of the palace just as he had taught her. He had seen her on occasion, expertly wielding the katath Aliz Nok had made for her, once again under the tutelage of Niharn. The old fencing master had many tricks to teach her, but Lukien knew they would not be enough. No one could fight a rass and win, not without years of training like the Jadori or the gift Lahkali's lineage carried in their blood. Or, perhaps, a magical amulet to keep them alive. Lahkali's cause was hopeless, and despite his promise to the girl to never give up, Lukien had surrendered the moment Jahan had died.

They traveled on for nearly an hour more, until at last they reached the foot of the mountains. Here, the trail petered off, surrendering to the rocks. The air grew cooler, too, and from where they stood Lukien could see the far-off city below them. At the end of the trail, a campsite had been cleared away, all of the rocks and brush set aside for travelers like themselves. To Lukien, it looked like the camp had been used many times over the years, though not for a very long time. He sat upon his horse, wondering why they had traveled so far. Above, the towering House of Sercin swallowed them in shadows.

'What's this?' asked Lukien. 'Why are we stopping?' He groaned as a dreadful thought entered his mind. 'Don't tell me we're going up there.'

Karoshin shook his head. Night was coming quickly, and the old priest

looked anxious, as though about to reveal a secret. The serpent tattoo he
bore bulged on his neck as he craned for a view of the holy mountain.

'What are you looking for?' Lukien asked. 'Not the rass, I hope.'

'Get down from your horse, Lukien,' said the priest. 'We will stay
awhile.'

'That's what I was afraid of.'

With a sigh of surrender Lukien dismounted, tying up his horse on an
outcropping of rock. Very soon it would be dark, but he already guessed
they would not be riding back until morning. Lukien supposed a surprise
was coming, or worse, a lecture. He also supposed that he deserved one,
and couldn't help but grin.

'All right, Karoshin, we're here,' he pronounced. 'Now . . . why?'

Karoshin kept his eyes on the peak of the tall mountain. With the sun
going down, the whole horizon began turning a blazing orange. They
would need a fire soon, and food, too, but Karoshin appeared
unconcerned. Something about the mountain fixated him.

'Stay, Lukien, don't look away,' said Karoshin softly.

Lukien followed his gaze skyward. 'What are we looking for?'

'You'll see.'

Intrigued, Lukien continued watching the peak. The House of Sercin
swept the range with majesty, so much taller than its brethren. At its
pinnacle Lukien could see clouds gathering, willowy mists swirling almost
invisibly around the pointed rocks and snow. They moved like spirits,
almost alive, circling unnaturally around the frozen summit. In the pale
light of the dying sun, the clouds began to shimmer.

'Look,' spoke Karoshin. 'Look . . .'

The clouds began to mingle, intensifying in their brightness, sparking
with light as the orange of the horizon caught them, setting them ablaze.
Lukien gasped, stunned by the fireworks as the rolling mists intensified.
For a brief, wonderful moment the land beneath the mountains glowed,
and in its heat Lukien smiled, mesmerized. And then, like a candle flame,
it vanished. The crimson twinkle eroded, but the clouds remained,
forming a darkening ring around the mountain peak.

'What was that?' asked Lukien breathlessly.

'A sign,' replied Karoshin. He was smiling. 'It's begun, Lukien.'

Lukien asked, 'What has?'

'The Great Rass, Lukien. That is the sign. Do you remember? When the
clouds gather around the mountain top, Sercin will return.'

'You mean that? I thought you meant clouds, real clouds! Those aren't
clouds, Karoshin.' Lukien looked up again, amazed. 'Those are like
spirits.'

There seemed no other way to describe them, because to Lukien they
looked alive, like angels holding hands as they danced around the

mountain top. The light had gone out of them but the mists remained, circling in perfect time around the place where Sercin dwelt. A thrill ran through Lukien. In all his days in Torlis he had heard the tales of the Great Rass, listening as a sceptic. Now, though, he believed.

'You brought me all this way to see that,' he whispered. 'I should probably thank you.'

Karoshin nodded. 'It is too far from the city to see,' he explained. 'You would see the light, but not the real beauty. And I wanted you to see the beauty. Do you understand, Lukien?'

'I think so. I've been a very poor teacher lately.'

'You've grieved enough,' said Karoshin. 'Now you must stop.' He pointed up at the mountain. 'Sercin has come, Lukien. Soon he will become the Great Rass. Soon Lahkali must slay him.'

'I know,' said Lukien. He looked around at the campsite, then at Karoshin's donkey. 'You brought supplies for the night. Is this where we're staying.'

The priest grinned. 'It is time to talk, Lukien.'

Karoshin had never been much for words, and so did not engage Lukien until long after the sun had set. He had done almost all the work in camp as well, making the fire himself and cooking the food, then gathering the metal cups they had used and taking them to the river for washing. It had all been part of his plan, Lukien knew, to make the mood between them easy and loosen Lukien's tongue. At first Lukien had resisted the notion of spending the night at the base of the mountain, but soon he saw the logic in Karoshin's plan, and admitted to himself that it was good to be out of the palace and away from the reminders of his dead friend.

Long after sundown, Karoshin finally settled down, making a pipe for himself by stuffing it with tobacco and lighting it with a twig from the fire. Lukien, already stretched out by the camp fire himself, watched curiously as the old man blew some rings. The habit struck Lukien as odd, because he had never seen a pipe of such strange design and because he had never seen the priest relax. Karoshin gave a contented sigh as he inhaled deeply and held it, letting the smoke dribble contentedly out of his nose. The night was wonderfully quiet, and reminded Lukien of the long trips he used to take in the desert around Jador, when he was on patrol against Aztar's raiders. Those had been moments of great peace for Lukien, at least when he wasn't fighting. He missed Jador now and everything about it. Karoshin, sensing his mood, nodded at Lukien.

'What are you thinking, Lukien?'

Lukien answered without hesitation. 'About home.'

'Which home? You have so many.'

'Sad, isn't it? You're right, though. I was thinking about Jador.'

Karoshin nodded. 'Tell me.'

'Oh, it's a fine place,' said Lukien. 'A beautiful city, or at least it was before the wars. Fine people, too, full of character and heart.'

'Desert people,' said Karoshin knowingly. 'They are like that.' His eyes crinkled. 'Like Jahan.'

'Yeah . . .'

'You should talk about him. You will feel better if you do.'

'I think about him all the time, Karoshin.' Lukien pulled a stick from the fire, watching its burning tip. 'He was such a simple man. All he wanted was to come and help me. He thought he owed me a life debt and he wanted to see Torlis. The Red Eminence! That was all he ever talked about.'

'Ah, so you gave him his wish, then,' said Karoshin.

'No. I killed him.' Lukien blew out the stick and tossed it back into the flames. 'I shouldn't have taken him with me. I should have known the danger. It was stupid.'

'You could never have left him behind. Jahan would have gone with you anyway. He was that kind of man. Loyal.'

Lukien nodded. 'He was loyal. He believed everything I told him, even though he thought I was some kind of savage sometimes.' The memory made Lukien laugh. 'And he taught me things! I don't think I would have made it this far without him.'

'But you have made it, Lukien, see?' Karoshin nudged Lukien with his foot. 'Listen to me, now – you have made it. You have come this far.'

'Yes, but for what?' Lukien argued. 'I came to find the Sword of Angels. And I'm no closer to it than the day I got here. Karoshin, I think it's time for me to leave.'

Karoshin's face was placid. 'Oh yes?'

'Yes. I've thought about it and it's time. I'll never find the sword and Lahkali won't ever give it up. I thought—'

Lukien stopped himself, then saw Karoshin looking pleased with himself.

'You thought that Lahkali would tell you the hiding place of the sword. Of course you thought that. She is just a young girl, and you are so clever.'

'No, that's not right . . .'

'It is what you thought. It was obvious, Lukien, and Lahkali knew that the moment you promised to help her.'

'But she let me help her anyway?'

'She is stronger that you think. The secret of the sword is very dear to us. I have to confess that I was afraid for her. Not that I thought she would just tell you what you wanted to know. But you are much bigger than she is, and you did spent a lot of time alone with her.'

'What are you saying?'

Karoshin sighed as though it were obvious. 'You could have hurt her to get what you wanted, but you did not because you are not that kind of man. I know that now.'

'Thank you for that, Karoshin,' said Lukien. 'But it's not important now. I've failed. I failed Jahan and all my friends. If the sword is here, I'm never going to find it.'

'So you're leaving?'

'I don't see that I have much of a choice! All of this has been a waste. And my friends still need me. I have to go.'

'And forget your promise to Lahkali? Maybe you did not want any of this, Lukien, but it is yours now. It is your responsibility to help Lahkali because that is what you promised her you would do.'

'I know, but it's not that way anymore. I fought a rass now. I know what it's like. Lahkali doesn't have a chance.'

The old priest's expression darkened. 'Don't ever tell her that. Not ever. She must believe in herself. Even Niharn knows that now. He has taken over her training because you have abandoned her.'

'Karoshin—'

'She's going to fight the Great Rass, Lukien. She's going to do it soon, and she needs your help.'

'But she doesn't have a chance,' said Lukien angrily. 'If she goes she'll be killed.'

'And if she doesn't go then everything else will be killed.' Karoshin bit down hard on his pipe. 'So she's going.'

'And I'm going too,' Lukien grumbled. 'I'm going home. You wasted your time bringing me here, Karoshin. Yes, the clouds were pretty. Thanks. But it doesn't change anything. No one can train Lahkali to kill the rass. Niharn was right the first time.'

It took a lot to ruffle Karoshin's feathers, but this time Lukien had done it. The serpent tattoo on his neck pulsed venomously. A storm brewed on his usually docile face. Lukien braced himself for an argument. Karoshin pulled the pipe from his mouth, ready to speak, but then said nothing. He took a breath to ease himself.

'I brought you here because I thought seeing the clouds would change your mind,' he said. 'I thought once you knew that Sercin had come . . .' He shrugged. 'But you are right. This is our problem. We should deal with it ourselves. An outsider should not be our saviour.'

More than anything the priest had said, that last bit hurt. But Karoshin gave Lukien no chance to reply. He rose and walked away to finish his pipe alone. Now the solitary fire sputtered, making Lukien stare into it. He had not wanted to hurt the old man, but his logic seemed perfect to him. He grieved for Lahkali, because she would surely die fighting the Great Rass. Karoshin was right about one thing – Lahkali was strong.

Lukien reached beneath his shirt and felt the Eye of God. Calling upon its magic had been the only way to save himself against the rass. The arrogant spirit inside the amulet still kept him alive for a reason Lukien could never quite fathom, allowing him to speak to Lahkali's people without even knowing their tongue. Lukien took the Eye from his chest and examined it. It was a remarkable thing, but he hated it. He had already lived far too long.

At the other side of the camp, Karoshin quietly smoked his pipe.

44

Jazana Carr returned to Koth three days earlier than expected. Her trip to the border was successful, mostly, but the bad news she had got from her loyalists soured the whole ride home. To Jazana, home now was Koth, and not the badlands of Norvor or her fortress at Hanging Man. Though she longed to return there, her place these days was with Thorin, and it was her love for the Black Baron that drew her back to him against the pleas of her dukes.

Jazana rode in silence, choosing a horse of her own for the long ride rather than a gaudy litter. Rodrik Varl rode beside her, in command of the hundred or so soldiers who had escorted them to the border. Sensing her poor mood, Rodrik remained as quiet as Jazana, allowing her time to think and collect herself before reaching Lionkeep. His face broke with sweat in the afternoon sun. The avenues around the royal residence filled with people as the news spread of the Diamond Queen's return. Jazana fixed a practiced smile on her face, waving to the folks who had come out to greet her. Mostly they were soldiers like Rodrik, but also a sprinkling of curious Liirians as well, who very rarely saw the woman who had conquered their nation and brought the frightening Baron Glass to the throne. Careful to seem approachable, Jazana grinned and waved her way along the avenue, graciously accepting the few flowers or baubles the bravest townsfolk offered her. Up ahead, she saw Lionkeep waiting and secretly groaned at the thought of a soft bed. She had been in Andola for only two days, but the ride there and back had taken more than a week, and her whole body ached with the effort of the trip.

Thorin had not wanted her to go to Andola, but he had not forbidden it either, and Jazana had been anxious to meet with her dukes, that hand-picked lot of loyalists she had put in charge of the major Norvan provinces. At her request they had come from miles for the meeting, all with the same bad news, and all begging her to return to Norvor at once. Jazana had done her best to pacify them. In the grand castle of the vanquished Baron Ravel, she told her dukes and counts that Thorin was still consolidating his hold over Liiria, and that he still had plans to deal with Elgan and take back Carlion, the Norvan capital. Whether or not they believed her, Jazana simply couldn't say. They were loyal, for now, and Elgan had yet to move against any of the northern cities. That alone gave Jazana solace. She blew a kiss to a teenaged boy, waving at her from the street, trying to put the worst of the trip from her mind.

'Jazana, we should stop here,' Rodrik Varl suggested. The dust from the road had made his brogue particularly thick. 'Don't hide from the Liirians. Let them see you.'

'They see me well enough.'

Varl shook his head. 'They love you, see? And they don't love Thorin.'

'Hush,' Jazana snapped at him. 'Watch what you're saying.'

'These people need you, that's what I'm saying. Look how glad they are to see you! Because they're afraid and they know you're not like him.'

It was true, but Jazana chose not to acknowledge the point. As word continued to spread of her arrival, more and more Liirians began to fill the avenue, relieved to see the sane half of the throne back safely. The pressing crowd made her more determined than ever to reach Lionkeep, however, and as they rode Jazana increased her pace, urging her horse onward. Her exhausted mercenaries kept up without grumbling, and by the time they reached the gates of Lionkeep the crowds had fallen away. Lionkeep itself was a rolling tor of green lawn and flowers, an ancient keep kept away from the busy streets of the rest of the city. As the gates opened for the returning queen, quietude swept in after her. Lionkeep lay at peace before her, its courtyard moving with efficient servants and lazily trotting horses. Varl called the company to a halt, letting them dismount and dismissing them. Behind her, Jazana listened as the gate of Lionkeep close shut behind her.

'Thank the heavens,' she sighed.

As was customary, a groom came forward to help her down. Jazana took the man's hand and daintily slipped from her saddle. Varl tossed himself down beside her, shouting orders to his weary men. Jazana ignored him, eagerly scanning the courtyard for Thorin. She had sent word to her lover of her early arrival. Though she didn't really expect to see him, she nevertheless felt crestfallen at his absence. The groom, a middle-aged Rolgan named Fellors, noted her disappointment. She had installed Fellors herself in his position, wanting people she could trust around her and Thorin. He had been with her in Hanging Man for years, and could read her moods instantly.

'So? Where is he?' Jazana asked. 'No, let me guess. He's at the library. Again.'

Fellors coloured as he took hold of her horse. 'No, my lady.'

'No?'

The groom grew circumspect. 'Uhm, no.'

Jazana stepped into his face. 'What are you hiding Fellors? Tell me or I'll cut your tongue out.'

Fellors barely flinched. He had been with Jazana long enough to know her moods, and over the years Jazana had threatened him with far worse. Still, he remained aloof, as if searching for just the right way to give her bad news.

'Baron Glass is with someone, my lady,' he said. 'He's gone riding.'

'Riding? With who?'

'A woman, my lady.' Fellors looked at Varl, who had overheard their conversation and now stepped beside his queen. 'She arrived here a few days ago. An old acquaintance of the baron. From Jador.'

Jazana felt her heart trip. Speechless, she could barely even breathe. She turned away from Fellors, hiding her face, which she knew must look pained.

'What woman from Jador?' asked Rodrik. 'What's her name?'

'Mirage is her name,' said Fellors. 'I don't know much else about her.' He paused, and Jazana could feel his eyes on her. 'I'm sorry, my lady.'

Jazana pulled down on her riding shirt and straightened herself. 'When did they leave?'

'An hour ago. A little more, maybe. The baron didn't say when he'd be back.'

'No,' Jazana growled. 'Of course not.'

Her mind raced with possibilities, all of them ugly. Thorin never spoke of his time in Jador, nor of any woman he had met there, but Jazana had a fine imagination, and now it ran away with her. The old jealousy wriggled insider her, making her burn. And the only thing she could think of was how many times Thorin had ignored her of late. Yet somehow, he had managed to find time for this Jadori slut.

'Jazana? Do you know this woman Mirage?' asked Rodrik.

Jazana rumbled, 'No. But I'm going to wait right here until I see them both.'

The first thing Thorin saw when he rode into the courtyard was Jazana. Stone-faced, she sat on a wooden chair within the shade of Rodrik Varl, who stood coolly and loyally beside his queen. It had been an excellent afternoon, and Thorin was in a fine frame of mind, but the daggers that shot from the Diamond Queen's eyes instantly killed Thorin's joy. Next to him, Mirage was riding and laughing, happy from the long trip they had made through the orchards. She had been with Thorin for three days now, lifting him from the darkness of despair with only her patience and her pretty face. Her presence had worked magic on Thorin, just like a charm, just like he knew it would. No one in Koth or anywhere else outside of Jador knew what it was like to have an Akari, and Mirage had spent long hours talking with Thorin, listening to him, caring for him in ways that Jazana never could. Now, though, the bliss of the last few days fell on Thorin like a rainstorm. He drew back his horse, bringing it to a stop and telling Mirage to do the same. As his mount whinnied backward, Jazana stood and crossed her arms over her chest.

Mirage stopped talking, seeing Jazana at once. Her smile disappeared. 'Who's that? Jazana Carr?'

Thorin nodded. 'She wasn't supposed to be back yet. Damn.'

Mirage sat up with a grimace. 'Should I go?'

'No.' Thorin started trotting forward again. 'She's not my keeper. Come and meet her.'

'I don't think so . . .'

'Come on,' Thorin ordered, and with all the innocence he could muster rode up to where Jazana was standing and looked down on her. 'Jazana? You're back already?'

'I'm sorry, Thorin,' purred Jazana icily. 'I didn't mean to interrupt your fun.' Her gaze fell on Mirage, and for a moment she looked stunned. 'And look at this beauty!'

'This is Mirage,' said Thorin. Sure he had nothing to hide, he bade Mirage forward. Mirage cautiously trotted her horse into view.

'My lady, I'm pleased to meet you,' she said, her voice shaky. 'It is an honour.'

'Is it? How wonderful for you.'

'Jazana . . .'

'Stop talking, Thorin,' Jazana hissed. 'I'm tired of your lies and all your ridiculous promises. I'm glad you weren't here to greet me after my long ride from Andola. It gave me time to think.' Jazana smiled up at Mirage. 'Mirage. What a pretty name! And such a lovely young thing. Have you been enjoying yourself? Thorin is quite a lover, isn't he?'

Mirage blanched and reared back. Thorin rushed to her defense.

'Keep your tongue, woman,' he growled. 'Mirage is no whore. She came to help me. She's from Jador.'

'Oh, a friend,' sighed Jazana. 'How sweet. Tell me, Mirage, how will you help him? He likes his back rubbed. You can start with that before you bed him.'

'That's enough!' Thorin got down from his horse, towering over Jazana and eyeing Varl sharply. 'You, take her inside,' he ordered. 'Mirage, go with Varl.'

Mirage hesitated. 'Thorin? Are you sure?'

'He won't do anything to you,' Thorin promised. He turned to her, smiling, and helped her down from her horse. 'Please, just go with him. Jazana and I must talk.'

Varl looked at Jazana. She nodded, releasing him. With only a passing glance at Thorin, Varl came forward and touched Mirage's shoulder, leading her away. Thorin and Jazana both waited until they were alone before saying anything more. Thorin fought down his anger, flexing the fingers of his enchanted gauntlet. In his mind he could feel Kahldris' displeasure. The Akari still distrusted Mirage, and had not approved at all of Thorin's time with her. More importantly, he warned Thorin everyday about the danger of alienating Jazana Carr.

Calm her, Baron, whispered Kahldris. *You still need her.*

It was advice Thorin did not need. He knew he needed Jazana and her fortune. More importantly, he loved her, and that was something Kahldris could never understand. He studied Jazana's face, hoping for an inch of comfort, but her icy façade remained, and the storm in her eyes didn't fade.

'Will you walk with me?' he asked.

'Why should I?'

'Because I have asked it of you,' said Thorin. He took her arm. 'Please.'

Jazana relented, but brushed off his touch. 'Go on, then.'

With a grunt of displeasure Thorin led the way, heading to a more secluded part of the courtyard, away from the curious servants and soldiers spying on them. He located a place near a stand of willow trees, properly shaded and invitingly secluded. Jazana followed him, her lips twisted in a pout. By the time they reached the willows she was eager to speak.

'Tell me who she is, Thorin,' she demanded. Again she folded her arms. 'And please don't tell me she's a friend. Men don't have friends that look the way she does.'

Thorin thought for a moment, unsure how to answer. He had never told Jazana much about his time in Jador, though she had already guessed at a lot of it. She knew there was magic in Jador and that his armour was part of that magic. Amazingly, she had accepted it.

'She *is* a friend,' said Thorin. 'She's from Jador, and that's not something I can explain to you. She's one of the people who understands the magic of my armour, the kind of strength I have.'

'What's she doing here?' asked Jazana. 'Why has she come to Koth?'

'To see me. To help me.' Thorin had trouble not looking away. 'She knows about the Devil's Armour. She thinks it is harming me, Jazana.'

For the first time Jazana's ire lifted. 'She's right, Thorin.' She looked around, and her voice dipped. 'I've told you this already, a dozen times.'

'And she's wrong, just as you are wrong, Jazana. I've tried to tell her this but she won't listen. She's convinced, as you are.' Thorin laughed. 'So you see? She's not your enemy, Jazana. You both are on the same side. The wrong side!'

Jazana didn't laugh. 'Look at you. You're happier than I've seen you in months. Are you telling me it's because you're just *talking* with that pretty young thing?'

'Yes! Jazana, you don't understand. You don't know what it means to have this magic, what it's like to carry it around and live with it. But Mirage – she knows. I can't tell you how or why, but she does. And when I talk to her . . .' Thorin glanced away. 'I feel better.'

Jazana looked pained by his confession. She, too, looked away. 'You love her.'

'No.'

'You do. You make time for her, you go riding . . .'

'To talk, Jazana, that's all.'

'Yet you shut me out every time I try to talk, Thorin.' Jazana stepped away a few paces, distracted by the low boughs of the willow trees. 'And now I come back and I have all this news to tell you, and I see you with that *girl*. And you're listening to her! You're riding with her, spending time with her . . .' Jazana shook her head. 'It's wrong.'

Thorin frowned. 'What's wrong? That I should speak with a woman?'

'You've ignored me, and everything I've wanted. It's enough now, Thorin. I'm going.'

'Going?'

'Back to Norvor,' said Jazana. 'I'm needed there, and I'm not needed here.'

Kahldris shot through the clutter of Thorin's mind. *No!*

'No, Jazana,' Thorin insisted. 'You can't go.'

'I have to. I can't wait any longer, Thorin. You've already broken your promise to me. I lied for you in Andola. I told all the dukes that you would soon ride to Carlion and deal with Elgan. That's a lie.'

Thorin felt stung. 'I can't go to Norvor, Jazana. I've told you.'

'Because you're waiting for the boy to come,' Jazana groaned. 'I know. So wait for him, then. Wait with your pretty new harlot and be happy. I'm going.'

'No,' flared Thorin. He took Jazana's arm forcefully. 'I forbid it.'

'I'm not your daughter!' snarled Jazana, tearing free of him. 'I'm the Queen of Norvor and I'm going home!'

'And what about all of this?' asked Thorin, sweeping his arm across Lionkeep. 'Look at what we've built! You're going to just abandon it?'

'What have we built, Thorin? Nothing! Your mad dream has only emptied my coffers and emboldened bastards like Elgan. He thinks Lorn is coming back. He's waiting for him right now! What happens if Lorn does return? What will you promise to do then?'

'Lorn won't ever return,' scoffed Thorin. 'He's gone forever.'

'And so is Carlion. It's gone, Thorin. Do you hear? My capital, gone!'

'I won't let you leave me, Jazana,' said Thorin evenly. He felt the power of the armour roiling through him, angering him. Then, in a calm voice, Kahldris was there to advise him.

No, Baron Glass. Sweet talk.

Thorin caught himself. Jazana was starting at him, looking afraid. He smiled.

'My love, listen to me,' he crooned. 'I know I've ignored you. I'm sorry. But Mirage isn't what you think. She's just a girl! While you . . .' He put his arms around her waist. 'You're a woman. The only woman for me.'

Jazana squirmed a little in his grip but soon relaxed, losing herself in his eyes. 'Thorin, stop,' she pleaded. 'I have to go.'

'No, Jazana, no,' he whispered. He kissed her. 'No . . .'

She bent to him, falling to his kisses, resisting only a little, giving off a string of whimpers. Her hands dropped limply to her sides.

'Stop it,' she sighed, turning her face away. 'You're in love with her.'

'I'm not,' Thorin promised. 'Just you, Jazana. Just you.'

Jazana gave herself to him, collapsing against his warm cheek. 'Take me away, Thorin. Take me somewhere else. Be alone with me.'

'Yes, my love, anything.'

'Just us, Thorin, all right? Just me and you. Just listen to me this once.'

'We'll go away, Jazana,' Thorin told her, pressing her close. It was real love he felt, he was sure of it. 'Just us.'

In the back of his mind Thorin glimpsed a flash of Kahldris, nodding happily.

45

The rains had come to Torlis, turning the sky to soup and the winding path up the mountain to mud. Through the steady drizzle of the day the sun struggled to light the way, up into the thinning air of Sercin's giant house. The morning had come and gone, dragging along a grey afternoon. A chilly breeze spun the clouds along the top of the holy mountain. Out of breath but determined, the four climbers paused to look up toward the peak, capped with snow that made rivers down the mountain's rocky face. Lahkali, dressed in red silk, led the way, her fist clenched around the katath the legendary Aliz Nok had made for her. She spoke not at all as she climbed, lost in doom-haunted thought. Behind her, Karoshin the priest and Niharn the fencing master kept pace, exchanging a few whispered observations. Far in the rear walked Lukien. Keeping his distance from the other three, the Bronze Knight watched Lahkali through the steady rain, admiring the courageous girl and considering the daunting task ahead of her.

They had left the palace the previous afternoon, riding for the mountain with a host of priests and warriors, all of whom remained camped at the bottom. Karoshin, Niharn and Lukien had been hand-picked by the Red Eminence to accompany her the rest of the way. It was a great honour, Lukien knew, but really just a ceremony. Soon Lahkali would leave them, breaking off to make the rest of the trek up the mountain alone. Alone, she would face the Great Rass.

It had not been hard for Lukien to stay. Karoshin had shamed him into seeing the truth. He had made a promise to the young leader, and in his life he had broken too many promises. This one, Lukien was determined to keep. He had done his best, and for that Lukien was pleased. Lahkali had turned into quite a scrappy fighter, good enough perhaps to join Jazana Carr's mercenaries. She lacked the instinct to kill, of course, but her body had been toughened and her mind focused, and as she silently climbed the mud-slicked mountain Lukien could tell that she had changed. She had been a girl when he'd first come to Torlis, but now she was truly the Red Eminence.

And today, she would almost certainly die.

Lahkali sensed this with a kind of reserved melancholy. Before leaving the palace, she had called the three of them to a special ceremony where tea was served and prayers were said, and where Karoshin had blessed her with the sign of Sercin. Like the priest himself, Lahkali now bore a serpent tattoo along her neck. According to practice all of her line before her had got such a tattoo before their first time facing the Great Rass. But more than the tattoo, all of her line had enjoyed the gift that Lahkali lacked, the one real weapon they took into battle against the serpent god. These days, Lahkali never spoke about the gift. She could do nothing to control the rass, and so had only her training and perfectly made katath to keep her alive.

Lukien knew they would not be enough.

He walked in silence, breathing hard like the rest of them, battling the rocks and mud and altitude. Beneath his damp coat and shirt, the Eye of God warmed him. Lately he'd been thinking long and hard about the amulet, and how it had kept him alive, sometimes against his will. When Minikin had given him the amulet, he had been staring death in the face. That was the first time he'd faced it, after his battle with Trager. The second was barely a year ago, when he'd fought Thorin. That was when the miracle happened.

Lukien trudged along, and as he did his thoughts were of Cassandra. Soon, if things went as he hoped, he might see her again.

Karoshin and Niharn had stopped talking by the time another few minutes passed. The old fencing master – who had become a friend to Lukien – looked back in surprise, urging Lukien to keep up. Lukien nodded and sped up a bit, though not enough to catch up with them. Master Niharn, who had taken over Lahkali's training while Lukien mourned for Jahan, had not changed his mind about the young Eminence's chances. He still put them at nil. Nevertheless, he had done his best, showing Lahkali all his tricks, staying up late with her to drill in the courtyard or in the forests beyond the palace. Because she respected him, and because she was grateful for his help, Lahkali had asked Niharn to join her on the mountain. The honour was not lost on the old man, who brought his own katath with him and vowed revenge on the Great Rass when it inevitably killed his ruler.

For Karoshin, though, it was a day of great joy. He was a priest of Sercin, after all, and now his mysterious god had taken form, coming to life as a serpent somewhere up on the mountain. As Karoshin climbed he seemed oblivious of the hard trek, never complaining, always bearing a peculiar smile. Unlike Lukien or Niharn, Karoshin refused to believe that

Lahkali had no chance at all. He was oddly confident in the girl, or at least pretended to be. Lukien supposed his confidence was for Lahkali's benefit, and for that reason he no longer questioned it.

But in his heart he knew the truth, and that was why he had made his decision. Lukien fingered the amulet beneath his shirt, touching its smooth gold and feeling the heat from its throbbing ruby. Because of the Eye he had survived against the rass that killed Jahan. Because of the Eye, he was immortal. But the artifact had done nothing to help him find the Sword of Angels, and the strange god within its metal remained silent and unhelpful, leaving Lukien to search like a blind man for the sword. For that, Lukien hated Amaraz more than ever. He would not miss the obstinate god at all.

At last Lahkali came to a stop. She turned to Karoshin, and the two shared a knowing look. Lukien quickly caught up with them. The land had flattened a bit, leaving a small trail winding up ahead. Above them lay a ridge, but beyond that Lukien could not see. At their feet the rivers of melting snow ran fast, swelled by the rains that had finally slowed to a stubborn mist. Niharn seemed to know why they had stopped. His face slackened. Lukien looked at him, then to Lahkali, who nodded at him.

'This is as far as any of you may come,' she said. Her voice remained remarkably steady. The katath in her hand did not tremble at all, yet in her eyes Lukien caught a faint hint of dread. 'Stay here. Wait for me.'

'We will wait, Lahkali,' Karoshin promised. 'We'll be the first to see the river turn. It will be wonderful.'

Niharn was rueful. 'Eminence, do not forget to drink the blood.'

Lahkali nodded. 'Of course.'

'Quickly, though,' added Niharn. 'Don't wait. Drink the moment the rass is dead.'

'I know,' said Lahkali impatiently. It was very unlikely she would ever get the chance to drink the serpent's blood, and being reminded seemed to irk her. 'If I can, I will.'

'You will,' said Karoshin. 'Just do not forget.'

Lahkali looked up into the sky, toward the spirit-like clouds still spinning around the mountain's pinnacle. They had all climbed so far, yet the clouds still remained tantalizingly out of reach. Lukien was grateful that the climb had finally ended. Much further and the cold would have made the trek more difficult.

'How much higher?' he asked.

Lahkali pointed to the ridge. 'Just up there.'

'How do you know the rass is there?'

'Because the Great Rass is always there,' said Karoshin with reverence. 'That is its lair.'

The statement chilled Lukien. He craned his neck for a better view, but

463

the ridge remained mostly out of sight, without the slightest hint of the rass. He paused, wondering how he should say good-bye to Lahkali or present his gift to her. He needed to prepare himself, yet the end had come so quickly.

'Rest first,' suggested Niharn. He glanced around for somewhere they could sit. 'I'll make a place for you, Eminence.'

Lahkali shook her head. 'I don't want to wait, Master. Now is the time.' She smiled at Niharn. 'Thank you for what you've done for me. I hope I was a worthy student.'

Master Niharn bowed, keeping his eyes to the ground. 'An old man has few such honours, Eminence.'

Next was Karoshin, who smiled warmly at Lahkali. Instead of bowing, he embraced her, kissing both of her cheeks. 'Remember,' he said as he traced his finger over her tattoo. 'You are the Red Eminence.'

Lahkali nodded, filled with emotion. She croaked a simple thank you to the priest, then turned finally to Lukien. Her pretty eyes sparkled.

'Lukien, I don't know what I can say to thank you,' she told him. 'You were a stranger. And now you are a friend.'

She was so young, and so willing to meet death. Lukien admired her.

'Wait,' he said. 'I have something you'll need.'

Reaching beneath his water-logged shirt, he pulled out the Eye of God. The others inhaled when they saw it, dazzled by its shining light. Lahkali shrugged, confused, studying the amulet spinning on its chain.

'Your amulet? I don't—' Then she gasped, understanding. 'Lukien, no.'

'It's the only way,' said Lukien. 'You can't defeat the rass without it, Lahkali. You know it. We all know it.'

Lahkali looked him in the eye. 'You'll die without it.'

'Maybe.' Lukien shrugged. 'I don't know. I've never taken it off before.'

'You do know,' Lahkali argued. 'I can't let you give it to me.'

'It doesn't matter if I die,' said Lukien. He gave a pleading smile. 'I haven't found the Sword of Angels, Lahkali. I've failed. And I'm tired. But if you fail then everyone else will die. The land will suffer and all of you will starve. You told me so yourself.' Still keeping the chain around his neck, he reached out for the girl's hand and placed it against the amulet. 'Please . . . let me do this.'

Lahkali angrily drew back. 'No! I know what you're doing, Lukien. You want to die. Jahan told me about your woman. You want to see her again.'

'And what if I do?' Lukien laughed. 'Don't I deserve it? Haven't I served enough gods and their whims? If I die I won't regret it, Lahkali. I'll have served you and your people and can go to death in peace.'

'Lukien, think a moment,' said Karoshin. 'What about your friends back across the desert? What will happen to them?'

'They don't need me, Karoshin. I've already failed them. Without the sword there's nothing I can do, and I can't find the sword.' Lukien spoke gently to Lahkali. 'Eminence, I was wrong about you. I thought if I helped you I could get you to break your vow and tell me where the sword is hidden. I'm sorry. You are made of much stronger stuff! I'm ashamed I even thought it of you. I'm not giving you this amulet for any other reason but to help you. I don't want a reward. You're right – by the time you come back I'll probably be dead.'

'And that's what you want?' asked Lahkali breathlessly. She was near tears now, her tall, strong wall finally crumbling. 'To die?'

Lukien grinned. 'No man wants to die, Eminence. But it's been so long since I've really *lived*. And I'm so tired of being alone.' Again he took her hand, gently placing it atop his amulet. 'I want you to take it . . .'

A thunder clap shook Lukien's mind. He staggered back, stunned, as an angry voice cried out in his head, splitting his skull in rage. Through his one good eye he saw Lahkali and the others staring at him. Lahkali was speaking, asking if he was all right. Lukien tried to keep his footing, but all at once he felt his body being lifted. The world turned orange, then a bright, sweeping white. Blinded by the glow, Lukien shouted, suddenly realizing he was being taken away. The violence of the light tore at him. His ears roared with noise, and for a moment he felt his insides coiling with pressure, as if a great, unseen fist had snatched him to carry him away. The others were gone, and all he could see was the rushing tides of light and wind, swirling up around him and pulling at his skin. He was flying now, up and into the great spreading light of his amulet.

Then, the noise ended. Lukien felt the ground turn firm beneath him. The light faded. He looked around in awe of his surroundings, remembering the place. Overhead was a ceiling, gigantic and soaring, with spirits in the rafters, looking down on him. The floor was stone, polished and smooth, the walls of the place alabaster. Lights and shadows mingled through the air. Lukien squinted to see ahead of him, bracing himself for what he knew he would see.

Out of the light formed a towering figure. Eyes of fire stared at Lukien from the ancient face. He was not a man but a deity, alive but long dead, with smoke for fingers and a chorus of lesser angels at his sides. He stood but had no legs, for light and mists obscured him, and when he rose up to his full height the spirits in the rafters fled. He was Amaraz, the spirit of the Eye. And when he spoke it was like storm.

'You're giving me away,' he bellowed, staring straight at Lukien through the haze. 'All my power and magic. To a girl.'

Lukien stood his ground, secretly delighted to at last be facing the Akari. 'So I have your attention!' he crowed. 'I should have known you'd try to stop me. What took so long, monster?'

465

Amaraz, friend to Minikin, looked puzzled and angry both. His enormous face floated closer to Lukien. 'The Eye of God belongs to you, but it is not yours to give away.'

'Oh, but it is,' said Lukien. 'It belongs to me, and as long as I give it willingly your power goes with it. You see, Amaraz? I remember all your little tricks. It's time for you to protect someone else now, someone who needs your help.'

'Do not give her the amulet,' Amaraz warned, shaking the walls around him. 'You are not done yet.'

'You mean you're not done with me, don't you? Sorry, Amaraz, but I'm done being your pawn.'

'The Devil's Armour still lives in your world!' thundered Amaraz. 'You must defeat it, and the demon who dwells inside it.'

'Yes, well, that would be very nice,' Lukien hissed, 'except that I have no idea how to find the Sword of Angels, and you're not helping me find it, are you?'

The great Akari looked regretful. 'You do not understand. Do you not remember? I said there is a way to defeat the armour, and so there is – you have only to find it.'

'How convenient for you,' snarled Lukien. 'Yes, that's very helpful, knowing there's a weapon but not knowing where to find it. You sent me here to the Serpent Kingdom. Tell me where to find the Sword of Angels!'

'I cannot,' said the spirit. His face shifted colours. 'It is yours to find, your destiny alone.'

The answer made Lukien irate. 'Do you see why I hate you? You are a cruel and terrible master, Amaraz, and I'm done with you. Lahkali needs your help to save her people. You're going to have a new host for a while. Get used to the idea.'

'I will not allow it,' said Amaraz.

'You have no choice! I wear the amulet. It's the one thing I have control over in my life. I wear it or I don't wear it. You can't stop me from taking it off.'

'And when you die, how will you help Baron Glass and the others? Have you thought of that?'

'I won't help them,' said Lukien. 'I haven't been any help at all to them. They won't miss me.' He stepped back from the spirit's fiery face. 'Now, send me back.'

For all his great power, Amaraz could not change Lukien's mind. His expression soured to remorse. 'You are not done yet,' he said.

'I don't care. I don't want to be a slave any longer. Send me back, Amaraz. Now.'

The great face turned away, and as it did Lukien felt the rush of wind and light again. Closing his eye, he waited for the magic to carry him back. This time, the wind was gentler, like the melancholy breath of Amaraz himself, and when at last he felt the ground reappear beneath his feet Lukien looked to see Lahkali just as he had left her. She was staring at him.

'Lukien? Are you all right?'

Lukien glanced at each of their faces, seeing the same amazement in them all.

'What happened?' asked Karoshin. 'You were here, and then you were not, but only for a moment.'

'Like you were asleep,' said Lahkali. Her face was troubled. 'Lukien?'

'I'm fine,' said Lukien. He was still holding out the Eye of God. 'Take it,' he told Lahkali. 'I know it will work for you.'

46

On the ridge below the peak of the mountain, a thousand years of wind and rain had carved catacombs into the rock. The ever-melting snow, dripping down from what seemed like the roof of the world, became gushing rivers in the rainy days of Spring, flooding the caves and turning ground loose and dangerous. Of all the countless, meandering catacombs, one stood out importantly from the rest, larger and grander than its ugly siblings, its mouth filled with tooth-like stalactites, its dark recesses thick with rolling mist. Just beyond its holy threshold, the world outside disappeared, devoured by the sounds of water and the hiss of rumbling vapour.

Lahkali entered the cavern knowing it was the one. There was no premonition in the decision. It was simply as Karoshin had described it – magnificent and unmistakable. As she crossed the ridge and stepped inside, she felt the warm breeze of unseen fires strike her face. The cavern glistened with green light, the incandescence of countless gem-stones glowing in the rock. Along the ground rushed a torrent of water, higher than Lahkali's ankles. Beneath it, her feet shuffled carefully across the gravelly floor. In both hands she held the katath out before her. The weapon trembled in her grip. She scanned the cavern without blinking. Her wide eyes caught every nuance of the place.

Beneath her rain-soaked gown of scarlet, the Eye of God pulsed against her chest. Looking down, she could see its red jewel behind the wet silk. She paused, trying to feel its unnatural power. The ruby burned against her skin, but that was all. Confused, she touched it with her hand, trying to summon the great god within its gold. Lukien had told her it would keep her safe, but Lahkali felt nothing, and now the warning the Bronze Knight had given came back to her quickly.

'You may feel nothing,' Lukien had told her. 'But when you need him, Amaraz will strengthen you.'

He had placed the amulet around her neck with his own hands, divesting himself of its power with an odd smile on his face. Together they had stared at each other, and Lahkali had watched the pain on his face as the old wounds crept back to claim him. Within minutes, he had been almost unable to stand.

'Go,' he had urged her. And she had. She had left him, and whether or not Lukien still lived Lahkali did not know. With tears in her eyes she had climbed the ridge, leaving him and the others behind to find the Great Rass. Now, touching the amulet, Lukien's kindness overwhelmed her.

'I'm here,' she told the spirit inside the Eye. 'Can you hear me?'

Her whisper echoed through the green haze, but the spirit of the amulet did not reply. Lahkali licked her lips. Her people were well-accustomed to spirits. It was a secret she had never shared with Lukien, or any other outsider. Because she herself had spoken to the dead, the thought of communing with the amulet's ghost did not frighten her. Rather, she was surprised not to hear its voice, not even silently, within her soul.

'Lukien tells me you are a great being,' she whispered, hoping to coax the spirit's trust. 'I need your help now, Amaraz. I know you're angry with Lukien, but he did what he thought was right. Will you help me, Amaraz?'

Amaraz did not reply. His silence unnerved Lahkali. She peered deeper into the haze, looking beyond the gems that twinkled along the rock walls. Beyond the mist was darkness, and from the darkness came the heat, like the breath of a dragon, striking Lahkali's face. She held tightly to the amulet, trying to glean some strength from it.

'I know you're inside,' she whispered. 'I know you are with me. The spirits of all my people are with me, too, Amaraz. I speak to them in the garden. Do you know that? Have you seen?'

She supposed there really were no secrets from a god like Amaraz, but if he had ever seen her in the story garden, he clearly had never told Lukien. She wondered why the spirit was so silent, not only to her but to Lukien as well. Her feet were leaden as she considered going further.

'Protect me, Amaraz,' she asked. 'I have to do this thing.'

Lukien felt the cold water running against his back, cooling the wound that bloomed like magic between his shoulders. The mud of the earth took away some of the pain, but the pain was growing now, coiling around him like the fingers of a giant. Fighting to control his shallow breathing, he imagined himself in a very different place, away from the cold rains of the mountain, back in the warm sands around Jador. He imagined the peace of the desert, and his heartbeat managed to slow. Overhead, he saw the troubled eyes of Karoshin, looking down over him the way a mother might a sick child. Next to the priest, Niharn knelt in the mud, staring peculiarly at Lukien. Niharn could not understand, but the sacrifice seemed to impress him. He nodded as Karoshin spoke, trying to comfort Lukien.

'. . . as soon as it is done. When you have the amulet back you will be well again, you'll see.'

Lukien only half heard Karoshin. The intensity of the wound on his back made listening difficult. He gulped the air, but somehow getting enough was impossible. He dug his fingers into the ground, feeling his nails scrape the stones. He was not afraid of dying, but death had not come the way he had supposed. He remembered now how Cassandra had died. Once the spell of the amulet was broken, her cancer had devoured her. Like an inferno, it consumed her. Lukien closed his eyes, searching for what had gone wrong. The wound along his back had been given to him by Trager. They had battled on a mountaintop and Lukien had won, cutting off his enemy's head and tossing it over the cliff side, but not before taking a mortal blow. Trager's blade had cut him deep, and when he collapsed Lukien had thought it would be his end, but then he had awoken, alive, with the Eye of God around his neck.

'What's happening?' he heard Niharn whisper. 'Why is he still alive?'

Karoshin shook his head. 'Lukien,' he asked gently. 'Is this right? Should it be this way?'

Lukien managed to raise his head, but Karoshin set it back down. 'No,' said the priest. 'Lay still. I'm sorry. Do not speak.'

Lukien grabbed his knee and dug his fingers into Karoshin's flesh. 'The spell,' he choked. 'The spell.'

Karoshin did not understand. 'All right,' he whispered.

'Breaking the spell killed Cassandra,' Lukien went on. 'That's it.'

In his frantic state of mind, he could think of no other answer. Though he no longer wore the Eye of God, the spell that had long protected him had not really been broken, the way it had with Cassandra. He had merely given the Eye away.

'That's it,' he gasped, laughing. 'But I die, Karoshin, to be sure!'

Karoshin's smile was kind. 'Stay awake, Lukien. Wait until Lahkali returns.'

'No . . .'

'You must,' said Karoshin. 'Why die?'

Lukien closed his eyes, and for a moment felt serene. 'To go to a better place . . .'

Deeper and deeper Lahkali went into the mountain, and the light of the gems did not diminish. Like torches they lit her way, beckoning her forward, urging her through the meandering cavern. No longer could she see the exit. Up above, the roof of the cave soared. She looked down and watched the water running past her feet, cold and crystal clear. And somehow, she was sure she had reached the Great Rass.

But Lahkali could not see the beast, nor could she hear or smell it either. She simply knew, because her fear took hold so deeply in her bones that her fingers ached and her tongue dried up. In her hands she held the katath, keeping it low the way Lukien and Niharn had taught her. In her lessons, she had learned how to bring it up quickly, thrusting that one, deadly thrust that might bring down the rass. She would have only one thrust, probably, because after that she would be dead.

'No,' she promised herself. 'I will not die today.'

Saying it strengthened her. She calmed herself. In her ears her heartbeat throbbed just a little quieter. It was, she realized, a majestic place, this House of Sercin, and like a tiny few before her she was going to face a god. The realization humbled her, and then the fear fled entirely. It was not so bad to die this way, in this place.

Lahkali walked on, slowly and in silence, picking her way carefully across the cavern. Her wide eyes scanned for any movement in the mist. Then, up ahead she saw the mists begin to part. A hot breeze spilled out from the gloom. She stopped herself, crouching low and ready, and waited. A shadow moved toward her, barely glimpsed. Lahkali strained to see. As the vapours ebbed, the green gems shined their light on the darkness ahead, revealing the rising figure of a hooded beast.

In the form of a serpent, Sercin still looked like a god. The creature made no sound as it slithered, its great head swaying hypnotically, its eyes filled with black, unblinking life. Its hood fanned out from the side of its head, swirling with colours that rifled along its scales. A creamy under-belly pulsed with breath. The rass stared at Lahkali, looking amused.

'Sercin . . .'

Sercin, the great god of Torlis, took his time contemplating the Eminence. Lahkali had seen rass before, many times, but they were so different from the thing that rose up now to face her. This rass – the Great Rass – gave her a look of intelligence and pleasure, as if it knew who she was and why she had come. The slits of its eyes fixed on her, unmoving, and Lahkali could not look away, even as the katath began to slacken in her grasp. On her chest, the Eye of God began to burn and flash, and the rass noticed this and grinned, its expression oddly curious. It was certainly the largest living thing Lahkali had ever seen, and yet she was not afraid of it. What she felt instead was awe.

'I am the Red Eminence of Torlis,' she declared. 'I've come for your blood, Sercin, to feed the land.'

Her voice sounded small. Sercin replied by opening his mouth and letting out his forked tongue. The long appendage curled unnaturally through the air, as if greeting Lahkali. In her mind she heard its cool, reptilian voice.

You are a child, and I cannot be beaten by a child. Go now, and bring a father or a brother to challenge me.

'I have no father and no brother to set against you, Great Rass. I say again – I am the Red Eminence.'

The serpent appeared disappointed. *You are a girl, and a tiny one. I could swallow you whole, like a bird.*

Lahkali nodded. 'That is right, but I have come prepared for you.'

Sercin's glowing eyes searched the amulet around her neck. *What is that you wear?*

'This is the Eye of God,' said Lahkali. 'It is magic, from a place far away. There is a god inside it, a god to protect me.'

Now Lahkali felt the serpent's enormous pleasure. *So then the challenge is real from you, girl. Summon your protector. Let me see him.*

'I cannot. But he is real, Sercin. He will keep me safe and I will kill you, and then your blood will feed the land.'

As it has always been, replied the rass. The scaly face looked satisfied. *I am ready to fight you.*

Lahkali drew a breath and brought up her weapon again. The Great Rass acknowledged her signal and tucked back its colourful hood. Then, like a cracking whip, it snapped toward her.

Karoshin watched Lukien's eyelids flutter as the whites of his eyes rolled back into his head. Lukien's body, still on the rocks, began to convulse and his throat let out a terrible wail. As consciousness at last slipped away, Lukien's face slackened. Thick red blood began to pool beneath him as the wound on his back opened, soaking though his wet garments. Karoshin, who along with Niharn had rolled Lukien onto his side, tore more of Lukien's shirt away as he inspected the wound.

It had come over him like magic, just as Lukien had said it would. At first it had only been a scar, but slowly it had opened, oozing blood and throbbing red around the edges. It was a clean wound, made by a expertly sharpened sword, cutting deep between Lukien's shoulder blades. Karoshin touched the wound lightly with his finger, then set his other hand atop Lukien's head, gently stroking his long blond hair.

'He dies,' said Niharn. The fencing master looked angry. 'This is stupid. Now they will both die.'

'Or Lahkali will live,' said Karoshin.

Niharn gave a grudging nod. 'It is not impossible.'

Beside them, Lukien's body started to shiver. He cried out again, lowly and with great effort, regaining a tiny hold on consciousness.

'The demon in the amulet should let him go,' Niharn growled. 'Look at this cruelty!'

'It is what he wanted,' Karoshin reminded him.

'It frustrates me.' Niharn studied Lukien's face with pity. 'Look – it is like he is dreaming. What is he seeing, do you think?'

Karoshin could not say.

It was only the fangs that Lahkali saw, like a blurring heading toward her. The head of the rass exploded forward, its mouth open wide, its long white teeth dripping venom. A rush of air blew Lahkali backward as she spun to avoid the darting head, which reached her in an instant then rose up fast to corner her. The voice of Sercin had left Lahkali's mind. She turned fast to keep the beast from her back. Her katath came up high for defense. The long body of the rass curled quickly around her, but she jumped, coming up with a roll on the other side. The cavern was giant, and Lahkali had room to move. So she ran.

The rass watched her, probed her, following her through the cavern without attacking. Lahkali reached a group of rocks and dived behind it. In an instant the rass was overhead, its tail to one side of her, its head coming around for another strike. Choosing the tail, Lahkali slashed to the left and freed herself, out in the open once again. The unscathed tail whipped quickly around to slither back behind the patient rass. The creature's head drew back, sizing her up. Lahkali raised her weapon. The yellowish scales of the serpent's underside caught her attention. There were the hearts, beating and ready.

Lahkali's twin blades twitched as she waited. With plenty of room, she bounced from one foot to the other, ready to spring. The rass came down fast, fangs bared, its long tongue darting out like an arm. Lahkali yelled and moved right, then slashed her blades across the hood, catching it and cutting it. As she spun away she heard the snake's painful hiss filling the cavern. Angrily it rose up, its black eyes glowing in disbelief. Aliz Nok's amazing blades had sliced easily through the serpent's flesh, making two deep rents that gushed bright blood.

You are fast, girl! complimented Sercin.

Hearing his voice made Lahkali's head swim. She struggled against its lulling tone. Already she was breathing hard, and all she had done was nick the beast. She had missed its breast entirely.

'Come and fight me!' she cried.

The rass obliged, balling its tongue into a tight fist and firing it forward. The blow caught Lahkali's chest, sending her sprawling. As she hit the ground the breath shot from her lungs. She rolled desperately to get away, scrambling through the water with her katath in one hand. Knowing she was vulnerable, she got to her feet and turned to see the Great Rass looking down at her. The strange tongue twisted in its mouth.

You are less than I hoped, said the rass. *Put your weapon down and I will end this for you. One strike. Death will come quickly.*

'No, I can't,' said Lahkali desperately. 'You have to fight me. I have to kill you!'

You cannot kill me.

'I must!'

The serpent's expression grew almost human, with a mix of anger and sorrow. It swayed confidently from side to side, watching Lahkali, sure in its ability to kill her. Lahkali stood her ground, prepared to run or strike or dance away – whatever was needed. Her knuckles were white around her katath. She realized with dread that the rass was blocking the way she had come.

But it didn't matter. She had come this far, and there really was no turning back. Lahkali raised her katath, knowing that this time there would be no running. This time, she had to fight.

'Amaraz!' she cried. 'Help me!'

The Eye of God flared, sending shards of red light through the chamber. The Great Rass hissed and thrashed its tongue, tasting the venom that dripped from its own fangs. Beneath the shadow of its spreading hood, young Lahkali summoned her courage.

This time the serpent came like thunder, screeching a hiss and tearing forward. Lahkali waited the split-second before the fangs were near, then stepped aside to work her blades. Expecting her to flee, the rass kept on, barreling into her katath. The hooked blades carved through its face and raked along its hood. Lahkali crossed to the side, lowered to a crouch, and watched the stunned creature lift its head. Blood gushed from the wound across its mouth. Its left eye popped with black ooze. Lahkali didn't wait. She sprang, unloading her katath with a scream and bounding for the serpent's breast. The weapon's blades found the beast's belly, going through its tough skin as easily as air. Lahkali held on, feeling the rass rise up, pulling her from her feet as an angry wail erupted from its throat. It's whole body rattled, shaking Lahkali loose. She fell, katath in hand, and looked up into the bruised eye of the Great Rass. From the wound in its gut came the most foul-smelling muck, a greenish-black jelly that rolled down its belly. Lahkali cursed, knowing she had not hit the beast's hearts.

There were no more words from the beast, no more of Sercin's playful voice in her head. There was only wrath. The long body of the snake snapped around Lahkali, quicker than a blink, wrapping around her and squeezing her instantly. She screamed, finding herself lifted again, locked in the powerful coils. Lahkali fought to hold on to her katath. Already blood filled her fingers as the pressure within her rose. Her head pounded as higher and higher the creature took her, bringing her face to face and licking its sabre-like fangs.

'Amaraz, please!' cried Lahkali. 'I can't hold on!'

The hot fire of the amulet burst with dazzling light. A new vigour flooded Lahkali's muscles. Flexing, she worked the fingers around her katath and straightened the weapon, poising it to strike. The hearts were high, she knew, just feet beneath the head. A little closer and –

Blackness. Lahkali screamed. Burning, spitting venom filled her face. Her eyes caught fire, filling with tears then the most unbearable pain. Blindness came quickly. Lahkali threw her head back, crying out for help. The skin around her eyes began to bubble.

Katath still in hand, she writhed blindly in the serpent's coils.

Lukien floated. Without a body, he swam effortlessly through a dark, warm sea, searching the endless horizon. Beneath him, somewhere in the world he had left, Karoshin and Niharn stood over him, watching with worry as the shell that had held him breathed its last, shallow breaths. But Lukien knew that he was dead, and the realization gave him peace. He had died once before, and now no longer feared it. To him, death was bliss.

Because he had no feet, he could not walk like a normal man, but could will his mind to take him anywhere, and so he moved through the darkness, searching for Cassandra. She would come to him, he was sure. Death had been the only way for them to be together, and now death had finally claimed him. He was a spirit now, like an Akari, living forever in a place without strife or the pain of physical bodies. Now he had two eyes again. Now he would be whole.

He imagined the orchard where they had made love, and where Cassandra had died. In her death place she had come to him when he himself lay dying. As he imagined it, the orchard bloomed around him, real and perfect in every detail. The sun was high and warm, filling the trees with its orange fingers. Apples fell gently to the mossy ground. In the distance sat Lionkeep, the way it had been on that wonderful day, unpolluted and filled with children, the flag of Liiria snapping overhead. But here in the orchard the noise of the castle was a world away. In the orchard, peace reigned.

Lukien walked the lanes between the apple trees, smiling at the creation his imagination had wrought. He had only to wait, he knew, and Cassandra would find him. Pulling a perfect apple from the nearest tree, he took a bite of the fruit and smiled at its freshness. It was fine to be dead.

Lowering himself against the tree trunk, Lukien sat and patiently ate his apple.

Lahkali screamed against the burning pain, thrashing in the rass' iron grip as the venom raked her eyes. Angry tears flooded down her face. She could feel the hot breath of the rass as it watched her, pulling her closer. She had somehow managed to hold tightly to the katath, but working the weapon was impossible now. Bound by the snake and unable to see, she could barely keep the katath in her failing hand. On her breast she could still feel the Eye of God, growing hotter and hotter, burning her skin as much as the venom. Her wet garments seemed to catch fire. The rass held her confidently in its tail, toying with her, but no longer squeezed the life from her. Lahkali, refusing to face the end, concentrated on the steady power of the amulet.

The heat grew around her. Even through her acid-laced eyes, she could see its dazzling light. A great burning filled the cavern. The rass hissed against it, shaking her in its grasp. Lahkali cursed the beast, letting the power of the amulet fill her. The pain of her wounds ebbed as hot blood pumped through her body. She could fill Sercin's disbelief. The glow was everywhere now, red like the sun, beating back the green light of the cavern's gems. As fire filled the chamber the water below began to hiss and bubble. Sercin tossed her back and forth.

'Amaraz!' called Lahkali. 'Bring your fire!'

She was strong again, strong enough to keep her breath and fight. Sercin swayed, falling back as the magic fires shook the cavern. As she struggled she felt his tail waver, then loosen. Gradually she brought up her katath, inch by inch, hoping blindly for one clear shot.

'More!' she cried.

Amaraz obliged, and the shock of his power stunned her. Fire leapt from her hair and dangling feet, burning but not harming her. The scaly hide of the serpent's tail scorched as it tried to hold her. A burst of flame and smoke erupted off Lahkali's body, sizzling the reptilian hide. Sercin jerked back, at last opening his coils, dropping Lahkali. She tumbled, blind and on fire, crashing against the flooded earth. Her hand opened and the katath skidded away. Nearby she could hear the serpent's anguished keen.

Water filled Lahkali's mouth. She raised her head out of the muck, then desperately began cupping the water with her hands, washing out her stinging eyes. The world was a blur, a cauldron of mist and fire. The flames that had burned away Sercin's grip had gone out now. Her body was hers again.

Find your weapon, said a voice in her head.

This time the voice was not the serpent's. Lahkali knew it to be Amaraz.

'Where?' she asked. 'I can't see!'

Just ahead of you. Find it quickly. I cannot make the fire forever.

Lahkali scrambled, searching for her weapon. Her fingers moved through the water, feeling the rocks and mud for the katath. Through her reddened eyes she could just make out the rass, hissing and thrashing as fire fell upon it. On hands and knees Lahkali hurried forward, spreading her arms wide so not to miss the weapon.

'Where is it?' she cried.

Straight on. Move, child.

'I am!' Lahkali shouted, then found it. With a victorious yelp she raised the weapon and got to her feet. 'I have it!' she said. 'What now?'

Now kill the beast.

'Amaraz, I can't see. How can I?'

I will guide you. Go to it now.

'Amaraz . . .'

Go, now!

Lahkali gripped her katath, prepared herself, then charged forward. Ahead of her she could barely see the flailing body of the rass, raging as it struggled against the fires. Heat and smoke choked Lahkali. The wet ground grabbed her boots. But she continued, faltering all the way, running headlong toward the serpent.

And then, her body lightened. Lahkali tried to pause, yet kept on going. Her hands flew forward, her legs filled with vigour, and suddenly she was launching herself, not knowing how, leaping through the air toward the rass. Sercin's wounded face turned to her. Seeing her attack he once more unfurled his tongue. The appendage stretched out, unspooling from the snake's mouth, reaching for the girl. Lahkali knew what to do. With Amaraz part of her, she brought her katath through a slashing cross, easily slicing through the pink muscle. The tongue fell away, the stump recoiling with a cry. Katath was falling now. Through the haze she felt the serpent beneath her, trying to escape. There was a moment left.

'The hearts!' she cried. 'Find the hearts!'

Amaraz became her eyes, guiding her. The giant body of the snake moved to evade, but Lahkali was already on it, fighting her way quickly towards the hood. Beneath the hood were the hearts, she knew, and the twin blades of her katath sniffed for them, gleaming hungrily. Blood spattered across Lahkali's face as Sercin spat and tossed, reeling back against the cavern wall. His wounded eye, his severed tongue, the two deep rents along his good, none of these had killed him. But the blood was everywhere, gushing from the creature, mingling with the mud and water.

Then, as Lahkali climbed his flexing body, Sercin stopped. The wide hood folded back and the chest swelled with air. His good eye watched her blackly, urging her forward. Lahkali squinted through the pain, barely glimpsing the beast. What little she saw spoke of surrender.

You have won, child. The voice was Sercin's again.

He could have struck her, but did not. He could have quickly coiled away, but he stayed. Stretching out his hood again, the Great Rass lowered and showed its breast to the girl.

Slowly, he urged. *No more fighting.*

Lahkali paused. The glamour of Amaraz began to fade. As it did the enormous pain of the serpent's venom took hold again.

'I am the Red Eminence!' she cried.

The Great Rass hovered closer. Weakened, bloody, it closed its ruined mouth. *You are the Red Eminence. Take my hearts. Drink my blood.*

Amaraz was gone. Searching her mind for him, Lahkali found no hint of the Akari. But still he sustained her, giving her strength. Lahkali put out her hand, wishing for all the world that she could see the face of the defeated god. When she touched him, Sercin did not pull away. His cool scales coloured at the graze of her fingertips. There was blood on her hands. Lahkali drew her finger through it then put her finger to her lips. At once her mouth filled with bitter heat, a fire that spread quickly from her mouth to all the tendrils of her body. She blinked, and her eyes began to clear. The sizzling pain of the serpent's venom eased from her skin. Slowly her sight returned, blurry but true. The face of the Great Rass waited in front of her.

Lahkali could not speak. There were no words for what she was about to do. Sercin's black eye gleamed with understanding.

It is our secret, he told her, *the secret of your line. I give myself to your people, Eminence.*

And then she understood. She had not really beaten him. He had surrendered. The katath felt unreal in her grip.

'I have to do this,' she said shakily. 'I am sorry.'

Both hearts, said the serpent.

Facing death, he looked serene.

In his dream, Lukien had fallen asleep against the tree. Just as if no time had passed, the sun was in the same spot in the sky when he awakened. He looked around, sure he'd heard his name called. He searched the orchard for Cassandra. Getting to his feet, he peered down the lanes of perfectly trimmed apple trees. Lionkeep was just as before, distant and contented. The rows and rows of trees stood at rapt attention. But Cassandra was gone, or had never been there, leaving Lukien to puzzle.

And then he heard the voice again, like the voice of an unseen angel, very far away and calling to him. And he knew.

'Oh, no . . .'

It seemed impossible. He was dead. He had to be dead.

'No!' he cried, staring up into the sky. 'I won't go back!'

The darkness came again, sweeping him away.

Lukien opened his eyes. When he saw Lahkali's face, he sobbed. He was glad for her, glad she was alive, but the pain of his wounds had gone and that meant only one thing.

'I'm back.'

'Yes,' said Karoshin brightly. 'You are alive, Lukien!'

Lukien realized he was laying on the ground. Glancing at his chest he saw the Eye of God. He put a hand to his mouth to stifle his sobs.

'Don't be afraid, Lukien, you're all right,' said Lahkali gently. 'I have killed the rass. Look, Lukien, look at the water . . .'

Around them the melting snow was the colour of blood, rushing down from the mountain to feed the valley far below.

47

Within hours Lukien had fully recovered from his wounds, but he spent the next few days in the palace, alone, wondering why Cassandra had not come to him. He was glad that Lahkali had defeated the Great Rass. All of Torlis seemed to be celebrating. It was a kind of miracle that he had witnessed, watching the holy river turn to blood and feed the lands around the delta. But he had been too shocked by what had happened to him to pay the miracle much attention, and now, though everyone else in the palace had taken the time to go to the river, Lukien had remained by himself. The great tear of flesh along his back had healed, leaving a scar that looked like it had been there forever. There was no more pain from his missing eye, either. All was just as it had been before he gave the amulet to Lahkali. Apparently, his cursed Akari was once again protecting him.

On the long trek back to the palace, Lukien had listened intently to Lahkali's tale. She was still horribly weak from her encounter with the rass, her face reddened from the serpent's venom. But she was so excited about what had happened that she refused Karoshin's orders to rest. Amaraz had spoken to her, she told Lukien. He had actually conversed with her, even guiding her hand in battle. To Lukien, this was the most amazing – and frustrating – part of all. How many times in his life had he asked, even begged Amaraz to speak to him? And always the spirit ignored him, coming to him only once to chide him. It was one more of the great mysteries Lukien could not unravel, and by the time three days had passed he was sure he had made the right choice.

It really was time for him to go home.

Lahkali didn't need him anymore. He had managed to keep his promise to the girl and she had done the rest, slaying a god to save her people. Thinking about her heroics brought a wide grin to Lukien's face. He stopped what he was doing long enough to conjure a picture of her, katath in hand, facing down the beast with Sercin's face. She was every bit the Red Eminence, every bit the leader her people needed. And with good men like Karoshin and Niharn around her, Lukien was sure she would succeed.

'And without me,' he said, looking around the room. There was very little he had accumulated during his stay in Torlis, and nothing he really wanted to take back with him. More than anything, he wanted to return Jahan's body back to his village, but that was impossible. His widow would have to settle for a story instead. He would hire a boat to take him back down the river, he had decided, just as he and Jahan had done to reach the fabled city. He would have to wait until the red tide receded, of course, but after that he would make haste across Tharlara, and with luck would reach Jahan's village in three weeks or less. From there he would trek back to Kaliatha, perhaps making contact again with Raivik, the dead Akari. Raivik loved stories, he remembered, and now he had so much to tell! It would be a fine reunion, Lukien imagined, but a brief one. It was time for him to get back to Grimhold.

With little left to do, Lukien decided to leave his chamber and take a walk through the palace's grounds. Usually he waited until nightfall to make his excursions, but the palace was quiet and he supposed no one would interrupt him. Karoshin was busy tending to Lahkali, who remained in bed despite her remarkable recovery, and Niharn had returned to his own home days earlier. Lukien was free, he realized, and could at last enjoy all the peace the palace offered. There were still gardens and paths he had yet to explore, so Lukien headed out of his chamber and into the hallway. Not surprisingly, the corridor was empty. A great, soaring ceiling made his boot heels echo on the marble. He made his way past the other apartments where men close to the Eminence resided, all of them grand chambers with multiple rooms and views of the city. Throughout his days in the palace Lukien spent very little time dealing with the men who called these rooms home. He was still a foreigner to them, even after all he'd done for their ruler, and Lukien was sure they would be pleased to see him go.

Lukien had made his way to the end of the corridor before seeing Lahkali. She had been heading toward his room but stopped when she saw him, giving him a knowing smile. She looked radiant, fully recovered. Her dark hair bounced happily about her shoulders. Around her eyes a bit of redness remained, a tell-tale hint of her encounter with the rass, but otherwise Lahkali looked fine, dressed in a golden royal gown that somehow fit her a little better these days.

'I came to see you, Lukien,' she said. 'I have been asking for you.'

'And I you, Eminence.' Lukien went to stand before her. 'Karoshin told me you were resting.'

'Karoshin has kept me a prisoner in my bed,' she joked. 'I have not even been to see the river! That's why I have come, Lukien, to take you there to see it.' She frowned at him with fake anger. 'Karoshin tells me you have been keeping to yourself again.'

Lukien nodded. 'It is time for me to leave soon, Lahkali. I have been making plans.'

The girl looked sad, but not surprised. 'There are no boats on the river to take you back now. You will have to wait.'

'I know. But soon.'

Lahkali took his hand, saying, 'All right, soon. But first come with me to the river. Let us see our miracle!'

The river of blood took Lukien's breath away. Along with hundreds of others, he stood with Lahkali near the bank of the river, watching in awe as the red water flooded the delta and nourished the silt with life. The houses standing nearest to the river had all been temporarily abandoned, the residents evacuating themselves to the tents that had sprung up along the shore to accommodate the milling spectators. For the people of Torlis the coming of the blood was exactly as Lahkali had described it – it was a miracle, and folks had come from miles to witness it and give praise to Sercin, whose blood it was that turned the river crimson. Lukien and Lahkali kept back a respectable distance, though they allowed themselves to step closer to the bank than anyone else. They had come with a group of soldiers and priests to protect the Red Eminence from the throngs of onlookers, but a remarkable hush had fallen over the gathering and Lukien knew that Lahkali was in no danger at all. Her people were in awe of her. To them, she was no less of a miracle, and so they did not pester her with questions or requests to touch her garments. Instead they kept their distance, offering only grateful smiles.

Among the priests accompanying them stood Karoshin, who looked out over the holy river in reverence. Dropping to his knees, he lowered his head in prayer. His acolytes quickly did the same. Lukien watched them, unable to hear their words. Overhead the sky was a brilliant blue, as if Sercin himself had cleared away the clouds just so they could enjoy the view. The air smelled sweet, not of blood but of flowers, and all the ferukas had been taken from the water, resting idle on the beach. Not a single fisherman waded through the scarlet waters. In the distance, the tower mountain that was Sercin's home had been swept free of the ghostly mists. The red tide that had gushed from its peak had already receded.

Lahkali was more at peace now than Lukien had ever seen her. She stood proud and tall, no longer like a girl but fully like a woman grown, casting her gaze out over the inexplicable river. To Lukien, who had seen magic in many forms through the years, the river was perhaps the strangest thing he had witnessed. He had not believed the tale when he'd first heard of it, nor any of the other incredible claims Jahan had made. But now, standing on the banks of a river made of blood, Lukien would have believed anything possible. As Lahkali slipped her hand into his, Lukien sighed.

'You were a fine student, Lahkali,' he said softly. 'I will miss you when I'm gone. I won't forget anything that happened to me here.'

'You are happy then, Lukien? You do not seem happy.'

'No, I am happy. I am have just been . . . thinking.'

'Of Cassandra? And why she did not come to you?'

Lukien grimaced. 'Yes.'

'Perhaps it was just a dream,' Lahkali suggested. 'Perhaps you were not dead at all, not even for a moment.'

'It felt like death to me,' said Lukien, remembering the bliss of floating and the perfection of the apple orchard. 'It is just how it was last time. Except . . .' He shrugged. 'She never came.'

Lahkali was silent for a moment. She kept her hand in Lukien's, giving it her reassuring grip. Soon the crimson would recede and the water would return to normal. In a few days time, the miracle would be over. Lahkali seemed determined to enjoy every minute of it, but her face drooped with concern over what Lukien had told her. She grew edgy.

'Do you have anything that belonged to her?' she asked suddenly.

Lukien looked at her. 'What?'

'Cassandra. Do you have anything of hers with you?'

'That's an odd question, Eminence.'

'I am wondering, that's all. Some men carry trinkets of their lovers with them. Do you have one?'

'No,' Lukien said sadly. 'Only this . . .' He patted the amulet beneath his shirt. 'Cassandra wore it before it was given to me. It reminds me of her constantly, but it's not the kind of good memory you mean.'

'Do you have anything else? A ring, maybe? Or a lock of her hair?'

'No, nothing. Lahkali, why do you ask?'

Lahkali did not look at him, but rather kept her gaze on the river. 'Maybe I'm just curious.'

'Or maybe not,' said Lukien suspiciously.

'What about a story,' the girl suggested. 'There must be a story about her that only the two of you know, something you both shared. Can you think of one?'

'I suppose I could if I tried. Tell me why.'

Lahkali laughed. 'You are mistrustful!'

'Lahkali, it's a strange question!'

'No, not here it isn't,' said the Eminence. 'That's how people talk about the ones they love here, Lukien – with stories.' At last she turned to him. Her eyes looked tired. 'We have been here long enough. Let's go back to the palace.'

'Already? We just got here.'

Lahkali let go of his hand and began to move away. 'It doesn't matter. Let's go to the palace, Lukien.'

The long ride back to the palace was punctuated mostly by silence. Lahkali rode in a litter carried by a dozen brawny, bare-chested servants, while Lukien rode behind her on a horse of his own, remaining with the soldiers and Karoshin's acolytes. The whole group seemed disappointed in the Eminence's decision to leave the river so soon, but when they arrived at the palace Lahkali gave all of them leave to go back if they wished. Confused, Lukien hurried up to Lahkali and asked for an explanation. The young ruler merely smiled and took his hand again.

'We should be alone,' she said. 'I want to show you something.'

She was acting strangely, almost giddy, but Lukien allowed her to guide him away from the others and along one of the palace's many flower-lined paths. It was late afternoon and the trees threw long shadows across the lane, providing needed shade and a hint of the coming evening. A few straggling priests who had not joined the others passed them along the way, bowing deeply to Lahkali and offering her words of thanks. They were in a part of the sprawling palace Lukien had never been before, and he took the time to marvel at the statues and high walls that rose up around them like a maze. The grounds became deathly quiet. Priests sat cross-legged under trees, deep in prayer, their lips barely moving as they lightly uttered chants. Lahkali kept to the path, walking slowly as she held Lukien's hand, not bothering to explain any of the interesting things they passed. A strange sense of dread dropped over Lukien, but he could not fathom why.

'Where are you taking me?' he asked in a whisper. He looked around, surveying the statues and the walls built of carefully laid bricks. 'Why is it so quiet here?'

'This is a place of prayer,' explained Lahkali. 'People come here when they want to commune.'

'Commune?'

'Wait,' advised Lahkali. 'You will see.'

They continued walking, turning left and right and left again, going deeper into the maze as if it had no end. The priests soon fell away, and up ahead stood a tall black gate with ornately twisted iron bars. Past the bars Lukien could see what looked like a cemetery, with long, rolling lawns and neatly trimmed trees. Dotting the grass were stones, some of them beautifully carved, others small and ugly. The gate was unguarded. It was also unlocked, as Lukien quickly learned when they reached it, watching Lahkali tug on it to pull it open. As she did she stepped aside, fully revealing the lovely space. Lukien peered his head inside. The tranquil setting brought a smile to his face.

The garden went on for acres, stretching past the visible end of the palace itself, all of it hemmed in with various walls that directed the eye to the many separate areas. Amid the stones and trees, Lukien saw small pockets of people gathered, many of them kneeling next to the carvings, talking or nodding happily. Even the ones who were by themselves were talking. The nearest person, a young man in plain peasant garb, lay on his side near one of the stones, laughing and chatting all by himself. Lukien stared at him in wonder, and suddenly he remembered a very similar looking rock that he had once uncovered by accident.

'Story stones,' he whispered. He looked at Lahkali for an explanation. 'What is this place?'

'We call it the Story Garden,' said Lahkali. Her face grew placid. 'Lukien, this is the greatest gift I could give you. I have no other worthy way of thanking you for what you did for me. I laid in bed for days wondering how to repay you, and this is the only way that made sense to me.'

'Lahkali, I don't understand.' Lukien peered into the garden. 'Is this a burial place?'

'No.' Lahkali took his chin in her hand and guided his gaze to hers. 'Listen to me now – this place is sacred to us. You spoke of the story stones. Do you remember?'

Lukien remembered perfectly. In Kaliatha, Raivik the Akari had come from a story stone. It was how his people communed with the dead, he had told Lukien. 'Tell me,' he urged. 'This place – can anyone speak to the dead here?'

'It is a secret,' said Lahkali. 'No one outside of Torlis has ever seen the Story Garden. Only you, Lukien.'

'Why me?'

'Because you mourn, Lukien. All these years, and still you mourn.' Lahkali took his hand again and stepped through the gate. The others in the garden paid them no attention. 'Look at all these markers, Lukien. They are what the Akari Raivik told you they are – story stones. They call the dead back to our world.'

Lukien was awestruck, drifting after Lahkali with his eyes like saucers. 'All of these stones? They are all for speaking with the dead?'

'In this place there are no boundaries between the worlds. The spirits of the dead can cross easily into our lives. The story stones summon them.'

'And all these people? They are talking with the dead?'

Lahkali smiled. 'Does that seem unbelievable to you?'

'No,' sighed Lukien. 'No. I want to believe. Tell me more, Lahkali. Tell me everything.'

As they walked Lahkali spoke, continuing to lead him deeper into the Story Garden. The iron gate fell far behind them as Lukien listened, enraptured by the girl's tale.

'Malator the Akari built this place for us,' she began, 'hundreds of years ago. His people have the knowledge of summoning the dead; you know this already, Lukien. When he came to us, he passed this knowledge on to us and created the Story Garden.'

Lukien nodded. 'You haven't mentioned Malator since I came here, Lahkali.'

'And you have not asked, Lukien.'

'What could I ask that you would tell me? He must have something to do with the Sword of Angels. Ah, but I don't care about that now.'

'You want to speak to your own dead lover, I know,' said Lahkali patiently. 'But listen to my story first.' She continued walking, tredding green grass with Lukien at her side. 'The Akari were angels to us. That is how the sword got its name. It is the Sword of the Akari – the Sword of Angels. Malator was kind to the King of Torlis, my ancestor. This garden was a gift for the king.'

'A gift? For what?'

'That doesn't really matter. Malator came here to ask our help, remember. In those days the Akari were warring with your people, Lukien. The Jadori were slaughtering them.'

'The Jadori aren't my people exactly, Lahkali. But go on.'

Lahkali slowed. Up ahead stood a small altar, weather-worn but sturdy looking, sitting alone near a tree. A handful of chisels and brushes lay across the altar. Stacks of stones lay near its base. They were the same small, ugly stones Lukien had seen dotted throughout the garden.

'Here,' Lahkali pronounced. She stood beside the altar. 'Later, when you are done here, I will tell you the rest of the story. But now there is something you must do, Lukien.'

Lukien looked at her helplessly. 'If there's any way for me to see Cassandra again . . .'

'Choose a stone.'

'What for?'

'So you can make a story stone for Cassandra. Take any of them, it doesn't matter.'

486

Lukien nervously picked up one of the rocks. Smaller than his head, it nevertheless made a loud thud when he placed it on the altar. His hands dithered as he brushed the dirt from its smooth surface. He stared at the stone, then at Lahkali.

'I'm afraid,' he confessed.

Lahkali's face filled with sympathy. 'Don't be, Lukien. Remember – this is what you've always wanted. You don't have to die to see Cassandra. You have only to come to this holy place.'

It seemed impossible, yet Lukien believed. In Torlis, where rivers turned to blood and gods came to life as serpents, what did it mean to talk to the dead? It was just one more miracle.

'What do I do?' he asked.

'Think of a story, anything that is special between you and Cassandra. Think hard on it, and then carve the words into the stone. Not the whole story, just a few words. Just something that she will remember. And when you do, *believe*.'

'Believe,' echoed Lukien. 'Yes, alright.'

He picked up one of the chisels, a small tool with a blade kept sharp by some caring grounds-keeper. He knew exactly what to carve into the stone, remembering those long ago days when he would send secrets notes to Cassandra. He always signed them the same exact way.

'When I first loved her she was the wife of my king,' said Lukien in a low voice. 'Every chance I had I sent her notes. It was our secret. She kept them, I know, and hid them from her husband Akeela. Lahkali, if I sign on this stone, will she know it is from me? Will it summon her?'

'Yes, Lukien.'

'But it's just a stone . . .'

'No. Not here in the Story Garden. They are markers. They summon the ones we love. You have to believe, Lukien.'

'Yes,' Lukien agreed. 'Alright.'

He steadied the stone with one hand and began to carve with the other. Lahkali assured him that it made no difference how beautifully he carved or how he spelled the words. It was only the meaning that mattered, she explained, and how deeply he believed. Slowly, carefully, Lukien carved the stone with the words he'd used to sign his love notes all those years ago. It took long minutes for him to complete, and when he was done he leaned back and showed his work to Lahkali, who read the inscription and smiled.

'Your Adoring Servant.'

Hearing her say it made Lukien colour. 'That's it. That's what I was to her. I still am.' He looked at her blankly. 'What now?'

'Now you choose a place for it,' replied Lahkali. 'Someplace quiet and pretty.'

The place Lukien chose was away from all the other story stones, beneath a tree that reminded him of the apple trees in Lionkeep's orchard. With Lahkali's assurance that the stone would be left undisturbed, he set it down near the trunk of the tree and leaned back to study it. Lahkali had already left, telling him that she would return in an hour or so. Lukien stared at the stone, unsure how to begin. In the distance he saw an old woman kneeling comfortably by a stone of her own, a much taller and grander stone that had been carved with runes and gently sloping sides. Her face was serene as she spoke, confidently conversing with some dead loved one. Lukien noticed her casual demeanour, wondering again if this was all some elaborate ruse. Perhaps the dead did not come to the living at all here. Perhaps it was all just some grand imagining.

Finally, Lukien placed his hand on the stone and thought of Cassandra. He had never summoned a spirit before, so he closed his eyes and concentrated, feeling a bit stupid.

'Cass? I'm not sure what to say. If you're here with me, please let me know.' His hand began to tremble. His fingers brushed the stone, gently caressing it. 'Maybe I was only dreaming up in the mountain, but it seemed so real to me. I was sure you would come, but you didn't. I don't know – maybe you never did come to me that one time.'

He kept his eyes closed, making a picture of her in his mind. The picture was static, quiet and unmoving. Without a background, it was colourless. Lukien grimaced, realizing it was hopeless. Until the picture moved.

It was not he who controlled it anymore. The image of Cassandra came alive on its own. Lukien's hand froze on the stone. When he opened his eyes, the picture remained.

'I can see you!' he gasped. 'Cass!'

'I can feel you, Lukien,' said Cassandra.

His whole body swelled with her warmth. Lukien stared into the distance, looking past the trees and rolling lawn to the figure in his mind. Cassandra reached out a hand. The touch was sweet. Lukien melted.

'You're here,' he sighed. 'Cass, you're *real*.'

Cassandra's face came clearly to him now, very close, as if she were laying next to him. She smiled serenely, her skin untouched by time or disease. 'I am still here, Lukien,' she said. 'I told you I would be. I told you I would always be with you.'

'Yes,' said Lukien, remembering. 'I've felt you close. I've tried to reach you, so many times!'

She could sense his agitation and quickly moved to calm him. 'My love, it is the way things must be.' She moved even closer, almost touching his nose with hers. For Lukien, there was nothing else in the world but her. 'I promised you this place, and you found it.'

'Yes,' said Lukien excitedly. 'We can be together now always!'

Cassandra shook her head. 'Not yet. I brought you here to find the sword.'

'I know, but I can't find it, Cassandra. They won't tell me where it is, not even Amaraz! But I can stay. Lahkali will let me. I don't have to go . . .'

'Lukien, no.' Cassandra's face twisted as though she were in pain. 'My love, you're not done yet.'

'But I am! I helped Lahkali. I came here. I did everything!'

'Except find the sword.'

Lukien stared at her. 'I don't want to know where it is. If you know, do not tell me.'

'I have to, Lukien. I must.'

'But how can you know? You never knew before! Cassandra, don't tell me, I beg you.'

Cassandra's hurt expression grew. 'I can feel the sword, Lukien. I can feel it very near.'

Lukien put up his hands. 'Damn it, no! I'm not a pawn anymore!'

'No, beloved, you're not,' said Cassandra gently. 'You're a man of honour. And you have a duty.'

'Duty?' laughed Lukien. 'Doesn't anyone have a duty to me? Not even Amaraz talks to me! Why, Cassandra? Tell me that, will you?'

Cassandra smiled. 'I have all the answers now, my love.'

'What?' Lukien fell backward. 'Why then?'

'Because the sword has an Akari. The sword is yours. The Akari is yours.' Cassandra closed her eyes dreamily. 'I can feel him, Lukien. I can feel Malator. He's waiting for you.'

Lukien refused to accept her words. 'No, Cassandra. You don't understand. You're not an Inhuman. I have an Akari. He's a damned menace, but he's mine.'

'You're wrong, my love.' The pain left Cassandra's face, and she opened her eyes with a smile. 'Malator is your Akari.'

Two hours later, Lahkali returned to the Story Garden. Beneath the tree where she had left Lukien, she found him still sitting alone. His eyes were open, but he was not speaking, and Lahkali knew that his conversation with Cassandra had ended. She took her time walking toward him, making sure not to disturb his contemplation, and when he turned to look at her he smiled. He looked tired, but also immensely pleased. Lahkali returned his kind grin.

'It happened?' she asked. 'You have seen her?'

489

Lukien nodded, then took the Eye of God out from beneath his shirt. 'You see this? Soon I won't need it anymore, Lahkali. I'm going to have an Akari of my own to keep me alive. A proper Akari.'

Confused, Lahkali asked, 'What do you mean?'

'The Sword of Angels,' replied Lukien. His face was serene. 'It's mine. It belongs to me, and I know where it is.'

48

As he walked with Lahkali across the rolling greens of the Story Garden, Lukien felt more than simple bliss. What he felt was indescribable, too much for words, and because he had no words he said nothing. Lahkali's voice was low and sweet, as though she were reading a sonnet to him. Lukien nodded politely, trying to listen, but his every thought was of his beautiful Cassandra and the brief, dream-like time they had spent together. She had touched him. From her place among the dead she had reached her hand across the void as though she were still alive. Her fingers burned with life and passion. Lukien thought of her and smiled.

Jahan had been right about Torlis. It was indeed a place of miracles. And Lahkali had gifted him with the greatest miracle of all, one that made the river of blood seem like a parlour trick. Lukien floated as he walked, not really caring where the girl was taking him. He had told her about the crypt at the other end of the Story Garden, and she had smiled at him with open pleasure. Cassandra, now part of this strange city, had known at once where the crypt was located, finally ending the maddening mystery. But to Lukien, the revelation was merely one more tiny blessing. He no longer really cared about the Sword of Angels, or about the tale Lahkali was spinning. He had seen Cassandra, and for him that was enough.

The sun continued to shine as Lukien and Lahkali made their way across the greens, over the hills and gulleys of the enormous garden. Lukien walked slowly, not really wanting to reach his destination. Just as Cassandra had told him, they were westward toward the sun, toward the tomb Lukien knew they would find there. Cassandra had told him everything, and he in turn had told Lahkali. The young Eminence seemed relieved as she told her secret tale.

'When Malator died the tomb was built to keep the sword. His body was burned and his ashes taken to the sacred river. Only the sword lies within the tomb.'

It was a remarkable story, and for Lukien, the end of a mystery. He nodded as he walked alongside the girl, not saying anything as she unburdened herself.

'I have kept this secret since my own father died, and he kept it most of his life, just as all the fathers before him, from the time of Faros himself. Faros was the first. He was the Eminence who befriended Malator. When Malator came he asked for Faros to help him. You know this already, Lukien. The Jadori were murdering the Akari, and Malator came here to find allies. But Faros refused.'

'Of course,' said Lukien. 'Why would anyone bring their people to war needlessly?'

'Ah, but Malator warned otherwise. He told Faros that the Jadori would one day come here to Torlis. One day they would conquer Torlis, just as they would conquer the Akari. That was almost a thousand years ago. We are still waiting!'

'The Jadori aren't like that anymore,' Lukien told her. 'They were, but no longer. They're good people. Peace-loving.'

'As you say,' agreed Lahkali. 'But in Malator's day they were blood-thirsty, and Malator was desperate. He begged the Eminence for help, but Faros always refused him.'

'And so the Akari were slaughtered.'

Lahkali nodded. 'Yes, but not all at once. Malator stayed for months here in Torlis, trying to win Faros over. And that's when he taught us how to commune.'

'Ah! Tell me about that. You said the Story Garden was a gift.'

'That's right, but the garden took time. Malator did not build it all at once. At first he taught only Faros how to speak to the dead.' Lahkali slowed a little and smiled at Lukien. 'Faros was like you, Lukien. He grieved for a woman he loved. Malator knew this and gave the magic of the story stones to Faros so that he could talk to his beloved wife again.'

'You mean he bribed him,' said Lukien dryly.

'And it almost worked! After months of trying, Malator had finally given Faros a reason to help him. But by then it was too late. By then the Jadori had won.' Lahkali paused, considering her own, heavy words. 'I don't know how Malator knew, but he did. The story doesn't explain that. I've always guessed it was his magic that told him what had happened to his people.'

'He was right, though, however he knew.' Lukien remembered what Raivik had told him of the slaughter. 'So what happened to Malator?'

'He never went back to his Kaliatha,' said Lahkali. 'He remained here in Torlis with Faros. He was bitter over what happened to his people, and too ashamed to go home and try to find anyone who might have survived. He spent the rest of his life here.'

'And he built the Story Garden,' said Lukien. 'Yes?'

'That's right. He worked on it the rest of his life. The story says that it was a gift to all the people of Torlis for being so kind to him.'

'A generous gift!' laughed Lukien. 'But what about the Sword of Angels?'

Lahkali shrugged. 'It's yours now.'

'That's not what I mean, Lahkali.'

'I know.' Lahkali continued walking, looking down at her slippers. 'Malator could have helped his people. He could have worn the armour that his brother Kahldris made for him. He told Faros of his brother, you see, and of all his evils. Kahldris placed himself into the armour to make a great weapon to defeat the Jadori, but his Malator shunned it.'

'Yes, that's right,' said Lukien anxiously. 'That's what Raivik told me. But he told me nothing of the sword, Lahkali, and so far you haven't either.'

Lahkali glanced ahead. 'We're almost there.'

Lukien nodded. Somehow, he could feel it. 'Cassandra told me that Malator would be my Akari.'

Lahkali smiled. 'That is a good thing, yes?'

'Yes,' Lukien replied. 'At least I think so.' Still, the notion made him wary. 'He's calling to me. I can feel him.'

'Malator?'

Lukien stopped walking. 'Tell me the rest of the story before we get there. Why did he make the sword, Lahkali?'

'To stop his brother, Lukien. Somehow he knew his brother would survive. Before he died he placed himself into the sword that he brought with him from Kaliatha. That's what the Akari do, yes? Place themselves into objects to make themselves more powerful? Like your amulet . . .'

'Yes, that's right,' said Lukien. 'But I never really understood it. It makes them live on in this world, our world. It makes them strong here.'

'Malator knew his brother would never die inside his armour, Lukien. He was old by the time he made the Sword of Angels, and so was Faros. He made Faros promise never to reveal the location of the sword to anyone. People who see Malator's tomb don't even know what it is. Only the priests know, and even they have no notion of the sword. It is a secret.'

'But you knew I'd come for it,' said Lukien. 'How?'

'Because that is what Malator told us would happen.' Lahkali laughed. 'They are so marvelous, the Akari! They see the future. They are truly like gods.'

'No,' said Lukien sourly. 'They aren't gods. They just think they are. They manipulate people into doing their bidding, and they never, ever explain themselves.'

'Be at ease, Lukien,' said Lahkali. She touched his hand gently. 'You have your answers now.'

'Do I?' Lukien wasn't so sure. He looked toward the west where he knew the tomb of Malator waited. The story stones were fewer here, spaced so far apart it was hard to see them, and except for himself and Lahkali, Lukien saw no one. A small bird in a nearby tree chirped when he saw them approaching. Lukien shook his head, angry that the oceanic happiness of seeing Cassandra had faded. 'They have all used me,' he grunted. 'Not just Amaraz but Malator, too. And we're all caught up in their ancient game. All right, so Malator will be my Akari now. But is that really a good thing?'

Lahkali grimaced. 'I don't know, Lukien. You already have the amulet to keep you alive.'

'But I don't want to be alive! Now more than ever, I just want to . . .'

He stopped himself, biting his lip. He felt Lahkali's hand tighten on him.

'Cassandra will wait forever for you, Lukien.' Carefully she pulled him forward. 'Come. We're close now.'

Lukien relented, giving himself over to her guidance. They walked quietly, neither of them speaking, cresting a hill of wildflowers until a little valley was revealed, laying in the shadows of birch trees. Among the shadows stood a stone tomb, not particularly grand, its grey surface overrun by moss and creeping vines. No bigger than a shack, the tomb had a single, iron door and a symbol hung over the threshold, carved of the same weathered rock. Lukien peered at it from the place on the hill, noting the symbol with a wry smile. It wasn't a blade that marked the sword's resting place, but a single, expertly carved torch with flames that leaped off the surface in relief. Lukien turned toward Lahkali.

'Life?'

'Eternal,' explained Lahkali. 'That must have been what Malator requested. The tomb has been here a thousand years, Lukien. It's built, rebuilt and repaired, but always the torch has remained.' She smiled at him. 'Are you ready?'

Lukien took a breath. 'I'm ready.' He hesitated. 'What now?'

'Now you go inside. The sword is waiting for you.'

'Inside? But how? That door must weigh a hundred pounds.' Lukien studied it from the distance. 'And look – it must be locked.'

'It is locked, Lukien. But you are here to claim the sword. If as you say Malator is waiting for you . . .'

Lukien understood without really knowing how. He had long ago accepted the Akari magics. Opening a long locked door was hardly a task for them at all. 'Will you come with me?' he asked.

'No,' said Lahkali. 'You've come a long way, Lukien. You should go the rest of the way on your own.'

She reached up on her tiptoes and put a kiss on his cheek, then retreated back with a smile. Lukien regarded her with open admiration. They both knew he'd reached the end of his journey, and that soon he would be going home. But there would be no tears from this strong young woman.

'Wait here for me,' he told her, then turned and started down the hill. The flowers crunched beneath his boots as he hurried, carried down by the gentle slope. At the floor of the valley he felt the cool shade of the birch trees touch his face, and for a moment he slowed, taking in the ancient tomb. It looked every day of its thousand years, crumbling in places, its rocks patched with new mortar, its roof slanted with age. The hinges of the iron door had long ago rusted shut, almost falling to dust. The portal itself seemed unmovable. Lukien sized it up as he approached the crypt. It would be impossible to move alone, he decided.

'But I won't be alone, will I?' he whispered.

This time, he wasn't talking to Amaraz. Behind the door waited Malator, and despite the thick iron between them, he could almost hear the Akari's voice, urging him onward. Lukien placed his hands onto the metal portal, feeling its cold sturdiness. There was no handle to the thing, and only the barest space between its edge and the stone. Confident, Lukien put his fingernails into the narrow gap, digging in as best he could.

'All right, Malator. I'm ready. Help me!'

Then, closing his eyes, Lukien pulled. His fingers slipped, but held just enough to move the door a fraction. Amazed, he tried again, this time getting a stronger hold, and when he pulled the door creaked open, giving a screech like a wounded animal as the antique hinges shattered. Lukien's muscles shook as he pulled, using his weight to pry the door open. He felt it grinding forward, crushing the earth beneath it. Lukien gave a triumphant shout, then used his shoulder to push the door aside. It fell with a loud crash to the ground, and suddenly the thousand year-old air rushed out of the tomb. Inside, shrouded in darkness, stood a single, plain looking altar, almost the twin of the one used to make the story stones. Dust had settled thickly over its smooth surface, obscuring the object sitting atop it. Lukien held his breath, taking one small step inside. As his sight adjusted to the darkness, he saw the point of the sword sticking out from the altar's edge.

The Sword of Angels rested in the dust of eons. It didn't glow or burn with fire. It didn't sing or call to him. Looking like an old, discarded weapon, it merely waited atop its humble altar, letting the years dull its shine. Lukien inched deeper into the tomb, gazing lovingly at the sword. Its simple workmanship touched his heart. Endless generations of spiders had weaved their silken homes around the crypt, and the air smelled foully of must. Amid all of this, the sword rested patiently, not complaining. Lukien reached the altar and hovered over it, his light breath disturbing the dust. He could see the sword clearly now, and knew it for its Akari craftsmanship. The blade was straight, long and slender and double-edged. The cross-guard, made of simple steel, curved upwards at the edges. The grip, so time-worn it showed the finger grooves of its master, had been made of something like onyx, still with a sheen despite the years of dust. But it was the pommel that caught Lukien's attention, the only grand part of the sword. Used as a counter-balance, this pommel had been perfectly formed into the likeness of a lion's head. Lukien stared at it in amazement. He had expected the Sword of Angels to take his breath away. Instead, it merely pleased him.

'Malator?' he whispered. He looked up from the sword, gazing around the chamber. 'I am Lukien of Liiria. I've come a long way to find you and your sword, and how I mean to claim it. Your brother is at work in the world again. He's very far away. You probably don't even know he's awake.'

Lukien paused, listening. Malator did not speak, yet Lukien could feel his presence all around him.

'I tried to defeat him,' Lukien explained. 'I wasn't at all prepared for it. Your brother has a friend of mine, you see. My friend – Baron Glass – he's a good man. He is, really, but he's taken the Devil's Armour for himself and now your brother Kahldris has corrupted him. Malator? Are you listening?'

He had only to ask, and the sword on the altar began to vibrate. Slowly at first, the steel of the blade began to hum, shaking the dust and singing with a strange, metallic music. Lukien laughed with delight.

'Malator! You see, Amaraz? It's not so hard to speak to me!'

He knew he should take the sword. He knew the singing was Malator's signal to him. Lukien prepared himself, unsure what would happen when he touched the simple hilt. The sword was his; Cassandra had promised him that. And now Malator too seemed to insist the same thing. Lukien reached out carefully and took hold of the sword, wrapping his fingers around the onyx grip and gently lifting it from the altar. It came up easily, weightlessly, slipping through the air without any effort at all. Lukien grinned at the blade's perfect balance, the way his hand moulded to its timeless contours. At once he felt the power of Malator coursing through him.

'I'm ready, Malator,' he declared. 'Show yourself to me, I beg you.'

Outside, the sky began to darken. Or was it just the tomb itself? Lukien turned toward the door and watched as the shadows from the birch trees crept up on the threshold, blanketing it until the chamber went black. Unable to see, Lukien waited, feeling the sword grow warm in his grip. Just as he had with Amaraz, he felt his head begin to swim. The ground beneath him turned to water, and the walls began to bend with light. Bracing himself, Lukien shut his eyes. When he opened them again the tomb was gone, and he was alone in the Story Garden.

He looked around, unsure if this was the same garden he had entered with Lahkali. Night had fallen, and the flowers had vanished. The birch trees remained but they were different somehow, with moonlight trickling through their leaves. Malator's crypt was nowhere to be found, yet it felt to Lukien as though he were in the same valley. Up in the sky a few tendrils of clouds moved across the moon. A steady breeze rambled across the green. Lukien looked around, confused but unafraid. He knew that this was Malator's doing, and that the dead Akari would soon appear. Still holding the Sword of Angels, he began to wander among the trees. The hill where he'd left Lahkali was still there, but of course the girl was gone. He was not only in Malator's world – he was in Malator's death world. Lahkali wouldn't be born for a thousand more years.

'Malator?' called Lukien. 'I'm ready to meet you. Please.'

From the corner of his eye Lukien glimpsed movement in the trees. He turned and saw a figure among the birches, almost hiding behind one of the trunks. The man wore a white shirt that flared out at the bottom, cinched with a wide belt of tan leather. A long coat hung from his shoulders, battered from years of riding. He leaned against the tree trunk, his green eyes shining, his lips curled in a shy smile. His hair was white, his face elfish and lightly boned. His spidery fingers clasped together over his belly as he watched Lukien wordlessly. Lukien stepped toward him, not really sure who he was seeing.

'I know,' said the man. 'You expected someone grander, didn't you?'

'I'm . . . not certain,' stammered Lukien. 'Are you Malator?'

'I am. And I don't look very much like my brother!'

'I've never seen your brother,' said Lukien, 'but I've seen his armour. And you're right – you're not what I expected.'

Malator grinned and stepped away from the tree. He walked with a lilt that surprised Lukien, but even in his shining eyes a hint of remorse remained. 'You found my sword,' he told Lukien. 'You wouldn't have come if you didn't need it.'

Lukien nodded. It was all so surreal, yet he couldn't help himself from telling the Akari everything. 'It's like I said in the tomb. Did you hear me? Your brother has a friend of mine under his spell. Call it magic, call it whatever your word is for it. I want to save my friend, Malator.'

'And you tried already? Tell me about that.'

'If I must. It's not a pleasant memory. I was told the armour was invincible, but I didn't believe it really. I do now. I was left for dead after the fight. Only my amulet saved me.'

Malator's eyes leapt. 'Yes, your amulet! I can feel the one inside it. He's very powerful.'

'He's an Akari, like you,' said Lukien. 'His name is Amaraz.'

'I know of Amaraz,' said Malator. His tone grew serious. 'He was a great summoner, even before I left for Torlis. He was far greater than I was, or my brother. May I see your amulet?'

Lukien removed the Eye of God from beneath his shirt, holding it out for Malator to inspect. 'It was given to me after a battle,' he said. 'It keeps me alive. It's the only thing that saved me after fighting the armour.'

Malator studied the amulet intently, leaning forward but not touching it. He was quiet for a long time, sometimes nodding, other times glazing over as if lost in thought. 'Amaraz speaks to me,' he said softly.

Lukien scoffed. 'Good. He speaks to everyone but me.'

'Do you know why? Have you figured it out yet?'

'I think so,' said Lukien. He stared at Malator. 'Because you're to be my Akari.'

'That's right. You won't need the Eye of God any more, Lukien. While you carry my sword, you will have life.'

'Incredible,' sighed Lukien. He looked down at his amulet, saw the red gem pulsing with light, and wondered what it all meant. 'If I take this off, will I live?'

'Take it off,' said Malator with a grin. 'Find out.'

Lukien laughed. 'You're a jester. You're the great warrior Kahldris thought would save your people? I can't believe it.'

'I'm stronger than I look,' joked Malator. 'I helped you move that door, didn't I? Go on – take off the amulet. You have the sword.'

'Ah, but this is the world of the dead . . .'

'It doesn't matter,' Malator insisted. 'In my world, in your world – it's the same. I will keep you alive, Lukien.'

Lukien accepted the challenge with glee. 'All right, then,' he grumbled, taking the amulet from around his neck. He let it dangle at the end of its chain. 'I don't want to live anyway. I want to die, once and for all!'

'Toss it away, then!' urged Malator.

'I will!'

With a shout Lukien tossed the amulet as far as he could, watching as the Eye tumbled toward the trees. He raised the Sword of Angels above his head and taunted the sky to strike him down.

'Hold on to the sword,' warned Malator. 'Keep it close.'

'What if I forget it one day?' asked Lukien, taunting him. 'What if I leave it behind and go for a ride?'

'It won't be that easy,' laughed Malator. 'If you don't renounce me, you'll live. Why are you so eager to die, fool?'

Lukien lowered the sword. He felt perfectly fine, and doubted it was just a trick. 'No man should live forever,' he said sullenly.

'I have,' countered Malator, 'and I have loved every moment of it.'

'Sure you have, because you're here in paradise. Nothing can touch you here. No one you love dies.'

Malator considered this with a frown. 'You have a story to tell me, Lukien? I would enjoy hearing it.'

'Maybe,' said Lukien, not really wanting to tell the Akari too much yet. He spied the trees where he had thrown the Eye of God. 'Back in the real world I'm still wearing the amulet, right?'

'That's right. But you can rid yourself of it, if that's what you wish. I told you – you have no need for it any longer. I'm your Akari now.'

'And Amaraz knew that all along,' said Lukien bitterly. 'He is a bastard not to have told me.'

'No, Lukien, that's not the way things work. Amaraz knew you would find me someday. That's is why he would not bond with you. But it's not his place to tell you the future. And what does it matter now? We will bond, Lukien, you and I!'

'That is a frightening prospect,' drawled Lukien. He let the sword droop in his hand. Looking around, he could not help but laugh. 'All of you Akari – all you do is play these games! What if I don't want to play anymore? What if I just want to walk away?'

Malator shrugged. 'You could do that. But you haven't done it yet, and I don't think you will.'

'Oh, I will, Malator, I promise you. Just as soon as we are done with your wicked brother. Then I will be done with you as well, and I can die in peace.'

'If that's what you wish,' said Malator, though Lukien's promise clearly concerned him. 'But you'll have to tell me why. I want to know all about you, Lukien.'

Lukien thought about the Akari's request. 'It's a long way back to my land,' he said. 'We'll have all the time in the world to talk.'

He should have been happy, but he wasn't. He had found the Sword of Angels, the means to defeat Kahldris at last. So why wasn't it enough? Malator smiled kindly at him, as if reading his mind.

'You don't want to go?'

'Not anymore,' said Lukien. He looked away. 'It's your Story Garden.'

'Oh,' sighed Malator. 'Now I understand.'

Lukien shook his head. 'No, Malator, you don't. You have no idea what I've been through to get here, or what I'm leaving behind. Someday you might understand, if I decided to tell you. But right now all I want from you is the means to save my friend. And I want you to take me back to the land of the living. Now, if you please.'

Malator stepped up to Lukien at last, putting a slender arm around his shoulder. 'I can do anything you want me to do, Lukien.'

'Can you defeat your brother?'

'Yes, I can do that. Or at least I think I can.'

'How?'

Malator's smile was mischievous. 'Let's save that for the long ride, all right? It's time for us to get to know each other, my friend.'

'We're not friends, Malator,' said Lukien.

'We will be,' promised the Akari. 'Once you get to know me, you'll be glad you did.'

'Take me back, please. Will you do that for me, *friend*?'

'Of course,' said Malator, and once again the world went dark.

49

King Baralosus of Ganjor sat at a table beneath the desert moon, balancing himself on a chair as it sank into the warm sand. Around him sat a bevy of advisors, all of them tired from the long day of travel. The sun had gone down hours ago, and the fourteen-hundred soldiers who had accompanied them from the city had begun to bed down for the evening, unwrapping bed rolls among the hastily erected tents. The drowa rested uneasily in the distance, their noise and smell carried to Baralosus by the breeze. He could hear the grunting of the discontented animals over the voices of his men. It had been a good day of travel, completely without incident, and Baralosus was pleased. He had not thought an army could move so effortlessly. Baralosus studied the faces of the men gathered around the table as they drank wine and filled their bellies with food. To the king's right sat Minister Kailyr, his old comrade. Though Kailyr was not a military man, he had insisted on accompanying his king. And he still insisted there would be no battle with Aztar. Kailyr picked up his goblet, listening to General Rhot's argument.

'He has no archers, either,' Rhot continued. 'Even if he does decided to fight, we can pick at him for hours if we choose.'

Rhot's man Kahrdeen nodded in deference, as did the others around the table. Minister Kailyr lowered his goblet and licked the red wine from his lips. He looked tired, but refused to let the argument lapse.

'How do you know he has no archers? That's not what Jashien said. Jashien said he didn't see any archers. Why would he? Do you think the Voruni can't use bows, General?'

General Rhot laughed like a sceptic. 'So maybe they do. How many could they have? Jashien saw only a few hundred people with Aztar. *People*, mind you. Not just men. Women and children, too.'

Kahrdeen, dressed in his black robes, looked peculiarly at Kailyr. 'What does it matter to you? You say he won't fight.'

'He won't,' said Kailyr confidently. He gave his king a sideways smile. 'Majesty, don't fret about it.'

'His Majesty isn't afraid,' said Rhot, speaking for Baralosus. 'His Majesty knows I've made a fitting army for him. If Aztar decides to fight, we will finish him quickly and there will be nothing left of him but his ugly, scarred hide.'

There was some laughing around the table as the soldiers joked at Aztar's expense. Kailyr, however, did not laugh. Nor did Baralosus. The king looked down into his wine glass, wanting to go home. He wasn't like these men, and knew he didn't belong with them. Like all of his bloodline he had trained in weapons and tactics, studying the arts of war like any good king. But they had been texts and mock battles only. His skills were diplomacy, manipulation, and greed, and these things he excelled at. They had made him a great king, fabulously rich, the kind of man who brokered deals for land and gold and women. Yet being with Rhot and his muscular friends made Baralosus feel small.

To form an army, to march it across the desert, to threaten his one time ally Aztar – all of these things had been thrust upon Baralosus by politics and his stubborn daughter. Salina had refused him, and because she was too beautiful to resist, Aztar had refused him, too, beguiled by Salina's brown eyes and smooth skin. Baralosus had offered Aztar land and title, but to his great surprise the desert prince had turned him down, sending back his men empty-handed.

'Tell them, Majesty,' said Kailyr.

'Eh?'

'What you offered Aztar. Rhot doesn't believe.'

Baralosus felt annoyed, caught off guard by the question. He shrugged, a little drunk, and snapped at one of the servants to fill his glass again. A boy, shirtless, hurried over with a pitcher and poured wine into the king's goblet. Baralosus shooed him away.

'A seat at the table,' he muttered. 'Kailyr, you know this . . .'

'Of course I do. You see, Rhot? Do you really think Aztar would turn that down?'

Rhot laughed. 'What does that mean to a man like Aztar? He lives in the desert. He's like a king to the Voruni who follow him.' He stopped himself, looking sheepish. 'Well, not a king. Not a king, no. But you see my meaning, Majesty.'

'I see your meaning, General,' sighed Baralosus with disinterest. The warmth of the wine began to loosen his tongue. 'But old Kailyr roped me into this, all of his nonsense. I don't want to kill Aztar. I have to.'

The men around the table glanced at each other. Rhot smiled.

'And we will, Majesty,' he promised.

Baralosus put down his goblet, leaned dangerously back in his chair, then let out a loud curse. His eyes burned from the day of hot sand, and the insipid talk between his aides had given him a headache. The air smelled of drowa dung and sweaty men. He felt like vomiting.

'We should reach the Skein in a day or two, yes?' he asked, addressing no one in particular.

'Yes, Majesty. No more than two days,' said Rhot.

Baralosus rubbed his eyes hard, then opened them to skewer the general. 'And you'll make quick work of Aztar? I want your promise on this, Rhot. No surprises.'

'There will be no surprises, Majesty. Aztar is weak. His men have no means to stand against us. When he sees what he is up against, he will give up your daughter.'

Baralosus wanted desperately to be assured. 'And if he doesn't, you will defeat him easily?'

'Easily, Majesty.'

Rhot's words came out with such confidence it almost offended the king. Of all of them, only Rhot took glee in the coming battle. While most of Ganjor admired Aztar, Rhot thought him a brigand. And a threat to Ganjor's throne. There was a glint of arrogance in Rhot's eyes as he sat across from Baralosus, a kind of gloating that silently said 'you should have listened to me, Majesty.'

King Baralosus took up his wine glass again and sipped at it, inviting the others to talk again. They all remained quiet. Kailyr, always the friend, offered Baralosus a smile of warning.

'What is it?' Baralosus grumbled at him.

'It's hot,' said Kailyr. 'You shouldn't drink so much.'

Baralosus belched and turned away. Throughout the camp he saw fires wavering, lighting the dunes with a pale flickering. His army moved around the fires, settling in for meals or sleep or quiet conversation. The moon seemed impossibly bright, huge and alabaster. The din of the army faded in the enormity of the desert.

'I'm tired,' pronounced the king.

'Yes, get some sleep,' agreed Kailyr.

'No,' said Baralosus, getting out of his chair. 'I mean I'm tired of listening to all of you. I'm going for a stretch. I need to breathe.'

'Breathe?' Kailyr stood up beside him. 'No, Majesty. Sit. Or let me take you to your tent.'

Baralosus shook his head. More than anything, he wanted to be away from his aides. 'You sit. Keep on arguing. I'm going.'

As Kailyr began to speak, Baralosus walked away from the little table. The guards around him started to follow, but Baralosus barked at them to keep back. All the attention was making him feel like a child. Pulling his garments around himself, he trudged along the sand to where the soldiers were bedding down, keeping his face in shadows. Because he'd known the trek would be difficult, Baralosus hadn't dressed in his usual finery. Instead a wore a gaka made of tanned drowa skin and a pair of riding boots that hiked up to his knees. A headdress of scarlet cloth spun around his skull, but his face remained uncovered. Still, it was nearly impossible to make out his features in the darkness, and none of the men bothered looking up as Baralosus moved through their ranks.

When he was a comfortable distance away from Kailyr and the others, Baralosus slowed a bit. He was unsure where he was going, and he knew that the wine he'd drank was playing tricks with his brain. He felt happy and deliriously sad both at the same time, on the verge of laughing and crying. His feet shuffled through the dirt, kicking up a tiny sandstorm behind him. The cooking fires carried the smell of meat to his nostrils. Baralosus took a deep breath of it. He looked around, sure that he was lost, but it didn't really matter. Anyone of these men could escort him back to his tent, if Baralosus didn't mind looking like a fool.

Then, from the corner of his eye he spotted a single, familiar figure sitting alone by a campfire. The man had a boot in his hand, carefully lacing it with long strands of gut. Baralosus paused, waiting for Jashien to notice him, but the man was too entranced by his careful work to look up. The others in Jashien's company had gone to their tents, leaving the fire for Jashien to enjoy. Around him the camp sparked with life, but young Jashien worked without regard for any of it, slowly looping the lace through each of the boot's holes.

Baralosus could not bring himself to leave. Watching Jashien reminded him instantly of Salina, and why he had come to this place at all.

Jashien continued working a few moments longer. Then, with that sense one always gets of being watched, he looked up at Baralosus. A hint of confusion crossed his face, then recognition. He stood, boot in hand.

'Majesty?'

Baralosus stepped closer, coming into the light. He wasn't sure what to say, or even why he wanted to speak at all.

'I'm wandering,' he said, then realized how silly that sounded. His voice slurred badly. He cleared his throat. 'I needed a stretch. Too much sitting about.'

Jashien smiled awkwardly. 'Yes. It was a long ride today.'

'May I join you?' asked Baralosus.

'Me?' Jashien looked around at his meagre camp. 'I haven't anything to offer you. I can fetch some food and wine . . .'

Baralosus put up a hand. 'No. I'm quite good.' He sauntered up to the fire, feeling its heat against his face. Jashien was staring at him. The king looked around, not wanting anyone to overhear him. There were things on his mind, the kind of things kings rarely talk about. For some reason, Jashien seemed the perfect foil.

'Sit,' he directed the young man. 'Go on with what you were doing.'

'I was lacing boots, Majesty.'

'Then go on with it,' the king insisted. He waited until Jashien sat himself back onto the sand. Jashien shrugged and placed his boot in his lap, but his hands moved distractedly this time. He grimaced uncomfortably.

'My lord has something he wishes to say?' he ventured. 'Your pardon, Majesty, but you look troubled.'

'Why would I be?' asked Baralosus. 'Because my daughter has left me? Because I have to go kill a hero? Because I have sand in my shoes that's making my feet ache?' He flopped down onto the ground and angrily began unlacing his own boots. He didn't care what Jashien thought of him or how ridiculous he looked. When he had his first boot off he tossed it aside, undid the other, then began massaging his feet with a sigh of utter satisfaction. 'I have been drinking.'

Jashien spoke carefully. 'Then you should rest, Majesty. Sit here with me.' He smiled. 'It is a fine night. Quiet.'

Baralosus looked around. 'Yes, it is quiet. Is it always so quiet out here, so far from the city?'

'Oh yes, Majesty, always. This is a good place for a man to come and think.'

'And to get bitten by a scorpion. Take no insult, Jashien, but I prefer my palace to all this sand and drowa dung.'

'But it is peaceful here, Majesty, and here you can get away from all the others. This can be a palace, too, if you know where to look. Even the moon is different here. Look how grand she is.' Jashien gestured toward the bright orb. 'It is like she has come out only for us. Don't you think?'

Baralosus stared at the moon. 'Yes . . .'

He felt old suddenly. He saw Salina's face in the moon.

Jashien put down the boot, setting it down beside him. He had come back to Ganjor twice with bad news, both times delivering it to the king himself. Baralosus knew him for what he was – a good man, loyal and devoted to the throne. But there had always been a hint of admiration in his voice when he spoke of Aztar. Aztar's strange glamour worked on men like Jashien, and Baralosus did not know why. The king stretched out his legs and leaned back against his palms, still looking contemplatively up at the moon.

'Kailyr and the others – they'll come looking for me soon,' he said.

'Not much time, then,' said Jashien. 'Will you tell me what troubles you, Majesty? I think that's why you came here.'

'I want to know about Aztar,' said the king. 'What do you think of him, Jashien?'

The question set Jashien off balance. 'Aztar? He is a fool, Majesty. That is what I think.'

'And what else?' probed the king.

'I think he has made a mistake.'

'And what else?'

'Majesty?'

'No, Jashien, don't do that. Don't tell me what I want to hear.' Baralosus sat up and glared at the man. 'I came to hear the truth from you. I want to know what you think of Aztar, and what you think he'll do.'

'Majesty, I can't say what is in the man's mind. Or in his heart. He does love your daughter. That is what I think.'

'Kailry says he won't fight. He says Aztar is merely playing games with us, still, and that he wants more from me than what I've offered.'

Jashien shook his head. 'No.'

'No?'

'Minister Kailyr was not there with me, Majesty. He did not see Aztar's face. Or your daughter's. There is real love there. He will fight for her.'

'He'll die if he does.'

'Yes,' Jashien agreed, as if there was no question of the outcome.

'So? Is he insane? He has no chance at all. If I have to kill him, what will Salina think of me? He is a fox. He has played me into a corner.' Baralosus frowned in frustration. 'And what will you think of me, Jashien?'

'Me, Majesty?' Jashien laughed. 'What should that matter?'

'I want to understand. I want to know why men love him. They follow him, you see, and not just the Voruni. You admire him, Jashien. I can see it when you speak of him. If I kill him . . .' Baralosus closed his eyes. 'I'll be the villain, not him.'

'You'll be the king,' said Jashien. 'Majesty, make no mistake – you are the King of Ganjor. No one hopes for Aztar to best you. He is like a myth, but that's all. He is a good story to tell. You worry what the people will think of you? If you do nothing, you look weak.'

'And if I come back with Aztar's head on a pole?'

'Yes,' said Jashien. 'That's what you must do! Take his head and hang it from the palace door. Then you will show the people who is the king and who is the brigand.'

'What? Really?'

Jashien nodded seriously. 'Yes, Majesty. Nothing less will do. Prince Aztar has offended you. When he is killed, go to him yourself and cut off his head. Take it back with you to Ganjor. Then show it to everyone. Show it like a trophy.'

'But Salina . . .'

'Majesty, you came for my advice, yes?'

Baralosus nodded. 'Yes.'

'Good. Now you know what you must do. It doesn't matter what your daughter thinks of you after this. You will have her back, and you can lock her in her room forever if you like. But Aztar has to die, and the people have to see that he is dead. If it turns your stomach, Majesty, then you should not have come here.'

Baralosus should have been offended, but he was not. 'I have a gaggle of advisors who tell me what I want to hear,' he said. 'I wrote poetry when I was younger. Sometimes I would read it to Kailyr. Always he told me how wonderful it was, but I was a horrid poet. Now he is doing the same thing.'

'Minister Kailyr is a friend, Majesty. He believes what he tells you, but he is wrong. Aztar will fight. So Aztar must die. You are ready for this?'

Baralosus tried very hard not to let the wine speak for him. He said in a clear voice, 'I am ready, Jashien. I will take Aztar's head myself. And when I have it I will show it to everyone, and they will know that I am king.'

With nothing left to say, Baralosus sat and looked at the moon.

Across the Skein, Prince Aztar knelt beneath the same giant moon. Atop the hill where he always went for prayer, he communed with his god, Vala, asking him for guidance. The Great One's voice was quiet but Aztar's heart was open, ready to hear anything the god might say. Alone and not speaking to anyone, he had neglected his evening meal so that he could talk to heaven. The hour had grown late and Aztar's body ached. The pains that followed him everywhere since the fire plagued him especially when he prayed, but he considered this a reminder of the things he had done wrong, and accepted his discomfort with grace. Aztar liked the solitude of the hill. Mostly, he went to it in the mornings, greeting the sunrise. Tonight, though, he needed Vala's presence. The Tiger of the Desert whispered his prayer aloud.

'. . . and I will do as you ask, Most Holy One. I will not flinch from it. Whatever you send to me, I will embrace it. Whatever your fate for me, I will take it.'

Aztar kept his eyes closed as he waited for Vala's reply. When the Great One spoke to him, it was not by words but with a simple touch on the heart. It was not easy for Aztar to describe this to others, but among the Voruni they understood. It was what made them devout. Aztar unclasped his hands and put them face down on the warm rock. Craning his neck, he looked up at the moon, and past it, toward the heavens. Why did Vala dwell in the sky, he wondered? Why not in the sand or in the life-giving plants? The answer came to him instantly, and he smiled.

So that He can see it all.

Tomorrow or the tomorrow after that, the hill would be taken from him. Very soon, he would go to face Vala. Aztar knew this with certainty and was unafraid. Living in his scarred body had become an ordeal. Living without Salina had torn his soul apart. Still, Aztar worried. He had sent Salina away to Jador, and so far she had not returned or even sent word to him of her welfare. She was well, though, and this he knew because his men had returned without her. The Witch of Grimhold had agreed to protect her, as had Jador's blind Kahana. For that, Aztar was grateful. For that, he had spent the night in prayer, thanking Vala. But there were others that Jador could not protect, and for them Aztar was frightened.

'Not for myself, Vala. Never for myself.'

He kept his eyes on the stars, desperate for wisdom. Not one of his people had fled the camp, not even now, when the Ganjeese army was so close. They would die, Aztar supposed, because he had spat on Baralosus and the king would have no mercy in his heart. But Aztar knew he deserved no mercy, not for himself. He had slain too many innocents for that. Now, Vala made him suffer for them.

'If they stay they will die. Shall I make them leave, Great One? Shall I face the Ganjeese myself? Salina will have no chance at all, then. I must take some with me to your presence. Yes?'

He waited, and the answer seemed obvious.

'Yes,' he pronounced. 'That is what we will do. For your glory, I will protect her. She is your servant, so much better than I ever was. And the people of Jador, your favoured. I will protect them, too.'

Was Vala satisfied? Aztar waited for the touch, and when it came it was good. With Vala's help he had made his decision.

Finally, Aztar lifted himself off his knees, stretching his knotted spine as he rose to his feet. The burns along his body screamed but he ignored them, smoothing down his robe and taking a deep breath of the good desert air. He loved the desert. All he ever wanted was to protect it. Did Vala understand that? He hoped so. It was not good for a man to die being misunderstood.

At the bottom of the hill, Aztar glimpsed a silent figure, waiting for him patiently in the moonlight. He took his time looking at her, admiring her and all she had done for him. She might have been there for an hour or more. Harani was loyal and never interrupted his prayers. With a slight wave he greeted her, then started his decent down the hillside. Because of his many aches he moved slowly, but when he reached the bottom Harani came to offer aid. Aztar took her arm gratefully, letting the young woman guide him toward smoother ground.

'How long have you been here?' he asked.

'Not long,' replied Harani. It was a standard answer. 'You told me to come as soon as Fahren arrived back, but I did not want to interrupt you.'

They walked together back toward the distant camp, neither of them hurrying. Aztar took his time before speaking again. He did not need to question Harani. He already knew what she would tell him. Whenever the news was bad, Harani's pretty face sagged. It was a small change, but Aztar knew her well enough to see the subtle creases. She held tight to his arm as they walked, not hiding her affection. He was her master, and she adored him. It was not at all a romantic thing. Really, it was so much more.

'Harani . . .'

The young woman stopped and looked at him. 'Master?'

'We are alone?'

The question made her blanch. 'Yes. Fahren could not convince them, Master. I am sorry. No one else will help us.'

Aztar nodded. It was the answer he'd expected. Asking for help among the other Voruni tribes had always been a gambit. They had no reason at all to stand up against Baralosus. 'Do not blame them for it,' he told Harani, seeing the disdain in her face. 'I asked too much of them.'

'We do not need them, Master,' said Harani confidently. 'We're still strong.'

'Not so strong,' laughed Aztar. He kept hold of her, refusing to go further. 'Harani, the Ganjeese are only two days away. There are at least a thousand of them. Many more, perhaps. When they come they will kill us. You do understand that, yes?'

Harani's expression turned serene. 'I understand, Master. We all understand. We are ready.'

'Ready to die?'

'Ready to go to Vala,' said Harani.

Her answer touched the desert prince. He opened his mouth to speak, then stopped himself. It would do no good to tell her to leave him. She would not free herself from the coming storm. Just like the rest of her people, she would stay with him until the Ganjeese came.

And then she would die.

50

Corvalos Chane walked alone through the halls of the forum, certain he would find his king inside. As it was on most days, the forum was deserted, and the animals that were sometimes kept in its many cages had been moved off to other places throughout the city. Chane's boots scraped quietly across the pebbled surface, not wanting to disturb his lord and master. Since returning to the city from Gilorin Court, Raxor had spent most of his time alone. Chane had barely seen his beloved king in the past week. Still in mourning over the death of his son and shaken by the defeat at the Kryss, Raxor had retreated into a private little hole, and without Mirage around to coax him out of it, the old man had become even more remote. Chane mourned, too. Not for Prince Roland, because he never really liked the red-headed loud-mouth. Rather, Chane mourned for Raxor, because the king he had known for so many years was really already dead. Between the two of them, all they could hope for now was vengeance.

And that was why Corvalos Chane had come.

When he reached the end of the hall, Chane stopped behind a pillar, peering around the stone edifice toward the arena. There, in the centre of the vast oval, he spotted King Raxor, standing in the centre of the arena with his two enormous pets. The bears were on their hind legs, prancing around Raxor as the king urged them on with treats. At their full height, the bears were a good deal taller than the big king, yet Raxor wasn't at all afraid of them. He had raised them from cubs and knew they'd never hurt him. Chane smiled, noting the pleasure on the old man's face. It was good to see him happy, if only briefly. Chane's grin sharpened, for he was sure his plan would please Raxor even more.

Chane did not want to disturb his master, but his news couldn't wait, and so he stepped softly onto the ground of the arena, making sure that Raxor saw him. The king looked surprised but waved him forward. The bears continued dancing as Chane approached, barely noticing him until Raxor ordered them down. They sniffed at Chane, knowing him immediately, and watched him with their beady black eyes. Varsha, the female of the twins, pawed up to Chane and nudged his hand with her nose in greeting. Chane took the beast's jaw and gave it a gentle squeeze. He had always liked the bear siblings, and they had always amazed him. Their loyalty to Raxor rivaled his own.

King Raxor knew immediately that Chane had come for a reason. He looked at his spy expectedly. Chane stopped playing with the bear and greeted his king with a bow.

'My lord, may I speak?' he asked.

'Tell me,' said Raxor at once.

'I have news, my lord. From Koth.'

Raxor perked up. 'Indeed?'

'Baron Glass is going to the old estate at Richter. He plans to leave in two more days. He's making ready for the trip, my lord. And he's taking Jazana Carr with him.'

Raxor was old but his mind was as sharp as ever. He seized on Chane's meaning at once. 'Interesting,' he mused. His hand rose to his mouth, rubbing his lower lip. 'How many are going with him?'

'Not many,' said Chane. 'That's the key, my lord. Baron Glass is having trouble with Jazana Carr, more so since Mirage went to him.'

'Jealousy?'

'So it seems. Glass means to make amends with her,' said Chane. Not all the details were in place, but he told his master what he knew. 'This comes from Jaron, my lord. From inside Lionkeep.'

'Then this is reliable? You're sure?'

'I think so, yes,' Chane answered. Raxor had spies everywhere, and Chane had his own connections. Of all of them, Jaron was among the best. He had posed as a mercenary to gain access to Jazana Carr. Later he had managed to work his way into Lionkeep itself, working as an outside guard. Jaron had a gift for small things, an uncanny ability to put puzzles together out of the barest scraps. 'He sent the news as quickly as he could,' Chane continued. 'But it's five days old, at least. Jaron says that Glass is planning on traveling with only a small contingent. He wants to be alone with his queen, no doubt.'

Raxor laughed with satisfaction. 'Mirage has had the same effect on him, no doubt! Jazana Carr is wise to be worried.' He looked at Chane. 'What of her? Anything?'

'Of Mirage? The same, my lord. She is well, that's all I can tell. She spends time with Glass. A great deal of time from what I'm told.'

A shadow of envy crossed Raxor's face. 'Baron Glass has everything a man could want, then,' he grumbled. 'He has taken my son and my woman both. He loves Mirage. I always knew it.'

Chane avoided looking straight at his king. He had not confessed his drunken advance on Mirage, that moment of weakness in Koth. The guilt of it gnawed at him. He said, 'Mirage is well, my lord. You should not worry about her. And this news is worth acting on.'

'Agreed.' Raxor sidled closer to Broud, the huge black male of the bears, and dug his fingers deeply into his thick fur. The bear responded with a grunt of pleasure. 'I have been to Richter,' said Raxor, 'years ago. That was when King Akeela was alive, when there was peace.' He thought for a moment, summoning the memory. 'It's very small. Not many staff. There are mountains around it, and I remember a lake. It's very high up. Secluded.'

'My lord, I've already sent some people there,' said Chane. 'Horatin and Kaprile of the Red Watch. A few others. They're already making plans, watching the layout. I had some ideas for them to take with them.'

'What ideas?'

'As you said, it's a small estate, my lord. And Glass isn't taking many men with him.'

'He doesn't need many men. He has the armour, remember.'

'Aye,' said Chane, 'I remember. But nothing is indestructible, my lord, and he can't wear the armour forever. Not to bed, certainly.'

Raxor looked intrigued. 'You mean to assassinate him.'

'Yes,' said Chane. Assassination was a specialty of the Red Watch. Chane had trained them himself. 'Six or seven of us should be able to get it done.'

'If Glass sees you, he'll kill you,' said Raxor.

'He won't see us, my lord. I don't intend to climb though his window.'

'What then?'

'I plan to burn him,' Chane replied. 'I've thought about this, my lord. If the doors were barricaded, no one would be able to escape. And if someone did manage to get out alive . . .' Chane shrugged.

'You mean to murder them all?'

'Baron Glass and Jazana Carr at least,' said Chane coolly.

King Raxor turned away, considering the plan. Chane stood very still, giving his master time to think. It would not be as easy as he'd hinted, but he desperately wanted Raxor's blessing.

'A chance like this won't come along again soon,' he said. 'Consider, my lord – both Glass and the Diamond Queen in the same small space. Not even the armour can protect Glass against an inferno. And if it does, we'll be there to finish him – all of us.'

'Even you won't be enough to stop Baron Glass, Corvalos. If you had seen him at the Kryss you would know what I mean. He's not just a man anymore. It's like Mirage said – he is possessed of a devil. And devils live in flames.'

'Then at least we will kill his queen,' Chane countered. 'My lord, there isn't much time. I have to get to Richter quickly and join the others. There are things I'll need to arrange. Baron Glass will have the jump on me either way.'

'I hear you, Corvalos, I do. But there are risks.'

'To myself and the others alone,' said Chane. He brought his lanky body closer to the king. 'Please, my lord, let me do this for you. Let me kill the man who killed your son.'

The bears had stopped ambling around. As if sensing the seriousness of the conversation, they looked up earnestly at Raxor. The king remained silent, his eyes glazing over.

'I'm not mad,' he said softly. 'I've heard others talking, Chane, the things they've said about me. But I'm not mad. I'm simply . . . troubled.'

'Yes, my lord,' said Chane gently. 'I know.'

The old man turned his eyes on Chane, full of love. 'Baron Glass must not know it is us. Do nothing to betray Reec. Dress as mercenaries. Make him believe it is Norvans, even. That upstart Elgan perhaps. But nothing must lead him back to us. We cannot have him march against us. Not yet. Not when we are so weak.'

'Of course, my lord.'

Raxor reached out and gripped Chane's shoulder. 'You have been so good to me for so many years. Let this be your last mission, Corvalos.'

'My lord?'

'We are old, my friend,' said Raxor with a grin. 'No one has served me better or longer than you have. You have given up everything for me. Even your birthright as a man.'

'I have not minded, my lord.'

'Haven't you? I have eyes, Corvalos. I saw the way you looked at Mirage, how you craved her. No, do not be embarrassed! She was a splendid woman.'

The revelation stung Chane. He dropped his head and sank to his knees. 'My lord, I'm sorry,' he sighed. 'In my heart I lusted for her. Forgive me.'

'There is nothing to forgive, my friend,' said Raxor, looking down. 'You're not a eunuch, after all. No man can expect to be without hungers if he is truly a man.'

'But she was your woman, my lord . . .'

'And you brought her to me and made me happy. Rise.'

Chane got to his feet but could not bring himself to look at his king. In his heart, he had betrayed Raxor. He had even tried to bed Mirage. Would his king be so forgiving if he knew that too?

'Let me show you my devotion, my lord,' he begged. 'Let me kill Baron Glass and his bitch queen. Say the word, please . . .'

'You have your leave, Corvalos. Do it and be well. And when you are done and Baron Glass is dead, your service to me will be over.'

'My lord, no . . .'

'It's time for you to live your life, Corvalos,' said Raxor easily. 'While you are young enough to enjoy a woman, you must find yourself one. Have children. Know that joy before you die. That is how you can serve me best.'

The offer overwhelmed Chane. Since he could remember, he had been in Raxor's service, first as a soldier, then as a bodyguard. He had devoted his whole life to the king and had never regretted it until he'd been alone with Mirage – when his own stupid drunkenness had made him forget his vow.

'My lord, I promise you – Baron Glass will not return from Richter. Let him call his demon. Let him summon all the devils of hell. They will not save him from me.'

51

In the waning sun of twilight, a tiny mass of two-hundred men wound their way through the dunes of the desert, watching the eastern horizon for their unseen enemies. They had ridden for most of the day, leaving behind loved ones in the Skein and the meagre homes they had made for themselves among the brush and blowing sands. Mounted on drowas, the men had dressed for battle, bearing scimitars at their sides and carrying the long lances they would use for the charge. Around their faces they wore dark wraps. Black gakas draped their bodies. They had no long bows for distant combat, but some brought smaller, nimble bows with them, the kind that could be fired quickly from the back of a galloping drowa. The mass moved with purpose across the soft earth of the desert, determined to meet their foes by sun fall, sure to a man that they would not see the morning.

Prince Aztar rode at the front of the force, sitting tall despite his pain and weariness, proud of the men he was leading to their deaths. They were Voruni, the hard and powerful nomads of the desert, and because he was their master they would follow him to hell. Without complaint, they had followed Aztar throughout the day, kissing their wives and children farewell and mounting their drowas to confront Baralosus' army. Scouts returning from the desert had told Aztar that the Ganjeese were no more than a day's ride from the Skein, riding slowly but undaunted toward Aztar's humble camp. And Aztar, determined to keep the bloodshed as far as possible from the children, had ordered his men to make ready to ride. It was, he determined, as good a time as any to die, and he was not afraid. He had prayed mightily for guidance and Vala had given it to him. This time, he was sure he was on the right side.

The plea he had sent to the other tribes had gone mostly unheeded, but in the last day before the march some fifty men had come to join him, bringing their own drowa and weapons with them. They had come from each of the five Voruni tribes peppered throughout the area, mostly lawless men who had no standing in their own tribes and who, like so many others, respected Aztar's stance. They knew that this would be the prince's last stand, and somehow that moved them. Knowing they would die, they could think of no better place to perish than at the side of a legend.

Aztar himself had no such illusions. He had already led men to slaughter, and because he had chosen his enemies so poorly Vala had punished him. He was not the myth so many thought he was, but rather just a man with troubles. Still, he rode with confidence in the waning light, eager to glimpse Baralosus' army. And because his brother Baraki had come he was not afraid at all. Bouncing atop his sauntering drowa, his scarred body burdened by heavy battle clothes, Aztar stole a glance at his brother Baraki, the man who had followed him into battle against Jador. Once, Baraki had been his most trusted Zarturk, but in the aftermath of battle he had fled with the others, sure that Aztar had blundered irreparably and unable to face him. Baraki had been one of the few who had survived the Jadori fire, and the magic had frightened him away. Aztar had never blamed him for that. But now, when Aztar needed him most, Baraki had returned. And Aztar, full of love for him, smiled at the man.

'Not much more,' said Baraki. He had lowered his wrappings to the cooler air of twilight, revealing his unreadable face. As always, his expression was a mask, but what feelings it hid Aztar could not say. Baraki glanced back at the men snaking behind them, riding quietly. 'Look how weary they are. We should stop now, Aztar.'

'We go on,' said Aztar. 'Before the sun rises again, I will speak to Baralosus and show him that we are not afraid of him.'

Baraki nodded tacitly. Only a pace behind him, the other Zarturks rode together, having fallen quiet as they too sensed the closeness of the Ganjeese. Fahleen, the oldest of them, kept his eyes on the east, his gaze unwavering. When Aztar turned to look at him, Fahleen raised his hand. Aztar did the same, then did so to the others as well, urging Rakaar and Adnah on with confidence. Rakaar grinned. Adnah did not. Rakaar was not afraid of anything. Adnah had left a wife behind. Together they would command the little army they had left, each of them taking fifty or so men. Once, Aztar's army had numbered far more, but the battle with Jador had decimated them. Now, the man who called himself the Tiger of the Desert had barely two-hundred men to face down Baralosus' much larger force.

Aztar continued to ride, ignoring the enormous pain racking his body, until his brother Baraki sidled up to his drowa. Baraki's beast was a large, black drowa, powerfully built with armour across its flanks and a gleaming brass bit between its yellow teeth. The drowa snorted unhappily at Aztar's mount.

'So?' asked Baraki. 'What will you say to him?'

'To who, brother?'

'Who,' scoffed Baraki. He lowered his voice. 'Baralosus, of course. What will you tell him? You haven't said yet. He will want to make a deal with you. He is a snake, remember.'

'He has had his time to deal,' said Aztar. 'He has already sent his dogs to me. Baralosus knows I cannot be brought.'

'Ah, but he will try! He will offer you anything for his daughter.'

Aztar glowered at his brother. 'I no longer have her to give. Our duty now is to protect her. You will remember that, Baraki, won't you?'

'I've come, haven't I? I know what you expect of me, brother.' Baraki grinned. 'And I cannot wait to see his pompous face when you tell him Salina isn't with you anymore. What will he say, do you think?'

'He will rage like the witch winds,' said Aztar, 'because his heart will be broken.'

There was no glee in Aztar's statement. Unlike Baraki, he had no real hatred of Baralosus, despite the way the king had used him. But there were things he wanted to say to Baralosus, things that men of honour should say face to face. Thinking of that now, he was glad once again that Baraki was with him. He could not take an army into the presence of the king, but he could take his brother.

'Keep your dagger close, brother,' Aztar quipped. 'You might need it sooner than you think.'

King Baralosus was reclining in his coach when the carriage came to a sudden stop. He opened his eyes, shaking off the daydream he was having of the new young maid he had hired for his staff, and blearily peered out of his open window. The coach was unbearably hot, pulled along the soft ground on wide, giant wheels made especially for desert travel. Outside, he watched as the men of his army – mounted and unmounted – slowly halted one by one. Commanders at the front of the column were shouting orders back to the rear. Behind his own coach, the smaller, less elaborate conveyance of his friend Kailyr also ground to a stop. With almost no light left in the day, Baralosus supposed General Rhot had decided to camp for the night, a notion that suited the king fine. They were less than a day's ride from the Skein now, and Baralosus wasn't anxious to face Aztar.

Then, someone up ahead shouted Aztar's name. Baralosus' heart began to charge.

'What is it?' he called out of the window. 'What's happening?'

His driver shook his head and called back stupidly, 'I don't know, Majesty. There's something ahead.'

'Something?' sputtered Baralosus. 'Don't move! I'm getting out.'

517

The driver kept the drowas firm as the king opened the door of his coach, not waiting for his groomsman. Flinging himself to the sand, he raced up to where his driver sat, scanning the dark horizon. The sun setting behind the dunes turned the west pink with its fiery decent. Past the rows and rows of his own weary soldiers, Baralosus saw something unfamiliar in the distance, something not very large but not insignificant either. He fell back at the sight, dread rising in his gut.

'Aztar . . .'

The Prince's army was unmistakable, staked out atop a large, unmoving hill of sand. With the last rays of the sun lighting their backs, they looked like ghostly silhouettes atop their battle drowas, the tips of their long lances pointed skyward. How numerous they were, Baralosus could not say, though an ugly feeling crept up his spine that they just might have blundered into a trap.

'Majesty?' called a voice from behind. 'Is it them?'

The voice was Kailyr's, and the Minister sounded troubled as he raced out of his own carriage to stand beside his king. A handful of soldiers were hurrying toward them out of the front ranks, among them Kahrdeen, Rhot's trusted commander.

'Majesty, you should get back into your carriage,' said Kahrdeen quickly. His drowa skidded to a halt before the king. 'That's Aztar, Majesty.'

'I can see that,' snorted Baralosus.

'What does he want?' wondered Kailyr. 'To talk? Or to fight?'

King Baralosus studied his enemy on the hill. If Jashien was right, Aztar would be able to field only two-hundred men, maybe slightly more. Even if they were hidden in the dunes, they would be no match for the Ganjeese army. The king thought very hard about his options, blocking out the shouts of men around him. All he really wanted was his daughter. If killing Aztar was the price, it mattered little now.

'Look at him,' whispered the king. 'Look how he sits there, so confident, so calm. He knows he has no chance at all. He must know that.'

'He knows,' hissed Kailyr. 'That's why he's come to face you, Baralosus. He must want to talk.'

Baralosus agreed. 'You are right. He is a man of honour, after all.' The king turned toward the waiting commander. 'Kahrdeen, get word to Rhot. I want to speak to Aztar myself. Make a drowa ready for me and an escort.'

'You're going out there?' screeched Kailyr.

'I have to face him,' replied Baralosus. 'I have to get my daughter back.'

In less than an hour, Rhot had sent word out to Aztar on the hill and Aztar had responded. With only one Voruni as an escort, the Tiger of the Desert rode within arrow range of Baralosus' army.

The king himself had picked Rhot and Jashien to accompany him to the talks. Night had fallen by the time they rode out of camp, protected by a dozen other men bearing arms and torches. Baralosus waited on the back of his personal drowa, a beast of impeccable bearing and breeding with golden cloth draped across its flanks and hammered, iron armour. He watched curiously as Aztar approached, the breeze stirring his long black garments. Neither Aztar nor his escort bore a lance. Instead, both men kept their scimitars safely at their sides, riding casually toward the much more heavily armed Ganjeese. Baralosus felt a twinge of fear, not really sure what he would say. He had nothing left to offer Aztar. Only the threat of death might convince the Tiger to let his daughter go. It was how things had to be, he told himself. He simply could not return to Ganjor without Salina. And Aztar's severed head.

If Aztar knew these things, his gait did not show them. He looked as fearless as ever as he rode forward, his face not obscured by his usual Voruni wrappings. Baralosus squinted for a good look at him. He had not seen the prince since his maiming, but according to Jashien he had suffered badly in the fire. It surprised Baralosus that the man could ride at all. His pain must have been enormous.

General Rhot kept his hands on the reins of his drowa. Mounted beside the king, his expression remained contemptuous. Slightly behind the general, Jashien waited with an uneasy grimace. The young soldier had been surprised by his king's invitation to join the party, but had not wasted any time at all riding forth. He was, Baralosus knew, the only man among them who could talk to Aztar at all. Twice he had managed to leave the Tiger's camp alive.

At last, Aztar was close enough to see clearly. Baralosus gasped a little under his breath. Even in the darkness he could see the terrible scars that had clawed through Aztar's once handsome face. His skin had a smooth quality, as if all the wrinkles had been burned away. The pain that Baralosus imagined showed now in Aztar's eyes, but the prince managed to tame it. Still, Baralosus could not imagine that Salina – a perfect rose of a girl – could love a man so damaged. As Aztar neared the king's party, he reined in his drowa, spinning the beast around a little to show its broadside. Next to him, his escort did the same. Baralosus recognized the man at once. He had thought that Baraki had abandoned Aztar.

For a long moment, Aztar and Baralosus glared at each other. Once, they had been allies, conspirators in a mutual game against Jador. They had eaten the same food and spoke the same rhetoric, and they had enjoyed each other at least a little. Now, though, the wall between them rose up high and fast. To Baralosus, there seemed only one thing to say.

'I've come for my daughter,' he pronounced. 'Give her to me.'

Aztar's face was firm. 'I cannot. She is not mine to give you.'

'Then why have you come?' asked the king.

'To speak with you,' the prince replied. 'To tell you that I cannot let you pass.'

General Rhot gave a throaty laugh. 'Who will stop us? You? That rabble on the hill? You forget yourself . . . *Prince*. You have no chance at all. Release Princess Salina to us and by the king's grace go on your way.'

'Princess Salina is not with me,' said Aztar. He spoke directly to Baralosus, ignoring Rhot completely. 'She has gone to Jador. They are protecting her now.'

Baralosus' jaw dropped. 'You lie . . .'

'Salina has not been in my camp for more than a week,' said Aztar. 'She is already safe within the White City, and they have vowed to defend her. As have I. You may be her father but—'

'I am her king!' Baralosus thundered. 'And I am yours! You filthy mutt, bring her to me!'

Aztar remained frustratingly calm. 'She is in Jador,' he repeated. 'I sent her there to be free of you. You are a serpent, Baralosus. You used me and locked up your daughter as though she were a slave. Once I was like you, but I have seen the warm light of truth. Vala is with me now. He has spoken to me, and this time I hear clearly.'

Baralosus could not believe his ears, or the audacity of the man before him. 'I'm here to talk in good faith,' he seethed. 'And you have sent my daughter away? You spit in my face, Aztar! I offered you everything!'

'You offered me slavery,' said Aztar. 'You meant only to make me one of your puppets. But Salina's love is not yours to grant. It is the only thing I want, and she has already given it to me.'

'Aztar, hold your tongue,' cautioned Jashien. He drove his mount forward a little to confront the prince. 'Don't you see? I warned you of this. Look at the army massed against you! Have you any chance at all? You do not. Call the princess back from Jador. Do it, please, and spare yourself.'

Jashien's plea surprised Baralosus, but he did not object. He looked hopefully at Aztar, but the prince was steadfast.

'I can't do that. Nor can I let any of you pass. Salina is blessed by Vala because she is righteous, as the Jadori are righteous. They are beloved by Vala, all of them.' Aztar looked mockingly at Baralosus. 'For once I am on the right side, Majesty.'

'Is that why you came to talk? To make your little speech?' hissed Baralosus.

'I wished to see you one more time, my old benefactor,' said Aztar. 'After all, it's all about politics, isn't it? That is why you are here – to kill me and keep your honour. So – I do what a man of honour does. I come to you, face to face. This is my threat, Majesty. I cannot let you pass.'

Baralosus felt his hope fade away. Like grains of sand, the last of it slipped through his fingers. 'I love my daughter,' he said. 'Whatever you may think of me, know that, Aztar. And she loves me. If you had not filled her mind with sweet talk and lies, she would be with me now, safe in Ganjor. She would be fed and clean and uncorrupted.'

'She would be your slave, dancing when you clap,' said Aztar. 'She is free of you now, Baralosus. As am I.'

'You are a dead man,' said the king. 'And I do not speak to dead men.' Baralosus spat at the ground then wheeled his drowa around and headed back to camp. 'Go back to your hill,' he called over his shoulder. 'Pray to Vala with all your might, Aztar. Very soon, you will see him face to face.'

52

Aztar and his brother had barely reached the hill by the time he heard the horn sound. Behind them, Baralosus' General was calling his troops to battle. Aztar urged his drowa up the hill, then swung it around to see the advancing army. His Zarturks hurried to his side. Baraki began calling out to their warriors, preparing them for the assault. The Ganjeese army came alive like a great, unified mass, spreading out across the desert as they took up their positions. Aztar watched them from the top of the dune, wondering about their tactics. He had riled Baralosus, surely, but he wasn't sure it would be enough. The king was angry but not stupid.

'They're coming,' said Rakaar excitedly. 'Look!'

The spreading stain of the Ganjeese army swarmed out toward them, moving slowly but perfectly to encircle the dunes. The hills were high and would protect them, Aztar knew, giving them a much needed advantage. With the sunlight gone, he would have a chance – if Baralosus made the hoped for mistake. Aztar continued to watch them as Baraki positioned their own troops. Most had already taken up positions in the dunes. Because of the size and arrangement of the hills, even Aztar could not see most of them, but he knew that his mounted bowmen had hidden themselves in the front, ready to fire at the advancing enemy.

'They're coming,' said Rakaar. 'We should retreat to the centre now, Aztar.'

Aztar agreed, and with a shout to his brother spun his drowa toward the undulating middle of the hills. There he passed the others who had already gathered, ordering them to spread out through the dunes and get ready for the fight.

'Be ready for them,' he called. 'They may come in the dark if we are lucky. If not they will wait until morning.'

'Baralosus isn't that stupid,' said Fahleen, the eldest of the Zarturks. 'He'll surround us until the sun rises. Then he'll come for us.'

There was arguing back and forth among them, Rakaar sure the

Ganjeese would attack, while young Adnah sided with Fahleen. But they all had their own men to command, and their wagging tongues angered Aztar.

'Get to your men,' he snapped. 'Rakaar, fire on anyone who comes close enough. They may test our front. If they do, kill them. Go.'

Rakaar nodded and went back the way he'd come, riding quickly toward the front of the dunes. He was the one with the most bowmen, the one who would take the brunt of the attack if the Ganjeese advanced as predicted. As for the flanks, they belonged to Fahleen and Adnah, each with barely fifty men. Aztar himself would remain in the centre with Baraki, commanding the battle from a tall dune until he could himself ride into the fight. He had already selected his position, and rode toward it now with Baraki and a handful of Voruni warriors. The ground yielded like mud beneath the hooves of their drowa, making the climb a chore. When at last they reached the top, Aztar looked out over his dark position and smiled.

Throughout the dunes his men had doused their torches, leaving them almost invisible in the moonlight. Far up ahead, Rakaar's men crouched in the dunes, some mounted, some standing near their drowa with bows in their hands. They were the short, quick firing bows, the only kind his men ever used, with small arrows tipped with iron that they carried in poaches on their backs. Rakaar's men had fanned out along the front dunes, keeping deep within the shadows but also using scouts to watch the approaching Ganjeese. Other scouts from each of the Zarturks took up positions on other dunes as well, so that their actions could be coordinated. Aztar took the time to give a little smile. Even though they had no real chance at all, what he saw impressed them. Any damage they could do would make things that much easier for Jador.

'Aztar, look there,' directed Baraki, gesturing toward Baralosus army. The great mass had begun to split. 'They mean to surround us.'

Aztar knew General Rhot to be a competent man, a leader with enough experience to know they shouldn't attack at night. Still, the manoeuvres disappointed Aztar. Rhot had obviously talked his king out of a night-time attack. His men moved cautiously as they began to fan out, unhurried. The bulk of them remained at the front while two smaller groups moved to flank the dunes. Each force contained rows of mounted drowamen with lances, which would probably do them no good. Aztar's men had already discarded their own lances, taking up javelins instead. But what made Aztar the most curious were the longbowmen. General Rhot, oddly visible in the moonlight, remained with them as they advanced and then halted, readying themselves for the assault.

'They can reach us from there,' Aztar whispered, studying the archers.

'In the dark?' Baraki shook his head. 'No.'

'Baralosus has all the gold he needs for arrows,' said Aztar. 'He'll waste them all night long if he must.'

Because his men had no shields, the thought of the archers worried Aztar. Even hidden in the dunes and darkness, his men would be vulnerable. He looked around, wondering how best to protect them, and realized that it would only be luck that let the archers find their marks.

But there were so many of them . . .

'We're vulnerable up here,' grumbled Aztar. 'And so are the scouts.'

It was a stupid mistake, the kind Aztar had expected Baralosus to make. With the bowmen raining chaos on them, it would be impossible for him to command his men. Aztar determined to wait as long as he could, sure that the barrage would not come too soon. Again he was wrong.

He heard the shout from the general first, then watched in dread as the archers drew back their longbows. Rows of them, perfectly tilted, aimed their weapons skyward and awaited the order to loose. Aztar called out frantically to his men, warning them of the attack just as the arrows flew. Instantly they disappeared into the dark sky, but against the moon Aztar could briefly see them, like insects quickly flying. At once he and his brother sought cover, riding their beasts back down the hill. A moment later the storm began. The arrows pelted the ground, landing with sharp thuds all around them. Aztar heard his men shout – then scream – as amazingly the missiles found some marks. Though the dunes were fine for hiding them, they did nothing to shield them from the heavens. Aztar galloped quickly from his hill, heading toward the front where the barrage seemed lightest. Turning back he watched as a single arrow fell from the sky and slipped perfectly through a man's eye.

'A night of this?' cried Baraki. 'This is Baralosus' honour?'

'Up front,' Aztar called back. 'That's where they'll come at us.'

'Now? They'll attack now?'

Aztar waved at his brother to hurry. 'They'll try to push us out of here. They'll try to wear us down. Come, brother! Why should we wait like women on a hill? To the fight!'

King Baralosus watched from his drowa as General Rhot ordered the archers to continue. Already the barrage had produced happy results, dislodging Aztar from his place on the hill and sending the scouts scattering. Baralosus imagined the chaos in the dunes, the terror as the darkness filled with death. If he listened closely, he could hear men screaming over the noise of his own moving army. The moonlight made the dunes shift with life. Aztar's men were hidden, mostly, but at the forefront of the dunes some of them peeked out their heads, making ready for the assault. Baralosus tried to calm himself. His words with Aztar had unsettled him, and the thought of his daughter in the hands of the Jadori made him seethe. Such an unimaginable turn of events – why hadn't any of his advisors warned him? All of them, especially Kailyr, had been wrong about everything. Only Jashien seemed capable of rational thought, and because of that Baralosus kept Jashien close, calling him out of his own regiment to be a personal guard. Jashien kept very quiet as he watched the battle begin. His expression looked peculiar. Near him stood Kailyr, also looking strange. More precisely, Kailyr looked embarrassed, and kept to himself after being proved so wrong. He stole a glance at Baralosus while the spearmen prepared to move. Baralosus smirked at him.

Kahrdeen galloped up to him out of the front lines. The young soldier had been back and forth the whole time, relaying messages from Rhot. He already looked haggard. 'Majesty, we're ready. General Rhot asks your permission to begin.'

'Tell General Rhot to do whatever he sees fit,' said Baralosus. 'Tell him that I want Aztar brought to me. He can be dead or alive, I don't care which. Just make sure his head is still on.'

Kahrdeen reared back. 'Majesty?'

'Just give the order, Kahrdeen.'

The soldier spun his drowa around and headed back toward the front. As Baralosus watched him go, he saw the spearmen making ready and knew it would be a long night.

Aztar had his hand on a wounded man's throat when he saw the first Ganjeese spearman. The man he was holding – a friend named Mulam – had taken an arrow in the neck and fallen from his drowa only feet from where Aztar had been waiting and watching. The blood sluicing through his wound told Aztar he would not live much longer. Aztar plugged the wound with his finger, cursing for Rakaar to hurry with the bandage.

'They're coming,' Rakaar hissed, tossing a glance over his shoulder as he fumbled with the cloth, tearing off a strip of his own gaka.

'I see them,' said Aztar. All he wanted was to get back on his drowa. He tried to smile at Mulam, who was gasping now for breath. It made no sense to dress his wound, really, but Aztar could not let him die. Not yet. Not in such a terrible way.

'Aztar come!' his brother cried. 'They're coming through!'

'Aztar go,' Rakaar told him. He was already working the bandage around Mulam's neck. 'I'll bind his wound and leave him be. What else can we do?'

With a last look at his loyal Voruni, Aztar sped toward his drowa, climbing quickly onto the beast and driving it forward. Passing a stand of javelins stuck ready in the sand, he reached out and snatched one of the weapons, catching up to his brother Baraki. Baraki and a band of others had taken up positions behind the leading dune, a great mass of loose sand that shifted in the evening breeze. The men, all of them mounted, had begun firing their bows at the coming spearmen, riding and ducking at the same time as they loosed their bolts. Overhead the air filled with another volley of Ganjeese arrows. Aztar saw them against the moon, bracing himself for the deadly rain.

'There are so many,' said Baraki dreadfully, peering out past the dune at the swarming mob. The spearmen were infantry, charging across the bare earth with their long weapons tucked beneath their armpits. Far behind them, General Rhot kept his drowas in reserve, ready to charge.

'They're testing us, that's all,' surmised Aztar. 'He won't send in his drowamen. Not yet. Not till morning.'

The prediction did little to ease Baraki's fears. He had fought with Aztar dozens of times before, but this time was different and both of them knew it. Baraki had the face of a man who simply knew his death was lurking.

'Remember,' Aztar told them all, 'this is for the glory of Vala.'

The men around him raised their javelins, cheering themselves, trying to stoke the fire that would make them fight. In the hills behind them, the other Zarturks endured the Ganjeese arrows, but these were the men who'd be first into battle. Aztar unwound the headdress from around his skull, flinging it aside, proudly displaying his entire, fire-scorched face.

'Come then, damned king!' he cried. The glamour was on him now, for all his men to see. He rode out of the cover of the dune, not needing to ask his men to follow, and called out to the coming spearmen. 'You are the whores of the world! We are righteous! We are not afraid!'

The spearmen came like a big black wave, breaking across the dune and spreading out against the opposing bowmen. One at a time some hit the dirt, felled by the arrows of the galloping Voruni. Still they came, undeterred, spurred on by Rhot's distant battle horns. Aztar sized up the coming men, knew them to be weaker, and rode for the fight, bringing down his javelin as though it were a lance and tearing gleefully into them. Spears flew against his head. His great beast bellowed and spit. And Aztar, full of fury, tackled a trio of spearmen, barreling past them as they reached for his clothes then bringing his weapon plunging down into the back of the nearest man. At once the soldier's chest exploded, run through by the javelin. Aztar ripped it free and continued on, again and again bringing it down against his enemies. Around him he heard Rakaar's men shouting, besting the spearmen, but not without casualties. They were stronger easily, but woefully outnumbered, and the spearmen seemed without end, two taking up where one had fallen. They were only the first wave and Aztar knew it. He had men enough to beat them back, but that would only expose them more, and he could not ask it of his warriors.

'Alone, then,' he said. Determined to see who would follow, he tossed his javelin into a coming soldier, took his shining scimitar from his side, and cried out for blood. He did not look back as he raced from the dunes – he saw only the wall of spearmen before him.

General Rhot sat atop his drowa, comfortably distant from the unfolding fight. Remaining near the lines where his bowmen were firing, he watched with detachment as his infantry advanced on the dunes, confident that his patience would easily win the day, or more precisely the night. Through the moonlight he could see his men steadily moving, helped by the barrage of their bowmen back in the ranks. Two more groups of warriors had already encircled the dunes, ready to move in at the first sight of sunlight. It would be a long evening, and probably unproductive, and General Rhot tried hard not to grow bored. He knew that Aztar was trying to draw him in, trying to make him fight in the dark dunes. The dunes did a job of concealing the Voruni numbers, but it was a desperate tactic and one that really didn't impress Rhot.

'They think too much of this man,' he sighed openly. At his side was young Kahrdeen, who nodded in agreement. 'See how stupid he is, Kahrdeen? Who would do such a thing?'

'And why?' wondered Kahrdeen. 'He could have had so much.'

There was a trace of regret in his commander's tone. Rhot didn't approve of it. 'Because he is a fool,' he shot back. 'Aztar is a zealot, and now it has ruined him. You should watch closely, Kahrdeen – I want you to learn from this day. Do not make a hero of fools.'

Kahrdeen did not argue with the general. Instead he focused on the battle ahead, leaning forward in his saddle curiously. For a moment he blinked, then smiled. 'General . . . look there.'

Rhot had momentarily looked away, but now turned his attention back to the dunes. What he saw confused him. 'Is that Aztar?'

The question needed no answer. There he was, plain as daylight, galloping through the spearmen, blade raised high, voice ringing through the night. Behind him came a stampede of Voruni drowamen, flooding out onto sand and hacking down Rhot's soldiers. Rhot began to boil.

'Get that ridiculous grin off your face, Kahrdeen,' he seethed, 'and send Zasif's men after him. Now!'

Kahrdeen snapped to attention and loped off, calling out for Zasif and his drowamen. Rhot sat in stunned silence, shaking his head.

'He wants to be hero,' he whispered. 'That's all the madman cares about.'

Then, realizing the turn of events, he wheeled his mount around and rode toward King Baralosus.

Aztar saw the cavalry riding for his position. Atop his drowa, he stayed very still for a long time, watching as they charged closer. Under their assault his men would stand no chance at all, not out in the open, but he wondered what Rhot was thinking and why he had sent them so soon. The spearmen had been sent to test them.

Hadn't they?

While Aztar puzzled, his brother rode up and pulled back hard on his tack. Around them the spearmen continued to swarm, but the Voruni riders had cut a wide swathe through them, leaving bodies scattered on the sands. Aztar himself was drenched in blood and sweat. A gory smear ran across his face. He wiped at it, frustrated by Rhot's tactics.

'Is he sending them in?' he asked. 'Or is this another ploy?'

'Does it matter? We should go, Aztar?'

Hoping the Ganjeese riders would follow them into the dunes, Aztar retreated with his men into the dark recesses of the shifting hills, battling their way through the remaining spearmen. In mere minutes they had cut down a hundred of them, but a hundred more remained and chased them relentlessly into the dunes, where covering fire from Rakaar's bowmen held them back. Once he reached the inside passage, Aztar rode back toward his command hill, ignoring the on-going hail of arrows from the tireless longbows. His men rallied to his side, peppering him with questions.

'They want a fight,' Aztar declared. 'We will give them our best.'

Thundering up the sandy slope, he glanced backward toward the Ganjeese lines. Higher now, he could see the advancing cavalry. Already it had slowed. Aztar cursed and checked the flanks, which remained quiet.

'Damn it,' he growled. He shook his head at Baraki, who had come up behind him. 'He's not coming. He's only driven us off like flies!'

Baraki took notice of the tactic, his face sour. Like his brother, his gaka clung heavily to his body, soaked with blood. His scimitar remained in his hand, gleaming with a slick of scarlet. The two brothers remained silent, listening to the restless sounds of night. Overhead, arrows whistled through the darkened sky.

'We must wait,' counseled Baraki. He turned to his brother. 'Aztar? Do you hear?'

Prince Aztar nodded wearily. 'I hear you, brother. The morning.' He took his scimitar and raised it high above his head, so that the blood dripped from its point down to its hilt. 'For you, Vala!' he cried. 'And in the morning, you shall feast.'

*

Baralosus spent the night near a campfire, eating poorly cooked food as he awaited word from his commanders. General Rhot continued to send him reports, all of which said the same uninteresting things. His men had the dunes surrounded. Aztar's forces hadn't moved at all. The bowmen on both sides stopped firing hours ago, leaving the night quiet.

But Baralosus did not sleep. His every thought remained on Salina, and by the time the sun finally arose he was eager at last to have his vengeance. Springing up from the sand, he called to his grooms to fetch his drowa. He had already discussed their tactics with Rhot and didn't want to miss any of the bloody action. Kahrdeen was waiting for him when he broke away from camp, ready to escort the king to the front lines. Jashien, who had remained with Baralosus most of the night, kept close to his master as he waited for his mount. The grooms quickly brought up the drowa. Looking rested and refreshed, the huge beast rolled its eyes at the king as Baralosus tossed himself into the saddle. Before snapping the reins he gave Jashien a knowing nod.

In the quiet of the small hours, the two had talked again of Aztar and the thing Baralosus needed to do. More importantly, he needed to be *seen* to do it. King and soldier shared a silent understanding before Baralosus rode off with Kahrdeen.

'You have been right about everything,' he told Jashien.

Jashien shrugged. 'It is easy to be right about a man like Aztar. He is predictable.'

'He's not stupid, if that's what you mean.'

'No, Majesty. I mean that he is devoted. Men like that are easy to figure out.'

Baralosus said nothing, but the reply rattled him. Aztar *was* devoted. Not just to Vala and to his Voruni, but to Salina as well. There had even been a time when the Tiger was devoted to the king himself. Suddenly, Baralosus regretted the turn events had taken. His whole life had been politics. Aztar had seen that in him. For the first time since coming to the desert, Baralosus felt regret.

'He lives in a world above me,' he muttered.

Jashien turned to him. 'Majesty?

Baralosus smirked unhappily. 'Just a thought. Stay close to me, Jashien.'

'Of course, Majesty.'

Together they followed Kahrdeen to the front of the army, where General Rhot still sat upon his drowa, directing the men who scurried around him. The long night had wearied Rhot, making his bearded face droop. Still, his eyes burned with determination, even pleasure that morning had finally come. He smiled a little at the approaching king.

'Majesty, we are ready,' he declared. 'On your orders, I will unleash hell on Aztar.'

Baralosus looked around. Out around the dunes, his much larger army surrounded Aztar's own, poised to enter the sandy hills and extract the prince. Atop the highest dunes a handful of the Voruni waited, scouting their enemies. It had no doubt been a terrible night for them all, and Baralosus was sure they would not be refreshed enough to fight their best. It would be a rout, a massacre even, and giving the order gave the king no pleasure at all.

'General Rhot,' he said softly, 'do what you must.'

The order went out, and the great army of Ganjor came alive like a huge, armoured beast.

Prince Aztar knew his time had come.

For the prince and his brother, it had been a bizarre evening. Knowing that the morning would bring their death had made the two siblings talk about things they hadn't spoken of in years, the kinds of things that old men discuss on their death beds. Prince Aztar had reflected on his life and was satisfied. He had made mistakes, but in the eyes of Vala he was cleansed now, with only one great task left before him.

To Aztar, it did no good to hide within the dunes. His task seemed as clear as the new daylight pouring over the sands. His enemies numbered over a thousand, but most of these were unimportant men, like game pieces moved about by a master. And like any game of skill, it was capturing the king that mattered most. Aztar had no illusions of his chances, but it was Vala's will that he try. And like a fool, Baralosus had come out of hiding to accommodate him, riding up to the front of the ranks so that he was plainly visible now atop his ostentatious drowa.

'He looks like a fat hen,' commented Baraki. 'Does he mean to fight?'

'And dirty his hands? No, never,' Aztar replied. He gazed out over the sand to where Baralosus waited near Rhot.

'Reaching them will be impossible,' said Rakaar.

'But glorious to try,' said Aztar.

Rakaar grinned. 'We are peculiar.' He laughed nervously. Then he looked up into the sky. 'For Vala, then.'

Aztar nodded. 'For Vala.'

Rakaar and his men had all agreed to ride with Aztar from the dunes. Their excursion against the spearmen the night before had filled them with fearlessness, and because the odds truly were impossible the thought of dying in hiding was abhorrent to them. The other Zarturks might fight within the hills – that was up to them. Aztar had given them autonomy to die as they saw fit. For him, though, and for his brother, dying meant living like a man, with the sun on his face and the sand of his beloved desert flying from his drowa. He gave one last look at the fifty men who would charge, then took the scimitar from his belt. Up ahead waited Rhot and his soldiers, a long line of drowamen ready to charge. Mingled among them were the spearmen, who would quickly run in after them. Aztar put their numbers in the hundreds.

He closed his eyes. He spoke a prayer. He thought of Salina and imagined her perfume. And then he was ready.

Scimitar raised, he called out to his men. 'For Vala!' he cried, and like a storm they bolted forward. Across the flat earth they tracked toward the drowamen, who slowly came alert. Behind them General Rhot turned toward the dunes, a great, stunned smile on his face. He was all fury suddenly, swinging into action with his men, galloping forward and leaving Baralosus behind.

'Do you see him, brother?' Aztar shouted. 'Do you see Rhot?'

Baraki, tucked behind the neck of his mount, nodded vigourously. 'He wants you, Aztar. Be ready for him!'

Aztar fixed his grip on his blade, ready to strike. Between him and the general stood at least a hundred men, but Rhot was riding forward furiously, eager to meet him. Aztar's men dispersed around him, clashing quickly with the cavalry. A moment later all was chaos. Beside him, Aztar caught a glimpse of Baraki, slashing feverishly with his sword, already surrounded by Ganjeese. The fighters tore at him, stabbing with their weapons and Baraki fought to free himself. A turn of his drowa and he was out, swinging around again to face them. Aztar brought his own beast around and joined the mêlée, then found relief in Rakaar's leaping attack. Rakaar fell upon the men, his drowa bursting through their ranks, his blade moving with impossible speed.

'I can't get caught here!' Aztar cried. 'I have to reach him!'

'Go!' cried his brother.

With more of their men coming to join them, Aztar pulled free of the fight and turned again toward the front lines. Amidst the madness he had lost sight of Rhot but a great mass of spearmen headed toward him. Aztar wiped at the blooming sweat across his brow. Over their head he could see the distant flag of Baralosus, looking hopelessly remote.

'Vala, help me,' he groaned. 'Help me reach him . . .'

The spearmen swarmed him. Aztar's drowa reared to its hinds. The beast kicked out, catching a man in the teeth with its hooves and clearing a tiny path for them. Aztar seized the chance, driving the drowa out of the swarm then turning to unleash his barrage. His scimitar found flesh quickly, carving its way through the nearest man's face. Another came, then another, and Aztar viciously dispatched them all, splattered by the blood that sprayed from their wounds. He was alone, he realized, with his nearest Voruni long yards away. And the spearmen kept coming.

'Where are you?' he bellowed, calling out for Rhot. 'General, I'm here!'

The sun spread hotly over the sands. Stinging sweat blinded him. Aztar rode wildly, unsure where to go, heading east toward the distant flag. Around him the battle swelled, carrying him forward, forcing his aching sword arm up again and again, each time to fall on an enemy's head. But the wave was relentless, and already Aztar's drowa panted, slobbering spittle from its lips. He had damned himself, Aztar knew, and a glance toward the dunes said there was no turning back. Somewhere in that mass of men his brother fought. Or maybe he had fallen. Aztar wondered a little too long . . .

His drowa fell beneath him. A second later he noticed the sound, as a trio of arrows slammed the beast's side. Its front legs collapsing, the drowa slid face first into the dirt, spilling Aztar over its head. The tumble loosened Aztar's grip on his sword. He was flying, heals over head, then landed with a jolt with his face looking skyward. His body tightened with pain. His lungs screamed for air. Catching himself, he rolled over, clutching the sand and raising his eyes toward the coming riders.

There, at their point, rode General Rhot, his face triumphant. He had picked up a javelin along the way and held it at his side, its steel tip gleaming. A dozen men rode with him; two dozen more circled around Aztar. The prince got unsteadily to his knees, looking back at his fallen drowa, sprawled uselessly in the sand, a groaning death rattle streaming from its mouth. Rhot ordered another company of men into the fight. Aztar knew why. Being so occupied, none of his men could come to his rescue. He got to his feet and stared at the approaching general, sure that none of his lackeys would deliver the death blow.

'You are a mighty fool,' crowed General Rhot. He reined in his drowa, his men taking up positions at his side. 'Here,' he told Aztar, then tossed the javelin to his feet. 'This belongs to you.'

It was indeed a Voruni javelin, one of the many they had used the night before. Aztar stooped to pick it up, hiding the pain that wracked his body.

'So? You are man enough to fight me alone?'

Rhot started to answer, then turned toward another group riding into the circle. This time, King Baralosus led the way. With him was Jashien, the young soldier who had come to Aztar's camp. Aztar recognized him at once, giving him a scowl. Baralosus' own expression was unreadable. He trotted up to General Rhot, regarding Aztar strangely.

'You wanted him, Majesty,' said Rhot proudly. 'Here is your prize.'

Baralosus frowned. 'You gave him that weapon. Why?'

'Speak to me!' Aztar demanded. 'You may best me, but I won't be ignored.'

Rhot sneered. 'A man like him should die on his feet, Majesty. You said that yourself. Look . . .' The general turned toward his men. 'All of you look at him! Is this your hero?'

No one spoke. Jashien looked away. Aztar hefted the javelin, took measure of the distance, and heaved it at Rhot. Amazingly, it struck his unprotected breast. Rhot's eyes bulged in astonishment. Baralosus gasped. The nearby riders closed the gap, supporting Rhot as he fell. And Aztar, as amazed as any of them, raised his voice toward heaven in praise.

'You see?' he told them all. He danced across the dirt, almost laughing. 'I am the hand of Vala! You defy him by riding for Jador!' He pointed at Baralosus. 'By following this toad!'

Rhot cried out, cursing as his breath faded. His men rushed in to help him to the ground. As he lay there dying, King Baralosus said nothing. The other commanders looked at him impotently.

Like Aztar, Baralosus seemed lost. He stared at Rhot, then at Aztar, then at nothing as the general died. The battle still raged in the dunes. It would go on for hours. But Aztar was finished. He knew it and did not care. Vala had guided him. He was happy.

'Vala watches over me,' he told the king. 'Everything I do is for him. And for Salina. Go back now, Majesty. Go back and beg for His forgiveness.'

Baralosus smiled sadly. 'I cannot. I cannot leave this place with you alive.'

'Then kill me,' said Aztar. 'You can do me no greater glory.'

Jashien rode quickly up to Baralosus. 'Do it, Majesty,' he urged. 'Do it yourself. Take his head back to Ganjor.'

Aztar laughed. 'Yes! Make a trophy of me, Baralosus! Let all the people see how good and just you are!'

King Baralosus called up his archers. Aztar watched them, then spread his arms out wide.

'I'm ready to receive your gift!' he told the bowmen. 'You send me to a better place!'

'No!' Jashien growled. 'Majesty, do it now! This is your chance.'

Baralosus shook his head. He said to Aztar, 'I love my daughter. I love her. And I will have her back.'

The bowmen fired. Aztar watched the arrows come. A stunning pain filled his chest. His punctured heart exploded. The sand rose up to greet him as he fell, and in his mind he saw the smiling face of Vala.

Vala looked pleased. Aztar was happy.

Baralosus got down from his drowa, then went to stand over Aztar's body. Death had come quickly; his marksmen were perfect. Red blood soaked the sand beneath the prince's corpse, spreading out like wine. The men encircling him were silent. Baralosus knelt, putting his hand on

Aztar's head. He had died with serenity on his face, and the king was glad for it. He himself had rarely known serenity, and always envied those who did. But Aztar deserved such peace, he believed, and with his death the king's hatred fled.

'My daughter is no closer,' he said to no on in particular. It was merely the truth. Aztar was dead. His men were being slaughtered. And still Salina was no closer.

'Majesty, take his head,' Jashien urged. 'The others must see you.'

King Baralosus scoffed. 'Let the vultures have his head.'

He rose, then glanced at the body of General Rhot. He had died so foolishly, so impossibly. It would be one more story added to Aztar's legend. 'Kahrdeen,' he called, 'you are in charge now.'

Kahrdeen nodded solemnly. 'As you say, Majesty.' He looked toward the dunes where the battle raged on. 'What shall we do with the rest of them?'

'Finish them,' said Baralosus. 'They mustn't follow us to Jador.'

'And the camp? What of that?'

'Women and children?' snapped the king. 'What shall we do with them?' He turned to Jashien. 'Shall we take their heads as well?'

No one had an answer. Baralosus sighed disgustedly. 'Kill the men for as long as they fight. If they surrender, give them leave. When you are done, make ready to ride.'

'For Jador?' asked Kahrdeen. 'Majesty, we should wait. We are not strong enough to fight the Jadori.'

'We should go back to Ganjor first,' said Jashien. 'When we have enough me—'

'Jador has my daughter,' the king thundered. 'We're not going to wait another day. Not another minute! We're going to get her back.' He took one last look at Aztar's body. 'You loved him,' he told Jashien. 'You bury him.'

Sickened by all he'd seen and done, King Baralosus retreated to the back ranks of his army, where the cooks and cowards waited.

53

A jagged blade of lightning cut across the sky, making the forest road glow for a brief, frightening moment. Across the glass of the coach's window, beads of rain fell hard and steady as Mirage pressed her nose against the glass, scanning the dark world for any signs of life. Up ahead she could barely hear the men above the storm's incessant din. Straining, she saw the white rump of a horse struggling against the rain. The constant clouds had smothered the moon and stars, and with no light at all to guide them the little caravan snaked its way through the hidden hills, on toward Richter and the promise of warm beds. Mirage braced herself against the thunder. Seated across from her, Thorin had fallen asleep in the plush bench of the coach. His slack face leaned against his enchanted arm, his head bobbing steadily. He had ordered his men to keep going despite the rain and darkness, sure that his estate at Richter was only an hour or so away.

That had been more than three hours ago.

Still, Thorin slept, unperturbed by the noise and unafraid of the lightning. His self-assured manner gave Mirage a measure of ease. They had spent nearly two days together in the coach, far from Koth's prying eyes, and except for the rain the trip had been wonderful. Without Jazana Carr and the pressures of kingship to hassle him, Thorin had become remarkably civil again, the way he had been when they'd first met in Grimhold. Amazingly, Kahldris had not come again either. Only once had he threatened Mirage, that first night when she'd come to Koth. Since then he had yet to rear his ugly face again, and Mirage knew it was because Thorin was controlling him. She knew she had come to Thorin at just the right time, and for that she was proud of herself.

Thorin's invitation to join him in Richter had surprised Mirage. For her first week in Lionkeep, she had done her best to stay far from Jazana Carr, letting Thorin mend his relationship with her. The trip was to be for the two of them alone, a way for Thorin to prove to Jazana that he loved her. At first it had worked, and Jazana had been happy. But then Thorin had broached the subject of bringing Mirage along with them, and a giant, dangerous freeze set in. Mirage still didn't know if she'd done the right thing by agreeing to come, but she was alone with Thorin now and that was good, surely. She had a mission to accomplish, and if she could save him from Kahldris it would all be worth the hurt. She knew that Thorin loved her again, the way he had in Grimhold. With her new, beautiful face, she was irresistible to him, and that was why he had willingly risked his relationship with Jazana Carr. He needed her, Mirage knew. He had almost begged her to come.

Just then, Thorin opened a single eye. He smiled at her. 'We're not there yet.'

'No,' replied Mirage. 'Not yet.'

Thorin sighed. 'And it's still raining.'

'Yes.'

'You were looking at me when I woke up.'

'I was thinking,' said Mirage.

'About me?'

Mirage nodded. 'I am happy to see the change in you. I am happy I came with you, Thorin.'

Thorin beamed. There were not many men to witness the look in his eyes; they had come with only a handful of guards. It was how Thorin had wanted it. For him and Jazana, going to Richter was to be a private affair, a way to rekindle the sparks that war and ruling had smothered. Then, Mirage had come and changed that. Already things were moving faster than she had imagined. She had a way with men now, a power she had never known until her face was repaired. Raxor had fallen under it, and so had Corvalos Chane. Now it was Thorin's turn to fall. This time, though, Mirage felt something different. She cared for Thorin. And she wasn't completely sure it wasn't love.

'You'll like the estate,' Thorin told her. 'It's simple, a sad little place. Very old.'

'And remote,' joked Mirage.

Thorin let his arm rest on his thighs. 'We'll be there by the morning.'

'That long?'

'I can't say. I can't see anything in this darkness.'

'But you can,' said Mirage. She gave him a knowing look. 'With your armour you can see.'

Thorin nodded grudgingly. 'Yes.'

'What else can you do with it? You haven't told me yet, Thorin. What is it like?'

'You want to know?' Thorin laughed at this. 'I remember, back in Grimhold – you warned me off the armour.'

'And I was right. Look how it's devoured you.'

Thorin grimaced. 'I'm stronger now. Because of you.'

They shared a moment of beautiful silence. Thorin leaned forward on the bench. Their faces stood only a few feet apart, and Mirage could feel his warm breath. Thorin's appearance was alternately grim and powerful. When she had first come to him in Koth, he had looked emaciated. Now, though, he seemed vital. Even youthful. The black armour encasing his arm gleamed with unnatural light.

'You are good for me,' he told her. 'It does not matter what Kahldris thinks of you.'

'What does he think of me?' asked Mirage.

Thorin sat back without kissing her. 'Kahldris is afraid. He fears anything that might come between him and me.' He patted his arm with a smile. 'I can feel him in me even now. He's grumbling.'

The thought frightened Mirage. Of all the Akaris she had ever encountered, he was by far the most powerful. 'He wants me dead,' she said. 'That's why he exposed me.'

'Kahldris wants only me,' said Thorin. 'And he has been good to me. You will see, Mirage – he is not the devil everyone thinks. Without him I would be nothing, just an old man with one arm. Instead I am a king! And Liiria is great again.'

There was room for argument in his statement, but Mirage let it go. She had made too much progress to fail now. Soon, she knew, Thorin would see the truth in her words. Kahldris was nothing more than a cancer. It time, she would convince him of that.

They rode on through the miserable night, unsure of the time even as midnight slipped away. Mirage fell into an untidy sleep as the lightning finally subsided, and groggily opened her eyes as she felt the coach come at last to a stop. Through blurred vision she saw the light of torches through the window, and bolted up for a better look. Thorin was making ready. Outside, the men on their horses began to dismount, and voices echoed across the night.

'Are we here?' Mirage asked hopefully.

Thorin went to the door of the coach. 'We are.' He undid the latch and pushed the door open, letting in a gust of wind. A sheet of rain struck his face, making him squint. 'Get your cloak,' he told Mirage.

Mirage quickly rummaged through the things beside her on the bench. She had taken very little to the estate, but her cloak was foremost among them. Clutching it in her hands, she waited until Thorin departed the coach before going to the door. Thorin, standing in the mud, held a hand out to help her. Mirage peered out and saw the looming estate, an ancient home of stone and wood brooding in the rain. The house was larger than Mirage had imagined, though only a small fraction of Lionkeep's size. The men that had accompanied them from Koth – all mercenaries –

waited in the rain with Thorin while a pair of servants hurried out from the house to join them.

'It looks better in the light!' Thorin assured her with a smile. 'Come on.'

Without hesitation Mirage took Thorin's hand. Jumping down from the coach, her boots hit the muddy ground with a splash. With her cloak over her head, she dashed for the warmth of the precious estate.

For Corvalos Chane, the ride to Richter was miserable, a lonely trek of muddy roads and never-ending rain. He had left behind his soft life in Hes nearly four full days ago, hurrying out of the capital to join his comrades near Baron Glass' remote estate, hoping to beat the baron and his lady queen. But the rain and mud had made that impossible, and Chane had pressed on through the misery, crossing over the border and taking the valley road north toward Richter. Because the road was rarely traveled, used mostly by huntsmen and trappers, it was overgrown in most spots and not really much use at all. Still, it provided an easy to follow map for Chane, who followed it all the way into the mountains until it disappeared. There was, he knew, a better way to the estate, but Chane couldn't risk it. The main road – the one the kings of Liiria maintained – would be the one that Glass and his people took to Richter. And because he wanted no mistakes, Chane avoided it.

Everything he did was meticulous. Corvalos Chane would take no chances. This one, wonderful opportunity to kill the Black Baron had fallen like a lucky star into his lap. Determined not to waste it, Chane worked over every detail with precision, confident that his plan would work.

Still, there was much that could go wrong, and as he made his way through the stormy night Chane considered the countless contingencies. Baron Glass might come late to his estate. He might not come at all. Worse, the men of the Red Watch might have already been discovered.

No, Chane told himself. That was impossible. He had trained the Watch himself, years ago. They didn't make mistakes like that. In the days before the peace with Liiria, when Raxor was Reec's War Minister, he had formed the Red Watch to assassinate the newly crowned Akeela. Years of attrition had convinced Raxor of the rightness of the move, but Akeela had proven to be more than anyone expected. The young king willingly gave Reec the river Kryss, and the Red Watch faded into obscurity, killing minor nobles and criminals instead. But they always kept their skills honed, and their loyalty to Chane was unshakable. Now they had been given another mission, this one far more difficult than any previous one. Chane knew that killing Thorin Glass would be difficult.

But he is just a man, he reminded himself. *And all men die.*

To Chane, it didn't matter that some called Glass immortal, or that he wore a suit of god-forged armour. He could not let himself be swayed by talk. This would be his last, most important mission. Corvalos Chane would not taste failure.

At last he came to the place he was seeking. After hours of darkness, he saw the fork in the valley road. To the east the road branched upward, almost invisibly toward the mountains. To the west it meandered aimlessly, flat and overrun with weeds. Chane slowed his horse and shook the rain from his face. Up behind the clouds he could just make out the shimmering moon, peeking weakly through the storm. Richter Estate was about a mile away. After days of riding, he had finally arrived.

Chane began to sing.

'Farewell to you, sweet lady of Torlna, farewell to you, sweet lady . . .'

He kept his tone measured, loud enough to hear over the rain. As he sang he trotted slowly upon his stallion, keeping an eye on the surrounding trees. Listening, he heard the slight rustle of the branches, then glimpsed a tiny movement up ahead. Then, a figure spilled out onto the road.

'Ah, sweet lady, there you are,' crooned Chane.

A big smile bloomed on the figure's face. A handful of men came out to join him.

'You must have ridden that horse backwards to get here so slowly,' said the man. He came forward to help Chane with the beast. 'Believe it or not, I was starting to worry.'

Chane slid down from his saddle to face him. His name was Kaprile. He was about the same age as Chane, with the same lanky frame. His balding pate glistened with rainwater. He was dressed like a mercenary, as were they all, bearing no particular colours or insignia that would give them away as Reecians. Each man greeted Chane warmly. There were six of them in all, seven including their leader, Chane. All of them took turns embracing Chane and kissing his cheeks.

'So?' Chane asked impatiently. 'Tell me.'

The man named Kaprile spoke first. 'Glass is already at the estate, Corvalos. He arrived last night.'

'What about Carr? Is she with him?'

'She is. We watched them from the trees. The rain gave good cover.'

Chane turned toward Horatin, a man with a haggard red beard and puffy blue eyes. 'You were supposed to get yourself inside. What happened?'

'Couldn't risk it,' said Horatin. 'Glass might have seen through the ruse.'

Chane was disappointed. He had expected at least one of the Watchmen to make it inside the estate, posing as a traveler in need of rest. 'You should have tried,' he said, not crossly. 'We need someone inside.'

'We don't,' said Kaprile. 'I've seen the place, Corvalos. It isn't big. Glass brought only a half dozen guards with him. He's cocky, for sure.'

'And how long have you been here?'

'We set up camp a few days ago,' said Horatin. 'Me and Kaprile arrived first. Robb and the others came a day later.'

'So, I'm the latest to the ball,' sighed Chane. 'I could use a fire.'

'We could all use a fire,' said Horatin, commenting about the rain. 'This way, Corvalos – let us show you something.'

Chane left his horse with Noan and Robb, two more of the Watch, and followed Horatin back toward the trees. Kaprile and the two others – Calan and Travor – followed close behind. Pushing aside the wet branches, Horatin led them toward their makeshift camp, a clearing cut away among the trees and cleaned of debris. Here, the men had hidden their horses and supplies, including one item that struck Chane at once – a wagon filled with leather containers. Guessing immediately what they were, he went to the wagon and inspected the containers. The rain had stained them, but they were sturdy and stable, and when he poked them they moved like jelly.

'You brought more than I thought you would,' said Chane, pleased by the discovery. 'Half this much should have the house burning.'

'It's the rain,' said Kaprile. 'We'll need more oil to get it to burn good.'

'True enough,' agreed Chane. He had asked them to bring enough of the flammable fuel to get a good blaze going. Usually, the oil was used for lamps, but this special, viscous variety had been made for the Red Watch. Because it was so sticky, it wouldn't wash away as easily as normal lamp oil. And it had very little odour, an advantage considering how they planned to use it. 'How are you planning to get it inside? Have you thought about that?'

Kaprile said, 'Once we take care of the guards we'll get it through the windows. We'll slit the bags and toss 'em in.'

'That'll do it?'

'The place is old,' said Horatin. 'Old drapes, old furniture. And there's plenty of wood to burn. Believe me, Corvalos – it'll go up like kindling.'

Like kindling. Chane tried to grin but couldn't. Things had worked out perfectly, but it was a terrible way to die.

'Even Glass won't be able to survive it,' he told himself. 'What about the door?'

'There,' said Kaprile. He pointed toward a pile of chains and padlocks. 'There are only three or four doors. Once we get those chains on, no one's getting out.'

'Three or four? Shouldn't someone make sure?'

'Can't,' said Kaprile. 'Not without getting closer.'

'All right. Crossbows for the guards?'

'Probably. We'll be able to get a shot at some of them. The others will have to be cut.'

Chane's thoughts went at once to the dagger at this belt. Every member of the Red Watch carried the same weapon, so sharp it made no sound at all when dragged across a windpipe.

'That's everything, then,' said Chane, satisfied.

Kaprile shifted and asked the obvious question. 'When do we go?'

Chane looked at the wagon full of oil sacks. If they had forgotten something, he couldn't think of it. 'Tomorrow night,' he told them. 'Sharpen your knives, Watchmen. Tomorrow we draw blood.'

54

By the afternoon of Mirage's second day in Richter, the rain had finally stopped. After the long deluge, it was good to see the sun, but Mirage continued to stay indoors. All the day before – when the rain had been relentless – she had stayed with Thorin inside the estate, letting him show her its quaint wonders and listening to his stories about how life used to be. Despite the downpour, the day went remarkably quickly, as did the following evening. Mirage had been given a splendid room on the second floor of the house, overlooking the impenetrable woods. The room was much like the one she had left behind in Hes, well appointed and quiet, with a huge, comfortable bed thick with downy linens and fine old furniture. Though not a large room, it was more than serviceable for the Mirage, who slept like the dead as the rain pelted her window, secure in the knowledge that Thorin and his Devil's Armour was protecting her.

That next morning, while the rain still fell, Mirage broke her fast with Thorin, seated in a room near the kitchen. The estate had a lovely dining room, but Thorin had not wanted to waste such splendour on their morning meal. Instead he told her that tonight his servants would treat her to a feast. Mirage had no idea of the romantic scene that awaited her. She spent most of the day away from Thorin, who decided to go riding. Alone with the quiet servants and the handful of bodyguards, Mirage enjoyed the tranquility of the estate, venturing outside only briefly to feed the ducks in the nearby pond. She ate her midday meal alone, napped in her giant bed, and when the day was over felt surprise at how quickly it had gone. By the time the maid Stella came to retrieve her for dinner, Mirage was extremely well rested. She set aside the book she was perusing – a volume of poetry Thorin had selected just for her – and went to the door to let Stella inside. The maid, who looked as though she had spent her entire life in the remote estate, politely averted her eyes.

'My lady, Baron Glass has returned,' she told Mirage. She wore a perfectly pressed uniform of grey and black, complimenting her salty hair. Mirage, on the other hand, had dressed for the evening, and looked radiant in a gown that Thorin had purchased for her. The surprise had been waiting for her when she returned to her room, including a note from Thorin requesting that she wear it for him. Made of silk and threaded with gold, the emerald gown fit her perfectly, and in it Mirage felt like a queen.

'Thank you, Stella,' said Mirage, still not sure how to address the servants. In Hes, she had become friends with the maids, and never liked ordering them about. Giving orders was counter to everything she had learned in Grimhold, a place that worshipped equality. Mirage stepped back from the door. 'How do I look?'

Surprised, the old woman raised her gaze. 'My lady looks lovely.' Then she smiled. 'You are beautiful.'

'Beautiful? Really?' Mirage still couldn't believe that word applied to her.

'Yes, my lady. Baron Glass will not be bothering much with his meal, I think. He will not be able to take his eyes off you.'

Mirage blanched. All the people in Richter seemed to think they were lovers, though they plainly knew of Thorin's relationship to Jazana Carr. 'Let's pray that the food is excellent, then,' laughed Mirage, 'for I myself won't be on the baron's plate.'

Stella looked rebuffed. 'No, my lady, I am sorry . . .'

'Do not be,' said Mirage gently. 'And thank you. I'll be down presently.'

Mirage waited another few minutes before going downstairs. Stella's comment had unnerved her. Throughout the long ride to Richter and all during the first day, she had felt Thorin's love for her, burning into her like a brand. He had treated her better than his own queen, talking sweetly to her and buying her expensive gifts, and she knew that tonight was a prelude to something more than she'd expected. When at last she went down to dinner and saw the elaborate dining room decorated with candles and gleaming silverware, she realized she had stumbled into a trap. And that she had done so willingly.

Thorin looked resplendent in a velvet jacket, brushed clean of every speck of dust. A vest tucked his white shirt neatly against his solid body. He had shaved for the evening, looking young and strangely handsome. And though he still wore the armour of his left arm, the sleeve of his jacket covered it almost precisely, custom tailored for his odd appendage. The enchanted gauntlet hung at his side, looking strange and out of place. Thorin kept it out of sight as he rose to greet Mirage. Behind him, a pair of smart-looking stewards waited to serve them. The smells from the kitchen grew in Mirage's nose. She drifted like royalty into the dining room, smiling and letting her gown twirl prettily behind her.

'A vision,' Thorin declared. 'That's what you are.'

'A Mirage, you mean,' said Mirage wryly.

'No,' said Thorin. He reached out and took her hand. 'That is not what I mean. That is never what I think when I see you.'

He led her to her chair at one end of the table, pulling it out for her and letting her sit. Then he went to his own chair, helped into it by one of the stewards. There were only a handful of servants in Richter Estate and Mirage already knew them all. These two, like everyone else in the house, performed multiple duties. Now they stood arrow-straight, waiting for Thorin's orders. Mirage looked around, marveling at the room. Over the table hovered an ornate iron chandelier, each one of its candles lit with a gently wavering flame. The table itself was polished to a mirror shine, covered with linens and expensive looking silver. At Thorin's request one of the stewards poured Mirage some wine. The red liquid shimmered in the crystal. Across the table, Thorin beamed at her.

He was like a boy again, happy, trying to impress her.

'Whatever they've cooked up for us smells wonderful,' Mirage commented. 'They fed me well just hours ago and already I am hungry again.'

'You see? I'll take care of you,' said Thorin. He unfolded his napkin and placed it over his lap with his one real hand, then self-consciously tucked his other hand out of sight. 'After we eat we can go outside and have our drinks. The night has cleared. It's beautiful now.'

'I was out by the lake this afternoon,' said Mirage. 'I looked for you.'

'I gave you some time to be by yourself. After all the time we spent getting here I thought you'd be tired of me by now.'

'No,' said Mirage. Her words felt awkward, and she groped for the right thing to say. Thorin came to her rescue.

'No,' he told her gently. 'Relax. We don't have to say anything at all. We can just eat.'

Mirage needed no more prodding. Instead of forcing herself into banter, she let the servants bring her meal, indulging herself with the fine food. Course after meticulous course came out of the provincial kitchen, stunning her. Even in Raxor's court she had not eaten like this, and for a moment she lost herself in thought, wondering how her old benefactor was faring. She missed Raxor.

No, she scolded herself suddenly. *Do not think of him.*

Kahldris was powerful, and could probably read her thoughts. She wasn't sure of that, but she suspected it. Still, the demon had been quiet since that first day in Koth. Had Thorin really tamed him?

Mirage didn't know, and wasn't willing to take the gamble. Instead she let the evening unfold, plate by plate, occasionally engaging Thorin in the most unimportant subjects, like the rains that had plagued them and his day in the woods. To this Thorin brightened, telling her that the forests and lakes around Richter were renowned throughout Liiria, a place of exceeding beauty that he insisted she see.

'Tomorrow we will ride around the lake, just you and I. Forget the ducks, my lady – there is a spectacular brood of herons on the east side of the lake. They fly in like angels. We can boat there, if you like.'

'Maybe,' said Mirage cautiously. 'That might be nice.'

The stewards moved gracefully around them as the dinner unwound, then finally came to an end. One of them, an old man named Jarel, produced a pipe for Thorin which he gratefully accepted.

'Come,' he said, pushing back his chair. 'Let's go outside. We can see the stars.'

Mirage hesitated. The night was going too quickly. Something told her to slow it down. 'No,' she declined. 'I think I'd rather stay inside.'

Thorin looked surprised. 'But you've been inside all day. Just a quick breath . . .'

'No. Thank you.' Mirage rose and put her napkin on the table. She smiled at him. 'That was wonderful. It was, really, but I'm tired now. I think I'd like to go upstairs.'

Thorin chaffed at this. 'So soon?'

'It's what I want, Thorin.'

The fingers of his gauntlet flexed. 'I had hoped we could talk some more tonight. In private. It's very quiet by the lake.'

She could feel him drawing closer, craving her. His eyes smouldered. Mirage carefully backed away, feeling her own resolve loosening.

'No, Thorin, no,' she said, more firmly this time. 'I have to go upstairs.'

He stalked closer to her, not menacingly. 'Let me walk you upstairs.'

She shook her head. 'No.'

'Yes, I want to.'

She put up her hands. 'I'm fine.' With a smile she added, 'Thank you.'

Thorin came to stand before her, towering over her. Sensing the moment, the stewards disappeared. The house became still. 'I think,' said Thorin, 'that you should let me see you upstairs.'

'Why?' asked Mirage, feeling weak.

'I see something in your eyes.'

Whatever he saw, Mirage could not hide. She swallowed, looking away, but his gaze fell on her like a shadow, suffocating her. She glanced around, checked that they were alone and wished to heaven for someone – anyone – to stop them.

'I can't,' she said breathlessly. 'Please . . .'

Thorin's hand came up to touch her cheek. 'What is this that you can't do? You can't make your own choices? You can't betray some misplaced loyalty? You came to *me*. Remember that, Mirage.'

'I remember,' said Mirage. Did she regret that now? 'I—' Her words trailed off.

'What? You want to tell me something – speak it.'

She looked squarely into his powerful eyes. 'I am a maiden, Thorin.'

She expected to see conquest on his face. Instead, he softened.

'What a sweet gift that would be, if you would give it to me.'

Mirage began to shake. Seeing this, he took her. His strong embrace propped up her failing knees. And then she was up, off of her feet and in his arms, sweeping out of the dining chamber toward the stairs. She put her arms around his neck, unable to speak, wanting to cry out for help.

But not a sound escaped her throat.

At midnight precisely, Corvalos Chane and his Watchmen broke camp. They took with them everything they needed for their task – their crossbows and daggers, their chains for the doors, and the flammable oil that would turn Richter Estate into a torch. The night was clear and cool, and in the light of the full moon it took less than an hour for them to get into position, staking out the woods around the estate and leaving their horses deep in the trees. The sacks of oil that they brought with them waited nearby, also hidden from view. The seven faces of the Watchmen peered invisibly out over the grounds of the estate, each two man team taking a different door. Because he was their leader, Chane remained near the front of the house, not far from the road that led up to the estate's circular drive. From his place in the trees he could see the Norvans patrolling the grounds. Stupidly, a foursome of them had clutched near the covered walkway leading to the kitchens. One of them puffed languidly on a pipe. Kaprile and Horatin, who crouched with Chane in the brush, noted the guards with hand signals.

Chane shook his head. Kaprile raised his crossbow, putting his hand out to lower the weapon. Kaprile was the best shot of the group, and the crossbows the Watchmen carried had all been specially made for strength and silence. Even in the darkness, it would be no problem at all for Kaprile to kill two of the guards. But not four.

There were other guards as well, and these too would be dealt with. Robb and Noan, who had taken up position near the back of the estate, had already determined from earlier excursions that there was one man posted there at all times. Probably, he was already dead. Calan and Travor had the most difficult task. They had each been posted at opposite ends of the estate. They had no crossbows, but were armed with knives. It was up to them to sneak in first.

Horatin kept one hand on the stout chain. Sweat beaded on his forehead. He did not look nervous, just determined. It seemed to Chane that things were going wonderfully well. They had taken up their positions without being noticed and ostensibly had the house surrounded. They had everything they needed in place.

Still, there were those four guards . . .

'There's no time,' whispered Chane, his voice so low he himself could barely hear it. 'We have to move on them.'

He knew that his men were waiting, and that Robb and Noan had probably already killed the rear guard. Other soldiers inside the house might come looking for him, and if he went missing things would get difficult fast.

'Horatin,' he said, 'with me.' Then he turned to Kaprile. 'When we get close, hit them.'

There was no need for either of them to speak. Kaprile readied himself behind his crossbow. Horatin followed Chane through the woods. They both had their daggers drawn, moving likes cats through the brush, finally emerging out of sight of the four guards. The walkway leading to the kitchens had a roof that shadowed the men, making it difficult to see which way they were looking. Chane watched the glowing pipe in the lips of the one man, turned sideways to the grass. There was no easy way to reach them.

Chane and Horatin lingered in the shadows, their backs pressed against the stone of the house. The four Norvans stood beneath the roof, talking and laughing, fifty feet away. For Chane, killing four men was easy. Unless one of them ran. Or screamed. He looked to the trees where Kaprile was waiting, hidden somewhere in the mesh of leaves. Raising his hand, he gave the signal.

The crossbow's silent mechanism fired.

Mirage lay awake, naked, her tattered clothes draped over the mantle where Thorin had thrown them. The sheets of her enormous bed lay in a tangle around her limbs. Through the window she saw moonlight slanting through the glass, striking Thorin's happy face. Half asleep, his arm draped over her breasts, he smiled at her and kissed her ruddy cheek. A strange pain ached between her legs. Her body felt taught, like the strings of an instrument. Against her skin she felt the hotness of Thorin and the cool touch of his metal arm, that magnificent appendage that had brought her magically to life. Wrapped in it, he had lifted her effortlessly from the bed, again and again while he thrust against her, filling her mind with visions. Mirage had never known ecstasy, and had never really understood the word.

Until tonight.

He had been gentle at first, sweetly whispering in her ear as he undid the buttons of her gown. She had feared him but did not stop him, and when the moment of his own nakedness came she had gasped, astounded by him. Passion had taken them both like a swift river, and when it was over the current began again. As though he were a machine, Thorin took her again and again, each time more surely than the last, the magic of his armour giving him the virility of men half his age.

No, thought Mirage as she lay against him. *Not a man. More like a god.*

For no man could do what Thorin had done, or done it so flawlessly. She was in the arms of an avatar, and finally realized why Jazana Carr had never left him.

She rolled her head over to face him. Thorin's heavy eyes opened a bit wider.

'Sleep now,' he said.

Mirage stared into his eyes. 'I cannot. I feel strange.'

'You are a woman now,' he whispered. 'You're no longer a child. Everything will be different for you now.'

Without understanding him, Mirage simply nodded. He closed his eyes, drifting away to sleep, and a moment later Mirage did the same. Outside her window, she thought she heard a sound, something odd that she did not recognize. Too tired to pay it much heed, she ignored it.

Out of the blue came the bolt from Kaprile's crossbow, streaking invisibly through the moonlight. A moment later, the man with the pipe fell to the ground. His head exploded so quickly that the others around him didn't know what happened. He was talking and then he wasn't, and the three remaining Norvans simply stood there, stunned. Chane and Horatin flew from the shadows, knives in hand, and by the time they had reached the guards another bolt came out of the darkness, this one felling the man nearest Chane. Changing tactics, Chane selected another of the doomed men, who was just turning around to face him. With his dagger in one hand, he grabbed hold of the man's hair, snapped back his head, and ran the blade silently across his neck. Next to him, Horatin did the same, and before five seconds had ticked away both Norvans were dead.

Chane quickly glanced around. He listened for any sound. Out of the forest came Kaprile, his crossbow discarded, his back burdened with the heavy chain and padlock. Horatin wasted no time in dashing back for the oil. Chane kept watch on the door as he ran toward it, then put his ear against the wood. Inside the house he heard nothing, not even the idle chatter of servants or the footfalls of guards. Sure that the other teams had done just as well, he helped Kaprile loop the chain around the door.

Mirage awoke to the noise of breaking glass. At first it seemed like a dream, distant and unimportant, but then she heard it again, louder, closer, and her eyes snapped open in alarm. Thorin, still asleep beside her, his face slack after their love-making, barely stirred. Mirage listened intently, afraid and not knowing why. She thought to wake him, but feared his anger. She tried to lift her head but his weight pinned her down. Somewhere in the house something fell, bursting with sound. Another followed then another, and suddenly someone screamed.

Mirage bolted upright, waking Thorin instantly. Naked, she spotted her clothing flung against the mantle. Thorin groggily came awake, rubbing his eyes in confusion.

'What is it?' he croaked.

'I don't know,' said Mirage. 'Something's happening.'

'What's happening? What?' Thorin tossed his feet over the bedside. He shook his head a moment, then looked alarmed. 'I smell fire.'

The word paralyzed Mirage. 'What?'

'Smoke.' He looked at her. 'Do you smell it?'

Then suddenly she did. All around her. Mirage leapt from the bed, dashing for the door. When she opened it a burst of heat gushed at her.

'Thorin!'

All the memories of that horrible day rushed at her, those far flung nightmares of burning. Mirage stood in the door, frozen by the flames, stung by the heat as Thorin rushed up behind her.

'Fate above, what's happened?' he gasped. He pulled her roughly from the door. 'Get back! Get some clothes on!'

Mirage stumbled to the mantle, finding her gown clutching it. The whole downstairs seemed to be in flames. Through the roar she could hear the cries of people burning.

'We have to get out of here,' Thorin told her. He looked around for a way. 'The window!'

He ran to it, breaking it open with his gauntleted fist and sticking his head outside to see. Mirage already knew it was impossible. They were too far up, even for Thorin to make it. As he cursed the danger, she saw him glimpse something troubling below them.

'You there!' he cried.

Mirage hurried toward him. 'What is it?'

'An attack,' Thorin grumbled. His face went suddenly. 'Great heaven . . .'

'Thorin, what's happening?'

He backed away from the window, his face pensive. Then he took her in his big hands. 'Listen to me – there are men here. They mean to kill me. They set the fire, Mirage. And they've locked us in.'

'No!'

'Don't be afraid. I can get you out of here.'

'You can't! We're on fire, Thorin!'

'The fire won't hurt me,' Thorin insisted. 'I'll carry you out.'

Mirage tore away. 'No!'

549

'Meriel, you have to trust me. I can protect you . . .'

'No you can't! I'm not like you, Thorin! I'll die!'

'You have to trust me,' he said, then grabbed hold of her arm and dragged her forward. She fought him, screaming, but he lifted her up in his arms, tucking her head against his shoulder and pinning it there. Mirage was sobbing, pleading with him to let her go. Thorin ran headlong for the door.

Chane and his men gathered on the main lawn to watch the fire. Robb, the last of them to arrive, ran up to Chane quickly to give his report. With Noan's help they had broken through most of the ground-floor windows, tossing in their containers of oil. Chane had helped on the other side of the house, lighting the oil with a tiny flame made by striking flint. He had been amazed at how quickly the oil had combusted, bursting into tall flames that quickly licked at the drapes and antique furniture. Now, as he massed with his Watchmen, Chane could hear the cries of the old wood beams, buckling and cracking as the fire consumed them.

'Listen,' Horatin directed. But it wasn't the beams that had caught his attention. He motioned toward the main door, the one Chane had helped barricade. On the other side of it, someone was screaming. An insistent pounding rocked the thick wood.

'Chane, I saw him,' said Robb, gasping for air. 'Glass.'

'What happened?'

'He looked down at me from one of the bedrooms. He broke the window trying to escape.'

'Was he alone?'

Robb nodded, catching his breath. 'He's still up there.'

Kaprile raised his crossbow. 'Maybe not for long.'

'He can't survive it,' said Chane confidently. 'No one can.'

He felt a surge of pride at what he'd done, and a wave of self-loathing. The battering at the door continued. A window shattered on the top floor. A man appeared, his clothes in flames, ready to leap. Kaprile raised his crossbow instantly, took aim, and mercifully killed him. The man fell backward, disappearing into the flames.

The pounding at the door died away.

Corvalos Chane, bathed in the light of the conflagration, imagined Baron Glass and his Diamond Queen, charred and dead within the house. Some twenty others had died with them, but to Chane the arithmetic seemed fair. How many men had Glass killed at the Kryss? How many more might he have killed?

The flames spread across the ground floor, leaping from the windows and scratching at the doors. Corvalos Chane bid his Watchmen to stand down.

'Get the horses,' he told them. 'I want to be ready to leave.'

Thorin ran naked through the flames, leaping over burning beams and corpses. In his arms, Mirage was screaming, begging to be saved. The heat that licked their bodies had torn the skin from her back. Near tears, Thorin peered through the choking smoke, ignoring the pain. The armour on his arm glowed ferociously, lighting a path, but the fire was everywhere, blocking his way. Thorin turned desperately, trying each direction, beaten back by the inferno every time. His ears rang with Mirage's pleas. She was dying, her hair on fire, her skin bubbling.

But not Thorin. The power of his armoured arm spread across his person, shielding him from the scorching flames. Enraged, he cried out to Kahldris.

'Save her!' he begged. 'Kahldris, get us out of here!'

But the demon was silent, never entering Thorin's mind. Confused, Thorin raced for nearest exit, passing the stairway as it collapsed. A shroud of burning curtains fell from the wall, sending up a storm of sparks. Mirage sobbed agonizingly into his shoulder.

'Let us out of here!' he bellowed. 'Let us out!'

The fire raged in answer. All around him now, the flames touched his naked feet, climbing up his legs. His hair singed and curled back. The enormous pain drove him onward. Remarkably, he did not falter, and he realized that he never would – nothing could stop him.

'Hold on to me,' he told Mirage. 'I'll get you out of here.'

On his shoulder, Mirage was silent. Thorin stopped running. Terrified, he glanced at her face and saw that she no longer moved. Her body drooped in his arms.

'No . . . Oh, no . . .'

With fire all around him, he laid her down on the floor, studying her lifeless face. Her skin had turned a frightening red. And all the scars from her old life were there, showing once again on her face. Her Akari had fled. Thorin knew it. Kneeling over her, both of them naked, he touched her face and thought she was beautiful.

Then Baron Glass rose and let the fire reach for him, effortlessly swatting back its deadly flames.

'Who has done this?' he hissed in rage.

Down in the cellar, safely locked away, his armour waited, calling to him.

Outside, standing on the great lawn of the estate, Corvalos Chane watched the burning, amazed by how quickly the fire had spread. The entire ground floor was engulfed in flame. The blaze had easily reached the top floor. He had watched the fire for nearly an hour, listening for any signs of life within the house. Happily, he heard nothing, just the screaming of the old timbers as they snapped and buckled. A great feeling of accomplishment came over the old soldier, bathed in the inferno's eerie light. He was sure the blaze could be seen for miles, if only someone had been around to see it. It had been great hubris that had killed the Baron and his Queen, thought Chane. A man should never think himself so powerful.

Chane toyed with the dagger in his belt, fingering its hilt. He was tired, and he longed to return to Hes and give his king the news. After a long life of service, Corvalos Chane was done. He might at last take a woman. He would retire to a quiet corner of Reec and be happy.

'Corvalos, I've cleaned up everything,' said Kaprile, coming up quietly behind him. Only the two of them remained. Chane had sent the others back to camp, telling them to get rid of any evidence that might link them to the deed. The danger had passed, after all, and now there was nothing left to do but wait until morning and retrieve the Devil's Armour. Kaprile, who read Chane's thoughts easily, asked the question on both their minds. 'Do you think it survived?'

Chane shrugged. 'They say it's indestructible.'

'It didn't help Glass much, though, did it?' chuckled Kaprile. He looked at his old comrade. 'We did good tonight, Corvalos.'

'Aye,' agreed Chane. 'We did good.'

They would stay until morning, when the fire finally died and they could make their way through the rubble. Glass' skull would make a fine trophy, and Chane hoped to find it in the ashes. The skull and the Devil's Armour were the only things he wanted from the ruins. He planned to leave behind everything else, especially his memories. Chane turned to say something to Kaprile, but as he did he saw the main door explode outward. He ducked the flying splinters and sparks, shielding his face with his hand and reeling backward in surprise.

'All the hells,' gasped Kaprile. 'Who's that?'

In the burning threshold stood a man, big like a mountain, flames clawing at his back. He held a weapon in his fist, a long, straight-bladed sword that shined darkly in the firelight. Gleaming metal encased his body, covered with spikes, flowing with life, while atop his head rested a huge, horned helmet with a face like a death mask and two haunting eye slits. He stepped out of the flames and on to the cobblestone court, little drips of fire falling from his armour. The horrible helmet turned toward Chane and Kaprile.

It was impossible. Yet there he stood. Monstrous. Alive.

'I am Baron Glass,' he declared. 'And I will make you pay for what you've done.'

Corvalos Chane stepped forward, drawing the dagger at his side. Kaprile raised his crossbow and took aim.

'You're a very hard man to kill, Baron Glass,' said Chane. 'I'm sorry to say, I can't let you go further.'

'You have killed my woman,' Glass cried, 'the most gentle creature on this god-cursed earth!' His voice broke with sobs. 'You are the worst kind of murderers. You deserve the worst kind of death.'

Kaprile fired his crossbow. The perfectly aimed bolt smashed into the baron's breastplate. At such a range the weapon should have punctured, but it did not. Against the strange metal, the missile simply shattered. Baron Glass shook his head as Kaprile loaded up and fired again.

'I wear the Devil's Armour!' he said.

Chane nodded. 'That may be, Baron, but I have sworn an oath to kill you.'

'You may try,' said Glass.

Kaprile tossed his crossbow aside and drew his own Watchman's dagger. He looked at Chane for guidance. It was hopeless, of course, but they had both sworn the same unending oath. Together, then, they would fight.

They both ran forward, daggers raised. Chane leapt for the baron, legs outstretched in a well aimed kick. Glass, unmoving, absorbed it easily, and Chane felt the bones in his leg crack instantly. He fell to the ground, crying out, rolling away as Kaprile launched his own attack. This time, Glass reached out with inhuman speed, snatching Kaprile from the air. By the neck he took the Watchmen, raised him off the ground, and popped his gasping windpipe. Chane, in agony, clawed away as Glass towered over him. The eye slits looked down upon him contemptuously.

'Watch, brigand, and see how you will die.'

Kaprile's body was like a doll in Glass' grip, lifeless and limp, pendulating as if from a Hangman's noose. Baron Glass held him out for Chane to see, then madly drove Kaprile's head against the spikes of his shoulders, driving the iron daggers through his skull. Blood and brains splattered across the metal.

And the metal came alive.

'You see?' taunted Glass. 'He feeds me.'

Spreading from the bloodied shoulder, the armour writhed and glowed, the figures and runes along it twisting and pulling from the metal until at last it wasn't really metal at all, but a black, impenetrable skin that stuck to Glass like his own. Glass held up Kaprile's body, showering himself with blood. Chane tried to look away, but the sheer horror of it kept his eyes pinned to the gory scene. His shattered leg burned with pain, and he knew he could not escape. All he could do was keep his secret, and take it with him into death.

When he was done with Kaprile, Baron Glass tossed aside his blood-drained husk, then glared insanely down at Chane. 'Mercenary,' he said, 'who sent you to kill me?'

Corvalos Chane grinned. 'Do you think I am afraid of you? I am not. I am not afraid of anything.'

'No?' Baron Glass stalked closer. 'It is well, then. Do not tell me your secrets. You will find no mercy in me anyway.'

Stooping down, he grabbed hold of Chane's broken leg, lifting him up by the ankle and dangling him like a fish. Chane braced himself but did not struggle. Closing his eyes, he said a prayer to the Great Fate and waited for the end to come.

55

Thorin rode throughout the night, riding a horse he had commandeered from the dead assassins sent to kill him. He left behind the burning ruins of Richter, heading south along the valley road toward Koth, a journey that would take him days but which also allowed him the time he needed to grieve. Haunted by his memories of Meriel, he took no time at all to rest or eat or drink from the river. Instead, Thorin brooded over what had happened and the great stupidity of it all. Still fully garbed in the Devil's Armour, he did not even try to make contact with Kahldris. Sensing his grief, the demon stayed far away from Thorin's mind. Thorin remained strong as he rode, refusing to give way to the sobs threatening to break him. His mind reeled with questions, but mostly he thought about Meriel and how his vanity had killed her.

Finally, when morning broke, Thorin found himself beside a placid lake. Birds sang their songs of dawn, and the trees filled with gentle light as the sun peaked its orange head above the hills. His exhausted horse would go no further, and Thorin guided it to the lake, dismounting and letting it drink. He took the helmet of the armour off his head, holding it in the crux of his arm and gazed out over the waters. Without food his horse would not take him all the way to Koth, but it didn't really matter. In the armour he could walk forever and never tire. Such was the power of the Devil's Armour.

'But it does not give wisdom,' Thorin whispered.

The rage he could no longer control boiled over, and he slammed the armour into the dirt. His metal fingers came up, clawing his face, and the sobs he had tried so hard to stifle overcame him in a torrent, shaking his body and driving him to his knees. There in the mud of the lakeside he cried, weeping, unable to stop himself until he felt Kahldris' cold touch on his soul.

'Why?' he groaned, lifting his face skyward. 'You could have saved her!'

Kahldris' voice was filled with sympathy. *I could not. I could only save you.*

'You lie!' Thorin sneered. 'I know how powerful you are! You could have saved her but you hated her! You wanted her to die, you jealous shit-eater!'

No, Baron, you are wrong. I know how happy she made you. That is why I left her to you. I could have harmed her any time, but I did not because she pleased you.

'And now she's dead,' said Thorin, his hands in the dirt. He shook his head, wanting to blame someone. 'Why'd they kill her? Who were they?'

They were mercenaries. You know that.

'Who sent them?' demanded Thorin. 'Tell me, Kahldris!'

Baron Glass, you think too much of me. I cannot be everywhere at once. I do not know who sent them. The demon paused as if he wasn't telling everything. *Who do you think sent them?*

Thorin looked up. 'What are you saying? Damn you, Kahldris, tell me clearly.'

Kahldris' tone grew annoyed. *Who has mercenaries to kill the woman you cared about? Who knew you would be in the house alone with her? Who hated the girl because you loved her? Who, Baron Glass? Who?*

Thorin thought for a moment, but the idea seemed impossible. 'Jazana would never do such a thing!'

Would she not? After how you've treated her?

'She would not!'

You stupid toad of a man. What is a woman but a warm place to lay? You have no need of any of them, yet you protect and believe their words. Why would Jazana Carr not want her dead, and you rotting next to her? Who else would send filthy mercenaries to burn you both alive?

It was unthinkable, too much for Thorin to get his mind around. He got to his feet, feeling faint and feeling angry. The demon's words were relentless, his logic cold and true. Meriel's tortured face muscled into his memory, and suddenly it made sense.

'Would that bitch do such a thing? Would she do it to me?'

What have you given her that she did not have herself? She wants to return to Norvor, Baron. She despises Liiria.

Thorin felt helpless. 'What shall I do?'

You can act like a man. These women – they are a distraction to you. Jazana Carr does nothing but hinder you. We needed her once. But no longer.

'No,' said Thorin desperately. 'What are you asking of me? Ask me to tear the flesh off my bones, but do not ask me this . . .'

She has killed the woman you loved, Baron Glass.

'No!'

Thorin hurried away, running along the edge of the lake, trying to escape. But Kahldris clung to him, refusing to let go.

Why do you run? Will you let that diamond-crusted bitch beat you? Listen to me, Baron Glass – you are a man! I have made you whole again!

His words drove Thorin back to his knees. Collapsing into the mud, he put his hands to his ears trying to silence the Akari. He hated Jazana suddenly, and hated himself for doing so. But the logic seemed so clear to him. How could he ignore it?

'She is a bitch and a whore and I hate her!' he cried.

Good! Now have your vengeance on her!

Thorin closed his eyes as tightly as he could, wishing for a better way. Killing Jazana would be a horror. He would see her in his dreams for the rest of his life. But he would also see Meriel, lovely, helpless. She had been like a flower, totally innocent, so very fragile. And Jazana had murdered her. He saw that plainly now.

'She is a woman who must be taught a lesson,' he rasped. 'When I return to Koth, she will feel the hand of Baron Glass.'

56

Through the blowing sand of a morning dust storm, King Lorn the Wicked bent low along a dune, his body pressed against the hot earth. Peering with squinting eyes, he saw the first signs of the Ganjeese army, slowly marching west toward Jador. Behind him, the kreels of his party kept hidden from view, warming their bodies in the sun and chittering nervously about the coming foreigners. King Lorn stretched his neck for a better look, his face peppered by wind-borne sand. From the looks of them, the army had camped for the night and had only recently resumed its march. Caravans of drowa burdened with supplies plodded unhappily behind the rows of fighting men. Baralosus' flag, clearly visible among the ranks, snapped vigourously as the dust storm tore at its fabric. In the east the sun was rising, painting the army with an eerie glow. Lorn strained for a better view. It had been a long night of riding, but their kreels had performed magnificently, seldom needing rest and spiriting them like winged horses across the desert. To the men who had accompanied Lorn, the feat was commonplace. But to Lorn, who had always harboured trepidations about the beasts, their speed was magical.

'How many, do you think?' Lorn asked Noor, the leader of the kreel riders. The question was rhetorical. Noor did not speak the language of the continent at all. Still, the Jador seemed to understand Lorn's meaning.

'Khaln a balin,' he replied. Crouched next to Lorn against the dune, his face covered with a gaka to shield away the sand, he looked at the king to share his meaning. Lorn read his expressive eyes and nodded.

'That's what I think,' he said.

He leaned back and contemplated the scene. Baralosus' army was smaller than they'd feared. Lorn put their numbers at just over a thousand. It was a goodly number, actually, because their own forces in Jador were so depleted, but Lorn had expected far more of the Ganjeese to come across the desert.

'Aztar. They must have beaten him.'

Noor nodded. He looked sad. 'Aztar.'

Princess Salina had promised them that Aztar would do his best to stop her father. Apparently, his efforts had failed. Lorn had no doubt that Aztar was dead, and most of his men with him. The Jadori all fell silent, honouring the Voruni's sacrifice. They had come with Lorn because time was growing short, and because they wanted to defend their homeland. Lorn had done all that he could to help rebuild Jador's suffering army, and to train its blind Kahana. Now, all that remained was to wait. And when the time came, to fight.

The blowing dust growled intensely. Lorn rolled over and covered his face with his hands until the worst of it had passed. At the foot of the hill the other scouts waited quietly for word. Noor signaled to them to be still, then looked expectantly at Lorn, who blinked hard to clear his eyes.

'Not too many,' he said to Noor. 'But don't be too happy, my friend. All that means is that Baralosus is determined.'

Noor grimaced, confused.

'He wants his daughter back,' Lorn tried explaining. 'He should have waited after he defeated Aztar. He should have brought more troops with him, but that doesn't mean they won't come.'

Noor made a fist and shook it. Lorn smiled.

'Maybe we can beat them. I don't know.'

White-Eye had done a remarkable job of rallying the city. Lorn was proud of her. The Night Queen, as the Jadori called her now, had asked every able-bodied man within the white wall to make ready for the fight. They had nearly a thousand men themselves now, and almost four-hundred kreel riders. Once, in Jador's glory days, that number had been far, far greater. Under White-Eye's father Kadar the Jadori army had been a force to reckon with, but two recent wars had decimated them, and without a proper king to lead them . . .

Lorn stopped himself. Jador didn't need a king. It had a queen. It had White-Eye, and she was strong. But what should he tell her when he got back to Jador? She was waiting for word about Baralosus, and had vowed to protect Salina from him. With the forces under her command she could probably defeat the Ganjeese. Noor, who had carefully been reading Lorn's expression, pointed out across the desert to the coming army. He looked sharply at Lorn and said a single, powerful word.

'Lhat.'

Lorn knew very little of the Jadori language, but had picked up bits of it during his time in the city. In Noor's tongue, the word *lhat* meant death. And to Noor, their path was plain.

'You're right,' said Lorn. 'We'll kill them.'

That's what he would counsel White-Eye. They had enough men and kreels for the job. There could be no other course. They would fall like death on the men from Ganjor, and they would slaughter them. And

Minikin? She was always counseling peace, but this time she was wrong. This time, war was the answer. He would have to convince White-Eye of its rightness.

'Let's hope the little lady stays out of my way,' grumbled Lorn, then slid down the hillside toward the waiting kreels. Noor did the same, and the two stood to face each other. 'We go,' said Lorn to his guide. He pointed east. 'Back to Jador.'

Princess Salina heard of Aztar's death from a man with a serving tray. She had been sitting alone in the garden of Jador's palace, occupying her troubled mind by counting the hummingbirds that came to the rose bushes. Behind her, hidden by a vine-covered trestle, a servant was talking in a loud whisper, oblivious to her presence. He spoke hurriedly, as if he knew his gossip was taboo, his voice strangely clear, the way one hears one's own name spoken in a crowd. Salina froze in her seat and remained there long after the man had gone.

Lorn had returned. King Baralosus and his army were nearing Jador. And, to Salina's great sorrow, Prince Aztar was dead.

The servant seemed to have no proof of this, but spoke of it as though it were clearly a fact. His voice dithered nervously, sure that he and his fellows would soon be called to defend the city. Salina held her breath, trying to stem the awful feeling twisting in her stomach. She should have expected the news, and yet it struck her like a thunderbolt.

For long minutes – Salina did not know how long – she remained in the garden, paralyzed among the flowers. Her mind skipped through images of Aztar. She remembered his touch, how soft his calloused hands had been on her body. She remembered his face and hoped the memory would never fade. But mostly she remembered his courage. He had sacrificed himself for her, for all of Jador really, and for that he had surely ascended to heaven. Salina managed to rise from her chair, lifting her face toward heaven. In the endless sky she felt him, and knew that he had died happy.

But guilt clamped down on Salina, forcing her out of the garden in search of White-Eye. Driven to find the blind Kahana, Salina searched the usual places in the palace, asking everyone she passed where she would find White-Eye. Most gave her apologetic shrugs, but after a while she found the young Jadori woman, massed with some Jadori soldiers in a large, darkened chamber near the palace's great hall. Surprisingly, no one stopped Salina as she skidded into the room, embarrassing herself with her clumsy entrance. The oil lamps along the long rectangular table had been dimmed; Kahana White-Eye always craved darkness. Among the handful of soldiers with her stood King Lorn, stooped over a map of some kind he had obviously drawn himself. The soldiers all looked at Salina, disturbing Lorn's attention. He shot the princess an angry glance.

White-Eye, seated at the head of the table, turned in Salina's direction. 'Who is it?'

Salina's voice constricted suddenly, looking into the anxious faces of the Jadori. The room filled with the awkward silence caused by her appearance. Caught off guard, Salina stuttered.

'Kahana White-Eye, it is me – Salina.' She went no closer to them. Her face felt hot. 'I am sorry . . . I was looking for you. I . . . would speak to you, please.'

King Lorn came forward, looking weary but not unsympathetic. 'Princess, now is not the time.'

'My father is coming, King Lorn? You saw him?'

Lorn nodded. 'Yes.'

'And Prince Aztar?'

It was the king who faltered this time, searching for the right words. But it was White-Eye who spoke up, saying, 'Princess, you are right. You should hear this. Come ahead.'

The men in the chamber backed away from the table as White-Eye stood to greet the princess. King Lorn guided Salina to a chair, but she did not take it. She looked into White-Eye's blank stare, confused and afraid. The kahana seemed to sense this, and firmly asked her men to leave.

'Take them to the parlour,' she told Lorn. 'Let me speak to Salina alone.'

Amazingly, the gruff king did as White-Eye asked, gathering up his map from the table and herding the soldiers out of the chamber. Salina watched them go, leaving through one of the many archways and turning a corner, leaving her and White-Eye alone in the echoing space. The feeble lamplight looked strange against the Kahana's blind eyes. To Salina, White-Eye looked steely. She waited until her men had gone, listening to their footfalls disappear before softening her expression, just a little.

'When were you going to tell me?' asked Salina pointedly.

White-Eye didn't blink. 'When I was done here.'

'You're making plans against my father. I saw Lorn's map.'

'Aztar is dead.'

The words struck Salina like cold water. For a moment, she could not speak. 'You are sure?' she managed.

'Lorn has seen your father's army, Princess. He has come across the desert and is no more than a day from Jador. Unless you think Prince Aztar fled from him . . .'

'Aztar would never run.'

'No,' White-Eye agreed. 'No doubt he stood and fought them.'

Salina took her meaning. Even without proof of his death, she knew that Aztar had perished. She could feel it, its ugly truth. The hole that had opened in her soul told her it was so. Suddenly, just standing took all her strength.

'He did this for me,' she said weakly, turning away from White-Eye's mysterious gaze. 'It is my fault he is dead.'

'Aztar chose to fight your father, Princess. It was his gift to you.'

'His gift?' Salina laughed. 'He is dead.'

'Yes. And soon, others will be dead as well.'

'My father – has he come with many men?'

'Not many,' said White-Eye. Pleasure flashed across her face. 'We had expected more. But he is determined. He wants you back, Princess.'

Salina gripped the back of the chair, her knuckles blooming white. The soldiers who had been with Lorn made the Kahana's plans obvious. They meant to fight, and from the looks of White-Eye they intended to win. What Salina did not understand was why.

'You're going to defend me?' she asked.

'We have promised you that,' said White-Eye. 'We are indebted to you.'

'No,' argued Salina. 'No, I . . .' She tried to piece her thoughts together. 'I don't want your people to die for me.'

White-Eye grimaced. She said nothing for a time, sitting herself back down at the head of the table. Her blank eyes froze on Salina. 'You don't want people to die,' she repeated.

'Kahana White-Eye, I am sorry. I never wanted things to get this far. I wanted only to go to Aztar.'

'And to teach your father a lesson. Yes?'

Salina nodded sheepishly. 'Yes.'

'Well, now he has come to teach us a lesson. For the second time, he means to destroy us, Princess. First he used Aztar to bring us to our knees, and now he comes himself. And you have given him the reason.'

The accusation stung Salina. She lowered her head. 'I'm sorry. Truly, Kahana White-Eye, I am sorry.'

Her grief overcame her, and she began to weep. 'I'll go to him,' she choked. 'He only wants me back. Once he has me it will be over.'

'You are not going to him,' said White-Eye.

Salina sobbed, 'What?'

'Aztar died for a reason, not just for you, Princess. He died to defend Jador because that is what he believed Vala wanted. He knew that he had wronged us and wanted to protect us.'

'But my father—'

'Your father has threatened us. He meant to have our secrets, our wealth, whatever he could take from us. He used your lover Aztar to get these things, but now he has come himself to defeat us.'

Salina still did not understand. 'Yes? So?'

White-Eye sat tall and straight in her chair. 'Your father has blundered. He has come with too few soldiers. We are not so weak as he thinks we are. Princess Salina, it is too late for you to go to him. If you did not want people to die, you should have stayed in Ganjor.'

As night fell and White-Eye could at last venture out of doors, she left the palace in search of Minikin, climbing the white wall that surrounded the city and finding the little mistress in one of the wall's few battle towers. There, among the battlements and lookouts and archers, Minikin leaned against the white stone, her head barely able to see above the crenellations. White-Eye approached the mistress slowly, climbing the stairs as quietly as she could, guided by a Jadori soldier who told the kahana everything. They spoke in whispers, and when she no longer needed the guide White-Eye dismissed him with only a wave, but she knew that Minikin could hear her. The lady's tiny, elfish ears were uncanny, and White-Eye had never been able to surprise her. As she plodded uncertainly across the tower, she smiled at Minikin, or at least in her direction. Then, out of the darkness came Minikin's voice.

'You are so confident now.'

White-Eye paused, not really sure where in the tower she was standing. 'Minikin?'

The lady's voice came from several yards away. 'When you lost your sight I did not imagine you climbing up here ever again. You make me prouder everyday, child.'

Her voice was weak, tired from hours of worrying. If she could see her face, White-Eye was sure she would see bags under her sparkling eyes. 'I have been looking for you,' said White-Eye. 'Why did you not come to meet with Lorn and me? We waited for you, but you never came.'

'You did not need me,' said Minikin.

White-Eye put her arms around her shoulders. The night was surprisingly cool. 'How long have you been up here?'

'Oh, not so long. I have been watching the warriors.'

From atop the wall, almost all of western Jador could be seen, from the huge gate that protected the city to the sparkling sands beyond. As a girl White-Eye had climbed the wall countless times. She could remember the sight perfectly, and still loved to think of it when she drifted off to sleep. Tonight, though, the scene had changed. Tonight soldiers patrolled the streets and positioned themselves in the desert, waiting for the Ganjeese to come. White-Eye paused, wanting to go to Minikin yet feeling afraid.

Since returning to Jador, the mistress had said very little about the way White-Eye had handled things, but White-Eye suspected she disapproved.

'Minikin, I wanted you to be there tonight. I wanted you to know what we have planned.'

Minikin stayed quiet a moment. Then she said, 'Baralosus is coming. I know what you have planned, White-Eye.'

'I have to stop him.' White-Eye took a few steps closer. 'I want to know you understand that.'

'You have to protect Jador.'

'Yes.'

'Come closer to me, daughter.'

White-Eye went to her, following her voice until she felt a tiny hand come out to help her. Minikin guided her to the wall. The cool breeze rolling off the desert brushed White-Eye's face. She could hear the commotion in the city, the uneasy chatter of people preparing for war. In the shacks just outside the wall, the northerners from all across the continent braced themselves for another bloody siege. White-Eye's loyal Jadori moved supplies from the city to the desert, preparing their weapons and their kreels.

It would not be like last time, White-Eye resolved.

'I can hear them making ready,' she said. 'Can you see them?'

'Oh yes.'

'We are strong this time, Minikin. This time we will not lose.'

Minikin's hand slipped away. 'King Lorn has taught you more than I supposed.'

'He has taught me to be a leader,' said White-Eye. 'Is that such a bad thing?'

'Will you talk to Baralosus?'

'Talk? No, we will not talk.'

Silence. White-Eye shifted in her blindness. Lorn had warned her, told her to be strong.

'They come to kill us, Minikin,' she stressed. 'Like last time. Only now Baralosus has made a mistake.'

'He comes for his daughter,' Minikin reminded her. 'Has Salina not told you she wants to return to him?'

'Salina does not know what she wants,' said White-Eye, though it was partially a lie. 'And even if she did go back to him, what would happen then? Would Baralosus suddenly forget his desires? I do not think so. And neither does Lorn.'

'Lorn.' Minikin's smile was obvious. 'You have taken his counsel to heart.'

White-Eye nodded. 'I have. He knows of these things, Minikin. He has made war before. He recognizes who our enemies are.'

Minikin's pause was icy. White-Eye feared she had offended her. But instead of arguing, the lady seemed to slump, sighing and turning away.

'He is right, I suppose,' she said grudgingly. 'So much war has come to us. And I have not been able to stop it. I am old, White-Eye. And what I did last time . . . well, I cannot do it again.'

'I know,' said White-Eye gently. She searched for Minikin's small shoulder, placing her hand on it. 'I would never ask such a thing of you.'

A year ago, Minikin had summoned the Akari fire, saving them from Aztar. The feat had decimated the Voruni, but had left Minikin hollow and depleted. Worse, she was still guilt ridden from the act, seeing it akin to murder. Over the months, White-Eye had tried to comfort Minikin, but nothing had really worked.

'Minikin,' she said, 'that is why you gave me to Lorn – to become strong. To learn the things you could not teach me. I have learned. I am ready to defend Jador.'

Surprisingly, Minikin embraced her, wrapping her arms around White-Eye's waist. 'You are ready,' she said. 'You are the Night Queen.'

57

For a full day more, Baralosus' army trudged through the burning desert, determined to quickly reach Jador. The king rode at the forefront of his army, abandoning his carriage and all his fine trappings for the chance to be seen and to show his demoralized men that he was not afraid. The memory of Prince Aztar haunted Baralosus as he rode. He saw the imprint of the prince on every shifting dune, and when he closed his eyes Aztar was there, faintly smiling, pleased to be doing the work of Vala. Baralosus knew now that he no longer did the work of heaven. He was a man possessed of a single, selfish mission, and no amount of grumbling from his underlings would deter him.

Minister Kailyr tried in vain to talk reasonably to his friend, working to convince him of the folly of his plan. They had ridden hard the past two days, driven by Baralosus's insatiable need to save his daughter. After battling Aztar, they had gone ahead to his camp, finding more than a hundred women and children there, all of them frightened and grieving for their fallen husbands and fathers. Kahrdeen, who had taken command of the army after General Rhot's death, had urged Baralosus to kill them, or to at least burn their meagre tents. Sure that Vala was watching him from heaven, Baralosus had refused, hoping to appease the angry god and gain his favour for the fight ahead.

Night was fast approaching, and in his bones Baralosus knew they were getting closer. The desert had flattened, its sun-baked earth turning hard and rocky. A strange quiet blanketed the world. Baralosus kept his gaze on the horizon, waiting for the first hint of the white city to peak above the sands. His skin blazed from the heat. His tongue ached for the water they had tried to hard to conserve. Behind him, his weary army muttered as they marched, sure that they were too few to frighten the Jadori. Baralosus, who was not a military man, did his best to rally them, but in their eyes he saw their fears. Despite their loyalty, they rued his decision to march on to Jador.

Next to Baralosus, sitting silently atop his drowa, the young Jashien rode wearily along, careful not to speak unless the king asked him questions. He too had been disappointed in Baralosus, a fact confirmed by his constant silence. Baralosus wondered if the soldier thought him a coward. He had not taken Aztar's head as Jashien had urged, nor wanted any other trophies from the dead to show the people back in Ganjor. Still, he kept the young man close, valuing his counsel. Like the rest of the disgruntled army, Jashien remained impeccably loyal.

Minister Kailyr spurred his drowa a little faster, riding up to Baralosus. Preferring the comfort of his royal carriage, he rode the beast only because his king had insisted. To Baralosus, every able man needed to be mounted, ready to fight. Long and reedy, Kailyr wasn't a warrior at all, and his only weapons were quills and ledgers. Still, he carried a scimitar at his side, checking it nervously from time to time. When he rode up to Baralosus, his face looked concerned.

'We should stop now, Majesty,' he softly urged. 'It will be dark soon.'

'We go on.' Baralosus gestured toward the horizon. 'We are almost there.'

'It can wait until morning, surely,' said Kailyr. 'Jador isn't going anywhere.'

'No? That's what you said about my daughter.'

Kailyr grimaced, then fell back a pace. Baralosus ignored him. His advice had been useless, and now he was just one more petty voice, complaining about the heat and the difficult odds. Being reminded of the tasks ahead of them was no use all to Baralosus. And nothing would deter him.

They rode on while the sun began to set, Baralosus sure that Jador was just ahead, hiding itself. Then, at last, he caught the first glimpse of the city. Its ancient spires collected the last of the sunlight and shined it back at them like a mirror. Against the backdrop of the darkening sky, the city's outline was unmistakable.

'There!' cried Baralosus. 'There, you see? There is Jador!'

His men went from muttering to oddly hushed. Kahrdeen rode from out of the ranks to be with his king. Jashien nodded, and Kailyr let out a low groan.

'Majesty, we should stop now, make ready,' said Kahrdeen.

'No, not yet,' replied the king. 'We go on. I want to get closer.'

'In the morning we can do that, Majesty, when there is light . . .'

'No. Tonight.' Baralosus bit his lip in thought. 'Kahrdeen, bring the woman. I want her to see this.'

The woman, as Baralosus called her, was the only prisoner they had taken with them out of Aztar's camp. Her name was Harani, a young, pretty thing whose husband had died in the battle. Staunchly loyal to Aztar, she had stood up to Baralosus and his troops when they'd entered her camp, ready to defend the others. Baralosus had liked her immediately, but not because she was pretty. Amazingly, she had claimed to know his daughter. That, along with her annoying streak of honesty, made her valuable to Baralosus. It had taken three men to drag her out of camp, but since then she had acquiesced. Still far from docile, she had stopped kicking and biting his men and had answered all of Baralosus questions.

Kahrdeen returned with Harani a few minutes later. Having given the woman a drowa of her own, she nevertheless rode tethered to Kahrdeen's own mount, a precaution Baralosus thought was unnecessary in the inescapable desert. He meant her no harm after all, and fully intended to free her once he was done with her. Harani's tight face regarded him coldly as she trotted up to the king.

'Look there,' he said to her. 'Jador.'

Harani was unmoved. Just two days ago, she had lost her husband, her friends and her home. Her lips curled in a look of utter disinterest. Baralosus shooed away his new general.

'Let her ride alone,' he told Kahrdeen. 'Let us talk.'

Kahrdeen let go of the rope and let it drag behind Harani's drowa, falling back so that his king could talk. Harani and Baralosus rode out several paces from the rest of the group, and when they were clear the king smiled at his captive.

'I want you to trust me,' he said. 'Nothing is going to happen to you. Do you believe me?'

'I believe that you are a devil. A devil cannot be trusted.'

Baralosus controlled himself. 'You're very loyal to Aztar. That's good. But your master is dead now, woman. I am your master now.'

'Then send me to some slave pit.'

'That's not why you're here.'

'Why, then?'

'To talk sense to the Jadori,' said Baralosus. 'That is all you need do, woman, and you will be freed. Tell them that I spared your camp. Tell them that your women and children are unharmed.'

'I will tell them that you killed my master,' said Harani. 'I will tell them the truth.'

'Yes, you Voruni are always so truthful, aren't you? Good. That's all that I want from you.'

Angered, Baralosus turned away. Harani remained next to him.

'May I go?'

'No you may not. You will stay with me until the Jadori come to meet us.' The king glared at her. 'I am not a butcher, woman, whatever your master may have told you. He stole my daughter from me, then sent her to live with the Jadori. He turned her against me, not I.'

Harani grinned. 'Who are you trying to convince?'

Baralosus sneered, 'Convince the Jadori, woman. Tell them Aztar is dead but that the women and children were spared.'

'And you think that will get your daughter back? The Jadori are not weak. They will destroy you.'

'They will try.'

Harani looked puzzled. 'No, they will not just try. They will win, King Baralosus, because you do not have enough men to beat them. You must know this.'

'I know,' said Baralosus. 'But it does not matter. What you think of me does not matter, what these men think does not matter. Nothing matters to me now. Only Salina matters.'

White-Eye sat upon a magnificent, emerald green kreel, feeling the power of the beast beneath her. Her long fingers made tight fists around the reins, compelling the creature to stay back. She could not see its fabulous skin, rifling quickly through different colours, but she could feel the reptile's anxiousness as they waited. Unlike the other kreel riders, White-Eye had no affinity for the beasts. She could not read its thoughts or use its eyes to see the way Gilwyn could. Still, she had practiced with the kreel. Under the tutelage of experienced riders, she had drilled long and hard. She was ready.

For the first time since hearing of the Ganjeese, White-Eye felt afraid. Night had fallen again, and Baralosus had stopped the march of his army just outside the city. From up on the wall, Minikin and others could see the foreign troops, spread out and ready for battle. King Baralosus himself waited at their point. According to reports, the king looked determined. His weary men had ridden long and hard and were in no condition to fight, yet Baralosus had thrown reason to the wind, defying the Jadori to come to him.

I am ready, White-Eye told herself.

Beyond the wall, her fighting men waited, mounted on kreels and on horses, their bodies trained and rested, their orders clear. Tonight, White-Eye would lead them. Tonight she would finish the bad business between Ganjor and Jador. Behind her waited twenty mounted men, all of them on kreels except for one. King Lorn rode a horse instead. At White-Eye's side, he waited very patiently and whispered to her gently.

'Kahana,' he said. 'We are ready.'

'Stay with me,' said White-Eye.

'Of course.'

She could not see him, and for the first time in weeks cursed her wretched blindness. He had taught her confidence and courage, and she had learned her lessons well. But tonight, her courage faltered.

'I can do this,' she said. Her voice sounded fragile, even to herself.

'Yes you can,' agreed Lorn. 'Give the order.'

Soaring above her, the giant doors of the city awaited her call, ready to open at her signal and usher her forth. She would ride through the gates and then through the outskirts of the Jador, past the shabby homes of the refugees toward her Ganjeese enemies. White-Eye steeled herself, then out of habit turned her blind eyes upward, toward the tower wall where she knew Minikin was watching her.

'Minikin,' she cried. 'Your blessing! Give it to me!'

She waited, desperate to hear the little woman's voice. It came like soft rain.

'Go with my blessing, daughter,' echoed Minikin's voice. 'Go and show these Ganjeese the metal you are made of!'

It was all the blessing White-Eye needed. Straightening up, she gave the order.

'Open the gate!' she shouted.

She heard the effort of the gate, creaking on its man-sized hinges as the men pulled it open. And then, to her astonishment, a cheer went up. Around her, the hundreds of gathered people cried out in approval, shouting in their native tongue the name they had lovingly bestowed on her.

Night Queen.

White-Eye, the blind Kahana, squeezed her legs and urged her kreel forward, coaxing the reptile through the gates. The noise of the men behind her told her all she needed to know as her troops followed her past the portals. At her side rode Lorn, close enough to hear his steady voice as he guided her along. Having found himself armour and a helmet, his big body bounced along noisily beside White-Eye, ready for battle.

'Straight on,' he told her. He paused, and a smile crept into his tone. 'White-Eye, if you could only see this.'

White-Eye could not see, but she could hear it all perfectly, the rousing voices of the men and women just outside the wall. Like her own Jadori, the northern Seekers had gathered to cheer her. Throngs of them lined the way. Her warriors had all left the city, taking up positions in the desert, but the Seekers would defend their homes as well, and as she passed them White-Eye could hear their boldness as they shook their weapons in the air, promising the Night Queen that they too would vanquish the Ganjeese. White-Eye steadied herself, swallowing the lump in her throat. She had not called these foreigners to help her, yet here they were, swelling the streets and defying Baralosus just as her own people did.

'I hear you!' she cried. 'Thank you!'

She said the words again and again, speaking the language of Gilwyn, and each time she called to them the cheers grew louder, shaking the ragged homes. Next to her, Lorn laughed gleefully.

'You are the Night Queen,' he shouted. 'You see how they follow you? Because you are strong!'

'I am strong!' White-Eye repeated. 'I am not afraid!'

She was afraid, but suddenly her fear no longer mattered. With Lorn at her side and the teeming Seekers, White-Eye felt truly like a kahana, and somewhere in heaven she knew her father was watching her. She rode on, confidently guiding her kreel while Lorn whispered directions to her, keeping her on course through the narrow avenues. As the minutes tripped away the cheers of the northerners died away behind her, and White-Eye knew she was nearing the desert. The breeze quickened, striking her face. The strange buzz of the Ganjeese army reached her ears like distant insects. Beneath her kreel, she felt the earth soften as the pavement of the city gave way to desert sand. Above her, the sky widened endlessly.

'Where are we?' asked White-Eye. 'Lorn, do you see them?'

'I see them,' said Lorn. 'Steady on.'

'They are not retreating?'

'They are not retreating. Steady on, Kahana.'

White-Eye did as Lorn directed, keeping her course as her tiny army snaked toward their brethren, positioned in lines opposite the Ganjeese. As she approached she heard the kreels of her own men approaching, kicking up sand in their wake. They greeted their Kahana boldly.

'What word?' White-Eye asked them, speaking Jadori.

It was Narjj who spoke first, his voice clear in the darkness. 'Baralosus awaits us,' he reported. 'He remains at the front of his army.'

Narjj, who had attained the rank of Hota among the kreel riders, had somehow survived the last two wars. That feat alone made him a natural leader. Narjj had taken command of the bulk of their forces, mostly because there was no one else more qualified to do so. Though young, White-Eye had confidence in him. More importantly, she had confidence in their kreels. Baralosus had probably never seen a kreel in battle.

With Narjj to guide them, White-Eye and Lorn and the others followed the Hota to the lines of kreel riders, positioned only a few hundred yards from where the Ganjeese waited. The enemy soldiers were remarkably quiet, unnerving White-Eye. She brought her kreel to a halt at Lorn's order, then turned to face her many men. For a moment, it saddened White-Eye that she could not see them. In the days when she had been with her Akari, her natural blindness had been no hindrance at all. He would have revealed the ranks of riders to her, looking frightful in their gakas, their long, curled whips hanging like serpents at their sides. In totality, her little army numbered around one-thousand, with hundreds of kreel riders among them. The chittering of the trained reptiles gave White-Eye a terrible confidence.

'Men of Jador,' cried White-Eye. 'Who calls you to battle on this eve?'

'Kahana White-Eye!' came the answer, high and strong. The kreels joined their masters' call, letting out a fluttering hiss.

'Look at the puppets who come to destroy us!' said White-Eye. 'See the big man who holds the strings? Twice now he has brought his dogs to devour us. Once they were defeated. Shall we defeat them again?'

The thousand men gave a unanimous reply. Like thunder their voices filled the desert air. White-Eye raised her hands. Expectantly, the army silenced.

'Will you follow me?' White-Eye asked them.

An explosive answer pushed White-Eye backward. She smiled triumphantly, steadying her kreel, then wheeling the beast around toward Lorn. 'Come with me,' she ordered. 'It's time.'

Lorn agreed instantly, then quickly told Narjj to join them. Narjj knew at once what to do, gathering up the riders who had come with White-Eye from the city and arranging them in a long line behind himself and Lorn. When he was done, White-Eye waited for the word.

'We're ready,' said Lorn.

White-Eye nodded. She fixed her face with the most determined expression she could muster, then led the way across the empty sands toward Baralosus. Darkness followed her everywhere, yet she rode with confidence toward her enemies, secure in Lorn's soft guidance. As her party crossed the distance, Lorn continued to instruct her.

'Baralosus has ridden out apart from his army,' he said softly. 'He has a few men with him. They haven't drawn their weapons.'

White-Eye nodded. 'What else?'

'He's tired. He hasn't slept. He's looking right at us.' Then, as if sensing her fears, Lorn added, 'He looks weak.'

White-Eye thought for a moment, then dismissed his assessment. She didn't want to kill Baralosus. It was merely a necessity. But cockiness was something she wouldn't brook. She nodded, giving Lorn the signal to stop talking, and rode the rest of the way toward Baralosus. When she was just ahead of him, Lorn loudly cleared his throat, and White-Eye reined her kreel to a stop. Behind her, the men accompanying her did the same. Next to her, she heard Lorn's reassuring breath. Unable to see her enemy, she nevertheless addressed him.

'King Baralosus, you should not have come.'

Up on the tower of the white wall, Princess Salina waited with Minikin and the archers, holding her breath. It was the first time she had seen her father in months, and his appearance shocked her. From so far away, he looked gaunt and bone-weary, barely able to remain erect on his horse. The army he had dragged with him across the desert seemed bedraggled from the journey, not at all like the proud warriors she was accustomed to back home. Salina gripped the stone rail of the tower until her fingers ached, but she was oblivious to the pain, squinting for the best view of the coming battle. Her father's forces looked woefully outnumbered, especially against the blood-thirsty kreels. The reptiles were easily capable of ripping open the stomach of a drowa. Her father knew that.

So why had he come?

'Look how out-manned he is,' said Salina desperately. She turned to Minikin, who along with her mute bodyguard had spent the entire evening up in the tower. 'Lady Minikin, I don't understand.'

Minikin smiled cheerlessly. 'Don't you? Your father has come for you. A father's love is like that.'

Salina stared at her father across the desert. 'Love?'

Was it love to lock her away? Was it love to keep her a girl when she was really a woman, and to kill the man she loved? Minikin gave her a peculiar smile.

'It is love to risk everything for someone else,' she said.

She didn't explain how she had read Salina's thoughts. She didn't have to. The catch in Salina's throat kept her from speaking, but the lady's words rattled in her mind. Confused, she looked back over the armies, hoping for a miracle.

'I want her back,' said King Baralosus. 'I've come for her and her only. We can make peace, or we can make war, Kahana White-Eye. Which one we choose is up to you to decide.'

In the blackness of her blindness, White-Eye heard Baralosus' voice like a drumbeat, steady and predictable. She sat like stone upon her kreel, unmoved by his words.

'Your daughter is safe within the walls of Jador,' she replied. 'There she will remain. She has sought protection from you, King Baralosus, and I have granted it to her.'

'You have been bedeviled, girl. You have listened to the likes of this one!'

'I am a blind woman, sir,' said White-Eye. 'Tell me of who you speak.'

'He's pointing to me,' growled Lorn from the darkness. 'King Baralosus, you are outmanned and out armed, and if you have never seen a kreel in battle than I pity your foolishness. You daughter saved these people from your own designs. Do not expect them to give her up to you.'

'I will not leave without her,' said Baralosus. The ire in his tone rose dangerously. 'Here, look at this woman. Listen to what she tells you.'

White-Eye heard another rider come forward. She cocked her head curiously. 'Who do you show me?'

'My name is Harani,' said a voice suddenly. Unexpectedly, the voice was a woman's. 'Kahana White-Eye, I am a Voruni woman. King Baralosus has killed my master, Aztar. He has brought me here as witness to his deed.'

'You speak the language of the continent,' said White-Eye, surprised.

'I am an educated woman. My father was a merchant and we spent time in Ganjor. Now I am the captive of this pitiful thing.'

'She is not a captive,' Baralosus corrected angrily. 'She is only what she claimed – a witness. Aztar is dead, Kahana. My daughter has no reason now to remain here. Give her to me. I demand it.'

'You may demand nothing from these people,' hissed Lorn suddenly. 'They know of all your treacheries.'

'And I know of yours, Lorn! You are the Wicked One, the butcher of Norvor!'

Baralosus moved closer, but Lorn was there to stop him.

'Keep your distance,' ordered the Norvan.

Baralosus bristled, 'Kahana White-Eye, you should know who you take counsel from. This man is an demon. His own people detested him.'

'I know all I need to know,' retorted White-Eye. 'King Baralosus, you are wasting time.'

'I have spared the lives of these women and children!' protested the king. 'I could have killed them all, but I did not. All that I want is my daughter back.'

His words were ranting, but also pleading. White-Eye felt her resolve start to crumble. Before she could respond, Lorn was speaking for her.

'Your daughter is Jadori now,' he said. 'And you have doomed yourself.'

'If you kill me,' said Baralosus, 'others will come. A proper army will avenge me, and you won't be able to stand against it. Save us all this misery. Give me back my daughter!'

Trapped, White-Eye's words failed her. Suddenly, battling this forlorn king seemed more like murder than any cause of glory. But she had made a promise, and she knew that Baralosus could not be trusted.

'Why have you come here?' railed White-Eye. 'Why can you not simply stay across the desert? Why, King Baralosus? Tell me, please!'

King Baralosus replied wearily, 'I cannot go back without her.'

'And I cannot give her to you! Damn you!'

Spinning about, White-Eye rode back the way she'd come, ending the conversation. She heard the startled reaction of Baralosus behind her, and then Lorn's surprised call.

'White-Eye, what are you doing?' he asked, galloping up beside her.

'He brought this on himself,' replied White-Eye angrily. 'Vala help me, he has damned us.'

Back on the wall, Salina saw White-Eye riding away from her father. The Kahana's face twisted in rage and sadness. Behind her, Salina's father turned and called his men to attention. The ranks of the Ganjeese came quickly alive. Amidst the rows and rows of Jadori, the army of the Night Queen prepared for battle.

'No,' Salina gasped. 'No, he'll be killed!'

Minikin's expression had lost all its usual mirth. Looking dour, she nodded. 'He has decided.'

'No!' Salina grabbed hold of Minikin. 'Mistress, you have to stop it.'

Trog tramped forward to defend his mistress. Minikin put up a hand to halt him. 'I cannot stop it, child,' she told Salina. 'It has already begun.'

'You can stop it, you can stop it with your magic! Please, lady, I beg you . . .'

'What can I do?' Minikin said desperately. 'Look, they are ready for battle.'

Down on the battlefield, Salina saw White-Eye riding among her soldiers, waving her arms, rallying them for the fight. Her father's forces settled down behind their drowas and raised their spears and scimitars. Baralosus himself had drawn a weapon, a shining, curved sword that gleamed in the moonlight.

'I can't let this happen,' groaned Salina. She needed to escape, to get down to her father at once. 'Mistress, let me go.'

'Child?'

'I have to stop them! Please, let me go to them.'

'You're not my prisoner,' said Minikin. 'But the battle had begun . . .'

'I don't care. I have to stop them.' Salina looked around frantically. The stairs leading down the tower were unguarded, and she knew no one would stop her. 'Mistress, I need a kreel. Can someone take me?'

Minikin grabbed her hand and hurried toward the stairs. 'Trog, follow us.'

King Lorn galloped behind White-Eye as she rallied her men, her long-toothed kreel turning a fiery red. The young kahana raised her voice above the din, signaling Narjj and the others to make ready for attack. Lorn's horse whinnied beneath him as he drew back hard on its reins, spinning the beast to face the Ganjeese. Baralosus had raised his scimitar, giving his own men the same battle cry. A thrill coursed through Lorn as he saw the drowamen prepare to charge. They had no chance at all, but they were certainly brave bastards.

He spurred his horse again, catching up to White-Eye. The kahana heard his cry and turned her kreel toward his voice, her blind eyes searching for him. Narjj and his men had unhooked their whips from their sides and began swinging them overhead. Their eager kreels clawed restlessly at the sand.

'White-Eye, I have to get you to cover,' said Lorn, taking hold of her reins.

White-Eye furiously shook her head. 'I have to stay!'

'You can't even see! You'll be killed!'

'I have to stay, Lorn!' she insisted. 'The others need me. You have to protect me.'

She had her own sword which she finally drew, holding it high so that her men saw it. Lorn let go of her kreel and cursed her courage.

'Kahana, they're coming,' he told her, and as he spoke the first charging drowamen surged forward. Amazingly, Baralosus was among them, leading the run toward Jador. Lorn at last drew his weapon, prepared to defend White-Eye. Narjj threaded through the kreel riders, shouting orders at the other Hotas. In small teams the kreels broke ranks and bore down on the Ganjeese riders. Baralosus, smart enough not to break up his forces, kept them together like one, lethal hammer, determined to spearhead his enemies. They came quickly, weapons poised, thundering toward the screaming kreels. Lorn braced himself, sure that at least a few of them would straggle though the lines. 'Do everything I tell you,' he shouted to White-Eye. 'And if I say run, you run.'

White-Eye stood her ground, facing the enemy, listening for the collision. A moment later, it reached them with a boom as the clashing armies met. Baralosus and his riders rammed their spears against the reptiles. The kreels leapt, claws barred and slashing like razors. The drowas charged, necks lowered, long legs tearing up the sand. A horde of Ganjeese fell instantly, pulled from their mounts by the insatiable kreels. But Baralosus, wrapped in a tight cocoon of fighting men, continued charging. Scimitar raised, he pointed toward White-Eye and Lorn, and his men ducked low to pursue. A band of Jadori saw the tactic, riding fast to White-Eye's aide. King Lorn the Wicked put his mount between the kahana and their enemies and braced himself for battle.

Out of the darkness they came with speed, spears lowered against the Night Queen's protectors. Lorn cried for White-Eye to retreat, then spat a string of obscenities as she ignored him. Too busy to argue, he took on the first of the riders to break through the kreels, batting aside the Ganjeese spear and driving his sword headlong through the man's throat. A kreel leapt across his vision, tackling the drowa and tearing open its gut. Lorn spun about, grabbed angrily at White-Eye's kreel, and yanked the rein away from her, pulling girl and beast back toward the city.

'Go!' he bellowed.

'I won't!'

Through the mêlée Lorn could see King Baralosus battling through the Jadori. Surrounded but undeterred, the king's men swarmed around him, swatting at the kreels and dodging the flailing whips. Another rider broke through, heading again for White-Eye. Lorn exploded after him, slashing his sword and hacking off his head. Confused, White-Eye called to him, and as Lorn turned he saw her riding toward him.

'You get back!' he railed. 'Damn you, girl, listen to me!'

'Tell me what's happening!' demanded White-Eye. Her kreel loped forward, landing at Lorn's feet and sniffing at the air with its tongue. White-Eye looked like a wild child on its back, her black hair flying, her milky eyes madly scanning the field. Lorn reached out for her again, snatching up the kreel's tack and spuring his horse back toward the city. This time the kreel resisted, pulling free. Lorn swore at the monster. 'Come with me!' he spat. 'It's not safe here!'

Over White-Eye's head he saw Baralosus. The king had spotted the kahana and fixed her in his sight. With his men tangled in kreels, Baralosus saw his opportunity and blasted forth, galloping for the defenseless girl. Lorn leapt after him, passing White-Eye and lowering his sword. He heard a commotion behind him, someone screaming. Ignoring it, he brought up his blade and collided his horse against Baralosus' huge drowa. The king's face burst with sweat and hatred. His big beast muscled back Lorn's steed. Lorn worked his sword, ducking the king's own as the silver scimitar flashed. The head of the drowa darted forward, smashing against Lorn like a ram. He collapsed, gripped hard on his reins and pulled himself upright. White-Eye was shouting. Another voice joined her. Unable to spare even a glance, Lorn slashed madly at Baralosus, trying to regain his momentum. The two kings crossed swords, again and again battering each other back. Kreels and drowamen crashed around them. A big man, Baralosus held his own, bolstered by his powerful mount. Lorn skirted around him, searching for a weakness, but the well-trained drowa moved with him, dancing on its gangly legs, avoiding every blow.

Then, another kreel slipped onto the field, barreling towards the battling kings. Again Lorn heard the unfamiliar cry, this time seeing Salina. She rode atop the kreel with Trog, Minikin's monstrous henchman. The kreel that carried the girl and giant sped across the sand. White-Eye's head swiveled quickly, hearing Salina's cry. King Baralosus saw his daughter and dropped his guard.

And there it was, the opening Lorn needed. He glanced at Salina, then at White-Eye. White-Eye was screaming, calling for him. Salina's arms flailed madly. Lorn raised his sword, cocked to strike.

'Salina!'

Baralosus cry rose out of him like a prayer, smothering every other sound. Stunned by his daughter's appearance, he forgot the fight, ignoring Lorn even as the Norvan's sword hovered. Lorn trembled, aching to loose his final barrage, but Salina's face filled his vision suddenly, tearfully pleading for peace. Baralosus bolted toward her, out of Lorn's range, and King Lorn the Wicked merely sat atop his horse and watched his quarry escape. Guided by Trog, Salina's kreel raced to meet her father. All around them the battle raged, but they were lost in each other suddenly.

'White-Eye,' called Lorn, 'it's Salina.' He lowered his sword, shaking his head in disbelief. 'Call it off.'

White-Eye's mouth fell open. 'Salina?'

'Call off your men,' said Lorn. 'It's over.'

Princess Salina jumped from the kreel and onto the battlefield, pleading with her father to retreat. King Baralosus reached down from his drowa, grabbed hold of his daughter's hand, and hoisted her onto the back of his mount. He turned toward his troops, shouting at them to break off their attack. Lorn galloped past them toward White-Eye.

'What's happened?' White-Eye asked.

King Lorn carefully shielded her from the battle. 'Your charge has changed her mind,' he replied ruefully.

'Salina?' A huge smile filled White-Eye's wild face. 'Thank Vala for that.'

'Baralosus is retreating,' Lorn told her. The scene left him oddly disappointed. White-Eye, however, was plainly relieved. She shouted as loud as she could for her Hotas, ordering the commanders to reform their lines.

'It's over, then,' she said wearily. Her eyelids closed with a giant sigh. 'Over . . .'

King Lorn smirked despite the turn of events. 'I am proud of you, Night Queen,' he said. 'Now you are truly Jador's Kahana.'

58

To Lukien, the Bronze Knight of Liiria,

How have the days passed for you, my friend? Are you well? Are you happy? So much has happened to me these past months, I have not the ink to write it all. The long days since our parting have exhausted me, but now I rest. I am in the company of Prince Daralor of Nith, and Nith is a very fine place. There is peace here, a kind of peace that I never thought to find again. The word from Liiria is terrible, but here at least I am sheltered from it. I have rested. And still I am waiting for you.

I am writing in the hopes that this correspondence will find you, Lukien, for I know not where you are or even if you still draw breath. With Daralor's help I am sending this note across the desert to Jador in the prayer that you are there. There is still great need of you, and the sword you quest to find. I still have faith in you. You must know that I do not wait here alone for you now. I have ridden the world it seems, and in all of its kingdoms I have found only two brave men. Prince Daralor has kept me kindly, and is ready to join us when we ride again to Liiria. My father still holds sway there. I have seen him, Lukien, and he has truly fallen into madness. I have fought him, too, and seen him now in battle. He is like a demon possessed of hell, and surely only the sword can stop him.

My news is this – in Nith I wait for you, but in Reec they wait as well. I have been to Reec and fought alongside King Raxor, and he too is ready to fight when you return. There is so much to tell you, Lukien, things that I should say to you in proper talk, face to face when finally we meet. Time is running short for us, and so I send this letter in the hopes that it will speed you north to Nith. I will be waiting here when you come.

Aric Glass paused, the quill in his hand stopping cold. His mind rambled with all the things he could tell his friend, the terrible confessions about Mirage or Roland or the battle at the Kryss. These things would have to wait, Aric knew. Still, his hand would not move. He stared at the last line he had written, wondering how long it would be until the knight returned. It took a mighty faith to believe in Lukien these days, when all chaos had erupted in Liiria and the Bronze Knight seemed nothing more than a quaint fable. Yet Aric forced himself to believe that Lukien would return. To think otherwise would make a waste of all his efforts.

I will see you again, he wrote finally. *My heart tells me you are coming.*

Aric signed the letter and released a sigh of melancholy. Outside the window near his little desk, the afternoon beckoned him into the sunshine. Nith's green hills shimmered. Aric dropped his eyes to the letter he had written, feeling cathartic. It had been weeks since he had come again to Nith, and he had spent his days luxuriating in the bosom of Daralor's hospitality. Guilt gnawed at him, for he knew that away from Nith's green borders the world of his father was in peril. But he had been so exhausted, and Daralor's people had been so kind to him.

'But I am rested now,' he resolved. 'And there is work to do.'

Before he could go in search of Daralor, before he could feel that precious sunlight on his face, Aric Glass had another letter to pen, and so he picked up his quill again and began.

An hour later, Aric was out of the charming little castle and walking across the green grass of the hunting grounds in search of Prince Daralor. Tall trees lined the ways, the forests ribboned with paths for the huntsmen and their dogs. A great field cut through the forest, still in view of the castle and canopied by the blue sky. The land rolled in gentle swales and the grass grew barely ankle high. Across the field, looking regal as he stood alone in the sunshine, Prince Daralor watched the sky, oblivious to the distant young man approaching him. Aric watched the prince carefully, not sure if he should disturb him. It had been a perfect day, the kind of day that always seemed to bless the tiny nation, and Prince Daralor had left the castle early after breaking his fast. His wife, a lovely blonde thing named Laurena, had told Aric where to find her husband. He was the kind of man that often went out on his own, enjoying a long ride with just the company of a fine horse. At times, he had invited young Aric to join him, and Aric had always eagerly agreed. To Aric's great surprise, he had found a friend in the enigmatic prince. It was one more reason why he yearned to stay in Nith.

A speck of something caught Aric's eye, sailing quickly through the air. Prince Daralor lifted his arm expectantly. Curious, Aric watched as the speck became a hawk and the hawk spread its feathered wings, flapping vigourously to hover before the prince before resting on his gloved hand. Daralor beamed at the bird and used his other hand to gently knead the feathers of its neck. The hawk's keen eyes turned to Gilwyn, alerting Daralor of his presence. Aric paused to wave at the prince, who happily waved him onward.

'Come ahead, Aric,' called Daralor. 'Don't be afraid of old Echo.'

Still, Aric hesitated. He remembered how his father had kept game birds when he was a boy, and he recognized the hawk at once. Bigger than a falcon, the hawk that Daralor held had speckled tail feathers and a bright ivory breast. Its dark eyes watched Aric carefully as he neared. Daralor grinned proudly at the bird. It was then that Aric noticed the mouse in its talons.

'She's nearly ten years old, yet she sees like a youngster,' the prince declared. He put out his bare hand, and the hawk opened its talons, dropping the grisly prize into its master's palm. Daralor dangled the dead creature before the hawk, letting the bird's beak snap forward to snatch it. Aric watched as the mouse disappeared down the hawk's gullet.

'She's beautiful,' Aric remarked. 'She reminds me of my father's birds. He had a kettle of hawks when I was a boy. I think of them sometimes.' He laughed. 'When I was young I was afraid of them.'

'There is nothing to fear from Echo,' Daralor promised. 'She would never hurt anyone, not unless I order it.'

'You mean she fights?'

'Oh, yes,' said the prince. 'All of my birds fight. That is what they are best at – fighting and hunting. When we go against your father, Echo will come with me. She's smaller than the others, though. A lot smaller.'

Aric, who had brought the letters he'd written with him, let the hand carrying them drop to his side. 'I should like to see that,' he said. 'I have never seen hawks used in battle.'

'You will see – Echo will protect me like one of her chicks. So will they all.'

'How many will you bring?'

'I have many birds like Echo,' said Daralor, admiring his hawk. 'I will bring them all.'

Aric nodded, not sure what to say. Unlike himself, Prince Daralor was already preparing for the fight against his father. The prince's determination shamed Aric, who had spent too long in Nith's soft valleys. Prince Daralor hoisted the bird above his head and gave the order for the bird to fly. In a great flurry of feathers the hawk lifted from his hand and ascended. Aric watched the bird wing skyward, smiling.

'Where's she going?'

'To hunt,' said Daralor. 'When I call her, she'll return.'

Daralor took the leather glove from his left hand, pulling it free with his right, wounded hand, the one missing fingers. The glove dangled awkwardly in the remaining digits as the prince watched Echo slipping into the blue. Not far from the field, the village of Nith rested quietly in its valley, looking sleepy, but in the field they were all alone and the silence soon engulfed them. Aric shifted, waiting for the chance to ask his favour.

Daralor had yet to comment about the letters in his hand, but Aric was sure the prince had noticed them.

'You were long in your chambers this morning, Aric,' said Daralor. 'I would have asked you here to hunt with me, but your mind was elsewhere, I could tell.'

'Aye, Your Grace,' replied Aric. 'I was occupied.'

'Pensive, I would say. These last few days I've seen you only seldom.' Daralor turned to study the younger man. 'My wife told you where to find me?'

Aric smiled. He had been caught admiring the lovely Laurena more than once. Surprisingly, Daralor didn't seem to mind. 'Yes, Your Grace. She was about the kitchens with the other women when I came to find you. She told me you were on the field with your hawk.'

'Discovered,' said Daralor with a grin. 'That woman gives me up too easily.'

'I can go, Your Grace . . .'

'Don't be silly. I joke with you, is all. I wanted you here. Did she offer you supper yet?'

'She did, Your Grace, but I will wait first, I think. She is very kind, your wife.'

Daralor gave him a wink. 'She is that and more, Aric. A fine woman like Laurena should be the goal of every man.'

'Yes, Your Grace.'

They watched the sky for Echo, who had flown to a great height to circle the field.

'What about you, then? When will you find a woman, do you think?' asked Daralor.

'Me?' Aric shrugged. 'Not for some time, I should say. There's so much to do first.'

'Your day will come,' Daralor assured him. 'Nightmares do not last forever, Aric. In time we wake, and a new day greets us.'

Aric laughed. 'You are optimistic, Your Grace. Thank you for that.'

'And you are not optimistic enough, Aric. You have brooded since you returned here. Tell me – what is in your hand?'

Aric cleared his throat. 'Letters, Your Grace. That is what I was doing this morning – writing letters.'

Daralor smiled. 'To whom?'

'This one is to King Raxor,' said Aric, handing that particular piece of paper to the prince. It was sealed in an envelope of parchment, and Daralor merely nodded at it. 'I thought it was time for me to tell him that I arrived here safely. He was a kindly man, and I'm sure he thinks of me.'

'Aric, it is very much past the time for you to have written this letter. I have wondered when you would do so.'

'I'm sorry, Your Grace,' offered Aric. 'I know you're right. I've just been . . .'

'Pensive?'

Aric nodded. 'All right, then.'

Daralor handed him back the letter. 'It is well. You have been through much, and no one here faults you, not after the things you have seen. I will have my messengers deliver your letter to Raxor.'

'Thank you, Your Grace.' Aric tucked the letter behind the other one. 'I have told King Raxor in my letter that I still await Lukien, and that you are ready to ride with us when Lukien returns with the sword.' He bit his lip uncertainly. 'It's been some time now, though. I hope Raxor still believes.'

'Have more faith than that, boy! You have told me that Raxor is a brave man, and I believe you. He has lost his son, remember. He will not forget, not ever, not even if you take a decade more to ride to him.' Daralor jabbed the thumb of his wounded hand into Aric's chest. 'You're the one that must believe, Aric. You're the one whose faith is flagging. I can see it. Raise yourself up, man! The Bronze Knight will come again.'

'Yes,' said Aric. 'I believe.'

Daralor gestured to the letters in his hand. 'And that other letter? That one is to Lukien?'

Aric's brows went up. 'You know? I'm too obvious.'

'It is time, that is all,' said Daralor. But he grimaced. 'You mean to have it taken across the desert?'

'Lukien will go to Jador and Grimhold first, I am sure,' said Aric. He looked down at the letter. 'I know it's asking a lot, Your Grace. Taking this across the desert won't be easy.'

'None of this is easy, Aric,' said Daralor. He brightened suddenly. 'This is a great quest, and from all the mortals the gods have chosen us for it. I have come to believe that, truly! The gods have their hands in all of this, for they know the evil your father has unleashed.'

'Is that why you're willing to help us, Prince Daralor?' It was the one question Aric had never really got answered, at least not to his satisfaction. In all the time they'd spent together, it was a subject Daralor rarely broached. 'I have wondered this, is all. You have more faith than I do sometimes, and it bewilders me.'

'Does it? It should not. The answer is all around you, Aric.' Daralor held out his falconry glove. 'Put this on.'

Aric did so without question, slipping the heavy leather glove onto his left hand.

'Good. Now hold up your hand,' directed Daralor. 'That's right. Just the way I did.'

With the two remaining fingers of his right hand, Daralor gave a powerful whistle, watching the sky for his hawk, Echo. Hearing the call, the bird wheeled around and spotted its master beside the stranger with the outstretched hand. Aric braced himself, knowing what was coming.

'Steady,' laughed Daralor. 'I told you, she won't hurt you. Just keep your hand strong for her. She'll land on it like a butterfly.'

The hawk bore down on them, folding back its wings to dive. Aric grimaced.

'A butterfly? The biggest damn butterfly I've ever seen.'

'Oh, they get bigger,' said Daralor. 'Steady . . .'

Despite his trepidation Aric kept the perch out for the bird. Gaining speed, the fabulous hawk drove through the air, making a perfect line for Aric. Then, when it was only yards away, its great wings flared out, striking Aric's face with their breeze. The talons stretched, the head reared back, and the beautiful bird lilted gently onto Aric's hand.

'Beautiful!' Aric exclaimed. Exhilarated, he raised the hawk above his head, turning his face slightly from the fierce wings. 'Echo, you are fabulous!' Aric turned to Daralor, who was smiling at him. 'That was amazing. Can we do it again?'

'I can teach you, if you like. We'll have time, I think, until that letter of yours reaches Jador.'

'Time? Oh, yes, Your Grace, a great deal of time.' Aric looked at him hopefully. 'Then you will have your messengers send my letters for me? Both of them?'

'Of course.' Daralor grinned admiringly at his prized hawk. 'This is a fine place, don't you think?'

'You mean Nith? Yes, a very fine place, Your Grace.'

'It's worth saving, isn't it?'

'Certainly.' Puzzled, Aric held the bird aloft. 'I'm happy here. It's a fine country. Peaceful.'

'Raise your hand quickly,' said Daralor. 'Like this . . .'

He made a fast gesture, snapping his hand upward the way he had before. Aric mimicked the act, sending the bird skyward again. Together the two of them watched Echo reach once more for the sun.

'I think I have answered your question, Aric,' said Prince Daralor.

Aric nodded grimly. 'Yes, Your Grace,' he agreed. 'You have.'

For now, it was enough just to watch the sky.

59

With Thorin away at Richter estate, Jazana Carr spent most of her time alone, drinking too much wine and pining for the love she knew she had lost. Lionkeep seemed to shrink without Thorin's enormous presence. The halls were too large, the tables too empty, and the faces of the many servants were just too damn unfriendly for Jazana to care. She had lost the man she loved to a woman who was much younger and prettier, and for Jazana Carr that was the worst of it. She had done her best to keep herself beautiful, sparing no expense in the care she lavished on her face and body. But the girl called Mirage had cast a spell over Thorin, stealing him, and Jazana knew she had lost him.

Still, she considered things while Thorin was away, hatching plans to win him back. Whatever the cost, she intended to please her lover again. It was her fault that Thorin had turned away from her, she decided. She had come to this realization over an expensive bottle of wine, sipping it alone in her private chamber as she counted the diamonds in a golden urn near her bedside. The urn overflowed with the gems, jagged little reminders of her life in Norvor, lost to her now. She had been a shrew to Thorin. Picking up the diamonds, she dropped them slowly back into the urn, counting all the times she had nagged and needled him. She talked incessantly about Norvor. She nagged him constantly about regaining her throne. And she had threatened to leave him. No wonder he sought refuge in Mirage's tender arms. She had driven him to her.

Of all the people left to her in Lionkeep, only Rodrik Varl had remained steadfast. Good Roddy, so loyal and true, the kind of man Jazana wished she could love. She had always fallen for cruel men like Thorin, but Roddy would have been the perfect mate. Drunk, she wondered what her life would have been like with him as her husband. Even now, with all her mercenaries siding with Thorin – mostly because they feared him – Rodrik stayed close to her, always checking on her welfare, never wandering far. Jazana leaned back in her bed, letting her head sink into the plush pillow, and stared at the dark ceiling. The taper by her bedside had burned down nearly to a nub, but it still cast shadows on the stone walls and tapestries. The hours had slipped away and Lionkeep was silent. Jazana could hear only her own breath and the breeze outside her window. She stretched out her arm, reaching again for the urn full of diamonds, casually letting them slip out of her hand as her eyelids grew heavy.

Sleep did not come easily for Jazana any more. Unused to sleeping alone, she preferred a man beside her, be it Thorin or one of her numerous suitors. And Lionkeep, despite its quiet, had hardly been a relaxing place for her. As she stared at the ceiling she wondered how things were in Richter, and if Thorin and his new woman were laying together even now, under the same dark sky. Like grains of sand, the diamonds slipped lifelessly through Jazana's fingers, a fortune in gems that no longer brought her happiness. Drunk, sullen, she rolled over and blew out the candle, encasing herself in darkness.

'I have no children,' whispered to herself. 'No lover to share my bed. I have no family, no kin, no one to carry on after I am gone.'

The words made Jazana feel hollow. Her father's face came to her in a flash, haunting her. He had been a vicious man, single-handedly teaching her to hate his gender. While she grew to womanhood he took her to his bed, and in her most despairing moments she could still feel his filthy hands on her. But she had shown him, hadn't she? Hadn't she made something of herself?

'The Queen of Norvor,' she said, then laughed because it meant nothing. 'Maybe you were right, Father. Maybe I am just a slut.'

When she was a child, Jazana would cry herself to sleep. But tonight she had no tears for herself, and so closed her eyes and hoped that slumber would take her soon. The wine did a good job of salving her, though, and in a few minutes she drifted off, her mind ripe with visions of her father and the mother who had died too young. Lionkeep's tomb-like silence lulled her as she slept, and the hours tripped languidly away. Eventually, even Jazana's dreams faded.

Then, a sound awakened her. Startled by the commotion, she shook the sleep from her eyes and sat up. In the hall outside her chamber she heard the noise of heavy feet stomping and a voice barking angrily.

Thorin's voice.

Jazana struggled to wake herself, fixing the straps of her elegant night-gown, wondering how and why Thorin had returned. But it was him, she was sure of it, and as he neared her room she realized he was shouting. The door to her chamber exploded open. Jazana jumped.

'Jazana!' he yelled. 'Where are you?'

The room with Jazana's bed was not near the door. Another chamber separated them, though the distance was not great and Thorin traversed it easily. Seconds later he appeared, bellowing over his shoulder for the servants to stay out. When he turned his eyes on her, Jazana saw the rage in them. The Devil's Armour swam angrily over his huge body, though he had doffed the frightful helmet. He flexed his gauntlets into a pair of metal fists. Jazana tossed her naked feet over the bedside and stood, staring in astonishment.

'Thorin?'

'Jazana, you treacherous old bitch,' he seethed. 'I—'

Shadows appeared in the room behind him. Thorin whirled to see a pair of maids, concerned and clutching their bedclothes. 'Get out!' he thundered. 'Or I'll burn you alive!'

The maids went scurrying, slamming the unseen door behind them. Thorin turned back toward Jazana and shook an angry finger at her.

'I know what you did, you jealous harlot!'

Stunned, Jazana tried to speak, her words coming out in a stutter. 'Thorin, what . . . ?'

'You killed her! Bitch!'

His open palm shot forward, catching her across the jaw. The jolt spun Jazana backward, splaying her across the bed. Stunned and gasping, she looked up at Thorin's maddened visage, tasting blood from her crushed lip.

'Thorin . . . what?'

'You sent your mercenaries after me, didn't you?' He stalked over to her. 'You killed Mirage.'

'What?'

'Stop saying that!' He grabbed hold of her leg and dragged her off the bed until she hit the floor. 'Whore! I know what you did!'

Jazana grabbed desperately at the bed, terrified and confused. Thorin's shouts rang in her ears, but his words were senseless.

'Why are you here?' she cried. 'What happened to you?'

He stooped and took hold of her hair, wrenching her up to her knees. Holding her, he put his spitting face against her own. 'Now you lie? You think I'm so stupid?'

Again he struck her, knocking her down. The pain of the blow made Jazana's skull shake. She clawed away, searching the darkness for escape. Thorin snatched up her wrist and yanked her bodily off her feet. Her blinking eyes fought to focus. Blood drooled down her chin. His mouth curled upward with a snarl as he held her.

'Let go of me!' she hissed.

'After all I've done for you, you repay me with treachery!'

'What are you saying?'

'Thorin!'

The shout came from behind him. Thorin turned to see Rodrik Varl in the threshold of the chamber. Still in his bedclothes, the fiery mercenary had a sword in hand.

'Let her go,' he ordered. 'Or can you only beat up on women?'

Thorin held fast to Jazana's wrist, crushing it in his iron grip. 'Of course you come to help her. Varl, you water-headed ass . . .'

'Let her go,' repeated Varl sharply. 'Now, Thorin.'

Like a doll Thorin tossed Jazana back onto the bed. She scrambled away from him. 'Roddy, don't!'

'Yes, *Roddy*,' taunted Thorin. 'Be a good boy and don't get hurt.'

'Roddy, he's raving,' said Jazana. 'Get away, please!'

'I won't leave you to be beaten like a dog, Jazana,' said Varl. He stood his ground, hefting his weapon. 'Thorin, go. Leave her alone and get yourself together.'

Thorin turned toward him, smiling as an idea lit his face. 'This is just right,' he mused. 'Perfect, even.' To Jazana he said, 'You took the woman I loved, bitch. And so I will take this man that you love, and our score will be settled.'

Jazana leapt from the bed. 'No!'

Thorin seized her by the shoulder and pushed her aside, then turned on Varl. 'Come and get your lesson, Norvan.'

'Roddy, don't! He'll kill you!' screamed Jazana.

'Yes I will,' said Thorin. He took a step toward Varl, holding up his armoured arm as his only weapon. 'How long have you wanted this, Rodrik? How long have you waited?'

'A very long time,' sneered Varl.

Wrapping both fists around his sword pommel, he unleashed his attack, slashing down ferociously at Thorin. Thorin's arm shot up to parry. The sword sparked as it slid from the metal. Jazana screamed, crying for help that wouldn't come. Varl hacked again and again, each blow blocked by Thorin's swift moves. To Jazana, the mêlée was a blur, swathed in the darkness of her pitch black chamber. The combatants danced noisily through the room, knocking over furniture and tangling in bed linens.

'Stop it!' begged Jazana.

Varl barraged Thorin, quickly raining blows, each one expertly parried. At last Thorin's hand shot up, catching the blade in flight. Varl tried yanking it free, but a flexing of the baron's fist shattered it like glass. Thorin tossed the remnants aside, leaving Varl with the weapon's useless stub. Before the mercenary could retreat he reached out and grabbed his neck, lifting him off the ground. Varl's hands flew to his throat to pry loose the iron fingers, gurgling helplessly as Thorin carried him toward the nearest wall.

'I loved her, Jazana,' Thorin moaned. 'I loved her!'

'Fate above, Thorin, don't!'

But the demon inside him had seized the baron completely. Jazana saw the madness in him, pure like crystal water. His eyes glowed red as he held Rodrik near the wall, cocking back his arm. Rodrik Varl sputtered hatefully, knowing what was coming. Thorin looked remorseless. His arm snapped forward, smashing Varl into the wall. Made of stone, it shattered his skull like a melon, spraying blood and smearing brains against the rough surface. Jazana Carr shrieked. Thorin dropped the twitching corpse to the floor.

'You may deny it all you wish, Jazana,' he said. 'But I know what you did.'

Jazana could not speak, not even to defend herself. Her gaze remained on Rodrik's body and the gory stream across the wall. Finally, a hint of regret showed on Thorin's face. He shook his head, studying the dead mercenary.

'He was loyal to you until the end. Why could you not be as loyal to me?'

'Madness,' groaned Jazana. Her broken lip continued dripping blood. 'You're mad.'

Thorin went to her bed and leered at her. 'What will you do? Leave me? You will never leave me, Jazana. I will never let you go.'

The lust in his face brought bile to Jazana's throat. 'Gods, no . . .'

He fell on her, stripping off her gown and driving her down into the bed, smothering her with his heavy body. Stripping himself, he forced her legs apart with his spiky gauntlet. Jazana's screams filled the chamber.

This time, no one came to help her.

When it was over, Jazana laid alone in her bed in shock and horror.

Thorin had gone an hour before, leaving her in her tattered nightgown to stare at the corpse of Rodrik Varl and endure the thousand bruises he had inflicted on her body. The keep remained unbearable quiet. The frightened servants, locked in their chambers, left their queen and her murdered mercenary to themselves. Jazana supposed they were waiting until morning. When they came, they would find her battered. She thought about this, about her bruised and bloodied face, and wondered what they would think of her now.

In the urn at her bedside, the jagged diamonds remained, undisturbed by the shattering events. Beside them rested the bottle of wine. Jazana picked it up and surveyed its half-full contents. Then, without hesitation, she selected a gemstone and placed it in her mouth, swallowing it down with a swig from the bottle. This she did again and again, each little gem cutting her throat as it slid down to her stomach. She knew her death would be an agony, but Jazana did not care. With Roddy's visceral remains spilled across her bedroom floor, a lesser death seemed cowardly.

60

Stay awake, Gilwyn, urged Ruana. *It's not much further.*

The Akari's voice coaxed Gilwyn to lift his head. Ahead of him, the forest road seemed to stretch on forever, with no hint of Koth except the marks made by carriages and horse hooves. Gilwyn licked his dried lips and swallowed, trying to stem the sickness overtaking him. The slow canter of his horse made him sway from side to side. The motion stoked his illness. Wanting to vomit, Gilwyn nevertheless swallowed it back. He had been this way for the past five days, exhausted and dizzy, brutalized from the long trip north. The rass venom that remained in his blood had plagued him the entire journey, but now, when his terrible trek was near its end, it threatened to knock him from the saddle.

'I need to rest,' he groaned. 'Just for a little while.'

You can't rest here, said Ruana. *It's not safe. It will be dark again soon.*

'But we don't know where we are.'

We are near Koth, Gilwyn. Don't you remember?

Gilwyn nodded, vaguely recalling the trees of the forest. He had been a boy in the city, and had sometimes ventured out of the library to be among the trees and wildlife here. Instinctively, he knew he was home, but the day's ride had wearied him and he longed to lay his head down and sleep. It had been weeks since he had left Roall, leaving behind the kind-hearted Kelan and his wife Marna. Gilwyn had been happy there, content to help them on their little farm in the valley between the mountains. Everything had been idyllic there. His troubles had seemed a thousand miles away. But Kahldris had shattered his peace, and Ruana had reminded him of his mission. Gilwyn had done his best to make it to Koth quickly, but his lame leg and the relentless sickness of the venom had slowed him to an almost embarrassing pace. He had begged for money in the towns along the way and slept in small villages where people took pity on him, but he had never given up, slogging all the way north to Koth.

To home.

'When I left here,' he gasped, 'there were always people on the forest roads. Where are they?'

Ruana had no answer for him, except to say the sad truth. *Things are different now, Gilwyn.*

'Thorin is no tyrant. I don't believe the things they say.'

He sat up, making a miserable face. All through his trip north, he had heard the stories about the Black Baron. They were calling him a demon, but Gilwyn knew the truth.

'He's corrupted. That's all.'

He will not be the man you knew, Ruana warned. *Gilwyn, you should prepare yourself.*

'I'm ready,' said Gilwyn. 'I know Thorin, Ruana. He won't hurt me.'

Deep inside his mind, Gilwyn could feel his Akari's discomfort. She was afraid for him.

You think on those stories we heard, said Ruana gently. *Soon you will see him. Soon you will see the truth for yourself. Do not refuse the truth because it is ugly.*

Gilwyn nodded, then took a deep, unsteady breath. His eyes drooped and his head swam, and it took all his strength just to guide the horse that Aztar had given him. The remarkable beast had taken him all the way from the Desert of Tears. Without complaint, the horse had borne him proudly. Gilwyn had named the beast Triumph, a name that had come to him in a flash of inspiration. After so many months spent with the stallion, he was almost as close to him as he was with his beloved kreel Emerald.

'Almost there, boy,' he told the horse, rubbing its neck. 'It's almost over.'

The thought of the journey's end gave Gilwyn the wind he needed to continue. Fighting back his nausea, he urged Triumph onward through the forest, following the narrow road that he knew would lead them to Koth. Ruana slipped back into the darker recesses of Gilwyn's mind, where he could feel her brooding. She had tried for weeks to reason with him, and he had always refused her counsel. Whatever else Thorin had become, he was still a friend, and Gilwyn was determined to help him.

Then at last Gilwyn glimpsed the end of the rest. Up ahead the canopy of trees thinned. The sky spread out above it, blue and beckoning. Cheered, Gilwyn hurried along the road until he reached a place where the trees parted. For the first time in years, he saw the city he called home. The breathtaking visage stunned him.

'Oh, Fate . . .'

His horse slowed beneath him. Ruana tiptoed from her hiding place. Together the travelers stared at the city sprawling before them, and the first thing they saw was the library on its hill, rebuilt and beautiful, glistening in the sunlight. Gilwyn's heart tripped at the sight. His mouth fell open in disbelief. Koth had changed. To him, the city seemed lifeless and twisted. But the great Cathedral of Knowledge remained, engendering a flood of emotions in him.

'Look, Ruana, look!'

I see it, Gilwyn. Remarkable.

'Isn't it beautiful? It's still there!'

Still, because the Baron has remade it.

'Yes!'

The sight swept the sickness from Gilwyn's mind. Suddenly, the only thing he wanted was to see his old friend Thorin. At the base of Library Hill, the rest of Koth crawled with shadows. People meandered through the streets, and the buildings of the royal quarter rose up from the sloping avenues. A distinct change had gripped the city, a kind of invisible pall that darkened the shops and gardens. But above it all, the library remained. Gladdened, Gilwyn hurried on.

The morning after Jazana's death, Thorin discovered her in her bed, naked and bruised. A pool of vomited blood lay at her bedside. Her dead face stared blindly at the ceiling from two pulpy sockets, her eyes clawed out from the pain. The discovery had sent Thorin to his knees, wailing like a child in the gory chamber. Near the wall furthest from the bed, the stain of Rodrik Varl's blood and brains remained, dripping down toward his nearly headless corpse. Not a single maid or scullery hand had come to clean the room, nor to help the Diamond Queen in the throes of her agony. Thorin, who had heard her cries and dismissed them, had ordered her left alone, sure that her rantings were for her dead paramour. Thorin spent almost an hour in Jazana's chamber, weeping, trying and failing to understand what had happened. Then, when he had finally collected himself, he left the room and closed the door behind him, ordering the servants to get to work cleaning the unimaginable mess.

Baron Glass left Lionkeep that morning and walked out to the orchards at the edge of the castle. Alone, he ordered that no one follow him or come to disturb him. It was a long walk to his destination, but Thorin did not care. Kahldris was with him, and he needed to be away from Lionkeep and wash himself in the river. The river that ran through the orchards cut a wavering swathe across the apple trees. Stones lined its bubbling banks. In the seclusion of the trees, Thorin stripped off his blood-stained clothes until he was naked, leaving only the armour of his magical arm. The water was cold but he submerged himself, dreading the possibility that no amount of water could clean him. There he swam for two long hours, climbing out finally to dry himself in the sun.

Staring up the sky, Thorin mourned for Jazana.

He had memories of her that could still make him smile. It had been Jazana who rescued him from exile, giving him a home in Hanging Man, where they fell in love. He had served her loyally in those years and she had repaid him with pampering and womanly affection. And she had always been beautiful, stoking such hunger in him that he could never refuse her. With Kahldris guiding his hands, his lust for her had been insatiable . . .

He closed his eyes, remembering with horror their last love-making. It had not been love at all, but an act of vengeance. She had screamed and screamed, and he had ignored her, taking her until she bled and his rage finally quieted.

What was wrong with him?

Thorin opened his eyes. Above him, the limbs of a tree obscured the sky, and in the tree a bird hopped from branch to branch.

'I am not myself,' he whispered.

Kahldris answered, *You are better than yourself alone. We are one now. We are strong.*

'We killed her,' lamented Thorin.

She is gone now, but we don't need her.

Thorin fought back a sob. 'We murdered her.' The thought was too much to bear. 'Last night a madness descended on me . . .'

Kahldris flittered above him, barely visible, like a ghost. He came as an old man, smiling down at the divested baron. 'We have killed our enemies, Baron Glass. But there are more of them. They still plot against us.'

'Who? Who plots against us?'

'The ones across the desert. The Jadori plot against us. And my brethren Akari.'

'You mean your brother?'

'I feel him, Baron Glass. He is in the world again.'

Thorin sat up. 'No.'

'The Bronze Knight is with him.'

'Lukien?' The news stunned Thorin. 'Why are you keeping this from me?'

Kahldris shimmered just of reach. 'The Bronze Knight has found my brother and brings him here to destroy us. Do you see, Baron Glass, how many hate us?'

'Even Lukien.' Thorin leaned against the tree, contemplating the problem. 'Where is he?'

'He comes across the great desert. He bears a sword. I have seen it.'

'This sword – can it break your armour?'

The demon darkened. 'I do not know.'

They were words Kahldris rarely spoke, and the admission shook

Thorin. They were in danger. Malator was more of a threat than Reec or any other of their enemies. 'How did Lukien find this sword?' he wondered aloud. Nothing made sense to him anymore.

'There is another thing,' said Kahldris. 'Another secret I have kept from you.'

'Tell me.'

'The boy, Gilwyn Toms. He has come for you, Baron Glass. He is here in the city.'

'Gilwyn?' Thorin leaned forward excitedly. 'The boy is here? In Koth?'

'At last, yes,' drawled the demon. 'Now he nears Lionkeep.'

Thorin leapt to his feet. 'Why do you keep these things from me? I must know these things, Kahldris!'

Kahldris smiled. 'To protect, my sweet friend. We must protect each other.'

'Yes,' Thorin agreed, 'but—'

'The boy comes to save you from me, Baron Glass. Just as all the others have tried.'

Thorin bristled at the hint. 'We will not harm him. I will not have it, demon. I love that boy.'

'No, we will not harm him,' said Kahldris. His grin was impish. 'We will keep him and adore him. Then he will use the machine and he will help us defeat my brother and the knight.'

'All right,' said Thorin, relieved. He looked around for his clothes, excited by the thought of seeing Gilwyn. 'We must get back to Lionkeep before he arrives. I want to see that boy at once!'

By the time Gilwyn reached Lionkeep, he was exhausted once again. Overwhelmed by the sights and sounds of Koth, the sickness from the rass venom had made his skin clammy and his eyes too blurry to see clearly. The sun was going down past the keep. Soldiers milled along the avenues, dressed in uniforms Gilwyn knew weren't Liirian. In his day, when King Akeela had been alive, Royal Chargers had paraded around the residence, but those days were long ago and only faintly echoed by the current occupants of Koth. Gilwyn kept his head down as he approached Lionkeep, careful to avoid eye contact. His whole body ached. His head split with the effort of riding. Triumph, smart enough to sense his master's distress, trotted carefully along the cobblestones, letting Gilwyn lean against his neck. Ruana lingered at the back of Gilwyn's mind, remaining quiet but plainly enthralled by the sights. Lionkeep, though damaged and neglected, remained an impressive structure, replete with sculpted figures and catwalks that tied together the many towers. In the courtyard of the keep, Gilwyn could see a handful of soldiers taking notice of him. He kept to the road, approaching unthreateningly, his clubbed hand barely holding the reins of his mount. Behind the men stood the main entrance to the keep, a big bronze portcullis crowned with spikes. The portal slowly began ascending as Gilwyn approached, a curiosity that puzzled Gilwyn. Alarmingly, the soldiers pointed at him.

'Ruana, they see us,' said Gilwyn weakly. Suddenly he was afraid. He began to shiver. 'I think I have a fever.'

Soon you can rest, said Ruana in her soothing voice. *Gilwyn, protect yourself.*

'What? Why?'

It is Kahldris. I can feel him.

The soldiers began coming toward him. Gilwyn slowed his horse. 'What do you mean? Where is he?'

He is coming, said Ruana.

The portcullis rose to reveal the inner darkness. Gilwyn strained to see. The soldiers were waving to him, calling out. Ruana braced herself. Gilwyn's skull began to throb as his heart raced. A mercenary hurried up to him. He was in the courtyard now, his eyes fixed on the open walkway.

'You boy,' said the mercenary. 'Are you Gilwyn Toms?'

Hearing his name surprised Gilwyn. He nodded, staring with blurry eyes. 'Yes, I am.'

'Get down,' the man ordered. He had stopped the horse and offered Gilwyn a hand. 'Let me help you. You don't look well.'

'Yes,' said Gilwyn haltingly. He began to shake. 'No, I'm ill.'

As he slid off Triumph's back he kept his eyes on the keep, waiting dreadfully for Kahldris to appear. His legs turned to jelly when his feet hit the ground.

'You're lame,' the mercenary commented. Other soldiers had gathered now. The man looked at Gilwyn oddly. 'How can you ride with such a hand? And what's that boot you wear?'

'Stop with your questions!' thundered a voice. 'That boy is twice your better and more!'

The men stepped away, leaving Gilwyn to gape. Out of the portcullis stepped a figure, big and terrifying and barely a man. His face was familiar, as was his voice, but it was a demon visage that came out to greet him, and Gilwyn weakened in his fiery gaze. Like a serpent, the man's left arm twisted with life, enchanted by some unholy metal. A grim smile upturned his thin white lips. He was the shadow of a man Gilwyn had once known, speaking with a voice stolen from another time. Stepping out into the courtyard, the wraith that was Thorin opened his arms wide.

'Gilwyn!' he cried. 'My boy, it is good to see you!'

Overwhelmed by the sight of him, Gilwyn fainted.

61

The moment Gilwyn awoke, he knew the bed was unfamiliar. The heaviness in his head began to lift. His eyes opened slowly. In his chest he felt the grip of panic, but the chains of his own lethargy kept him pinned to the downy pillow. As his blurred vision focused, he saw the ceiling, dark and tiled with ornate metal. Wood and velvet covered the walls. A window on the other side of the room revealed the blackness of night, draped with open, scarlet curtains. Gilwyn took a breath and held it, his eyes darting around the chamber. Very slowly his memory returned. He remembered the gate rising and the figure coming from the shadows.

Thorin!

Ruana's gentle touch was on him instantly. She whispered into his troubled mind. *You are safe, Gilwyn. Don't be afraid.* And then she told him, *He is with you.*

The room was dark but for small candle burning on a distant table. Gilwyn's eyes went to it, then saw a figure seated near it, its two big hands clutching the arms of a high-backed chair. The face met his, the red eyes softened, and the grimacing smile animated the mask, bringing the visage to life. Gilwyn stared, mesmerized, his heart galloping. A gleaming hand of living metal rose to gesture.

'You're awake, my boy?'

It was Thorin's voice, and yet it was not. Gilwyn broke down when he heard it.

'Gods above,' he moaned. 'What's happened to you, Thorin?'

Thorin Glass rose from his chair and took two big strides to Gilwyn's bedside. His face was wraith-like, shadowed by the night and lit by his two burning eyes. His brows lifted in concern.

'You have slept long,' he said. 'How do you feel?'

Gilwyn stared at him in dread. 'Where am I?'

'You are in Lionkeep. You came here, remember? You fainted.'

'Yes,' groaned Gilwyn, 'I remember.' He licked his dried lips, still in disbelief. 'Thorin?'

'It is me, Gilwyn,' assured Thorin. 'Do not be afraid of me. I beg you, please.'

Behind the crimson eyes, Gilwyn saw a spark of love, a tiny of hint of Thorin's humanity locked behind the madman's mask. He recognized it unmistakably. Wearied, he could not help the tears from falling.

'It is you,' he choked. He looked away and brought up his hands. 'I didn't believe it. They told me but I didn't believe.'

'Don't look away from me, Gilwyn, please.'

'But I see madness in you!' Gilwyn cried. 'Oh, Thorin, what's happened?'

Thorin knelt beside the bed. 'You have come to save me. My appearance is too much for you. I know I have changed. But I am Thorin, my boy, and it gladdens my heart so much to see you that I could weep.'

Gilwyn struggled to control his sobs. The thousand challenges of his long journey caught up to him at last. He felt like a little boy suddenly, lying sick in some huge bed. And Thorin, like a father he'd never known, gazed down at him helplessly. Gilwyn forced himself to look at Thorin, studying his twisted features. The Devil's Armour had poisoned him.

'It has maddened you, Thorin,' Gilwyn groaned. 'I had heard it but I didn't believe. Look at yourself!'

'I have seen myself, Gilwyn,' said Thorin gently. 'I am fearsome to behold, I know. I have done things, horrible things. But you must look at me. I am begging you to see me!'

'I'm looking, Thorin,' said Gilwyn, holding his gaze. 'And what I see scares me.'

Thorin keened as though his heart was breaking. 'See me as I was, not as I am. Remember who I was, Gilwyn, when I was your friend.'

'It's the armour,' said Gilwyn. 'The armour did this to you.'

Thorin nodded. 'I am one with Kahldris now. This is the price of it.'

'You can fight him.' Gilwyn struggled to sit up. 'You can beat him, Thorin.'

'Hush.' Thorin put a hand on Gilwyn's shoulder. 'Lie back.'

'No . . .'

'Lie back, boy,' Thorin ordered. 'You are sick. Rest and tell me what has happened to you.'

Gilwyn took a breath. Fighting was no use, so he sank back against his pillow, feeling the pain of an enormous headache. 'It was a rass,' he said. 'When I first left Jador. It found me in the desert. Its venom did this to me.'

'You're very weak. Has it been this way since then?'

'Yes,' said Gilwyn. 'Sometimes worse. When I get worn out it comes back. It was such a long ride home, Thorin.'

Thorin smiled, faintly reminiscent of his old, fatherly grin. 'And all for me. You are too good, boy. I am not worth your efforts.'

'I didn't come just for you,' confessed Gilwyn. 'I came because of White-Eye.'

Thorin avoided the subject, saying, 'How long were you on the road? It has been months and months since I left Jador.'

'Months,' sighed Gilwyn. 'It seemed like forever.' He closed his eyes to beat back the nausea. 'I should have made the trip faster.'

'A lame boy like you?' Thorin laughed. 'No.'

Gilwyn opened his eyes. 'Where is Kahldris, Thorin?'

Thorin hesitated. 'He is part of me. As your own Akari is part of you, Gilwyn.'

'He came to me, Thorin,' said Gilwyn. 'Weeks ago, when I was in Roall. He goaded me here. That's why he hurt White-Eye, to make me come here.'

Again Thorin shifted the conversation. 'You must rest now, Gilwyn. You are here now and have nowhere else to go. We will take care of you here.' He smiled. 'How good it is to see you.'

'Thorin, tell me what happened to you,' said Gilwyn. He was full of questions and refused to let Thorin avoid them. 'When I was in Marn I heard what happened with the Reecians. They say you slaughtered them and that you killed their prince.'

'Yes,' said Thorin, his face darkening. 'Sit back, Gilwyn.'

'Tell me,' said Gilwyn.

Thorin sighed distractedly. He rose from his place at the bedside, then went and dragged his chair closer. Sitting down again, he watched Gilwyn with his enigmatic gaze, as if sifting through all his horrible history.

'It will be morning soon,' he said. 'And the things I've done would take longer to tell than that. I've heard the same stories as you, Gilwyn. What do they say in Marn? That I am a tyrant? Very well. If tyranny is what it takes to throttle Liiria back to greatness, then I am proudly guilty. Yes I killed the Reecians. In the armour I was like a god! No man could stop me. And I won the Kryss back for all of us. Did they tell you that in Marn?'

'Thorin?'

'Yes?'

'You've gone mad.'

Thorin smiled then and nodded. 'I have.'

Silence. The two friends stared at each other. Could a madman know such a thing about himself, Gilwyn wondered? Suddenly, he no longer feared Thorin. Rather, he was grief-stricken. Tears came again to his eyes.

'No, do not weep for me,' Thorin counseled. 'I am well enough to know the choices I have made. I do not regret taking the armour, Gilwyn.

Liiria needed me. She still needs me! She is weak, but I am strong. I have beaten nearly all my enemies. Kahldris has been good to me.'

'Good for you? How can you say such a thing when you know that you are mad?'

'Because I have chosen,' said Thorin. 'All of this was my own design. Did you see the library when you rode into Koth. I have rebuilt it! And when you are better you can take your place there, my boy, and you can run it and bring all the scholars to your side. You will make it great again.'

'Thorin, stop.' Gilwyn pushed himself up again. 'Kahldris did not lure me here to run the library and you know it. Tell me why he wanted me here.'

Thorin's face saddened. 'It was necessary.'

'So then, you know what he did to White-Eye? He blinded her, Thorin.'

'I did not know this until it was over,' Thorin insisted. 'Believe me, please. Kahldris needed you, and how else could he have got you here? But I swear I would not let him hurt you, Gilwyn. I will never let him hurt you.' Thorin leaned forward earnestly. 'I will protect you.'

Amazingly, his promise heartened Gilwyn. After so many months of loneliness, of fending off animals and running from highwaymen, the thought of Thorin's protection was like a warm blanket.

'He hurt her,' he said. 'And you let him. Why, Thorin? Tell me.'

'I will tell you,' said Thorin. He leaned back. 'But not yet.'

Frustrated, Gilwyn looked around the room. 'Where are my things? I had saddle bags with me.'

'They're here,' said Thorin. With his chin he gestured to the other side of Gilwyn's bed. 'And your horse has been taken care of too.'

Gilwyn leaned over the bed and saw that his bags were indeed there, lying just out of reach. 'I need them,' he said, too weak to get them. 'Please, Thorin, will you get them for me?'

Thorin rose with a sigh. 'You should rest, Gilwyn. We can speak again in a few hours.'

'Thorin, please . . .'

'All right,' lamented the baron, then went to the bedside and stooped down to retrieve the bags. 'Which one?'

'That one,' said Gilwyn, pointing weakly to the smaller of the two leather bags. They were both badly worn and sun-bleached, but that one in particular bag held an item of great value. 'Look through it. You'll see what I want.'

Thorin looked puzzled but did as Gilwyn asked, setting the bag down on the bed at Gilwyn's feet. He began rummaging through the few items within it, stopping quickly as his eyes seized on the item.

'What is this?' said Thorin, pulling it out and holding it up for inspection.

'That ring belongs to King Lorn of Norvor,' Gilwyn said. He watched Thorin's face for a reaction. 'He came to Jador. He helped me, Thorin. When he knew that I was coming here he gave that ring to me to show to Jazana Carr.'

Thorin's face went suddenly white. 'Jazana.'

'Lorn's still alive, Thorin. I promised him I would give that ring to Jazana Carr to prove to her he would be back for her. He wants Norvor back.'

Thorin sighed peculiarly. 'Does he so?' Then he shook his head and placed the ring in Gilwyn's lap. 'You may keep this ring, Gilwyn.'

'No. No, I have to give it to her. I made a promise, Thorin.'

'It's a promise you can't keep, boy,' said Thorin darkly. 'I . . . have something to tell you.'

He moved away from the bed and stalked toward the window, staring out blankly at the dark night. Gilwyn could tell at once something terrible was on his mind. He picked up the ring at his lap, rolling it anxiously in his fingers.

'Thorin? What happened?'

'You can't give that ring to Jazana,' said Thorin. 'Jazana's dead. She died last night. She killed herself.'

The ring fell out of Gilwyn's hand. 'What?'

'She was plotting against me, Gilwyn. That's something you need to understand. You're going to hear things while you're here. True things, about how I beat her and drove her to it. But she tried to kill me.' Thorin struggled with the story. 'I am sorry for her death. She was good and loyal until she turned on me. I loved her.'

'Thorin, I don't understand. What happened?'

'I was in Richter. Do you know that place?'

Gilwyn nodded. Most Liirians knew of the royal estate. 'I know it, yes.'

'I was with another woman, and Jazana took the chance to have me killed. She sent mercenaries there to burn me alive. They locked the doors of the house and set in on fire, but I escaped. The woman I was with did not.' Thorin turned from the window to look at Gilwyn. 'The woman was Meriel, Gilwyn. From Grimhold.'

'Meriel?' Gilwyn bolted upright. 'She came here with Lukien.'

'She did. And I battled Lukien and nearly killed him. After that she wandered for months before coming back to me. She loved me, Gilwyn, just as she did in Grimhold.'

The story made no sense. Gilwyn urged Thorin to go on. 'What happened to Lukien? Where is he?'

'Meriel seldom spoke of him. He left her to go and find a sword to defeat me. He abandoned her, Gilwyn, and she came to me!'

'Thorin, I don't care,' Gilwyn shouted. 'Tell me what happened to Lukien!'

'Bah! Have you not heard what I've said, boy? I have lost two women who loved me in less than a week!'

Gilwyn shrank back. 'I'm sorry,' he said, knowing he had to tread carefully. 'You're right, it's terrible news.'

'I thought I was all alone in the world again,' said Thorin. 'But then you came to me.' His expression filled with bitter-sweet emotion. 'The things I've done no man should speak of, Gilwyn. Jazana and Meriel both spoke to save me. They called me a madman, just as you have. Now I know that I am mad, but I cannot change. I have made enemies, too many to turn my back on.'

'Kahldris has driven you to this, Thorin. It wasn't you that killed Jazana – it was him.'

Thorin shook his head. 'No, Gilwyn, it was I. I am not separate from Kahldris. I am him and he is me, and that is what has become of me.'

'Thorin, tell me about Lukien.' Gilwyn shifted painfully in the bed. 'Please.'

'He came to stop me, Gilwyn.'

'I know he did. But what happened to him?'

It was a story Thorin didn't care to tell. He moved from the window as a hint of dawn began to light his face. 'He came here with Meriel,' he said finally. 'And joined the others at the old library. My son Aric was with them.'

'Your son? He's still alive?'

'Maybe he is dead now. I do not know. He fought with Lukien and the others, but Jazana and I defeated them easily. Lukien came to rescue me, just as you have done, Gilwyn. I begged him not to stand in my way. I begged him!'

'Did you hurt him?' Gilwyn asked pointedly.

'Yes. I had to. I left him for dead just outside the city.'

'But he's not dead . . .'

'No. He left to find this sword.' Thorin came again to kneel beside the bed. 'It is called the Sword of Angels,' he whispered. 'It is the means to destroy me, Gilwyn. Lukien has found it. Now he is coming to kill me.'

'How do you know this?' asked Gilwyn.

'Because Kahldris has told me so,' said Thorin. 'Because it is his brother that lies within the sword. That is why we brought you here, Gilwyn – to help us find his brother, Malator.'

Gilwyn shrugged, confused. 'But how could I have helped?'

602

'You knew Figgis better than anyone. He built that infernal catalogue machine to answer mysteries like this.'

'No, Thorin, that's not so.'

'It is. It is a thinking machine. You told me this yourself.'

'Yes, but it doesn't work like that . . .'

'The machine helped Figgis find the Eye of God. Did you not tell me that?'

Gilwyn nodded reluctantly. 'Yes, I did.'

'Then surely it can answer the questions I need answered,' said Thorin. 'And you must help me, Gilwyn. You must use the machine to find out how to stop Malator. If there is a way, the machine will know. The contents of the library have every useless bit of knowledge mankind has ever learned! I have spent hours on end reading the books your master Figgis collected, but they are too many. I need the machine to help me find the answers. I need you, Gilwyn.'

Gilwyn's head began to reel. He leaned back against the pillow, averting Thorin's wild eyes. 'I cannot use the machine. I don't know how.'

'Surely you must remember something, though. You spent your life in that place with Figgis. He must have taught you.'

'I don't remember, Thorin! It was so long ago. And the machine is so complicated.'

'But you must try, Gilwyn!' Thorin got up and sat next to him on the bed. 'Lukien was a friend once. I warned him to stay away, but he comes again, just like all the rest of them. They all want me dead, Gilwyn.'

'Lukien wants to help you—'

'No!' Thorin jumped up and stomped the floor. 'He means to kill me, don't you see? Just like Jazana and the Reecians and everyone else! If you don't help me he will succeed, Gilwyn, and then there will be chaos in Liiria. Is that what you want?'

Gilwyn closed his eyes and groaned. 'There already is chaos, Thorin. You've killed Jazana Carr, you've slaughtered the Reecians. Now everyone is afraid of you.'

'But they obey me,' declared Thorin proudly. 'They know I am their master. Have I not rebuilt the library? I can rebuild all of Liiria. I can make it great again, if you'll help me, boy.' He calmed himself, looking down at Gilwyn. 'Will you help me?'

Sick in his bed, Gilwyn could barely speak. Even thinking made him ache. His mind mulled over the things Thorin had told him. It all seemed impossible, but somehow he knew the stories were true. He wanted to help Thorin – he had come so far to rescue him. Perhaps the old man needed time. Perhaps in time, Gilwyn thought, he might be able to reach him.

'I'm very tired,' he said. 'I need to rest.'

'Yes, of course, you must rest,' agreed Thorin. He put his fleshy hand onto Gilwyn's forehead. 'I have women here that will attend to you. They will bring you food and drink and when you are ready they will bathe you. But Gilwyn, I must have your answer soon. Rest now, but think on what I have said to you.'

He turned to go, heading for the door. Before he reached it Gilwyn called to him.

'Thorin, wait.'

The baron lingered, his hand on the door handle. 'Yes?'

'Thank you for taking care of me.'

Thorin smiled. 'I will always take care of you, Gilwyn. For as long as you remain in Lionkeep, I will protect you.'

He opened the door and left the room, closing off Gilwyn again in darkness. Gilwyn remained very still, listening to the baron's footsteps disappear down the hall.

'Ruana,' he whispered. 'Did you hear?'

I heard, said Ruana, her voice sad. *I am sorry, Gilwyn. I tried to warn you.*

'He's mad.'

In his mind, Ruana nodded. *Yes.*

'I want to help him.'

You will not be able to reach him, Gilwyn. It is up to Lukien now.

'But I have to try,' resolved Gilwyn. 'You see how he cares for me? He might listen to me.'

He will destroy you, Gilwyn, because he is a jackal now and that is what jackals do.

'No.' Gilwyn shook his head, refusing to believe it. 'No, I see the man he was, still inside him. If I can wait, pretend to help him, maybe Lukien will come in time.'

Lukien is coming to kill him, Ruana pointed out. *Not to save him.*

'You don't know that.'

The Akari sighed. *You are hopeless.*

Gilwyn rolled over onto his side, facing the window. Outside he could see the morning light struggling through the sky. The vision heartened him. 'It's never hopeless, Ruana,' he said. 'We just have to believe.'

PART THREE

ARMOUR
AND SWORD

62

The dead city of Kaliatha rose out of its sandy tomb, glowing purple in the cloudy light of day. A westward breeze whistled through its crumbling spires, portending a storm, and ghosts of dust flittered through the empty avenues. Darkened windows in the lifeless towers stared like black, unblinking eyes, forever watching the desolate horizon, and in the cracks along the ancient pavement the weeds grew up like serpents, indomitable amidst the sad and speechless city. The foreign sound of horse hooves echoed along the main thoroughfare as a single horseman rode through the city, his head spinning from the awesome sights. Lukien had seen Kaliatha before, months ago, and he had dreamed of it since. The impression it had left on him was like seeing a massive grave. He did not speak as he trotted through the city, nor direct his comrade to any particular sight. Next to him, the Akari spirit Malator walked in stunned amazement, rendered mute by the image of his forlorn home. It was the first time since Lukien had met the Akari that Malator was lost for words, and the oddness of it struck Lukien. They had ridden together from the grand city of Torlis, through the villages and swamps of Tharlara and across the desolation toward Jador. And all the while, Malator had been full of quips and questions, barely sparing Lukien time to sleep. Now, though, Malator's tongue was still. His glowing eyes filled with the likes of ethereal tears.

'Here I was a boy,' he said in a whisper, 'and then a man and a soldier and a summoner. I have thought of almost nothing else in the countless years of my death but Kaliatha. But I never thought it would look like this.'

Lukien had tried to warn Malator. A hundred times, he had told the spirit that the city of the Akari was nothing like he'd left it. It had fallen to ruin a thousand lifetimes ago, torn by the teeth of storms and ravaged by the claws of the relentless sun. Day by day, year after endless year, the glory of the city had been peeled away, fading to a shell full of memories and almost nothing else. Malator, a child-like optimist, had merely nodded at Lukien's description of Kaliatha, assuring him that he understood the depths of what had happened. Had he lied, Lukien wondered? Or was it just too much for the spirit to imagine?

'It still stands, Malator,' said Lukien. 'It's still here for you to see, after all these years. That's something good, at least.'

Malator nodded, but grudgingly. Because he had no real body he did not tire the way Lukien did, and so he often came out of the sword to walk beside Lukien while the knight rode. They had spent hours telling each other about the lives they had lived, even laughing at times at each others jokes. Malator had surprised Lukien from the very start, looking not at all like the great warrior destined to defeat Kahldris. He was tall and reedy and even foppish at times, with a grin that seemed better for a jester than a soldier. He was entertaining company, always prepared to use his wit to disarm the sceptical Lukien. Seeing his new friend – his Akari – so broken-hearted made Lukien wilt.

'You have no idea how grand this place was once,' Malator continued. 'And I treaded the world like a prince when I was alive. All of Kaliatha knew my name, and my brother's. They looked to me for help.' Malator trembled. 'For help, Lukien.'

Lukien smiled reassuringly, understanding Malator's pain. 'You did what you could for them. You tried to help. Now you can explain that to them, Malator. That's why we are here.'

'We are here because there is no other way to your land of Jador, Lukien. If there were, I would not be here.'

'You dissemble, my friend. Nothing would have kept you from seeing Kaliatha and you know it. And it is good that you see it. Look at it! You see ruins. I do, too. But I see glory here, still. I can imagine what a world your people made.'

'Can you?' Malator appeared heartened. 'Then your one eye is clearer than my two.'

Lukien did not rise to Malator's bait. He had the right to mourn for his city, Lukien supposed, and nothing he could say would assuage the spirit's feelings. The Sword of Angels rested at Lukien's hip, keeping him alive and filling him with vitality. The Eye of God still hung from his neck, but Lukien could no longer feel the presence of Amaraz within himself, and he knew that the great Akari had vacated his body, leaving the job of sustaining him to Malator, his one, true, Akari. Throughout their trip together, Malator had stayed close to Lukien, assuring him that he need not wear the sword at every moment. Eventually, Lukien had come to trust the spirit.

Still, the long ride from Torlis had been bittersweet. Without Jahan, the lush landscape of Tharlara seemed empty, and Lukien spent many hours of the trek mourning his kind-hearted friend. He missed Lahkali and Karoshin. He even missed Niharn. But Jahan he missed most of all, and he knew that he could not pass by his village without telling his wife what had happened.

Oddly, his ride through the dead city reminded Lukien of that moment now, and in the high spires of deceased Kaliatha – a city Lukien knew Jahan would have loved – he saw the wonder-filled face of the villager. The memory put a dagger through his heart. He had told Jahan's family that their beloved husband and father had died valiantly, saving him from a rass. He made sure that the children believed their father was a hero, and took pains to praise him and tell how much he missed him. Even in their crushed expressions, Lukien saw the love they had for him.

'You are thinking of your friend?' asked Malator.

Lukien grinned. He was not used to having an Akari who could so easily pick at his brain. 'This is what Gilwyn warned me about,' he jibed. 'Yes, Malator, I am thinking of Jahan. He would have understood what you cannot. He would have seen the glory that's still here in Kaliatha.'

'Always on the past is your mind, Lukien,' said Malator, shaking his vapourous head. 'I grieve for a city, a whole world of people! You grieve for one man, though I have assured you that he lives on, not just in your memory but in a very real world beyond this one. Do not lament for him so.'

'I know what you have told me, Malator. But it is hard.'

'But you have seen the truth yourself, in the Story Garden!'

'I have seen it, yes,' said Lukien. Cassandra, too, he thought of often. And yet Malator never questioned him about her, as if he already knew all he needed to know. 'You have been dead too long, my friend, not to know what it is to lose someone. Not a city, mind you, just one special person.' He looked at Malator and shook his head. 'I pity you for that. Truly, I do.'

Malator was not offended. His elfish ears perked up a little. 'I see there is still so much to teach you, Lukien. I value life more than you think. More perhaps than you ever have yourself. Ah, but I do not want to argue with you!' The spirit looked around, floating on his ghostly legs. 'I want to see my city, Lukien, and I do not want the moment ruined.'

'No,' Lukien agreed. 'No . . .'

Together they continued through the deserted streets, Malator taking the time to notice every tiny detail, Lukien gently guiding him toward their destination. Though he had only been in Kaliatha briefly, Lukien easily remembered the way toward the house where Raivik had lived, and where the dead man's story stone still resided. He intended to repay every kindness that had been granted him on his long journey to Torlis, and that included the dead as well as the living. Raivik had been the first to tell him the truth about Malator and his brother. He had set Lukien's feet on the right path. In return, Raivik had only wanted to know about the world of the living. Because he had been in too much of a hurry to indulge Raivik's craving, Lukien had left the Akari after only one brief night together. Now, though, he had something very special to give Raivik, the greatest gift anyone could give to an Akari.

Malator.

'He will want to know what took me so long to return,' said Malator. 'He will question me incessantly.'

'Get out of my head, Malator.'

'I'm not complaining, Lukien. It will be good to tell my people the truth finally.'

Lukien shot the spirit a sceptical glance, then continued onward. His horse rode gamely through the city, exhausted beyond anything a horse should have to endure. Lukien knew his mount needed rest and water, and neither of these were plentiful in Kaliatha. But there was a stream a day's ride away, and if they rested well tonight they might reach it by tomorrow's end. Until then, the water they had brought with them in skins would have to do.

As the afternoon sun dipped below the highest towers, Lukien at last saw Raivik's home. The dilapidated building had been a splendid home once, with a sprawling garden and high walls of stone that looked down imperiously on the structures around it. Long overrun by weeds and varmints, the garden nevertheless continued to produce a few wild roses from its thorn-covered bushes. Lukien slowed his horse as he reached the garden gate, a desiccated tangle of metal ready to crumble at his touch. The story stone was hidden among the weeds. He remembered its place precisely. In the shadow of the ancient house he dismounted his horse and stood at the edge of the garden, patting the Sword of Angels and smiling. The city of ghosts comforted Lukien. He felt at home among the countless bones. Beside him, Malator had once again lost his boyish grin. He was all seriousness now.

'Malator, are you ready for this?'

The spirit sighed. 'They know I am here, Lukien. I can hear them.' He rolled his eyes about their surroundings. 'So many voices . . .'

Lukien listened but heard nothing. 'Can you hear Raivik?'

'No. There are too many.' Malator laughed. 'They greet me, Lukien.'

'I am glad for you. Welcome home.'

Malator smiled then entered the garden, not waiting for Lukien. The knight followed quickly at his heels, but Malator needed no guidance, homing in precisely on the story stone. Surrounded by tall, tangled grasses, the stone rose up only slightly from the lumpy earth. Malator studied the thing that looked like a grave marker and gently reached out his misty hand to touch it. When he did, the figure of Raivik appeared at once. Lukien stood back, amazed by seeing the dead man rise.

'Miracles,' he said. 'Everyday, more miracles.'

Raivik knew him at once, and beamed excitedly at Lukien. But he did not speak, turning instead to stare at Malator. Raivik's jaw dropped in reverence. His skin was the colour of a living man, flushing with excitement. Raivik, who had told Lukien all that he knew about Malator and his brother, now gazed dumbstruck at the ancient legend. Then, as if realizing all the millennia that had passed, he closed his mouth in a grimace and sadly shook his head.

'Do you hear?' Raivik asked Malator.

Malator nodded grimly. 'I hear them.'

'They wail for your return, like they wailed when you left us.' Raivik's tone was reproachful. 'Look around you and see what you have wrought.'

'No,' said Lukien, stepping forward. 'That's not right, Raivik, and you know it. The Jadori destroyed Kaliatha, not Malator.'

Raivik turned to Lukien. 'I thought to never see you again, Lukien, or to ever be called once more from my stone.' He glanced down at the sword at Lukien's belt. 'You have found it.'

'It is the sword that contains the soul of Malator, Raivik,' Lukien explained. 'I found it in Tharlara. It was just as you said. That's why I've come back, to thank you and to tell you our story.'

'A story.' Raivik grinned. 'You remember me well, Lukien. But this is more than a story! You cannot hear my people because you are not one of us, but the city cries all around you.' He turned back to Malator. 'I will listen to your story, Malator. Tell us where you have been.'

Malator sat himself down on the tall grass next to Raivik's story stone, looking strange as he crossed his unreal legs beneath himself. He cocked his head to hear, and Lukien knew that he could hear the countless voices of the dead ringing through Kaliatha. He had agreed to explain himself to Raivik, and in so doing make his peace with what he had done.

'You believe that I abandoned you,' he said to Raivik. 'If you listen, I will tell you the truth.'

Raivik floated closer to him. 'Will you tell me why you never returned? When Kaliatha needed you most?'

'There was nothing left for me to return to,' said Malator. 'By the time I could have come home, the Jadori had already ruined us.' He bade the old man's spirit to sit beside him. 'Let me tell you my story,' he said. 'And then, when I am done, you may judge me.'

Lukien watched as Raivik sat down before Malator, agreeing to hear his tale. It was a long story, Lukien knew, and he had already heard it. He was also powerfully tired, and unlike a spirit he needed rest. Backing away from the Akari pair, he left the garden and went to his horse, unpacking the things he needed for his well-earned rest.

All the next day, Lukien rode alone. He had spent the night in Kaliatha under the clouded sky, and by the next morning he felt refreshed and eager to go on. Malator had returned to residing within the sword, and though Lukien fully expected the Akari to appear walking next to him, Malator never did. Even so, he could feel the presence of Malator inside him, nestled warmly in a little corner of his brain. As Lukien rode through the familiar territory on his way to Jador, he decided not to bother Malator by calling him forth. Obviously, the spirit's conversation with Raivik had drained him, leaving him as quiet as when they'd first entered Kaliatha.

Lukien was glad to leave the dead city behind. At last, after weeks of riding, he was nearing the familiar world he had left. Soon, he would at last return to Jador, and the thought of seeing all of his old comrades heartened him. There was still much left to do, still hundreds of miles yet to go. And his next battle with Thorin loomed over Lukien like a terrible shadow. But he kept these blacker thoughts far from his mind as he rode along the dusty earth, preferring instead to think about Gilwyn and Minikin and all the others he missed so sorely.

The day went quickly for Lukien. The weather co-operated and his tired horse at last slaked its thirst properly as Lukien located a stream he had forgotten from his first ride through the area. Mountains to the north poured down their melting snowcaps in gushes of crystal clear water, inviting both man and beast to enjoy its pure taste. Lukien took his time filling up his water skins as his horse drank and rested. The remarkable beast had taken him miles more than any steed should ever endure. Horses were rare in Tharlara, and this one had been a gift from Lahkali. She had promised Lukien that its heart was stout and its legs strong, and she had been right. Lukien thought about the girl as he dipped his water skins into the stream. He missed her, and wondered if he would ever see her again.

After he and his horse had rested, Lukien continued on, still without the company of Malator. The Akari remained silent the rest of the afternoon, and then into evening as Lukien stopped riding for the day and made a camp in the shadow of the mountains. When he had tended his horse and prepared him for the night, Lukien made a fire to stave off the coming chill, settling down in front of it and staring into its jumping flames. He quieted his mind with a few deep breaths, letting out a sigh that traveled through the camp. Next to him, the Sword of Angels lay in its scabbard. Like his horse, the scabbard too had been a gift from Lahkali. Lukien reached over and picked up the weapon, pulling it free of its scabbard. He laid the blade across his lap and admired it. The ancient metal glowed warmly in the firelight. He touched its smooth surface, knowing that Malator dwelt within it. And within himself.

'Will you stay in there all the way to Jador?' asked Lukien. 'I hope not. I can use your company.'

In the back of his mind he felt Malator shuffle. The spirit was uneasy.

'We made good progress today,' Lukien continued. 'Tomorrow should be a good day, too. With luck we will be in Jador in a week or two.'

Still Malator did not appear, nor answer wordlessly in Lukien's brain.

'I would have you show yourself, Malator,' said Lukien. 'To know that you are not cross with me.'

'You try to shame me?' Malator's voice appeared before the rest of him. His face shimmered into being on the other side of the campfire. His body came last, sitting in the same relaxed manner as Lukien. 'I am not cross with you, Lukien. I have been thinking, that is all.'

Lukien gently kept his fingertips on the blade of the sword, making the bond between them stronger. 'I did try to tell you what it would be like, Malator,' he said. 'And you could not have expected Raivik to welcome you like a hero.'

'I did not expect that,' said Malator. 'And now I have made my peace with my people. I should thank you for that, Lukien. It was a burden I carried for too long.'

'And now they know where you were, and they can be at peace as well. You see, Malator? It is good. Now you can go on.'

Malator nodded in agreement. The familiar grin returned to his elfish face. 'You could go on as well, my friend. I have told you this a hundred times. You have don't need as much rest as you give yourself. I'm here to give you strength, Lukien, but you must take it from me.'

'I rest as much for the horse as I do myself, Malator,' Lukien pointed out. 'Unless you have another sword for the horse to wear, a little dagger on a chain perhaps . . .'

'You know what I mean, Lukien.' Malator gestured at him. 'And look – you still wear the Eye of God around your neck, even though I have promised you there is no need for it.'

Lukien replied, 'An old habit. I wear it for safe keeping now, Malator. I know that it is you who gives me my vitality. When we get to Grimhold I will return it to Mistress Minikin.'

'And what will she do with it?' asked Malator. He was always curious about the Akari and their relationship with the Inhumans. Even though he was an Akari himself, he knew nothing about their covenant with Minikin's people, only the little that Lukien had told him. 'Will she give it to someone else? Keep them alive forever?'

Lukien shrugged. 'That's a weighty matter for her to decide, not me. The amulet is hers to do with what she wishes.'

'I am fascinated by these things you say, Lukien. To think that the Jadori are peaceful now! It is unbelievable to me. And now they protect the Inhumans and Akari. The world has surely changed while I was gone.'

'It has indeed, Malator. And the Inhumans will have questions for you, no doubt.'

'Let them ask whatever they wish,' said Malator. He leaned back on his palms and studied Lukien. 'And let you ask the questions on your mind, Lukien. I know you have them.'

There was no way to hide anything from Malator, and it frustrated Lukien sometimes. He had tried to mask what he was thinking, but had easily been discovered. 'Very well,' he said. 'I want to know how you plan on beating your brother. You have told me just about everything else about yourself, Malator. You have talked me nearly to death! Now tell me the thing I most need to know.'

'Why Lukien, I will fight my brother, just as you have fought Baron Glass,' replied the Akari. 'What else would I do?'

'No,' said Lukien, growing angry, 'don't dodge me. Tell me how you're going to beat him. Will this sword break his armour? Is that all there is to it?'

'Think on what I have said, Lukien. I will fight my brother because I am a soldier. You will fight Baron Glass because you are a soldier.'

'Malator, that makes no sense to me.'

'Why doesn't it?' Malator leaned forward. 'You expect some conjuring from me, is that it? Do you think I will cast a spell upon my brother and that all will be done? No, Lukien. My brother was a great summoner, but he was also a general, and he did not get that rank by being weak in battle. He was renowned for his abilities, but so was I, and when we settle this thing it will be with blades.'

'But how?' asked Lukien. 'You are not even in this world. Not really.'

'That's right. I don't intend to battle Kahldris in this world, Lukien. This is your world. Kahldris and I will fight in ours.'

'In the world of the dead, you mean.'

Malator smiled. 'Now you get it.'

'And Thorin and I? We are to battle again, here in this world?'

'That will bring us all together, Lukien. When you cross blade with Baron Glass next time, you will have my sword with which to defend yourself. And when the metal of my blade touches the metal of his armour, Kahldris and I will meet again.'

'And then I will be able to crack his armour? I must be able to crack it, Malator . . .'

'When I have beaten Kahldris, you will breach the armour, Lukien. But not until then.'

'Oh.' Lukien grew pensive. 'And if you don't beat him?'

Malator laughed and said, 'You have no confidence in me!'

'Well, it's just that . . .' Lukien struggled for the right thing to say. 'Malator, you hardly look like a soldier.'

'That may be, Lukien, but I was a fine soldier, finer than Kahldris some say. Find some good in me, Lukien, please.'

'I'll try,' said Lukien unconvincingly. 'But you have to admit, you look . . . out of practice.'

Malator bristled playfully at the insult. 'You are such a sceptic, my friend. I will simply have to convince you.'

'Yes,' said Lukien. 'Because if you can't, Kahldris will beat us both.'

63

In the township outside the white wall of Jador, the days were long and filled with boredom. The drudgery of daily subsistence occupied most of the time, as the Seekers from the northern continent settled into the unending routine of the southern desert. Because they were unused to the sun and heat, most Seekers spent whatever time they could indoors, relaxing in the shrana houses or playing card games under the tin roofs of their shabby homes. For most Seekers, hope was something they had given up a long time ago. They had come across the Desert of Tears seeking healing, and had got a slum instead, a bustling conglomeration of tongues and skin tones that had once been a place of vibrant commerce, but had swelled to the world's largest camp for refugees. And though Kahana White-Eye did her best to make the lot of the northerners easier, despair was the thing they had most in abundance. Returning north was out of the question, and gaining the magic of Grimhold was impossible. And so they were stuck in the netherworld between both, unable to go in either direction.

King Lorn loved the shrana houses. They were an import from Ganjor, a place where the desert folk – and now the Seekers – could enjoy a lively conversation over a stiff pull of hot, black shrana. Shrana was an acquired taste that almost everyone acquired late, but Lorn had learned to love the drink. In the shrana houses, he was no longer the counselor to the great Kahana, and the people there referred to him as a kind of good-natured jibe. For Lorn, who had been in Jador for more months then he could remember, the shrana houses were a strange whiff of home.

Tonight, Lorn relaxed as a pretty serving girl brought him and his comrades another pot of steaming shrana. He had spent the day in the township, helping the Marnan brothers repair their ramshackle home, replacing the sun-burned roof with another layer of thatch. Harliz, Garmin and Tarlan had all come to Jador with the same empty hope, wishing to be cured of the blood disease that made their bones ready to snap. Because none of them could climb a ladder, it had fallen to Lorn to do the bulk of the work, which he had done with aplomb and a smile on his face. White-Eye was a queen now. She had taken to her role like a fish to water, and rarely needed Lorn's counsel any more. The rise of confidence had left Lorn feeling like a proud father's whose child moves away.

'I think,' said Tarlan as he watched the pretty servant walk away, 'that we should have some food now.' He turned to his brothers with a sly smile. 'Let's get her back here, yes?'

'You're a letch,' commented Harliz. He blew on his steaming cup. 'And ugly, in case you haven't noticed.'

'Leave her alone,' agreed Garmin.

Lorn grinned, amused by the bickering brothers. Neither of them were remotely handsome, but that rarely stopped Tarlan from flirting with every girl he passed. His wandering eye constantly annoyed Harliz, leaving Garmin to make peace between them. Lorn tasted his shrana, burning his lips on the hot liquid. He never sweetened his shrana with honey or cane, liking its raw, bitter taste. Tonight, after his long day of labour, the shrana tasted particularly fine.

'I'm going to talk to her,' Tarlan decided. Making a great effort, he pulled his stooped body away from the dark table and meandered through the crowded chamber toward the serving girl. Harliz shooed him away with annoyance, plainly glad to be rid of him. Garmin, ignoring both his brothers, looked at Lorn instead.

'What about you? Shouldn't you be getting back?'

Lorn nodded. 'I should.'

But he kept right on drinking.

'Lorn, you've got your own pretty girl back inside the wall,' Garmin pointed out. 'And your child, too.'

'Yes,' Lorn drawled. 'But Poppy will be sleeping when I get back, and Eiriann spends nights with her father. He's not well at all, and I don't like to keep them apart.'

'And Kahana White-Eye doesn't need him anymore,' said Harliz playfully.

'So?' Garmin pressed. 'What will you do? Become a roofer?'

Lorn laughed, but their jibes stung him. 'Let me tell you – I am happy White-Eye doesn't need me any more. She stood up to Baralosus and saved Jador, and that's no less than any king or queen could ask. But, I have been thinking . . .' He rolled the little cup between his palms. 'I've been here a good long time now. Poppy is happy, and so is Eiriann. She's a good woman, the second good woman I've had, and that's saying a lot for a man like me. I didn't deserve my first wife and I'll be damned if I deserve Eiriann. Poppy doesn't even know she's not her mother.'

Garmin smiled. 'What are you saying, Lorn? What's on your mind?'

Harliz answered the question first. 'He's restless. He wants to go home.'

'To Norvor?' Garmin studied Lorn. 'Is that it?'

Lorn shrugged. 'I think about it. Of course I do. Look, we all came here to get a healing out of Grimhold, and none of us are any closer. Minikin will never take Poppy into Grimhold and I'd be a fool to hope otherwise. There's no room for her. The mistress had made that plain. So what am I to do?'

The brothers glanced at each other. 'What can any of us do?' said Harliz. 'We're stuck here, Lorn, all of us. That means you, too, king or not.'

'Aye, and it's maddening,' roiled Lorn. 'I thought I could rest here and grow old and be content to see Poppy safe and happy. Oh, but Norvor calls to me! She does, and I miss her so.'

Harliz starting to say something, but his brother stopped him, putting up a hand. 'Let's just drink,' suggested Garmin. 'Let's not talk about the past.'

For all the Seekers, the past was a subject of little interest, and Lorn was grateful to end the conversation. He made an effort to bring the talk to lighter things, commenting about the work they had done that day and about how crowded the shrana house was tonight, and soon they had all forgotten about the past once more. They had forgotten about Tarlan, too, who had disappeared somewhere among the crowd. Lorn assumed the man had found game somewhere or a benefactor willing to share some tobacco. Another hour passed. The light from the dingy windows on the other side of the shrana house had long gone dark. At last, Lorn decided it was time to leave. He said his good-byes to his unusual friends, left a couple of coins on the table, and headed toward the door. Suddenly, he was eager to see Eiriann and find out how her father Garthel was doing. Garthel was old and feeble, and though the desert air had done him good he was still fairing poorly. Tomorrow he would spend the day with them all, Lorn decided, and forget this nonsense about Norvor. But before he could exit the shrana house he heard Tarlan excitedly calling his name. Tarlan was coming through the beaded door, shouting for Lorn and dragging a stranger along behind him. His eyes bulged excitedly as he glimpsed Lorn.

'There he is,' he said excitedly, turning toward the stranger. The man with him had a circumspect look. 'That's Lorn.' Tarlan quickly closed the gap between them. 'Lorn, wait. This is someone you need to meet.'

Lorn stopped by the beaded entrance, stepping aside to greet his friend. Tarlan hurried them together. Lorn spied the man, then Tarlan. 'Who's this?'

'A Nithin!' Tarlan laughed giddily. 'A Nithin, Lorn, come all the way from Nith!'

'A Nithin?' Lorn again focused on the man, this time more precisely. 'Is that so?'

Nithins were known to be proud and rare like diamonds, and in his whole life Lorn had never met a single one. In all of the township, not one of the Seekers were Nithin, and so Tarlan's surprise seemed appropriate. The stranger, a man of substantial bearing, wore riding clothes and a bright green cape caked in desert dust. He had been long on the road, that much was plain. His brown hair hung in dirty tangles around his unshaven neck.

'My name is Alsadair,' he pronounced. 'You are King Lorn of Norvor?'

Lorn straightened. 'I am unaccustomed to that title these days, sir. But yes, I am Lorn. And you are from Nith? Truly?'

'I am,' said Alsadair, 'and I have just at last come across the desert with a Caravan from Ganjor. I am on a mission, King Lorn, and in this horrible little village they speak of you as the man to see.'

'Do they?' Lorn looked to Tarlan for answers. 'Where'd you find him?'

'He just come across, just as he says,' replied Tarlan. 'Started asking all kinds of questions, looking for a way into Jador. People told him to come looking for you. I ran into him outside while having a pipe.'

By now, Harliz and Garmin had noticed the little commotion, coming up to stand beside Lorn. They quietly eyed the stranger, listening intently to their brother's explanation. Lorn, not liking the gathering attention, directed all of them back outside, pushing Tarlan toward the beaded curtain. The Nithin followed him out, trailed by Lorn and the Marnan brothers. At once the cool night air struck Lorn's face. He pulled the Nithin away from the shrana house, speaking to him in a measured tone.

'What is your business?' he asked. 'What do you want in Jador?'

'To deliver a message,' said Alsadair. He brushed the dust from his fine green cape. 'I am a herald of His Grace, Daralor, Prince of Nith. I bear a letter with me from His Grace.'

'A letter?' asked Lorn. 'For who?'

'For the Bronze Knight,' said Alsadair. 'For the Liirian named Lukien.'

The name was instantly familiar to Lorn. 'Lukien?' He looked at Tarlan. 'Did you know this?'

Tarlan shook his head. 'No. He just said he was looking for you, and I told him we was friends.'

'This letter you carry – it's from your Prince?' Lorn asked Alsadair.

'The letter is from a charge of the prince,' said the Nithin. 'I cannot tell you more. It is private, and for the eyes of the Bronze Knight only.'

'Lukien isn't here,' said Lorn. 'I don't know where he is, and neither does anyone else.'

Alsadair replied stoically. 'It does not matter. He will return here, and when he does I will give him the letter.'

'What? What makes you think he'll be coming here?'

'Because that is what I have been told, King Lorn. That is what the author of this letter has told my prince.'

Lorn was thoroughly bewildered. And intrigued. 'This author – is he a boy?'

Alsadair looked surprised. 'Why do you ask that?'

'Because a boy named Gilwyn Toms left here some months ago. He was a friend of Lukien.'

Alsadair shook his head. 'Then I will not keep you wondering, King Lorn. The one who penned this letter is not named Toms. But I cannot tell you more. I can speak only to the man in charge of this city.'

'There is no man in charge of the city,' said Garmin. 'If you mean the township, we have no ruler.'

'I mean Jador,' said Alsadair. 'Who rules there?'

'A girl,' said Tarlan.

'The Kahana,' said Lorn. 'Her name is White-Eye.'

An hour later, Alsadair the Nithin got his audience with White-Eye. In one of the palace's many open-aired chambers, the messenger of the Nithin Prince explained the long trek he had endured, and why he had come to Jador. With White-Eye seated imperiously before him, Alsadair delivered his tale standing, holding the letter he had carried with him for hundreds of miles. Lorn stood off to the side, allowing the Nithin to make his case and studying the letter clamped in his hands. The envelope of ivory-toned paper bore the wax stamp of Daralor, the Nithin ruler. Although Alsadair had been offered food and drink, he had remained standing in the chamber the entire time, waiting for the blind Kahana to arrive. Upon hearing the news of the Nithin's request, White-Eye had come to him quickly, a favour for which the messenger seemed grateful. A pitcher of beer and some food lay on a table near him, but Alsadair's eyes never wandered to them. Instead, he watched White-Eye as he spoke, his voice reverential and practiced.

'. . . and from Dreel to Ganjor. In Ganjor I found the caravan that took me here, Kahana. When I came to the village – the township, you call it – I asked for a man who could help me. Someone of importance. The people there pointed me to King Lorn.' Alsadair glanced briefly at the letter in his hands. He seemed unbalanced by White-Eye's blindness, as though she was not only blind, but deaf to his words as well. 'By my accounting I have been on the road for four weeks. I have expired many horses in my haste to get here. And now that I am here I ask your peace, Kahana. This letter may only be given to the Bronze Knight. I may not even give it over to your safe keeping. That is my mission.'

'I understand your mission, Sir Alsadair,' said White-Eye mildly. 'And you are welcome to stay here within Jador for as long as you wish. But be aware, Sir – your stay with us may be long indeed. We have no knowledge of Lukien's whereabouts, and only hope that he will come to us again.'

'My lady, I have been promised that he will come here, and if it takes all of my life to wait for him, then that is what I will do.'

White-Eye grimaced in Lorn's direction. They were both thinking the same things, he could tell.

'Sir Alsadair,' began White-Eye, 'You have seen the way Jador is bursting with northerners. We of course have room for one more. We welcome you, and we wish only good relations with your Prince. But . . .'

Lorn spoke up. 'But you vex us. You have a letter for Lukien? Good. Then deliver it when he comes. But you cannot keep us in the dark. You must tell us more. Who wrote the letter?'

This time, Alsadair did not hesitate in his answer. 'This was only a secret to the men you were with, King Lorn. I meant no offense by keeping things from you. Aric Glass is the name of the man who wrote the letter. He is in Nith even now, waiting for Lukien to return.'

'Glass?' Lorn almost laughed. 'A relation to Baron Glass, I suppose?'

'His son,' said Alsadair. 'He claims to have fought with Lukien against the baron in Koth, and now he waits for Lukien to return to the battle.'

'That amazes us, Sir,' said White-Eye. 'We hear almost nothing of the battle for Liiria. What else can you tell us? Have you heard of a young man named Gilwyn Toms?'

Lorn shook his head. 'I'm sorry, White-Eye, I asked him about Gilwyn. He has not heard of him.'

White-Eye suppressed her obvious sadness. 'Any news would be welcome, Sir Alsadair.'

'My news is at least two months old, Kahana,' said Alsadair. 'I know only what Aric Glass has told my Prince. Koth still lays in the hands of Baron Glass. So too does the rest of Liiria.'

'And Norvor?' asked Lorn. 'What about Norvor?'

'The Diamond Queen rules Norvor.'

Lorn frowned. 'You are sure?'

'As I told you, my news is old. But they are a formidable team, the Diamond Queen and Baron Glass. It is not likely that anyone has toppled them. King Raxor and his Reecians have tried, and they have paid heavily for it.'

'They have warred?' asked Lorn.

'They battled at the river Kryss,' said the Nithin. 'And the victory for Baron Glass was unarguable. Raxor's son was killed in the battle. Thousands of others, too.'

'The armour?' asked White-Eye.

Alsadair nodded gravely. 'The baron's armour is relentless, lady. It knows no blade that can harm it. That is why the Bronze Knight quests, to find a sword that can best the armour.'

'What sword?' Lorn asked.

'Aric Glass says it is called the Sword of Angels. He had told us the knight Lukien seeks the sword in the Serpent Kingdom, a land beyond this one. That is why he will return here. When he finds the sword, he will come home to Grimhold first.'

For a moment White-Eye was too stunned to speak. Lorn watched her, seeing understanding dawn on her face. 'There is a place of serpents,' she said softly. 'An ancient land very far from here. It is called Tharlara, but most Jadori do not know of it. I know because my father taught me these things.'

'And Minikin?' asked Lorn. 'Does she know of it? Does she know of this sword?'

'She must,' said White-Eye. 'Or if she wished to, she could find out.'

'Then why didn't she tell us?' Lorn asked angrily. 'How could she keep something like that from us?'

White-Eye turned to him, freezing him with her stare. 'We should wait to speak of this.'

Lorn caught himself. 'Yes,' he agreed. Embarrassed, he cleared his throat. 'I am sorry.'

'Kahana White-Eye, King Lorn, I can tell you only what I know myself,' said Alsadair. 'It does not even matter to me if this sword exists or not. I have my mission, and that is all that concerns me. With your leave I will wait here for the Bronze Knight to return.'

'Yes,' said White-Eye distractedly. 'Of course . . .' Then she caught herself and turned her face up at him. 'Tell me one more thing, Alsadair. What news can you give us of Ganjor?'

'Ganjor? I'm not sure what my lady asks . . .'

'Anything,' said Lorn. 'How did Ganjor seem to you? Was it at peace?'

'Oh, yes, King Lorn. A beautiful city. I had nothing to trouble me there, and I had heard that northerners were not always welcome in Ganjor.'

White-Eye smiled broadly. 'That is well, Sir. Isn't it, King Lorn?'

Lorn agreed heartily. 'It is well indeed.'

'Take your rest, Sir Alsadair,' directed White-Eye. She rose from her chair. 'We will make a place for you. But now, eat. And drink! You must have a thirst.'

'I do, my lady,' sighed the Nithin. 'Thank you.'

White-Eye bade him toward the beer and food, then picked her way toward Lorn, offering the old king her arm so he could guide her. Lorn knew what was coming, and so walked the kahana gingerly toward the other side of the gigantic chamber, out of earshot of the eating Alsadair. Long shadows filled the room, cast by candlelight from the jumping tapers. White-Eye did not search for a place to sit, but rather stood, biting anxiously on her lower lip.

'Lorn, I must explain something to you,' she said. 'You are troubled. You are right to be. But whatever Minikin might know about Lukien or about the sword or even about Gilwyn, she may not tell us.'

'Why not?' demanded Lorn. 'There is too much at stake for her to keep secrets.'

'Because it is not our place to know everything. Minikin may summon knowledge from the Akari, but they live in the world of the dead, and their knowledge may change the way we in this world live our lives. It is a great burden that she carries – and a great temptation.'

'I understand that,' said Lorn, 'but this *is* life and death we're talking about. Surely if she can look into some talisman—'

'No,' said White-Eye. 'And I will not ask it of her, not even to find out Gilwyn's fate.' Her face softened then, and she said to Lorn, 'You have taught me so much. Now, will you let me teach you how things are done here? We are still a mystery to you, I can tell.'

'Yes,' sighed Lorn. He glanced over his shoulder at Alsadair, who was gulping down great mouthfuls of beer. 'Do you believe him, White-Eye?'

'Should I not believe him? You can see his face, Lorn, and I cannot. Do you think he lies?'

'No,' replied Lorn. 'I think everything he's told us is true. And it troubles me, White-Eye.'

'Yes, I can feel that,' said the girl. 'He reminds you of home. Of Norvor.'

Lorn nodded. 'Aye.'

White-Eye felt for his hand. 'You think of Norvor too much these day. Your home is here now, with Eiriann and Poppy.'

'Yes.' Lorn smiled faintly. 'Of course it is.'

'It *is*, Lorn.' White-Eye squeezed his hand. 'You can be content here, if you try.'

'Ah, to be content!' Lorn lifted her hand and kissed it. 'Let me tell you something about men, Kahana. Men are never content. Their hearts are restless rivers, always running.'

'Always running away, perhaps?' suggested White-Eye.

Lorn didn't like her perception. 'You see very clearly,' he said sourly, 'for a blind woman.'

64

After the death of Jazana Carr, things slowly returned to normal in Koth. Word of what had happened to the Diamond Queen traveled quickly through the capital and then throughout the surrounding countryside. The people – who had learned to love the odd harlot from Norvor – mourned for her as if she were a Liirian. Great crowds gathered outside of Lionkeep, desperate for word of her demise. And Thorin, distraught over her death and rightfully blaming himself for it, walked among the throngs to speak to them and tell them how much he missed Jazana and how beloved they were to her. Not wanting a circus for a funeral, Thorin ordered Jazana's body burned, cremating every beautiful bone of her in a blazing pyre that lit the courtyard. Norvan and Liirian soldiers kept the crowds far from the fire, and Thorin stood alone as he watched the smoke take Jazana's remains to heaven. Two days later, he rode out alone to the apple orchard and spread her dust amid the winds.

Gilwyn watched the crowds gathering around Lionkeep from the safety of his high bedchamber. And when the pyre had burned to ashes, he watched the crowds disperse, returning to their sad lives without their Norvan patron. In the few short weeks he had been in Koth, Gilwyn had heard the remarkable tales about Jazana Carr and how generous she had been to the people of the city. The maids and stable boys of Lionkeep spoke of her with reverence, and everyone seemed to have a story about a kindness she had done for them. It was hard for Gilwyn to think of Jazana Carr like that, because he himself had met her once, years earlier in Norvor, and he not seen the side of her that so many people now worshipped. Still, he lamented her death, mostly because it had effected Thorin so badly, and while he recuperated in his bed Gilwyn was careful not to say anything that would bring his friend Thorin bad memories.

Aside from the excitement of the funeral, very little happened to Gilwyn those first weeks. He grew stronger, naturally, resting in his comfortable bed and eating the warm foods the kitchen provided in abundance. He had lost considerable weight during his trek across the continent, and was now determined to put back every single pound. At first he remained weak, the rass poison reasserting itself in his bloodstream. But as the days progressed he felt less and less of the lethargy that had plagued him for so long, and under the watchful eye of Lionkeep's maids he soon grew strong again.

But Gilwyn was careful. It would be weeks or even months until Lukien returned again, and that meant he needed time. So Gilwyn kept to his bed for as long as he could, convincing Thorin that he was far too weak to start work in the library, or to even think about using its complicated catalogue machine. He whiled away his hours in his bedchamber, sometimes venturing out into Lionkeep's halls, always keeping up the pretense of illness and lassitude.

Even so, the day finally came when Thorin decided that fresh air was all that Gilwyn really needed. It was nearly four weeks from the time Gilwyn had collapsed at the threshold of Lionkeep, and the day was sparkling and cool. That morning, Thorin came early to Gilwyn's bedchamber, insisting that he dress himself and take a hearty breakfast. They were going riding, Thorin told him, and that meant he needed to be strong. Puzzled, Gilwyn did not argue with Thorin but instead did exactly as the baron requested. He pulled on the fine clothes that had been provided for him and slipped his feet into the boots that made walking with his clubbed foot possible. Downstairs, he found a steaming breakfast of eggs and bread waiting for him, which he quickly devoured. Then he went outside and found Thorin in the courtyard, waiting for him along with a pair of newly brushed geldings. There were no soldiers to accompany them, none of the Liirians who had been conscripted into service or the ubiquitous Norvan mercenaries, most of whom had stayed with Thorin even after the death of their queen. A sprinkling of stable hands moved in the distance, and that was all. With Thorin's help, Gilwyn made his way into the saddle of his horse, then followed the baron out of Lionkeep.

Less than an hour later, he was staring up at the great library.

A stiff wind blew his curls into his eyes, but Gilwyn quickly brushed them aside. He wanted nothing to obscure his view. Knowing this, Thorin stood aside, watching him proudly, unveiling the magnificent structure he had destroyed and then rebuilt. Work had mostly stopped on the library, but from the outside it had been fully restored to its lost glory, and its shadow loomed over Gilwyn, striking him dumb. He had never thought to see this place again, and all the memories of all the years he had spent within its walls flooded over him, choking his voice and bringing a lump to his throat. Whatever other things Thorin had done – whatever wickedness he had occasioned – his new-found love for the library was obvious. He had spared no expense in returning it to glory, and the endless hours of toil showed. Gilwyn gazed up at the awesome edifice, the breeze whistling in his ears, and all at once he felt at home again.

'It's real, Gilwyn,' said Thorin. 'You should say something.'

There was only one thing Gilwyn wanted. 'Can we go inside?'

'Why would I bring you here if not to let you inside?' said Thorin. 'Of course, boy!'

He tossed himself off his horse, then helped Gilwyn down from his own mount, using his real, fleshy arm to guide him from the saddle. Thorin had not worn the entire suit of armour since Gilwyn had arrived, but had not once removed the parts of his enchanted arm, either. Gilwyn knew the armour gave Thorin strength, keeping him forever connected to Kahldris. And Thorin was careful not let anyone touch the black metal, especially not Gilwyn. With Gilwyn following close behind, he went to the great doors and pulled them open effortlessly, a feat that should have taken more than a little sweat. At once the candlelit interior of the library greeted them, calling to Gilwyn with its polished ceiling and walls of glowing marble. The scent of the place had changed, thought Gilwyn, but as he rushed up through the threshold he saw at once that it was just as before. Newer, perhaps, but mostly unchanged, honeycombed with reading rooms and staggered by rows and rows of dark wood shelves, all of them lined with precious books. Gilwyn moved like a dream through the main hall, his eyes wide, his head swiveling to take in every marvelous nuance. He laughed, giddy from the sense of homecoming.

'It's wonderful, Thorin!' he called, racing ahead of the baron. 'I can almost hear Figgis calling me!'

The sconces on the wall flickered with soft light. They had all been lit, every one of them, making a constellation along the smooth walls. Thorin beamed, proud of his accomplishment, and of the surprise he had been able to gift to Gilwyn. He followed Gilwyn through the hall, but not so close that the young man could not go exploring, peaking his head into every little cranny of the place and pulling manuscripts from the infinite shelves. Gilwyn could barely control his glee. It took him spinning through the library, his mind racing with happy memories. He shouted in the hall just to hear his voice echo. In the giant western study chamber, a place where he'd once seen an Andolan scholar fall asleep in a bowl of soup, he stood up on the table just to reach the highest shelves, balancing on his clubbed foot and pulling down a book of ancient maps with his badly fused hand. The book tumbled out of his buttery fingers, spilling to the floor, and like the good librarian he used to be Gilwyn hurried down to retrieve it.

'Leave it,' said Thorin. 'There are people who clean up here now, Gilwyn.'

'No,' Gilwyn argued. 'No, I can't.' He stooped, then smiled at the baron. 'These are books, Thorin. Where did you get them all? I thought they were all lost.'

'No, not all of them,' said Thorin. 'Too many, but not all. You see, Gilwyn? I have spared nothing to bring this place back to life.'

'Yes,' agreed Gilwyn, surveying all the new workmanship. 'I can see that.' He placed the map book onto the table. 'But why, Thorin? I don't understand. You never wanted the library built. You opposed Akeela when he built it.'

'I did,' said Thorin. He sauntered into the room, taking books nonchalantly from the shelves only to glance at them. Gilwyn watched a peculiar smile twist his face. He laid his hand on the smooth wood as if checking for warmth. 'But I see now what a fine place this always was. You opened my eyes to it, Gilwyn, with all your stories! I never wanted it destroyed.' Thorin made sure to get Gilwyn's attention, going to stand in front of him. 'It's important to me that you believe that. I never gave the order for the library to be attacked. I gave orders for it to be protected!'

Gilwyn nodded, though he had his doubts. 'I believe you, Thorin.'

'I hope you do, boy. I would never want to harm this place, knowing how much it means to you.'

'All right.' Gilwyn managed to hoist himself onto one of the reading tables, letting his legs dangle. The quiet chamber soothed him, a good place for a serious talk. 'But I still don't understand why you rebuilt it. I mean, I've heard others talking about it. They say you want to bring Koth back to glory. But I want to hear it from you, Thorin. Make me understand.'

'There is truth in those rumours you've heard,' said Thorin. He stood before Gilwyn like a felon, letting the boy question him. 'Koth cannot be great again if the library is not reborn. The library is the symbol of Koth, of all Liirian greatness. It must be reborn so that Liiria can live again.'

Gilwyn grinned. 'Now you sound like Akeela himself!'

'It's not a joke, Gilwyn. The land bleeds. And the people have been hollowed out by war. There's nothing left inside of them, just rottenness and helplessness. They have to believe in themselves again. They have to believe in *me*.'

'I think I see your meaning,' said Gilwyn. 'But it's going to take more than gold, Thorin. You can make this place a palace. You can fill it with every word ever written, but people won't come unless there's peace. And if people don't come . . .'

'I know,' Thorin lamented. 'And there will be peace. Just as soon as my enemies are done with, Liiria will have peace. A thousand years of it!'

There was madness in the old man's eyes, the kind Gilwyn hadn't seen too much lately. Thorin had been better the past two weeks, looking less like a madman than he had that first night. Gilwyn decided not to press him.

'Show me the rest,' he said, sliding down from the table. 'Show me the painting Lucio did for you.'

'Ah, yes,' crowed Thorin. 'It is magnificent. He is still working on it. Still, Gilwyn! The man is a genius, but slow.'

Gilwyn laughed, heading back toward the hall. He had heard of the fabulous ceiling the legendary Lucio had done for Thorin, a gift to the people of Liiria, and was anxious to see it. But before Gilwyn could turn toward the chamber, Thorin's words stopped him cold.

'After you've seen the ceiling, we'll go to the catalogue room.'

Gilwyn paused. 'The catalogue room?' He turned to face Thorin. 'Today?'

'Why not today?' asked Thorin. 'You are well enough, I think, and time is running out, Gilwyn.'

'No,' said Gilwyn. He made a grimace of pain. 'I don't think I should, not today, Thorin. I'm not ready for it.'

Thorin seemed disappointed. 'Gilwyn, you did promise me . . .'

'I know, Thorin. And I will help you. I'll do my best for you, but not today. Not yet.' Gilwyn stalled, searching for an excuse. 'You know how complicated it is,' he said. 'I'm not well enough to start trying to figure it out.' He put his hand to his head. 'My head still hurts terribly, and I'm not seeing well at all.'

'You're not?'

'No.' Gilwyn sighed, then coughed. 'I didn't want to tell you. I didn't want you to worry. I'm fine, really, but . . . tired.'

'Tired.' Thorin gave a sceptical frown. Then, as if someone were speaking in his ear, he cocked his head to listen.

'What are you doing?' Gilwyn asked.

Thorin hesitated. 'Kahldris. He does not believe you, Gilwyn.'

'No? Was Kahldris ever bitten by a rass?'

'Kahldris thinks you should be well enough by now,' said Thorin. 'And in truth, you should be.'

Cornered, Gilwyn grew defensive. 'I can't work with the catalogue today, Thorin. It doesn't matter what Kahldris thinks. I'm telling you I'm sick.'

In all the days that Gilwyn lay in bed, Kahldris had never come to him, not even at his weakest. He had expected the Akari to appear, to threaten him or cajole him out of his sickbed, but Thorin had forbidden it, Gilwyn supposed. It was a good sign, and Gilwyn knew Thorin was making progress. But he needed more time.

'All right, Gilwyn,' said Thorin gently. 'You don't have to look at the machine if you're not ready.'

Gilwyn smiled. 'Thank you, Thorin. I will look at it, just as soon as I'm able.'

Without another word, Thorin turned and headed back the way they'd come. Gilwyn followed him, his good mood deflated. Obviously, they were going back to Lionkeep without seeing Lucio's painting. Gilwyn knew he had to play along and not make a fuss. But before they made it halfway to the entrance, he detoured himself into one of the smaller reading chambers. Annoyed, Thorin called for him to come out, but Gilwyn refused. There were a dozen chairs in the little room, each of them exactly the same, crammed among the books so that scholars could study peacefully. Gilwyn chose one of the chairs, faced it toward the entrance, and sat down to wait for Thorin. The baron came in after him, pausing in the threshold.

'We're going, Gilwyn.'

Gilwyn shook his head. 'Not yet.' Sullen, he asked Thorin, 'Is that why you brought me here? Just to get me to work on the machine?'

'Certainly not,' said the baron. 'I thought you were well enough to see what has been done here. It's important that you see.'

'Why?' asked Gilwyn.

'Because,' said Thorin, sauntering into the room, 'this will be your library soon.'

Gilwyn sat up. 'Say that again?'

'The library needs someone to run it,' said Thorin. 'I can't do it. Neither can anyone else. That's your job, Gilwyn. It's your destiny.'

'What? No! I mean, I can't—'

'Why can't you?' said Thorin. 'Because you are promised to White-Eye? I have considered that already. It does not matter.'

'But it does matter, Thorin. Of course it does! I love White-Eye. And someday I'm going to return to her.'

Thorin's face darkened. 'I know you think that.'

Gilwyn studied him. 'What aren't you telling me, Thorin? There's something . . .'

'The library needs you, Gilwyn. This is where you belong. Not in Jador. You were born to this place.'

'Thorin, White-Eye needs me too.'

'No,' said Thorin. 'You may think she does, but she does not.'

'She's blind, Thorin,' argued Gilwyn. 'Your demon made her so. Do not tell me that she doesn't need me. She does, more than ever now because of Kahldris.'

Thorin turned away, hiding his face. 'Gilwyn, there are things you still haven't worked out. You mean to save me from Kahldris. I understand. Others have tried, and believe it or not I am grateful to them all.'

'But you are better now, Thorin,' said Gilwyn. He went to the old man, speaking soothingly. 'I have seen the change in you in just the past few weeks.'

'I am better,' Thorin admitted. 'I am myself again, because I am happy you are here and because I have learned a little how to placate Kahldris. But it is not what you think, Gilwyn. I belong to Kahldris.'

'No,' spat Gilwyn. 'I don't believe that. You're nothing like Kahldris, no matter what he makes you do.'

'If you think that, you are a fool.' Thorin's eyes blazed. 'Look at me, boy. I have my arm again, and all my manhood. I have my vigour back and a kingdom to rebuild. I have returned home. These are fabulous things, and it was Kahldris who bestowed them on me. I owe him a debt.'

'He gets to live through you, just like any other Akari,' retorted Gilwyn. 'He uses you to walk through this world. He has drank a river of blood thanks to you, Thorin. You don't owe him anything.'

Pain pinched Thorin's face. 'Will you take what I offer you, Gilwyn? The library is a great gift. You can be happy here.'

Gilwyn hesitated. 'Thorin, I don't know. I don't understand what you're saying.'

Thorin put his hand on Gilwyn's shoulder. 'I want so much to give you the things you lost when you left here. Can't you see? I'm trying to rebuild all of it. And when you returned, you put something good in my heart.'

'You're scaring me, Thorin. I'm not going to let anything happen to you.'

'But you can't stop it! This is what I'm telling you, boy. Lukien is coming to kill me. What will you do when he gets here? You mean to stall until he arrives. That's your plan, I know it is. You're well enough to use the machine! Any fool can see that. You're just waiting, hoping that something good will happen.'

'All right,' said Gilwyn, flushing with embarrassment. 'So it's true. But I've seen the change in you, Thorin. I have! I am reaching you. Don't deny that; I see it too clearly. And if Lukien is coming to kill you, then I won't let him. I'm going to stay with you, no matter what. Do you understand that?'

There was real warmth in Thorin's touch as he tightened his hand on Gilwyn's shoulder. 'One day soon I'll have to stop calling you 'boy.' You're a man now. When did that happen, I wonder?'

'Tell me what you're keeping from me,' pressed Gilwyn. 'Why are you giving me the library? Why can't I return to Grimhold?'

'The reason should be obvious. What do you think Kahldris wants from me, Gilwyn?'

Gilwyn thought for a moment. 'Your body. That's what all the Akari want, a chance to be among the living.'

Thorin shook his head. 'No. Think deeper. Think like a demon.'

'Thorin, I don't want these riddles. Tell me what he wants from you!'

'Revenge!' Thorin spun away, laughing mirthlessly. 'Imagine a lifetime locked in that armour. A thousand lifetimes! Imagine the horror of it. Kahldris made the armour for his people and they shunned him. Not just his brother, but his whole damned race. They had the means to defeat the Jadori in their hands, and instead they let themselves be slaughtered like sheep.'

Finally, terribly, Gilwyn understood. 'He wants revenge against the Akari.'

'That's right,' said Thorin. Madness crackled on his tortured face. His voice became a twisted whisper as he stuck his nose close to Gilwyn. 'I'm just a puppet on a string,' he said. 'So are you. So are all of us. Thank you for trying to save me, boy, but it's already too late. Because once Kahldris takes care of his brother, he's going back to Grimhold. And then he will destroy it.'

65

Lukien saw a distant kreel, its legs propelling it across the shimmering sands. The rider caught no sight of him, disappearing quickly through the dunes that led in a meandering line toward the white city. Lukien squinted against the powerful sun. His neck burned from long days on horseback. He stopped himself, leaning back in his saddle to admire the fleeing kreel, knowing he was home. The tall towers of Jador's palace twinkled in the orange haze, stark and beautiful against the desert backdrop. The high wall surrounding the city blinded, its polished rock sending shards of sunlight in all directions. A great, wistful smile twisted the knight's blanched lips. He had come across the world and back again, and the weight of his journey made his shoulders slump with exhaustion. Beneath him, the horse that had given him everything threatened to collapse, its legs made brittle from the impossible trek from Tharlara. Lukien patted the beast's lathered neck.

'You can rest forever now, my friend,' he rasped. 'That is home.'

Within him, Lukien felt the thrill of his Akari, Malator, as the long-dead spirit watched the city through the eye of his host. In Kaliatha Malator had mourned, but now his feelings soared like an eagle, buoyed by Lukien's own indescribable joy. It was enough for the spirit to share the happiness, and Lukien honoured the moment by falling silent himself. So far, none within the city or on its walls had seen him approaching, the ragged knight in his bedraggled clothes, his face heavy with beard. Not even the fleet-footed kreel had smelled him. But soon they would know he had come. He was Shalafein – the defender – and they would feast and celebrate his homecoming. Lukien's mind turned to the good foods and fine wines and the faces of his friends, and summoning the last fibres of his horse's mettle he drove the weary mount onward to the city, through the sands that sucked at its hooves and along the dunes that swept dust into their eyes. The glorious city loomed ahead, growing ever taller as Lukien approached.

Together the silent trio approached the outskirts of Jador, and Lukien noticed for the first time the changes wrought in the city. How long had he been gone? A year, perhaps, he reasoned, and yet he saw a newness to the ancient wall. Battlements had been constructed along its length, and he knew these things did not belong. Puzzled, he drove on, and soon heard the murmur of the city. The populace in its hidden streets buzzed with mid-day business. Lukien steered his horse toward the palace, the grand structure clearly visible beyond the wall. When at last he reached the white edifice, he looked across its length to find egress, knowing there were gates built within it, the largest of which stood at the front of the city. Because he was miles away from there, Lukien waited, patiently trotting along the sands until he came at last to a gate manned by a trio of Jadori guardsmen. The gate was open, allowing kreel riders and people of commerce to flow in and out as they wished. The guardsmen, looking unconcerned, turned unexpectedly toward Lukien as he rode up to them. Not recognizing any of the young men, Lukien nevertheless smiled at them.

'I am Lukien,' he declared. 'And I have returned.'

Word of the Bronze Knight's return spread quickly through the city, reaching White-Eye in the palace while she and Lorn were playing with Poppy in one of the palace's numerous alcoves. Eiriann, who had been mending garments with the other women, had been the first to hear about Lukien's arrival, and had raced into the alcove to tell the news. Lorn stood up with Poppy in his arms, staring at the amazed White-Eye as they listened together to Eiriann's tale. Lukien had entered the city, she told them, and was heading for the palace. Hearing this, White-Eye had hurriedly dispatched a contingent of men to fetch him and bring him to her. Now, as excitement buzzed within the royal residence, White-Eye and Lorn waited for Lukien in a shaded terrace of the palace, a sprawling area of polished flooring with a fountain that bubbled continuously and a low ceiling to protect White-Eye from the powerful sun. The terrace echoed with the excited voices of those who had gathered to greet the returning knight. More than two dozen Jadori – soldiers and citizens both – clamoured for a chance to see him. White-Eye stood apart from them, straight and regal, her blank eyes looking out over the encroaching garden. Lorn, still holding the two-year old Poppy, kept close enough to the queen to seem like one of her advisors, yet far enough away to give her the importance she deserved. Lorn's beloved, the young Eiriann, stood next to the old king, as excited as any of them to be seeing the legendary Lukien.

'What will he look like, do you think?' Eiriann wondered, holding Lorn's elbow. 'I heard he was handsome once, but no more.'

Lorn smirked. 'Should I worry?'

She laughed and pecked his rough cheek. 'You are handsome. But are you not curious?'

'I am. Don't I seem so?'

Eiriann did not reply, giving Lorn a taste of her recent aloofness. It had been easy for the perceptive woman to sense his dissatisfaction the last few weeks. Ever since the retreat of Baralosus and his army, Lorn had felt less and less useful, and Eiriann had tried to ease his unrest. Now, though, she keened like the rest of the crowd, eager to glimpse the returning Lukien.

'There's much he doesn't know, don't forget,' rumbled Lorn lowly. 'He'll be expecting to see Gilwyn.'

None of these things seemed to worry White-Eye, however. The Kahana had taken the time to brush her hair and change her dress for Lukien's return. She looked proud and glamourous in the shade of the protective terrace, her back as straight as her pretty jet hair, her face flushed with anticipation. Even Poppy, deaf as she was, could feel the vibrations of the place, bringing a smile to her cheerful face. Lorn held his daughter close, unable to help himself from bristling. He had heard stories about the Liirian knight for years. Lukien had even helped his nemesis, the hated Jazana Carr, serving as one of her mercenary dogs for years with Baron Glass. As he waited for Lukien, Lorn prepared himself for the natural animosity he was sure would spring up between them.

Amid the chirping birds and gathered voices, Lorn soon heard the approach of men. The crowd went hush. A statue of a women holding a pitcher stood at the edge of the chamber's floor, where the smooth stone met the sand. Lorn watched the statue as the outline of the men appeared behind it. First came a Jadori warrior, smiling. The man bowed hurriedly to his queen, then waved at the others to come into view. Poppy squirmed in Lorn's arms as he craned for a better look, suddenly glimpsing a man come into view. The tall northerner turned toward the chamber of the queen, looking momentarily bewildered. His skin, red from the sun, bore the marks of a life lived hard. A black patch of cloth covered his eye, and his once golden hair hung now with streaks of grey. He wore plain, unadorned riding clothes and a beaten leather coat, giving him the look of a brigand. At his belt dangled a formidable looking sword. He paused at the edge of the terrace, his sole eye searching the crowd. It came to rest finally on White-Eye, followed by a wide, wolfish grin. Somehow knowing he had arrived, White-Eye stepped forward with her arms outstretched.

'Lukien?' she probed. 'I can feel you!'

The Bronze Knight of Liiria paused, studying the girl. A trace of dread crossed his happy face. 'White-Eye . . .' He looked puzzled as he searched her sightless eyes. 'I'm here.' He took another step toward her, ignoring the hushed crowd. 'Can you see me, girl?'

White-Eye shook her head, remaining cheerful. 'No, Lukien, I cánnot. But I hear you and I know it is you! Come to me, Shalafein, come!'

Like a loyal servant, Lukien went to her, falling to his knees before the Kahana and bowing his head to the floor. A rush went through the crowd. Eiriann gripped Lorn's arm. The show of dedication made the hardened Jadori soldiers sigh, as White-Eye put her hand atop the knight's sun-burned head and gently stroked his hair.

'I've come back to you, my lady,' said Lukien.

'Rise, Shalafein,' said White-Eye, her voice breaking with emotion. 'Look at me.'

Lukien rose, meeting her sightless gaze with a look of heartbreak. His hand came up to touch her, falling just short of her pretty face. 'White-Eye,' he said softly. 'What has happened?'

Lorn could tell it took effort for White-Eye to speak. 'I have lost my Akari, Lukien. I am blind now.'

'How is that possible?' Lukien asked. 'How can you lose an Akari?'

'The story is long, Lukien. I will explain it.' White-Eye tried to brighten. 'But you are home! That is what matters' He put her hands to his face, running them over his skin with a great smile. 'Oh! You are different. You have a beard now, and you are thinner. Lukien, I must hear everything!'

Lukien took her hand and kissed it. 'You will, Kahana, I promise.' He looked purposefully at the gathered faces. 'Where is Gilwyn?' he laughed. 'Has he forgotten me already?' Then he stopped himself. 'White-Eye, why are you here at all? Why are you not in Grimhold?' He glanced around in concern. 'Is Minikin here?'

'Lukien, you have questions, I know,' said White-Eye. 'Let me answer them for you my own way.'

'What's wrong?' asked the knight.

White-Eye hesitated. To Lorn, she looked more frightened now than when she had confronted Baralosus. The old king fought the urge to stand beside her.

'Minikin is in Grimhold, Lukien,' said White-Eye. Her voice went brittle. 'And Gilwyn is not here.'

Lukien started. 'Is he all right?'

'I do not know, Lukien. He has left Jador. He followed after you to Liiria.'

'Liiria?' the knight erupted. 'Why? Damn the Fate, White-Eye, tell me what's going on.'

White-Eye shook her head. 'Not here, Lukien. Please . . .' She gestured to the crowd, all of whom had been so pleased to see the Liirian return. 'They're here to see you, Lukien.'

Lorn watched Lukien carefully as the knight struggled to control himself. The news about Gilwyn had overwhelmed him. 'I want to talk now,' he said softly. 'Away from these others.'

'I will tell you everything I can, Lukien,' said White-Eye, 'but first tell me this – did you find the sword you quested for?'

Lukien seemed surprised. 'How did you know about that?'

'Did you find it?' pressed the girl.

'Yes.' Lukien dropped his hand to his side to touch his sword. 'But you can't see it . . .'

White-Eye grimaced. 'No.'

'It's called the Sword of Angels.' Lukien's tone fell flat. 'It's the means to beat the armour, White-Eye.'

'I want to know all about it.'

'And I want to know what's happened to you,' said Lukien. 'And to Gilwyn.'

Something in Lukien's tone made Lorn snap. He didn't like the arrogant knight at all. Still holding Poppy, he stepped out to defend White-Eye. 'Gilwyn left of his own accord,' he said sharply. 'White-Eye had nothing to do with it.'

The probing, single eye turned to Lorn angrily. 'Who in all the hells are you?' he growled.

White-Eye put up her hand. 'Lorn, don't . . .'

'I am Lorn, King of Norvor,' declared Lorn. 'And for a knight so devoted to his queen, you speak like a peasant.'

'What?' sputtered Lukien. He laughed in disbelief. 'You are Lorn the Wicked? I say prove it.'

'Lukien, stop now,' ordered White-Eye. 'He is who he claims. He is Lorn.'

Lorn held his ground. 'The King of Norvor.'

'The King of Norvor is dead,' hissed Lukien. 'Run off his throne by Jazana Carr.'

'He is Lorn!' spat Eiriann.

'Stop this!' White-Eye shouted, getting between them. 'Lukien, you do not understand. You have been gone; you don't know what has happened.'

'Then tell me!'

'Lorn came to us with others across the desert,' said White-Eye. 'He helped us. He helped me, Lukien!' The Kahana carefully took Lukien's hand again and gently led him away. 'Let me explain it all to you.'

'What do you mean, he put Lorn in charge?' Lukien blared. In the tiny,

636

private chamber, his voice boomed. 'I don't believe it. Gilwyn is smarter than that.'

White-Eye remained standing before him. All of them stood, in fact, including Lorn, who stayed close to White-Eye as he stared angrily at Lukien. With the three of them in the chamber, the room was hot with emotion. White-Eye had remained remarkably calm. Lukien, on the other hand, could not believe his ears.

'Gilwyn saw no other choice,' White-Eye explained. 'Jador needed a leader, and I could not do it. Not then.'

'Why not?' Lukien pressed. He had never seen White-Eye so confident. She seemed the perfect queen. 'You are your father's daughter, White-Eye. Jador is your birthright, not *his*.'

Lorn bristled as Lukien jabbed a finger toward him. 'I've made no claims on Jador.'

Lukien ignored him. 'Explain this to me, White-Eye, because I'm starting to think I am dreaming all of this! You were blinded by Kahldris, so Gilwyn went after him?'

'He wanted revenge,' said Lorn.

'And you let him seek it?' Lukien turned with a hiss. 'I know you, Lorn. I fought against you when Jazana Carr had you running with your tail between your legs! You're a brigand and a butcher. Of course you would encourage a boy like Gilwyn to seek revenge. Of course you would!'

'I did no such thing,' said the Norvan. He was a big man, who despite his age still looked capable of combat. 'Nor did I ask for the task of training your queen. Minikin herself asked me to do so.'

'Minikin asked you?' erupted Lukien. It was too unbelievable. 'Why would she do that?'

'Because I needed him!' said White-Eye. 'Because I was broken by my blindness and no one else could help me. Lorn was a king once. He knew what I needed to do to protect Jador.'

'Ah,' sighed Lukien, 'now I see. Those battlements along the wall – he did that, didn't he?'

Lorn stood his ground. 'Jador was like a lamb ready for the wolves,' he said. 'The city could barely defend itself. Someone had to change that.'

'And you're just the man to make a city ready for siege,' snarled Lukien. 'White-Eye, this man is using you! He's duped you, and Gilwyn. But I can't believe he's fooled Minikin, too.'

'We know Lorn's history, Lukien,' White-Eye assured him. 'But you don't know what he has done for us.' She paused, preparing herself. 'Aztar is dead, Lukien.'

Lukien softened. 'No one told me that,' he said. 'What happened?'

'He had changed,' said White-Eye, her face brightening with a smile.

'He helped Gilwyn across the desert. He defended us from Baralosus of Ganjor. That is how he died.'

'Aztar did that?' The claim was unbelievable to Lukien, who had fought the minions of the desert prince many times. 'I don't understand. Why would Baralosus attack?'

'Because he had designs on Jador from the starts,' said Lorn, openly contemptuous of Lukien's ignorance. 'And because his daughter Salina came here for sanctuary.'

'We would not give her up, Lukien,' added White-Eye. 'She helped us too many times for us to turn her over.'

'So? What happened?'

'Your Kahana stood up to them,' declared Lorn, sounding surprisingly proud. 'You see? She is not the little girl you left behind, Sir Lukien. And Jador is not the same, either.'

Lukien fought to stem his simmering temper. Too much was coming at him to make sense of, and Lorn clearly had the advantage. White-Eye's adoration of him was frightening.

'White-Eye, listen to me now,' he said, mustering his calmest voice. He took the girl aside to press his point. 'Your blindness has frightened you. And from what you've told me of Minikin, she is too distraught herself to be much use to anyone. But I tell you what I know in my heart – this wretched man is not the saviour you want him to be. Let us touch the bottom of this swamp and see the truth! I fought against him for years. I was in Norvor and I *know* him.'

'But you do not, Lukien,' said White-Eye sadly. 'You have been gone.'

The accusation stung Lukien. 'Yes,' he admitted. 'I've been gone too long. And maybe I should never have left you. If I'd been here to protect you—'

'Stop.' White-Eye found his face and put a finger on his lips. She smiled at him. 'You could not protect me. No one could. What Kahldris did to me was beyond anyone's power to stop. I tried to tell that to Gilwyn, Lukien. I never wanted him to go.'

The profound loss in her voice proved her wounded love. Confused, Lukien relented.

'I have to much to tell you,' he lamented. 'I wanted this homecoming to be a happy one.'

'It is, Shalafein,' said White-Eye. She pulled him down to her, kissing his forehead. 'My Shalafein. I never doubted you would come back. And we will celebrate! We will feast and you will tell me everything that has happened to you.' Her hand slipped down to his belt, feeling for his sword. 'This is it. This is the sword.'

'Yes,' said Lukien darkly. 'The Sword of Angels.'

White-Eye grinned. 'I wish I could see it.' She turned to Lorn. 'Lorn, is it very grand?'

Lorn eyed the weapon at Lukien's side. 'It is sheathed,' he said sourly. There was a trace of envy in his tone.

'Will you let me touch it, Lukien?' asked White-Eye.

Lukien hesitated. 'White-Eye . . . no. Not yet. I want to speak with Minikin. She should be the first to see it.'

White-Eye retreated from him. 'I have sent for her. She will want to speak to you as well.' Her blank eyes searched for the sword at his belt, then filled with sadness. 'When will you tell us what happened to you, Lukien? We have waited so long.'

Her sincerity overwhelmed him. 'I have come so far,' he groaned, turning away from them both to stare at the stone wall. 'All of this you've told me – I didn't expect any of it.'

'But you have the sword,' Lorn pointed out.

'So? What of it?'

'You have found what you quested for. Now you have the means to defeat Baron Glass.'

'What?' Puzzled, Lukien stepped toward Lorn. 'Why would you know about the sword anyway? No one in Jador knows I was looking for it.' He searched White-Eye for an answer. 'How did you know?' He thought for a moment. 'Was it Minikin? Did she find out somehow?'

White-Eye was clearly keeping something from him. Lorn shifted toward her. 'You should tell him,' he suggested.

'Tell me? Tell me what?' queried Lukien.

'Lukien, there is someone else here to see you,' said White-Eye reluctantly. 'A man from Nith. He came to us some weeks ago, bearing a letter from Aric Glass.'

'Thorin Glass' son,' said Lorn.

'I know who he is,' snorted Lukien. 'I fought with him in Koth. White-Eye, what's in the letter? What does it say?'

'I do not know, Lukien. The messenger who brought it has orders not to give it to anyone but you. He said that you would return here. He was sure of it.'

Lukien grinned at the news. 'Because Aric knows about the sword. That means he's still alive.'

'Alive, and waiting for you in Nith,' said Lorn. The old king looked grave. 'He thinks you mean to march on Koth again. Do you?'

'Of course.' Lukien patted his sword confidently. 'I have this with me now.'

Lorn drew a breath of anticipation. 'Then I want to go with you, Sir Lukien.'

White-Eye's face collapsed. Lukien looked at Lorn in shock.

'Why?' he growled.

'To fight with you, to help you free your land and my own,' said Lorn. 'Jazana Carr usurped me, Sir Lukien. She stole my soul from me.'

Lukien laughed. 'For revenge, then? Forget it.'

'But I can help you! I can fight, and there are still men in Norvor who would follow me. I can call them to your side.' Lorn grew excited. 'Even if you have the sword, you'll still have to fight an army to get to Baron Glass.'

'You forget yourself, King Lorn,' Lukien mocked. 'These Jadori may not know you, but I do. I would never let you have Norvor again. Better that Jazana Carr should let it rot.'

Thunder flashed across Lorn's face. 'You cannot keep me here,' he seethed.

'Would you leave us so easily?' asked White-Eye, hurt by Lorn's words.

'Not easily,' said Lorn. He softened as he looked at her. 'White-Eye, look at you! You are a queen now, a real Kahana! You don't need me anymore. Let me go with your blessing.'

'It's not up to her,' said Lukien. 'It's up to me, and I say no.' He moved toward the exit, angry suddenly and no longer wanting to talk to either of them. 'White-Eye, I want to speak to Minikin,' he said.

Looking forlorn in the light of the lanterns on the wall, White-Eye nodded. 'She will be here. Perhaps tomorrow.'

'Good,' Lukien snapped. 'I don't want to be bothered until then.'

Not really sure where he was going, Lukien left the tiny chamber, his long-anticipated homecoming ruined.

66

In the main pool of the palace bathhouse, Lukien luxuriated in the warm, perfumed water, his arms stretched along the marble edge, keeping his chin just above the surface. Steam rose up from the placid pool, disappearing in wisps as it floated toward the domed ceiling. Tall columns lined the walls of the vast chamber, and the pool itself licked at them, surrounding them and stretching out to the dark edges of the bathhouse. There were five pools of crystal water in the house, but this one – the main pool – was by far the largest. Here, the water ranged in depth from many feet to just a few inches, so that the youngest members of the royal household could enjoy a bath as well. Lukien rested somewhere in the middle, still able to feel the bottom of the pool on his backside. He had forgotten how good it felt to relax and do nothing. The waters of the bathhouse washed away cares and woes as easily as desert dust.

Architecturally, the bathhouse was splendid, like everything in the palace. Kahan Kadar had never spared expenses while building his home, and the bathhouse reflected his good taste. Usually, the baths were filled with people, but today they had abandoned the warm waters, leaving them for Lukien to enjoy. The solitude did not bother Lukien in the least. He had only been in Jador for a day, but already he longed to be alone.

No, he told himself, closing his one eye and sighing. That wasn't quite true. He had missed White-Eye and all the others, but her news had left him distraught and he no longer cared to speak with her about his long trek across the world. All the things he had seen and done – these were things to share with Gilwyn. But Gilwyn wasn't here. Lukien let his naked body float in the steaming pool, feeling the warm waters untie the knots in his weary muscles.

His eye opened, and Lukien saw the dark end of the bathhouse shrouded in shadows. Around him, gurgling water soothed him with its music as it tumbled over fountains and rocks. The mosaic patterns on the ceiling calmed him with its colours of gold and coral. Protectively, he glanced over to where his clothing sat in a nearby pile. Along with his shirt and trousers lay the Sword of Angels, looking unloved in its battered sheath. Within an arms length of Lukien, the sword still managed to keep him alive, unlike the Eye of God which he still wore around his neck. Thinking of the amulet, Lukien lifted it off its chest and held it up, dripping wet. He saw his face reflected in the gold, wavy and curious, lit by the light of its ever-glowing ruby.

'Amaraz,' he said, 'are you still there?'

As always, there was no answer from the Akari. Lukien laughed.

'It doesn't matter. Soon you'll be back in Minikin's care. And I will be done with you forever.'

The prospect made him strangely sad. He had never liked Amaraz, nor really appreciated the gift the spirit had given him. Now, though, the thought of parting with the great spirit made him pensive. He let go of the amulet, letting it sink back onto his chest. Like the rest of him, the skin of his chest bore numerous scars. Looking at his naked body, Lukien grimaced. There were battles yet to fight, still more scars to bear. But he was almost done.

'Almost,' he whispered drowsily. 'Almost . . .'

His eye began to close again, then he caught a glimpse of something at the other end of the bathhouse. A figure moved through the shadows, peering out its little head toward him. The unmistakable coat swam with colour, and the pointed ears twitched. Minikin stepped out from behind one of the columns to grin at him. Lukien smiled back at her, pleased beyond words to see the mistress.

'I'm not wearing anything,' he warned jokingly.

Minikin snorted at his modesty. 'Please, Lukien. You are still a baby to me.'

'Come ahead, then,' he bade. 'If you don't mind getting wet.'

Moving like a cat, Minikin picked her way along the edge of the pool, avoiding the puddles of water that had collected on the marble. Her colourful coat shined as the tones of the water reflected in its strange fabric. Her quick movements gave her a bouncing look as she loped toward him. Lukien, unmoved by his nudeness, merely sat up a little to greet her, not bothering to cover himself at all. It was true what she had told him – despite his age, he was a comparative infant to the ancient Minikin, and there was nothing about a man's physique she hadn't seen a thousand times. There were no benches in this part of the bathhouse, no place at all for the little woman to sit. When she reached Lukien, she stood over him, smiling.

'I've been waiting for you,' said Lukien. 'Forgive me if I don't get up. Believe me, it is good to see you, Minikin.'

Her happy expression filled the sparkling chamber. 'I came as quickly as I could. Lukien . . .' She stooped and put her hand to his face. 'Sweet Shalafein. I cannot tell you how my heart leapt to hear you had come back.'

Lukien choked back his melancholy. 'I ache, Minikin. I have been to every part of this world, and now all I want to do is lie here.'

'Then do that,' she said soothingly. 'Take your ease.' She went to her knees, ignoring the water soaking through her garments, and ran her fingers through his hair like a mother might. 'I've spoken to White-Eye. She told me what has happened to you.'

Lukien nodded. He hadn't told White-Eye everything, but enough. 'Did she tell you I've been here all day? I'm soaked through my skin and I still don't want to get out.'

'White-Eye is afraid you have a stone in your shoe over her,' said Minikin. 'You are angry, I can tell.'

'No. Well, yes!' Lukien sank deeper. 'Shouldn't I be? I came home expecting things the way they were. Things have changed and I don't like it.'

Minikin sat back on her haunches. 'You were gone a very long time, Lukien. White-Eye did the best she could without you here. So did I. So did Gilwyn.'

'I'm still angry,' muttered Lukien.

'And you wanted to unburden yourself on me. Very well. I am here.' Minikin kicked off her shoes and began rolling up her pant legs. Positioning herself at the edge of the pool, she let out an exclamation of pleasure as she dipped her small white feet into the water. 'Oh, that's *good.*'

She looked comical sitting there, threading her fingers through the water and glowing ecstatically. Lukien knew she meant to soothe his anger.

'You look different, Minikin,' he said seriously. 'Even you've changed. You look older. To be true, I didn't think that was possible.'

'I have been through a journey of my own, Lukien,' said Minikin. 'Without ever stepping foot out of Jador.' She considered her feet as she spoke, unwilling to look at him straight. 'Aztar is dead. You know that already. And White-Eye told you of how he attacked us?'

Lukien nodded. 'I should have been here. Aztar was always after me. He was scum.'

'No,' said Minikin. 'His heart was hard, but it changed. He was burned in a fire at the battle, and he was sure the fire came from Vala. He was sure it was a sign that he had wronged us and that we were favoured by Vala. But the fire didn't come from Vala. It came from me. It was Akari fire, and I summoned it. I had to save Jador; I know that. And yet . . .' She closed her eyes. 'It plagues me, Lukien. It was heinous.'

'It was necessary, Minikin,' Lukien assured her. 'White-Eye told me all about it.'

'Necessary, yes, I know. But you see, that doesn't mend my heart.' Minikin looked at him as though pleading for an answer. 'It was a slaughter, and no matter how many days go by I cannot forget it.'

'I think I know that feeling,' said Lukien gently. 'I would be lying if I told you it will pass. But it does get better, Minikin. With time.'

'I have less time than you think, Lukien. I am old. Look at me!'

'I am looking,' said Lukien cheerfully. 'I still think you're beautiful.'

Minikin laughed, even blushed. Then she saw the pile of clothes and the sword placed gently upon them. 'So, that is it. You haven't told White-Eye much about it. Will you tell me, Lukien?'

There was so much to tell, Lukien wasn't sure where to begin. So he blurted out, 'Cassandra told me about the sword. It's just like you told me all those months ago. We don't just disappear when we die. We go on.'

'Cassandra came to you?' Minikin was truly interested now. 'When did this happen?'

'When I fought Thorin,' said Lukien. 'When he nearly killed me! He could have killed me easily, but he left me dying in the road. That's when Cassandra came to me.'

Minikin's almond eyes widened. 'I believe you, of course. And she told you about the sword? She told you to go to the Serpent Kingdom?'

'She did,' said Lukien, then settled back to tell Minikin everything. The little woman listened, enthralled, as he told about his trip to Kaliatha, the dead city of the Akari, and how he had come to know the spirit of Raivik. He told Minikin about Jahan, too, and how his friend had gone with him to Torlis and about his wretched end in the mouth of a rass. But most importantly, he told Minikin about Lahkali, the Red Eminence who he trained and who he missed terribly now. And finally, about the Story Garden. 'Cass is there right now,' said Lukien, 'waiting for me.'

Minikin was enchanted. She regarded him with astonishment, wanting more. 'That's beautiful. Lukien, I am so happy for you. To know that Cassandra still lives! I told you that, but to have it proven, well, that must amaze you.'

'I have been amazed so many times since meeting the Inhumans, I don't know what to feel anymore. Except to say that I miss her. I *miss* her, Minikin.'

'I know,' said the mistress gently. She looked at the sword again, eager for Lukien to unsheathe it. 'And what of Malator? When will I meet him?'

'That should be easy for you. Can't you feel him?'

Minikin concentrated. 'Yes. He is strong, like Amaraz.'

'Malator is my Akari now, Minikin, in a way that Amaraz never was.

Still . . .' Lukien picked the amulet up from his chest. 'I will miss him. He never spoke to me. Well, he did, but only when I meant to give him to Lahkali. I enjoyed seeing him angry, I'll tell you that!'

'And this Malator – tell me what he is like.'

Lukien smirked as he recalled Malator's boyish face. 'He's hardly what I expected. He acts like a child sometimes. He's not at all like Kahldris, I don't think.'

'But he can beat Kahldris?'

'That's what he claims,' Lukien sighed. 'I have to believe him.'

'Good,' said Minikin. 'It is like that when you have an Akari – you must believe in him. And you will not be alone when you head north again. Alsadair the Nithin will be with you, and Ghost, too.'

Lukien perked up. 'Ghost? I haven't seen him yet. Not that I would! He's probably listening to us right now. He means to go with me? He told you that?'

'He begged me, and I agreed,' said Minikin. 'We are all at risk from Kahldris. If there is anyone else you want to go with you, you have only to ask. I was thinking of Greygor.'

'No,' said Lukien. 'I appreciate that, but Greygor should stay here to protect Grimhold.'

'Baron Glass will still have an army to face, Lukien. You should consider that.'

Lukien did consider it. He had thought of little else, in fact. But Greygor was the guardian of Grimhold, a sacred duty. 'I won't take him away,' said Lukien. 'But I will take Ghost with me. And Alsadair, too.'

'What do you think of him?' asked Minikin.

'Well, he's loyal, that's for sure. He brought me that letter at his own peril. I tell you, Minikin, I can't wait to see Aric again. He's the way his father used to be. He reminds me of Gilwyn, even.'

'White-Eye tells me there will be an army of your own waiting for you in Nith. Do you believe that?'

'I believe Aric,' said Lukien. 'He wouldn't have written me anything that wasn't true. And you know what else? I believe in Malator.' At last Lukien removed the amulet from around his neck. 'I don't need this anymore, Minikin. It's time you took it back.'

But Minikin did not take the Eye of God from Lukien. She merely studied it as it spun on its chain. 'Giving it back to me must feel like a great burden being lifted.'

'It does. Take it, please.'

'It's caused you so much trouble. But it's also brought you life.'

'I know. I'm thankful for that.'

'And yet you still think of returning to Cassandra.'

Lukien lowered the amulet. 'I didn't say that.'

'Nor did you have to. Lukien, you wear your thoughts on your sleeve even when you're naked! You mean to return to her when you are done with Baron Glass, is that so?'

'Yes,' said Lukien, unashamed. 'Why shouldn't I? I'm done being a pawn of demons and gods. After I've dealt with Thorin, I'm going to make my own choices.'

'What will happen to the sword then? What will you do with it?'

Lukien looked away. 'Does it matter?'

'If you get rid of it, you will die.'

There was an ugly pause between them. Lukien held out the amulet again. Again, Minikin refused it.

'I want you to keep it,' she told him. 'Take it with you to Liiria.'

'Why? Malator will keep me alive.'

'Keep it,' Minikin advised. 'There's a battle brewing, Lukien. Even if you don't need it, someone else might.'

Thinking of his friend Ghost, Lukien saw the mistress' logic. 'If that's what you want,' he said, and tossed the amulet unceremoniously onto his pile of clothes. 'I'm going to do my best, Minikin. Malator thinks he can beat his brother. I promise you, we will try. And hopefully find Gilwyn there in one piece.'

'I think,' said Minikin, 'that Baron Glass will not harm Gilwyn.'

'He's a madman now. There's no telling what he'll do.' Lukien tried to curb his tongue, but couldn't. He added, 'You should have known better than to let him go, Minikin. And then you let that snake Lorn take over for him!'

'Lukien—'

'No,' Lukien snapped, 'let me have my say. Do you think you know Lorn? You don't. I don't care how many roofs he's put up for the Seekers or what a good teacher he was to White-Eye. That all might be true. But if you knew his history, really knew it, you would never have taken the chance you did. You're lucky to all still be alive.' Lukien sank back broodingly into the pool. 'A lot of Norvans weren't so fortunate.'

He expected Minikin to argue with him. She did not. Instead she rose from the edge of the pool, took off the coat that always covered her, and dropped the fabulous garment next to his own clothes, exposing the Eye of God that she wore around her neck. Hers contained Lariniza, the sister of Amaraz, but looked identical to Lukien's amulet in every way.

'What are you doing?' asked Lukien.

'Making myself comfortable,' said Minikin. She began rolling up her sleeves.

'How long are you planning to stay?' Lukien quipped.

'That depends on you, Lukien. You see, I am not leaving until you change your mind about Lorn.'

'No, Minikin!'

'Oh, don't misunderstand. You don't have to like him. I'm not expecting that. But I want you to take him with you.'

'Fate above, no!'

'You're being petulant,' crooned Minikin. She sat down at the poolside again, returning her white feet to the water. 'Lorn doesn't belong here. He is restless. He needs to return north.'

'What about his family?'

Minikin darkened a little. 'They will remain here.'

'Even his daughter?' prodded Lukien. 'I know about her, Minikin. White-Eye told me. Lorn wanted her to have a place in Grimhold.'

'There is no place for her,' said Minikin sadly. 'But we can care for her here. Lorn cannot. He is a restless tiger, and Jador is a cage to him. He must return home to Norvor.'

'And then what?' raved Lukien. 'Fight Jazana Carr for power?'

'He must do what he must do, Lukien. That is not for us to decide.'

This time, Lukien pulled himself out of the pool nearly completely. 'I won't do it,' he said. 'I won't help Lorn get his throne back.'

'He is a fighter, Lukien. Let him help you.'

'He's a butcher, Minikin!'

'What if he's changed?'

'Come on,' scoffed Lukien. 'Men like him don't change.'

'No?' Minikin grinned as she kicked water at him. 'Some people said the same about you once, Lukien.'

Her words cut him, making him drift back into the pool. 'That's different. I never did the things Lorn has done.'

'I know,' said Minikin softly. 'But you were not here to see the way he helped us. When Aztar attacked, he was there to battle with us. And when White-Eye needed him, he taught her what it means to be a ruler. He stood up to Baralosus, right alongside the rest of the Jadori, ready to die for the city. I had the same doubts about him once, Lukien. That's why I am asking you to trust me.'

'Minikin, please . . .'

'Can you do that, Lukien? Can you trust me?'

'I always trust you. You know I do. But this . . .' Lukien clamped his fists together. 'It makes no sense to me. None of this does!'

'Lorn will leave here, with or without you, Lukien. Even now he prepares to leave us. Better that it should be with you, don't you think so? It will give you a chance to know him better.'

The last thing in the world Lukien wanted was to know King Lorn the Wicked. The prospect of riding north with him made Lukien's teeth hurt. And yet, there was nothing he could do to change Minikin's mind. Despite her stature, she was made of steel.

'This is going to be a very long trip,' he groaned. 'Do me a favour, will you please?'

'Anything, Shalafein.'

'Will you let me have this bath in peace?'

'Of course,' said Minikin, then picked up her coat and left.

67

Lorn moved cat-like through the darkened chamber, past the form of the sleeping Eiriann toward the little chamber where his daughter slept. The hour ticked past midnight, and the halls of the palace groaned with hollowness. With the long day behind him, Lorn stifled a yawn, longing to lay himself down to bed. It had been an eventful day, full of planning, and his eyes watered with sleep. He paused, hoping his squeaking boots would not wake Eiriann, who slept soundly in the sheets, looking beautiful as a shaft of moonlight caressed her face. Eiriann, young and perfect, had taken to his bed without shame, leaving behind the mores of her past life and adopting both Lorn and Poppy into her world. She was a fine woman, so much like the wife Lorn had buried, and he wondered at the good fortune that had brought him such a lovely lady. Full of fire, Eiriann had refused to speak to him the last few days, angered by his decision to head north with Lukien and the others.

Why couldn't she understand?

Lorn looked at her, admiring her. She was always such a vocal woman, it seemed strange to him to see her so silent. He noticed her more closely now, in ways he had never stopped to see before. Her neck pulsed with every breath. He eyes flittered, deep with sleep. She would be fine without him, even if he never returned. But what of Poppy?

Lorn turned back to the nursery, tip-toeing toward his daughter's alcove. The nursery sat just across from their main chamber, a comfortable little nook perfect for the baby girl. There was no door to the chamber, just a curtain that separated the two rooms. Lorn pushed the curtain aside, closing it behind him as he entered. Poppy slept inside her wooden crib, a crib he had made for her himself not long after arriving in Jador. She had grown long since then; she could walk now, though not well. Her blindness and deafness – the very ailments that had driven Lorn to Jador in the first place – still persisted, frustrating Poppy as she grew more aware. Tonight, though, his daughter didn't fuss. She slept angelically in the crib, her slack, pretty face up toward the ceiling. Like a doll, her smooth skin glowed with the chamber's tender light. Her small chest moved almost imperceptibly with the in and out of her tiny puffs of breath.

Lorn hovered soundlessly over her crib, staring down at her. There were so many things he wanted to tell her, but she was far too young to understand. She was remarkable, strong like her mother. She had survived the long trek across the desert because she was made of steel. Even deaf and blind, she would grow into a fine woman someday.

'I want to tell you all those things,' Lorn whispered carefully. His voice barely carried down to the sleeping girl. 'I want you to know me, and that I thought the best of you.'

In Norvor, when he had been a king, some had argued for her murder. She was a burden, his advisors had told him, and could never be anything more. What kind of princess could she possibly make? Lorn remembered those words now, and how blithely he had said the same himself of other unfortunate infants. They were weak, weren't they? They couldn't be Norvans, because Norvans were strong.

'But you are strong, little Poppy,' said her father. 'Never let anyone tell you otherwise. Never think yourself the weaker. You are my daughter. Your blood is my blood, and my blood is like fire. You are born to greatness.' Lorn placed his palm lightly on the girl's chest. 'Don't forget me.'

Poppy slept, undisturbed by her father's words. He turned, and to his surprise saw Eiriann standing near the curtain. Her eyes drooped sadly, watching him. She shook her head in sorrow.

'Why are you leaving us?' she asked.

She had yet to confront him, but could no longer resist. Inexplicably, she loved him. To Lorn, there seemed no good answer to her query, nothing that could make her understand the need he had to go and fight for Norvor. He shrugged, almost an apology.

'I am a leopard who cannot change his spots,' he said.

Eiriann waited for him to say more. When he did not, she nodded and closed the curtain.

68

Gilwyn sat in the windowless catalogue room, pondering the massive machine sprawling out before him. His oil-covered hands drummed absently on the wooden desk, the portal that unlocked the machine itself. The hard chair beneath his rump creaked as he leaned back in it perilously, just as he had seen his mentor Figgis do a hundred times before. A bank of hastily lit candles illuminated the machine, setting its rods and pulleys aglow. For days now Gilwyn had tinkered with them, trying to figure out the ingenuity of their design. Now, thoroughly vexed, he let out a mumbling groan, not really hearing himself as he stared at the miraculous, confounding catalogue.

'What in the world makes this thing go?'

The mystery of the machine made the young man bite his lip, mightily wishing he had paid Figgis more attention. Over their years together, Figgis had tried to teach Gilwyn the machine's intricacies, but Gilwyn had always given up in frustration, sure that only the brilliant Figgis could understand its complexities. The machine had sprung from the genius' own mind, like a dream made real. He had built the thing with his own feeble hands, somehow cobbling together the remarkable pieces from all across the continent. The catalogue machine was more than just a marvel. Some believed it could actually think, but Gilwyn knew better. To truly bring the machine to life had been the greatest part of Figgis' ambition, and one he had never achieved. Still, the myth of the catalogue lived on.

For weeks now, Gilwyn had spent time stalling, pretending to try and work the machine in those hours he did not spend with Thorin. Thorin seemed to believe his endeavours, mostly. At least the old baron seemed satisfied. They had been good weeks for both of them, and Gilwyn had tried his best to keep Thorin's madness at bay. But the catalogue machine still loomed over both of them, a nagging reminder that Malator was still on his way.

'I think,' said Gilwyn, 'that this thing should have died with Figgis.'

He straightened out his chair, lowering his head to the desk and resting his chin atop his clubbed hand. It was hard for him to imagine Thorin ever killing White-Eye, or any of the other Inhumans. Yet that was the baron's bleak promise. Claiming no choice in the matter, Thorin had told Gilwyn that the Akari – and their hosts – needed to pay for what they had done to Kahldris.

How did one kill a spirit, Gilwyn wondered? Really, wasn't that what Thorin wanted? The Akari were already dead, and yet somehow Kahldris wasn't satisfied. He wanted them removed forever from the earth, and there was, of course, only one way to do so. The Akari lived among the living because they had living hosts. Kill them, Gilwyn supposed, and the Akari would flee, leaving the world forever in the hands of the demon Kahldris.

At first, Thorin's horrible proposition had kept Gilwyn awake for weeks. Thorin – who had once been so gentle – openly planned to do Kahldris' bidding, surrendering bodily to the spirit. First, though, they would deal with Malator. And that alone gave Gilwyn hope. It gave him time to plan.

'We'll find a way, Ruana,' muttered Gilwyn.

The great, inscrutable machine stretched out before him. With Thorin's help he had managed to make the machine move, starting up its apparatus so that now it clanked and whistled with life. But that was all, and it frustrated Gilwyn. He did not really believe that the catalogue could help him find a way to stop Kahldris, but he had so few other options. He had combed the library for any scrap of information that might help him, but in all the books and scrolls there was almost nothing about the Akari, just vague references to spirits that might – or might not – live across the Desert of Tears.

Gilwyn, you are tired, said Ruana. *Stop now and rest.*

Gilwyn spied the food he had brought with him, sitting at the edge of the desk. He had not eaten for hours, and the smell of the cheese drew him to it like a mouse. Karlina, the woman who ran Lionkeep's kitchen, had taken good care of him over the weeks he had been in Koth, fattening him on hearty cooking and tempting him every night with baked treats. Thinking of her now, Gilwyn smiled.

'There'll be raisin cake tonight,' he said cheerfully. 'Too bad you can't have any, Ruana. You don't know what you're missing.'

You'll eat enough for both of us, retorted the Akari.

'I will,' Gilwyn pronounced, then sat up to stretch his aching back. He realized that he had already been in Koth for nearly two months, and in that time had made many friends among Lionkeep's prodigious staff of servants and stable hands. His arrival had lightened Thorin's mood considerably, that's what they all claimed, and because of it they were happy to have Gilwyn with them. Karlina was fond of saying that Gilwyn was their charm, like a talisman to ward off the baron's black moods. Over the weeks he had kept his promise to Thorin, deciding not to abandon him no matter how bad things got. They would get bad, Gilwyn knew, but not yet. For now, life in Koth was good again, and even Thorin seemed better every day.

You are pleased, said Ruana, smiling in Gilwyn's mind. *You should be, Gilwyn. I am proud of the way you have handled Baron Glass.*

Gilwyn nodded, feeling proud himself. 'He is better, isn't he, Ruana? He really is. I knew he would be. I knew I could reach him.'

Ruana paused. *Gilwyn . . .*

'I know. There's still a lot to do. But I am reaching him, and we still have time. There's no way Lukien could get here before another month or so. By then, who knows?'

I know, Gilwyn. And you know. And Baron Glass knows, too. He has surrendered to Kahldris. He told you so already, many times.

'I have to hope, Ruana,' countered Gilwyn. 'It's all I have.'

Ruana understood, graciously letting the matter go. *You know him better than I do, Gilwyn. If you say that he is better, then it is so.*

'It's the time we spend together,' Gilwyn pointed out. 'It makes him remember the way he used to be. You saw him when we were riding yesterday, Ruana. He was like a kid!'

A very big, demented kid perhaps.

'No. He's the way he was, before all of this happened to him.' Gilwyn sighed, fondly recalling their ride through the countryside. Thorin had even sung while they rode. 'When was the last time that he sang, do you think?'

A long time ago, Ruana conceded.

'That's right. And Karlina and the rest of them have seen the change in him. He hardly ever speaks of Kahldris any more. I tell you, Ruana, his grip is slipping.'

Ruana was quiet, which was really her way of saying she disagreed. Not really caring, Gilwyn collected his bag of food and left the catalogue room, happy to be out of the dark chamber. He stepped immediately into the light of a stained glass window, putting his face to the sunlight with a smile. The day was mild and pretty, a good day for being outside, but Gilwyn still had work to do. First, though, he would break his fast. Out in the hall, he pointed himself quickly to one of his favourite reading rooms, a little nook that let the afternoon sunlight splash through its windows. Bag in hand, he left the catalogue room far behind, happy to forget about it for an hour or so. As usual, the library was empty. While he worked with the machine, only a handful of artisans and carpenters had come to finish up their reconstruction, and today Gilwyn had the entire, massive building to himself. He had long ago grown accustomed to the eerie quiet of the place and it never frightened him, not even at night. To him, the library was always a place of fabulous peace.

Reaching the reading chamber, Gilwyn put down his bag of food beneath the window, then scanned the polished shelves for something promising to read. It didn't really matter to him what he selected, because he found all of it fascinating, and after the dearth of books he'd endured in Jador, even the worst tome of poetry delighted him. Eventually, he selected just such a book, a collection of ancient prose from long-dead Marnan writers. Gilwyn paged through it as he made his way back to the window and sat down, absently opening up his bag of food and pulling out some fruit and cheese, which he nibbled happily while he read. The sun coming through the glass touched the ancient book, lighting the dust particles that took flight as he turned the pages.

As they always did when he read, the minutes ticked away unnoticed.

Gilwyn ate his fill, settling in for a long read which stretched well beyond his planned hour. When he realized how long he'd been away, he closed the book and leaned his head against the darkly paneled wall. Ruana was in his mind, skimming quietly across its surface. Something puzzled him. He glanced back at the book and remembered the last story he had read, about a man who would not tell his daughters the names of the princelings he had sent them to marry. The secret struck him as strange, and he didn't know why. For some reason, he thought about Kahldris.

Kahldris hadn't come to him again, not in all the long weeks he'd been in Koth. The demon had visited him only once, and only then when he was far from Koth, safely away from Thorin. Gilwyn chewed his lip pensively, sure that something plain was being overlooked. In the story, the man was frightened of his daughters, and so never told them of the princes they'd be promised to. The story made no sense to Gilwyn, and neither did his suspicions. His pensiveness snagged Ruana's attention.

She asked him, *What are you thinking, Gilwyn?*

'I'm thinking about Kahldris,' said Gilwyn, still unsure why. 'He still hasn't come to us again. Don't you think that's odd? I mean, I expected him to, didn't you?'

I'm sure he has nothing to say to either of us.

'But isn't that strange? He was the one who wanted me here, and now he ignores me. I thought for sure he'd be after me about the catalogue.' Gilwyn set the book aside and stared blankly across the chamber. 'It makes no sense.'

Thorin is protecting you from him, perhaps.

'That's what I thought, but . . .' He shrugged. 'He hasn't even mentioned Kahldris to me, which means that Kahldris isn't pushing him.'

That's good, then. Ruana thought for a moment. *Isn't it?*

'I don't know.' Gilwyn glanced at the book again, and then it came to him. 'I think he's afraid of me, Ruana. I think he's afraid of the influence I have over Thorin. Remember? You told me that the first time he came to us in Roall. You were right, but he didn't even know it then. Now he sees how Thorin feels about me.'

He stood up, then started pacing. His theory made sense. He was sure it did.

Yes, Ruana agreed after a moment. *He knows that if he harms you, Thorin will be angry with him.*

'Right! So maybe he doesn't have such a stranglehold on Thorin after all.'

Gilwyn's mind was racing suddenly, thinking through the possibilities. He had been working like a madman to find out about Malator, any little scrap that might help him defeat Kahldris. Now, it seemed Kahldris himself was afraid of him. Surely that meant an opportunity.

'I can drive them apart,' he mused. 'That's what he's afraid of.'

No. Ruana's voice was adamant. *Forget what you are thinking, Gilwyn.*

But Gilwyn had already convinced himself. 'Let's see how tough he is, Ruana.'

No!

'Yes! How can I know how to beat him if I don't know anything about him? I have to face him!'

Gilwyn picked up the remnants of his lunch and hurried out of the chamber. There was a lot to do, a lot to plan. Somehow, he needed to tempt the demon out of hiding.

Gilwyn spent the next several days spending all the time that he could with Thorin. Rarely leaving the baron's side, the two took every meal together, rode for long hours in the crisp countryside, and whiled away their time at the ponds that surrounded Lionkeep. Thorin, who still wore the arm of his Devil's Armour everywhere, nevertheless ignored the subject of Kahldris completely, focusing instead on the progress he had made in Koth the last few months. Since Gilwyn's arrival, Koth had prospered, he explained ecstatically, and for the first time in a long while Baron Glass seemed very much like the man Gilwyn had known before. They were good days, full of laughter, but Gilwyn had his own reasons for spending so much time with Thorin. Slowly, he wedged himself between the baron and the demon that controlled him.

On those rare times when he wasn't with Thorin, Gilwyn carefully badmouthed Kahldris to anyone who would listen. He found a willing – even fascinated audience in Karlina – who listened intently as Gilwyn told her about how weak he thought the armour really was, and that the demon who dwelt within its metal was a coward. When he told this to the stable boys, he had them enraptured, and when he repeated this to the maids they were scandalized. Gilwyn was cautious, however, and never let Thorin hear what he was saying. He knew, however, that Kahldris heard everything. Day by day, he made it his mission to criticize the unseen spirit, sparing no insult in his attempt to rile Kahldris from his hiding place. After a week, however, Kahldris still had not appeared to him. Gilwyn kept up his verbal assaults, but knew that he needed to take a more direct approach.

Though he was certainly older than most in Lionkeep, Thorin rarely slept these days. The armour gave him unnatural strength, along with the ability to go for days on end without slumber. Gilwyn waited patiently for exhaustion to overtake his friend, knowing Thorin needed to be asleep for what he planned to do. Finally, on a night when rain clouds overtook the glorious day, Thorin retired late to his bedchamber, leaving Gilwyn on the other end of an unfinished game board. Gilwyn watched as Thorin excused himself, then waited an hour more to be sure the baron was asleep. At nearly midnight, the entire castle fell silent, leaving Gilwyn free to explore the cellar where he knew the Devil's Armour waited.

He had prepared himself for the encounter, yet now felt a pull of fear holding him back. Ruana, who had never cared at all for his plan, muttered to him in his brain, warning him. Gilwyn ignored her counsel; he had made up his mind. There was only one way to find out the things he needed to know, and that was from Kahldris himself. The catalogue had proved useless. So had the library and its awesome stock of books. Not even Ruana knew how to defeat Kahldris. If he had any weaknesses at all, only he knew what they were. But getting him to reveal them was the challenge.

Remember, don't let him into your mind, cautioned Ruana as Gilwyn made his way to the cellars beneath the keep. *And never forget, he can kill you. No, wait – you have forgotten that. You must have.*

'I have to do this, so hush,' snapped Gilwyn nervously. He peaked around the corner, making sure no one saw him. As expected, the corridors of Lionkeep were empty, and the doors leading down to the cellars stood unguarded. Amazingly, Thorin had never thought to post a guard to protect the Devil's Armour. He claimed the armour needed no protection. Besides that, everyone in the keep was terrified of the enchanted suit, and could only rest knowing it was buried safely away in the bowels of the castle. Thorin, realizing how uneasy the armour made his servants, gladly tucked it away from sight. As long as he wore the pieces of his missing arm, he had no real use for the rest of the armour, except in battle.

Gilwyn went to the doors, twisting the ancient latches and pulling the portals open. The rusty hinges flaked and screeched, alarming Gilwyn as he hurried past them. He had brought a lantern with him, balanced expertly in his fused hand. As he closed the doors behind him, he saw the huge, curving staircase come darkly into view, spiraling down and disappearing in the murk. The light from the lantern bounced eerily off the stone walls, giving the descent a hellish quality. He moved carefully down the stairs, slowly working the boot of his clubbed foot so as not to slip. There was no hand rail for him to grip, just the wall that curved alongside the stairs. Gilwyn felt the coldness of it on his fingertips, a hundred years of grime and filth. His eyes adjusted slowly to the darkness, stretching out the time so that it seemed to take forever to reach the solid ground. Finally, as he stepped off the last riser, he looked around at the chamber, noticing dusty crates of wine piled high atop each other. Moving his lantern, he let the feeble beams of light crawl across the cellar, illuminating the tools and odd bits of metal that littered the walls. Across the floor he saw an archway leading into another chamber, and crossing through it he found more of the same. Gilwyn looked around despairingly, afraid he'd be lost forever in the endless catacombs, but as he shuffled further along he noticed one more chamber in the distance, this one glowing with peculiar light.

'That's it,' he whispered, studying the dark radiance. The chamber dazzled him with its dancing light, a kind of black glow that might have been moonlight on a stormy night. He inched toward it, feeling Ruana's trepidation.

I feel him, she warned. *Protect yourself.*

'He can't hurt me,' Gilwyn reminded her. 'He won't.'

At least that was his theory. But now that the time had come to test it, his feet moved leadenly toward the glowing chamber. When at last he reached the archway, he peered inside to see the source of the marvelous light, frightened into stillness by the image of the armour. It hung upon a tiny dais, suspended there in perfect form without a hint of ropes or wires to hold it erect. The horned helmet gazed at Gilwyn as if upon a living head, but there was no man inside it, just the essence of the great Akari. The left arm was gone, of course, but the right one rested easily at the figure's side, the fingers of its gauntleted hand open. The magnificent metal shined like black liquid, throwing off its strange light in all directions. Gilwyn lowered his lantern to the ground, having no need of it in the presence of the armour. He studied the evil suit, enthralled by its pulsing life-force.

'He's inside it,' he said, putting up his hand to feel the cold, almost imperceptible breeze coming from it. 'It's just like when he came to us in Roall.'

Gilwyn stepped closer to the armour, feeling dwarfed by its enormity. He had practiced what he would say, and for a week he had done his best

657

to anger the demon. Now it was time to draw him forth. Suddenly, all the fear that had accompanied him down the staircase gathered on his shoulders. His mouth went dry. Summoning his courage, he folded his arms over his chest.

'I've been waiting for you,' he said. 'Why haven't you come to me?'

The armour pulsed quietly atop its dais.

'You've been watching me, I know. You've been listening. I'm surprised you haven't tried to stop me yet.'

Still, Kahldris was silent. Gilwyn began to circle the dais as he spoke.

'When you came to me in Roall you said you wanted something from me. But now you don't, do you? I figured it out, Kahldris. It took me a while, but now I understand. The catalogue is useless to you now. Your brother is already on his way. That's why Thorin hasn't been pushing me to learn it anymore. It's too late. You wanted to find your brother but Lukien found him first.'

Almost imperceptibly, the breeze from the armour grew. The metal glowed a little hotter.

'Yes, you are listening, aren't you?' Gilwyn smiled mockingly. 'Why don't you come and face me, Kahldris? Are you afraid? I've never had someone be afraid of me before. To be honest it feels pretty good!'

Gilwyn, be careful, advised Ruana.

But Gilwyn continued, 'You know I'm getting to Thorin. I'm reaching him, Kahldris.' He paused in front of the armour, staring up into the glowing eyes of the helmet. 'That's what you're afraid of, isn't it? You're afraid I'm going to win. That's why you haven't come after me, because you know Thorin wouldn't allow it. You're not in control of him after all!'

Again the armour seethed, the light bending as the metal flexed.

'I've been telling everyone what a coward you are. They couldn't believe it at first, but now they're seeing that they don't have to be afraid of you. You don't control them anymore, either. They have you locked down here in this cellar like some rusty old tool. You might never see the light of day again!'

That, at last, was enough to make the demon snap. The fleshless armour exploded to life, jumping down from the dais. Shocked, Gilwyn turned toward the exit, but the armour beat him there, clanking across the floor to block his out. The death's head helmet leered at him as the metal feet stalked forward. Gilwyn backed away, wild-eyed as he stared at the possessed thing. The one hand came up, making a shaking fist, and suddenly a horrid laugh ripped from the mouthpiece.

'Do you want me, *boy*?' it taunted. 'Here I am!'

The hand went up to pull away the helmet, revealing the visage of the withered Kahldris. Just as he had been in Marn, his face was old and leathery, topped with long white hair and fixed with two blazing eyes that pinned Gilwyn in place. Kahldris opened his mouth to hiss his curses, showing his rows of yellow teeth.

'You are a damnable little troll, Gilwyn Toms. Why have you come here, you lying shit-eater?'

Gilwyn stayed his ground, managing to hold the demon's gaze. 'At last you have the stones to face me.' He faked his own mocking laugh. 'So now, what will you do to me?'

'Shall I tear you into bits and eat you? Shall I spill your guts to the floor? There are a thousand things I could do to you.'

'No, there's nothing you can do,' countered Gilwyn. 'Because if you did, you'd lose your host. And you're nothing without your host, Kahldris.'

Kahldris clamoured one stop closer. 'You value yourself too highly, boy.'

'I don't think so,' Gilwyn challenged. 'I've figured you out, Kahldris.'

The demon's face creased angrily. 'Do not presume to frighten me.'

'But I do! You're scared of me,' said Gilwyn, refusing to back away. 'You should have killed me back on that farm in Roall, before Thorin ever had a chance to see me again. Now it's too late. You've seen how he cares about me. If anything were to happen to me, he'd know who to blame.'

Kahldris cocked his head, his lips feigning a pout. 'Oh, thank you, boy,' he crooned, his voice sickly-sweet. 'Your warning warms my heart. Have you not seen how the baron does my bidding? He is mine, body and soul.'

'No, not anymore. He's changing. And you can't stand that, because then all your plans for revenge will be finished, and you'll have to go back to living in a cage.'

Kahldris' face began to boil. 'Why are you here?' he demanded.

'To put you on notice, demon. I'm done being afraid of you. I'm going to keep telling everyone what you really are, and I'm going to show Thorin that he doesn't need you. He's remembering the man he used to be!'

'Do that, and you will pay,' spat Kahldris.

'You can't hurt me, Kahldris.' Gilwyn relaxed, sure of his hunch. 'If you do, you'll lose everything.'

Kahldris smiled. 'You are tasking me. But let's not play this game. Tell me what you want. It is something, surely. Something you want me to reveal, perhaps?'

His guess unbalanced Gilwyn. Feigning disinterest, Gilwyn shrugged. 'You're not going to reveal anything you don't want to,' he said casually. He turned and rounded the dais again. 'Anyway, I think you know you're in trouble. Your brother is on his way, and you can't stop him. You wanted me to help you find him, and now it's too late.'

'I will deal with my brother,' Kahldris rumbled. 'Happily.'

'You'll have to, because he's coming. And until you do you won't be able to have your revenge on the other Akari.'

'But I have patience, Gilwyn Toms! Don't you know? I have been entombed for eternity. I can wait.' Kahldris put his gauntlet to his heartless chest. 'And what will happen to your precious White-Eye then, do you think?'

Gilwyn saw his move and countered. 'You may kill her, I know that. But it's the same problem. Anything more you do to her will hurt me, and Thorin wouldn't like that.'

Kahldris snorted. 'You are very brave. And stupid. You may not be afraid of me, boy, but you should be.'

Gilwyn shook his head. 'Nope, no longer. I'm here to tell you that the challenge is on, Kahldris. From now on I'm going to do my best to win back Thorin's soul. I'm not leaving him. Who knows? By the time your brother Malator gets here, Thorin might already be rid of you.'

'Stop talking about my brother, you wretched imp!'

'Look at you,' Gilwyn taunted. 'You're afraid of him, too. Why?'

'You horrible little toad . . .'

'Everyone says what a powerful summoner you were, what a great general! I don't believe them. You can't be all those things and still be so afraid of a single Akari!'

Before Gilwyn saw it, the metal hand shot out and struck him hard across the face. He fell backward, skidding along the floor, his head striking the dais. Dazed, he looked up into Kahldris' maddened face, and knew he'd hit the right note. With a grimace of pain he touched his crushed lip.

'Go on,' he said, staggering to his feet. 'Hit me again!'

This time, Kahldris backed away. 'Do not speak of my brother.'

'Why? What's he going to do to you? Why can't you beat him?'

Kahldris was about to erupt, then stopped himself. His eyes turned to shrewd little slivers. 'Oh, you clever little boy.' He clenched his fist, holding back his rage. 'Now I see what you've been up to. The library hasn't been much of a help to you either, has it?'

Gilwyn smirked. 'What are you talking about?'

'You've been trying to find a way to defeat me, but you haven't yet. And you won't, because there is no way. I am indestructible!'

'I don't believe you,' said Gilwyn. 'Your brother has the means.'

'Then you'll just have to wait for him,' snarled the demon. 'Because I won't help you.'

Gilwyn knew his ploy was over. Angry, he stepped up to the Akari. 'You're still being challenged, Kahldris. I may not find a way to beat you, but I may not have to.'

'Do not talk against me to the baron, boy,' Kahldris warned. 'I have other ways to harm you.'

Gilwyn began to walk past him. 'I'm not listening to your threats anymore.'

Kahldris put out his arm to block him. 'You should listen,' he said with a grin. 'I can turn you inside out with fear.'

For a moment Gilwyn paused, remembering Ruana's warnings. He had seen what Kahldris had done to White-Eye, driving her madly into the desert, chasing a phantom that didn't exist.

'Good-bye, Kahldris,' said Gilwyn calmly. 'You can battle me for Thorin's soul, but you'll lose.'

The demon lowered his arm for Gilwyn to pass. 'Don't forget what I've said here tonight. Don't forget that it's you who've challenged me.'

The lantern burned on the floor, beckoning Gilwyn. Kahldris stepped aside. The armour would find its way back to the dais, Gilwyn knew, and no one else would know what had happened between them. Sure that he'd let a cobra out of its basket, Gilwyn picked up his lantern and left the chamber.

69

Gilwyn blew the dust off the row of books, smiling as he read the titles printed along the spines. Carefully balanced on his step stool, the branches of a birch tree tapping at his window, he ran his fingers lovingly along the top of the manuscripts, comforted by their permanence. The library had been destroyed and then rebuilt, but the words within its books were forever, and Gilwyn took care with them now that he was home again, treating them as though they were his own precious children. Tucked in his belt rested a feather duster, dirty from the morning's work. He had spent hours alone in the rotunda, cleaning up the debris that had settled on the woodwork and books from all the recent construction. Once, the rotunda had been the library's grandest reading room, and had been remarkably unscathed during the bombardment from Norvan catapults. Under Thorin's direction, the wood paneling and plaster ceilings had all been carefully restored of cracks and blemishes, and nearly all of the books and manuscripts remained, just as they had been when Figgis was alive.

For Gilwyn, his work in the library was a joy, one he had never dared hope to have again during his long stay in Jador. He awoke early this morning, eager to return to the huge chore of getting the library back in order. If it was to ever reopen to the public – which was Thorin's promise – it needed to not only be repaired, but also restocked and returned to its original order, and only Gilwyn knew how to do that. Figgis had taught him much in their years together, and Gilwyn remembered everything. Whenever a book was out of place, he knew exactly where it belonged. And so he worked diligently but carefully, using his stool to reach the higher ledges as best he could and wishing his friend Teku could help him. In the days when Gilwyn had been Figgis' apprentice, the little monkey had helped the crippled boy with everything, even fetched books off the highest shelves. She had been given to Gilwyn by Figgis, but she was always meant to be more than a pet. She was more than a friend, even. Teku had made the challenge of working in the giant library a possibility for Gilwyn, and even seemed to sense his moods and needs. As his eyes absently scanned the shelves, Gilwyn thought about Teku. He missed the little beast, just as he missed everyone in Jador.

His mind began to wander.

Another week had passed since he had confronted Kahldris in the cellars. Despite the demon's dire pledges, it had been a wonderful seven days. Kahldris had remained quiet and aloof, allowing Gilwyn to continue bad-mouthing him, and Thorin gradually continued his slow-climb back to normalcy, taking interest in the small things in life again. He and Gilwyn continued to go riding almost every morning, and each night before he went to sleep Gilwyn made sure to spend an hour or so with the baron, usually playing cards or sampling from Lionkeep's wine stores. Ruana continued to caution Gilwyn about Kahldris, but even she was forced to admit that the Akari's threats had baffled her. He had done nothing to harm anyone, and soon Ruana, too, began to believe Gilwyn's claims that they were untouchable.

Heartened by the recent events, Gilwyn spent more and more time in the library, imagining himself at the helm of the great edifice. When he had arrived in Koth, Thorin had offered the job to him, saying that the library needed him. It did, Gilwyn knew, but he still had a life and a lover to return to in Jador. Nevertheless, he daydreamed about remaining in Koth and reopening the grand 'Cathedral of Knowledge,' returning both the city and its icon to its glory days. How proud would his mother be to see him now, he wondered? She expected great things from him. Before she died, she had told him to reach for the stars.

Gilwyn pulled the duster from his belt, stretching to feather the higher books. Had he disappointed his mother? He thought so. But then, everyone in Koth was disappointed, because the city had fallen into ruin over the years, breaking all the dreams of it populace. The young face of Gilwyn's mother burned brightly in his memory, and he held it while he dusted, unaware of the melancholy smile curling his lips. She had died young but he remembered her perfectly, and the memory of her gentle touch was never far from his mind. Thinking of her now, his hand stilled. His eyes drifted blindly from the books, seeing nothing but the image of her smiling face.

'Oh . . .'

He caught himself with a sigh, stepping down from his stool and laying his duster down on a shelf. He rarely felt alone in the huge library, but now the solitude of the place unnerved him. It was almost noon, he was sure, and he promised Thorin he would be back in Lionkeep for midday meal. He glanced around the rotunda, proud of the work he had done, and then glimpsed a tiny movement near one of the many long reading tables. He pivoted to see it better, catching sight of a bit of tawny fur. Still in his dream state, he grinned when he realized it was Teku.

And then froze.

Impossibly, unimaginably, Teku jumped from one table to another, stopping to chatter at him from across the room. The monkey who he'd left in Jador gave him her familiar grin of little teeth. Gilwyn barely breathed, trying to make sense of what was happening. His eyes scanned the chamber, but everything else was the same, without a hint of distortion.

'Teku,' he said softly. 'You can't be here.'

As she always did, Teku gave her little monkey bark, then climbed up onto one of the shelves, wrapping her tail around a pole of wood to support herself. She dangled down from the long appendage, urging Gilwyn forward.

'It's not you,' said Gilwyn. 'It can't be.'

Teku frowned in annoyance. Always remarkably intelligent, her human-like expressions left no doubt to her thoughts. Pulling herself up again, she hopped to a bookshelf closer to the exit, then jumped up and down excitedly. In her language, that meant for Gilwyn to follow her, but Gilwyn shook his head.

'Whatever you are, go away,' he told her. He glanced around the rotunda. 'Do you hear me, Kahldris? I know this is your doing. You're in my mind.'

Teku seemed not to hear him. The monkey leapt to the floor, clapped its tiny hands together, then loped out of the rotunda, looking back at him to follow. Her chattering went with her out into the hall, where she screeched for Gilwyn to come. Sure that he was being duped, Gilwyn nevertheless went after her. Ruana touched his mind instantly.

Don't, she urged. *That's not Teku.*

'I know,' Gilwyn assured her.

You're doing just what Kahldris wants. Don't follow her.

Too curious to ignore the monkey, Gilwyn stepped out of the rotunda and into the corridor. Fleet-footed Teku was already well down the dim hall, but chattered happily when she saw Gilwyn following. Again she started off, heading down the corridor toward the private living chambers. The darkness of the hall gave Gilwyn some pause. He had spent very little time in that part of the library since returning, and still didn't care to see the places where he and Figgis had lived. Teku, disappearing around a bend in the hall, called insistently for him to proceed.

'What does he want?' Gilwyn wondered. There was no sense of Kahldris in the air, yet he knew the spirit toyed with him.

To frighten you.

'With a monkey?'

To Gilwyn it made no sense at all, and the puzzle of it propelled him down the hall. With Ruana's cautions ringing in his mind, he hurried down the corridor after the monkey, catching glimpses of her as she continued rounding corners. Gilwyn's clubbed foot ached in his special boot, trying gamely to keep up with her. Very quickly he was in the living area, a much less grand part of the library marked by plain stone walls and small, narrow chambers. This was where he had spent his adolescence, where he and Figgis had shared their lives, and the ghosts of the place were all around him suddenly, flooding him with memories. With only the light from the clouded windows to guide him, Gilwyn struggled to see where Teku had gone, peering into the many chambers to find her. Her chattering voice was coming from everywhere at once, and like a hall of mirrors the corridors all took on the same, confusing greyness. Gilwyn realized with dread that things were not exactly as they were before. The halls were impossibly narrow, and not because they'd been rebuilt. Just as he had when he'd come to Gilwyn in Roall, Kahldris was changing the landscape.

'We should go,' he told himself, but turning around did him no good at all, because the way he'd come was blocked. A wall that shouldn't have been there had sprung up in seconds, and the only way out was forward. The panic of being trapped gripped Gilwyn. He forced himself to stay calm.

Wait, said Ruana. *He means to trap you, Gilwyn. This is a game, but you don't have to play.*

'Don't I? There's no way out now.'

Whatever he would find going after Teku, it had already been ordained. Gilwyn stiffened his resolve, refusing to let Kahldris best him. He took a resolute step forward. Teku's calls stopped instantly. Silence engulfed the hall. Up ahead, a chamber beckoned, pouring out orange candlelight. Vaguely he remembered the room, calling it up from his past. Not a room from the library, this one was from Gilwyn's first home. The place he had been born.

'Lionkeep . . .'

Things had changed in Lionkeep over the years, but he was back there suddenly, nearly two decades in the past. Shadows grew in the chamber's threshold, the frantic throes of a woman in labour. It was his birthday, and in that room he was being born.

Inching forward, the illusion became complete as he heard his mother's cries, screaming as the midwives consoled her. The agony of his birth drove her cries through the hallway. Gilwyn pushed himself onward, unable to look away as he neared the chamber. At first he saw Gwena, the midwife who had delivered him, half hidden behind a woman's bloodied thigh. Gwena stared intently into the woman's womb. Another woman – a girl, really – stayed beside Gwena, looking frightened as the one on the bed continued to scream. She was Beith, Gilwyn's mother. Gilwyn could see her contorted face now, streamed with tears, the veins on her neck bulging with effort. Gwena urged her on, coaxing her to push the baby from her body, its head beginning to crown between her legs. Fluid rushed from the womb, staining the sheets. Beith screamed for it to end. Gilwyn reared back, the surroundings swimming and changing as the library more and more became Lionkeep. Then, inexplicably, his mother turned to look at him. When their eyes met, she scowled.

Gilwyn couldn't move. Like his mother, he wanted to scream, but even breathing became difficult as he forced himself to watch his own bloody birth. With one last momentous push, the infant that was him came tumbling out of Beith's body, wet and wailing, the cord connecting them pulsing pink with life. The midwives looked at the infant and all at once their happy faces shrouded in dread. The baby – baby Gilwyn – writhed in its own wet bounty, its hands hooked, its fingers fused to clubs. Gwena shrieked at the hideous thing and the girl at her side fainted away. His mother was sobbing, somehow knowing the monster she had birthed. Gilwyn shook his head wildly, falling back.

'That's not how it was!' he shouted.

Beith's wails followed him as he turned and ran down the shifting corridor. He was crazed by the vision and desperate to get away, and the hallway stretched out before him, changing in the darkness as he hobbled, part Lionkeep, part library. The screams of his mother fell away behind him as he manoeuvred through the coil halls, turning corners only to see another unfamiliar wall. Soon he was exhausted, and resting against the wall he caught his breath, trying to banish the horrible images. Ruana was talking to him, begging him to breathe. The long hall lead to darkness.

At the end of the corridor, an apparition waited. Gilwyn turned toward it with a moan. His mother Beith waited there, dressed in saffron, her face tranquil and beautiful. She smiled at him, raising her gentle hand to call to him. Gilwyn gripped the stone wall. She was as she had been when she was healthy, before the cancers had eaten her flesh. Like sea foam she floated toward him, the hem of her saffron dress trailing silently across the floor. Gilwyn pulled himself from the wall and drifted toward her, fascinated by the image Kahldris had conjured. He knew she wasn't real, but in every way she was his mother, picked from his memory and gloriously remade. He remembered the dress she wore, her favourite, and the way she kept her hair, straight and long around her shoulders. The serene expression on her face spoke only of her love for him, the child she missed so sorely.

'Mother . . .'

Beith met him in the centre of the hall, reaching out to take his hands. Her warm touch brought him to tears.

'My Gilwyn,' she said, her voice a perfect likeness. 'I've come back to you.'

'It's not you,' sobbed Gilwyn. 'You're not real.'

'I live on, Gilwyn. You know that. I watch you. Everyday I am with you.'

He knew that spirits walked the world; he had learned that much at least in Jador. And the touch of his mother's soft fingers made her seem so real to him.

'No,' he argued. He closed his eyes against the pain. 'You're the trick of a demon. I know you are!'

His mother leaned in closer, kissing his cheek. 'What a fine man you are now! I am so proud of you, Gilwyn.'

'Stop,' he begged, falling into her embrace. 'No more . . .'

But his mother held him closer, taking him to her bosom the way she had in his youth, and later in all those dreams when she was dead. Gilwyn sank into her, surrendering, knowing she was made from smoke but unable to resist. So sorely did he miss her, so much had he missed in those years when she was gone. Sickness had taken her, but she was back now, and for a moment he believed.

Gilwyn, stop! cried Ruana. *She is a phantom!*

Her shout broke his spell, and he pulled himself from the visage of his mother. Looking at her, he watched her eyes began to bubble in her head, the skin on her face falling off in clumps. She screamed, clawing at her body as Kahldris' magic ravaged her. Bones popped through her skin. The ivory complexion turned to dust. Then, in a heap of wailing flesh, she fell to the floor and shattered to bits.

'No!'

Horrified, Gilwyn ran. The long halls of Lionkeep became the library again, but he hardly noticed the transformation. Driven by the ghastly images, he dashed from the hall as quickly as his shriveled foot allowed, leaving behind his dead mother and the taunting laughs of Kahldris.

70

One day's journey south of Nith, in a valley not unlike the tiny principality itself, Lukien and his cohorts from Jador had reined in their horses
to bed down for the night. Dusk had settled over the surrounding hills,
casting the long shadows of twilight across the road. In the nearby
meadow, only a handful of trees obscured the flat landscape, inviting
them to rest themselves and water their horses at a lake of clear water.
Alsadair, the most anxious among them to reach Nith, agreed reluctantly
to stop for the night, and as he and Lorn watered the horses Ghost and
Lukien prepared the fire. The young albino worked fast and diligently,
and by the time the others had unpacked their things he had the fire ready
for them all, just in time for the encroaching darkness. The four of them
went through their usual routine with ease, well-practiced in the tasks of
making camp. They had ridden together for many long weeks, and over
that time had developed a rhythm to things, each of them taking on their
own set of duties. And in less than an hour, they were ready to eat.

Amazingly, cooking their rations fell to Lorn, the only one of them
with a genuine talent for it. Despite a lifetime spent being pampered by
servants, the last few years of the deposed king's existence had been
marked by doing things for himself. He knew his way around a frying pan
like an expert, and whatever meats or vegetables they had managed to
find for themselves found their way into Lorn's oddly capable hands. He
was, Lukien had discovered, a man of many surprises.

Tonight, Lukien remained unusually quiet, made thoughtful by their
closeness to Nith. Alsadair, who had guided them all the way north, bore
an unmistakable smile of anticipation. He had been gone from his
homeland for months, but he was near enough to smell it now, and had
spent the day regaling them all with the big history of little Nith. And
Ghost, who almost always played his flute while they rode, made up
ditties about Nith that had them all laughing.

All but Lukien.

The campfire leapt and crackled. On the other side of it, Ghost and

Alsadair played cards while Lorn finished making the meal. Lukien watched them through the orange glow, glad that they were with him. In Jador, before he had left to rescue Thorin, he and Ghost had been fast friends. He was more than a companion on their mission – he was a confidant, and the only one of the three that Lukien really trusted. Lukien had grown to like Alsadair during their time together, but Ghost was an Inhuman, and because of that there was a special bond between he and Lukien. They understood the magic of Grimhold better than the others. It made them like brothers.

Lukien relaxed, quietly watching Lorn as he tasted the stew simmering in his iron pot. The old king gave a nod of satisfaction, then caught Lukien staring at him. Without a word Lorn went back to his work. The two of them rarely talked, though to his credit Lorn had tried. It was Lukien who kept the Norvan at arm's length, because he neither liked Lorn nor trusted him, and he wanted no misunderstanding about that. Lorn had proven useful on the long journey, not only as a cook but also as a scout and a lookout and all the other talents martial men learn. He could fight, too. There was no doubt about that, and having his sword with them gave them all an added sense of security. Still, Lorn had only one mission in life, and it was not to free Thorin Glass.

Above all else, it was this that made Lukien uneasy tonight, and it was this that lead him to step away from the fire. Beside him lay the Sword of Angels, resting inconspicuously in its battered sheath. He retrieved the weapon and got to his feet, eager to be away from the others. Ghost was the first to notice him leaving.

'Lukien? Where you going?' he asked, lowering his cards. Alsadair swiveled to give Lukien the same puzzled look.

'I have something to do,' replied Lukien vaguely. 'Eat without me.'

Lorn looked up from his pot but said nothing. Ghost crinkled his white nose. Now that the sun was down he had taken off his protective wraps. His grey eyes danced with firelight.

'It's dark out there!' he shouted after Lukien.

'Thanks, Mother,' said Lukien. 'I'll be careful.'

It wasn't lack of appetite that drove Lukien out to the field. He was famished, as they all were, but a nagging feeling sent him away, one that he could not share with the others. So far, he had only spoken with Malator once on the long ride north, just before leaving Ganjor. His Akari had been as silent as Amaraz over the past few weeks, leading Lukien to worry. Now that they were nearing Nith, it would only be a couple of weeks more until they met Kahldris. And then?

Lukien didn't know, because Malator had done little to give him solace. And solace was what the knight needed more than anything this evening, more than food or friendship. He needed to see the face of his Akari and be told that everything would be alright. Leaving behind the light of the camp, Lukien walked through the tall weeds of the meadow, brushing aside the cattails and switches of grass. The ground was damp beneath his feet but solid. He could hear the rustle of wildlife from the nearby lake. Overhead, the moon glowed big and bright, lighting his way. He walked until the voices of his companions fell away and he could no longer see them. For what he was about to do, he needed privacy.

Finally, near the centre of the sprawling meadow, Lukien stopped. He took a breath, glancing around then pausing to stare up at the moon and the stars that had come out to greet him. He saw the great sweep of milky cosmos, feeling small beneath it and confused. In his hand he held the Sword of Angels in its sheath, and through his fingers felt the pulsing of its steel, alive with Malator. The spirit in the metal sensed his trepidation, but said nothing. Lukien pulled the sword from its sheath and held it high toward the moon, not really sure if it was a ritual or not.

'Malator,' he said, 'I need you. Show yourself to me, please.'

It took only a moment for the spirit to respond. Shimmering into being, the figure of Malator came to stand before the knight, dressed as he had been that first time they'd met in a simple shirt and trousers. Malator, youthful and confident, smiled at Lukien, clearly reading the trouble on his host's face. Lukien lowered the sword and looked at him, still amazed that a ghost accompanied him everywhere.

'You don't have to do that, you know,' said Malator wryly.

'Do what?' asked Lukien.

'Summon me like that. There's no trick to it, Lukien. If you want me, just ask. I'm always with you.'

A little embarrassed, Lukien put the sword back into its sheath. 'I wanted to speak to you away from the others,' he explained. 'You haven't come to me in a while. I was concerned.'

'I know when you are concerned, Lukien, and when you are happy or tired or hungry. I know what you're worrying about.' Malator looked around, absorbing the night air into his ethereal body. 'It's cooler here,' he said. He looked back at Lukien with a flash of mischief. 'Almost time.'

'It is almost time,' agreed Lukien. 'Are you ready? Have you been preparing yourself?'

Malator studied him. 'It's not me that needs to prepare himself. It is you, Lukien.' As though he were one of Lukien's riding cohorts, Malator sat down cross-legged on the ground, a peculiar sight considering the ethereal state of his legs. He looked up at Lukien expectedly. 'Talk,' he directed.

Lukien took his meaning, but knew not where to begin. He had a hundred worries running through his mind, and no way to quell them. Instead of sitting down in front of Malator he paced around him with his sword in hand.

'This is Nith,' he sighed. 'We're a day out. Soon I'll be seeing Aric again, and then we'll be riding for Liiria. Your brother, Malator.'

'I know,' said Malator. 'I can feel him getting closer.'

'But you haven't spoken to me about him,' argued Lukien. 'You haven't said a word about how you plan to fight him, nothing beyond what you've already told me. I want to know if you're ready, Malator.'

'And I want to know if you are ready, Lukien.' Malator's tone was surprisingly stern. 'I have all the talents I need to fight my brother. What do you want from me? A promise that I will defeat him?'

'That would be very nice, yes!'

'Well I can't give you that. So you can go on gnashing your teeth all you like. All I can do is go with you and do this thing you ask of me. But what I need is a host who won't lose his nerve.'

'What?' Lukien stopped to stare at him. 'My nerve is as steely as ever, Malator.'

'No,' said the spirit. 'I don't think it is. I've been in your head, remember. I've felt what you've felt. You see, I can't do my best unless the one who wields the sword is prepared. And all you've been doing is thinking about your last battle with Baron Glass. You're afraid.'

The words struck Lukien hard. He made to strike back, then stopped himself.

'Let me force you to face it,' Malator went on, 'since you won't admit it yourself. I'll be that little voice in your head that tells you when something's not right.' His eyes pierced Lukien, never blinking. 'When you can't sleep at night, it's because you remember lying in your blood in the middle of the road. You remember what it was like to have your muscles set on fire. And all you could do was let Glass toss you around like a doll and hope he wouldn't kill you.'

Lukien stopped breathing, confronted by his own nightmares. In the meadow it seemed that time had collapsed, bringing him back to that awful moment in Koth when Thorin held his life in his hands like so many grains of sand. Malator's hypnotic gaze held him, refusing to let him look away. Lukien shuddered.

'There's nothing I can hide from you, is there?' he whispered. 'You see me too clearly.'

'It is good to be afraid, Lukien,' said Malator gently. 'And if you cannot tell the others, then you can tell me because I know already.'

Lukien lowered his head. 'I have never been afraid like this,' he said. Even his words frightened him. 'Never in my life. I have seen death a thousand times. Hell, I have craved it! But this . . .' He groped for an explanation. 'Facing Kahldris was worse then death. Like being eaten by a dragon, slowly bit by bit.'

Malator was plainly moved. His face twisted with sympathy. 'When he and I were boys, even our mother was afraid of Kahldris. And then when he became a general, his men thought he was a demon and they were right. They followed him because he was strong and fearless, but they never loved him. No one ever loved Kahldris, because no one ever could. He gathers fear around him like a cloak, Lukien. He has had a thousand years to learn the craft. You are brave even to face him again.'

'I don't feel brave,' whispered Lukien. 'I feel like a little boy.' It was hard for Lukien to face Malator. He raised his eyes slowly. 'You are right about me, Malator. I'm afraid, and I do not know what I will do when I face him again.'

'You will fight, I have no doubt of it,' said Malator. 'But you must be as strong as Kahldris, Lukien. It will not be easy for me to battle him. You will need all your skill to give me the time I need. That means you must be there completely. If you are afraid, they will sense it and use it against you.'

'But I am afraid,' said Lukien hopelessly. 'And I cannot shake it.'

Malator rose and floated closer to Lukien. Despite his slight frame, there was a tautness to him that gave Lukien confidence. 'Then I will be strong for both of us. You must trust me.'

'I do.'

'Perhaps you do a little, but it must be complete.' The Akari laughed to leaven the mood. 'I have not been doing nothing, you know! I have been thinking, and I know I can beat my brother. I need you to believe in me, Lukien.'

Lukien gave a wan smile. 'I'm hungry,' he said miserably.

'Go back to your friends,' said Malator. 'And know that I am with you.'

The Akari disappeared then, blinking out of the world as quickly as he'd come. Lukien stared blankly at the place he had been, feeling lost.

71

By the time the Bronze Knight reached the castle, Aric Glass had already learned of his arrival. It didn't take long for the rest of the keep to spring into action, either, as the servants who regularly took care of things prepared for their new guests. Sentries at the castle gate reported that the quartet had entered the courtyard, where they were waiting for someone – anyone – to greet them. Aric, who had been occupied in his chambers when the news of their arrival came, pulled on a pair of boots and ran down the hallways of castle Nith, eager to see his old comrade. As bad luck would have it, Prince Daralor was not in the castle. The prince had been gone the last few days, visiting a cousin in a nearby province. His ministers, however, were already falling over themselves to see to the needs of their new visitors. As Aric raced toward the courtyard, he found Daralor's trusted aide Gravis waiting for him, dressed in royal finery and just as anxious as Aric to meet the newcomers. He waved at Aric to hurry.

'They're waiting in the courtyard,' said Gravis nervously. 'They're asking for you.'

'Alsadair is with them?' asked Aric as they walked briskly together through the hall.

'Alsadair is with them!' pronounced Gravis happily. He laughed, hardly believing it. 'That wily bastard – he found them!'

Aric could barely contain his glee. How many months had it been since he'd parted with Lukien? It seemed a lifetime ago, and more than once he had doubted to ever face his friend again. He had a thousand things to tell Lukien, but right now all he wanted was to see the knight and embrace him. As a curious crowd began gathering around the main hall, Aric and Gravis pushed their way toward the courtyard, at last stepping through the castle's portcullis into the cobblestone yard. At least a dozen Nithin soldiers were already there, all of them chattering as they crowded around the centre of the yard where – presumably – Lukien and his cohorts waited. Aric craned his neck for a better view, but all he could see over the heads of the people were a group of horses, their saddles empty. He cleared his throat to no avail, asking politely for the soldiers to move aside. Annoyed, Gravis made no such attempt.

'Out of the way!' barked the minister, grabbing one man by the shoulder and shoving him aside. 'Clear off!'

Whatever magic his voice held, the soldiers parted when they heard it, moving to the sides of the courtyard to reveal a foursome of bewildered men. Aric grinned when he saw them, his eyes falling immediately on Lukien, who looked around with confusion. At last the knight's probing gaze fell on Aric, and all at once a giant smile lit his face.

'Aric!' he cried. Gleefully he bolted forward, arms outstretched. Behind him, the Nithin soldier Alsadair was laughing. Lukien rushed to Aric, grabbing him in both hands. 'Aric! Gods above, it's you!'

'It's me, Lukien,' laughed Aric. He let Lukien's strong arms encircle him. 'I can't believe you're here!'

The two men embraced for a long moment, each of them choked with surprising emotion. To Aric, Lukien looked like a changed man, wearied by whatever quest had taken him away. When at last they pulled apart, Aric stole a glance at Lukien's weathered face. The knight nodded solemnly.

'It's been a hard road,' he said.

Aric sighed and touched his shoulder. 'You're here now. You can rest.' He smiled at Lukien's companions. 'All of you.'

Alsadair pushed the other two forward. One was an older man, big and fierce looking. The other, smaller man, wore desert wrappings around his face and gloves along his wiry hands. Only his two grey eyes peered out from his scarves, jumping with excitement. Aric studied them both, thinking them equally peculiar.

'Welcome,' he told them. 'I'm Aric Glass.' He gestured toward Gravis, still beside him. 'This is Minister Gravis. He runs things here for Prince Daralor.'

Gravis bowed to them slightly. 'Welcome to Nith,' he said smoothly. 'We have been waiting for you.'

Alsadair stepped up to them, bowing to Gravis and losing his giddy grin. 'Gravis, this is Lukien of Liiria. These others are his companions, from Jador.'

Gravis smiled at him. 'Well done indeed, Alsadair. We have waited for you as well. We are proud of you.'

Alsadair swelled at the compliment. 'I should like to take them to Prince Daralor myself,' he said.

Gravis shook his white head. 'The prince is in Yaroo province,' he said, 'and won't be back until the morrow.'

The news deflated Alsadair. 'Oh . . .'

'It doesn't matter,' said Aric cheerfully. There was nothing that could spoil his good mood. 'You're here now, that's what matters.' His gaze dropped to Lukien's belt. 'And you found the sword.'

As though they all knew what Aric meant, the crowd fell quiet. Lukien gently patted the weapon at his side, a great blade resting in a threadbare scabbard. 'I have found it, Aric.'

Aric felt a charge. 'The serpent kingdom?'

'It exists,' said Lukien. 'The sword was there, waiting for me.'

'Amazing,' Aric sighed. 'I must see it. But first . . .' He gestured for the others to come closer. 'Introduce your friends, Lukien.'

'I am Ghost,' said the one with the head scarves. He bounded forward like a child. 'And I am not a Jadori.'

'No?' said Aric, confused. 'What are you, then?'

'I am an Inhuman,' pronounced the man, who Aric guessed was young. 'Do you know what that means?'

'Easy,' counseled Lukien.

Ghost laughed. 'Oh, let me show them, Lukien. These brave people are helping us! Let them see that we are not ourselves helpless.'

Lukien sighed as though he had seen the young man's performance before. 'Very well,' he said with a wave. 'Watch him closely, Aric.'

Aric puzzled over the young man, waiting. The rest of the crowd did the same.

'They call me Ghost,' declared the stranger, 'because I can simply disappear.'

And then he was gone. Aric gasped. Astonished, the crowd stepped back. The stranger's laugh bounced through the courtyard.

'What's going on?' asked Gravis. His serious face turned red with anger. 'What's this trickery?'

'No trick,' said the young man's disembodied voice. 'Magic!'

The astounded soldiers looked at Alsadair, but the Nithin merely smiled. 'It's what he does,' he offered sheepishly. 'Amazing, isn't it?'

'It's witchery!' said Gravis.

Lukien rolled his eyes. 'Show yourself, Ghost,' he ordered.

The stranger popped back into view, this time standing right beside Aric, who jumped as he felt his arm around his shoulder.

'What?' Aric blurted. He looked at Lukien then back at the stranger. 'What is this?'

'Don't be afraid,' said Ghost with an audible smile. 'I'm an Inhuman. Surely Lukien has told you what that means.'

Aric had only a vague idea. Uncomfortable, he squirmed out of the man's grasp, then looked at the older man. 'And what do you do?' he asked. 'Fly?'

The crowd laughed, even Minister Gravis. But the man with the fierce eyes merely shrugged. 'Nothing so extravagant,' he said. His answer left mystery in the air. Lukien stepped between the man and Aric.

'This is Lorn,' said Lukien. 'I'll tell you about him later.'

'Alright,' agreed Aric. He laughed again, too pleased from seeing his old friend to let anything worry him. 'Let's go inside. You need to rest.'

'And to eat,' said the one called Ghost. 'We've had nothing but Lorn's cooking for months.'

Two hours later, Lukien found himself seated at a long table beneath a chandelier lit with glowing candles. The table had been set with fine silverware and crystal goblets full of wine and beer. Platters of steaming food and breads covered the linen tablecloth. Lukien and his cohorts had rested, the Nithin servants falling over themselves to make the strangers comfortable. Alsadair had said his goodbye's to them, rushing off to see the family he had left behind so many months earlier. While Lukien and the others refreshed themselves, Aric disappeared until their supper was ready, reappearing in the splendid banquet hall to unveil the treasures the kitchen had cooked up for them. Minister Gravis, sure that the old friends wanted to be alone, excused himself from the feast, leaving just the four of them – Lukien, Ghost, Lorn and Aric – to enjoy the meal and catch up on all the news they had for each other.

Lukien revelled in the meal and Aric's company. After so many weeks on the road, just having a roof over his head was a treat. The banquet room itself was an elaborate confection, full of expensive artwork hung on its mahogany walls and lit by a trio of wrought iron chandeliers that made the chamber glow with warmth. The long, striking table seemed to reach from wall to wall, surrounded by a collection of high-backed chairs, all of them richly upholstered in red velvet. The servants that darted in and out of the chamber paid no attention to the conversation, doing their best to keep the wine flowing and the good food hot. Ghost flirted with the prettiest servants, flashing his wolfish grin as he held out his tankard for more beer. Because they were inside and out of the sun, he had removed the cowl from around his face, smiling flirtatiously to any girl who would pay him attention.

Lorn, meanwhile, listened cagily to everything that Aric told him, breaking a mutton joint in his hands and eating slowly, never saying a word. Like Lukien, he sat diagonally across from Aric, who had placed himself at the head of the table. Lukien glanced at Lorn occasionally, taking in the sly way the old king hung on every word. So far, none of them had told Aric about his true identity, and Lorn didn't seem to mind the pretense. With endless patience, he listened to Aric tell his story, relating every detail about his life since he had parted with Lukien in Koth a year earlier. Lorn chewed his food carefully, never making too much noise, always waiting for any mention of Norvor or his hated nemesis, Jazana Carr. Lukien knew this and did not mind. He would have to tell Aric the truth about Lorn, he realized, but saw no hurry in ruining their reunion.

Lukien leaned back in his chair, sipping on his wine as he listened to Aric tell of his days with Raxor of Reec. In years gone by, old Raxor had been an enemy of Lukien's. More than once had the two of them met on the battlefield, but that was long ago, before the peace between Liiria and Reec. Lukien hardly knew Raxor at all now, but listening to the story of his son's slaughter made the knight wistful.

'And then I went to the bridge and saw my father,' said Aric. His face grew dark, the memory of the day souring his mood. Young Aric lowered his eyes to stare into his wine goblet. 'They told me he wasn't a man any more,' he said softly. 'I don't know what I was thinking when I rode to the front. At first I couldn't even see anything. It was all just a black swarm. And then I saw him on the bridge. I tell you, Lukien, he looked like a demon, sitting there on his horse. And the river was choked with bodies. *Choked.*' Aric shook his head as if he still couldn't believe what he'd seen. 'After that I rode back to Raxor and begged him to retreat.'

The men around the table fell silent. Ghost had stopped grinning, and Lorn had pushed his plate aside. Lukien groped for the right thing to say, but nothing could erase what Aric had endured.

'What happened then?' Lukien asked. 'You went back to Reec with him?'

Aric nodded. He hesitated, as though he were hiding something. 'I didn't stay with him long,' he said. 'By then he knew about Nith and wanted me to come back here and wait for you. He said that he'd be ready if the time ever came, and that he'd stand with us when we returned.'

Lukien was intrigued. 'Do you believe him, Aric?'

'I do, Lukien. I tell you, I have seen such strange things this last year! Raxor is a good man. He's nothing like I'd thought he'd be. He's as crusty as an old loaf of bread, but his heart is good and I trust him. He'll be ready for us when we return, I know it.'

'We'll need him,' said Lukien. 'You say Daralor has only a few thousand men to bring with us?'

'I don't even think it's that many, really,' said Aric.

'And Raxor? He's already been beaten by Thorin. He can't have that many men, either.'

'Reec is still strong,' said Aric confidently. 'But it's not about numbers, Lukien. Raxor could have thrown everything he had at my father, it wouldn't have mattered. I'm telling you, you had to have seen him!'

'I did see him,' Lukien reminded Aric. 'I fought him, remember.'

Aric grimaced. 'I remember. But he's changed even since then. He's much worse now, Lukien.'

'And he's had time,' said Lorn, finally breaking his silence. The big man looked at all of them seriously. 'Without Reec to bother him he's had all the time he needs to build up his forces, to call up reserves from Norvor. Tell me, Aric, what about that? You have hardly mentioned Norvor or Jazana Carr.'

Aric shrugged. 'I have no news, not since leaving Liiria. Travelers don't come here to Nith.'

'Then we must assume the worst,' Lorn concluded. 'Baron Glass will be waiting for us, and Jazana Carr's dogs will be surrounding him.'

Lukien nodded at the deduction. 'When Daralor returns, we should speak to him, ask him just how many men he can muster for this.'

'Lukien, it won't matter,' Aric insisted. 'Three thousand men or a hundred thousand, my father could take them all if he wanted. Everything he told me about his armour is true – he's invincible in it. Only your sword can stop him now.'

Leaning against Lukien's chair rested the sword. If he listened very closely, he could almost hear its rhythmic humming. The awesome responsibility for bringing down Thorin rested with the sword now, and with the man who would wield it. Aric didn't need convincing. He was sure that only Lukien and his magical sword could save them.

'I think,' said Lukien, 'that I should like to speak with Daralor when he returns. Sword or not, I will still need to get to Thorin, and that will take men. He's not just going to come out of Lionkeep and fight me this time.'

'Then we'll draw him out,' said Lorn, 'and his bitch-queen with him.'

Aric bristled at his tone. 'Sir, it's time you did explain yourself . . .'

'No,' said Lukien. He smiled. 'Forget him, Aric. I want to know more about what happened to you. Where did you go after I left?' He paused, hoping Aric would take his meaning. 'Where did everyone go?'

Young Aric blanched. 'Oh. I think I see what you mean.' He glanced at the others uncomfortably. 'How much do you want me to say, Lukien?'

It was plain that Aric had bad news. Lukien braced himself. 'What happened to her?'

'Lukien, I haven't told you this yet. I don't know if I should.'

'Tell me, Aric,' Lukien insisted. 'What happened to Meriel?'

Aric shifted. 'She's in Reec, Lukien. With Raxor.'

'What?'

'I know it's hard to believe. I didn't even believe it myself at first! She was captured, Lukien. She meant to go to my father as she threatened, but Raxor's spies in Koth found her and brought her to him in Hes. When I went there, I saw her.'

Lukien's mouth hung open in shock. 'Aric, you left her there?'

Aric nodded, looking ashamed. 'I had no choice. I spoke to her. We argued. I don't know if she's still there with him, but he wouldn't let her go and I don't think she would leave him, either.'

'So you left her there.' Lukien fought to still his anger. 'Like she was just some harem girl, you left her behind.'

'I had to, Lukien. I had to get back here, to tell Daralor what had happened and to wait for you!'

'You should have demanded Raxor let her go!'

'I did!' snorted Aric. 'But he loves her, Lukien. And I'm not sure, but I think she loves him, too. He's a broken man. She's all he has.'

'She's not a slave,' Lukien rumbled. 'She's being kept as a prisoner.' He pounded his fist on the table. 'You should have stayed with her, Aric. You should have made Raxor let her go!'

'You weren't there!' Aric shot back. 'You went off without her, remember? You're the reason she wanted to go to my father in the first place!'

Both Ghost and Lorn shrank away as Lukien got to his feet. With a face like thunder, Lukien said, 'I brought her across the desert because she wouldn't make a move without me. She hung around me like death because she loved me. I never wanted her love, but I never wanted her discarded, either.'

Aric remained seated, staying as calm as he could. 'It's not like that, Lukien. Raxor is good to her. He doesn't treat her like a slave or plaything. He's kind to her. Kinder than you were, probably. And you know what else? She was happy there!'

Lukien was about to erupt, then stopped himself. He reached for his chair as he stared at Aric – and at Aric's accusations. 'I'm supposed to trust Raxor now?' He laughed. 'I'm surrounded by men like that!' He looked with disdain at Lorn. 'Tell him who you are, Lorn. Let Aric have a good laugh.'

Lorn got up from his chair. 'Sit down, Lukien. You're drunk.'

'Drunk! Yes!' cackled Lukien. 'All my enemies are here to help me. And why? To kill my best friend!'

'What enemies, Lukien?' said Ghost. 'We're not your enemies.'

'Raxor is my enemy!' roared Lukien. He picked up the sword, and with a swipe of his arm sent the plates and glassware near him flying off the table. The crash of dishes brought the servants running, but Lukien ignored them, pointing his sword – still in its sheath – at Lorn. 'And this hideous pig of a man – he's my enemy. He's everyone's enemy! I'm just Minikin's messenger boy, bringing him back to Norvor!'

'Lukien, that's enough,' hissed Ghost.

Aric stood puzzled, looked between Lukien and Lorn. 'I don't understand,' he said. 'Lorn?'

Lorn, staring down Lukien's sword, declared proudly, 'I am Lorn, the rightful king of Norvor. I'm going home to reclaim my throne.'

'You're not,' sneered Lukien. 'I won't have it.'

Lorn looked almost serene. His expression infuriated Lukien. 'I'm the rightful king,' he said. 'You know I am, Lukien.'

'You are a butcher and a tyrant,' spat Lukien. 'Minikin must be out of her mind to let you go.'

'Minikin owes me. I lived up to my part of our bargain.'

'Bargain?' Aric piped up. 'Lukien, I don't understand this.'

'Your bargain was with her, yes,' said Lukien to Lorn. 'Not with me.'

'So what will you do?' challenged Lorn. He stood his ground, looking unafraid of the crazed knight.

'I should put you down like a sick dog,' hissed Lukien.

'You may not find that so easy,' said Lorn calmly.

'Oh, I knew this was coming!' cried Ghost, who jumped onto the table between them. He turned to Lukien, making sure to push the tip of the sword aside. 'Put it down,' he directed. 'You don't want to fight here, Lukien.'

Lukien's hand began to tremble as he stared into Lorn's hard face. The Norvan was icy calm as he returned the glare. Aric hurried to Lukien's side.

'Put it down, Lukien,' he echoed angrily. 'I don't care what your grievance is with Lorn. This is Daralor's house!'

'Right,' sighed Lukien, at last relenting. He lowered his sword without ever having unsheathed it, shaking his head miserably. 'Aric, do you want to know this man's history? Ask him. He'll tell you everything. He's proud of it.'

'It doesn't matter,' said Aric, holding his gaze. 'We're all going to Liiria.'

'That's right,' chirped Lorn.

'Shut up,' Ghost snapped at him.

Lorn withdrew with a scowl. He began to leave the banquet chamber, then stopped to glance at Lukien. 'Sooner or later you'll have to trust me, Lukien.'

Lukien shook his head. He said to Ghost, 'Go with him.'

Reluctantly, the albino followed Lorn out of the chamber, taking the stunned servants with them. Lukien laid his sword on the table, sorry for the things he had said to Aric, the scene he had caused. Aric waited a long moment before going back to his chair. But he did not sit down. He merely paused there expectantly.

'I did care about her,' said Lukien.

Aric nodded. 'I know you did. I did what I could for her, Lukien, just like you.'

'When you see Raxor again, you must try to get her free.'

'I'll try, Lukien.'

The awkwardness between them was intolerable. Lukien looked at Aric and smiled. 'I'm drunk.'

They both laughed.

'King Lorn the Wicked?' said Aric. 'Is it him, really?'

'Aye,' lamented Lukien. 'Truly, I am cursed.'

Aric began to laugh more loudly, taking his seat. He licked his lips as if he still had a secret. Lukien eyed him, knowing the man too well.

'What are you laughing at?' he asked.

'Lorn.' Aric stopped laughing abruptly. 'Maybe it's nothing . . .'

'What? Tell me, Aric.'

'It's really just a rumour.'

'What?' pressed Lukien.

Aric looked around to make sure no one was listening. 'He's going to hear it from someone, it might as well be you. I didn't mention this yet because it didn't seem important, not until we started talking about Norvor. There's something you should know, Lukien.'

'Aric,' groaned Lukien. 'Tell me!'

'It's about Jazana Carr,' said Aric. 'We do get some news here in Nith. Lukien, we heard she's dead.'

72

Old King Raxor knelt on the dirt floor of the arena, his face buried in warm, brown fur. Broud, the big male bear, wrestled him playfully, using its powerful jaws to tickle his shoulder and its big, clawed paws to leverage him aside. As Varsha looked on with mild interest, waiting for her own turn to entertain her master, Raxor lifted Broud to his hind paws, then let the bear dance backward, loudly calling out his approval. Broud, who seemed to get bigger every time Raxor saw him, remained upright for Raxor's pleasure, balancing expertly the way he had been taught. Raxor clapped his hands and laughed, letting the bear fall gently forward, then called his sister forward.

'Varsha, up,' said Raxor, and with a wave of his hand brought the female upright. Varsha stretched her muscled body skyward, prancing the way she'd seen her brother do. The bag of treats at Raxor's side brought a quick reward. 'Good,' praised Raxor happily. It would be the last he would see of his two beloved bears, and he wanted to remember them perfectly.

Above the open-air arena, the morning waned quickly into afternoon. Sunlight leaned heavily on Raxor's weathered face. He sweated in his velvet garments, not at all dressed for a day with his pets. Where he was going, he needed to look the part of a king, but his heart was here with the siblings, and he knew he would miss them horribly. One at a time he tossed the bears the bread balls from his bag, taking his time. He had asked General Moon to wait for him, and the old soldier had relented to the request, yielding to the king's idiosyncrasies. There was a long march ahead of them and all was ready, prepared for months as Reec simmered from its many loses. Reec was hardly the country Raxor remembered. It had changed so much since he'd returned from Liiria.

'Why do things have to change?' he asked his bears. 'Why do men have to get old?'

Broud and his sister ignored the question, more interested in the treats being tossed into their snouts. Their silence reminded Raxor why he had come to the arena today. Today, he needed the solace of the place, the simple companionship of the bears. In all of Reec a storm was brewing, but not so in this peaceful place. As it had been for so many years, the arena and its inhabitants were a refuge for Raxor. His country had gone mad. Too many mothers had lost sons in Liiria, and too many fathers were crying for revenge. Raxor himself had lost his son, and the heart-break of that gave him insight into the madness of his countrymen. He had tried to keep a lid on the boiling pot, to wait until Aric and their Nithin allies arrived, but he had heard nothing from Aric in months, not since getting his letter, and the rage of his Reecians would not be quelled.

'Only blood,' mused Raxor with a sigh. 'That's the only thing they want.'

Raxor himself wanted blood. He wanted Baron Glass on the end of his lance for what had happened to Mirage. For weeks, the news of her death had spiraled him into depression, and when he had awoken from it the lament of his people had become too much to ignore.

Raxor felt around in his bag of treats. It was empty. He looked at the bears apologetically.

'That's it.'

Broud looked sad. His sister Varsha came up to nuzzle Raxor's leg. Between them both, they had left a slick of brown hair on his fine garments. Seeing it made Raxor smile. His people loved him, but thought he was mad, and he did their bidding now because they demanded it. Raxor was not afraid of facing Thorin Glass again. He had hoped to do it with Nithin help and the aid of the enchanted sword, but those things had never happened, and wounded Reec could wait no longer.

It was time for Raxor to go.

He said his good-byes to his beloved twins, then turned to make his way down the corridor that would lead him to the street. In the shadow of the corridor he saw General Moon. The general nodded, realizing the king was ready, then escorted him out of the arena. Raxor could see the sunlight beckoning at the end of the rounded hall. General Moor moved stiffly as he walked. Like Raxor, his mood was morose. He was, however, a military man, and would do his duty no matter how distasteful. Raxor took the lead as the two of them moved out into the sunlight, stopping at the edge of the street to see the passing parade.

The avenues of Hes were choked with marching soldiers, all the men that she could muster. Thousands of them, armed and gleaming, snaked their way past the king. West they marched, toward Liiria, toward the looming unknown of battle. King Raxor's horse waited for him, surrounded by loyal bodyguards. General Moon motioned Raxor toward his mount.

'If you're ready, my lord,' he said.

Raxor was ready. For Roland and Mirage, he would once more face the Black Baron.

73

Alone in the library, a pile of unread books spread out before him, Gilwyn paged through the yellow leaves of a dusty tome, trying vigourously to read the foreign penmanship. His eyes stung as his mind wandered through the words. He had never been able to decipher the strange tongue of Marn, at least not as well as Figgis could, but this one book intrigued him and he continued, occasionally picking out a word he recognized. He read by sunlight, waves of which came though the big windows of the reading room. The empty library echoed with his tiny sounds as he gently turned the pages. It had been nearly two weeks since he had returned to the library, and he did so today only reluctantly. But time was running out and Gilwyn knew it. If he was ever to find a way to break the bond between Thorin and Kahldris, he had to do so quickly.

Gilwyn leaned back with a doleful sigh, exhausted from his morning with the books. Nothing, not even the obscure texts from Marn, told him what he wanted to know. He gave a little curse for the catalogue machine. That vexing collection of rods and pulleys had been no use to him at all. Nor had the endless volumes of manuscripts. Nothing had helped Gilwyn unlock the secret he needed. He began to feel defeat creeping over his shoulders.

Keep going, urged Ruana. *Don't give up.*

'It's hopeless,' Gilwyn rumbled. He slammed closed the book from Marn, sending up a cloud of dust. 'I can't even read it.'

You're tired. Rest a bit. Then try again.

'No,' said Gilwyn. He grit his teeth. 'All right, yes.'

Ruana smiled in his mind's eye. *If it's here, you'll find it.*

'Ah, but what if it's not here? What if I'm wasting my time?'

There is an answer, Gilwyn. You're close.

As tired as he was of reading through the book, Gilwyn was even more tired of Ruana's encouragement. In all his life he had never met a more cheerful soul. To Ruana, every puzzle had a solution. Being an Akari herself, she should have known how best to beat Kahldris, Gilwyn thought. But she did not. She knew only as much as Gilwyn himself, and they had already been over that tired knowledge a hundred times.

A noise outside the window snagged Gilwyn's attention. He bolted upright with alarm, then realized it was the wind.

'Damn it.'

Calm yourself, Ruana urged.

But Gilwyn could not. His feud with Kahldris had frazzled him. It was not enough that the demon had made him face his mother in the library that day, and every day since. Now his dreams were filled with poison. He woke up sweating every midnight. More than once Kahldris had turned his broth to blood and filled his shoes with maggots. They were illusions, but they were all too real for Gilwyn, so that now every small sound made him jump. He had endured Kahldris' conjurings for two unendurable weeks. Keeping himself awake at night to avoid the nightmares had made him as brittle as an old branch. His hands shook and his eye twitched at the corner. He waited frantically for his mother's agonized face to appear in every pool of water. Sometimes she spoke to him, other times she simply wailed, giving off a glass-shattering lament.

Gilwyn closed his eyes, trying to refocus his mind. Kahldris had played the game well, and had driven Gilwyn to the edge. But the last two days had been blessedly quiet. There had been no nightmares, no unwanted visitations from his past. It was as if a truce had been called between the two of them, and Gilwyn had honoured it. He had not gone to Thorin or bad-mouthed Kahldris to Lionkeep's staff. He had simply enjoyed the respite.

Still, he had work to do. He surveyed the stack of books awaiting him, unsure where to start again. They were books on varied subjects, but all with an underlying theme of death and the spirit world. The fact that none of them even mentioned the Akari no longer bothered Gilwyn; he had given up on that tack. Now, all he wanted to know was how the bond between man and spirit was formed. And how it could be broken.

He thought of White-Eye again, and how she had lost her beloved Akari, Faralok. It was pain that had driven him away from her, the intense pain of the desert sun. According to Minikin, the pain had shattered the bond between human and Akari forever. It seemed a simple enough plan, but how could anyone inflict such pain on Thorin Glass? When he wore his armour, he was invincible. And he had lost an arm in battle years ago. He knew pain already, and how to cope with it. To Gilwyn, the notion of inflicting such pain on Thorin seemed hopeless.

'White-Eye was young,' he mused aloud. He considered this, and how little pain she had really endured up until she lost Faralok. 'She didn't know pain until then, not really.' He rubbed his temples distractedly. 'And if I'd been there to protect her . . .'

Stop, said Ruana. *There's nothing to be gained.*

Gilwyn nodded, but in his heart felt the emptiness. It was good to be back in the Koth, among his books and his own people, but more than anything he wanted to see White-Eye again. He told himself that soon this nightmare would be over, and that Lukien would return to save Thorin from himself, but he didn't really believe it. Too many months had passed. And he could not leave Thorin, not after the promise he had made to him.

'I have to save him, Ruana,' he whispered desperately. 'It's up to me.'

Then, like a cold breeze, he felt Kahldris roll into the room. At first he did not see the demon. There was only the chill on his skin and the strange sense that they were not alone. Frightened, Gilwyn looked to the threshold of the chamber, then saw a shadow growing beneath the archway. The shadow poured itself like treacle, rising from floor to ceiling into the black shape of a man. A dark maw opened to speak.

'There once was a boy named Gilwyn Toms,' came the booming voice, 'who thought he could save the world.'

'Fate above,' Gilwyn gasped.

The black mass congealed and solidified, changing suddenly into Kahldris. The demon stood in the doorway, smiling, holding a book in his hand. The book opened effortlessly, the pages turning. Kahldris shook his white head.

'You can look and look forever, boy,' he taunted. He snapped the book closed and tossed it into the room where it landed near Gilwyn's table. 'What have you found? Anything? Is there anything at all in this whole cursed place that's any help at all?'

Gilwyn rounded the table to face the spirit. 'You finally decided to come yourself, eh? No more apparitions of my mother?'

'Your mother tires me,' sighed Kahldris. 'Don't worry, boy – I will think of other nightmares for you.'

'Go ahead,' challenged Gilwyn. 'I'm still here. You can't frighten me away, no matter what form you come in.'

Kahldris floated into the reading chamber. 'I have frightened you. You haven't come back here for days. My little trick scared you, didn't it, boy?'

Gilwyn hardened. The way Kahldris had turned the familiar library into a labyrinth had indeed frightened him, but he would never admit it to the demon. 'You can't keep me away from here. Somewhere in here there's a book that will tell me what I want to know.'

'You're wasting your time,' said Kahldris. He waved his ethereal hand at the books on the table. 'All this superstition and nonsense, writing of shamans and charlatans. What do you hope they will tell you? Your own Akari can't tell you how to beat me!'

'Get out,' Gilwyn thundered. 'Go, get away from me.'

Kahldris looked hurt. 'Oh, now you're angry. What will you do? Tell Baron Glass? Go run to him like a little boy? You haven't done that yet, and you won't because he won't have anyone speak against me. Don't you see? You're losing him.'

Infuriated, Gilwyn stood his ground. 'If I was losing him, you wouldn't be here. You're the one who's afraid, Kahldris. That's why you're here to threaten me.'

'No, indeed, Gilwyn Toms,' said Kahldris. His expression was mischievous. 'I'm here to warn you, that's all.' He cupped a hand to his ear. 'Listen . . .'

Against the silent backdrop, Gilwyn heard footfalls suddenly. His heart tripped. 'What's that?'

'A surprise,' said Kahldris.

'Another of your tricks.'

'Not a trick,' said the demon. He stepped aside so that Gilwyn could see down the hall. 'You have visitors.'

Gilwyn heard voices rolling down the corridor, the rough sounds of men. He looked around suspiciously, but so far nothing in the library had changed.

'I assure you, it is not my conjuring,' said Kahldris. 'Go and see for yourself. And remember what I said, Gilwyn Toms – you are losing Baron Glass.'

As quickly as he'd come, Kahldris disappeared, blinking out of the chamber, leaving Gilwyn alone and bewildered. From the corridor outside, he heard the voices nearing, swarming through the library on booted feet. Alarmed, he hurried out of the chamber toward the noise. It wasn't Thorin, Gilwyn knew – he would have recognized Thorin's voice immediately. But Thorin hadn't told him about any visitors to the library, and as Gilwyn rounded a bend in the hall he was stunned by what he saw at the other end.

A man was moving through the library, backed up by a dozen Norvan soldiers. More soldiers moved behind them, fanning out through the halls and varied chambers. As Gilwyn came to a halt, the man caught sight of him and stopped, and suddenly a wide grin cut his rocky face. He was dressed like a nobleman, his vestments velvet and expensive looking, his black boots polished to an ebony shine. A blue cape drifted off his wide shoulders, flowing down his arrow-straight back. He acknowledged Gilwyn immediately, summoning him forward like a stable hand.

'You, boy,' called the man. 'Come here.'

Gilwyn hesitated. The soldiers were Norvan; he could tell by their dark uniforms. Norvans were common in Liiria, but he had never seen the stranger before. 'Who are you?' he asked. 'What are you doing here?'

The man in the blue cape strode toward him, followed directly by his bodyguards. 'Your name is Gilwyn Toms, yes? I expected to find you here. Baron Glass told me to find you.'

'Thorin? What's he to do with this? Who are you?'

'I am Duke Cajanis,' the man pronounced, as if offended Gilwyn didn't know. 'You are Gilwyn Toms, aren't you?'

'Yes,' said Gilwyn cautiously. He had heard the name Cajanis before, mostly among the Norvans who protected Lionkeep. 'Duke Cajanis, from Hanging Man?'

'There is no other Duke Cajanis, boy,' laughed the nobleman. Like sycophants, his bodyguards laughed, too. 'Why do you look so surprised?'

Gilwyn wasn't sure how to answer. 'I wasn't expecting anyone here today, my lord. I was working alone when I heard you and your men.' He shrugged. 'I don't understand why you are here.'

Duke seemed puzzled. 'We're here to protect the library. Don't you know that?'

'Protect the library? No, my lord . . .'

'Yes, boy, yes,' Cajanis insisted. 'We're here to see what's needed.' He looked over his shoulder, saying to his men, 'It should be easy to defend. Frial, go with your men. Have them go around the back of the hill. I want to see if there's any other way up here.'

One of the man nodded and broke away. Another offered his own appraisal. 'We can dig in on the road, my lord. And barricade the courtyard. We can station archers in the towers to keep from being charged.'

'What?' Gilwyn blurted. 'What's going on here?'

Duke Cajanis turned on him, annoyed. 'I told you, boy, we're here to start defending the library. There's a lot to do, you know, and you'll just be in the way.'

'Duke Cajanis, I don't understand,' Gilwyn pleaded. 'No one told me anything about this. I wasn't expecting you or anybody! Please tell me what's going on.'

The duke's eyebrows knitted, seeing Gilwyn's distress. He told his men to go about their business, then put his big hand on Gilwyn's shoulder as he led him down the hall. 'Gilwyn Toms, you can help me,' said the duke. 'Baron Glass says you know this place better than anyone.'

'Baron Glass hasn't told me a thing about this!'

The duke guided Gilwyn away from the others. 'I see that,' he said, not unsympathetically. 'How old are you, boy?'

'Nearly nineteen,' replied Gilwyn.

'Nineteen? Then you are man enough to know the truth. Liiria is in danger. The Reecians are on the march again, and word from Marn is that Nithins are coming, too. They're making ready to war on us, and we're making ready to defend ourselves. That's why I'm here.'

Gilwyn was shocked. 'Thorin didn't tell me about this . . .'

'Baron Glass likes to keep you in the dark, it seems. No matter. You'll know it all soon enough. He sent for me and my army to help defend Koth. The rest of them will be coming in the next week or so. We're going to make sure nothing happens to the library this time, so don't be afraid.'

'No, this can't be right.' Gilwyn reeled away from the duke. 'Thorin would have told me!'

Duke Cajanis stiffened. 'Ask him yourself if you don't believe me. War is coming, Gilwyn Toms. The Reecians have already reached the Kryss. There are five-thousand of them, and no telling how many Nithins are on the way.'

It was all too much for Gilwyn, who could barely believe what he was hearing. If the Nithins were on their way, that meant Lukien might be with them. But what about the Reecians? Hadn't they been trounced already? Gilwyn tried gamely to keep calm, wondering just how much Thorin had withheld from him, his heart breaking with the thought.

'Duke Cajanis, what's going to happen now? I mean, what is Thorin planning?'

'Planning? What he's always been planning, boy! To kill his enemies.'

'Yes,' said Gilwyn with a nod. 'His enemies . . .'

'They're all coming now. They mean to take Koth for themselves. Norvor too, if we let them.' The Duke put his hands together, cracking his knuckles. 'But we're stronger than they think.'

'Yes.' Gilwyn grimaced, knowing the duke was infected by the same paranoia as Thorin. 'So Thorin sent for you, then. He told you to come here to the library?'

'This is where we'll make our stand,' proclaimed the duke. 'Not in Lionkeep.' He smiled at Gilwyn with warm insanity. 'This time, we're going to make sure nothing happens to the library.'

Speechless, Gilwyn could only watch as Duke Cajanis turned back to his men and began shouting orders. The Norvan soldiers swarmed through the library, checking through the windows for good vantage points and sizing up the thick walls. As the duke walked away, he waved for Gilwyn to join him.

'Come along, Toms,' he chirped. 'You can help us.'

But Gilwyn couldn't move. Distraught and deceived, he thought only about Thorin and all the good times they'd spent together. Had he made progress? He had thought so, but now he knew the truth. Then, like a flickering candle, Kahldris' face flashed across his mind.

You see? the demon whispered. *You are losing.*

As he followed after Duke Cajanis, Gilwyn's ears rang with Kahldris' laughter.

74

Between the principality of Nith and the vast country of Liiria, only the city-state of Farduke stood as a barricade. For the army of Prince Daralor, that meant only a week-long march between home and their enemies, with only Farduke to stand in their way. The princes of Farduke had seen the army coming from their towers of bronze, having been made aware of the Nithins days before by Daralor's heralds. Word had come back from Farduke's rulers that they would not join the crusade to oust Baron Glass, but neither would they obstruct the Nithins in their march. Prince Daralor, who had openly voiced his disgust for Farduke during the trek north, laughed when his heralds returned with the news, and told his men to be careful when crossing Farduke territory.

'Don't crush the flowers,' Daralor ordered his lieutenants.

It was the kind of contempt Lukien had come to expect from Prince Daralor, a man with so many contradictions he was impossible to predict. He kept to himself, surrounded by his council of trusted advisors, but he spoke openly and warmly with Aric Glass, treating the young man like a little brother. At times, he barked fierce orders at his men, hissing at them to keep their pace or to better groom their animals, but every night while the army camped Daralor made sure to visit every campfire and see that his men were all right.

For such a small country, Daralor had arrayed an impressive army. Besides his cavalry, which numbered close to a thousand, there were twice that many infantry marching alongside the horses, proudly displaying the green flag of Nith above their armoured heads. Daralor's kennel masters had also brought with them nearly a hundred fighting dogs, great, hard-headed beasts with skin like leather and wide, slobbering jaws filled with sharp teeth. Lukien, who had fought against dogs in battle before, made sure to keep well away from the barred wagons that housed them. At night, when the men bedded down, Lukien could hear the soulful howling of the dogs. More than a few Norvan soldiers would lose their throats to the monsters, he was sure, but it was hawks that truly intrigued Lukien.

Prince Daralor had an obvious affinity for using animals in battle, and so had brought three dozen trained hawks with him to use against Thorin. Aric had explained to Lukien that Daralor was a master hawker, and that his flying pets would make awesome adversaries in battle. The birds, which were kept in giant mesh cages, looked at Lukien peculiarly as he trotted alongside them. Like the dogs, they frightened Lukien, because he could not understand how their little brains worked or what they were thinking. They were a mystery to Lukien, like Daralor himself, and whether or not any of them could be trusted still alluded Lukien.

Lukien had spent very little time with Daralor since meeting him in Nith. A few days after reaching the principality, Lukien, Ghost and Lorn were quickly on the march again, this time heading for Liiria with Daralor's army. The prince himself had not taken the time to meet with Lukien privately. He was cordial to Lukien, seemed impressed by him, and that was all. In the brief exchanges they had at the castle, Daralor explained to Lukien how important it was that Baron Glass be stopped, and how much he detested the cowardly kings of Farduke and Marn and Jerikor, all of whom had spurned Aric Glass' pleas to join them. Yet Daralor did not elaborate on his reasons for joining the crusade. He simply said that it was necessary, and that was all, leaving Lukien to wonder about his motives. They were pure, Lukien was sure, but that did not keep him from being curious.

Aric, on the other hand, seemed completely at ease with Daralor. Daralor was a man of principle, Aric told Lukien, one of only two such rulers on the entire continent. The other ruler was Raxor, of course, who Prince Daralor himself called a 'courageous old fool.' Now that they were nearing Liiria – and the border with Reec – Aric was looking forward to his reunion with Raxor. Rumours abounded that Raxor's army had already taken up positions near the river Kryss, ready for his rematch with Baron Glass. Aric chaffed a little when he spoke of it, openly worried about the old king. Like the rest of them, he was eager to reach Liiria and find out what was really going on.

Out of all of them, however, Lorn was the most anxious to return home. As they drew farther north, the rumours about Jazana Carr's death continued to grow. Some said she had killed herself. Others, amazingly, claimed Baron Glass had killed her. And to confound them even more, some people they met on the way north told them nothing at all about Norvor or the Diamond Queen, completely ignorant about both. To Lukien, the rumours were fascinating, even frightening. But to Lorn they were intoxicating, tantalizing him with the notion that he just might be able to win back Norvor without a fight. Lorn and Lukien had spent very little time together since leaving Nith. Day by day, Lorn became more withdrawn, keeping to the rear of the army as it snaked its way north and rarely joining others at meal time. Mostly, the Norvan brooded, and while he rode his mind was a thousand miles away, his steely eyes hiding the dark workings going on behind them. No one in the company trusted Lorn, especially not Prince Daralor, but no one had forbidden Lorn to accompany them, either. He was a willing sword in the fight against Baron Glass, for that reason alone Daralor accepted him.

Lukien had spent a good part of his over-long life on the road with soldiers, and so it was easy for him to fall into the natural rhythm of the march. Even with his homeland looming ever-nearer, he managed to remain calm and appreciate the long days and quiet nights. He had almost given up on ever getting to know Prince Daralor, until at last the enigmatic prince called Lukien to his tent. It was on the second night out of Farduke. The army had marched for miles that day, making good progress in the cooperative weather. Men had begun to bed down for the night, and cooking fires were already roiling. Lukien and Ghost had prepared their own places for the night. Because both of them were famished, they waited in line with the other Nithins while the cooks prepared supper. Lorn, as usual, waited alone, not joining the line. As Ghost passed a comment about their quiet friend, the ubiquitous Alsadair made a surprise appearance, taping Lukien on the shoulder.

'Prince Daralor wants to see you,' he said. He looked at Ghost. 'And you, too.'

Ghost perked up. 'What's this?'

'A meeting,' said Alsadair. He was uncharacteristically stiff as he spoke, his tone without humour. 'We'll be at the border soon. It's time.'

'Time for what?' asked Lukien curiously.

'He wants to speak to you,' said Alsadair. 'He'll tell you why when he sees you. Bring Lorn, too.'

'Aw, do we have to?' groaned Ghost.

But Alsadair was already waving at Lorn, summoning him forward. Lorn put down the boots he was shining and sauntered over to the group. When he heard about Prince Daralor's meeting, a grin bloomed on his wolfish face.

'What's it about?' he asked.

'Just follow me,' said Alsadair, herding the men out of the food line and guiding them toward Daralor's tent. As usual, Daralor's pavilion had been hastily erected at the rear of the encampment, close to the river they had been following north. It took Daralor's men less than half an hour to erect it, practicing the feat to perfection every night of their journey. A handful of guards milled outside the entrance to the tent, stepping aside as the newcomers approached. Lukien recognized most of the guards, soldiers he had got to know during their journey. Inside, he heard the eager voices of others who had already gathered. Alsadair pushed aside the flap of the tent and stepped inside, revealing the big, stark interior. Though the sun had already gone down, the tent glowed with warm lamplight. A long, flat table had been brought in to accommodate Daralor's guests, all of them his closest advisors. The men spoke nervously among themselves as they passed along the pitchers of wine and beer. Among them sat Aric, abstaining from the drink. Young Aric brightened when his eyes caught Lukien's, motioning for him to sit in the chair he had saved for his friend. At the head of the table sat Daralor himself. The prince looked imperious, not saying a word as his gaze jumped from man to man. He greeted Lukien and the others with a cursory nod, his maimed hand awkwardly cupping a tankard. On the right side of Daralor sat Trayvor, his trusted lieutenant. Daralor rarely made a move without Trayvor. On the left side of the prince sat a man Lukien had never seen before. From the looks of him he was not a Nithin, either. As Lukien took his seat beside Aric, he noted the man's heavy red beard and puffy blue eyes. The man looked exhausted, his grim clothes dirty from riding. To Lukien, he had the dangerous look of an assassin.

'Who's the stranger?' Lukien whispered as he sat beside Aric.

'Don't know,' said Aric. 'I just got here.'

Ghost took the seat beside Lukien. 'What's this about?'

Aric shrugged. 'Don't know that either.'

Lorn found an empty chair on the other side of the table, directly between two of Daralor's aides. He spied the red-bearded stranger suspiciously, refusing a drink offered by the soldier to his left. The old king looked uncomfortable, as if dreading Daralor's news. Lukien felt a similar shiver. None of them spoke, waiting for the prince to explain things. At last Daralor cleared his throat and got to his feet.

'You want to know why you're here. You can probably imagine why. We're just days out of Liiria now. It's time to plan.'

There was steel in Daralor's voice. Every man around the table straightened.

'By the end of this week we will be at the border. We've marched for miles and our journey is nearly ended. We are strong and we are ready to fight, and it's time for all of us to get right with our hearts and with our heads.' Daralor looked around the room at each of them. 'We're not all coming back.'

The men nodded quietly. At his side, Lukien felt Malator squirming within the Sword of Angels.

'Horatin, stand up, please,' said Daralor. He gestured to the stranger with the red beard. The man stood, his arms at ease at his sides. Daralor continued, 'You've all noticed him. His name is Horatin. He's a Reecian, a member of Raxor's Red Watch.'

The prince waited for a reaction. It came quickly in gasps from the men. Lukien reared back a little, stunned. As one who'd fought the Reecians for years, he knew a thing or two about the Red Watch. They were indeed assassins, and the best spies on the continent. At once a hundred questions leapt to Lukien's mind. Daralor stayed them with a raised hand.

'He came this morning, in secret,' said Daralor. 'From Raxor himself. The Reecian King has prepared himself for battle.' Prince Daralor gave a smile to Aric. 'He's kept his promise to us.'

'I knew he would,' Aric whispered faintly.

'Horatin has risked his life to come here. Others of the Red Watch weren't so lucky. He's brought news with him from Liiria you all need to hear.'

Ghost leaned into Lukien's ear. 'He must be a good spy,' he chirped. 'I didn't see him come in. You?'

Lukien shook his head, hushing Ghost. Daralor turned to the Reecian, bidding him to speak. In his weary voice, Horatin began, 'My king sends his greetings, and his thanks. He is grateful to brave Nith. My country and king have suffered greatly, and we are grateful to have your help. I left my king three days ago. His army is at the river Kryss, waiting to cross the border into Liiria.'

'He doesn't know about us yet, not for certain at least,' Daralor piped in. 'But news of our army coming north has reached Liiria.'

'Right,' said Horatin. 'We heard about you not even a week ago. My king sent me down to find you, and to find out if you were really coming north.'

'King Raxor has been waiting for us, apparently,' said Daralor, a bit ruefully. 'And not very patiently, either. Horatin has told me that his king is . . .' The prince hesitated. 'Let's say he's unwell.'

Horatin grimaced at the description. 'King Raxor has lost his son. And thousands of other men, too. The people of Reec demanded he move against Baron Glass. They love Raxor and have rallied to him. He's ready to die for them, but now he waits to see if the rumours of Nith coming to help are true.'

'So he's ready to fight?' Lukien asked.

Horatin looked at him, then at Daralor. The prince said, 'You can answer him.'

'Yes, my king is ready,' said Horatin to Lukien directly. 'What is your name, sir?'

Lukien stood. 'My name is Lukien of Liiria.'

Recognition flashed on Horatin's face. He grinned wildly. 'I thought as much.'

A charged moment passed between the two old adversaries. Daralor put himself between them quickly, saying, 'I've told Horatin about all of you. Even you, King Lorn. But we will get to that. More importantly, Baron Glass has been making ready for us. He has his armies dug in around Koth, especially around the old library.'

'Glass is obsessed with the library,' said Horatin. 'He's making every effort to protect it this time.'

'That makes sense,' said Lukien. 'Library Hill is better fortified than Lionkeep, and a lot higher. Aric and I have fought from Library Hill. It'll definitely give Thorin an advantage this time.'

Aric nodded uncomfortably. 'That's right. Horatin, how many men does my father have?'

'It's hard to tell,' replied the Reecian. 'We've had spies in Koth, but too many of them have been captured or killed. Not many Liirians have come to Glass' banner. They're Norvans, mostly. And there's a new man with Thorin, a duke from Hanging Man named Cajanis.'

Lorn grunted in disgust. 'I know him. He's loyal to Jazana Carr.'

Horatin said, 'He's brought an army of at least three thousand with him, and more are on the way.'

'And what about Jazana Carr?'

The question, of course, came from Lorn, who could not contain himself any longer. Horatin turned to Lorn, seeming to recognizing him. Daralor nodded as if to confirm the Reecian's suspicions.

'You are King Lorn,' said Horatin. 'Then you most of all will want to know this. The rumour you have heard about the Diamond Queen is true. She is dead.'

Lorn sat frozen in his chair. 'Dead. You are sure?'

'There is no doubt of it. I myself was sent to kill her at Richter, along with Baron Glass. But the queen wasn't with him, and Baron Glass discovered our plot. Two good men of the Red Watch died that night by the baron's own hand.'

'And Jazana Carr?' pressed Lorn. 'What of her?'

'A few days later she was dead,' said Horatin. 'When Baron Glass returned to Lionkeep he beat her. I don't know why; no one knows why. After that she killed herself.'

'You're sure of this?' asked Lukien.

'There is no doubt of it, Sir Lukien.'

The news left Lukien strangely empty. In the years he had spent in Jazana's service, she had always been kind to him. Her conceits were legion, but her heart was bigger than her brain. Seeing Lorn's glee over her death angered Lukien.

'This is great news,' said Lorn, sighing as though he had slipped into a warm bath. 'Without Jazana Carr, Norvor has no leader. They will welcome me again.'

Lukien gritted his teeth, holding back an insult. Daralor steadied Lorn's excitement.

'Your Norvans follow Baron Glass now, King Lorn. Until he is gone, you still have no kingdom.'

'Excuse me, Prince Daralor, but Baron Glass is not a Norvan, and I think I know my people a bit better than you do. Baron Glass has the bitch-queen's fortune, no doubt, but not her blood. The people need a rightful ruler.'

'Maybe,' said Horatin sharply, 'but Baron Glass won't let go of Norvor easily. The dukes of Norvor flock to him still, because he is powerful and they are afraid of him. Listen to me, all of you – not one of you really knows what we are up against.'

'I do,' Aric spoke up. 'I've seen my father close up, Horatin.'

'As have I,' said Lukien. 'Your words are well meaning, Reecian, and I respect them. But I don't need to be taken to school about Baron Glass or what he has become.'

'And the rest of you?' queried Horatin. He scoffed in their faces. 'Be cocky at your peril.'

'We are Nithins, Watchman,' chastened Daralor. 'We do not frighten easily.'

'That is good,' replied Horatin, 'because once you see Baron Glass in his armour, you will know what hell looks like.'

'Baron Glass is near his end,' predicted Lorn. He pointed at Lukien. 'The Bronze Knight holds the means to his undoing.'

'Fate above, who knows?' said Lukien, shaking his head. 'I have the Sword of Angels. You've heard of it by now, Horatin. Whether or not it can beat Baron Glass, even I cannot say.'

Daralor appeared disappointed. 'Lukien, you will not be alone. We will all be fighting to beat Baron Glass.'

Aric shrank at this. Lukien put a hand on his shoulder and said to him, 'And some of us will be trying to save him.'

'Baron Glass is our mutual enemy,' said Lorn. 'I have no problem with that. When he is done, I will return to Norvor as king.' He looked pointedly at Lukien. 'And then I will send for my family, just as I promised them.'

The barb bounced off Lukien, who was wholly disinterested in the argument. 'Horatin, tell us what else you know,' said Lukien.

Daralor took up a rolled parchment leaning against his chair and laid it flat across the table. 'With what Horatin knows we can start planning our movements.'

'I'm sorry, Prince Daralor, that's not what I meant,' said Lukien. 'I have a personal question, if I may.'

'Personal?' said Horatin.

Lukien leaned forward. 'It's about Baron Glass and Koth. There was another of us from Jador who went to north to Liiria, a boy named Gilwyn Toms. Have you heard anything about him?'

'Ah, the boy!' Horatin laughed. 'He is Glass' obsession.'

'He's alive?' asked Lukien.

'He is. Baron Glass protects him. He's given the boy the library to run. He's like a son to the baron. From what our spies have told us, the two of them are inseparable.'

'I knew it!' crowed Lukien. 'I knew Gilwyn would still be alive!' He clapped his hands together gleefully. 'And if Gilwyn is alive he's been trying to reach Thorin. Aric, there's hope for your father yet.'

Aric smiled grimly. 'Maybe. But if there's not and he must die, then that is how it should be.'

But Lukien was in too good a mood to think such dour thoughts. Just hearing about Gilwyn had lifted his spirits out of the doldrums. Daralor continued to speak, tracing his finger over his map and quoting figures to his aides. The back and forth continued for nearly an hour. Lukien listened to all of it, satisfied that the prince had done his best. They would likely be outnumbered when they got to Koth, and Thorin would have the advantage perched high on Library Hill. Still, the Nithins had the heart and the charisma of Daralor to lead them. The Reecians had something even more powerful – a thirst for vengeance.

Finally, when Daralor had said his peace, he glanced across the table at Aric, who had listened to the back and forth without adding a word. 'Aric,' said Daralor gently, 'it's time you went back to King Raxor. Horatin will be leaving in the morning. I want you to go with him.'

Aric nodded, giving no complaint. 'If that is best, Prince Daralor.'

'We'll need to ride fast,' said Horatin. 'My king still doesn't know for certain that your army is coming north to join him. He has to have this news quickly.'

'I can ride fast,' Aric assured him.

'Good,' said Daralor. He gave Aric a warm wink. 'We'll be behind you, just as quick as we can. The rest of you, make yourselves ready. In a few days, we'll be at war.'

They were being dismissed, and Daralor's aides knew it first. The Nithin officers got to their feet and began filing out of Daralor's tent. Ghost and Aric did the same. Lorn lingered a bit longer, catching snippets of conversation on his way out, as did Lukien. Horatin took his time, still talking with Prince Daralor as the meeting broke up. Lukien watched the Reecian, hoping for an opportunity to speak with him. There was still one question pressing in his mind, a matter even more personal than that of Gilwyn. Deciding not to be rude, Lukien left the tent to wait for Horatin outside. Ghost and Aric had already headed back to the food line, while

Lorn had cornered two of the Nithin officers, peppering them with questions. The camp had fallen silent as most of the army had settled down for a night's rest. Daralor's bodyguard's outside the tent eyed Lukien but did not shoo him away.

Finally, Horatin emerged, looking haggard and hungry. He walked past Lukien without noticing him until the knight hurried up behind him.

'Horatin, wait,' called Lukien. 'I have a question.'

The Watchman paused and turned toward him. 'Yes?'

Lukien was careful to keep his voice low. 'It's about your king. Aric Glass told me about a woman he keeps, a foreigner. Her name is Mirage.'

Horatin drew back. 'What of her?'

'Do you know her?'

'I know of her,' said Horatin. 'Why?'

Lukien decided to tread carefully. 'Horatin, I know she is your king's woman. Aric told me about them. I just want to know how she fares.'

'She is a friend of yours?'

Lukien nodded. 'Yes.'

'I see.' Horatin averted his eyes. 'Sir Lukien, the woman Mirage is not in Reec. She left my king some time ago to be with Baron Glass.'

'She did?' Lukien was stunned. 'But I thought King Raxor was in love with her.'

'He was indeed,' lamented Horatin. 'That did not stop her. Nor did my king stop her, either. He gave her leave to go the baron.'

'So what then?' asked Lukien. 'Have you had any word from her?'

Horatin's discomfort grew. 'We have had no word from her, no. Sir Lukien, I did not tell you all of my story about our attack on Richter. Jazana Carr was not there. We were mistaken.'

'So?'

'The woman Mirage was at Richter with Baron Glass, not Jazana Carr. I'm sorry, Sir Lukien. Mirage is dead.'

Lukien stared at Horatin, his breath stopping in his throat. 'Dead?' He swallowed, feeling his legs grow wobbly. 'Mirage is dead?'

Horatin's blue eyes filled with pity. 'She died in the fire. No one made it out of Richter alive. Only Glass.'

'A fire.' Something inside Lukien crumbled. 'A fire . . .'

He turned, walking off and shaking his head. Horatin was saying something, but Lukien heard none of it. All he could think of was Mirage, and how she had burned to death. She who could control flame, who had given up that gift for a mask of beauty.

'Just so I would love her,' said Lukien, and went numb with horror.

75

Since the arrival of Duke Cajanis, Library Hill had become an armed camp.

Gilwyn hardly recognized his beloved library any longer. The emptiness – the solitude he had come to worship – had been replaced by the constant clang of metal and the shouts of armoured soldiers. Nearly every room of the place had been turned into barracks for the Norvans and Liirians who poured through the great doors, all of them bearing weapons and provisions and other things for the siege ahead. Books, scrolls and manuscripts had been carefully laid aside, packed into the cellars while the shelves were lined with swords and the oiled book cases burdened with clothing. Even the fabulous entry hall had been stuffed with bunks and bed rolls, so that the men lucky enough to sleep there for the night could look up at the magnificently painted ceiling as they fell away to sleep.

It had taken nearly a week for the transformation to take hold, but now it was nearly complete, leaving Gilwyn bewildered and displaced. Surprisingly, Duke Cajanis had been kind to Gilwyn during the changes, even sympathetic. The Norvan noble was careful not to upset the young librarian too much, and made sure that Gilwyn always was consulted when books were moved or rooms commandeered. It was in fact an orderly transformation, done with military precision, and Duke Cajanis was proud of his quick accomplishment. Now, when one looked out from the library's many windows, the sight of the road leading up to the hill was fortified with men and battlements and the courtyard filled with weaponry. The library had swelled into a formidable fort under Cajanis' hand, and the soldiers who milled about its grand halls readied themselves for the coming assault.

Rumours abounded in Koth these days. Norvan spies returning from the border spoke of Raxor's army, an impressive force of many thousands said to be waiting to cross the river Kryss. Raxor himself led the forces, just as he had done the first time, determined to finish the job he had started months earlier. Retribution was in the air, said the Norvan spies, and King Raxor was ready to avenge his fallen son, telling all who would listen of his intention to slay Baron Glass. Rumours from the south were no less ominous, telling of the Nithins who marched freely up from Farduke with their fighting hawks and broods of battle dogs. Prince Daralor had summoned every able man in his tiny country, claimed the rumours, and had given orders that none of them were to return home while Baron Glass remained alive. Gilwyn listened to the rumours with interest, frightened and exhilarated by them, but one claim in particular had him galvanized – the Bronze Knight was returning.

Even Thorin knew this one rumour to be true. Through Kahldris, he could sense the approach of Lukien and his magic sword, and had told Gilwyn that the final battle was nearing. After days without seeing each other, Thorin had called Gilwyn to him in his little parlour in Lionkeep, looking haggard from the endless hours of preparation. By the light of the crackling fireplace, Thorin had leaned forward in his big leather chair as if to tell a terrible secret.

'Our days are numbered now, Gilwyn.' Thorin's tone bespoke his misery. 'Lukien comes.' He shook his head as if there could be no doubt. 'And we will certainly battle.'

Gilwyn did not question Thorin that night. Since Cajanis had arrived, the two of them had slipped the bonds of friendship growing strong between them, growing apart instead as the demands of war took Thorin further away. And though Gilwyn had not yet given up his hopes of reaching Thorin, he realized now that Kahldris' hold on his friend was stronger than he'd imagined, and that only the supernatural power of Lukien's sword might be able to break it. Along with Ruana, Gilwyn had racked his brain to think of a way to shatter the demon's grip on Thorin, but he had always come back to the same, impossible puzzles. Intense pain could sever the bond between host and Akari, but Thorin no longer knew pain. Ensconced in his enchanted armour, he was truly untouchable.

Twelve days after Cajanis' arrival, Thorin finally called all of his commanders together. Using the finest of the library's grand meeting chambers, he ordered the shelves removed and rows of chairs placed in their stead, along with a table he could use to speak from. Duke Cajanis organized the event, and with his usual aplomb had the meeting scheduled sharply at noon. By a half hour prior to the hour, the great chamber swelled with officers, all of them eager to hear the words of their benefactor, Baron Glass. Gilwyn, who was surprised to be invited to the event, sat not far from Cajanis himself, occupying a chair in the very first row. Because it was a formal meeting, no drinks or food were provided at all. The ranks of officers sat sombre-faced in their chairs, chatting quietly to each other. Norvans made up the bulk of the audience, though there were many Liirians in the crowd as well. Thorin had done an impressive job over the past months of bringing the Liirian military back to life and had openly declared himself their supreme commander, a boast no one dared challenge. Among the Liirians were soldiers who Gilwyn had got to know during his time in Lionkeep, including the good-hearted commander Kilvard. Kilvard, who was not a handsome man like Cajanis, wore a hang-dog expression as he waited for Baron Glass. Unlike most of the soldiers, Kilvard had no interest in the diamonds that kept the others loyal to Thorin. He was a true nationalist, motivated by the need to protect his country. He was loyal to Baron Glass because no one else had taken control of the chaos engulfing Liiria, and that was all. Gilwyn eyed Kilvard curiously as he sat back and waited. The pipe in the old man's mouth spouted patient puffs of white smoke.

At noon precisely, the big mahogany clock at the end of the chamber announced the hour. A moment later, Thorin stepped into the room, even the clock seemed to go dead.

He had dressed for the occasion, donning the Devil's Armour, which shined with blinding. His enormous figure filled the doorway, his steps heavy from his armoured feet. The skin of metal clung to his muscles, fitting perfectly to them, flexing with life at every breath. Thorin's eyes scanned the room, his smile wide and frightening. He wore no helmet, but rather left his head bare, displaying his white yet youthful hair. His two big fists rested at his sides, covered in spiky gauntlets. Stepping into the chamber, he paused to the gasps of the gathered, swelling at their astonishment. Duke Cajanis was first to his feet. Taking one step forward, the Norvan clapped at Thorin's arrival, first alone, then joined by others until at last the gathering was up and cheering. Gilwyn looked around, shocked at the outpouring of affection. He knew it was fear that motivated most of them, and could not help but pity them all. Thorin strode proudly to the table, waiting for the cheers to die away. His eyes met Gilwyn's with a twinkle of approval that Gilwyn did not return.

'Sit, all of you,' boomed Thorin.

He raised his hand to quiet the crowd, repeating his request until the noise relented and the soldiers took their seats. Thorin took a deep, satisfying breath, his hands resting palms down on the table. Behind him, two huge flags were draped side by side along the wall, one Liirian, the other Norvan. The scene appalled Gilwyn. Just months ago, Thorin had murdered Norvor's queen.

'Friends,' began Thorin, 'you honour me. You are the saviours of Liiria, and of Norvor too. Together we will do great things, but first we have a challenge. Once again our enemies are upon us. Once again we are called to fight and to sacrifice.'

There was nodding within the crowd. The most loyal of the soldiers vocally agreed. Others, Gilwyn noticed, squirmed a little.

Thorin continued, 'On our eastern border, our enemy Raxor has returned. Last time we were merciful. Last time, we let Raxor and his army flee our land. And how do they repay us? By threatening us once again. Once more they seek to take what is ours.' The baron clenched his fist. 'But this time, we will not be merciful. This time, we will crush them utterly.'

The chamber rang with dutiful applause. Duke Cajanis cheered the bellicose words.

'Raxor comes with another great army,' Thorin went on. 'As large as his last one. He is beloved by his people and we are sorely hated by them. They fear our strength, and that is wise of them. But they are not alone. This time, they have allies.'

'Nithins,' spat Cajanis.

'Aye,' Thorin agreed. 'What could possibly tempt the Nithins from their long hiding if not madness? Do you see? Madness grips our world! This hatred for our nations – for Liiria and Norvor both – is a jealousy that compels the world to hate us. Look how the nobles of Farduke have turned on us, too. With not a word of complaint they have let the Nithins soil their land just so they could come to conquer us. In Marn they are just as silent, and in Jerikor too. Does anyone come to our aid? Has any one of these nations sent their ambassadors here? Have they offered the smallest kindness to us? No they have not.'

It went on like this, Thorin laying out his case for war, the officers of his combined armies nodding in agreement. Gilwyn listened, disgusted by the speech, sure that it was Kahldris stoking Thorin's madness. The man who had once been so kind to Gilwyn had vanished, and in his place stood a ranting lunatic, fanning the fires of suspicion. Thorin's big voice rose and fell, filled with emotion as he worked the crowd. He told them about the force of the Nithins coming toward them, and how they numbered in the thousands. They had their creatures with them, he said, their slobbering dogs and their fierce birds of prey, merciless monsters both. And with them came Jadori, Thorin claimed, foreigners who had joined the alliance against them. Here, Thorin's words had special meaning to Gilwyn. Thorin actually seemed saddened.

'Who knows what baneful magic they bring against us,' he lamented. 'I have been among them. I know they are powerful. They are good and decent, too, but they have joined against us and so they too are our enemies. Perhaps, when we are done with this grisly work, we will settle the score with Jador as well.'

Gilwyn sat bolt upright at this. They were Kahldris' words, without a doubt. It was Kahldris who threatened Jador, Kahldris who hated the

Jadori and their alliance with the Akari. Gilwyn shook his head vehemently at Thorin, but the baron ignored him. Before he could protest, however, another voice joined the fray.

'What of your son, Baron Glass?'

The question shattered Thorin's oratory. He searched the room for the culprit, fixing on a Liirian officer in the second row.

'What?'

'Your son, Baron Glass. What about Aric?'

'What about him?' Thorin growled.

The officer held fast. 'It is well known that your son was in league with the Reecians at the battle of the Kryss, and that he was one of the Royal Chargers defending the library when you invaded Koth with Norvor. I'm asking only what part he might play in the coming battle.'

The crowd held its breath. Stunned, Gilwyn watched as Thorin's face twisted with discomfort. He almost never spoke of his son Aric, and certainly never in such a public forum. His suffering looked unbearable.

'My son has decided to defy me,' he said. 'He will ride against us when the time comes, I have no doubt.'

'Will he rejoin the Reecians?' asked the officer. 'I ask because that might make a difference in our plans. We may attack Raxor's forces, but none of us has the wish to harm your son, Baron.'

Thorin shrugged off his concerns. 'When the library fell to us, the Royal Chargers who were left alive melted away. They are brigands now. Some will join with the Reecians, certainly, others with the Nithins. And others will not have the courage to join either one. My son has courage, but it makes no difference.'

The reply confused the audience, prompting Duke Cajanis to speak. 'Baron Glass, if your son goes to Raxor's side, then the man unlucky enough to slay him in battle will have your doubts to deal with. How can you assure us that it matters so little to you? He is your flesh and blood.'

Thorin said simply, 'If my son chooses to join my enemies, then it is his conscience that should be troubled, not mine.' He clamped his hands together and smiled. 'That is all I have to say. We are done.'

They had their orders, and the officers of Thorin's armies rose and took up their noisy conversations, some thanking Thorin for his time, others shaking their heads. Gilwyn remained seated, unsure what to do next. Duke Cajanis was always in need of him these days, but the duke was one of the first to exit the chamber, off on one of his many errands. Thorin stayed at the table for a long while, shaking hands and making promises to the sycophants in the crowd. Eventually, the chamber thinned of people. Gilwyn stood and watched them go, waiting for his chance. Finally, when the last of the stragglers left the room, Thorin strode softly toward Gilwyn.

'I'm glad you came,' he said warmly. 'It is important that you know what we're up against.'

Gilwyn tried hard not to look the way he felt – angry and dejected. 'You asked me to come, so I came,' he said.

'What did you think?'

'You were very . . . spirited.'

Thorin nodded. 'To lead men in battle, one must have spirit, Gilwyn. These men need to see that I am committed to them completely.'

'Oh, I'm sure they saw that,' sighed Gilwyn.

'You are upset with me.' Thorin put his hand on Gilwyn's shoulder and led him back to his chair. They both took seats facing each other. 'I know I have not spent much time with you lately. I'm sorry.'

Gilwyn laughed. 'Is that why you think I'm angry? No, Thorin.'

'No? Then what?'

'All of this!' Gilwyn swept his arm across the chamber. 'All the things that have been done to the library. The war, Thorin!'

'Ah, the war. Yes, of course. Gilwyn, how many times have I told you this day would come? I never lied to you. I could not have been clearer.'

'I know,' said Gilwyn. 'You did tell me. But I thought—'

'You thought to save me from Kahldris! Yes.' Thorin stood up, exasperated. 'Have I not told you a thousand times that I owe Kahldris everything? And look! Did he not prophesize all of this? My enemies are coming for me, Gilwyn, just as Kahldris said they would. Just as I told you they would!'

'I know!' cried Gilwyn in frustration. 'But you've given up on yourself! You don't even want to think that I might be right, that maybe somewhere inside of you is the man you used to be.'

Thorin said calmly, 'That man is a memory now.'

'Like Jador, you mean? Have you forgotten them, too?'

His accusation stung Thorin. 'Jador should no longer concern you. You're here now, with me.'

'Yes, I am, but I'm still a person of Jador, Thorin. And you are too, like it or not. How can you turn on them? How can you even think of such a thing?'

'I am the ruler of Liiria. I do not have time for sentiment.'

'No,' said Gilwyn bitterly. 'Not even for your own son.'

'My son? You have no idea how my son has broken my heart, Gilwyn. He's not like you. You came here to save me. Aric comes to kill me.' Thorin turned away. 'But he is still part of me, damn all. I won't let Raxor take him from me.'

Gilwyn looked up. 'What do you mean?'

'I mean,' said Thorin, 'that I will not let anyone claim him for their

705

own. He already has a father who is a king, he does not need to look to Raxor for that.'

'You can't stop him, Thorin. He's probably already there.'

'I have no doubt of it,' grumbled Thorin. 'But he cannot remain with Raxor. I will not allow it.' Thorin smiled suddenly. 'But let's not talk of that now. Gilwyn, I am afraid for you. Things will not be safe here much longer. You cannot stay.'

Gilwyn was startled. 'What?'

'It's too dangerous here in Koth.' Thorin touched his shoulder again. 'I am grateful for your loyalty, boy. You are braver than most. But this is no place for a librarian.'

'Thorin, it's a library.'

Thorin laughed. 'Not anymore. Until the battle is over it is a fortress. And you are a civilian.'

'But where will I go?'

'I've already made arrangements. You'll leave in two days for Borath. There's a farm there where you'll be safe. You'll have bodyguards to protect you. When this is over I'll send for you.'

Gilwyn got to his feet. 'No.'

'Yes, Gilwyn.'

'No,' said Gilwyn adamantly. 'I'm not leaving. I told you I'd stay by you. You're not pushing me away, Thorin.'

'You're being stubborn . . .'

'I don't care.' Gilwyn folded his arms over his chest, living up to the accusation. 'I made a promise to you, Thorin. You can't make me break it.'

Instead of looking angry, Thorin beamed. 'You are brave,' he crowed. 'Stupid, but brave. Very well, then, Gilwyn, you may stay.'

He started toward the exit. Gilwyn called after him.

'Thorin?'

'Yes?'

'What about your son? What are you going to do?'

The baron thought for a moment, then replied, 'I'm going to do just what you're trying to do, Gilwyn. I'm going to get him back.'

Then he left, leaving Gilwyn behind and bewildered.

76

Through the hard sheets of rain, Aric glimpsed the village nestled between the mountains, surrounded by Raxor's resting army. The village was called Kreat and it had taken Aric and his cohorts four days to reach it, riding through the never ending rain and the sad, familiar terrain of Liiria. Raxor's army had been too big to keep a secret, and in fact the old king had not even tried to hide his presence. In all the towns they crossed to reach Kreat and all the travelers they questioned on their way, the five riders heard the same predictable tale. King Raxor's army had come across the border days earlier and had made camp in Kreat, waiting for their chance to march on Koth. No one had challenged them, either, not a single of Baron Glass' men. In the midnight rain, Aric could see the sleepy village ensnared like a noose by the rolling encampment, smothered by the countless Reecian soldiers. Pinpoints of light glowed from smouldering campfires, and in the little homes of the village candles flickered against the night. Aric blew into his hands, frozen now from the chill and breathing a sigh of utter relief. The last few days had been an agony, a break-neck trek across Liiria that had tested all of them, even Horatin. Next to Aric, the trio of Nithin bodyguards let their own relief show on their wet faces. Cold and hungry, each of them longed for the peace of the village.

'No one's seen us yet,' said Horatin. Of the five, the Reecian was the most understated, and seemed disappointed at the lack of fanfare. The lateness of the hour had most of Raxor's army asleep, and it had been Horatin that had insisted on the night-time ride. 'Stay with me,' he instructed the others. 'Don't say anything – let me do all the talking.'

Aric and the Nithins happily agreed, driving on their weary mounts. Despite the desperation of their pace, it had been a mostly uneventful ride through Liiria, and the quiet had unnerved them. They had all expected to encounter trouble, especially Aric, but the countryside had been unusually silent and only once had they encountered any soldiers. That had been two days ago, when Horatin had spotted a platoon of Norvan mercenaries marching north toward Koth. The encounter had forced them into a detour, taking them further out of their way, but they had ridden hard and fast to make up the time, and had reached the Reecian border in short order. Amazingly, they discovered the truth of the rumours they'd heard. Raxor wasn't on the border – he had already crossed it.

Tucked into the side of his horse's tack, Horatin carried a small, unlit torch, its head wrapped with old fabric. As they neared the village he pulled the torch free and turned to his Nithin comrades.

'Trace,' he said, 'let me have your lamp.'

The bodyguard named Trace kept an oil lamp in his hand as they rode, containing a tiny flame that helped to cut the dark night. Even in the rain the glass lamp had managed to retain its flame, but now they needed a signal to announce them. Trace, who was not much older than Aric, handed the lamp to Horatin, who unceremoniously lifted the glass portion and touched the flame to his torch, setting it quickly ablaze.

'That should get their attention,' quipped Aric. 'It feels good not to be hiding anymore.'

The five men rode purposefully toward the encampment, Horatin holding aloft his torch, waving it from side to side. The rain poured down from the black heavens, blinding Aric and stinging his face. He longed for a warm place to spend the night, but the size of the homes and the many men already camped outside told him how unlikely that was. Horatin called out to his fellow Reecians, and before long they were sighted. Men began climbing out of the sodden bedrolls or mounting their horses to greet them. A trumpet sounded somewhere in the darkness, and all at once the camp roiled to life, undulating like a big, black mass. Aric kept close to Horatin as the Watchman had instructed. Trace and the other Nithins crowded around to protect him.

'It is I, Horatin of the Red Watch!' bellowed Horatin. 'I have returned!'

Men gathered around them as they reached the outskirts of the huge camp, squinting to see them through the darkness. A few bold soldiers drew their swords to challenge them. Horatin quickly reined in his horse, holding up both hands.

'Hold,' he ordered the soldiers.

'It's him,' someone mumbled, and then the others quickly agreed. Another man, an officer, shouldered through the crowd.

'Horatin?' he queried.

Horatin peered through the rain, unsure of the voice alone. When at last he saw the man's face clearly he laughed.

'Corvat, it's me,' said Horatin. 'I found them – I found the Nithins!'

'Living Fate, did you?' The Reecian spied Aric and laughed. 'Just the four of them?'

'There are many others,' said Horatin. 'Where's the king?'

The man named Corvat pointed toward the village. 'In the house by the river,' he said 'I'll take you.'

Horatin agreed, and let Corvat lead them through the throngs of men, shouting out orders to make way and inform the king of Horatin's return. Aric and his companions remained on their horses, trotting slowly through the rain under the curious gazes of the soldiers. Corvat shouted at them to disperse, ordering them back to bed, and soon the way ahead was clear. At last Aric could see the flapping flags of the Reecians through the gloom. The chimneys of the village houses belched smoke into the air. It occurred to Aric as they rode that he was still shrouded by the darkness and rain, and that no one had yet recognized him. Horatin picked up on this immediately, leaning over to whisper to Aric.

'Say nothing,' he said lowly. 'I'll get you into see the king. It will be our surprise.'

They rode on, passing a number of small houses and farmsteads, some of which still were occupied by Liirian families. Aric could see them through the windows, toiling with housework even at midnight. Surprised, he wanted to pepper Corvat with questions, wondering why the villagers had not fled. He supposed they were being held prisoner by the Reecians, a notion that infuriated him, but he held his tongue as they continued on toward the river, where a small, pretty house of cobblestones rose up from the rolling green grass, surrounded by a fence and a yard filled with soldiers. The men in the yard all stood, obviously awaiting them.

'That's it,' said Corvat. The soldiers dragged his palm across his forehead to wipe away the rain. 'He'll be waiting for you by now.'

'Tell me, Corvat, how does he fare?' asked Horatin.

'Some days better than others. You'll see what I mean. Just don't expect too much of him. It's late.'

'He'll want to talk about what I have to tell him. You should gather your officers.'

Corvat agreed, and as Horatin and the others dismounted the Reecian started giving orders to the men in the yard. A captain came forward, introduced himself to Horatin as Grenel, and offered to take them inside while Corvat gathered the other officers. Aric and his Nithin bodyguards got in line behind Horatin. Captain Grenel looked them over, but did nothing to question them or Horatin's judgment. Horatin, whose reputation obviously proceeded him everywhere, told Grenel firmly to take them to King Raxor.

'He's waiting for you,' said Grenel. 'This way.'

The little house was warm and quaint, and the moment Aric stepped inside he felt its homey embrace. Typical of Liirian farmsteads, it had one main room where the family gathered, furnished sparsely with wooden chairs and chests and a table where the occupants could take their meals. Because this home was slightly grander than the rest, it had an open-air hallway leading to the kitchen, a common way of keeping fires at bay. Aric could see the kitchen across the covered walkway, noting an older woman working there over the fiery pots. Hearing them come into her home, she shot a glare at Aric, who quickly looked away.

The newcomers had barely taken two more steps when out of the adjoining chamber stepped Raxor, startling them all. Raxor paused when he saw Horatin, looking immensely pleased. Horatin bowed quickly to his king.

'My lord, I've returned,' he told his liege, and in his bow revealed the young man behind him. Raxor's old eyes danced quickly from face to face, then stopped dead when he spotted Aric.

'Great Fate above,' he gasped. His weary face broke with emotion. 'Aric . . .'

Aric quickly parroted Horatin's bow. 'King Raxor,' he said solemnly, but there was more than ceremony in his tone. Straightening, he smiled broadly at the king. 'I'm back.'

Raxor went from exhausted to glowing. 'And it is good to see you back, boy! Horatin, you surprise me!' The king stepped forward, surmising Aric's bodyguards. 'And Nithins, too! You've brought the news I want, then?'

'I have, my lord,' reported Horatin happily. 'These are Prince Daralor's men, my lord. They came with us to protect Aric Glass, and to prove to you their prince has come.'

All the Nithins bowed to Raxor, but it was Brenor, the eldest who spoke for them. 'Prince Daralor sends you greetings, King Raxor. He is honoured to be joining you in your struggle against Baron Glass.'

'Is he?' Raxor asked. 'That is well. Your prince is a brave man, far braver than the cowardly kings who've turned their backs on us. Where is your prince now, Sir . . . ?'

'My name is Brenor, my lord, of the Green Brigade. This Trace and Jason, both under my command. We've come to tell you that Prince Daralor is on the march as well. His armies have crossed the border by now, I am certain, and march toward Koth.'

'As do we,' said Raxor, pleased by the news. 'Your prince and his army will have little resistance. These Liirians are like sheep this time. No one has even tried to stop us.'

'Yes, what about that?' Aric asked. 'We didn't expect to find you this far from the Kryss.'

'I will tell you about it,' said Raxor, 'but first . . .' He turned to his Watchman, Horatin. 'You have things to tell me, my friend, I'm sure.'

Horatin nodded. 'Corvat is gathering the others, my lord.'

'Good. Then there is time. Grenel, see to their needs. Horatin, all of you, rest now.' Raxor sidled up to Aric and put his arms around the young man. At last, Aric could smell the heavy liquor on his breath. 'You and I will talk first, boy.'

'My lord?'

'Come with me,' said Raxor, turning Aric toward the adjoining chamber. 'It is private this way. We can talk.'

Horatin surprised Aric by not saying another word. Instead he herded the Reecians back toward the main chamber, telling them to feel at ease while Raxor and Aric disappeared. Aric glanced over his shoulder as Raxor guided him away, not sure what the drunken king wanted from him. His Nithin companions, relieved to be out of the rain, seemed unperturbed as they began removing their wet coats and heading for the hearth. In the next chamber, Aric saw a table and a handful of plain wooden chairs. On the table sat a bottle of wine and an iron goblet, half-filled. Food had been prepared for the king, also half-consumed. A map and a few other documents lay across the table. Most striking of all, though, was the other occupant of the room, an attractive young woman dressed in a plain frock, her blonde hair brushed straight down her shoulders. She was collecting dishes off the table, but stopped when she saw Raxor reappear.

'That's fine, Alena,' said Raxor. 'Leave it. Go and bring some hot food.'

The woman – a girl really – made sure not to meet their eyes completely. 'Yes, my lord,' she answered curtly, then scurried past Aric to leave the room. Aric watched her go, confused.

'Who's that?' he asked.

'Alena lives here,' said Raxor. He motioned toward the chairs. 'Sit, Aric.'

Aric began taking off his coat, laying the sodden garment over one of the chairs. His whole person was similarly soaked, and the little fire built for Raxor in the corner of the room felt fine on his wet skin.

'I'll have dry clothes brought for you,' said Raxor. Seeing Aric's predicament, he dragged two chairs close to the fire and sat himself down.

'I'm soaked to the bone,' said Aric. Taking his chair, he started pulling off his boots, freeing his icy toes. 'My lord, I'm not sure I understand your meaning. That girl lives here?'

'This is her home, along with her mother and younger brother. There's no father.'

'They didn't flee? When they saw you coming, I mean?'

'Some did,' Raxor recounted. 'Others saw no need. We're not mistreating anyone here, Aric. They're taking care of us and that's all. We needed a place to stop and this was as good as anywhere.'

'But they're Liirians.'

'So? They hate your father as much as we do, I think. It's as I said, boy; we've had no resistance. And I'll wager your Prince Daralor has none either. We're on the march toward Koth now. That's where your father is making his stand.'

'We heard that,' said Aric. 'Horatin told us. He's holding up at the library.'

'Just as you did last time,' said Raxor with a grin. 'A good enough tactic, though. He doesn't really care about the rest of Liiria anyway. Just Koth. And that blasted library.'

Aric sat back. 'That's a painful thing to hear, my lord.'

'It's like a plague that's swept the whole world. Liiria is dispirited, Aric. And Reec, too. We are all ruined. And only tiny Nith has come to save us!'

'But I don't understand,' Aric protested. 'Why are you here at all? You were going to wait until you had word from us. Why make war before you even knew the Nithins were coming?'

'Because it is the time for war, Aric. Because it is forced on us. On *me*. I knew you would be wondering, that's why I wanted to speak with you.' King Raxor paused, then sat back to prepare himself. 'Your friend Mirage. She is dead, Aric.'

The confession seemed to tear the old king apart. His words trembled. 'Horatin told us,' said Aric. 'I'm sorry. For her and for you, my lord.'

'I know what your father is like, Aric,' said Raxor. 'I let her go to him even so. That is shame enough.'

'Is that why you're here to fight him? Because of Mirage?'

'No. Some people think that but they're wrong. It is not just Mirage that brings me here. Not even Roland. Oh, I want my vengeance, yes, but it is Reec whose heart is broken. The people demand this war, Aric, and I cannot resist them.'

Raxor poured himself more of the wine and began to drink. His hands shook as he held the goblet. Looking at his eyes, Aric could see how bloodshot they were.

'The world has gone mad,' Raxor went on. 'These men that follow me – they know what carnage they're up against. It's hopeless yet they yearn for it.'

'They yearn for death?'

'Aye, because they have nothing else! Your father took a thousand sons at the Kryss. Have you ever heard the wailing of a thousand mothers, Aric? No one can stand against that kind of noise. So now they send their husbands with me.' King Raxor looked blackly into his wine. 'I'm sure their fate will be the same.'

'Not this time,' said Aric. 'My lord, I have good news. It's not just the Nithins who've come to join you. Lukien comes with them.'

Raxor smiled. 'Ah. And what about that fairy tale you told me? About the sword?'

'It's no fairy tale, my lord. The sword is real and Lukien has it. He's come to fight my father again. This time he can win.'

Raxor scoffed, 'No one can win against your father.'

'You don't believe that,' said Aric. 'If you did you wouldn't be here.'

'Look into my eyes, Aric.' Raxor opened his eyes wide. 'Tell me what you see there.'

Aric looked, and to his deep regret saw nothing, not a hint of the twinkle he had always found there.

'Do you see hope in me?' asked Raxor.

'No,' admitted Aric. 'I don't.'

'Nor will you.' Raxor leaned back again, annoyed. 'Only a fool would believe that Baron Glass can be beaten. I'm not a fool, Aric. I'll fight him gladly. I have no use for hiding in Hes any longer. But no one will beat him. We will all die. Even your vaunted Lukien.'

Raxor's certainty riled Aric. He was about to speak when the girl named Alena returned, this time bearing a tray full of hot food. The temptation of the food distracted Aric, but only half as much as the pretty girl. Alena quietly floated into the room, setting down her tray and waiting for Raxor's orders.

'Alena, this is Aric,' said the king. 'We'll need clothes for him and a place to sleep.'

Alena looked surprised. 'He'll sleep here, my lord?'

'Yes. Make a place for him.'

'Yes, my lord,' agreed the girl, then turned and left the room. Raxor waited until she was gone before speaking again, keeping his voice low.

'Aric, your father means to keep Koth at any cost. He's already forsaken the rest of Liiria. Norvans are pouring over the border to help him because even they know how strong he is.'

'You don't know, Lukien, my lord,' said Aric icily. 'He's strong, too.'

'Yes, I know you think that,' said Raxor. 'But do not forget what you saw that day at the river. Remember?'

Aric remembered. He remembered far more than he could ever forget. It was the stuff of nightmares.

'My father may not exist any more,' he admitted, 'but he is still just a man behind all that armour. Surely you see that, my lord. You must, or you wouldn't be here yourself.'

Raxor glanced thoughtfully at his wine. 'Aric,' he said softly, 'I do not believe we will best your father. For most of us, this will be the end.' He looked at Aric, emphasizing his meaning. 'I have crossed into Liiria now. I will not be going home this time.'

The admission hit Aric like a thunderbolt. For a moment he was speechless. He saw the certainty in Raxor's eyes and did not know how to counter it.

'No, my lord,' he said cheerfully. 'You will live! Don't think such black thoughts. Believe what I tell you – Lukien has the Sword of Angels.'

'Bah!' Raxor pushed his goblet aside. 'An army of angels with an army of swords – that's what we need to defeat your father.'

'No, my lord,' Aric insisted. 'You can't go into this fight thinking that way. You need to lead! Where's that bear-hearted king we all remember? That's the Raxor that will make my father tremble!'

'That Raxor is old,' groaned the king. 'Old and afraid.'

'Not so afraid.' Aric gently poked him. 'He's brave enough to face death.'

'Death is what old people have to look forward to,' laughed Raxor. 'But all right, boy, you've made your point. I wouldn't have come here to face your father if I wasn't ready.'

'Good,' Aric pronounced, 'because I'm ready to face him too.'

The king got to his feet. 'I'm glad to hear that, because we'll need you. I won't keep you from the battle this time, Aric. Now eat and get some rest. Soon we'll be marching again.'

As always happened when the king left the room, a great emptiness swept in after him. Aric glanced around, stunned by everything that had happened. Exhaustion began to creep over his body, but the pull of the food on the table was greater than the pull of sleep and so he dragged his chair to the table and began to eat, slowly at first, then ravenously. As he reached for the wine, the girl named Alena reappeared, this time bearing an armful of clothing. She paused in the doorway, waiting for Aric's invitation. Aric stopped eating and stared at her.

'Come in,' he said clumsily.

The girl's face was stern but pretty. She avoided looking at Aric as she came forward. 'I did not want to disturb you.'

'This is your house,' said Aric.

Alena seemed amazed. At last she met his eyes directly. 'It is.' Catching herself, she held out the clothes. 'These are for you.'

Aric stood up. 'Thank you.' He took the offering with a smile. 'I'm truly grateful for this. I think I'll have to burn what I'm wearing!'

Alena didn't laugh. 'If you don't need anything else . . .'

'No.' Aric hesitated. 'I'm fine. Just a question – why are you still here?'

The question surprised the girl. 'My lord?'

'I'm a Liirian,' said Aric. 'I know this is your home. But these men are Reecians. Your mother and you . . .' He shrugged. 'I don't understand.'

'King Raxor's men have not been cruel to us,' said Alena. 'They have taken nothing from our home, only our food and service, and have paid us for both.'

'But they're invaders,' said Aric, still not understanding. 'They mean to kill your king, you know.'

'What king?' spat Alena. 'Baron Glass? He is king in name only. And we will all be better off when he is gone.' She made a face at Aric that was almost pitiful. 'You must have been gone from Liiria a very long time not to know this.'

'Yes,' admitted Aric. 'I have been.'

Alena laughed, not unkindly. 'Then you will see what I mean. There is no love in Liiria for Baron Glass. We welcome the Reecians. Anything would be better for Liiria.'

Without another word, the girl turned and left the room. Aric sat and watched her go, sure that his world was upside down.

77

At the edge of Koth, on a ridge of hills overlooking the sleeping city, Lukien paused amidst the rolling fog to ponder the place he had long called home. The rain that had plagued them for days had finally stopped, leaving the night sky clear and star-filled. A great, bare-faced moon hung overhead, shining with milky light. Down in the valley, tucked safely away from the Nithin army, Koth rested uneasily as it waited for the morning. The armies ringed the city like vultures, but old, enduring Koth seemed unafraid. The streets of the ancient city yawned with quietness. High on its hill, the great library loomed above the homes and shops. In the yards around the hill, Lukien could see the unmoving brigades of Norvan soldiers, still asleep as morning neared, their numerous war machines and horses poised for the coming battle. They were so far away, and yet like a great dragon Lukien could hear them breathing. Lights gleamed in the tower of the library. Inside, Thorin waited with his demon, and the sword at Lukien's side pulsed with unease.

Far behind him, the army of Prince Daralor slept, too. It was hours yet until dawn, when all of them would march for Koth. Amazingly, the coming battle had kept only handfuls of them awake. The rest of them – exhausted from the long trip north – slept soundly in their bedrolls. The dogs slumbered in their makeshift kennels while their keepers slept just outside, the keys to the long leashes jangling at their belts. Horses clopped at the earth, snorting in the cool night air. Like the armies of the Norvans occupying Koth, Daralor's army stretched deeply into the darkness, lit by smouldering campfires and torches. The Nithin flag snapped in the breeze, standing tall atop Daralor's distant pavilion.

Tonight, it seemed to Lukien as though the whole world had gathered at this one place, for on the other side of the city, barely visible even through the clear sky, glowed the pinpricks of another army. Raxor's forces had marched for Koth, too. Two days ago they had arrived. Daralor and the Reecian king had already sent emissaries to each other, sharing what they knew about the forces poised against them. Just like the Nithins, the Reecians had met no resistance either, marching effortlessly toward the Liirian capital. Now, though, the numbers of their foes showed themselves at last. Lukien paled as he considered them.

I can feel him, said Malator in his silent voice. He directed Lukien's gaze back toward the library. *Your baron is restless tonight, Lukien. My brother speaks with him.*

Lukien was immediately intrigued. 'What are they saying?'

Malator thought for a moment, then replied, *They are together. That's all I can tell.*

'Well, then, they're not the only ones who are restless.' Lukien put his hand on the sword, as if to put his Akari at ease. 'They can plan all they want. It won't change what's going to happen tomorrow. They should never have let us get this far.'

And yet we are still far away, Malator reminded him. *My brother is not stupid, Lukien. Look how he protects himself in the library.*

'Even the library isn't impregnable, Malator. They can't hide in there forever.'

Get us to Baron Glass. That is all you need to do.

Lukien nodded, but the task was daunting indeed. They were out-numbered, and would have to fight their way through the streets and the all the ranks of Norvan soldiers first. As he looked over the city, a thousand memories – happy and unhappy – flooded over Lukien. He had a been a boy in those streets, struggling to survive, and later he had risen to knighthood, though never to nobility. Those had been good days, when Koth had been at peace. When Koth had been great. She was not great anymore. Now she was an old cripple, groping her way through the world, decrepit and soiled, spoiled by war and corruption. And she had been torn apart by battles. Thinking of that, Lukien remembered that time not so long ago when last he had stepped foot inside the city. The memory made him shudder.

Do not think of it, Malator advised.

But it was impossible for Lukien not to remember, and he could not pull his eyes from the city or forget the faces of those he had fought with there. Breck and all his other friends, dead or scattered to the winds, and all because of Thorin's mad designs. And then, without wanting to, Lukien thought of Meriel.

His throat tightened. A grimace of pain gripped his expression. Malator eased closer to him, sensing his loss.

Listen to me now, Lukien. It's not your fault.

Lukien nodded. 'Right. I know. But . . .'

She is gone. Remember what Horatin told you. She went to him of her own accord.

'Yes. I know,' Lukien sighed. 'It's just . . .' He considered Meriel and all the others. 'There are so many who might still be alive if not for me.'

Malator started to speak, then stopped himself. His alarm jolted Lukien into turning around, revealing a figure coming toward him through the mist. At first he thought it was Lorn, but then he noted the royal garb and the confident gait and realized with surprise that it was Daralor. The prince paused a moment, regarding him.

'May I come ahead?' asked Daralor.

Startled, Lukien did not know what to say, so he waved the prince forward. 'Yes,' he bumbled, 'of course.'

Prince Daralor glided soundlessly to the edge of the hill, standing beside Lukien and taking the time to look out over Koth. Lukien eyed him curiously, not sure why the prince had come at all. So far, Daralor had never bothered to speak with Lukien alone. He had a thousand other things to do, and dozens of advisors to deliver his messages. Through the long ride north he had treated Lukien with respect, but that was all, preferring to get close to Aric. Now, though, Daralor Eight-Fingers didn't wear his usual, unapproachable air. He seemed calm, which was normal, but also oddly melancholy.

Neither man spoke for a few long minutes. Daralor, preoccupied by Koth, imbibed every tiny detail of the city. Then, at last, he turned away from the scene, anxiously rubbing the stump of his missing fingers.

'When it's near time for battle I walk among my men.' Daralor smiled strangely. 'It's been a very long time since I've been in battle.'

Lukien was unsure of his meaning. 'Your men are brave,' he offered. 'They'll make you proud, I'm sure.'

Daralor nodded in thanks, then looked out past the city toward the far-away lights of Raxor's army. Tomorrow, probably, they would join the Reecians and lay siege to the library. And then the real battle would begin.

'Even with the Reecians we are not as many as the Norvans,' said Daralor. 'How will they fight, do you think?'

'They're mercenaries, mostly,' said Lukien, 'but they're loyal enough.'

'Loyal to Baron Glass, or loyal to his gold?'

'To his diamonds,' Lukien corrected mildly. 'They're afraid of him, and they know no one can defeat him. He's not just the ruler of Liiria. He's the lord of Norvor now and they know it.'

Daralor considered this. 'Than he must be got to quickly.' His eyes met Lukien straight on. 'We will make the way for you, Lukien, but the rest will be up to you. And your sword.'

'I'm ready,' said Lukien.

Daralor smiled. 'Are you? Your pardon, Sir Lukien, but I see fear in you. I have seen it since we met, and I saw it grow when you learned about the woman Mirage.'

'What?' Lukien bristled. 'Who told you this? Lorn?'

'No,' said Daralor gently. 'Though King Lorn has his suspicions of you. You're not surprised by that, certainly.'

'No,' Lukien spat. 'Lorn saw me one night, speaking with the spirit of the sword. I should have trusted him to keep what he heard secret.'

'He has told me nothing, Lukien. My doubts are my own.'

'Do not doubt me, Prince Daralor.' Lukien's tone hardened. 'I have looked into the eyes of this demon before. I'll do it again and I won't flinch.'

'Then my men and I will do my part for you, Sir Lukien. You have my promise. Stay alive long enough to reach Baron Glass. That's all you need to do.'

'Ah, well then, that will be easy enough,' said Lukien darkly. 'For there is no way for me to die, even if I wished it.'

Daralor looked at him through the mist. 'Some say you do wish it, Bronze Knight.'

The accusation made Lukien grin. 'Believe what you want, Prince Daralor.'

'Tell me, what will you do when this is over?' Daralor eased away from the vision of Koth, smiling at Lukien. 'Will you go back to Jador or will you remain here?'

Lukien shrugged. 'I don't know yet.'

'No?' Daralor motioned toward the sword at Lukien's waist. 'And what of that? Will you keep it?'

'If I don't I'll die.'

'Yes. You will.'

The two men understood each other, but Lukien wanted no part of it. He told the prince, 'Whatever I decide after we are done here is no matter to you or to anyone. Tomorrow or the next day, when Thorin is free or dead, I will have finished my service to the gods that have ruled me. My life will be mine again.'

'To live it?' asked Daralor. 'Or to end it?'

His questions irked Lukien. 'To decide for myself,' he said icily.

Daralor seemed satisfied with his answer. The prince looked back toward his waiting army. 'They want you to stay alive until they can get you to Baron Glass. The rest is up to you.'

He said no more, ending his visit with those final words and going back toward his men. Lukien waited, perturbed, trying to figure out why the prince had come to him at all. Was he being tested? Did Daralor not trust him?

'You needn't worry, Daralor,' Lukien muttered after him. 'I'll do my part.'

Afraid or not, he was prepared to meet Thorin on the morrow.

Lukien remained alone on the hillside, but his daydreams had been ruined and he knew that rest was necessary. Abandoning the private spot, he walked slowly back toward camp, passing men and horses as he picked his way back to his own bedroll. Night had settled like a mantle over the camp, filling the air with the sounds of slumber and anxious animals. Lukien greeted a few soldiers on his way, giving them a casual nod until at last he had returned to the campfire he had made with Lorn. There, he saw the old king sitting by the fire, warming himself and gently sharpening his sword. The weapon gleamed in the jumping firelight. Lorn's eyes shined with anticipation. He looked up at Lukien as the knight approached, then glanced away again without a word of greeting. The two men had barely spoken at all during the past few weeks, the rift between them growing ever wider. For a reason he could not quite comprehend, Lukien regretted that now.

And yet, he could think of nothing to say to Lorn. An apology certainly wasn't in the offing; he still believed Lorn was a butcher. There was too much history to change his mind about that. He wanted only an understanding between them before tomorrow, when they rode together into battle.

'Lorn.'

His voice – the only voice – sounded loudly through the camp. Lorn cleared his throat with disinterest.

'Yes?'

Lukien sidled closer to him. He searched for the right words. They came to him out of nowhere. 'Gilwyn is a smart boy. He may be young, but he's smart.'

Lorn grumbled, 'What?'

'Gilwyn,' said Lukien, fumbling. 'He trusted you enough to help him. So did Minikin.'

'That's right,' said Lorn. He didn't bother looking up at Lukien, but rather ran his sharpening stone carefully across his blade. 'So did White-Eye. What's your point?'

'Did you tell Daralor what you saw that night when I was speaking with Malator?'

'No I did not,' hissed Lorn. 'Did he tell you I did? If he did he is a liar.'

Lukien quickly shook his head. 'No. He . . .' He paused. 'Never mind.'

Lorn stopped his sharpening. 'Sit if you want.'

It was the first kind gesture either man had offered the other since Lukien could remember. He seized on it, sitting down on the hard earth next to Lorn. The warmth of the fire felt good. It seemed like forever since Lukien had enjoyed a proper bed.

'Lorn,' Lukien asked quietly. 'Why aren't you asleep?'

'Can't sleep.' The old king took a deep breath. 'I'm too close now to sleep.'

'Too close?'

'To Norvor, Lukien. To home.'

Lukien stared into the fire. 'This was my home once. Maybe it can be again.'

'Oh?' Lorn turned toward him. 'You'll stay here, then?'

It was the same question Daralor wanted answered. 'Tomorrow you'll have a chance to prove yourself,' said Lukien, changing the subject.

'No,' Lorn grunted. 'I have proven myself, again and again. Tomorrow, Lukien, will be *your* chance, not mine. Whatever happens tomorrow, my conscience is clear. If we win, Norvor will be mine again. Then I can send for my daughter and Eiriann and return to my life. My real life.' Lorn looked imploringly at Lukien. 'That's all I want. Don't you see?'

Lukien did see. Finally, it was clear to him.

'We all want that,' he replied. 'Just to be home. To be with a woman we love. We all want that, Lorn.'

It was a single, simple point of agreement, but for Lukien it was enough.

78

Like a slithering tentacle, Kahldris' words wrapped themselves around Thorin as he stood by the window. The great expanse of the city lay beneath them, brightening in the rising sun. On the grasses on the outskirts of Koth, the army of their Nithin enemies watched the coming dawn, poised for battle. The sight thrilled Kahldris. The old general within him stirred, filling Thorin with his unholy passions.

'Today I will watch you shine, Baron Glass. Today your life will change forever, and the whole world will know you are its master.'

As he had done so frequently lately, Kahldris did not hide himself within Thorin's mind, but rather stood next to him bodily, his figure dressed in his ancient battle garb, his form shimmering in the weak light coming through the window. From their place within the library's tower they could see the entire west side of the city, its houses and store fronts locked up tight against the coming mêlée. Green Nithin flags waved in the breeze. Men and dogs scurried through the ranks of cavalry, preparing to march into the city. At the forefront of the army sat its leader, the strange and stately Daralor, barely visible at such a distance yet somehow unmistakable. Thorin let his gaze linger on the prince and the men around him. His preternatural eyesight – like a hawk's or better – spied their tense faces. Among them sat Lukien, stoic and one-eyed, his blond hair slowly greying, his weathered face full of pain. It should have been impossible for Thorin to make out such detail, but it was not. Kahldris' magic swelled in him, filling his mind's eye with the image of his old friend.

'He bears the sword,' said Kahldris. 'Look . . .'

Through the wavy glass Thorin could see across the miles, could see in the hand of his good old friend the weapon of his demise. Crude and plain, the sword seemed no more than the Akari sword Thorin himself would wield today. He closed his eyes to see it better. Letting the demon's magic guide him, he saw the weapon perfectly, then felt Kahldris shutter madly. The potent force within the sword shook the spirit.

'Your brother,' Thorin muttered. He opened his eyes and expelled a sigh. 'I can feel him. He's powerful. Like you.'

Kahldris nodded his ethereal head. In the darkened chamber, he gave off a ghostly light. 'He has found a willing ally in your friend, Baron Glass. You are sentimental about the knight Lukien. I warn you, do not be. Great things are undone by such feelings.'

Thorin stared out across the city. On the eastern side of Koth, invisible from his westerly perch, Raxor and his Reecians had gathered for the siege, weighing in from the farmlands to press against the city. His army had swelled considerably in the last few days, bolstered by loyalists ready to die for the old king. Because they were so near their own homeland, their supply lines had been easy to maintain. Raxor's men were rested and well fed, and armed with everything they could drag across the border. Thousands of men, most on horses, had heeded Raxor's call to battle, eager to avenge their dead Prince Roland and regain the pride Thorin had stripped from them. It had been an awful miscalculation, letting Raxor live that day. Thorin saw that now. He should have pursued his adversary across the Kryss and ended things. He should have cut the old man's heart out and eaten it.

Why hadn't he, then?

'I was covered in blood,' he mused aloud, addressing Kahldris without turning toward him. He felt grossly alone suddenly, the chamber echoing and empty. Beneath him, his own armies massed around Library Hill or spread out through the city, ready to defend him. They too numbered in the thousands, and yet not one of them loved him. Not the way they loved Lukien. Or Daralor. Or Raxor. Only Gilwyn loved him now, and that was a mystery Thorin could barely understand.

'Baron Glass?' Kahldris was staring at him now. Amazingly, he smiled. Putting his hand on Thorin's shoulder, he said, 'Thorin. Do you believe in me?'

Thorin looked at him but could not return his grin. 'I am grateful to you.'

'That is not enough. Not today.' Kahldris pointed out the window. 'Those men come to kill us. Your friend, Lukien – he comes to destroy you, not to save you. He is not Gilwyn, with all his stupid innocence. He and the rest of them want to take what you have fought so long for, Baron Glass.'

'I've killed so many . . .'

'It does not matter!' thundered Kahldris. 'Their blood fed us, made us strong!'

'No,' said Thorin, unable to shake the nightmarish memories. 'They are men, not goats to be slaughtered.' He stepped back from the window. 'Will today be like that again?' He glanced down at the armour covering his person. Like Kahldris, he was dressed for battle, every inch of him shielded in his shiny black suit. The hideous helmet with its upturned horns waited on a nearby table. Kahldris followed his gaze to the helmet.

'Take up the helmet, Baron Glass.'

Thorin shook his head. 'Not yet.'

'It is time. The sun comes quickly.'

'I have questions,' said Thorin softly.

Kahldris looked surprised. 'Now? It's not the time to be pensive.'

'I want to know things. Before I become a butcher again, I want to know what you know, Kahldris.'

'You know everything I know, Baron Glass. I have never hidden anything from you.'

'No, it's not so simple.' Thorin stalked back to the window, biting his lip as he looked toward the horizon. Already Daralor's forces were on the move, slowly cantering into the city. The start of the march made Kahldris uneasy, but Thorin held firm. 'I am unstoppable in this armour, but they will try to stop me anyway,' he said. 'And I'll be forced to kill them. You will blind me to their agonies and I'll feel nothing, but right now my mind is clear, Kahldris, and I know what they are facing.'

Kahldris' old face twisted. 'Get on with your question.'

'My question is this – what will happen to them?'

'You know what will happen,' growled Kahldris. 'They will die. Why do you care? They come to kill you, Baron!'

'No,' Thorin argued, 'that's not what I mean.' He looked imploringly at the spirit. 'I mean what will happen to them after they die?'

Kahldris reared back, looking thoughtful. 'Ah . . .'

'I need to know this, Kahldris. Ease my conscience. Tell me what will happen. They will live on, yes? I send them only to their glory?'

'Is that what you have believed?' The Akari's tone was slightly mocking. 'All our time together, and now you want enlightenment.' He shook his head doubtfully. 'I wonder, Baron Glass, if you have truly looked outside that window.'

'I know what we're facing,' said Thorin calmly. Truly, it hardly mattered to him. His mind was full of questions, because his hands were full of blood. 'I killed Jazana and all those others. What's happened to them? They live on, yes?'

Kahldris smirked with impatience. 'Yes, they live on. You know this already.'

'Where do they live on? In a world like this? Or in the kinds of worlds you've shown me?'

'The world of the dead is different for everyone,' said Kahldris.

'But they do live on. Minikin told me that once. It's not just Akari who go on.'

'Why do you ask me this now?'

'Because I'm going out *there!*' Thorin raged. 'Because I'll kill a thousand men today. Do I send them to hell or to heaven? Tell me, Kahldris, please.'

Kahldris glanced away, turning from Thorin to stare contemplatively out the window. The pull on him was mighty; Thorin could see him struggling. 'My brother is coming,' he whispered. His voice cracked with nervousness. 'There's just no time to unravel this mystery for you. It is unknowable.'

The answered vexed Thorin. 'How can that be? You exist in their world. Do you not see them, encounter their spirits?'

'I am in your world as much as their worlds,' Kahldris explained. He put his unearthly hands to the window, leaving no mark at all as he looked longingly at the armies ready to clash. 'Let us go, Baron Glass.'

'How is this unknowable? You have said there is a world beyond this one.'

'Yes, yes . . .'

'And what is beyond that? What gods are there? What angels or heavens?'

'It is unknowable!' shrieked Kahldris. 'I have no answers for you! I live, and that is all. Those you kill will find their own worlds. Or they will not. I cannot know everything!'

Thorin stared in amazement. 'You don't know what lies beyond your world? What gods rule you?'

'I rule myself,' said Kahldris, desperate to end the talking. 'You rule yourself. We are our own gods! We decide who lives and dies. Do you not see that? That is the power I have given you' He fixed on Thorin, trying to make him understand. 'Today, you will be the only god who matters to those men out there. Forget the Great Fate, Baron Glass. This day, you are a god.'

His awesome words left Thorin dumbstruck. It was a terrible gift he had taken from Kahldris, one that had rotted his mind and his morals both. There was no turning back from it; he knew that plainly. Liiria still needed him. There was still good he could do in the world, surely. Suddenly, more than anything, he wanted to see his son again. Thorin swallowed down the questions plaguing him, glancing one last time at the vision through the window. Kahldris, satisfied that he had convinced Thorin, dissolved into the air. His wordless voice rippled through the baron's mind.

Now, Baron Glass. It's time.

Thorin agreed reluctantly. Despite everything he'd done, only Kahldris had carried him so far. It was time to repay the demon's kindnesses. As Thorin turned from the window, however, he spotted Gilwyn at the end of the chamber, the boy's face partially hidden in shadows. Thorin had not heard him come in. Gilwyn stared at Thorin with a hopeless frown. His empty hands hung at his sides. Every other man in the library was dressed for battle, but not Gilwyn. Attired in his usual shirt and trousers, his boot with the special hinge wrapped around his clubbed foot, he looked as if the day was like any other, to be spent studying the library's vast shelves. His gaze told a different story, though, penetrating Thorin with his odd mix of love and shelter. Despite Kahldris's insistence, the baron could no longer rush away.

'You shouldn't have come,' he told Gilwyn gently. 'This is my quiet time. I won't have any more of it today.'

'It's dawn,' said Gilwyn. 'I had to come.'

Thorin made his way to the table where his helmet waited. There he paused, reaching for it then stopping. The death's head face of the thing leered at him, taunting him to pick it up.

'I wish you had listened to me,' said Thorin. 'I wish you had gone when I told you, left when you had the chance. Now . . .' He shrugged. 'You're stuck here.'

'I'm not afraid,' said Gilwyn. He managed to smile at his old friend. 'I told you, I'm not leaving you.'

'You should have given up on me, instead of trapping yourself here,' Thorin groaned. 'I can't change, and the dead are dead.' Finally, he picked up the helmet, holding it by one shining horn. 'After all this, how can you still see the good in me?'

Gilwyn's face darkened with sadness. 'I remember it. So I know it's there. But I failed you, Thorin. I thought I could break the hold Kahldris has over you, but I can't. I tried to find a way in the library, but . . .' He shrugged hopelessly. 'Maybe there is no way, not if you don't help me. You have to fight him. You have to want to give him up.'

'Then I am doomed,' said Thorin with a crooked smile. 'No matter how I try to explain this, I don't think you could ever understand. I cannot give up Kahldris, Gilwyn. He's part of me now.'

Gilwyn made no effort to argue with the baron. Instead, he simply stepped aside and let Thorin leave the room.

Dawn's light splashed colour on the yard of Library Hill, illuminating the men gathered there for Thorin's arrival. A huge, black charger awaited the baron, held by stable hands whose mouths fell open as Baron Glass entered the yard. Duke Cajanis, patiently waiting near his own horse and surrounded by Norvan bodyguards, straightened to attention as Thorin approached. Dressed completely now in the Devil's Armour, his head encased in the frightful helmet, Thorin's visage froze the waiting men. The long road leading up to the library bristled with men and weapons.

At the base of the hill a thousand Liirians were positioned, ready to defend the stronghold. Throughout the city other divisions were scattered, all carefully positioned to rebuff the Nithin and Reecian advances. A cool breeze reached Thorin through his armour, which rested on his body as lightly as a feather. Kahldris pumped magic energy into his blood and muscles. His sword, an Akari weapon he had stolen from the cellars of Grimhold, bounced at his thigh. Thorin wasted no time as he bee-lined to Duke Cajanis.

'Report.'

Cajanis said confidently, 'We're ready. Arand is waiting for us at the west end and Karris' men are in Chancellery Square. The Reecians have started to move down on him. Lothon and his Liirians will stay at the hill. They'll take care of anyone who makes it through.'

At the base of the hill Thorin caught a glimpse of Lothon as he rode slowly amongst his men, Liirians who had joined with Thorin to remake their army. It was a small band, only about a thousand men, but the terrain of Library Hill made their job of defending it much easier. Lothon was an old man now, a friend of the baron's from the old days when Akeela had been king. Long retired, he had been one of the few to see the hope of a better Liiria. As Thorin spied the old man far below, he felt a pang of sorrow. Things hadn't turned out the way either of them had hoped, and yet Lothon had stayed loyal to him.

'Make sure no one gets through,' Thorin told Cajanis as he headed for his mount. 'If Lothon dies today, I'll make sure you do as well, Duke Cajanis.'

Cajanis chuckled as if Glass was joking. 'Not much chance of that, Baron Glass. Once the Nithins see you in your armour they'll know they have no chance.'

'They won't be seeing me yet,' said Thorin. Without the help of the stable hands he hoisted himself onto his horse. 'You'll be in charge of Arand and his men. I'm going to the square.'

'What?' puzzled Cajanis.

What? erupted Kahldris.

'Chancellery Square,' said Thorin. 'That's where Raxor will be. That's where I'm going.'

Cajanis began to sputter. 'But Baron Glass, the Nithins!'

Thorin spun his horse toward the road. 'Go, Cajanis. You know what to do.'

Duke Cajanis stared at Thorin as the baron rode away. Passing the scores of soldiers positioned on the road, Thorin hurried down the hillside toward the waiting Liirians at the bottom. Lothon, hearing the commotion, looking skyward at the racing baron, raising his glove in greeting. But Thorin had no time for sentiment. Barely acknowledging his comrade's wave, he focused on Chancellery Square instead. From the hillside he saw it, choked with tall buildings and Norvan mercenaries, its parade ground dotted with lancemen. Coming out from the distant hills toward the square, Raxor and his Reecian army slowly bore down on the Norvans.

What are you doing, Baron Glass? asked Kahldris angrily.

'To do some good,' Thorin replied. 'To get my son back.'

My brother is with the Nithins!

'Your brother will wait. First I have to rescue my son.'

No! Kahldris raged. *Go west, Baron! West!*

Thorin ignored the demon's orders. At the bottom of the hill, he rode quickly through the amazed ranks of Liirians, passing Lothon and his lieutenants and heading for the heart of the capital where the spires of the old chancellery buildings stood.

'I'll kill for you today, Kahldris,' he cried as he galloped through the open lane. 'But first I want my son back!'

79

On a field filled with ghosts, Lukien and his comrades faced the city of Koth. In the shadows of the capital the Norvan mercenaries poured from the streets, lining up to fight for the duke that led them. Lukien, seated stoically atop his horse, watched as their enemies formed their ranks. Next to him, Prince Daralor minded his own men, calmly ordering his soldiers to hold their position. A great, green flag unfurled above him. Stately armour gleamed on his person, shining like copper in the new light of morning. His army stretched out proudly behind him, silently awaiting the coming battle, while dozens of war dogs strained at the leash, barely held back by their burly keepers. Deep in the ranks, the battle hawks stood tethered to their perches, madly screeching as they sighted the Norvans. Their cries scratched at Lukien's ears. On a horse beside him, Ghost swiveled anxiously in his saddle, his arms and face covered in a Jadori gaka to protect his pale skin from the sun. Ghost's grey eyes turned to slivers as he watched the Norvans. His hand twitched as he gripped his thin sword.

They had strategized and planned, and now they were ready, and Lukien saw confidence in Daralor's men. They had marched to this foreign land to follow their beloved prince, and still Lukien wondered why. Daralor had puzzled him with talk of honour and of men living free, and now that the hour of battle had come, he saw that Daralor had meant every word of it. With his face shadowed by his high-flying flag, Daralor looked like a hero to Lukien.

Duke Cajanis was easily recognizable in his blue cape and long golden hair. At the front of his army, his horse prancing as if in a parade, he looked both fearsome and foppish as he entered the field. The force of Norvan mercenaries that followed him impressed Lukien with its numbers. Norvan regulars loyal to Cajanis peppered the group. Despite Jazana Carr's death, her legacy lived on, and Lukien knew there was only one reason why so many men still followed Thorin. He was the big dog in this part of the world, and now had claim to Jazana's vast fortune. He was also indestructible, which meant no one could challenge him.

'Except today,' he whispered.

Ghost heard his words and flicked his gaze toward Lukien. The young, cloud-coloured eyes sparked with fire. Of all the Inhumans, Ghost was certainly among the best fighters. Only Greygor, Grimhold's guardian, was more frightening to behold in battle, and that was because Greygor was more monster than man. But Ghost wasn't the only spirit on the field, and as Lukien watched the Norvans approach he remembered another time, not so long ago, when he had fought on this very same soil. Then, it had been Thorin who was the invader, leading these same Norvan whores to sack the city. It had been a brutal battle and his confrontation with Thorin had left Lukien near death, and remembering that made him shudder now.

No, Lukien, came Malator's soothing voice. *Do not be afraid.*

At Lukien's side the Sword of Angels burned against his body. Malator essence glowed within it, setting the blade strangely alight. There seemed to be no fear at all within the Akari, and the calmness he felt helped to soften Lukien's mood.

'I don't see him,' said Lukien, as much to Malator as to the others. 'I don't see Thorin.'

'He has to come,' said Daralor. 'He knows you're here, Lukien.'

But looking past the ranks of Norvans, no one could see Baron Glass or the slightest hint of his terrible armour. Lukien pondered Library Hill, clearly visible above the city.

'He's in the library, maybe,' he surmised. 'He doesn't need to come and face us yet.'

'He lets his hirelings do his dirty work,' grunted Ghost. 'He thinks he has us bested already.'

Baron Glass is not in the library.

'Eh?'

My brother is with him, Malator explained, *and they are not in the library. Baron Glass goes to find his son, Lukien.*

'Oh, gods, no . . .'

'Lukien?' asked Daralor. 'What is it?'

'Thorin's not here. He's going after Raxor first,' replied Lukien.

No one asked how he knew such a thing. The magical sword at his side gave them their answer. Even the Eye of God, still burning against Lukien's chest, bespoke of the sorcery Lukien commanded.

'This changes things,' said Ghost.

Daralor shook his head. 'It changes nothing. You still must reach Baron Glass, Lukien.'

Ghost protested, 'But he's on the other side of the city . . .'

'No, Daralor's right,' said Lukien. 'It doesn't matter where he is, we have to get to him.'

Daralor grinned at the young albino. 'That shouldn't be a problem for a man who can make himself invisible.'

His levity broke the tension, and his lieutenants gave a laugh. Lukien nodded.

'We'll reach him,' he promised Daralor. 'We'll find him once you loose the hawks.'

It had been agreed, and Daralor said nothing more about it. They had all approved the plan, even Lorn, who waited unseen within the ranks of Nithins, ready to appear at the proper time. Lukien put his hand on the pommel of his sword, letting Malator's strength course through him as Duke Cajanis at last came to a stop. The duke's army halted with amazing precision, spears and lances tipped skyward. At Cajanis' flanks rode two men, one a mercenary Lukien remembered, one a Norvan nobleman. The mercenary, a man named Thon, smirked at Lukien distastefully.

'You know him?' whispered Ghost.

'I know him,' grumbled Lukien. 'I was one of them, remember.'

He had spent years in Jazana Carr's employment, and Lukien knew most of the mercenaries of any importance. Thon was from Jerikor, and like the warriors of that land he never wore armour or any coverings at all over his arms, preferring instead to display his many tattoos. He was an unsavoury character and Jazana had never liked him, but he was good at his work and so had earned a place in her vast army. Lukien was not surprised at all that he had remained with Thorin. Thon, like many mercenaries, cared only about money.

Duke Cajanis wheeled his horse to face his men. He had arranged his army so that his cavalry came first, just as Daralor had, with foot soldiers scattered among them. He had brought no archers with him, though they were surely stationed at the library, Lukien reasoned. Cajanis spoke loudly to his soldiers, rallying them, and his bold words were echoed by lieutenants in the ranks. Then, when he finished his speech, the duke turned around again toward the Nithins. Amazingly, he broke away from his army and began riding forward, accompanied by Thon and the Norvan noble.

'Terms,' spat Daralor in disgust. 'Lukien, Godwin, come with me.'

Leaping at the chance to return the insult, Daralor broke from his army and trotted out toward Cajanis with his aide, Godwin. Lukien followed, leaving Ghost behind and sure that Lorn, hidden among the Nithins, was watching and fuming. Prince Daralor rode out grandly, his head held high, then reined his stallion to a halt just feet before Cajanis. The two leaders locked glares for a moment, until Cajanis noticed Lukien.

'You are the Bronze Knight I have heard so much about,' said the duke mockingly. He glanced over at Thon. 'From what you told me, I expected more.'

Thon cracked a toothy grin. 'You look old, Lukien.'

'Do I?' Lukien reached beneath his breast plate and pulled out the Eye of God. As the amulet hit the sunlight it blazed furiously. 'I don't feel old, Thon,' he said, dropping the Eye against his chest. 'I feel immortal.'

'We've been warned of your magic, Lukien of Liiria,' said Cajanis. 'In truth it matters not. You already know what you're up against. You don't have a chance, not even with your pretty bauble.'

Daralor bristled at the duke's arrogance. 'You're a man of big words, Duke Cajanis. I have found in my dealings that men of big words have the smallest stones. I can already see the fear in your eyes every time my war dogs bark.'

'A thousand war dogs won't bring down the Black Baron, Prince Daralor. You would be better off slaughtering them yourself. Do it humanely and they won't suffer. Let me take pity on you, sir. I come to speak to you as a favour, to warn you of what will happen. This is not your fight, and you cannot win it.'

Lukien at last pulled free his sword. As he did, the blade burst with light. 'I have the means to best your baron, Norvan. Behold!' A ripple of surprise went through the Norvan ranks. Lukien pressed his advantage. 'I know you men!' he shouted to the mercenaries. 'Listen to me now. The reign of Baron Glass is over. I have come to undo him!' He laughed, full of malice suddenly, and looking straight at Cajanis hissed, 'And I have not come alone.'

Lukien lowered his sword, pointing it at the rows of Nithins behind him. The signal caused the soldiers to part like a curtain, revealing a single rider who trotted out from the crowd. King Lorn the Wicked had dressed for the occasion, looking as princely as Daralor himself in a silver breastplate and gleaming chainmail, his arms covered in scarlet fabric, his head crowned with a feathered helmet that left his hard-bitten face naked. He held an axe in his hand with a sword at his belt, his white horse garbed in golden armour that reflected like rainbows on the field. His appearance stunned and confused Cajanis. The duke frowned as he tried to make out the rider's identity.

'That's an old man,' spat Cajanis, then began to chuckle. 'It's that your champion, Prince Daralor?'

Lorn held up the axe in his meaty fist. 'I am Lorn,' he declared. 'And I live!'

As though they were arrows his words shot the men through, stunning Duke Cajanis and his soldiers. Whispers and shouts ran through the Norvan ranks. Cajanis, too shocked to speak, looking dumbly at his aide, and from the rows of mercenaries a cry went up.

'It's him!' said the single, distant soldier. 'That's Lorn!'

Lorn drove his horse to a gallop, hurrying to Lukien's side. To Lukien, he had never looked more like the manic king of legend. His rock hard eyes froze Cajanis in his glare as both Thon and the nameless noble drew back.

'I am King Lorn of Norvor, rightful ruler of our land, and you Cajanis are a usurper's lapdog. Save your warnings, coward. We are deaf to them.'

'You can't be Lorn,' sputtered Cajanis. 'Lorn is dead!'

Lorn tossed back his head and gave a shuddering cry. 'I live!' he shouted, half-mad with laughter. 'And I've come back for my throne and to kill all who defy me. Look at me, wretched duke! Call me a ghost one more time and you will die first today.'

Duke Cajanis struggled with his horse. Behind him, his usually orderly soldiers had broken into gossip. He turned to Lukien, spitting with anger.

'You've made an unholy alliance for yourself, Bronze Knight. You bring a devil back to Norvor!'

'Yield to us now, Duke Cajanis,' Lukien ordered. 'You cannot kill me, and once the dogs are loosed you'll have no chance of it. I have prayed for death and been denied it by heaven, and no Norvan fop will be the end of me.'

'Don't bargain with these piss buckets, Lukien,' said Lorn. He forced his horse closer to Cajanis. 'You may run from me, but wherever you go I will find you, Cajanis. And when I have my throne again you will be my jester.'

'They taunt you, Cajanis!' grumbled Thon. 'Who are they? Look at them and look at us.' The mercenary scoffed at Lukien. 'You shouldn't have come back, Lukien. You're over.'

His filthy grin drove all the fear from Lukien's mind. Now, like the old days, he hungered for a fight. 'Well, Cajanis?' he asked. 'Which will it be? Will you let this pile of shit speak for you? Or will you use your brain and yield to us?'

Cajanis was frothing now. 'You are outnumbered! Even without Baron Glass you have no chance against us.'

'Shall I lose my war dogs, then?' asked Daralor casually. 'The kennel masters have kept them hungry.'

'Damn your war dogs, you eight fingered freak.' Duke Cajanis pulled his reins up. 'Let them lose and we'll show them what Norvan blades are made of.'

The duke swiveled his horse quickly about, barking at his comrades to follow him as he returned to his army. Before Lukien and Daralor could turn themselves back, Lorn heaved his axe after Cajanis, missing the duke by inches. Cajanis roared in hatred.

'You are dead, old man!' the duke promised. 'Today Norvor will be free of you at last!'

'Come and kill me, then!' Lorn challenged. 'The moment you're man enough.'

Daralor had heard enough. The time for talk was over. He did not ride back to his army or tell his men to wait. He merely glanced at his lieutenants and with a nod gave the order to unleash the dogs.

80

In all his life, Aric Glass had only been in battle twice before. On both occasions others had protected him from the worst of it, but not today. Today, as a volley of arrows sailed overhead, the full stink of death singed his nose and the terrifying cries of dying men shook his skull. It had all happened so quickly, Aric had barely seen it coming. First there were the trumpets, the martial music of his Reecian comrades. The Norvans had seemed so far away, like toy soldiers on their horses. Then they had come like a wave across the battlefield, sweeping Aric into combat. His sword was up and his horse was charging with the rest of them, carrying him headlong into the clash. Beside him, the Nithin bodyguards Trace and Brenor rode at his flanks, into the teeth of Norvan lances. The stampede of cavalry shook the ground. And Aric was in chaos.

The world around him blurred. From atop his horse he saw Norvans and Reecians and his own slashing sword, blindly shooting out to parry. Time slowed and had no meaning, and though he heard the voices of the Reecian captains, he could not understand them over the din. Toward the rear of their ranks, King Raxor rallied his soldiers, shouting as he held a battle axe aloft. Horatin and others members of the Red Watch swarmed around him, protecting him as Norvan riders strained to reach him. Aric pivoted, trying to find his comrades in the mêlée. Trace and Brenor, distinctive in their green Nithin garb, battled back the curved blades of a band of tattooed mercenaries. Aric had seen their likes before, in his first clash against them, each of them dark-skinned and crazy-eyed. Trace barreled his stallion into them, disappearing for a moment as a single, pony-tailed brute rose up in Aric's sight. His blade fell quickly, knocking Aric back as he blocked it. The horse beneath him whinnied, then spun to help its master, letting Aric return the blow. The mercenary's own horse reared, kicking dirt into the air as Aric broke away. He had no shield to slow him down, and when the big man's horse came down Aric's blade was there, mercilessly slashing its neck. Its rider cursed as the horse collapsed, falling headlong into a swinging Reecian mace.

'Aric, watch yourself!' Brenor screamed. It was his mace that had split the man's skull. He sidled up to Aric through the battle.

'I can look after myself!' Aric shouted.

'Stay close! That's what we all do!'

Already another band of Norvans were breaking toward them. Trace emerged from the crowd, fighting his way back to Aric and Brenor, his emerald armour splashed with blood. As he reached his comrades an arrow plunged down, piercing his shoulder. He roared, spitting obscenities, and with two hands forced the pommel of his sword through the eye of a coming mercenary. Aric hurried toward him. Other Norvans had sighted Trace. Bearing down on the young man, they had almost reached him when the Reecian catapults began. Fire filled the sky as the burning missiles arced toward the Norvans, exploding like sunbursts amid the frenzied horses. Aric and Brenor pressed the distraction, and joined by charging Reecians forced the Norvans back. The slashing sword and flying spears blinded Aric but he kept on, faithfully fighting the way he had learned, the way his own father had once taught him. So far the battle was only minutes long, but Aric had not even taken a scratch, and a glamour of invincibility fell on him. He cried out in gleeful triumph, sure they would win the day, sure that his Reecian friends would easily best the dogs of Norvor . . .

Until Trace fell.

Aric was laughing, cocksure and strong, and he had not even seen the lanceman's charge. The weapon came from nowhere, like a cobra out off the crowd, striking Trace dead in the chest and blowing him backward. Aric's laugh died in his throat as the Norvan lance carried off the impaled Trace, and as though a gentle rain had fallen, his spraying blood struck Aric's face.

Dazed, Aric let his guard down. He stared dumbly at Trace as the Norvan shook the corpse from his weapon. 'Trace?'

'Damn all!' roared Brenor. 'Aric!'

His cry broke Aric's stupor. The Nithin glared at him. 'Brenor, Trace—'

'He's dead, now pay me some heed! Forget him and fight, Aric!'

Aric shook himself, lifting his sword again. Trace's blood tasted salty on his lips. He looked around, not sure where to go, the battlefield swollen with friends and enemies. Brenor was calling him, waving him on. Aric steeled himself again. Then, he heard a distant trumpet sound behind him, calling the Reecians soldiers' attention. Something was happening, confusing Aric. The Reecians grew pale-faced. The Norvans cheered.

'What's happening?' Aric asked.

Then, he saw him. Baron Glass. His Father.

Alone on his black charger, galloping toward them, his body glistening in living metal, Baron Glass drove toward the battle, towering over the men around him. The Norvans drew back, surrounding him at once, but Aric's father remained clearly visible, like a giant, shaking his fist and shouting.

'Fate alive, what's he doing here?' Brenor asked.

The clash around them softened as Norvans and Reecians both looked to their captains. At the rear of his army, King Raxor had seen the Black Baron enter the fray. The old monarch's face twisted with rage. Captain Grenel flew to his side, then barked orders at his men to regroup. Norvan leaders did the same, and soon the battle reignited. Aric and Brenor both fell back, sure that things had changed. Amazingly, King Raxor was riding forward.

Then, realizing what was happening, Aric reined back his mount. Looking toward the Norvan line, he saw his father madly scanning the field.

'It's me,' he said, coldly certain. 'Brenor, it's me.'

'What?'

'He's here for me, I know it,' said Aric.

'Well you're not going to him, that's for sure.' Brenor positioned himself between Aric and the Norvans. 'Head to the rear, Aric. I promise, I won't let him take you.'

'No,' said Aric, then turned his steed to fully face his father. 'I'm staying.'

'You're *not*!'

Brenor reached out and snatched the reins of his horse, jerking him forward.

'Let me go, Brenor,' argued Aric. 'Let me face him!'

Before Brenor could speak again the battlefield filled with Glass' voice. *'Raxor! I have come for my son!'*

Impossibly, the voice squashed every sound, effortlessly reaching over the armies. Already Aric's father was cutting his way forward. Reecian soldiers swarmed to stop him, forgetting their private skirmishes. The baron's mercenaries fanned out to meet them. Unsure what to do, Aric watched as his father churned toward him, his crazed voice ringing from his helmet. The Devil's Armour swam on him, the tiny figures on it writhing with life. A Reecian spear crashed against it, splintering. The strange sword in his father's hand pointed its way toward Raxor.

'My son, Raxor! Give him to me!'

King Raxor and his captains galloped forward. The old man raised his axe hatefully at Baron Glass.

'You'll not take him! You've taken a boy from me already, monster. You'll not have this one!'

His pledge brought a cheer from the Reecians, who surged forward again to fight. From the rear the catapults renewed their fire, tossing up their burning missiles. Reecian archers drew their beads, loosing their arrows against the baron. One by one the shafts bounced off Glass' breastplate. Aric's father took the blows, raising his strange sword high in the air and cursing Raxor's cowardice.

'King Raxor, stay back,' said Captain Grenel. 'Take the boy with you, back to the rear.'

'No, I won't run from him,' swore Raxor. He looked at Aric. '*You* stay, hear me?'

'My lord, no!'

'Stay put,' said Raxor. He hefted his battle axe and prepared to ride. 'I won't let him take you.'

'He'll kill you!'

'Let him. He's taken my son and the woman I loved. He's taken everything from all of us.' The old king took a deep breath and smiled sadly at Aric. 'I told you, I wasn't coming back from this one.'

The argument was lost and Aric knew it. Raxor ordered Brenor and his Watchmen to stay with Aric, then galloped off with Captain Grenel toward the Norvans. Aric moved to follow him, but Brenor and the others held him back. All he could do was cry for Raxor to come back.

The old king heard him, Aric was sure, but he rode off anyway, toward a fate of certain doom.

Thorin had cleared the first wave of Reecians, easily batting them back. His body roared with burning energy as the magic of the armour filled his muscles. Eye-sight and endurance, vigour and strength, all were enhanced by the Devil's Armour, which hung nearly weightlessly on Thorin's frame so that he moved more like a cat than a soldier. His Akari sword flashed menacingly, too swift for the normal eyes of his enemies. Just as he had been upon the bridge that day, he had become a killing machine. Unstoppable.

Look! Kahldris' voice exploded in his head. *He comes!*

Without needing to look up, Thorin saw the king approaching. He had brought a band of bodyguards with him, all dour-faced men eager to bring the baron down. Past them, Thorin could make out the figure of his son, Aric, struggling to join the fight. Other men, Watchmen, surrounded him.

'Let him go!' Thorin thundered, and without knowing how he heard his voice carry across the field. 'Aric! Son, I'm here for you!'

'No!' Raxor shouted. 'You won't take him!'

The king's men cleared a path for him, letting him ride into Thorin's view. Thorin held his own men back, ordering them to let the Reecian come. Around them the battle raged on, but in that small space a circle was cleared, allowing the rivals to tangle.

'You won't have your son today, Baron Glass,' said Raxor. 'By all the gods, you won't.'

Thorin trotted closer to his nemesis. Aric was shouting in the distance, begging Raxor to come back.

You see, Baron Glass? He taunts you! Kahldris was in a rage, and in his rage drove Thorin mad. *He keeps your son from you, your flesh and blood. He has turned your son against you!*

'Come, then, damn Reecians!' bellowed Thorin. He fought the temptation to tear the helmet from his head and spit at Raxor. 'Finally you are man enough to face me, old man!'

King Raxor jerked his horse to a halt. He wore no helmet himself, only a golden crown of kingship. He looked remarkably calm as he studied his opponent.

'*Murderer.* You have slain my son and taken the flower of Reecian manhood. Be warned, Baron Glass, we will not leave the field today until you are dead.'

'Then it will be a long day of butchery,' said Thorin wearily. He knew that Kahldris was driving him, and yet he barely cared. All he wanted was his son returned. After that, he would be the demon's plaything. With the finger of his gauntlet he waved Raxor closer. 'Come and face me, old man.'

Raxor's men surrounded him, preventing him from riding closer. But the king ordered them away.

'Back away, all of you,' he said. 'Let me face him alone.'

'Yes, let them see how a real man dies,' said Thorin. He shook his head, almost pitying his rival. 'You have no chance at all, Raxor.'

'And you have no heart, but it matters not, Baron Glass. My death will be an example to the others.'

'A martyr? Fine,' sighed Thorin. He slid down from his horse, stepping into the empty circle. The arrows had ceased firing, but the sky still whistled with catapult shots. Behind him his men scattered to avoid the burning blasts. 'Man to man, Raxor. Just you and me.'

King Raxor did not hesitate. Against the calls of his men he dropped from his mount and, axe still in hand, prepared to face the baron. Around him his men fell back. The fighting closest to them ceased as soldiers on both sides watched. Many yards back, Thorin could see his son Aric struggling with the Watchmen, shouting as he tried to break free of them. As their king closed in on his opponent, Aric's protectors faltered, too fascinated by what they were seeing. At last Aric broke away and began galloping toward his father.

'Look, Raxor,' said Thorin gleefully. 'My son comes to me!'

'He comes to save me,' Raxor gloated. 'Not to help his father.'

The accusation stung Thorin, and he lashed out at Raxor, just enough to clip the old man's armour. Raxor stumbled back, dazed by the blow. Thorin stalked after him, spreading his arms wide and dropping his defenses.

'Here I am, Raxor,' he declared. 'Put your axe through my heart!'

Raxor screamed and bolted forward. With two hands upon his axe he plunged the weapon down, catching the unmoving baron squarely in the chest. Thorin felt the blow the way a mountain might, hardly feeling it as his magic armour repelled the blade. Raxor cried out, dropping his axe and staggering backward as the power of the armour numbed his arm. This time, Thorin didn't use his sword. With only his gauntlet he struck the man across the face. Blood burst from Raxor's lips as he tumbled to the ground. This time, his men rushed in to help him. The circle closed all at once as men on both sides took up the fight.

Don't let him get away from you this time, Kahldris insisted. *Kill him.*

Thorin craned his neck over the surging crowd, looking for his son. 'Where is he?'

Listen to me, Baron Glass. Your enemy is at your feet. End him!

A lurching rush of power flooded over Thorin, clouding his mind and strangling his judgment. Through the haze of Kahldris' rage he saw Raxor on his knees, blood covering his face as he struggled to his feet. Aric was coming; Thorin could feel him. The thought of his son and the way he'd been stolen maddened Thorin.

'You took him from me,' he seethed. 'You turned him against me.'

Before the king could rise again Thorin reached out and lifted him from the ground, hoisting him bodily into the air. Raxor tried to grab his sword but Thorin's gauntlet stopped him, grabbing his wrist and crushing the bones.

'He was all I had,' Thorin groaned. He was shaking suddenly, overcome by emotion. 'My only family . . .'

'He despises you,' Raxor spat. 'And everything you stand for now . . .'

'No!' Thorin shook the king, snapping back his head. 'He's my son, not yours!'

'Father!'

Thorin turned to see Aric blazing toward him. The boy had his weapon raised. The blade shot out, smashing hard on Thorin's helmet. The surprise shot opened Thorin's grip, dropping Raxor to the ground. As the king rolled away Aric turned again to face his father. His horse reared up, and Aric's sword pointed hatefully at the baron.

'Enough! You want me, I'm here!'

Raxor staggered to his feet. 'No! I won't let you take him,' he cried, and finally drawing his sword came crashing back against Thorin. Again the blow did nothing and again the old man fell back. Thorin spun and kicked at him, pulling the blow.

What are you doing? asked Kahldris frantically. *Kill him!*

His rage unbalanced Thorin. His screaming rattled Thorin's skull.

They're your enemies, said the demon. *All of them. Even your son tries to kill you. I'm your only friend.*

'Aric,' Thorin cried. 'Leave here!'

The armour moved on its own now. Thorin knew his mind was not his own. Raxor was coming again, the sword slicing down. Thorin brought his arm up, staying the blow, but the old man kept coming. He glanced around, searching for Aric and saw his son racing toward him. This time, Thorin acted. His sword was out in an instant, instinctively, and when Aric was upon him the great Akari blade broke through his son's own sword, shattering it on the way to Aric's chest. A stunned look of terror filled Aric's face as he tumbled from his horse, his breastplate crumbling and filling with blood. He hit the earth hard.

And did not move.

Thorin stood for a moment, frozen. The Akari sword dropped from his hand. He stared at Aric, unable to speak. He could only scream. From deep within him, his agonized wail rocked the battlefield. Raxor, broken and defeated, stumbled and fell to his knees.

'You've killed him,' Thorin heard him say. The old Reecian started to weep.

'I've killed him,' Thorin cried. 'I've killed my son!'

His keening continued as he faltered backward. The battle went on around him, but Raxor and his bodyguards were still, and all the mercenaries who followed Thorin looked at him in shock. Aric's body lay in blood, his chest ripped up from the massive strike. His lifeless eyes stared blankly skyward. In his mind, Thorin could hear Kahldris speaking, urging him to fight on. The words fell deafly on the baron's ears.

'No,' he stammered. He raised his hands in surrender. 'No . . .'

His horse still waited where he'd left it. Thorin ran for it. Ignoring Kahldris' spite-filled orders and the shouts of his own men, Baron Glass mounted the beast and quickly pointed it back toward Library Hill. Behind him, he heard Raxor's hateful calls, swearing vengeance. Thorin buried his head against the neck of his galloping horse. All he could see was Aric, dead and helpless, and the image drove him on, back to the safety of his library.

81

Amid the mass of men and horses, Lukien and his cohorts rode through the heart of the Norvan enemies, their bodies slick with gore as their weapons swung overhead. The wild cries of war dogs echoed through the battlefield as the beasts ran between the legs of the startled horses, bringing down the steeds in ravenous packs. Daralor's army numbered in the thousands, and Lukien was surrounded by them. He had ridden on the heels of the dogs, using them as shields as they tore through the front ranks. With Lorn and Ghost at his side, he had ridden right past Cajanis and his hireling Thon, stabbing at the heart of the Norvans in his mad bid to reach the other side. Prince Daralor was too far away to see now. All Lukien could see behind him were soldiers, the familiar scene of chaos as the battle engulfed him. The roaring in his ears told him that the Nithins had engaged, charging the Norvan lines with their lances, their foes softened by the mad jaws of the war dogs.

Lukien had seen dogs used in battle before, on both sides of the fight, and always been frightened when he'd seen the canines coming toward him. So he flinched a little now when he watched the beasts leap on the mercenaries, launching themselves against the horsemen to tear their throats out. It was a horrible way for a soldier to die, and watching it around him sickened him a bit. Just yards away from Lukien, Lorn fought like a man possessed, shouting the dogs on as he pushed his way deeper through the Norvan ranks. It had taken nearly an hour for them all to get this far, and the numbers of the war dogs had dwindled down to dozens. Along with the corpses of men and horses, the broken bodies of the deadly pets smothered the ground. Lukien did his best to add to the body count. With the Sword of Angels writhing in his grip, he slashed his way across the field, swaying from side to side as he cut down all-comers. The Eye of God tumbled on its chain, bouncing from his chest and burning with red fire. The power of it flooded him, mingling with the strength of his own Akari, and in his mind Lukien could hear the voice of Malator, spurring him onward. The enchanted blade was everywhere, blocking every blow, and those few that did get through dealt him only glancing strikes, cuts so minor that the magic of his two great artifacts healed them instantly. Lukien cried out in bloodlust as he muscled past the mercenaries. Sweat and blood flew from his face.

'Keep going!' he bellowed to his comrades. 'Stay with me!'

Lorn was clearly visible beside him. The axe he had tossed at Cajanis had been replaced by a sword. The old man rode expertly, like a cavalry-man half his age, using his weapon in every conceivable way, stabbing and striking and holding the blade in his metal-garbed hands to block the Norvan attacks. His face shone with a frightening glamour as he gutted his foes, mercilessly avenging his stolen kingdom.

Ghost, however, was nowhere to be seen, yet his handiwork was everywhere. The albino had used his magic early in the charge, horse and rider both disappearing as if slipping into a mist. He said nothing as he fought beside Lukien, not wanting to break the spell that kept him hidden, yet his sword worked quickly and dangerously, stabbing out from the ether to slay his unsuspecting enemies. Word spread quickly through the Norvans that a demon was among them, and men fell back as they sensed him approaching, noting the severed limbs that seemed to come from nowhere. With the dogs to help them and Ghost's invisible blade, Lukien and Lorn had progressed halfway across Cajanis' army. The thunder of the battle from the front of the line reached them like waves against a distant beach.

'We wait for the hawks!' shouted Lukien to the others.

When at last the deadly birds were released, they would make their final charge. Lorn grunted in understanding, his face red with exhaustion. They had done a miraculous thing in getting this far, but they needed the help of Daralor's other pets to get through the rest of the army.

Just as Lukien turned to see what was happening with the Nithins, a single rider came galloping out of the crowd, heading for Lukien with his sword raised. The bare, tattooed arms and bald pate were unmistakable. Thon's charge came like lightening, catching Lukien unaware. He raised his sword a moment too late and felt the flat of Thon's blade smash across his face. Dazed, Lukien nearly fell from his horse. He twisted blindly to the side, groping for Akari strength. The power came to him at once, and as he rose in his saddle he spat hatefully at Thon.

'You stupid troll,' he bellowed. 'The likes of you could never kill me!'

Thon cried out, unleashing a hacking barrage, his big horse muscling back Lukien's own. The Sword of Angels took each blow, singing with Malator's irate voice.

'You're a traitor and a whore-monger!' railed Thon. 'You'll bring ruin to us!'

743

Lukien parried his attack, playing with the man. Lorn and Ghost were at his back, keeping the other mercenaries at bay. 'You'd follow a tyrant just for his gold,' accused Lukien. 'You're a plague on Liiria!'

Thon came again, enraged by Lukien's words. 'I'll end you!' he cried. 'I'll—'

The words died in a gurgle as Lukien's blade slipped through his gorget. Thon's eyes widened with horror, knowing he was dead. As Lukien pulled free his sword, Thon's body fell forward, spiraling down from his horse. Lukien looked at him as he hit the earth, feeling nothing but contempt.

'Too easy,' he whispered, frightened by the power his sword and amulet gave him. Across the field, Nithin soldiers were at last reaching his location, their green, feathered helmets bobbing up from the sea of bodies.

Throughout the battle, Prince Daralor had waited among his reserve soldiers, watching his war dogs and lancemen penetrate the enemy lines. For nearly an hour he had sat imperiously upon his horse, quickly calculating his army's every move while his captains and lieutenants fed reports to him and the forces of Duke Cajanis scrambled to reach him. For the duke, the hour had not gone as hoped, but Prince Daralor wasn't at all surprised. Accustomed to his Nithins being underestimated, he had already supposed he would win the day, despite the Norvans' superior numbers. They were mostly mercenaries, after all, and mercenaries had very little to fight for once the tide began to turn. It was easy to turn the tide with war dogs. Daralor had learned that a long time ago, in his war against Marn. In the ensuing years he had perfected the breed, making them bigger, more fearless. That, along with having truth on their side, made his army the certain victors today.

Not far from where Daralor waited, the hawkers prepared their giant birds for battle, having opened the huge wooden cages. One by one the birds were unhooded, kept tethered to their perches by little collars around their talons. Daralor turned from his captains, spying Glok, the head keeper. Near Glok, on one of the many wagons brought onto the battlefield, a single hawk waited on its perch. Daralor nodded to Glok and the keeper undid the bird's collar. The Prince then raised his arm, summoning the bird, and the hawk took wing, instantly sailing toward its master. Daralor smiled as his pet settled onto his forearm, gently digging its talons into his leather gauntlet. She was much smaller than the other hawks, but she was beloved by the prince nonetheless. It amused Daralor to think that Cajanis and his men expected birds the size of Echo.

'Call your brothers and sisters now, Echo,' Daralor crooned, his lips pursed like he was talking to a baby. The bird cocked back its head and released a peculiar cry. At once the bird's lament was picked up by the others. Prince Daralor did not have to tell Glok to let the war hawks loose. Echo had already done it for him.

Still in the thick of the Norvan army, Lukien and his comrades managed to hold back the coil of mercenaries closing around them. Nearly all the dogs were dead or too badly wounded to keep up the fight. Fifty yards back, Nithin soldiers advanced through the Norvans. Duke Cajanis had taken up a command position on a nearby hill, returning to safety from the worst of the fighting. Through the crush of swords and swinging maces, Lukien could see the duke frantically surveying the battlefield. He still had the advantage of numbers, but the chaos of the fight baffled him, and his men suffered for it. The seasoned fighters sensed the weakness in their leader, but the Norvan regulars among them drove them on, shouting commands. In a moment, Lukien knew, they could easily regain their momentum. Unless one side called retreat, the battle could continue on for hours.

'Lukien, look!'

The voice was Lorn's, and when Lukien turned to him he saw the king pointing westward, toward the Nithin lines. Toward the sky. What Lukien saw there made him reel.

Over the heads of the Nithins, the blue sky darkened with wings. A storm cloud of talons rolled over the field with a pitched, unearthly screech. Daralor's hawks filled the air above the soldiers, shooting up like arrows, their enormous wing spans blotting out the hills behind them. They moved swiftly toward the Norvans, sailing high at first then diving down with outstretched claws. They came in a tide, washing over the field, picking out the choicest flesh and digging their talons deep. Horses whinnied in terror, tossing off their riders while men dropped their swords to cover their heads. But the big, relentless birds took hold of them, working in teams to pull them from their saddles. Seeing this, King Lorn stared in amazement, his mouth dropping open.

'Incredible.'

'Yes, incredible. And they're coming this way!'

This time it was Ghost who spoke. The sight of the war birds made his magic falter, and he reappeared in the middle of the field only yards away from Lorn and Lukien.

'It's time to go,' he said with his usual wryness.

Lukien nodded, made almost mute by the sight of the freakish birds. They had only a few minutes before the shock of the attack wore off. Luckily, the Norvans around them were heading for cover.

'Malator,' said Lukien aloud, 'is Thorin still at the square?'

The Akari was silent for a moment, removing himself from the battle and stretching his mind out to touch his brother. A jolt of surprise went through him.

No, said Malator. *He's left the square. He's riding to the library, Lukien.*

The answer made no sense to Lukien, but he wasted no time. Raising his sword, he called to Ghost and Lorn.

'Follow me!' he cried, and with renewed vigour cut his way through the Norvans.

82

Thunder collected in Thorin's skull as he raced back to the library. He had left behind his men, giving them over to their enemies, but the real guilt that plagued him came from the blow he'd given Aric. It had all happened far too quickly; Thorin could barely remember it. But nothing could expunge the image of Aric laying dead at his feet, twisted and broken and staring wide-eyed at nothing. Thorin choked back sobs as he rode, Kahldris' angry voice ranting in his mind. The demon was screaming, demanding he return to the battle. Thorin girded himself against the assault, too consumed with thoughts of Aric to pay the spirit heed.

Up ahead loomed Library Hill, its winding road and flat yard dotted with soldiers. At the base of the hill milled Lothon and his Liirians, confused by the sight of the lone rider blazing toward them. With his face still hidden behind his grotesque helm, Thorin knew his men could not see his tears, but neither did he think he could control himself. Every twitch he made came with effort as Kahldris worked to turn him around.

'I won't go back!' Thorin railed.

He drove his mount into the crowd of soldiers. Lothon, who had been watching him, hurried up on foot to meet him.

'Baron Glass, what's happened?' asked the old nobleman. He looked genuinely concerned.

Thorin jerked back the reins of his stallion, trying to get it under control. He could barely speak. 'My son,' he stammered. 'Lothon . . .'

Lothon took the horse forcefully by the tack. 'Steady,' he commanded. 'Easy. Baron Glass, tell us what's happened.'

All Thorin wanted was to get away, to climb up into the library and hide. His whole body began to shake. Lothon and his soldiers noticed the quaking instantly – and distastefully. The armour on Thorin's body still writhed with life.

'Fate above, Baron Glass – what's happened to you?' asked Lothon.

Thorin's voice came out like a strangled cry. 'He is taking me!'

'Who?' Lothon demanded.

Thorin wailed, then reached up and pulled the helmet from his head, tossing it hatefully to the ground. With chattering teeth he tried to explain what had happened, but found he could no longer talk. The muscles of his face contorted horribly, making the men stagger back. Lothon grimaced in disgust. He looked at his fellow Liirians in confused horror.

'Look at him, he's mad,' said one of them.

'Let him go,' suggested another.

The baron ripped the reins from Lothon's hands. This time, his old friend made no attempt to stop him. Pulling his horse around, Thorin squeezed his legs together, driving the horse onward and headed for the hill.

Gilwyn had not left the chamber where he'd said good-bye to Thorin. As the battles raged around Koth, he kept his quiet vigil high up in the library, away from the soldiers and staff, brooding as he wondered what was happening. He knew that Lukien was coming for Thorin, yet that happy fact didn't hearten him. Thorin was lost to them, and not even Lukien could save him now.

The sun had reached the apex of the eastern hills, and as Gilwyn stared out the big window he could see the Nithin forces as they battled against the Norvans. From where he stood, Gilwyn couldn't tell how the sides were faring. He supposed it would be a long and bloody day, and full of grief when it was over. Gilwyn touched his hand to the frame of the window. It felt good and solid on his fingers, the way Figgis had intended.

'That was a long time ago,' he told himself.

Ruana had been strangely quiet throughout the morning, sensing Gilwyn's many regrets. Together they had tried to work the catalogue machine, to make it give up its arcane secrets and to find a way to best Kahldris. They had struggled to discover any weakness in the Devil's Armour, but they had failed, and Ruana shared Gilwyn's misery about it. Kahldris was too strong for them. In many ways, they were lucky to still be alive.

Gilwyn?

Ruana's voice surprised him. He replied with a sigh. 'Yeah?'

Look down below.

'Huh?'

There was a commotion going on at the base of the hill. Mostly the Liirians were hidden from him, but Gilwyn could see something was afoot. Some of the men were riding off, toward Chancellery Square. Others were arguing amongst themselves. Gilwyn cursed himself, wondering what he had missed in his daydreaming.

It's Thorin, said Ruana suddenly.

'What about him?'

He's here! Gilwyn . . . he's coming.

Gilwyn raised himself as high as he could, craning to better see out of the locked glass portal. 'I don't see him.'

No, I mean he's here. In the library!

'What?'

Gilwyn pulled away from the window, then heard the stomping footfalls. Someone was coming, and he knew instantly it was Thorin. An unmistakable chill went through Ruana, icing Gilwyn's blood. A moment later the door burst open and Thorin stumbled in. Gilwyn jumped back, shocked at the sight of him. The Devil's Armour was glowing on him with a furious black light. Blood stained his breastplate, feeding the living figures molded there. Thorin's eyes were wild as he searched the room, his jowls sunken, his skin a sickly white. Veins along his neck and forehead bulged as he gave a guttural howl.

'Thorin!'

Thorin spotted Gilwyn across the room. His hands shot up to hide his face. 'Don't look at me!'

At once he stumbled toward the window, spitting obscenities at the sunlight. His hands clawed the heavy curtains, frantically pulling them closed. Then, like a wounded animal, he sank to the polished floor, dissolving in moans. Gilwyn stood frozen, astounded and appalled. Thorin began chattering to himself, making no sense as he looked at some unseen phantom. His rapid-fire words came spilling from his lips.

'I know what you want and I won't do it. I won't do it, I won't do it . . .'

'Thorin!'

Gilwyn's shout broke the baron's stupor. Thorin gasped as he looked Gilwyn, helpless. He raised a gauntleted hand, stretching out his metal fingers toward the boy.

'Gilwyn,' he rasped, 'I killed Aric.'

At first Gilwyn didn't understand, so stunned was he by Thorin's appearance. Slowly, though, the words sank in, and horror dawned on Gilwyn's face.

'Thorin, no . . .'

'I killed him, Gilwyn.' Thorin began to weep. 'He's dead.'

Suddenly the armour began to glow again, this time with a strange white light. As the glow intensified Thorin shrieked, clearly in agony. The image of Kahldris appeared, swirling like a mist around Thorin, strangling him with tendrils of ether. In the mist Gilwyn saw the shape of the demon's face, hissing hatefully into Thorin's ear.

'Leave me alone!' Thorin bellowed.

The enormous pain of it made the muscles of his face contract. Gilwyn had never seen such agony on a man before, and certainly never on Thorin. This time, the Devil's Armour could not protect him.

Gilwyn, look at him, insisted Ruana. *Look at his pain!*

'I see it,' said Gilwyn.

No, you don't understand me. He's in pain, Gilwyn!

Then at last Gilwyn did understand. His eyes widened with the idea. 'Yes!'

Quickly he considered the gambit. Only pain could sever the bond between Akari and host, just as it had broken the bond between White-Eye and Faralok. In all their musings, Gilwyn and Ruana had yet to figure out a way to cause Thorin so much pain, yet now the means was right before them.

Not pain of the body, said Ruana. *Pain of the mind! His son is dead. He killed him, Gilwyn.*

Gilwyn shook his head. 'Ruana, I can't . . .'

Yes you can! You have to do it now!

Thorin was writhing, his arms wrapped around himself as he fought off Kahldris' attack. Man and demon both roared curses at each other, Thorin batting at the air as the insubstantial body of Kahldris clawed at him. They were in a battle Gilwyn scarcely understood, and he was to insert himself between them. Warily he stepped toward Thorin, crouching down close to him. His old friend's eyes, shot through with blood, danced insanely in their sockets.

Do it, Gilwyn, urged Ruana. *Talk to him. Make him feel it.*

Gilwyn licked his lips, hating himself. How could he poke at such a wound? Yet the notion made sense to him, and he knew it was his only chance. And Thorin's too.

'Thorin, tell me what happened,' said Gilwyn. 'Tell me what happened to Aric.'

Thorin stopped squirming and stared at Gilwyn. Kahldris' ghostly essence swarmed over him. He shook his head desperately.

'No. I won't tell you,' he huffed.

'You killed him,' said Gilwyn. 'You killed Aric. That's what you told me.'

Tears squeezed from Thorin's eyelids. 'Yes.'

'Your own son!'

'Yes!'

'He loved you,' said Gilwyn relentlessly. He put his face right up to Thorin's. 'Don't you remember? When he was a boy – he adored you!'

'He loved me,' Thorin echoed. He closed his eyes, his lips trembling. 'And I loved him. My little boy . . .'

'And you killed him.' Gilwyn spoke carefully now. 'Because of Kahldris, Thorin. He's done this to you. He's the one that made you kill your son.'

'Yes . . .'

'Get rid of him, Thorin!'

'*Yes!*'

'*No!*' shrieked Kahldris, pulling free of the armour and forming his figure out of the mists. He looked accusingly at Gilwyn. 'Look at him, Baron Glass. He's just another one who comes to harm you!'

'I'm not,' Gilwyn insisted. 'Listen to me, Thorin – you know me. I'm here to help you, just like Aric wanted. And he's dead! He's dead because you killed him!'

Thorin could take no more. Balling himself up like a child, his buried his face in his arms, screaming at them both to stop. But Gilwyn did not stop. Without mercy he pursued Thorin, peppering him with accusations, driving his pain to a fever. Thorin began seething, blathering to himself, while over him stood Kahldris, swearing in a tongue Gilwyn couldn't understand. Gilwyn stayed close to them both, knowing Thorin was on the brink. Just a little nudge more . . .

Gilwyn . . . Ruana's voice sounded strange. *Easy now.*

'Tell me how you did it, Thorin,' Gilwyn went on. 'Tell me what it felt like!'

'Leave me, boy! Go!'

Gilwyn knelt down next to Thorin. 'I can't Thorin! I want you to know what it felt like to kill your son!'

Gilwyn, stop!

'No!'

The fist shot out too fast to see. Gilwyn glimpsed the gauntlet, a spikey blur flying toward him. A blast of pain filled his chest and he was falling, tumbling back into blackness.

Baron Glass realized what he had done. Through the haze of rage and despair, he saw Gilwyn slide across the floor, then lay still on the stone tiles. Like Aric. The baron stopped breathing. At his side, the figure of Kahldris saw what had happened and was silent. The demon looked at his host. Thorin sat motionless, staring at Gilwyn, unable to speak. He had emptied himself of tears, spending them on Aric, and yet somehow this was so much worse, a thought so horrible that tears seemed inadequate. Thorin's mind snapped like a twig. He got to his feet, glaring hatefully at Kahldris.

'This is our work,' he said, his voice breaking. 'This is all we have ever done!'

Running from the chamber, screaming like a madman, Baron Glass tore at the latches of his Devil's Armour, desperate to shed its unholy grasp.

83

The way to Library Hill was remarkably empty. Lukien, Lorn and Ghost rode on the outskirts of the city, avoiding the populated streets and sticking to the meadows and farmlands that surrounded Koth. Because the hill was clearly visible from almost everywhere in the city, Baron Glass' hideout was plain to the companions as they rode, as was the small army of Liirians he had positioned at the bottom of the hill. The sight of them made Ghost groan. They had already fought their way through one army, and now it seemed Baron Glass had evaded them again. King Lorn looked dour, sizing up their situation.

'It's too late to turn back,' he said, sensing Ghost's wariness. 'They've already seen us.'

Common sense told them all to slow down, bringing their horses from a gallop to a canter. The Liirians milled under their own flag, looking disorganized. There were at least a few hundred of them, men who Thorin had somehow convinced to join his cause. Far too many for the three of them to fight through, Lukien knew. Already those soldiers closest to them were pointing, calling to their comrades. Some wore the midnight blue of Royal Chargers, though that fair breed was long extinct.

'We have to go back,' said Ghost, 'wait for the others.'

'The others may not get here at all,' Lorn reminded him. 'It's up to us to get to Baron Glass, remember?'

'Well I can get past them but what about you?' challenged Ghost. He said to Lukien, 'If I could make you invisible I would, my friend.'

Lukien studied the men ahead of them. 'They're Liirians,' he mused.

Ghost shrugged. 'So?'

'He's one of them,' said Lorn, guessing at Lukien's meaning. He asked the knight, 'Will they listen to you, Lukien?'

'Look at them – they don't even know what they're doing here.' Lukien shook his head. 'Something's wrong. Why has Thorin left the battle? Why isn't he out here with his men?'

'If he knows you're here, perhaps he fears you,' Lorn suggested. 'The demon in him senses the sword no doubt.'

Lukien closed his eye, concentrating on his Akari. Malator was already probing the library.

'Malator? What do you feel?'

Emptiness, replied the spirit. Lukien could sense his confusion. *Baron Glass is still in the library, but my brother . . .*

'What?'

I do not know, Lukien. He hides himself from me. He knows we are here, and yet . . . I can't tell.

'Lukien?' Ghost asked anxiously. 'What's he telling you?'

Malator's words worried Lukien. He told the others, 'He's in there. Malator can't tell anything else.'

Lorn braced himself as they neared the Liirians, who were crowding closer for a better look at them. Liirian riders were preparing to run them down. 'Time to decide, Lukien. If we're going to head back we have to do it now.'

'It's too late anyway,' said Ghost as he drew his weapon.

Lukien said firmly, 'Put it away.'

'Eh?'

'Both of you, don't do anything. Just follow me.'

Lorn and Ghost shared a worried glance but did as Lukien asked, riding at his flanks as the knight led them toward the hill. As the soldiers started to gather, a smaller group coalesced at its centre, all of them on horseback. A single man of rank stood out among them, looking weary beneath his flag. He and his captains waited for the riders to approach, ordering the hundreds of other soldiers to move aside and let them see. Lukien studied the man carefully. Once, he had known every man of rank in the Liirian military, but time had changed that and made them all too old to recognize. Still, it was obvious to Lukien that the man in charge was a Liirian, and that meant they had a kinship. Careful not to threaten them, Lukien remained relaxed in his saddle. Guards sprang out of the crowd to confront them. Near them, crossbowmen aimed at the trio. Ghost leaned over to Lukien and groaned.

'This was a great plan, Lukien. Really.'

'Go on, then disappear,' snarled Lorn. 'Any time you're ready.'

'Shut up, both of you,' snapped Lukien. He took a moment to prepare himself, and before the guards could utter a word shouted, 'My name is Lukien of Liiria! Brothers, hear me!'

The mere utterance of his name sent a ripple through the army. For a moment the crossbowmen faltered. Lukien seized on it.

'We're not here to fight!' he promised. 'We're here to help you!'

The nobleman near the centre of the army came charging forward. 'I know you, Lukien!' he proclaimed with ire. 'Do you not remember me?'

He was still difficult to see so far away. Lukien shook his head. 'I don't know you,' he said. 'Who are you, then?'

'I am Count Lothon. You should remember your betters, Sir Lukien. We all remember you, the one who bedded the king's wife and left us all to rot here. How dare you show your face among us?'

'I am Liirian, just as you, Count Lothon,' replied Lukien. He did now remember the man, a member of the House of Dukes when that body held sway. That was many years ago, and time had not been kind to Lothon. 'And just like you I've come here to save Liiria, not to bury her.'

Count Lothon's men began to bristle, wondering what was happening. Lothon himself came trotting out to face Lukien under the cover of his bowmen. The count stayed their weapons with a wave of his hand and the bowmen backed off a bit. The entire army seemed to have its eyes on the three riders.

'Who are these you bring with you?' Lothon asked.

'Friends of Liiria,' said Lukien. 'Like myself.' He said nothing about their identities, especially Lorn's. 'They ride with me because they want to rid us all of a tyrant. Count Lothon, I beg you – listen to me. Baron Glass is not the man you remember. You've seen him yourself, you know this to be true.'

For the first time, Lukien noticed the object dangling from Lothon's saddle. The count nodded as he saw Lukien's expression darken. The thing was a helmet.

'Baron Glass has been here today,' sighed Lothon miserably. 'And I will not lie and say he is anything but what you claim, Sir Lukien. He is a tyrant, true. And a madman now, too.'

'I can stop him,' Lukien promised. 'You know my prowess, Count Lothon.'

'Aye, and I know you bear the Sword of Angels. It does not matter, Bronze Knight. We are pledged to Baron Glass, all of us.'

'You're pledged to Liiria, first and always.' Lukien addressed them all, letting his voice carry through the ranks. 'Will you let the Norvans take everything from you? Your manhood, even? Baron Glass is no Liirian, not anymore. He's as foreign to this land as Jazana Carr and the mercenaries she brought with her. The creature inside Baron Glass has no loyalty to you at all. It's using you, all of you, to get its revenge on the people of Jador. That's it. That's all it's ever wanted.'

His words fell heavily on Lothon. The count hefted the helmet wearily from his side, unhitching it from the tack. He held it out disgustedly. 'I despair to even touch this thing,' he told Lukien, 'but by no means is Baron Glass finished. He wears the armour still.'

'Does he? You have seen him?' Lukien asked.

'I have not followed him into the library. None of us have,' said Lothon.

It was obvious to Lukien how much the men disliked Glass now, but the count seemed reticent to explain what had happened.

'Then let me pass,' said Lukien. 'Let me end it, for us all.' He put up his hands in a gesture of peace. 'You know me, Count Lothon. You knew me before Liiria was the ruin it is now. Baron Glass left Liiria too, but you found forgiveness for him.'

Lothon's aides shot him worried glances. The nobleman stared with a grimace at the helmet in his fist. The army was hushed as Lothon considered Lukien's proposal. Even the soldiers lining the long road up the hillside stood unmoving, wondering what was happening.

'He's mad,' said Lukien sadly. 'You said so yourself.'

'Aye, mad,' admitted Lothon. 'Because of this wretched thing.' His eyes filled with pity. 'He was a good man once, you know. He loves Liiria dearly even still. But it's a twisted love.' He held the helmet out for Lukien. 'Take it. Destroy it with your sword.'

'You'll let us pass?'

Lothon nodded. 'Do what you must, Bronze Knight, but do it with mercy.'

Then he gave the order to his aides, calling to all of them to let the riders past. The word was quickly passed throughout the ranks, rising up to the hillside and the soldiers stationed there. Amazingly, the soldiers cheered. Lukien could not contain his smile, so relieved was he to have won his gambit. He rode up to Count Lothon and placed a hand on the man's shoulder.

'I will best him,' he promised, 'and Liiria will be free again for men like you.'

Lothon said nothing, overcome with regrets, and handed the helmet of the Devil's Armour to Lukien. The metal felt cool in Lukien's hand, but the death's face was no longer alive, nor was the black surface glowing. Still, to hold the thing made Lukien shudder. He looked grimly at Lorn and Ghost.

'Ready yourselves,' he told them. 'This isn't over.'

To Lukien, it seemed like a lifetime had passed since he'd last been inside the library. Then, it had been the Liirians who had held the place, holding it against the twin tides of Baron Glass and Jazana Carr. Hundreds of men had died that day, brave souls all, many of them friends. Under the punishing bombardment of Norvan catapults, the library had collapsed in places, but it had all been rebuilt with Jazana's fortune and Thorin's obsession, and as he walked within its great hall Lukien could not help but marvel at the way it sparkled. Thorin had spared no expense in remaking the library. It was every bit as fabulous as it had been in its heyday, or so Lukien supposed. He had never actually seen the place in its glory days. He had been away, in exile.

'Everyone's gone,' Ghost whispered.

It was as the servants in the yard had told them. They had seen Baron Glass stumble into the library like a drunkard, raving insanely, and had rightfully been afraid of him, abandoning the place for the protection of the soldiers outside. Count Lothon had known this but had not revealed that important bit of truth, a fact that made Lukien smile at his cleverness.

'Lothon is a fox,' he said with a nervous laugh. 'Now he has us to do his dirty work.'

'Never mind,' said Lorn. 'Where's Glass? Lukien, can you tell?'

Lukien listened for Malator. The Akari was out ahead of them, searching the halls with his mind. The sword that held his essence burned in Lukien's fist, thrumming musically through the hall. Ghost and Lorn had drawn their weapons as well.

I can feel my brother, said Malator. *There was a trace of awe in his voice. He's here.*

'Where, Malator? Take us to him.'

Not precisely knowing what he would do when he found Thorin, Lukien let Malator guide his steps. The three men moved cautiously but with purpose, leaving the grand hall for another, smaller one, then finally up a long flight of winding steps. Like the main hall, the others were deserted as well, lending a sad aura to the place. Lukien remained as patient as he could, his heart galloping in his chest as he tried to bury the memories of his last encounter with Thorin. That one had left him near death. He glanced at Ghost and saw the same spark of dread in the young man's eyes. Amazingly, Lorn showed no such fear. He was resolute as they rounded the halls, as hard as ever, like iron.

Then, Malator spoke again. *He's here.*

Lukien stopped. 'Where?'

Up ahead. Malator seemed to sigh. *Don't be afraid, Lukien. It's over.*

'Over?' blurted Lukien. 'What . . . ?'

Go on. See for yourself.

Torchlight lit the way, guiding them through the hall. They were in the highest part of the library now, in the tower where Lukien himself had spent hours, laying plans for the hill's defense. He knew that a chamber lay ahead, a kind of meeting room with a great view of the city. Before the chamber was another hallway, dimly lit. It beckoned to them as they turned a corner. When they did, all of them saw what Malator had seen already.

756

Balled up against the wall beneath a flickering oil lamp was Thorin, his face buried in his one remaining arm, his knees pulled up tightly to his chest. His shoulders shook; his legs and hands trembled. His white hair hung in limp, filthy strands down his back. Hunched like an animal, he took no notice of the others, nor of the suit of armour discarded in a pile beside him. Lukien gripped the Sword of Angels tightly, then let his grasp wane as pity overtook him. Ghost mumbled a prayer.

'Thorin,' Lukien said gently, 'it's me, Lukien.'

Slowly, Baron Glass lifted his head. His glassy gaze met Lukien, blood-shot and full of pain. He was barely recognizable, a withered shell of a man. Once again, there was only a stump where his left arm had been. His wizened face showed off his insanity, a mask of twisted muscles and thin, pale lips. Like a dog he began to pant when he saw Lukien, as if unable to speak. Lukien hurried over to him and dropped to his knees beside his old friend.

'It's over, Thorin, it's over,' he said, trying to comfort him. 'Listen to me now, I'm here. Everything is all right now.'

Thorin's haunted eyes widened. 'Lukien . . .'

'Yes, Thorin, it's me.' Lukien attempted a smile. 'Just me.'

'Lukien . . .'

'Don't speak too much, Thorin. Just tell me – where's Gilwyn? Is he here with you?'

A shaking groan came out of Thorin then, his hand clutching Lukien. 'Gilwyn and my son . . . I . . .'

'Thorin?' Lukien held him tightly. 'What?'

The baron's boney finger pointed to the chamber down the hall. 'In there,' he stammered. 'Dead.' He began to sob. '*Gilwyn.*'

Panic seized Lukien. He sprung to his feet. 'No. No . . .'

Ghost dropped his weapon at once. 'I'll go see,' he said quickly.

'No!' Lukien steeled himself. 'Stay with him. Both of you, just stay with him.'

It was something Lukien wanted to face himself, because he knew what would happen if he saw Gilwyn dead. He would weep like a woman, and for that he wanted no audience. His legs like water beneath him, he made his way down the corridor, toward the chamber where Thorin had pointed, leaving his companions behind with the maddened baron. The Sword of Angels still rested in his hand, but as he reached the open doorway he sheathed the weapon, pausing at the threshold before peering inside. The chamber was quiet, and as big as he remembered it. A huge window – its curtains drawn – dominated an entire wall. In the feeble light it was difficult to see, but Lukien saw Gilwyn at once, not far from the window, sprawled and broken-looking on the tiles. Blood smothered his chest, collecting on the floor beneath him.

Lukien began to cry like he were a child.

'Gilwyn . . .'

He went to him, stooping over him, looking down at his white face, the blood drawn from it. The wound in his chest ran deep, a jagged gash like one might get from a morning star. Lukien wiped his eyes with his fingers, then knelt down next to his beloved friend. He put a hand on his face and felt its chill. The moment he did, Malator popped into his mind.

He's not dead!

'What?'

He's alive, Lukien, barely.

'Alive? Are you sure?'

His Akari has not left him. I can feel her, Lukien. She clings to him still.

Lukien groped frantically for an idea. 'How can I save him? Look at him, Malator!'

Lukien, the amulet. Give it to him. Put it on him quickly.

Instantly Lukien reached under his shirt and pulled out the Eye of God. 'Will it work?'

You give it to him freely, Lukien. The magic will keep him alive.

'Oh, Amaraz, I beg you,' Lukien pleaded. He place the amulet on Gilwyn's bloody chest, holding it there and praying to the Akari inside the Eye to spare his friend. 'Bring him back to me, Amaraz, please. Heal him. Keep him alive.'

Keep it on him, Lukien, said Malator. *You don't need the amulet any longer. I will keep you alive.*

Without a thought for himself, Lukien pressed the Eye hard against Gilwyn's motionless chest.

Out in the corridor, King Lorn stood apart from Ghost and the broken Baron Glass, staring at the heap of black armour laying uselessly nearby. The helmet of the armour had been left upright, deposited next to the rest of the metal suit by Lukien in his haste to save his friend. Doing just as Lukien had asked, Ghost remained with Baron Glass, kneeling next to him and comforting him. Glass himself was a pitiful mess, barely able to speak much less control his womanly tears. At first, Lorn had pitied him. But then he'd heard a voice.

The voice echoed inside his skull and was not his own. Lorn stared at the helmet. The helmet stared back. The voice spoke gently, like a lullaby, talking to him about his kingdom and all he had lost, and about the many people who had wronged him in his life. Somehow, Lorn knew instantly that the voice belonged to Kahldris. Yet he was not afraid. The demon's words were so sensible.

*

For long minutes Lukien knelt over Gilwyn, pressing the amulet against his chest and waiting for any tiny sign of life. Malator assured him that his young friend was still alive and the Akari had not yet left his body, but Lukien could sense only the barest warmth within Gilwyn and a heartbeat he wasn't even sure was there. The war that raged outside the library had flown from Lukien's mind, forgotten. Now, he thought only of Gilwyn and the amulet, and did his best to will Amaraz to save the boy.

'Amaraz, please,' Lukien whispered, his hand trembling on the Eye of God. Gilwyn's blood soaked his fingers. Lukien could feel the wound beneath the ruined shirt, the jagged bits of flesh torn, he supposed, by the spikes of Thorin's gauntlet. Malator hung over him, watching and hoping with his host, assuring Lukien that Amaraz was up to the task and that the boy would live.

He has saved you twice now, remember, said the Akari.

'I was never this bad,' Lukien retorted. 'Not like this . . .'

Malator did not argue. He was there for Lukien, and that was enough. His presence comforted the knight. As the moments ticked away, Lukien kept up his vigil, mumbling pleas to Amaraz and holding the Eye of God fast to Gilwyn's body.

Then, at last, Gilwyn breathed. He took a great gulp of air, shouting, his shoulders bunched with pain. Lukien reared back. Still holding the Eye, he laughed joyously.

'It's working!' he exclaimed.

Beneath his fingers he could feel the wound begin to close, the ragged flesh miraculously knitting together. The blood began to bubble through Lukien's fingers as Gilwyn's heart grew stronger, and soon a warmth swept his body. Overjoyed, Lukien grinned as Gilwyn began to pant.

'Thank you, Amaraz,' Lukien cried. 'Thank you!'

He began to place the amulet's chain around Gilwyn's neck when he heard a noise at the threshold. Someone was coming. Lukien called to the person over his shoulder.

'He's alive! Thorin didn't kill him!'

'Lukien . . .'

Alarmed, Lukien spun toward the door. 'Ghost?'

The albino clung to the door, staggering as he tried to hold himself upright. Blood sluiced from a wound at his temple. Lukien leapt to his feet.

'Ghost!'

Somehow Ghost managed to stumble into the chamber, falling into Lukien's arms. 'Lorn,' he gasped. 'The armour . . .'

Lukien helped his friend to the floor, letting him lie still on the tiles, then quickly began fumbling with the folds of his gaka so he could breathe better. 'What happened, Ghost?'

Ghost's hands clawed the tiles as he gulped for air. 'I don't know . . . Lukien, he has the armour.'

'He attacked you?'

The albino nodded, squeezing his eyes closed. 'I'm sorry,' he moaned. 'Damn him . . .'

'What about Thorin?'

Ghost turned his face away in misery. 'Lukien . . .' He hesitated. 'I think he's dead.'

Lukien rose to one knee, furious. 'Lorn did this?' he seethed. 'Lorn did this!'

He wanted to go after him, to take the Sword of Angels and plunge it through the Norvan's heart. But Gilwyn was only barely alive, and Ghost was badly wounded. And then, he thought of Thorin. He got to his feet, knowing that his old friend was dead. Malator did not have to tell him so. He could feel the emptiness of the world without Baron Glass.

'I have to go get help,' he told Ghost. 'Don't move.'

'Don't worry,' promised Ghost. He turned his head to look at Gilwyn. 'Gilwyn . . .'

'He'll live,' said Lukien. All the joy had left him. 'But King Lorn the Wicked will not.'

84

Along the rough terrain to Norvor, King Lorn rode on a borrowed horse toward his homeland, marveling at the feel of the Devil's Armour on his body. He had ridden without rest for more than a day and he was not fatigued at all. He had no food or water with him, yet his person craved neither, nourished instead by the strange magic of the demon Kahldris. The south had been blessedly uneventful, and Lorn had exhausted more than one mount in his bid to get home, eventually stealing horses where he could find them from unsuspecting riders. Now, though, the badlands of Norvor stretched out in front of him, just beyond the swiftly running river. Here the hills rose up like sentinels, grey and wind swept, shaped by eons into twisted giants. There were no homesteads for Lorn to raid now, only the siren-song of his homeland playing on the breeze. The dust of the earth struck his face, peppering his skin. He had removed the armour's helmet almost immediately after fleeing Koth, preferring instead to feel the air on his hair and beard. King Lorn examined the hills, choosing a single, rugged plateau from which to make his stand. The perch would afford him a view of both Norvor and the enemies he knew were chasing him.

'There,' he pronounced, not really speaking to anyone, though he knew that Kahldris shared his every thought. The odd union with the spirit had unbalanced him at first, as had the soaring power of the Devil's Armour. Night was coming. Already the sun was starting to dip, making shadows grow. Lorn looked longingly at Norvor, knowing that just beyond the river his throne awaited him. It would be a struggle to reclaim it from Jazana's loyalists, but with the armour his triumph was assured. 'We've paid in blood for this,' he sighed.

Getting out of Koth had not been easy. Once again, he had earned the title 'wicked.' Ghost had tried to stop him first, and then the weakling Baron Glass. Too withered to stand the blow, Glass' skull had cracked like an eggshell. Ghost, Lorn supposed, had survived. He wasn't at all proud of the things he had done, but it had all been for a reason, and he rehearsed now what he would say to Lukien when the knight finally came after him, going over all the reasons in his mind, telling himself that Lothon's men had died because they were fools. Surely they should have known they couldn't stop him, and yet a dozen of them had tried before the old count himself had called them off. Lorn shook his head, genuinely disgusted with himself, and started up his horse again, beginning to climb the hillside.

When night finally came, Lorn found himself staring at the death's head helmet by the light of the fire he had made. Finally, he allowed himself to feel tired. Reclining against his elbow, he considered the helmet, which he had propped up opposite him like a companion. Kahldris had spoken to him very little since leaving Koth, and when he did it was always gently, as though the two had known each other forever. Lorn knew the demon's treachery however. He had seen what Kahldris had done to Baron Glass and had no intention of becoming such a lunatic. Picking up a small stone, he tossed it at the helmet, pinging it against the faceplate.

'You there,' he snapped. 'Listen good. You're pretty pleased with yourself, I'd bet. You think you found yourself a new fool to take you where you want to go, don't you? Well, forget it. I'm not some weak-minded fool like Thorin Glass, and you've already given me what I want most. I'm home, demon. Finally.'

Kahldris said nothing. The lifeless helmet merely sat there.

'Let's understand each other,' Lorn continued. 'You're going to help me get my kingdom back. It's mine. It belongs to me, and so do you now. I'm the master and you're the slave, and if ever I find you toying with my brain I will lock you in a dungeon so deep even the worms won't ever find you. I didn't want to kill Baron Glass or those others, and I don't intend to be your plaything. If you need blood to stay strong I'll slaughter some chickens for you. Right?'

Again the spirit did not respond. Annoyed, Lorn tossed another pebble at it.

'Nothing to say? All right, then. We understand each other. Lukien will be coming for us. He'll never let us rest. So we're going to face him, right here. And when that's done we're going to Carlion to get back my throne.'

A saucer-like moon hung above the plateau. Lorn smiled up at it, satisfied. He was weary, tired of so much traveling. He had been on the road for months now, so long his journey seemed endless.

'Enough talk,' he said. 'Get some rest, demon. Tomorrow we have work to do.'

Lukien looked ahead to where the river cut across the terrain, finally noticing the familiar landscape of Norvor. His weary horse snorted beneath him, caked in the dust of the road and nearly lame from lack of rest. The sun had come up hours ago, marking their third day on the road to Norvor. They had ridden without stopping the entire morning, and all the horses of the company were faring no better than Lukien's. Count Lothon and his men – ten of them in all – scanned the horizon dotted with rocky hills. Lothon himself rode close to Lukien, staying at his side the whole way while the other Liirians trailed out in a long tail behind them. Lothon took his water skin from the loop at his saddle, offering it first to Lukien. When Lukien declined, the old man took a miserly pull from the skin, conserving its contents out of habit alone. With the river so close, they could water the horses and fill up their skins, but Count Lothon took only mild notice of the waterway. Like all of them, his eyes were fixed instead on Norvor.

'Ugly,' he pronounced. 'How did you ever manage to spend so much time there?'

'I had no choice, remember,' Lukien said, mildly annoyed. 'And not all of Norvor is like that. Those are the badlands.'

'Hanging Man.'

Lukien nodded. 'Yes.'

He thought about his days with Jazana Carr, the years they had spent together at Hanging Man with Thorin. He would not be seeing the fortress again, though. Lorn hadn't got that far, nor was he still on the move. It had been an easy thing to track the traitor, because Malator could sense his brother and because King Lorn did nothing to hide his tracks. He expected them to come after him. He wanted them to come.

'He's close now,' mused Lukien. 'Another hour maybe. Maybe less.'

Lothon grimaced at the prophecy. 'I have had my fill of magic and demons. Pardon me if I say I do not trust yours, Lukien. He is sure of this?'

Lukien's gaze narrowed on the horizon, where a rise of plateaus hung above the flat earth. On one of them, Lorn waited. 'Positive.'

There was no doubt of it, not to Malator, and the fact made Lothon and his men grimace. After what had happened back in Koth, Lothon had insisted on going after Lorn with Lukien. He had lost five men when the Norvan had burst from the library, garbed in the Devil's Armour in his hurry to flee. More would have died with them if Lothon hadn't ordered them to stand down. They had let Lorn go, because Lothon knew they couldn't stop him.

Word had spread quickly about Thorin's death. In the east, Duke Cajanis' army collapsed, routed by Daralor and his Nithins and dispirited over the death of their benefactor. In Chancellery Square the same had occurred, where the Norvan mercenaries had first seen Baron Glass abandon them. King Raxor and the Reecians did not slaughter the Norvans, however, but rather pulled back from the city so that the Nithins and Lothon's troops could take control. The city was still in chaos, but Gilwyn and Ghost were both safe within the library. Ghost's wounds, though far less serious than Gilwyn's, would take a long time to heal. Gilwyn, on the other hand, had healed miraculously. Already Lukien could not wait to return to his young friend. After so many months of separation, they had once again been separated. And because Gilwyn now wore the Eye of God, there were things Lukien needed to explain to him. When he had left the boy, he had seen the uneasiness on his face.

For Lukien, the death of Baron Glass was the like the end of hope. All through his journey to Tharlara and back again, he had dared to imagine saving Thorin, bringing back the man he had once been. Instead, he had seen a shambling mound of humanity, with barely a hint of the once great and proud Thorin. But in the end, he had saved himself. That, at least, brought a sad smile to Lukien's face.

Count Lothon continued on without speaking, confident that soon they would find King Lorn. He was an old man now, but canny and fearless, with the same sense of righteousness Lukien remembered from years ago. Lukien was grateful for the noble's company, but all of them knew they could do nothing against the Devil's Armour. That bad business fell to Lukien alone, and to the sword slapping at his thigh. For Lukien, Malator had been like a bloodhound in leading them to his brother, but now the real battle was about to begin. As the plateaus began to rise up above them, Malator's presence trembled with anticipation. The Akari spoke once again, his voice cool and certain.

Lukien, he's there, on the ledge ahead of us.

Lukien looked up, and as he did the image of Lorn appeared, leaning out over the ledge. Lothon gasped, pointing up at him.

'There he is!'

The riders stopped immediately. Lukien put his hand on the pommel of his sword. Malator's energy charged through him. Lorn gazed down and gave a small nod of regard. The helmet of the armour rested in the crux of his elbow. On his chest and arms, the black metal gleamed. He raised his chin and shouted down at his pursuers, his voice spilling down the hillside like a waterfall.

'I'm here, Lukien,' he declared. 'I'm ready. To your left there's a way up the hill. I'll wait for you here.'

Then he was gone, disappearing back behind the ledge. Lukien looked left and saw that there was indeed a grade to the hill, one that he could easily climb without his horse. The setting put him in a mind of another duel he had fought, just a few short years ago. There was no more time to rest or prepare himself. He had come this far with a purpose, and before he could ever return to Cassandra there was one more battle ahead. Knowing there was little he could do for the knight, Count Lothon once again took out his water skin and handed it to Lukien. This time, Lukien accepted.

'We'll be here. We won't leave you,' said the count.

Lukien sipped at the water, then licked his sun-cracked lips. He handed the skin back to Lothon with thanks. 'You're a good man, Lothon, and you have good men following you. Whatever happens to me up there, remember to take care of Liiria.'

'I have faith in you,' said Lothon, smiling. 'You've been dead more than once, but somehow you keep coming back again.'

'It's a curse,' said Lukien. He slid down from his saddle. 'No man should live forever, Count Lothon. Especially not King Lorn the Wicked.'

'His head would make a fine trophy for my study. If you don't mind . . .'

'I'll oblige if I can,' said Lukien, then turned and headed toward the grade.

At the top of the plateau, Lorn waited with the helmet in his hands, quietly contemplating the view to his homeland. He regretted the need to kill Lukien, but was sure the knight would never relent. Kahldris began to speak to him, whispering in his mind, telling him about the greatness that awaited him in Carlion. They would rebuild Norvor together, said the demon. They would be invincible. It made no sense to mourn the death of a single man, Kahldris explained. Lukien and Malator were just two insignificant souls. In the great design of things, they mattered not at all.

'Enough,' Lorn muttered, shaking his head. 'You are like a bad breakfast that won't stay down, spirit. Get out of my mind.'

The feeling of Kahldris faded from his brain, but not the energy he gave. Lorn flexed his fingers in their metal sleeves. He had never felt stronger, not even as a young man.

'I'm not a man any more,' he told himself. 'I'm more than a man.'

Silently he watched the edge of the plateau, waiting for Lukien to come.

Lukien took his time climbing the grade, keeping the Sword of Angels sheathed to his side. Sweat dripped down his nose onto his boots as he walked, and he cursed himself for blundering so quickly into Lorn's rocky lair. He should have waited, he supposed, and rested for the fight as Lorn had. But in the end Lukien didn't really care. He wanted things to be over, and if that meant losing . . .

No, he told himself. I will not lose. *For Thorin's sake, I will have my vengeance.*

He reached the top of the grade a moment later, stepping onto the flat surface of the plateau and staring straight into Lorn's eyes. The king surprised him by sighing.

'You're a mountain lion, Lukien,' said Lorn. 'I knew you'd find me wherever I hid.'

Lukien looked around. The sky remained perfectly blue. 'You picked a nice place to die, Lorn. You know what the Akari say – the place you die is where you spend eternity. I hope you like it here.'

'Let me extend you a courtesy, Lukien. I know you won't listen, but honour begs me to try. Turn around and go home. Go back to Liiria and find a hole to bury that sword. I don't want to fight.'

Lukien stepped closer. 'But I do. You've taken something dear to me, Norvan, and now I can't get it back.'

Lorn stood his ground. 'Baron Glass tried to stop me, Lukien. Ghost, too. I am sorry Glass is dead, but he's better off, I think.'

'Maybe,' said Lukien. 'The demon inside that suit of armour turned his brain to porridge. He'll do the same to you unless you give him up.'

'I can't do that, Lukien. I can't be king without the armour, and I can't live without being king.'

'And your daughter? What about her? What about the rest of the people in Jador and Grimhold? Once you get your kingdom back, will you ride against them next?'

'I'll send for my daughter and Eiriann once Carlion is mine again. With the help of the armour that should not be long.'

He was still the Lorn that Lukien knew; there was no trace yet of Kahldris' corruption. The old king was as hard and resolute as ever, and Lukien was sure there could be no reasoning with him. At last he drew his sword.

'Then we are done talking.'

Lorn frowned. 'Regrettably, yes,' he said, and placed the horned helmet over his head. Then he drew his own sword, not the Akari blade Thorin had used but the same one he had battled with against the mercenaries. As he stalked closer, he took the sword in both fists, making little circles in the air.

Lukien parroted his dance, moving side to side, waiting for the first blow. Quickly he searched his mind for Malator, asking him the only question that mattered.

When?

Malator replied, *When the metals touch, I will meet him in our world.*

'All right,' said Lukien aloud, 'get ready!' and launched himself against Lorn. He was in the air, flying at the Norvan, and quickly plunging down his sword. Lorn moved just as quickly, but only with his forearm. Astonishingly, he released his sword with his right hand, bringing up his arm to block the Sword of Angels. Black and silver metals clashed, showering the men with sparks. Lukien felt the charge of it throughout his body like an icy rain. His sword skidded down the metal with a shriek, and he knew that part of Malator had left him, flying off to the world of the dead.

Malator emerged headlong into the dead place, stepping into being as if born from a mist. Around him, he saw the place where he had died in Tharlara, full of story stones, the sky overhead pink with twilight. The serpent people who had sheltered him were nowhere to be found, but he was not alone in the garden. Ahead of him was Kahldris, looking youthful and fit, dressed as the general he had been in life. Resting in his fist was a hoka, the long sword with a slightly curved blade he had always favoured. Malator glanced down at his own hand and found the same type of blade there, emblazoned with the crest of their family. Unlike his brother, Malator did not wear the heady garb of a general. He had chosen to come to this world the way he had lived his final days, dressed in the simple garb of the Tharlarans. Kahldris, looking grand in his armour, smirked at Malator's choice of uniform. The reunion between them had been ages in the making. Yet Malator could not think of a single thing to say. When they were alive, Malator did not hate his brother, and so did not hate him now. It was more important to fear Kahldris, Malator knew. The key to Kahldris was the depths of his obsessions.

Kahldris' smile widened as he studied his surroundings, looking completely out of place in the peaceful setting. 'This is where you came,' he said with a deep breath. 'This is what you left us for. It reminds me of you, Malator. You're like the flowers here – weak and pretty.'

His brother was much as Malator remembered, larger in every proportion and much fiercer looking than Malator. Kahldris took after their father, also a man of the Akari military. Their delicate mother had gifted Malator with her bones, making him light on his feet, like a dancer. The older Kahldris had always envied his sibling's speed. Where Kahldris was the thinker of the pair, a military mastermind, it was the smaller, slighter Malator who was the better with a sword – and in combat. Kahldris seemed not to remember that, however, looking supremely sure of himself. He touched the point of his hoka lightly with his finger, preparing himself for the battle.

'Tell me, brother – did you find what you were looking for here? Were these sweet-minded gardeners willing to come to your aid?'

'They were,' said Malator. 'They were brave and kind to me and they would have helped us in Kaliatha.'

'But we were out of time,' Kahldris reminded him angrily, 'because you ran away. I made the armour for you, brother, and you turned your back on it, on all of us.'

'And you've believed that lie forever,' said Malator. 'I pity you, brother. You've wasted your eternity hating me.'

Kahldris grinned. 'I'll feel better once you're gone. Then all the obstacles will be out of my way.'

Flexing his hoka, Malator sprang toward his brother, bouncing on the balls of his feet. He was done talking. The time had come at last.

The Sword of Angels screamed as it cut through the air, a glowing tail of flames stretched out behind it. Each time it cracked against the Devil's Armour, fire flew from its blade. Lukien's hand burned with its power; his fingers coiled perfectly around its hilt. Like the living metal of Lorn's black suit, the weapon came to life in Lukien's grasp, writhing and stretching as it sang its magical tune. Lorn had withstood every blow, blocking some while others snuck through his defenses, ineffectually smashing the armour but nevertheless driving him back. He was a fine swordsman, nearly Lukien's equal, and the Devil's Armour made him fearless. His black limbs were everywhere, spinning and kicking, forcing Lukien to move like lightning to avoid his heavy blows. Time slipped from Lukien's mind, meaningless. Had it been a minute since he'd climbed the hill? An hour? In the heat of the mêlée, only movement mattered, the deadly ballet of combat.

Fire erupted from Lukien's sword as he swept low for the mid-section. Lorn moved faster than any man could, pivoting to smash the sword aside. The death's head he wore was ablaze with rage, its skull-like features changing with its wearer. Lorn moved in, butting Lukien with his shoulder and sending him sprawling. The concussion knocked the wind from his lungs. He rolled back and sprang to his feet, summoning the magic from his blade.

'Malator, help me send this beast to hell!'

He had only to speak the spirit's name to feel his other-worldly muscle. It flooded him, scintillating down the length of the sword and into his arm, filling his body with strength. Again he sprang, growling like a tiger and threading the sword past Lorn's own, straight for the hateful helmet. Blinded by sparks of fire, Lorn staggered. For the first time his weapon came up clumsily, nowhere near Lukien. Pressing the advantage, Lukien slammed the flat of his weapon against Lorn's head. Amazingly, he shouted, not in pain but in frustration.

In the world of the dead, Malator too pressed his attack, smashing his own weapon against his brother's armoured shoulder. No fire flew from his hoka, no magic music came off the blade. There was only the old-fashioned screech of steel as the siblings crashed again and again, trading blows and the advantage, each of them growing fatigued. It didn't matter that they were dead already or that they had no bodies to exhaust. Here in this corporeal state, they had chosen to focus their hatreds, making them real. No one would die here in the dead place, but one would be vanquished even so, and in the world of the living they would perish, expunged from that realm forever. Both knew the stakes were impossibly high, and both Akari gave no quarter. Kahldris slashed relentlessly at Malator, using his greater strength to wear his brother down. Always too quick, Malator danced away from his brother's hoka, spinning and jumping and then coming again to attack.

'I'm your better, brother, face it,' spat Malator. 'We can fight forever and you would never win.'

'Then let it be forever!' Kahldris roared. He broke off his attack, fading back to catch his footing. Around them the world began to change. Slowly, others popped in to being, the ghostly bodies of fellow Akari coming to see the siblings duel. Unnerved, Kahldris looked at him with spite. 'Cowards! I gave you all the means to save yourselves!'

The spirits did not answer him, they simply kept coming, rising up from the story stones or drifting down from the sky until there were hundreds of them shimmering in the light of the undead sun.

'They know you, Kahldris,' said Malator. 'They remember you for the madman you were.'

Kahldris kept his distance from his brother, unable to look away from the accusing Akari. 'They let themselves be slaughtered because they were too afraid,' he said. His face showed more than loathing now. A hint of regret glimmered in his eyes. 'Why were you such sheep?' he asked them, looking up as more of them descended. 'All I wanted was to save us all!'

'That's a lie,' said Malator. 'Every Akari knows the truth. You were a butcher, brother. You were depraved and they were right to fear you. Now they come to see your end.'

Kahldris shook his head. 'They are wrong, and so are you. No one knew my heart. Tell me I wasn't right about the Jadori, Malator. Tell me they weren't animals! They came and massacred us, and you were nowhere to be found.' He turned to his unwanted audience, shouting as he spun to see the whole garden. 'You hate *me*? He was the one who abandoned us!'

Throughout the story garden, the spirits were silent. Enraged by them, Kahldris came again at his brother, screaming and raising his weapon. This time, though, his attack seemed slower. His maddened face twisted with a new kind of anguish. Malator ducked left, easily dodging the attack. His brother turned as he blew by, snarling into Malator's face.

'End me!'

Malator reared back. His brother lowered his sword, looking pitiful.

'I can't beat you,' Kahldris groaned. 'And I can never win their hearts.' The ancient general tossed his sword at Malator's feet. 'Damn you for being better. For being loved when I was hated. Damn you forever, Malator.'

For a moment Malator was dumbstruck, too astounded to move. The audience of his fellow Akari moved in to circle the siblings, waiting for the end.

'Send me back,' said Kahldris. 'Send me back so I never need look at them again.'

Malator understood. There was no place so peaceful as that private place of death. Malator's was this garden. Kahldris' was a tomb-like temple full of stone and moss. Despite its coldness, he longed to return there. The old general no longer seemed young to him. To Malator, he was as ancient as the world, his face poisoned by rage and madness. He refused to look at his fellow Akari as they closed in around him, staring instead at the brother he despised. Even now, Malator realized, Kahldris hated him.

'I do this out of mercy, brother,' said Malator. He raised his hoka. 'Not out of spite.'

The blade came down at Kahldris' neck, delivering a perfect killing blow. If Kahldris had been alive, his head would have split from his body in a fountain of blood. But in the world of the dead, he simply disappeared.

Lukien fought until his arms and legs burned, until exhaustion turned to agony and his breath came in gasps. He had fought and given it his all, and he knew that no matter how much he gave he could never make the armour yield nor the man inside it submit. Lorn, too, seemed depleted from the fight, kept erect only by the Devil's Armour, which still gleamed with unblemished perfection despite a hundred well-placed blows. Hopelessness took hold of Lukien. Down at the bottom of the plateau, Lothon and his fellow Liirians were watching, sure that the end was drawing near. Knowing he could not go on yet refusing to yield, Lukien wound back for one more attack. As he did, he felt Malator rush back into his sword.

The tidal wave of new found strength dazzled Lukien. All at once his aching muscles filled with vigour. Holding high the Sword of Angels, he saw Lorn drop back, as if struck by some unseen force. Instantly the light of the armour died away. The skull-shaped helmet froze, lifeless. Lorn, clearly stunned, raised his eyes to Lukien and the sword hanging high above him. This time, the Norvan gave no defense.

It was over. In the netherworld, Malator had won and both men knew it. Lorn, however, made no plea. Before the blade could fall he reached up and pulled off the helmet, looking death full in the face. He seemed to know it was deserved.

Lukien thought only of Thorin. He brought down the sword, bringing an end to King Lorn the Wicked.

PART FOUR

THE LAST ADVENTURE

85

Ghost tore the gaka from his face when he saw Jador, shouting in triumphant glee. He held the long stretch of fabric high above his head, waving it like a flag, bouncing happily on the back of his drowa as the desert sun beat down on his pale pink skin. Ahead of him, barely visible in the blinding light, the white structures of Jador appeared, peeking over the dunes. Ghost let the howl trill from his throat, turning to see Lukien and Gilwyn. Lukien said nothing. The deep satisfaction of seeing Jador again was beyond words. Gilwyn too, was silent, his mind clearly on White-Eye.

'There she is!' cried Ghost. 'I told you, Lukien. Did I tell you? We'll be there before nightfall!'

Lukien lumbered up to him on his drowa, happy to admit he was wrong. Neither he nor Gilwyn had thought they would reach Jador before the day ended, and had already began preparing themselves for another night in the desert. It had been four long days since they had left Ganjor, and the prospect of one more night spent beneath the stars did nothing for Lukien's mood. Now, as he saw the city growing on the horizon, he knew his long journey was at an end.

At last.

You're home, Lukien. Malator sounded almost melancholy. *And so am I, I suppose.*

Lukien smiled, understanding his Akari's – his friend's – meaning. It was impossible to keep secrets from him, so Lukien never tried. This time, though, there was nothing to answer. Before he could reply to the spirit, Gilwyn sidled up to him, raising his eyebrows at Lukien.

'Will she be waiting for me, do you think?'

The boy's mind was forever on White-Eye. White-Eye had been a major point of conversation on the long ride south, and Gilwyn had big plans for the two of them. Mostly, though, he just wanted to see her again.

'I think,' said Lukien wryly, 'that she would walk across the desert to find you.'

Gilwyn puffed, looking supremely confident. 'I can't wait to see what she's like now. When I left she was more of a girl than a queen.'

'She's Kahana White-Eye now,' said Lukien. 'I think you'll be pleased.'

Ghost whipped around, scolding, 'Come on, already! Enough talking. Let's ride!'

They were in no hurry, though, and so Lukien merely waved at Ghost, telling him to lead the way. After so many months trekking across the world, Lukien had learned a few things about patience. Instead of rushing, he was satisfied to savour the last leg of his journey, if it was in fact the last. His drowa loped slowly after Ghost. The remarkable beasts had been given to them by King Baralosus. Upon entering Ganjor, the king and his daughter Salina had welcomed them, letting them rest in the palace before setting off once more to Jador. They had spent four lavish days there, pampered by Baralosus' servants and listening to Salina's stories. She had greeted them like heroes, and Baralosus, who had kept the peace with Jador, had encouraged them to stay, even sending messengers to Jador with word that the three were alive and would soon be returning home. Lukien liked Baralosus. Some still thought him a tyrant, but Lukien had known real tyrants in his life and saw Baralosus more like a benign despot. His daughter, of course, was the real jewel of Ganjor, a beautiful girl with a sterling heart. She still grieved for Aztar and it showed, making her pretty face sad when it should have glowed with joy. During their time together, Lukien had found a moment to share a special truth with her, telling her that true love never dies.

Thinking of Salina turned Lukien to thoughts of Cassandra once more, then to Gilwyn and his love for White-Eye. He stole a glance at his happy friend, noting the Eye of God glimmering beneath his shirt. The wound that Thorin had given him months ago had healed completely, leaving only a faded scar, and Gilwyn claimed he felt no pain from it at all. Adjusting to life with the amulet would prove far tougher, Lukien knew. So far, Amaraz had been as silent to Gilwyn as he'd always been with Lukien, but the aloofness of the great Akari gave Gilwyn no offense. The boy already had a spirit of his own, one to whom he was willingly bound. Amaraz had merely one duty to Gilwyn – to keep him alive.

'How long will I live?' Gilwyn had asked Lukien upon his return to the library. He was in a bed, looking frail and frightened, and Lukien had just returned from battling Lorn. He had no answers for his friend. He still did not. All he could do was beg Gilwyn's forgiveness for saving him and cursing him with immortality.

Hanging from Lukien's drowa, a drab burlap sack bounced against the creature's side. Inside, Lukien carried a gift for Minikin, one that he had brought with him all the way from Liiria. He would explain to her how Lorn had died, and he supposed he would have to tell Eiriann, as well. He barely knew the young woman, but for some reason she had loved the salty Norvan. Things were different in Liiria now. Not better, really, at least not yet, but at last the country had a chance, a start at a new day. Count Lothon and his small army of Liirians had begun the work of reconstruction, and King Raxor of Reec had pledged to help them, to protect them from Norvan bandits while that poor nation slid deeper into chaos. It was Lorn's sad legacy that Norvor no longer had a leader. Once again, civil war and madness ruled there.

But for Lukien, the fate of Norvan no longer mattered, and he had only small interest in the goings-on in Liiria, too. He had said his last farewells to his homeland. He had done the things he had promised to do, fulfilling every duty, every small point of honour. Now, at last, his time had come. For the first time in a long time, his destiny was his own.

By the time they reached the outskirts of Jador, word had already spread of their arrival. The narrow streets of the ramshackle town outside the white wall had filled with onlookers, many of whom knew Lukien by name and shouted to him as he entered the city. Gilwyn, too, received accolades, many from young girls who had grown up adoring him. He blushed a little as they blew him kisses, while Ghost jealously shook his head. Having replaced the gaka around his face, the albino had returned to anonymity. The crowds, however, were happy to see them all, and as they made their way across the township they returned the waves and shouts, basking in the warmth of their countrymen.

The people of the town followed them as they rode on toward the white wall, becoming a long train of humanity by the time they reached the tower and its big brass gate. As expected, the gate was open wide, and the people of Jador had spilled out into the avenue, mingling with the town's people. Near the gate stood Minikin, a little hunched over and supporting herself with a cane. Some of the Inhumans from Grimhold stood around her, and as always her bodyguard Trog was there, casting his giant shadow over the little woman. White-Eye stood close to Minikin, smiling excitedly as she heard the crowd approaching. Gilwyn saw her and cried out a greeting, lifting himself off the back of his drowa. Ghost tossed up his hands, waving at everyone, while Lukien simply smiled stoically, glad to be back. His happiness faded, however, when he saw Eiriann standing behind Minikin. Her father was with her, as were some of the other Seekers she had come with to Jador. In her arms she held Lorn's daughter, Poppy. The child was much bigger than when Lukien left, squirming in Eiriann's arms, sensing the excitement despite her blindness. She watched the men returning, her disappointment evident. In the message he had sent from Ganjor, Lukien had mentioned nothing of Lorn's death, only Thorin's.

Riding up to the gate, Lukien stopped his drowa and got off the animal's back. Gilwyn and Ghost did the same, Gilwyn running at once to White-Eye. While Ghost greeted Minikin and the others, Lukien undid the sack from his saddle. The crowed stilled as he turned and walked toward Minikin. The little lady smiled at him. Eiriann grimaced. Lukien reached into the sack and pulled out the helmet of the Devil's Armour. He held it out for the mistress to see.

'For you,' he said.

Minikin took the helmet in her tiny hand. It was much heavier than it had been when it was alive, and she struggled with its weight as she balanced on her cane. She was frail-looking now, much weaker than Lukien had ever seen her before. Not even the Eye of God could keep her alive forever, he supposed. She passed the helmet to Trog, then looked up at Lukien.

'Lorn?'

Lukien shook his head. Instead of answering Minikin directly, he went to Eiriann. The young woman looked at him, bravely stifling her tears.

'I'm sorry,' Lukien told her. 'It was what had to be.'

As if feeling his voice, little Poppy turned her face toward Lukien. Eiriann held the girl tightly against her bosom. She seemed to understand Lukien's meaning, but didn't ask the dreaded question. Rather, she asked him something else entirely.

'Did he die well?'

Lukien thought for a moment. 'He died quickly,' he told her.

Eiriann nodded, then turned to her father, who put his arm around her and led her back into the city. Lukien watched them go, lost in the woman's grief. He had never grieved for Lorn, and still couldn't believe such a pretty young girl saw anything redeeming in him. He had cast that spell on others, but never on Lukien. Why then, Lukien wondered, did he miss the Norvan now?

'Minikin,' he said wearily, 'I'm glad to be back.'

Minikin took his hand, squeezing it. 'You are welcome here, Shalafein. For as long as you will stay with us, you are welcome.'

Hand in hand, the two of them entered Jador.

86

Gilwyn spent the next few days in the palace with White-Eye, rediscovering the woman she had become during his long absence. She was everything Lukien had described to him and more, strong and confident, and more lovely than he remembered. She was truly her father's daughter, and in the quiet hours they spent together Gilwyn fell in love with her all over again. White-Eye abandoned her royal duties for a time, spending long afternoons strolling through the gardens with Gilwyn and asking him about the adventures he had experienced while away. She, of course, had her own adventures to talk about, particularly about her days with Lorn. So much had happened to both of them over the past few months; they had both changed. But they had not grown apart, and for that Gilwyn was grateful.

On the morning of his fifth day back in Jador, Gilwyn went alone to the garden, choosing a spot so that he could enjoy the solitude with his pet monkey, Teku. Like White-Eye, Teku had missed him, and had also changed during his absence. She was a bit slower now as age caught up with her lithe little frame, but she still liked to crawl up his arm and look for treats in his collar. Gilwyn sat beneath a tree, its wide, leafy canopy shading him from the sun while Teku ate dates out of his palm. He had no definite plans for the day but knew he would soon have to speak with Lukien. And with Minikin. Things were not the same in Jador anymore, and Teku wasn't the only one who had aged. Everyone could see the change in Minikin, even White-Eye, blind though she was. Time was catching up with the nearly-immortal mistress. The injustice of it made Gilwyn sad.

And too, thinking of Lukien saddened him as well. The weeks they had spent together on the road, first returning to Nith with Daralor and his men and then riding on to Ganjor had been some of the happiest Gilwyn could remember. They were both at peace at last, and the inevitable decision ahead of Lukien seemed a hundred years away. Now, though, they were back in Jador and Lukien's quest was over. He was still Shalafein, but White-Eye no longer needed a protector.

'But how can I ask him?' Gilwyn wondered aloud. He directed the question to Teku, who looked up at him inquisitively as she gnawed a plump date, holding it in her furry digits. 'I don't even want to think about it.'

All Gilwyn wanted was to be here in Jador, at peace, sharing his life with his friends and the woman he loved. Why couldn't Lukien feel like that?

The answer struck him as obvious.

'Because his woman is dead,' he sighed.

There could never be another Cassandra, not for Lukien.

An hour went by and Gilwyn remained beneath the shade tree. He was out of dates for Teku but the monkey didn't mind. Instead she had climbed up the tree to explore its many limbs, occasionally calling down to Gilwyn to assure him she was all right. Gilwyn looked straight up into the canopy, then noticed Minikin coming toward him through the garden. He made to stand, but the mistress bade him to sit. Oddly, she had come alone, without the ubiquitous Trog. Her little legs, helped by her cane, carried her quickly over to Gilwyn. Catching a glimpse of Teku in the tree, she smiled.

'May I sit?' she asked Gilwyn.

Gilwyn laughed. 'You never have to ask my permission, Minikin. I'm glad you're here. I was thinking about you. And about Lukien.'

'Ah, then we are thinking alike today, Gilwyn.' Minikin lowered herself to the ground a bit awkwardly, laying her cane on the ground beside her. She used her spidery fingers to caress the soft grass. 'This is a good place you've chosen for us to talk.'

'Huh?'

'You knew I'd come sooner or later. We have things to talk about, you and I.'

Gilwyn nodded. He put his hand beneath his shirt and pulled out the Eye of God. 'You mean this.'

'That and other things, yes,' said Minikin. She leaned forward, stretching her back. 'Oh, the aches and pains of old age. I hope you feel better than I do when you reach my age, Gilwyn.'

'And how old is that?'

'I'll never tell.'

They laughed, but Gilwyn knew her business was serious. He settled back against the tree trunk, encouraging her to speak. Minikin, who liked to take her time with things, did not hurry but rather enjoyed the garden for a spell, noticing the butterflies collecting around a patch of wildflowers. While she watched them, she spoke to Gilwyn at last.

'You are thinking about Lukien,' she said, 'and what will happen if he leaves here. He did not tell you, then?'

'No,' said Gilwyn. 'And I didn't ask him.'

'No? Not in all the time you spent together riding back to Jador?'

'I couldn't.' Gilwyn shrugged. 'Maybe I didn't want to know his answer.'

Minikin nodded. 'It will be a great loss if he leaves us, but the decision is his to make, all alone. I am glad you haven't tried to sway him, Gilwyn.'

'I want to, believe me. I want to beg him to stay here with us. He has the sword to keep him alive. He doesn't have to give it up.'

'You're right, he doesn't have to. Life is all about the choices we make. And I have made a choice too, Gilwyn.' Minikin took his hand, not the strong one but the clubbed one, holding it gently in her small palm. 'This is the fist of a powerful young man. A good man to wear the Eye of God. Amaraz and his sister have helped the Inhumans for centuries, Gilwyn.'

Gilwyn stopped her. 'Minikin, I know what you're going to say. Please don't.'

She grinned wickedly. 'See? You have my gifts already!'

'No, I don't,' Gilwyn insisted. 'I can't read minds and I can't summon the Akari and I can't do any of the things you can do. Grimhold needs you, so please – don't think about dying or passing things on to me.'

'We all die, boy,' said Minikin. There was not a trace of fear in her tone. 'Even you'll die someday, even with the Eye of God. I do not know why the magic doesn't last forever, but I feel it weakening in me, and Lariniza has told me my time is growing short.'

'No, Minikin . . .'

'Yes.' She held his hand firmly and looked straight into his eyes. 'When my time comes, you will lead the Inhumans, Gilwyn. You will be the Master of Grimhold. And White-Eye will be your queen. When I die, take the amulet from around my neck and give it to her.'

'What?' Gilwyn felt a shock of panic. 'I can't do that.'

'You can. She has already agreed to it.' Minikin's eyes twinkled. 'As they say, she is her father's daughter.'

'Minikin, I don't want this . . .'

'No,' Minikin interrupted. 'No more talk. It is done.' She picked up her cane and struggled to her feet. 'This is a good place to think. So think on what I have said. You will see the rightness of it, Gilwyn.'

Gilwyn got up after her. 'You're going? Just like that?'

She turned and hobbled back through the garden, waving over her shoulder. 'Think on what I've said,' she ordered. 'I have other business to tend today.'

On the other side of the palace, Minikin at last found Eiriann. She was playing with Poppy in one of the common areas that surrounded the royal residence, where everyone in Jador was welcome to enjoy the splendour of the palace. Here, a bubbling pool of crystal water fountained up from the ground, surrounded by beautiful brick work that invited children to come and play. Today being a typically perfect day in Jador, mothers from around the city had brought their children to frolic in the fountain, cooling off in its sparkling cascade. Eiriann held little Poppy beneath a spray of water, supporting the naked child under the arms. Poppy burbled with laughter at the sensation. She could not see or hear the water, but the feeling of it on her skin was enough to make her giddy. As Minikin spied Eiriann and the child from the outskirts of the common area, she mourned for Lorn and all the things he had stupidly left behind.

Eiriann and Poppy had been a pleasure to have in the palace, but Lorn's death had changed things. Things would be different now for both of them. Minikin prepared herself to give them the news, smoothing out her coat and fixing a smile on her face. Well-wishers greeted her, happy to see the mistress among them, and as Minikin approached the fountain she nodded politely to the people, not inviting conversation. Eiriann pulled Poppy away from the fountain, then brought her over to the warm grass to dry in the sun. When she saw Minikin coming toward them, her breath caught. She laid Poppy down on a square of fabric, blotting the water from her smooth skin. The child's blank eyes searched the shadows above her.

'Hello,' the girl offered awkwardly.

Seeing Poppy made Minikin glow. 'Hello to both of you,' she said warmly. 'How is the little one today?'

'Fine,' said Eiriann. 'Just fine.'

'And you? How are you, Eiriann?'

Young Eiriann made a brave face, shrugging off the question. 'I'm well.' She paused, then glanced up at the mistress. 'As well as I could be, I guess.'

'You've had quite a time, I'm sure,' said Minikin gently. She squatted down beside Poppy using her cane for balance, and with her free hand traced her finger over the babe's smooth belly. 'Have you thought about what you will do now?'

Eiriann's face tightened. 'You have been so kind to us. I know we can't remain here in the palace now, but perhaps we can find a place in the town outside the wall. I was hoping Kahana White-Eye might know of a place, or one of her people.'

'Hmm, yes, that might do,' said Minikin, trying to hide her mirth. 'You understand why I could never take the baby into Grimhold, don't you?'

Eiriann nodded. 'I understand. Lorn was mistaken; we all were. But it's all he ever wanted for Poppy, to be healed. To be like these other children.' Her gaze flicked momentarily toward the children and their mothers, all of them normal, none of them possibly understanding what it was like for Poppy. 'He wasn't just a bad man, Minikin. He was a good man, too.'

'Some people don't believe that,' said Minikin. 'But I do.'

The young woman looked at her strangely. 'Yes,' she sighed. 'I believe you. He liked you, Minikin. I think it's because you saw the real him. The good one underneath the bad one, I mean.'

'He loved his daughter, certainly. And he loved you.'

'And he loved Norvor,' said Eiriann sourly. 'And that's what killed him. I don't blame Lukien for what he did; he probably thinks that, but I don't. Lorn was obsessed; I know that. But he was good to me and my father.' She smiled at Minikin. 'I'm glad I'm not the only one that saw the good in him.'

Minikin put her finger into Poppy's palm. The little hand closed on it immediately. 'And he left you this little one to care for. It's a big job. You'll need help with her, probably more than you can give her.'

A shadow crossed Eiriann's face. 'I'll do the best I can for her. I'll work for money. Maybe I'll find a man who'll take care of us. I don't know . . .'

'You know,' Minikin began mischievously, 'I may know a place for her. There's a family not far from here that can take good care of her, teach her the things she needs to know to survive.'

'Really?' Eiriann was stunned. 'Who would do that?'

Minikin grinned. 'Who do you think?'

For a moment the girl did not understand, but then the realization dawned on her. She could not speak.

'King Lorn fought and risked his life for us,' said Minikin softly. 'He knew I was weak and never took advantage. He was true to his word to Gilwyn, right to the end, and he made a kahana out of White-Eye. Whatever else he might have been, he was never an enemy to Jador, or to Grimhold. We owe him a debt but we can never repay it because he is gone. But his daughter . . .' Minikin stroked Poppy's face. 'She belongs here. She can be one of us now.'

'You'll take her into Grimhold?' asked Eiriann breathlessly. 'How?'

'Every now and then I choose a child to enter Grimhold. It only happens seldom because there are very few Akari. But when an Inhuman passes, the Akari is free to find another host.'

'Passes? Who has died?'

Minikin shook off the question. 'It doesn't matter. There are many Inhumans. You did not know her. What's important is that there is space for Poppy now . . . if you'll let me take her.'

Eiriann looked heart-broken, and also hugely glad. She looked down at Poppy with tears welling in her eyes. 'She's like my own,' she choked.

'I know,' Minikin agreed. 'And that's why you'll let me take her, because you want the best for her.'

'She'll be normal in Grimhold? She will see and hear, like normal children?'

'No, not like normal children, dear.' Minikin got that impish look. 'She'll be better than normal. She'll be an Inhuman.'

87

Lukien lay in the steaming water, his wet hair dripping into his one, half-closed eye. His naked body had given itself over to the warmth, falling into an almost trance-like relaxation. Overhead, the mosaic ceiling of the bath chamber dazzled him with intricate colours. His arms spread out on the ledge of the pool, holding him at chin level in the water. As he floated, sleep crept ever closer. He watched his toes break the surface then sink back down. The hair on his body moved like in a breeze. Alone in the vast chamber, Lukien heard the slow ebb and flow of his breath and, if he listened closely, the calm rhythm of his heart.

Time did a wonderful disappearing act here in the baths. It had been morning when Lukien had entered, but he was no longer sure the sun was even up anymore. On the stone floor behind his head, the Sword of Angels lay on the moist surface, strangely impervious to getting wet. Though the weapon still sat near him, Lukien could barely sense Malator in his mind, the Akari having backed off. It was a small gift but Lukien was grateful for it, and had in fact enjoyed it for a week now. Since returning to Jador he had spent most of his time alone, with little contact with anyone, including Malator. He had done too much over the last year, traveling too many miles and watching friends die. Lukien never wanted to think again. All he wanted now was to drift away, high up to the colourful ceiling like the mist.

Today, however, a visitor interrupted his bathing. From time to time Jadori soldiers would enter the chamber, sliding down silently at the other end of the pool. On occasion, mothers brought their children to the baths as well, laughing while the naked babes were carried through the water, splashing and giggling. Lukien enjoyed the solitude but never expected it, and in fact he liked when others joined him in the baths, even when he never said a word to them. Lukien simply wanted to relax. And not to talk at all.

Still, it did not surprise him when Gilwyn entered the chamber. He heard the boy before he saw him, the distinctive clip-clop of his special boot dragging on the echoing stones. As Gilwyn turned the corner he peered into the pool chamber through the mists, seeing Lukien floating in the water. Lukien's eye widened a little. Was he glad to see Gilwyn? He didn't know, though he supposed the time had come to tell of his decision.

'Don't just stand there gawking,' he told his friend.

Gilwyn made a face before stepping around the corner. 'You looked like you were sleeping.'

Lukien's eye widened as he saw what Gilwyn was wearing. Not at all ready for the baths, Gilwyn sported his usual shirt and trousers, his special boot buckled up the length of his calf. 'If you try swimming like that you'll sink like a rock.'

Gilwyn smiled a little sheepishly, making his way across the edge of the pool. The way was narrow where Lukien floated, and Gilwyn was careful to keep his balance on the slick stone. Lukien watched, ready to help the boy if he needed it but Gilwyn did not, finally coming to a stop near Lukien's sword.

'I can't see you if you stand behind me,' said Lukien. 'Take your shoes off at least. Dip your feet in the water; that's what Minikin does.'

'No, thanks,' said Gilwyn. It was obvious there were things on his mind. 'I didn't come for a bath.'

'Still, I prefer you didn't stand there. Sit at least. Get comfortable.'

It was an effort for Gilwyn to sit himself down, but he found a spot that wasn't too damp over Lukien's left shoulder. He lowered himself to the stones, using his good hand for support. Then he looked around, admiring the chamber. They had the entire place to themselves.

'I've been waiting for you,' Lukien confessed. 'I should have talked to you sooner. I'm sorry. I've had some things I needed to consider.'

'I know,' said Gilwyn. 'I could leave if you like.'

'No.' Lukien tilted his head back and smiled at him. 'We should talk. But first, tell me – how are things with White-Eye?'

Gilwyn got that dreamy look. 'Perfect.'

Lukien laughed. 'That's it?'

'What else is there? She's perfect. I'm happy, Lukien.'

'Yes, I can see that.' Lukien enjoyed teasing him, but when he noticed the amulet beneath Gilwyn's shirt he got serious. 'And what about that?' he asked, gesturing with his chin. 'Any problems?'

'No. Not yet anyway.'

'It's a big adjustment, Gilwyn. Maybe you're not telling me the truth, huh?'

The boy looked frightened. 'Maybe. But what can I do? If I take it off I die, right?'

'That's right. But are you ready to live forever?'

'Is anybody?'

There was silence between them, awkward enough to make Gilwyn change the subject. He said, 'I dreamt about Thorin last night.'

Lukien sank deeper into the water. 'I dream about him sometimes.'

'He's alive somewhere,' said Gilwyn. 'Maybe he's talking to us.'

'I'm not sure I like that idea.'

'Why not? It means he's free.'

'Yes.' The thought made Lukien happy. 'Free.' Behind him, he sensed the Sword of Angels. He knew, too, that Gilwyn was staring at it. 'Go on,' he said. 'Ask your question.'

Gilwyn hesitated. 'I just . . . I wanted to know what your plans are. I mean if you've decided yet. If you haven't . . .'

'No,' said Lukien. 'I've decided.' He didn't turn to face his friend. 'I can't stay here, Gilwyn. I'm going.'

The silence between them rose up again. Lukien could feel Gilwyn's twisted expression.

'It's what I have to do,' he hurried to add. 'I'm going to Tharlara.'

A great sigh rushed out of Gilwyn. 'To the Story Garden.'

'That's right.' Lukien hesitated. 'I know what I said, but . . .' he stopped himself, unsure how much to tell.

'You can live with the sword,' said Gilwyn. 'And still see Cassandra again.'

'Yes. Yes, that's right.'

'I'm happy,' said Gilwyn. He shifted a little closer. 'I was afraid for you.'

Lukien still could not look at him. 'Well, that's all right then,' he said. 'I'm just going to Tharlara. I'll be all right.'

'Right,' Gilwyn chirped. 'If you keep the sword you can go on, just like me. I know how much you miss Cassandra, but you don't have to die for her. You can still be with her this way. It's like she's still alive.'

'She is alive,' Lukien reminded him. 'And she's waiting for me. In Tharlara.'

Gilwyn leaned down. 'Lukien?'

'Yes?'

'I'm going to miss you.'

Looking at Gilwyn before had been difficult, but now it was impossible. A lump rose in Lukien's throat. 'I'm going to miss you too, Gilwyn. I'm going to miss everything about this place.'

'But you can come back someday,' said Gilwyn.

Lukien nodded. 'Yes. I can come back.'

Gilwyn's face flushed with hope. He had never known his own father, but often he looked at Lukien the way a son might. Or a wise big-brother. It had been so easy for Lukien to lie and spare his feelings. Gilwyn started to his feet again, careful not to slip on the damp stones.

'I'll leave you alone now and let you think,' he said. 'Maybe we can all eat together tonight?'

Lukien, floating, nodded slowly. 'All right.'

But as Gilwyn turned to go he stood up quickly, splashing the water around him. 'Gilwyn, wait . . .'

Gilwyn stopped. 'Yes?'

Standing naked in the pool, Lukien stared at Gilwyn, searching for words. Gilwyn's hopeful glow disippated.

'What is it, Lukien?'

Perched on the very ledge of the truth, Lukien could not stop himself from tumbling over. 'I'm not going to Tharlara,' he said quickly. 'I'm sorry, but I lied to you.'

Gilwyn inched closer with concern. 'What do you mean?'

'I'm going somewhere else, Gilwyn, but I can't do it alone.' Lukien looked pleadingly at his young friend. 'I need your help.'

88

Two days later, Lukien found himself at the edge of a stream heading west. Around him, the desert had succumbed to moss-covered stones and leafy trees, and the stream bubbled as it rolled across its rocky bottom. Lukien sat by the edge of the stream, drinking of its clear water and eating the food he had packed for himself. Yards away, his horse waited, lashed to a tree. On the road to Tharlara, the stream had beckoned to him, offering the perfect place for rest and reflection. As Lukien ate, his mind filled with images of his friends. It was impossible for him to explain himself or the depths of his love for Cassandra, and yet Minikin and Gilwyn had somehow understood. The Sword of Angels lay in the grass beside him, sparkling like the river, close enough to its owner to keep him well and alive. In a way, the weapon had made his dreams come true. If he had never found it, he would never have found Cassandra.

For that, at least, he was grateful.

Lukien took his time finishing his meal. After so long a wait there was no real reason to hurry. When at last he was done he stood, taking a deep breath and admiring his surroundings. Looking west, he could see the stream continuing on, as did the grass and trees and all the lovely shade. The place was perfect. The day was perfect. Over his shoulder, almost out of sight, Gilwyn waited, patiently giving his friend the time he needed to prepare himself. With the boy had come Emerald his kreel. The reptiles head bobbed behind the branches. Gilwyn looked at Lukien through the leaves, then quickly turned away. He had said almost nothing on their ride to this place. Truly, there was nothing left to say, and Gilwyn had at last stopped begging Lukien to reconsider. At last, he had agreed to be here with him for one last adventure.

It was impossible to do alone, Lukien had decided. He could have walked away from the sword, he supposed, but he did not know how long he would linger or how far he would get. More importantly, he could not just abandon Malator after all the Akari had done for him. Gilwyn would take the sword back with him to Grimhold. If ever it were needed again, it would be in his safe keeping.

'You deserve to be home, Malator, among your people again.' Lukien spoke lightly to the spirit. 'How does that feel?'

I would rather be with you, replied the spirit.

Lukien knelt down on the soft earth and gently picked up the weapon. An image of Malator filled his mind. The Akari was not smiling, but neither was he angry.

Are you ready?

Lukien nodded.

Then call the boy.

Somehow Gilwyn knew the time had come. Leaving Emerald in the trees, Gilwyn emerged from the branches, looking resolute and pale. The Eye of God beamed upon his chest. He came to stand before the kneeling Lukien, his hand shaking as he touched the knight's shoulder. Lukien comforted him with a smile.

'I can feel her,' sighed Lukien. 'She's here with us.'

Gilwyn glanced around, looking for the invisible Cassandra. 'She's in the Story Garden too, Lukien. You can go to her there.'

'She's always with me, Gilwyn, but it's not the same. It's not like really being with her.' Lukien lifted the sword and kissed its shining blade. 'Malator, take care of them,' he said. His fingers wrapped gingerly around the weapon. The enormous power of Malator flooded through him one more time. Gilwyn stepped back, in no hurry to take the life-giving blade from Lukien. Lukien shut his eye, holding the blade out before him, summoning Cassandra like a prayer. 'My love, take me to paradise with you.'

His hands began to shake. He gripped the blade more tightly, feeling its edge bite into his flesh. He could feel Cassandra upon him, in his mind and body. Her face shimmered just out of reach. Agony seized Lukien when he saw her, shaking her raven-haired head, his eyes full of sadness.

'No,' Lukien gasped. 'Don't refuse me.'

Malator had moved away, leaving room for Cassandra's ghost to reach across the void between them. Lukien struggled to hear her, snatching up bits of her beautiful voice. She was barely audible, yet to Lukien her meaning was clear.

'No!' he bellowed, crushing the blade until blood from his fingers. His whole body shook with grief. 'I want to be in paradise. I want to be with you!'

Cassandra at last breached the gap between their worlds. Reaching out, she touched his face with her ethereal hand. In the darkness, all he saw was her, and all he heard was her voice, heart-broken by his choice.

We have forever, she told him. Live your life.

It took all her strength to breach the worlds, and then she was gone, floating back across the void, the feeling of her touch lingering on Lukien's cheek. He didn't want to open up his eye again, but try as he might he could not summon her again. Slowly his one eye opened, revealing Gilwyn's shocked face.

'Lukien?' Gilwyn was kneeling in front of him. 'Your hands . . .'

Lukien stared at the sword. His fingers burned with pain from the cuts of the blade. Instantly, Malator went to work, healing him.

'She doesn't want me,' he gasped. 'Not yet.'

'Cassandra?' Gilwyn hurried a handkerchief out of his pocket, dabbing gently at Lukien's bloodied hands. 'You saw her?'

Lukien raised his eyes and saw the Eye of God dangling at Gilwyn's neck, and suddenly the enormity of things struck him.

'She wants me to live my life,' he said. 'But if I have this sword . . .'

Gilwyn stopped him. 'No, it's not like that,' he said quickly. He could barely keep the happiness from his face. 'No one lives forever, Lukien. Not Minikin, not me – not even you with the sword. Listen to what Cassandra's telling you, Lukien.'

'What?' Lukien looked hopefully at his young friend.

'You'll see her again, Lukien. You'll have eternity together. Someday.'

'But the sword . . .'

'The sword won't keep you from her, Lukien. She's always with you, remember?'

Overwhelmed, Lukien remained on his knees, holding the Sword of Angels and letting Malator heal his lacerated fingers. Magically, the blood ebbed. The wounds began to close.

'Is this how it will be, Malator?' he asked with dread. 'Will I live forever here or not?'

Malator, like Gilwyn, hid his pleasure poorly. *Forever does not have the same meaning in this world, Lukien.*

Lukien scoffed at the Akari's vagueness. 'You're being slippery, Malator. Answer my question.'

'No, Lukien,' Gilwyn interrupted. 'It doesn't matter what he answers. It's still your choice.' He handed off the soiled handkerchief to Lukien. 'It's your life and it always will be. If you want to end it, give me the sword. I'll bring it back to Grimhold, just as we planned. You can go to Cassandra, if that's what you want.'

Lukien looked at Gilwyn in surprise. Unlike Malator, Gilwyn was not playing games. The perfect day had been sullied by blood and terrible choices, and Lukien did not know what to do or even how to get up off his knees.

'What will I do if I choose life?' he asked.

'What, don't you think we need you?' Gilwyn smiled. 'There's still so much to do in Jador. And what about Liiria? You could go back there if you want. You can help Lothon and the others rebuild. And even if you don't, there will always be a place for you here, Lukien. Remember – you are Shalafein.'

His words brought something deep within Lukien back to life. Slowly, he managed to rise to his feet. Glancing around, he heard the stream again and the rushing of its water. Once again he felt the warm light of the sun on his face. He had chosen a special place to die. In a way, it was a kind of paradise.

'Yes,' he said softly. 'I am Shalafein.'

The Protector.

THE END